Men of the Otherworld

"The intriguing tales, originally published as serials on Armstrong's website, unfold so fluidly that they read almost like a novel, providing a good introduction to new readers and a real treat for fans."

—*Publishers Weekly*

"It truly is a treat, even for those not familiar with Armstrong's previous work. . . . No matter which man is narrating . . . Armstrong creates a distinct and engaging voice and depth of character while maintaining her own sophisticated style." —*Winnipeg Free Press*

Made to Be Broken

"*Made to Be Broken* is a keeper. This novel proves Ms. Armstrong is a literary talent in any genre she chooses to write." —A Romance Review

Living with the Dead

"As Armstrong readers have come to expect, this book is balanced between likable characters and the creepy evil that they fight, all wrapped together with nonstop, edge-of-your-seat action." —*Library Journal*

"Rarely is the ninth book in a series as fresh and entertaining as the first, but this Women of the Otherworld volume defies the odds." —*Booklist*

Personal Demon

"A page-turning thriller. Fans of the paranormal will delight in the eighth Women of the Otherworld yarn, with its ass-kicking, Bollywood-beautiful, former-socialite heroine and full complement of sorcerers, witches, werewolves, and other paranormal beings."

—*Booklist*

"Better than sex and chocolate, Kelley Armstrong draws readers back into the Otherworld with a slam-dunk new story. . . . Nonstop action with just the right amount of romance and, without a doubt, a winner! Five blue ribbons." —Romance Junkies

"Another great read from one of the masters of urban fantasy. Fast-paced plots and concise, well-drawn characters define Armstrong's work. Her world-building and continuity are flawless. I never miss one of her stories." —Fresh Fiction

"Armstrong is a master of combining romance, mystery and the paranormal in one addictive package. And this latest addition to her series is no exception. Armstrong keeps providing new, fresh and interesting characters who inhabit a dangerous world filled with shades of gray." —*The Parkersburg News and Sentinel*

No Humans Involved

"Paranormal and show-business power struggles make for hard-to-put-down entertainment." —*Booklist*

"Armstrong brings a new twist to the necromancer mythology [and] romance fans will be delighted with the inclusion of a quiet but meaningful romance. [The] books, at their best, are about more than just a really cool supernatural world and this one delivers with action, emotion, sexiness and suspense." —*USA Today*

"Armstrong doesn't do anything in small measures. . . . Another great story you won't want to miss!"

—Romance Reviews Today

"Armstrong's intensity and talent never quit. This book will make you laugh, cry, sigh, scream and beg for more." —*The Parkersburg News and Sentinel*

Exit Strategy

"Original, dark, and gritty, with enough humanity to keep you caring about its anti-heroes and enough suspense to keep you turning the pages."

—CODY MCFADYEN, author of *Abandoned*

"Armstrong's expert plotting never falters, and she's able to keep ramping up the intensity throughout more than 500 pages—no easy feat—making this a top-notch entertainment sure to seduce fans of tough heroines."

—*Publishers Weekly*

"A perfect ten! Armstrong pulls off a miracle. [Her] ability to mesmerize with exciting action while making flawed characters sympathetic is enormous."

—Romance Reviews Today

"*Exit Strategy* is a perfect suspense novel. . . . It is fast-paced and high in action with a colorful cast of characters that will leave you wondering who you can trust. Four stars." —Curled Up with a Good Book

Broken

"This is a book we've all been waiting for, and let me tell you, Kelley Armstrong does not disappoint. . . . Sit back and enjoy a howling good time with Elena and the Pack." —Romance Reviews Today

"Action abounds as old characters and new ones run with a plot full of twists, turns, and enough red herrings to keep the most persnickety of readers entertained. A vastly entertaining read!" —Fresh Fiction

Haunted
"Another fantastic adventure in the Women of the Otherworld series . . . Kelley Armstrong is an author to be lauded. . . . Many writers in her position simply rest on their laurels, but Armstrong has instead decided to create something entirely different." —SF Site

Industrial Magic
"Breakneck action is tempered by deep psychological insights, intense sensuality and considerable humor." —*Publishers Weekly*

"Dark, snappy and consistently entertaining . . . Armstrong knows how to keep the reader constantly engaged. . . . There's never anything that could be described as a dull moment or filler." —SFcrowsnest.com

"Armstrong's world is dangerous and fun, her voice crisp and funny. . . . A solidly engaging novel." —*Contra Costa Times*

"One of Armstrong's strengths is the creation of plausible characters, which is a real bonus in a series based on the premise that there are supernatural creatures walking and working beside us in our contemporary world. . . . *Industrial Magic* is a page-turner and is very hard to put down."   —Bookslut

Dime Store Magic

"[A] sexy supernatural romance [whose] special strength lies in its seamless incorporation of the supernatural into the real world. A convincing small-town setting, clever contemporary dialogue, compelling characterizations and a touch of cool humor make the tale's occasional vivid violence palatable and its fantasy elements both gripping and believable."   —*Publishers Weekly*

"From the first page, *Dime Store Magic* captures the attention and never lets go. . . . First-rate suspense, action-packed, and an all-round terrific read. I highly recommend *Dime Store Magic* and proudly award it RRT's Perfect Ten!"   —Romance Reviews Today

"After only three books, Kelley Armstrong has proven her talent in creating a truly imaginative and trendy realm. If you're into supernatural stories with a fresh twist, *Dime Store Magic* is just what you're looking for."   —BookLoons

"Kelley Armstrong continues to dazzle. . . . With such crisp, stylish writing and a tautly suspenseful, well-crafted plot, this new installment in the Otherworld series showcases Kelley Armstrong at her best."
—Curled Up with a Good Book

BY KELLEY ARMSTRONG

* Available from Bantam Books

TALES
of the
OTHERWORLD

KELLEY
ARMSTRONG

BANTAM BOOKS • NEW YORK

Tales of the Otherworld is a work of fiction. Names, characters, places, and incidents either are the product of the author's imagination or are used fictitiously. Any resemblance to actual persons, living or dead, events, or locales is entirely coincidental.

2011 Bantam Books Mass Market Edition

Copyright © 2010 by KLA Fricke, Inc.

Published in the United States by Bantam Books, an imprint of The Random House Publishing Group, a division of Random House, Inc., New York.

BANTAM BOOKS and the rooster colophon are registered trademarks of Random House, Inc.

"Rebirth," "Birthright," *Beginnings,* "Expectations," "Ghosts," "Wedding Bell Hell," and *The Case of El Chupacabra* all originally appeared online at www.kelleyarmstrong.com

Originally published in hardcover in the United States by Bantam Books, an imprint of The Random House Publishing Group, a division of Random House, Inc., in 2010.

ISBN: 978-0-553-59330-3
eBook ISBN: 978-0-553-90742-1

Cover illustration: Katarina Sokolova

Printed in the United States of America

www.bantamdell.com

9 8 7 6 5 4 3 2 1

Bantam mass market edition: April 2011

CONTENTS

INTRODUCTION

Years ago, when I first launched my website, I wanted to do something that would thank readers for their support. I decided to try my hand at e-serials—writing a novella and posting chapters as I went. I asked readers what they wanted, and they said "a story about the guys." The result was *Savage*, a prequel to *Bitten* covering the rather unique childhood of the male lead, Clayton Danvers.

The e-serials became an annual tradition. I'd poll readers, then write them a story. *Savage* was followed by a sequel, *Ascension*. Then that was followed by another prequel to *Bitten*, *Beginnings*, which tells the story of how Clay met Elena. In 2005, I changed tracks and instead offered twelve short stories, again on topics or characters chosen by readers. The next year was my first "non-prequel" novella: *The Case of El Chupacabra*, an investigation by my spellcasters Paige Winterbourne and Lucas Cortez.

As much as readers seemed to appreciate the online fiction, the number-one question I got was: When will they be in book form? I said that I'd only publish them if I could make it a charitable endeavor. I expected it would take years before I'd be in a position to do that, but in 2007, my publishers made me an offer.

The first volume, *Men of the Otherworld*, was all about my werewolf Pack guys. This is volume two, *Tales of the Otherworld,* and it covers a lot of the stories that readers heard mentioned in the books, but never got a chance to see. There's a new story, too. I polled readers for their choice of characters to narrate the new novella, and the winner was Eve Levine. *Bewitched* tells the tale of her romance with Kristof.

All of my proceeds from these volumes are going to World Literacy of Canada, a nonprofit voluntary organization dedicated to promoting international development and social justice (www.worldlit.ca). The stories were originally intended as a gift to readers and now they'll be "re-gifted" to a worthy cause. And there is still plenty of free fiction on my Web site and maybe more to come in the future!

··REBIRTH··

Aaron stumbled from the tavern and gasped as the first blast of cold air slapped him. He paused in the doorway and took a deep breath. Geoffrey jostled him from behind, and Aaron gave him a good-natured shoulder that sent his friend staggering back.

"Move it, you big ox," John said, kneeing Aaron in the rear.

"Just push me out of the way." Aaron shot a grin over his shoulder. "Or maybe you should squeeze past instead. You're skinny enough."

Aaron stepped onto the cobblestone street and grimaced. So much for fresh air. The narrow street stank of shit—horse shit, dog shit, human shit; that's what came of living so close you couldn't take a crap without piling it on someone else's. Give him farm life any day. Plenty of shit there, too, but at least there was room to spread it around.

He squinted up and down the street, his ale-soaked brain struggling to remember which way they'd come. That was another problem with towns. You couldn't see a damn thing. The buildings not only crowded your view, they crowded out the moonlight, and the lanterns dotting the street added more smoke than light.

"Inn's this way," Geoffrey said, smacking Aaron's arm. "Come on before the mistress locks the door."

She *had* locked them out the last time, and it had been

a long, cold night on the street. Aaron and Geoffrey came to the city every other month, bringing goods to market. They'd finished their work this morning, but their families didn't expect them back until Sunday night, knowing that any young man who stayed home to help his parents on the farm deserved time to sample the cosmopolitan treats he was forgoing.

One of those "treats" peered out from a side street as they passed. She met Aaron's gaze and batted her lashes in what he supposed was meant to be a come-hither look, but seemed more like soot caught in her eyes. She couldn't have been more than twelve, the bodice of her dirty dress stuffed to simulate the curves she wouldn't see for another few years . . . if she lived that long.

Aaron walked over, and pressed a few coins into the whore's palm. A look—part relief, part trepidation—sparked in her eyes, then they clouded with confusion as he returned to his friends.

John bumped against him. "How drunk are you? You forgot to take what you paid for."

"Oh, Aaron never has to pay for it," Geoffrey said. "When a tart sees him coming, she closes her purse and opens her legs."

"If you don't want it, I'll take it."

John started to turn, but Aaron grabbed his shoulders and steered him forward.

"What?" John grumbled. "It's paid for."

As they stumbled past an alley, a whimper snaked out from the darkness, followed by the crack of a fist hitting flesh.

Aaron stopped.

"Ya gotta have more than that," a voice rumbled. "Find it . . . or I will."

"Aaron . . ." Geoffrey said, plucking Aaron's sleeve. "It's none of your business. And, for once, let's leave it that way, or we'll spend another night on the street."

Aaron brushed his friend off and strode into the alley. As he walked, his steps steadied, the effects of the ale sloughing off as he focused on the voices. He pulled himself up to his full height and peeled off his jacket. That was often enough—tower over the thug and flex his muscles, and most decided they really didn't need that few pence tonight after all. As he approached the black-haired lout and quaking shopkeeper, his gaze went to the ruffian's hands, looking for a weapon. Nothing. Good.

Aaron grabbed the man's shoulder. "You want to rob someone? Try me."

The lout's hand slammed forward. A flash of metal. *Where had that come—?*

The blade drove into his chest. Aaron shoved the man away and staggered back. His hands went to his chest. Blood pumped out over his fingers. The man came at him again, but the sound of running footsteps made him think better of it and he ran off into the darkness.

"Aaron? Aaron!"

Aaron tried to take a step, but faltered and hit the wall. He stood there, knees locked, forcing himself to stay upright. Then he crumpled.

Aaron twisted in his bed. The damned thing dug into both of his shoulders and butted against the top of his head and bottoms of his feet. Inns. Cram as many people into a room as they can, and if you're more than average height, well, that's not the inn's fault.

Eyes still closed, he took a deep breath. Flowers and a faint musty smell. The mistress probably set out fresh blooms to cover the stink, so she wouldn't have to change the bedding more than once a month.

He should open his eyes. He knew that—but he also knew that first blare of morning sun was going to feel like Satan's imps stabbing his eyes with pitchforks. He shouldn't drink so much. He wasn't used to it, and he paid for his folly every morning after.

Speaking of folly . . . He let out a groan as he remembered the man in the alley. Next time he decided to rescue someone, he'd take an extra moment to make damned sure the lout wasn't concealing a knife. Now he *really* didn't want to get up. He'd been stabbed in the chest once before, and it had taken him weeks to recover.

The last time, he'd been unable to lift anything heavier than a piglet for a month. His father had to do all the chores, and he'd kept sighing and muttering "Aaron, Aaron, Aaron," his weathered face wrinkling. But he kept his gaze down when he said it, to cover the pride in his eyes.

"A big strong boy with a good heart," he'd boast to the neighbors when he thought Aaron couldn't hear. "What more could a father want?"

"God gave you strength," his mother always said. "Always remember that it's a gift, and gifts from God are to be used in his service. Help those less fortunate than you, and you'll please him."

Helping others, though, did not mean getting stabbed and being unable to help his father. His mother would be very firm about that.

"Be *careful*, Aaron," she'd say. "You're too quick to act. Take a moment to *think* as well."

Maybe he could persuade one of his brothers to come back home for a month and help. Even as the thought occurred, though, he dismissed it. They had their own families and jobs and farms. He was the only one left. His father relied on him.

He groaned again.

Enough of that. Time to grit his teeth and get up.

He pulled up his knees and they struck something with a hollow thwack. He opened one eye. The wavering glow of candlelight cast a dim glow in the dark room. Was it still night?

He reached sideways to brace himself as he sat up, and his hand smacked against wood. A bed with sides on it? Had Geoffrey and the others dumped him in a horse trough again?

He opened the other eye. Then, grabbing the sides, he heaved himself up, bracing for the throb of pain through his chest. It didn't come.

Had he dreamed the stabbing? His fingers moved to his chest. It felt fine . . . fine and whole. That damned cheap ale was giving him nightmares now.

He sat up and blinked. He was in a dark, empty room, lit only by a few candles. It looked vaguely familiar. There was a board across his boxlike bed, pushed sideways away from his head and chest; that's what he'd hit his knees on. A black-robed figure sat near his feet, head bent forward in sleep.

Aaron rubbed his eyes. Where the hell was he? It looked familiar. Then he blinked as the memory clicked. It looked like the inside of the family mausoleum. Well, not really a mausoleum; it was made of rough-hewn wood. A mausoleum for a farmer's family was ridiculous, as every neighbor had at some point whispered to another. But that was the condition of marriage his mother had made.

"My children must be buried aboveground," she'd told his father. "It is our way."

His father hadn't argued. Who knew *what* her ways were? She was a Jew and a foreigner, and all he knew was that this beautiful young woman he'd met in London was willing to marry a forty-year-old bachelor and bear his sons. She could have said she wanted him to build her a tower to the moon, and he'd have done it.

As for why Aaron was waking up in the mausoleum . . . well, obviously the ale was giving him nightmares. Damn. He'd really hoped the *stabbing* part of his evening had been the dream, not the waking.

He went to lie back down when his knees knocked the board again, this time sending it clattering to the floor. The figure in the chair jumped up, her hood falling back, and he saw a dark-haired woman, gracefully sliding into middle age—his mother.

"Aaron!"

She rushed to him, hands grabbing his shoulders, fingers digging in. Her face loomed over his—blotchy with tears, eyes swollen, hair bedraggled.

"Say something," she whispered. "Please."

"I drank too much. Again."

Her arms flew around him, head going to his chest, burrowing in, shoulders convulsing in a silent sob.

"I prayed it would be you," she whispered. "I know it's not right for a mother to have favorites, but I always hoped that if God chose one of my children for the blessing, I hoped it would be you. And then after . . ." She hiccuped a sob. "I prayed, Aaron. I *prayed* you'd be the one."

"What one?" He pulled back to look at her. "I really think I drank too much. Maybe if I go back to sleep—"

He tried to lie down, but her fingers dug into his shoulders.

"No! There's no time. Your father wants to seal the coffin. It's been three days. It must be sealed."

"Seal? Coffin?" Aaron looked down. "I'm sleeping in a coffin?"

His mother took his hand and pressed it to a spot above her breast. "What do you feel, Aaron?"

His fingers almost trembled with the beat of her racing heart. Before he could answer, she moved the fingers to his own breast . . . and they went still.

"Now what do you feel?"

"Noth— Bloody hell!" He jumped, almost tumbling back into the coffin. "What—"

"You're *alive*. A different kind of life, Aaron, but you are alive, and that's all that matters."

"All that—? I'm not breathing! I don't have a—"

"You died, and you've been born again. It's a gift of my blood, told to each woman before she weds. Every generation, only a few are blessed. They die, and return to live again . . . to live and live, and nothing can kill them. A blessing beyond measure."

"So I'm alive?" He chewed his lip, then nodded. "All right. But what do we tell Father?"

Her gaze dropped. "We can't tell him, Aaron. You can't ever see him again." She hugged him again. "I'm so sorry, but he wouldn't understand. What you are . . . they have a name for it. They do not understand it."

"What am I?" he asked slowly.

When his mother didn't answer, he reached up, wrapped his hands around her upper arms, and pulled her away from him, his gaze going to hers.

"Mother, what am I?"

She wouldn't look him in the eye. "They call it a . . . a vampire, Aaron, but they don't understand—"

"A *vampire*?"

"It is not what they think, Aaron. You are not some soulless demon. You are still my son—still as good and as God-fearing a man as you ever were."

He forced her chin up, to meet her eyes. "And the blood-taking, Mother? Is that a lie, too?"

"You must feed, yes. On human blood. But it is only feeding, like taking milk from a cow or eggs from a hen. You'll do no harm."

"So I don't need to kill?"

A long hesitation before she hurried on, words tumbling out, almost incomprehensible. "Only once a year, before the anniversary of your death."

"And if I do not?"

Her gaze met his then, eyes blazing. "You must, Aaron. You must!"

"Kill another person to prolong my own life?"

She hesitated again, and the struggle in her eyes sliced him to the core—the conscience of a moral woman at battle with the ferocious instinct of a mother.

"You can make careful choices," she said softly. "Find those who are dying, and relieve them of their suffering. It is only once a year, Aaron. There are people—many people—who are not long for this earth. Take their lives and do some good with it. Honor God in that way, and he will understand."

God? Aaron bit back the word before it flew from his mouth. He suspected God had very little to do with this "blessing," but if his mother had convinced herself that it was so, then he would not destroy her faith by questioning the origin of this taint in her blood. And, as he sat there, holding her, listening to her cry, he knew he would not destroy her hope either. He'd been a loving, loyal son in life, and so he would be in this nonlife.

She said he couldn't see his father, which meant she'd expect him to leave. If he were to decide his new life lay in the New World before the year was up, she would understand.

He had a year. A year of feeding on the blood of men. But if she was right, and it did them no harm, he could stomach that. He would visit her, and feign contentment for her, and before the year was up, he would leave and let her believe he was still walking this earth, somewhere. That much he could do for her.

Aaron slunk through the alley looking for passed-out drunks. *Like a stray dog rooting for scraps in the trash.* He'd been a vampire for nearly a month now, and it wasn't getting any easier. Instinct showed him how to feed, but he despised every second of it.

It didn't seem to have much effect on the humans—his mother had been right about that. Yet skulking through alleys like a scavenger, preying on the weak . . . It made his stomach churn. Or it would, if his stomach could still churn. The only thing his gut did these days was complain when he wasn't paying it enough attention.

As a human, he'd always been able to skip a meal or two during harvest, to work from dawn until dusk and eat when he had time. But now he was at the mercy of his appetite. If he was but an hour or two late, his whole body revolted, turning sluggish and slow, leaving him stumbling through back roads looking for food.

As he walked, a cry came from the dark end of an adjoining alley. He went still, the old urge taking over, homing in on the sound like a cow hearing the bawl of her calf. *Though these days, it was more like a hawk hearing the squeal of a mouse,* he thought. From savior to predator. A blessing indeed. He kicked a stone into the wall and watched a rat scurry off. Then the cry came again. His head lifted, the old instinct refusing to buckle under the new order.

He stopped in midstep and tilted his head. And why should it buckle? Was he not impervious to harm? So his mother had claimed. Perhaps the time had come to test that. What was the worst that could happen? He'd get another blade between the ribs and be free. But if he couldn't die, then there was nothing to keep him from doing the same thing he would have done a month ago . . . and, this time, claim a blood bounty from the would-be predator.

The thug snarled something to the woman in his grasp, and Aaron's lips parted, canines lengthening.

He ran his tongue over them. This was one meal he wouldn't mind taking.

Six months later, Aaron slid along the darkened road, his feet making no sound. He'd learned that his new body came custom-made for hunting. Ahead of him swaggered a man. *Proud of yourself, aren't you,* Aaron thought. *It takes a brave man to beat a whore.*

The world was full of predators. If you knew where to look, you could find one any day of the week, and with very little effort. Aaron no longer worried about the effects of his blood-taking. If one of his victims suffered a bruised neck or a day or two of weakness, he wouldn't feel guilty. It was a world of difference from slinking through alleys. He had his power back, and his pride.

His mother had noticed the change almost immediately.

"See," she said, when he visited her. "You are adjusting. You are *living.*"

And he would continue to live, for another half-year. He'd already begun hinting about traveling to the New World, and his mother was pleased, seeing this as a sign that he was planning for his future.

A couple rounded the corner and headed Aaron's way, and his bearing changed, shoulders lifting, stride shortening, the smooth glide vanishing. A friendly smile and tip of his head as the couple passed. He walked another half-dozen steps, glanced over his shoulder at them, then swung his gaze around, slow and careful. When he was certain he was alone, the predator returned.

As Aaron drew close enough to hear the clomp of the man's boots, his fangs began to extend. An automatic reaction, like salivating. He forced himself to think of something else—of where he'd spend the night—and the canines retracted.

When his quarry hit a T-intersection at the end of the

lane, Aaron closed his eyes to test yet another developing skill. He counted to twenty, then looked. The man was gone. *He turned left,* his gut said. He hurried to the crossroad and looked each way. There, ten yards to the left, was the man.

Aaron smiled. It'd been weeks since he'd guessed wrong. He hadn't figured out how he could track people. It seemed like a sixth sense, being able to "feel" a presence, as if the pulse of life were vibrating through the air. Lately he'd even begun to be able to separate presences, and could track a target through a small group.

As he drew closer to his quarry, he slid into the shadows. No real need to hide. He was, after all, impervious to harm. Still, there was no sense in calling attention to himself. A slow glide through the shadows, then, once he was close enough to smell the man's unwashed body, he'd swoop out and snatch him up, and his victim would be unconscious before he was even sure he'd been attacked. *Like a hawk diving for a mouse.*

Something whispered behind him. Aaron swung around and focused on the sound with a speed and precision that still astounded him. Yet no one was there. He didn't need his eyes and ears to tell him that. He sensed it—or, more accurately, *failed* to sense anyone.

He replayed the sound in his mind. The whisper of leaves? The rustle of blowing paper? Both logical explanations . . . except that he'd been plagued by these odd noises behind him for days now. Aaron took a harder look around. Every sense told him there was no living being there, and yet . . .

He shook off his unease and loped off to catch up with his dinner.

Aaron took one last gulp of blood, shivering as the heat of it streamed down his throat. Then, with more reluctance than he cared to admit, he ran his tongue over the puncture wounds to stop the blood flow. He lifted his head and eased back on his haunches.

"You can take more than that."

Aaron whirled. There, less than a foot away, stood a woman, one who gave off no sense of life; who had slipped up on him as quietly as a phantom. Her dark green woolen cloak blended into the shadows, only accentuating her copper red hair and pale skin. Under the cloak, Aaron caught a glimpse of a dress as finely made as the cloak, spun from the kind of cloud-soft wool he'd only ever seen in shops.

She wasn't beautiful, and she had to be almost as old as his mother, but there was something about her that dared him to look away. Maybe the piercing stare of her green eyes or the arrogant tilt to her sharp chin or the bemused smile on her lips—or maybe it was all of those things, challenging his brain to figure out what the combination meant.

"You can take more than that," she said again. When he only stared, she arched her brows. "Well?"

"You're a vampire," he said slowly.

A slight roll of her eyes. "I should hope so. Do you have many humans popping 'round to give you pointers on blood-taking?"

"You've been following me."

A graceful shrug of her shoulders. "Curiosity. The curse of our race. Live long enough, and anything new tickles your fancy. And you certainly are new. Hereditary, I presume?"

When his brows knitted, she said, "Vampirism is in your bloodline?"

"Is there any other way?"

"Yes, but you don't strike me as the kind of young man who would choose such a thing."

His lip curled. "Who *would* choose such a thing?"

Another elegant shrug, then she waved at the unconscious man. "You can feed more without killing him. Quite a bit more. It's easier that way, so you don't need to hunt every night." Her gaze met his. "Unless you like to hunt every night?"

When he didn't answer, she continued. "Whether one enjoys the hunt or not, nightly can be taxing and inconvenient. Continue feeding, then, and I will—"

"I don't want to kill him."

An exasperated sigh. "May I finish? I was about to say that I will show you how to stop before you pose any danger to his life." An arch of the brows. "Acceptable?"

He nodded, but did nothing.

Her lips twisted in a smile. "Here, let me turn my back and give you some privacy."

He waited until she'd turned around, then repositioned himself on the other side of the man so he could see her while feeding. Several times he stopped drinking, not trusting her to tell him when to cease. With exasperated patience, she had him continually check the man's pulse. When it finally fluttered, she told him to stop.

He closed his eyes, and luxuriated in the warm heaviness of a full stomach.

"Better?" she said.

He opened his eyes to see her watching him. He blinked, forced his fangs to retract, and got to his feet.

"I can teach you more," she said, voice almost a purr.

"Thank you, but no. I don't—won't—need it."

He expected her to press for an explanation, but she just studied him, then nodded—that same infuriating half-smile on her lips.

"You don't intend to make your first kill," she said. "That would be quite a waste, don't you think?"

He didn't answer.

"Well, perhaps then, if you are in your final months, you could use some companionship. It's difficult talking to people now, always worrying that they'll see what you are, never quite able to stop thinking about what *they* are."

"I'd prefer to be left alone."

A polite nod. "As you wish."

With that, she walked away.

As the months passed, Aaron found himself thinking of the red-haired vampire. He'd be feeding and imagine her voice, telling him how to watch for signs that he'd drunk too much. Or he'd be darting through a busy market, always nervous about getting too close to humans, and he'd wonder if such caution was necessary. Could they see that he wasn't breathing? Would they sense that his heart didn't beat? She could have eased his anxieties with tips for blending into the human world.

Mostly, though, he thought about her when he was sitting in the corner of a bar or waking in an inn, surrounded by strangers, not daring to say more than a word or two. For a man who'd always valued the company of others, this was the worst part of his new life: the loneliness.

Now and then, he'd hear a whisper or a rustle behind him, and he'd turn to look for her. Then he'd see the newspaper blowing past or the dead leaves scraping against a windowpane, and he'd tell himself that what he felt was relief.

As the anniversary of his death approached, Aaron's resolve didn't falter. He enacted the final step of his plan, telling his mother that he was setting out for the New World, which she'd come to expect after his months of talking about it. Once gone, he couldn't send a post and risk his father recognizing his handwriting, but his mother understood that, and bid him farewell with only a few tears.

He hated deceiving her, but given the choice between lying to her and breaking her heart, he supposed God would forgive him the falsehood. As for whether God would forgive the rest . . . well, Aaron refused to fret over it. He'd done the best he could with the hand fate had dealt him and, if God condemned him for his choices, that was his decision.

He was sitting in a tavern, enjoying an ale—a *good* ale, in a *good* tavern; surely he deserved that much in his final days. Most of what he'd earned doing odd jobs over the last year he'd given to his mother. One of his brothers had moved his family home to help with the farm, but Aaron still liked to contribute. On his last visit, though, his mother had given the money back and told him to put it to good use in the New World. So he'd donated most to charity, and was indulging himself with the remainder.

As the tavern door swung open, the tavern's patrons turned to gawk and Aaron turned with them. The moment he saw that flash of copper hair, he couldn't help smiling. He covered it with a gulp of beer as the red-haired vampire swept toward his table.

She cast a suspicious glance at the stool and brushed it off before sitting.

"Ale?" he said, lifting his mug.

She only arched one brow, as if she couldn't believe he'd ask.

"They might have wine," he said.

"If they do, I'm quite certain I don't want it." Her gaze locked with his. "You haven't changed your mind, I see."

"Nope."

Again, that keen stare. "You aren't brooding, are you?"

"Nope."

"Good, because there is nothing duller than a brooding vampire." She adjusted her skirts. "Since we are to drink together, introductions are in order. Cassandra DuCharme."

"Aaron." He hesitated, then grunted. "Darnell. Aaron Darnell."

She nodded and waited while he polished off a quarter of his mug, then said, "What if I were to offer you a way out?"

"A way out of what?"

"That vexing moral quandary you've mired yourself in. A way to take a life without feeling guilty about it."

"It's not guilt—"

"Yes, yes." She fluttered her hands. "It's wrong. Morally reprehensible. Violates the Sixth Commandment and all that. But what if there was a loophole? A way to continue living?"

"Not interested."

Another soul-searching stare, then a sigh. "You are a stubborn one, aren't you? Better than brooding, I suppose. Humor me, then. I believe I have found a way for you to live; at least do me the courtesy of hearing my suggestion, as payment for my earlier assistance."

"It won't change my mind, but you can tell me if you like."

She recited an address. "Go there and take a look. I believe you'll see something that would interest you. How much longer do you have before your anniversary?"

"Eight days."

"Perfect. Take three. Spend some time at that address. Then meet me here again, at midnight."

Three days later, she was already in the tavern when he arrived, and had a mug of ale waiting for him.

"Well?" she said.

He shrugged.

"What? You did see what I meant, didn't you? It's the home of a grave robber. One who supplies corpses to the medical schools. Very fresh corpses."

"He kills people and sells the bodies."

"And that doesn't give you any ideas?"

"If you mean killing him, I might as well. If I'm already damned, there's no harm in it, and if God has forgiven me for the rest, he'll forgive me for that. Either way, the world will be better off."

"Good," she said, settling back in her chair. "So you'll kill him and—"

"Oh, I'll kill him. But as a man, not a vampire."

The red-haired vampire slumped forward, looking ready to beat her head against the tabletop, and Aaron almost choked on his beer, as he struggled not to laugh.

"Sorry," he said. "But I said I am resolved."

"No, you're stubborn, and I don't know why I'm wasting my time trying to change your mind."

"Because you're bored? Looking for a challenge?" His lips curved in a slow grin. "Or because I look like something you might want to decorate your bed with?"

She gave an unladylike snort. "My tastes don't run to farm boys."

Aaron only leaned back, stretching his legs.

"Explain this, then," she said, leaning closer. "You obviously feel compelled to do these acts of . . ." A shrug. "Charity, I suppose, perhaps through guilt or a misplaced sense of altruism. But you do them and you enjoy them. You will kill this grave robber to help others, yet you refuse to do it in a way that would prolong your life, and allow you to *continue* helping others. Does that make sense?"

He sipped his beer and gave a soft grunt.

"No, it does not." She slapped her gloves on the table. "I would propose, then, that you take this grave robber's life, as a vampire, and live for another year, since you already intend to kill him."

Again, Aaron only grunted. After a moment, he agreed to give it some thought.

Two days later, Aaron was in the grave robber's house, kneeling behind him, draining the last dregs of blood from his body.

"Make sure you take it all," Cassandra said. "If you leave any, it won't work."

He did as she said, then leaned back, closed his eyes, and shuddered.

"And so you have another year," she murmured.

He opened one eye. "But that's it. Just one more."

"Yes, yes, of course," she said. "Now, come. All this bloodletting has made me hungry. Hunt with me."

He watched her walk away, then rose and followed her into his new life . . . at least for another year.

··BEWITCHED··

THERE ARE MANY LIFE LESSONS MY mother never taught me, including how to deal with assassins. I'd been operating in the supernatural black market for less than a year, and already I had a bounty on my head. I hadn't yet decided whether that was a sign of success or stupidity.

I'd spent the afternoon teaching defensive spells to suburbanite teen witches who'd be better off learning karate. Given that it took them five minutes to cast a successful binding spell, I really hoped they never got cornered in a dark alley. But their mommies wanted them to learn—and were too busy to teach the girls themselves—so I obliged . . . for a price.

But as happy as I was to leave the Stepford-family world of suburbia behind, it was a lot safer than my own neighborhood, where daytime gunfire added a nice touch of ambiance, but also meant that my corpse in the middle of the sidewalk wouldn't be all that out of place. In the last few days, I'd discovered every alternate route to my apartment, and knew which would be cloaked by shadows at every time of day.

I took one of them now, casting sensing spells as I went and using my Aspicio powers to peer through corners before I stepped around them.

Each cautious step drove nails into my ego. If I was under siege, I had to fight back. And I would, if it was just some guy who mistook me for a helpless young woman. But this was Terrance Foley, boss of the nastiest half-demon gang in Chicago. When he wanted a supernatural dead, most of them just picked up a gun and saved him the trouble.

I wasn't stupid enough to piss off a guy like that. Just stupid enough to do business with him and expect a fair deal.

He didn't seem to have sent any goons after me so far. From what I'd heard, it was a closed contract, meaning he wouldn't pay an enterprising freelancer to kill me. Which at least narrowed it down a little.

I was about to step out of the alley when a black BMW sedan pulled up in front of my building. I pulled back into the alley and watched the car through the wall. I'm a dual-parentage supernatural—a witch on my mother's side, and an Aspicio half-demon thanks to my dad. If I had to pick one, I'd keep my witch blood—spells are a lot more versatile. My half-demon power is limited to sight, including a weak form of X-ray vision. Handy at times like this.

The rear passenger door of the BMW opened and a man stepped out. Midthirties, about six foot two. Broad shoulders not quite concealed by a perfectly tailored suit. Blond hair and bright blue eyes. An imposing figure. Good-looking, too, if you went for the cool Germanic type. I didn't.

I'd never seen the guy before, but I knew who he was—or who his family was, at least. The Nasts. Leaders of the premier North American Cabal—a cutthroat corporation whose business practices made Terrance Foley look like a schoolyard thug.

I knew the Nasts had an office in Chicago. But while they might control the black market, they never dirtied their hands with it personally. And now a Nast was walking into my building. Without an entourage. Without even a bodyguard.

I was tempted to stroll in after him and satisfy my curiosity. But caring to live another day, I decided I really wasn't *that* curious, reversed course, and headed back the way I'd come.

I'd just made it to the street behind mine when yet another black car pulled up to the curb, this one a Lincoln and a few years older than the Beamer, meaning someone a few rungs lower. And indeed, the guy who stepped out was a few rungs lower—on both the social and the evolutionary scale. Big bruiser. Ill-fitting suit. Steroid-induced acne.

He spotted me before I could back up.

"Eve Levine?" he called. "Mr. Foley would like to speak to you."

The thug opened the back door and waved me in. I strode forward, but stopped short of "grab and abduct" distance.

"Did he lose my number again?" I said. "Here, let me give it to you. Got a pencil?"

"Get in the car."

"I would, but the question is whether I'll get out of it again. Tell Mr. Foley if he wants to talk to me, he can take me to dinner. Anthony's. Five blocks over. I'm sure your driver can find it."

His left eye twitched. Could just be a tic. Could be a half-demon tell, too, meaning he was about to launch his power. A binding spell kiboshed that plan. He froze, scowl and all.

"Don't," I said. "I may be the new kid on the block, but Mr. Foley knows I'm not stupid enough to get in that car. If he told you to make me, then apparently you're expendable. My guess, though, is that he just told you to give it a shot. You did. I put up a fight. You decided that a public meeting was a reasonable alternative. Safe for me, and safe for Mr. Foley."

I released the spell. He grunted something that could be agreement and got back into the car. I waited until it drove off, then hailed a taxi. An extra expense I couldn't really afford, but under the circumstances, I'd budget it under health insurance.

Anthony's was an Italian restaurant on the boundary between my neighborhood and respectability. Not fancy, but nice enough, with good home-style cooking. The kind of place once frequented by Al Capone. Foley looked right at home.

He started to stand as I approached, then stopped himself as he remembered that I was six feet tall and he wasn't.

"Eve," he said, and motioned for his guard to pull out my chair. "Gorgeous as always."

I wasn't gorgeous. I was young, and Foley was at the age where the two terms were interchangeable, which was where the problem had started.

His gaze slithered over me. "You should wear green more often. It brings out your . . ." He struggled for a way to end the compliment. Since I have dark hair and dark eyes, there's no way to finish that line, so he settled for "beauty."

"Uh-huh." I sat and folded my hands on the table, leaning toward him and lowering my voice. "Still not interested, Mr. Foley. As I've said before, don't take it personally. I don't mix business and pleasure. Ever. If you've done your homework on me, you know that."

"But our business has concluded."

"No, when you finish paying me for that amulet, our business will have concluded."

He leaned toward me and smiled, all teeth. "When you stop being such a stuck-up bitch, I'll finish paying for it. If you're going to charge that much for a cheap piece of jewelry, then I expect more in the bargain."

"The Amulet of Bathin is a one-of-a-kind relic that'll give your shamans enough juice to astral-project past the best Cabal security. I offered it at fair market value and you agreed to my terms. If it's not performing as promised, then I'll take it back and return your deposit."

"I've misplaced it."

My hands clenched under the table, nails digging in, reminding me to keep my cool. That's never easy. I don't deal well with authority. Never have, starting with my mother. She'd been seduced by a demon and forced to bear his child. At least, that was the story she told the Coven. Once, when she'd popped a few too many Valium, she admitted to me that she'd summoned my father herself, wanted his child. A single act of rebellion, quickly regretted, leaving me to pay the price.

Not surprising that I didn't have much respect for my mother after that. Not surprising that I hadn't seen much point in following Coven rules. Not surprising that I got kicked out on my ass as soon as I was old enough to leave. Not surprising that my mother didn't lift a finger to help me when I did. And, not surprising that when every black market contact had told me not to do business with Terrance Foley, I ignored them. I was Eve Levine, dark-magic prodigy and daughter of the lord demon Balam. I could handle a middle-aged half-demon thug like Foley. Only I couldn't. And if I wanted to live long enough to smarten up, it was time to swallow my pride.

"Maybe it *was* overpriced," I said, as calmly as I could.

He smiled, victory sparking in his eyes. "It was."

"All right then." I stood. "You keep the amulet, and I'll keep the deposit. We're square."

* * *

Would he leave it at that? I didn't know Foley well enough to tell. Which meant I hadn't known him well enough to do business with. At least I was a fast learner. Next time I found something that valuable, I'd rinse the dollar signs from my eyes and find a buyer I trusted. Well, one I trusted well enough to do business with.

Foley didn't have his goons follow me from the restaurant, which I supposed was a good sign. I hightailed it back to my apartment, though. I'd make a few calls, see if word on the street changed and, if not, it'd be moving day. That didn't bother me; I never stayed in one place long. It was the running-away part I hated.

When I reached my apartment door, I cast a sensing spell. It came back positive. Someone was inside.

I readied an energy bolt, then moved against the door, bringing my face closer. A spot cleared, like a dirty peephole. Inside, I could see . . . gray cloth.

The door opened. My hand flew up, spell ready.

"Ms. Levine."

I looked up into impossibly blue eyes and felt a double shot of recognition. The first told me he was the Nast I'd seen earlier. The second said he was a sorcerer—a racial warning system. Witches and sorcerers have never been the best of friends.

"Come in," he said, moving back.

I hesitated, then stepped inside. "Something tells me we're doing this wrong, considering it's my apartment."

No hint of a smile warmed those icy eyes. He only dipped his chin, acknowledging the point. "My apologies for breaking in. There were some unsavory characters in the hall. This seemed wiser. I used a spell so I wouldn't damage the lock."

"You know witch magic?" That's rare for sorcerers. Rarer still for Cabal ones.

He shrugged. "A little. Very little, I'm afraid, which is why I'm here." He extended a hand. "Kristof Nast."

Now my internal warning system screamed louder than a banshee's wail. This wasn't just some Nast VP, second cousin twice removed. It was the CEO's oldest son, the heir to the empire. I couldn't even imagine what he was doing in my apartment. I was pretty sure I didn't want to find out.

When I didn't respond, he just stood there, hand out, waiting until I shook it.

"Look, whatever you think I've done—" I began.

"I'm not Terrance Foley, Ms. Levine. If you'd done something to displease my Cabal, I would hardly show up myself."

So he knew about Terrance? What had he heard? I was tempted to ask, but wisely kept my mouth shut until I could venture a calm "How can I help you, Mr. Nast?"

"I want training. Witch magic training. I believe you offer that?"

I headed into the living room, taking a moment to compose myself. He couldn't even be bothered to come up with a credible lie? I was in serious, serious shit. I racked my brain to think of something, anything, I could have done to piss off a Cabal. But on the scale of badasses, I ranked about a four. Okay, maybe a three, but I was working on it. Still, I'd done nothing to warrant the attention of any Cabal, let alone the Nasts. Which meant someone was spreading stories.

"What have you heard?" I said as he took a seat on my couch.

"That you're a good teacher. Not the best, but that's understandable, given your youth. You're discreet, though, which is my most important requirement."

"You really want witch training?"

Those cool eyes met mine. "That's what I said, isn't it?"

"I know your Cabal has its resident witch. Olivia Enwright. She's decent enough. Why come to me?"

He gave me a look that said if I was honestly asking, then maybe I wasn't as bright as he'd hoped. No Cabal sorcerer would ever admit that he saw value in witch magic. Not openly, at least, meaning he couldn't use a Cabal witch's services.

"I'm a mediocre spellcaster," Nast said. "My position doesn't require any particular knowledge or aptitude in that area. However, there are facets of witch magic I could use in other areas of my life."

"Such as?"

That cool look again, handsome face impassive. He didn't say "None of your damn business," but I heard the words loud and clear.

He went on, "Corporate headquarters are in Los Angeles, as I'm sure you know. If I could persuade you to relocate there temporarily, that would be ideal. It's not required, though. I have monthly meetings at our office here. We could schedule our lessons then. I'll ask, though, that we meet in a hotel. If we are seen, it'll be presumed I'm having an affair, which no one will question."

My gaze dropped to his hand.

"I'm not married," he said. "Nor am I in a relationship. I meant affair in the broadest definition of the word. Now, if that is acceptable, we should discuss terms."

I shook my head and stood. "Not interested. Sorry. I appreciate that you considered me. I'm grateful for the offer. Blah-blah-blah. But no."

"And your objection is?"

"Everything."

I headed for the door. When he didn't follow, I went back to see him looking out the window as he tucked his pager back into his pocket, having presumably called for his car.

"Yes, the view sucks," I said. "If you're going to point out that my apartment is a shitty hole, I already know that. If you're going to suggest that I could afford better with your offer, don't bother. I like where I am and I don't want an upgrade—not in apartments, not in clientele. I already tried that, and I learned my lesson."

"I'm not Terrance Foley, Ms. Levine."

"No, you're a whole other level of scary. Now, if you'll excuse me . . ."

"Will you walk me down?"

"Elevator on the left. Door straight down the hall."

He turned that icy gaze on me and, to my shame, I felt my gut chill under it. As much as I wanted to tell him to go to hell, I didn't dare.

"Fine," I said. "I'll walk you out."

When we stepped from the building, there was indeed a car waiting. For me, not him. Foley's goons sat in their idling Lincoln.

I stopped dead, then backed up into the shadows of the doorway.

"You son of a bitch," I said.

His brows lifted. He didn't hear that one a lot, I suppose. Not to his face anyway.

"Is this a threat?" I said.

"Of course not. I merely asked you to walk me down—"

"Because you saw them waiting. You're telling me I'd better agree to your terms or they won't be the worst of my problems. Or maybe they will. Turn you down and you'll turn me over." I glowered up at him. "I dealt with you fairly. You brought me an offer. I refused it politely and respectfully."

"You did. And I'm asking you to reconsider."

"Go to hell, Nast. I—"

"I'm not threatening you, Ms. Levine. I'm simply pointing out that this isn't a one-way deal. Yes, you can help me, but I believe I can help you as well." He glanced at the goons, who'd turned to gape at us through the tinted glass. "Would you like me to take care of this problem for you?"

"No."

Another brow arch. "I think you would. In fact, I think you'd like it very much."

"And, in return, I'd owe you. I may be young, but I'm not an idiot. I'm not about to get into anyone's debt, especially yours."

I walked back into the building.

I packed my bags and moved out that night. In this life, you learn to rent only furnished apartments. And you learn to budget for the occasional forfeit of that "last month's rent" paid in advance.

I checked into a hotel. A decent Holiday Inn. I'd earned enough from my deal with Foley to afford it, even if he hadn't paid full price. A bigger move—straight out of the state—was a definite possibility, but a last resort. I still had a few irons in the fire in Chicago, not to mention that very sweet teaching gig with the suburban witchlings.

I woke up at eight to my pager beeping. Two calls. One was from the Coven leader, Ruth Winterbourne. The other was John Weiss, a necromancer I'd done a job with a few weeks ago. I walked a block to a pay phone before calling Weiss back.

"Eve. I got you. Good." He sounded out of breath.

"What's up?"

"I owe you money."

"Huh?"

"That last job. The spells I sold for you. You thought

I took more than my cut. I was sure I hadn't, but I was just doing some banking, and I realized I screwed up. I owe you three hundred. I'm so sorry."

"Okay . . ."

"Can I send the money the usual way? Western Union? You'll have it by noon. And, again, I'm really sorry. It was an honest mistake. I hope we can work together again soon."

"Okay . . ."

We talked for another minute. After I hung up, I stood there, wondering what that had been about.

I'd been sure Weiss had screwed me over with the pay-out. I'd called him on it, but it hadn't been a big enough deal to cause trouble over. Just another lesson learned, and I'd moved him off my list of contacts.

Did he have something he needed help with now? Realized he shouldn't have burned this bridge so fast? Yep. I was pretty sure I'd get another call in a day or two, with a new job offer. Whether I took it remained to be seen.

I called Ruth next. She had a council meeting in Illinois next week. Was I still in Chicago? Could she drop by and see me? Paige was coming and she kept asking about me and they'd love to see me if I was free.

I said I wasn't in Chicago anymore. That lie came harder than any I'd told in months. I wanted to see them—God, I wanted to see them. I missed babysitting Paige. I missed talking to Ruth. But I couldn't let Ruth see how I lived now. I wasn't ashamed of it—I just didn't want to upset her. She didn't deserve that.

Growing up in the Coven as a half-demon was an experience I wouldn't wish on my worst enemy. The Coven prides itself on using only white magic—when it uses magic at all—and I was the embodiment of everything opposite. Or that's what my mother told me.

Looking back now, I'm not sure how much of it was unwarranted prejudice, and how much of it I earned.

My mother tried to "warn" me in hopes of curbing my powers and turning me into a docile little witch who would make *her* look good. Her witch sisters already treated her with suspicion for having had a demon's child, willingly or not. So she wanted me to prove that there was nothing wrong with me. I was just like every other Coven girl. And in expecting me to react that way, she'd proven how little she'd known her only child.

The Coven witches did treat me differently. I didn't imagine that. My earliest memories were of sitting alone at Coven meetings, watching the other girls play, knowing that if I went over, their mothers would whisk them away. They didn't mistreat me, but I knew they were watching, waiting to see what effect the taint of my demon blood might have. If I'd been the good little girl my mother wanted, maybe they'd have come to realize there was nothing wrong with me. But I couldn't be that girl. They expected me to be bad, so I complied.

On the scale of bad children, I'd have rated about a four. I misbehaved. I disobeyed. I caused trouble. But I was hardly the embodiment of demonic evil. When the adults shunned me, though, the other girls saw an easy target for every bad impulse *they* had. They tormented me and bullied me and blamed me for everything that went wrong, even stealing things just to plant them in my room.

The worse they got, the worse I got. I had only one ally in the Coven. Ruth Winterbourne. But it wasn't enough. Her influence was too little, too late, and I grew up knowing that the only person I could trust—really trust—was myself.

By the time I was a teenager, I was trolling the black markets of Boston, buying—and often stealing—darkmagic grimoires, immersing myself in that side of our world. The Coven kicked me out and I'd found myself adrift in a world with only one tool for survival: magic. I was a powerful witch and half-demon, and that was how I would survive.

After breakfast, I headed over to the Lincoln Park campus of DePaul University. No, I wasn't a student. I'd gotten my high school diploma and knew better than to push my luck. I had a coffee date with Molly Crane, a witch a couple of years younger than me, who *was* a DePaul student. Also a first-rate spoiled brat and second-rate spellcaster, but with the kind of connections that meant I could spare an hour for a weekly coffee with her. I even picked up the tab sometimes.

When I found Molly outside our usual spot, she was sitting with her aunt, Lavina Crane, Chicago's most notorious dark witch. A former teacher, Lavina now traded in the black market. She'd still take on the occasional student, though. Very occasional. Lavina Crane was the reason I'd moved to Chicago. I'd practically offered myself into indentured servitude for a chance to train under her. She'd taken one look at my résumé and told me to come back in five years.

"Eve!" Molly said, leaping up. She embraced and air-kissed me, bangle bracelets chattering. "Aunt Lavina drove in from Kenilworth this morning to talk to you."

"That'll be all, Molly," Lavina said, dismissing her with a wave.

Molly motioned that she'd be inside waiting.

"You've done the impossible, Eve Levine," Lavina said when Molly was gone. "You've impressed me. That's rare for any witch. But a Coven witch?" Her plucked brows disappeared under her hair. "I never thought I'd see the day. I take it you're still interested in training under me?"

I gaped, then cleared my throat. "Sure. I mean, of course. I'd be honored."

"Good. We'll start next week. My house. Two o'clock Wednesday. Same terms as before. You'll run errands for me—courier my goods about, convince debtors that delayed payment isn't good for their health, that sort of thing. Agreed?"

I nodded. She handed me her card, with her home address and phone number, and penciled me into her Day-Timer.

I found Molly inside, changing cassette tapes in her Walkman.

"When do you start?" she asked as I sat down.

"Next week."

"Damn, you're so lucky. I'm her sister's kid and I'll be lucky if she agrees to train me. You'll pass along what you learn, right?"

"Sure." I sipped my coffee. "I don't know what you told her about me, but thanks. I owe you."

Molly grinned, her pixie face lighting up. "I'll take the IOU, but I didn't do more than put in a good word for you. You did all the work on this one. Hot damn, did you do the work. I know you've got nerve, Eve, but this was ballsy, even for you."

"How did you hear about it?" I asked carefully, having no idea what she meant.

"From Aunt Lavina, when she called and asked to set up a meeting with you. She says she got a call before she even picked up the newspaper. The second it hit the newsstands, the grapevine was popping."

"Newspaper?"

I saw a folded *Chicago Tribune* two tables away. I went over and grabbed it.

"You didn't know it made the news?" Molly said as I

spread the paper. "Not major city news, but for supernaturals, it might as well have been the front page."

When I tried to flip through, she took the paper and turned to an article. "Local Businessman Electrocuted." Terrance Foley, fifty-eight, had died in his home last night, the apparent victim of an electrical malfunction. . . .

"Electrical malfunction." Molly chortled. "No malfunction there. Your energy bolt works just fine. Setting the scene to look like an accident, though? Genius. And getting past his security? Aunt Lavina was totally blown away. That's the kind of thing a Cabal can pull off, but a lone witch?" She whistled. "You showed 'em, Eve. With one strike, you jumped clear into the ranks of 'don't mess with me, motherfucker.' "

I nodded, still staring at the article. I guess that explained Weiss's behavior this morning.

"And everyone knows it was me?" I said.

"Duh. The missing Amulet of Bathin? With a cursestone left in its place? Kinda gave it away. Take credit for the killing, get that amulet back, and collect your assassin fee from the Nasts. One sweet deal."

"Assassin fee."

"You didn't think anyone would know about that? I'm sure that's what the Nasts were hoping—that no one would connect them to this—but Foley's men saw you talking to Kristof Nast yesterday." She grinned. "Is Kristof as hot as they say?"

"I wouldn't exactly use the word *hot*."

"Mmm, power is always hot. He's single, too. Did you know that? His wife took off a few years ago. Left him with two little boys. Single daddy. Sexy older guy. Multimillionaire tycoon." She sighed. "Too bad he's a sorcerer."

"Tragic." I checked my watch. "Whoops, gotta run. Same time next week?"

"Absolutely. Better yet, let's do lunch. My treat."

She beamed at me like I was her new best friend. Which I suppose I was. Not my choice for a bosom buddy, but Molly was useful, so I agreed we'd get together next week.

I walked around the campus, trying to decide my next move. Every supernatural knew where the Nasts' Chicago office was—on prime downtown property. And if I walked in there, I'd be kicked out on my ass so hard I wouldn't be able to sit down for a week. I could do it to make a statement, let him know I was looking for him. A bold move, but not necessarily a bright one.

I was pacing a walkway between two buildings when a shadow stretched out beside mine. I glanced over to see Kristof Nast and tried not to look surprised.

He kept pace beside me for at least a minute, then said, "You're welcome."

"I didn't thank you, and I'm not going to. I never asked you to do that for me. And if you think that puts me in your debt—"

"It doesn't. The gift came with no strings attached."

I snorted. "Right. I don't know what your game is—"

"My *game* is business. The wooing of a potential contract employee, hired to train me in basic witch magic."

He'd stopped walking, meaning I had to stop and turn to face him.

"Terrance Foley was becoming a nuisance," he continued. "My father has wanted to be rid of him for years. I found a way to do it without clearly laying his death at our door. Mr. Foley's colleagues may believe I hired you to kill him, and I'm sure my father will realize it, but *our* colleagues will never believe a Nast would enter into such business with a witch. You helped me and, in return, I freed you from a dangerous situation and cemented your local reputation. One could argue that I gave more than I received, but for me, that's a standard business practice when dealing with reluctant potential employees."

"Killing their enemies?"

An elegant shrug. "If necessary. It's usually simpler than that. Make their legal problems disappear. Resolve their debts—monetary or otherwise. Send them on an overdue vacation with their spouse. All I expect in return is their attention and consideration. They don't particularly wish to work for me, so I'm trying to change their mind."

"And if you don't?"

"Then I chalk it up to the cost of running a business. But I'm hoping that won't happen here. I can be very useful, Ms. Levine, as you've seen. I think you could use a little of my help and, even more, a little of my experience, because the lack of that is clearly what got you into trouble in the first place."

"What got me into trouble was doing business with a lech who wouldn't take no for an answer."

"Exactly."

I glanced up at him sharply.

He waved to a bench. "May we sit so I can explain where you went wrong with Mr. Foley? I know you don't want my advice, so it comes at no cost or obligation."

I strode to the bench and sat.

He took the other end. "I presume Terrance Foley showed an interest in you from your first meeting? Made a pass? Complimented your appearance? Flirted?"

"Yes, but if I refused to work for every guy who did that—"

"I'm sure it would greatly reduce your clientele pool. However, what you failed to consider was Mr. Foley's pride."

"If you're saying I led him on, I didn't. I was clear from the start. I don't mix business and pleasure."

"Which only increased the challenge and the value of the conquest. The harder you resisted, the greater the humiliation. It was no longer a matter of wanting to bed you. He had to."

I could say that was totally unfair and I shouldn't have to deal with shit like that just because I was a young woman. But he had a point.

"Furthermore," he continued, "when the situation became dangerous, you should have struck. Fast and hard. He double-crossed you in a business deal, and everyone was waiting to see how you'd handle it. Running away?" He shook his head.

"I—"

"You resisted your natural urge to fight back and did what you thought was the sensible thing." He glanced over at me. "Am I right?"

I said nothing.

"Your first instinct was correct. Act on it next time."

"Kill anyone who double-crosses me?"

Those cool eyes met mine. "Is that a problem?"

"No."

"I didn't think so. Initially, yes, you'll have to use lethal force. After that, you can rely on your reputation, show mercy where it's warranted."

His pager went off. He looked at it, frowning, then stood. "I'm afraid I need to cut this meeting short. Warning you against doing business with powerful men isn't, I suppose, the best way to convince you to work for me. However, as I'm sure you've noticed, you won't have the same problem with me as you did with Mr. Foley. You're an attractive young woman, but . . ."

"I'm a witch. Therefore, off the menu."

He shrugged. "I don't share the common prejudice against witches. But, like you, I don't mix business and pleasure. This is business. So, may I suggest a trial run? A single lesson when I return for next month's meeting?"

He took out a card and wrote a number on the back. "That's my private line, unmonitored by the Cabal. I'll ask that you use it—and only it—to contact me. If it rings through to the answering service, hang up. I'm in town on the twentieth. I'd appreciate a call the week before."

I took the card.

As much as I chafed at getting career pointers from a sorcerer, I could use the help. The supernatural underground was a tricky place to maneuver, and an easy place to get lost.

When I'd marched out into the world, I'd discovered I wasn't nearly the badass I thought I was. I had the instinct, as Nast said, but not the experience to use it.

Lacking that experience, though, I knew better than to leap into bed—even figuratively—with a guy like Kristof Nast. So in the weeks that followed, as I set myself up in a new apartment, I discreetly asked around about him, and what I got only confirmed my own impressions. The two words that came up most often were *ruthless* and *fair*. Exactly the qualities I wanted in a business mentor.

Everyone agreed on something else, too—that even if he hadn't been the CEO's eldest son, he'd have been the Cabal's best choice for its future. He didn't coast on his birthright. He worked his ass off and earned his position. I respected that.

A week before he was due to return to Chicago, I called and set an appointment.

The morning of our first lesson, Nast couriered a hotel key to my new apartment. He didn't tell me not to saunter over there, flashing my key through the front lobby, but the fact that he sent it, rather than having me pick it up at the desk, conveyed the same message. He was fine with people thinking he was having an affair. Not so fine with them knowing a witch was on the other side of that hotel room door. That was fair. I didn't want anyone thinking I was sleeping with him either. It wouldn't do our reputations any favors.

So I used cover and blur spells to get into the hotel and up to the room. It was a good hotel, of course, with a suite, which I figured he'd chosen intentionally, sparing the awkwardness of working together in a room with a huge bed. A nice touch, as were the cold drinks and sandwiches he'd had brought up before I arrived.

Our appointment was for seven. He arrived two minutes early, knocking before letting himself in. He took off his suit jacket, but left his shoes on and didn't loosen his tie. He was dressed for business, and this was an extension of that.

He greeted me and asked how I was. Did I have any trouble finding the hotel? Was it satisfactory? Were the snacks to my liking? Nothing remotely personal.

"Before we begin, we should discuss compensation," he said.

"What did you have in mind?"

"You may set the price."

I laughed. "What if I say ten grand a lesson?"

He took out his wallet. "I presume cash is satisfactory? I'd prefer not to leave a paper trail."

As he counted off bills, I tried not to gape. I'd never even *seen* thousand-dollar bills.

"You're kidding, right?" I said. "I'm good, but I'm not that good."

"No, I'm sure you aren't." He held out the money.

I eyed it. "If I take that, then I owe you, don't I? Overpay me and I'm in your debt."

"Naturally."

I plucked one bill from the bunch and pocketed it.

"Never give anyone the chance to place you in his debt," he said, folding the remaining bills back into his wallet. "And never miss the opportunity to put him into yours. Now, I believe the next lesson is mine, Ms. Levine."

"Eve, please. I know you're just trying to be respectful, but every time I hear Ms. Levine, I think my mother's around."

"All right then. I'll return the informality. It's Kristof."

"I bet no one ever calls you Kris, do they?"

"They don't."

"Do I dare ask what happens if they do?"

A hint of what could be a smile. "You'd have to try it and find out."

"Something tells me that's a lesson I don't want to learn."

I waved him into the living room.

I agreed to continue the lessons. There was no reason not to. He was exactly the kind of student I'd expected—hardworking, if not terribly adept. He was like the kid in class whom I would have ignored. Never late. Never off sick. Never overeager or enthusiastic, but dedicated, polite, and respectful, plowing through the work on sheer determination. Boring as hell, with the personality of a department store mannequin.

I shouldn't say that. Ruth would have said it was cruel and he didn't deserve that. I'd take a hundred of Kristof Nast over one of the suburban brats I was teaching. Still, there were times when I wasn't really sure I was teaching an actual person. Every now and then I'd catch a shimmer of wit or character under that frosty exterior, but it always vanished so fast I was convinced it was just my mind playing tricks.

The spells Nast wanted to know were simple ones. Too simple. Basic protective magic and healing potions. It made sense to choose easy magic—with his weak spellcasting powers, he wasn't going to be able to cast stronger witch spells—but this wasn't the sort of magic needed by a guy with a team of bodyguards and a whole Cabal hospital at his disposal. I began to suspect I really was being wooed as a potential employee—one who does more than spellcasting lessons. Nast's father had thought he was clever, hiring a witch assassin. Was that his real goal? Groom me as a sleeper agent?

If it was a killer he wanted, he'd come to the wrong woman. I didn't have a problem with the concept, but there was a big difference between killing a thug who was already gunning for me and killing a stranger for cash. That's where I drew the line.

For now, I was content to teach him simple spells, especially at a grand a pop. The professional advice was a huge bonus. While I appreciated Lavina's teachings, we didn't share a similar worldview. Nast's style was more my own.

He'd begin or conclude every lesson by giving me one of his own. That's what he was doing one summer afternoon. He had an important business dinner at eight, so he'd bumped our appointment up to four. He'd walked in and said, "I hear Lavina wants to wrest control of Dhamphir from the Granville family. I suppose she expects your help with that."

Dhamphir was a black-market magic shop that fronted as a nightclub, and both incarnations were very successful. I didn't ask how Nast heard that. I wasn't surprised, though. He was like the lion sunning himself on the highest rock, watching all the lesser beasts scamper around the water hole. He never involved himself in their daily business, but no part of it escaped his notice.

"It goes above and beyond your contract with her," he said.

"I know. She said it'd be a separate job. Paid employment."

"Good. And the job itself?"

"I don't know enough about Dhamphir yet to agree. It sounds easy. The Granvilles aren't what you'd call a force to be reckoned with, which makes me wonder why someone hasn't wrested control from them yet. I'm guessing there's more to it."

"You'd be guessing right. The Granvilles are backed by another investor. You'd have to dig hard to find it, though. The Cortez Corporation."

"Ah. That makes sense, then. If the Cortez Cabal is bankrolling Dhamphir, I don't want anything to do with—"

Nast's pager beeped. He checked the message and got up so fast, I jumped.

"I need to take this," he said, and strode into the bedroom.

I helped myself to the room service he'd ordered and tried not to eavesdrop on his conversation.

When he came out, he headed straight for his coat.

"I'll be missing my lesson today," he said. "The payment is yours, of course."

"We can reschedule for tomorrow. I'm free."

"I'm heading home immediately. One of my sons was in an accident."

"Shit. Is he okay?" I grabbed his briefcase for him as he looked around, distracted. "No, I guess that's a dumb question if you're blowing off the meeting to get back there."

"No, it's not— He had a game this afternoon and was

hit in the head with a baseball. A possible concussion, but nothing serious. I just . . . I should be there."

He started for the door, then stopped. "My car. I need to page—"

"A taxi will be faster. I'll call one. You head down."

He nodded, got halfway out the door, then glanced back. "Thank you, Eve."

"Go." I shooed him out and went for the phone.

In all the time I'd been training Kristof Nast, I'd never stopped seeing him as a Cabal sorcerer. He was a means to an end, nothing more. But when he tore out that door to fly to his son's side, he became something more. He became a person, maybe even someone I wanted to know better.

Nast called me the next day to reschedule. His son was fine. Just a bad headache.

"Do you remember the brew for that?" I said. "We went over it last month, or I could send you some."

"I'd appreciate it. I don't think I'll get a chance to pick up the ingredients. You can courier it to the L.A. office."

"I'll put Lavina's name on it as the return address. Will that work?"

"Yes, thank you. As for our next lesson, I'll be in town next week for that meeting I missed."

He gave me the details and asked if that would work. I said it would. As he was about to hang up, I said, "Kristof?"

"Hmm?"

"About your sons. That's why you want the healing and protection magic, isn't it? For them."

I swore the line frosted in the silence that followed.

"I'm not prying," I said. "I'm only asking because there are other spells I can teach you. Other potions, too. Specifically for children, childhood illnesses and whatnot. Some of the others might be a little strong. If that's why you want them, we should discuss that."

"It is."

"Good. I'll go make a batch of headache brew and send it out."

A week later I was kicking back in a hotel suite, eating sandwiches and eyeing the bottle of Perrier with suspicion. I knew it was the fashionable thing, but I really didn't get the point of bottling water. Give me a Coke any day. And none of that new Diet Coke either. I like my sugar straight.

It was 7:05 when Nast rapped on the door. I had to double-check the clock. He was never late—not even by a minute. When he came in, I could see why.

"Is your son okay?" I asked, standing.

"Hmm?" He took a second to focus on me, those bright blue eyes bleary. He ran his hand over his face and straightened, pulling himself together. "Yes, thank you. He's fine."

"You look like you got hit by the El train," I said.

He glanced up, giving me something that could have been a small, tired smile. Very small. Very tired.

"Rough day, huh?"

"Hmm."

"Come in and sit before you fall over. And no, I won't ask what's wrong. I know the rules. No personal stuff."

"Is that a rule? If so, I don't believe I set it."

"You don't need to. The Keep Out sign can't be missed. Neon letters, ten feet tall and flashing. I'm pretty sure I heard sirens, too."

"Oh." He gave me an odd look, then said, "Yes, I suppose so."

He moved into the living room.

"You look like you could use home cooking," I said.

"Can't help you there, but I'm handy with a room service menu."

He hesitated, and looked ready to tell me not to bother, then nodded, "Soup if they have it. And Scotch. A double. Single malt." Another hesitation. "Unless you'd prefer I didn't drink before a lesson."

"Something tells me you don't make a wild drunk. A double single malt Scotch it is."

"Get something for yourself, too."

I grinned. "I intend to."

Nast wasn't in any rush to start his lesson. He wanted to talk about my dilemma with Lavina and Dhamphir . . . or, I'm sure, wanted to listen to me talk about it, so he could rest. I explained that I'd dug up the evidence I needed to support the Cabal link and presented it to Lavina, who'd brushed it off. When the food came, he downed his Scotch in one gulp, with a shudder that said it wasn't his usual drinking style.

He picked at his soup, stirring it more than eating it, not saying a word until, gaze still on his bowl, he said, "My father didn't appreciate me jetting home last week. It was an important meeting and . . ." A one-shouldered shrug. "A bump on the head is hardly life-threatening."

"It could be," I said. "I'm sure your son was happy to have you there."

"His name's Sean. He's seven."

"Then he definitely would have wanted his dad there. You did the right thing. Not that you need me to tell you that, of course. I'm just saying—"

"I know. My father was fine with it last week. Groused a little, saying that's what nannies are for, but that was all. Then today, he found out one of the companies he acquired is losing money, so I got an hour-long telephone tirade about my lack of responsibility last week."

"Did you have anything to do with buying the company?"

"I advised against it. My father overruled me. But *that* had nothing to do with me going home last week. He was angry about the loss and wanted to vent, so suddenly he decided I'd been irresponsible last week, giving him a target." He leaned back on the sofa. "That's par for the course with my father. He's not an easy man to get along with. I didn't particularly need that tirade in the middle of the day, when I was already running behind, and I'd barely hung up when my youngest called. He got a birthday card from his mother today."

"Oh. That's good. Isn't it?"

"His birthday was last month."

I didn't know what to say to that. *Then she's a stupid bitch* came to mind, but it didn't seem to be an appropriate response.

Nast was obviously trying to open up to me—hence the quickly downed Scotch—and I wanted to say something. But what? Rumor had it that his wife had been the one to leave. Had he fought it? Did he want her back? None of my business, but not having a clue about the situation meant I couldn't respond to this without risk of jamming my foot in my mouth and shutting his for good.

So I said, "Oh," and sat there, like an idiot.

"Bryce—that's my younger son—wasn't even two when she left," he went on. "Everyone said that was good, that he'd be too young to remember her, and that Sean was the one I had to worry about. But it's the opposite. Sean's fine with it. They weren't close, as odd as that may sound. She seemed like she'd make a good mother. That was important. But I suppose she *knew* it was important—part of the deal—so she played her role until the kids actually arrived. Anyway, Sean got over her leaving. Bryce hasn't. There's really no substitute for a mother."

"If you're blowing off important meetings for them, then I'd say you're doing a damn good job of substituting."

His nose wrinkled, sloughing off the reassurance. That wasn't what he wanted. What did he want? Just someone to talk to, I think.

"I'm going to take Bryce out when I get home. Just the two of us. Overcompensating, but . . ." He shrugged. "It might help."

"It will."

He moved his now-cold soup aside. "We were going to talk about tailoring the spells and potions to children."

"Right. I brought a couple of books. Let me grab them."

Things changed after that. Kristof relaxed enough for me to start thinking of him *as* Kristof, not just calling him that to his face.

The key to getting him to relax, not surprisingly, was his kids. And that was the key to getting me to see him differently, too. The more he talked about his sons, the more respect I had for him. It was like seeing a mythical being come to life—a real parent, the kind I'd heard existed, but never met. Certainly never had myself.

When he came for his lessons, I'd ask about his boys, and he'd talk about them for a few minutes before we got down to work.

I guess a guy like Kristof Nast had learned not to let his guard down. The world has to see him as a cold, cutthroat corporate leader, not a single dad juggling play dates and baseball games. I was a safe outlet for that—someone who wouldn't think less of him if he had to interrupt our lesson to call home and see how his son did on his math test. Someone who was too low on the totem pole to ever use that weakness against him.

So he relaxed. Nothing drastic. The tie came off, the collar was unbuttoned, there was a little more conversation. The occasional smile. Even, once or twice, a laugh.

A couple of months later, as fall was setting in, I was the one calling him to reschedule a lesson. I was running an errand for Lavina—a courier job that had gone sour. I'd avoided an ambush by the client, who'd decided he didn't want to pay for the goods and brought along two buddies to support his point of view. When I called Lavina, though, she wanted me to trade in my messenger cap for a pair of brass knuckles.

"Teach him not to mess with me, Eve. Then bring back my scroll and the payment."

"Sure. I'll do that tomorrow, when he's lowered his guard . . . and gotten rid of his guards."

"No, you'll do it now."

I'd argued. I'd warned her that I thought this new client was trouble. And I was annoyed that in spite of my warnings, she seemed to be pushing ahead with the Dhamphir project, and not happy that I refused to help out. Besides, though I didn't say it, I had a more pressing—and better paying—engagement that evening, with Kristof.

When I balked, she threatened. So I did my best. By the time I had payment in hand, though, it was six thirty. I still needed to take the goods to Lavina, go home, and clean up.

I explained to Kristof. He said he'd be at the hotel. I could come by if I felt up to it, or skip it if I was too tired. I promised to be there by eight.

I walked in to the smell of spaghetti. A pot of sauce was bubbling on a hot plate. Kristof was in the living room, reading a business magazine. He walked into the kitchen behind me.

"I thought you could use dinner," he said.

"Where'd you pick this stuff up?" I asked.

"The grocery store."

When I turned to gape, he arched his brows. "I have children. The ability to cook isn't an option."

I could point out that, for him, it *was* an option—one that came with being rich enough to hire chefs. I could also point out that, from what I'd heard about his wife, she wouldn't have exactly been baking cookies for the kiddies either. It wouldn't matter. To him, being a proper parent meant knowing how to cook.

"I'll get the pasta going," he said. "Go sit down. Get something from the minibar."

I grabbed a beer and went to sit. There was nothing to read, so I picked up his magazine, which looked about as interesting as a dishwasher manual. When I picked it up, though, something fell out.

"*MAD* magazine?" I said as I walked back into the kitchen, waving it. "Are you planning to take over the company? Doing your background research?"

"It's for my sons."

"The seven-year-old? Or the four-year-old?"

"They're very advanced for their ages." He fixed me with that cool look he did so well. "I hope you aren't suggesting that *I* was reading it."

"And I hope, by stuffing it in *Fortune*, you aren't suggesting that I'd give a rat's ass *what* you're reading."

"True. Habit, I suppose." He took the lid off a pot of boiling water. "Spaghetti or linguini?"

"Do you think I'd know the difference?"

"Linguini, then. Not appropriate with the sauce, but I prefer it."

I stayed in the kitchenette, watching him cook and drinking my beer.

"So, are you going to talk to me about what happened today with Lavina?" he said after a minute. "This isn't the first time she's done this."

"She's punishing me for not helping her with Dhamphir. She said she was fine with my decision, but then she keeps pulling this shit." I took a long draw on the beer. "I think the way she's doing it bugs me more than what she's doing. It's sneaky. Underhanded."

"As a master of the underhanded business maneuver, I beg to differ. It's spiteful. Sneaky is the sign of a clever manipulator. Spiteful is the sign of a petty one."

"Point taken." I finished the beer.

"Grab another," he said. "Dinner will be a couple of minutes."

"Nope, one's my limit." I crushed the can and tossed it into the trash.

"She's not going to give up on Dhamphir," he said. "You know that. By associating with her, you're setting yourself up for trouble, even if you stay out of the deal. And I suspect she won't let you stay out of the deal."

"I'm not budging on that. She knows it. Still, I think I'm going to have to break it off with her. Which I hate. I came to Chicago just for her."

"Then maybe it's time to leave Chicago." He stirred the noodles. "Come to L.A. Work for me."

When I didn't respond, he looked over. "You knew that was coming eventually. Yes, I wanted to learn those spells for the boys, but as I'm sure you've guessed, I've reached the limits of my talents in that regard. There are still a few things I'd like to work on, but . . ." That elegant shrug. He lifted a noodle and offered it to me to try.

"Not enough to keep coming by every month for a lesson," I said. "So this is the big moment, then. Come work for you or bye-bye training—yours and mine."

His lips pressed together, the old chill creeping into his

eyes. "I wouldn't do that, Eve. I'd think you'd know that by now."

Did I? Not really. Kristof may have loosened up, but I never doubted that once I outlived my usefulness, he'd be gone.

When I didn't answer, he turned his back and pulled the pot off the stove, shoulders and jaw set, not a glance or word my way.

"What do you want me to say?" I asked when he handed me a plate of pasta. "You came to me for training. You stayed in hopes of cultivating a future employee. I'm a professional asset. I know that."

Those cool eyes lighted on mine, holding my gaze for a moment before he said, "I don't cook dinner for my professional assets, Eve."

I took a deep breath, then let it out. "Okay, I'm sorry. I just— Wait. Why am I apologizing? Who's the guy who told me never to mistake a business relationship for a social one? Keep my distance. Be on the lookout for the angle, because there's always an angle. You just admitted you've been hanging around because you wanted to hire me. That's an angle, isn't it?"

A moment's pause, then: "Yes, I suppose it is. *I* will apologize, then."

He took his own plate and gestured at the living room. We went in and sat, plates on our laps.

After a few bites, he said, "I would like to hire you, and I think it's a wise business move for you. You've learned enough from Lavina. Time to do something else. Leave her. Leave Chicago. Come to Los Angeles. I'll rent you an apartment—"

"Uh-uh. I don't need—"

"It's convenience, not charity, Eve. If you work for me, meeting in a hotel once a week won't do. I'll find a decent building where I can get two apartments. One for you and one, presumably, for myself, to conduct my affairs in privacy. My family will approve of the discretion and won't bother me."

"I don't want to move to L.A. Lavina isn't the only contact I have here. I don't want to work for one person either, Kristof. That's too . . ." I shifted. "It's not me. I need other work. Other jobs. Balance, you know? So I keep my fingers in. I've built a rep now. I won't lose it by dropping out."

"Your reputation will follow you to L.A. I'll make sure of it. As for taking on other jobs, that's fine. But I really think you should move."

"No. I've built a life here. Okay, maybe a year isn't exactly your idea of permanency, but for me, it is. If working for you means moving, then the answer is no."

He ate a few mouthfuls of pasta, then nodded. "All right. I'm not pleased about it, but I'll agree to your terms. You can work out of Chicago and work for others as well as for me. The first task I had for you is in Chicago anyway. Detective work. I need to track down . . ."

After we parted I realized that he wasn't "displeased" with the arrangement at all. I'd done exactly what he wanted—agreed to work for him. Throw in parts he knew I'd balk at—moving and having one exclusive employer—and by the time we were done haggling, I'd forget I hadn't been sure I wanted to work for him at all. Sneaky bastard. Can't say I wasn't warned, though. Kristof got what he wanted, by any means necessary. Had to admire that in a guy.

So I started doing jobs for Kristof. Most of it was intelligence and legwork. Find this scroll for me. Find this person for me. Find out more about this person for me.

With Lavina, while I'd made it clear from the start that whatever rumors she'd heard, I was not an assassin for hire, that didn't keep her from having me play the heavy now and then, roughing up slow-paying clients. Kristof never asked for that. He knew that if I was going to use violence, it was for my benefit—spell-blast someone who'd screwed me over, not someone an employer *said* screwed her over.

His monthly lessons stopped, but his monthly visits didn't. Now we needed to discuss business. That could have been done by phone, but neither of us suggested it. We followed the old routine with the hotel suites, only now those visits included dinner—cooked or room service, depending on the hotel—and usually stretched on long after business was concluded.

As we relaxed with one another, the discussions got more spirited. Heated, even. Only on one matter, though, did they spill over into outright argument: the subject of Lavina.

He'd been right. She was still pursuing Dhamphir. She hadn't pestered me for my involvement, but I knew that if she got in trouble, I'd suffer by association. I'd decided it was time to slide out of this relationship—preferably before the Cortezes came after her.

So I'd stopped getting her training. The relationship could have ended there, because I'd been careful to keep our books balanced, never taking lessons I hadn't already "paid" for in service. But I recognized that Lavina was a valuable contact to keep, so I still did a few jobs we'd already discussed.

I tried to make it clear, without being rude, that I considered this a favor, yet she seemed to think it was her due, like charging someone for a hotel room if she leaves halfway through her stay. Kristof wanted me to cut ties then, saying she'd only keep pushing if I didn't. But I couldn't risk my reputation, so I said I'd finish up.

He was right . . . again. Even after the jobs were done, she kept finding little things connected to jobs I'd done earlier, insisting they were part of the original task. She was cunning about it, though, not pushing me too hard, giving me only small jobs, easily done. Keeping me on the line. Keeping that last string attached. Keeping control.

Eventually, I said to hell with it. If she drove me out of Chicago, that was her loss. When she called, I'd ask how much the job paid. She got the message. If she wanted it badly enough, she did pay. Finally, that winter, when I told myself I'd be done with her in a job or two, she called and wanted me to do something a whole lot bigger.

"I'm meeting with Nico Tucci to discuss a partnership in the Dhamphir matter," she said.

"I don't—"

"—want anything to do with taking over Dhamphir. I know that, Eve, and while I think it's a mistake to be so skittish around the Cabals, that's a lesson for another teacher to impart. What I'm asking is only for your bodyguard services at the meeting."

"Because Tucci is a sorcerer? With a history of double-crossing his partners?"

"Exactly. But I also know that he does so only sporadically, suggesting he can be trusted under the right circumstances. He came to me on this matter, which is a good sign. And I intend to proceed with caution, which is why I'm asking for your help. You'll accompany me to this meeting, but take no part in the negotiations."

"Hired gun only?"

"Yes. For one evening's work, I will pay you five hundred dollars, which is more than reasonable. After this, I won't bother you again. Your debt is paid."

My debt had been paid months ago. I didn't say that, though. She was obviously desperate, and this was just the opportunity I needed to part on good terms.

"Where and when?" I asked.

* * *

Lavina led me to an abandoned warehouse. I think that at some point someone decreed that all clandestine meetings must be held in one. Woe to the criminal overlord who lives in a city thriving with commerce, with no empty warehouses to be found: He probably needs to build one, just to have a place to arrange late-night meetings.

I suppose the allure is that combination of enclosed and open. You're hidden from prying eyes, yet within a cavernous space, making an ambush difficult. Still, there's nothing to stop you from being jumped as you walk in or out of the building. Or being attacked from all sides once you're in there. A flawed concept, and one I was painfully aware of as I moved into the lead.

As I was casting my sensing spell, my pager buzzed. I silenced it and checked the display. Kristof. His third page since late afternoon. I should have called him back, but he had a sixth sense for knowing when I was up to something. I shut off my pager.

I cast sensing spells and got two pings, one on either side of the doorway. I motioned for Lavina to wait. Then I slid soundlessly to the warehouse and cleared a peephole. A thick-necked thug leaned against the wall, arms crossed. Standing watch, not lying in wait. Same with the guy on the other side.

I motioned Lavina toward the door, then cast a binding spell on the first thug before walking through. It was just a precaution, and I released the spell when his partner greeted us with a grunt and waved us through.

Tucci stood in the middle of the room with another bodyguard. A quick sensing spell revealed two more at the other side of the building. I flashed five fingers to Lavina.

"Five bodyguards?" she said, her voice ringing through the empty building. "Really, Nico. I know I said

I was bringing Eve, but you're giving her ego a boost it doesn't need. Two would be quite sufficient."

When Tucci hesitated, I held up three fingers.

Lavina sighed. "All right, three. Do you see what you're creating here?"

Tucci agreed to three, which is what Lavina and I had agreed on earlier. He sent two of his goons out. I followed them halfway to the door, cast a sensing spell and shook my head.

"If she can still detect them, they're too close," Lavina said. "Send them back to the car."

He radioed instructions. I waited, then cast again and nodded.

"All right," Lavina said. "Let's talk. You want Dhamphir. I want Dhamphir. The only thing standing in our way is—"

Tucci tossed a photo at my feet. As I bent to pick it up, he threw another, then a third, all facedown. I gathered them, straightened, flipped them over, and swore.

Lavina waited, hand out. I gave them to her one at a time. In the first, Richard Granville lay in his bloodsoaked bed, staring empty-eyed at the ceiling. In the second, Rick Jr. was facedown in his spaghetti, sauce and blood spattering the white tablecloth. In the third, his brother, Alan, floated at the bottom of his tub, electrocuted.

"I thought you'd like that last one," Tucci said to me, pointing to Alan and smiling.

I didn't smile back. I looked at Lavina. She calmly surveyed the photos, then stacked them.

"Messy," she said. "I suppose what they say about your family's connection to the mob is true. That could be a problem."

"*That* could be a problem?" I said. "Hell, I don't care how he killed them. He slaughtered a family with direct ties to—"

"The Cortez Cabal," she said with a sigh. "So you insist. I've failed to see the evidence for that, Eve."

"I showed you the evidence. You won't believe—"

Her look told me I was out of line.

"You let your bodyguard give you business advice?" Tucci said. "*That* could be a problem, Lavina."

"Former bodyguard. This is Eve's last job with me. As you see, her mouth is a bit of a problem. A weakening in the spinal column doesn't help matters."

She gave me a withering look. I wasn't withered. There was a difference between ballsy and suicidal, and killing the Granvilles had crossed it.

"Sorry, Lavina, but you knew how I felt about this. My employment ends here. If you want a bodyguard, I'll escort you to your car now."

I turned to go. She launched a binding spell, but I was ready, ducking fast and hitting her with a knockback. She stumbled back, her spell disrupted.

"Show some respect, Eve."

"I am," I said. "Otherwise, I'd have used my energy bolt. You knew my limits. You crossed them. I'm still offering to finish this job by escorting you—"

One of the thugs slammed a fist into my jaw. I didn't see that coming and it hit full force, teeth rattling, blood spraying as I staggered back. I launched an energy bolt. He flew halfway across the warehouse, letting out a squeal of shock and pain. When the next one ran at me, I doubled the power and he dropped on the spot, howling, the smell of burning flesh filling the air. The third took a step toward me. I lifted my fingers. He stopped.

I turned to Lavina. "May I leave now?"

"Go," she said. "And I'd suggest you keep going, Eve, because I'm not going to forget this."

I met her gaze. "Neither will I."

* * *

I didn't make it out that easily. Tucci still had two guards within radio distance. They tried to ambush me. I was ready, but I still ended up with a second-degree burn on my arm from the one who was a fire half-demon. I killed the other. I could have incapacitated him and run, but we were beyond that point. Come at me with five thugs and I can't leave them all standing.

The one in the warehouse probably wouldn't survive his injuries either. I don't regret that. They'd have done the same to me. Two deaths would only bolster my reputation. I didn't do it for that reason, but it was a factor.

That first blow had left all my teeth intact, thankfully, but my split lip and bloody nose meant I was covered in blood. No taxis for me. I didn't care, I could use the walk. It gave me time to reflect on my mistakes. *Reflect* isn't quite the right word, I suppose. I'd screwed up, and I knew it. I gave myself proper shit for it and spent the walk thinking of all the ways I could have handled it better.

I was heading into the alley behind my apartment building when a black BMW rolled to the curb. The passenger window buzzed down.

"Get in, Eve."

Kristof leaned over and flung open the door. When I didn't move fast enough, he opened his side, ready to come out and get me. I slid in and shut the door.

"How—?" I began.

He handed me a handkerchief and motioned to my lip.

"Don't bleed on the leather, right?" I said.

He gave me a look that said that wasn't what he meant. I nodded and pressed the cloth to my lip.

"As I said, I suspected Lavina would make a move on the Granvilles. So I decided to monitor the situation and received word this afternoon that Rick Granville had been found dead. By the time I was on the plane, his brother and father had followed him to the afterlife. I tried to contact you."

"Sorry," I said. "I got the page, and I meant to call back . . ."

"No, you knew you were making a risky choice, and you preferred not to speak to anyone who might talk you out of it."

True.

A loud ringing made me jump. Kristof motioned to the glove compartment. I opened it and found a telephone the size of a brick. A mobile phone. I'd heard of them, but never seen one. I handed it to him. He answered, listened, said a few words, then hung up.

"As I suspected, you won't be returning to your apartment tonight."

"Tucci's men were waiting for—?" I stopped. "No, not waiting for me. Setting me up to take the fall for the murders."

"Yes, but it's been taken care of. I sent a team there earlier to wait. They'll deal with it."

"Is that safe? Involving the Cabal?"

"Safer than letting you take the fall—after being rumored to have completed a similar assignment for me. My father will be happy to be rid of the Granvilles—and happy not to care too much about how it was done, as long as I've taken care of any potential link back to us."

"Thanks, Kris." When I realized what I said, I backtracked, "Kristof. Sorry."

"Kris is fine."

"No. If you don't like it—"

His brows lifted. "Did I say that?"

He hadn't. He'd just said no one ever called him Kris. I nodded and said, "Thank you. And I'm sorry. I screwed up."

"Which you always realize and never repeat the same mistake. That's all that matters. However, if this were to make you think twice before ignoring my advice again . . ."

"You aren't *always* right, you know."

He arched his brows, looking so shocked that I had to laugh. When I did, my lip split, blood gushing. He handed me another handkerchief and pulled into a parking lot, then twisted to inspect my injuries. When his fingers slid under my chin for a better look at my lip, I jumped, head banging against the roof.

"Sorry, just . . ."

"Not used to being touched," he murmured.

I nodded, cheeks heating. Sure, I did the one-night-stand thing, and that obviously involved physical contact. Beyond that, though, I avoided it. My mother hadn't been affectionate and I'd grown up keeping my distance. In a lot of ways, I guess.

"May I?" Kristof said, motioning at my lip. "It might need stitches."

I nodded. His fingers slid under my chin again. Smooth fingers. Warm skin. My heart started to race. I closed my eyes and let him check out my lips, then my nose, and even when he let go, I could sense him there, feel the heat of his body, smell his faintly minty breath, hear his breathing. As my heart pounded, I blamed a long dry spell between those one-night stands, but I knew it was more than that.

I was falling for Kristof Nast. It didn't matter, though, because he wasn't falling back, and that meant it was safe. I've never thrown myself at a guy. Never even made a pass at one. As long as he kept it business, everything would be fine.

"We'll get the lip looked at," he said. "Your nose is fine, though. Anything else?"

I opened my eyes and shook my head.

"Nothing?" His look told me to save the bravado for someone else.

I lifted my arm. He examined the burn and said that it, too, needed checking. He'd take me to a doctor he knew—not a Cabal one, but another, where he could drop me off and wait outside.

He backed the car from the lot. "As for Lavina . . ."

"I need to strike back. I can't let her get away with this."

He nodded. "I have a few ideas on that."

"I don't doubt it. In this case, though, I think I've got the situation under control." I reached into my waistband, took out a minirecorder, hit rewind, then play. My voice filled the car.

"—*killed them. He slaughtered a family with direct ties to*—"

"*The Cortez Cabal,*" Lavina replied. "*So you insist*—"

I hit stop and looked at Kristof. "Good?"

"Excellent."

"I may screw up, but as you said, I'm capable of learning. And, unfortunately, what I learned is that I'm not going to be able to stay in Chicago, even with this tape."

"I know you don't want to move to L.A., but closer would be easier. San Diego? San Francisco?"

I shook my head. "If I'm going to move, that's just silly. Is it easiest for you if I'm in L.A.?"

"It is."

"Then that's where I'm going."

Los Angeles wasn't my kind of town. Too phony. Too sunny. Too blond. But it had a thriving supernatural underground, if a more tightly regulated one, being in a Cabal home city. Still, it was a change of pace, and I liked it well enough. Or maybe I just liked seeing more of Kristof. It didn't matter. Nothing had changed.

Well, it did change a little. Kristof found me an apartment in a decent building. I paid for mine and he got a second one in the same building as a discreet bachelor pad. Being in the same city meant we got together more than once a month—at least weekly, and not always for business. It was only friendship, though, and I was good with that. He needed a place to kick back with someone he could be himself around. I needed that, too.

Once I moved, our meetings shifted to afternoons, leaving evenings open for his kids. I'd been there just over two months when he called wanting a rare evening get-together. Rarer still, he didn't want to hold it at the apartment.

"I have an engagement until ten," he said. "Would you be able to come by and meet up with me after?"

"Is that safe?"

"It isn't business," he said. "It's a personal engagement."

Personal? As in, a date? My gut did a weird little flip. I wasn't sure I wanted to see Kristof after a date with another woman. In fact, I was damned sure I didn't. Which was all the more reason to say yes. Squash any romantic hopes while they were still at the squashable stage.

"Sure. Where is it?"

He gave me an address and I said I'd be there at ten.

I drove to the address Kristof had given me. Yes, drove. In a city the size of L.A., you'd think public transit would be the way to go, but it'd taken me about two weeks to realize that if I wanted to work efficiently, I'd need a car. In this case, it was a good idea, because I'd hate to have footed the cab bill.

The address was almost an hour outside L.A. And when I pulled into the parking lot, I had to double-, then triple-check it. And, even then, I was convinced I'd copied it down wrong.

I was at an ice rink. Indoors, of course. There's no ice

in Southern California. When I circled the lot, though, I found Kristof's car. When he'd said personal, I'd jumped to the conclusion he was on a date, but with Kristof, the more obvious answer would be that he was with his boys. If so, I'd need to be careful. They were too young to recognize me as a witch, I thought, but I couldn't take chances. Kristof would expect discretion.

So I went in the back door. It was locked, but a spell fixed that. Inside, I followed the blast of a whistle and the *skritch-skritch* of skates until I found the rink.

If Kristof's boys had been here, their ice time was over. A hockey game was in progress. I like hockey. Well, marginally more than I like other sports, which is not at all, so I suppose that's not the most ringing endorsement. I'd never buy tickets to a game, but I could fathom the appeal more than I could with things like golf or tennis. Hockey combines skill, strategy, and good old-fashioned brute force. I could relate to that.

I just started for the front when a crash rang out as a player deftly shoulder-checked another into the boards. A whistle blast, and the referee signaled and waved the player off the ice. As the tall, broad-shouldered offender skated away, I admired the rear view.

He gracefully leapt over the boards into what I presumed was the penalty box. As he sat, he pulled off his helmet and shook out his blond hair. And I laughed.

I suppose shock should have been the correct response. Kristof Nast, scion of the Nast Cabal, playing *hockey*? Six months ago, I would have presumed he had a twin brother. Now I just looked at him, sitting in the penalty box, and thought, *I should have guessed.* Skill, strategy, and good old-fashioned brute force. That fit Kristof to a tee.

As I watched, he watched, too—gaze fixed on the doors at the far end of the arena. Looking for me. Frowning. Checking the clock. Waiting. Hoping.

I saw that and I knew he hadn't invited me here because it was a convenient place to meet. There was a reason he was playing hockey almost an hour from L.A. No one else knew about it. In bringing me here, he was throwing the door open as wide as it would go. This is me. This is the real me. This is the me no one else gets to see. You don't do that with someone you consider just a friend.

No. I had to be wrong. Kristof had never given me so much as a lingering glance. He just needed someone in his life who didn't expect him to play the role he'd been born to. That's all I was.

I stayed at that far end of the ice, watching him as he watched for me. When his penalty ended, he leapt out of the box and back into the game, playing with that same ferocity he showed in business. The same, yet different, too. Here he could pull the punches himself, and as I watched him skating around, blue eyes glowing behind his mask, I knew he loved that. The chance to get in the game, not just call the shots from the sidelines.

The game ended a few minutes after he left the penalty box. Then he finally saw me.

As the others streamed from the ice, he skated over to where I stood by the boards. At the last moment he sheared off to send a wave of shaved ice my way. I laughed and jumped back.

"Just get here?" he said as he hit the boards.

"Nope."

"Snuck in the back, huh? I should have guessed. So, surprised?"

"Pfft. Kristof Nast likes playing games where he gets to throw his weight around. Big shock there. Though I bet getting sent to the penalty box for it is a new experience."

He grinned. "It is. Nice in a way, though, to actually be called on my transgressions once in a while."

He pulled off his helmet and a glove and ran his fingers through his hair. Then he leaned against the boards and looked at me, still grinning like a little boy, face alight, and I knew I wasn't just falling for Kristof Nast. I'd fallen. Hard. And as he looked at me, I felt my cheeks heat and his smile widened.

One look at his face and I knew I hadn't been wrong about why he invited me here. One look at mine, and he knew he hadn't been wrong to invite me.

I should have run screaming from the arena. Well, excused myself and fled at least. I'd spent the last few months saying it was okay to fall for Kristof because there was no danger of him reciprocating. But now there was. And I didn't care, because when it came down to it, there was only one question to be answered. Did I trust him enough to take a chance? The answer was yes. I trusted Kristof more than I'd ever trusted anyone in my life.

We stood there for a minute, just looking at each other, until I cleared my throat and said, "Your teammates will be looking for you."

He leaned farther over the board and I thought he was going to reach for me, but he just said, "There's an empty changing room at the end of the hall. It's locked, but I'm sure you can fix that."

"I can."

I paced around the empty changing room. What if he didn't make the first move? I'd never made the first move. I had no problem with the general concept, but I've never chased a guy in my life—my ego couldn't stand the rejection.

I was supposed to be this tough, knows-what-she-wants, gets-what-she-wants girl. Maybe he'd expect me to make a move. How? What if I was wrong? I'd let Kristof see me make a fool of myself more than once, and I was fine with that. But this was different. Screw this up and—

The door opened. Kristof stood there, only his skates off, the hockey uniform now paired with a pair of thousand-dollar Italian loafers. At any other time, I would have laughed, but now I just stood there, staring at him.

"Is this still business?" he said.

I shook my head. "It hasn't been business for a long time."

He crossed the room in three strides and swept me up in a kiss that sent any last doubts flying. A deep, light-my-insides-on-fire kind of kiss—one I returned like I'd never returned a kiss in my life, arms going around his neck, body pressing against his, legs wrapping around him as he pressed me into the wall.

We kept kissing, gasping for quick breaths, neither pulling back long enough to breathe properly, let alone say a word. He managed to get my T-shirt off with only a split-second break. I didn't have nearly as much luck with his hockey uniform. With a little help, I got his shirt off, then the pads, and by then we were on the floor, still kissing, grappling to get out of our clothes as fast as we could. We were down to the bare essentials when he suddenly pulled back.

"—need—better," he said between pants.

"Sorry, but I don't get better than this."

He laughed, breath still heaving. "I mean, you deserve better. No changing-room floors. A hotel. I'll take you somewhere. Anywhere."

"Huh?"

He disentangled himself and backed up. "Where do you want to go? Someplace special. You deserve special."

"I do?"

His gaze met mine. "You do."

I stretched out on the floor and considered it. "Bali, then. Or Monaco. No idea where either one is, but they sound special."

He laughed again. "Both then. Bali first. This weekend. The best hotel I can find."

"That's very sweet." I toyed with the front clasp on my bra. "But the weekend's kind of far away, don't you think?" I slipped out of my bra. "Three days. Four if we can't get away until Saturday." I tugged my panties down over my hips. "How many hours is that?"

"Sixty-five," he said, his voice hoarse as he watched me. "If I can get away early Friday afternoon."

I laughed. "Already figured it out? Well, then, if you can wait that long . . ."

His gaze lifted, with some difficulty, to my eyes. "Not really, but I want—"

"—to be a gentleman. Treat me right. Which is probably the sweetest thing a guy has ever done. Under the circumstances, though . . ." I slipped off my panties. "Making *me* wait doesn't seem very chivalrous."

The corners of his mouth twitched. "You have a point."

"I absolutely have a point. And, while I do appreciate the sentiment, the most thoughtful, considerate thing you could do right now would be—"

He covered the distance between us and cut me off with a kiss, then showed me just how considerate he could be.

We still went to Bali that weekend. Monaco followed a month later. Both were just overnighters, but that was fine. If Kristof had turned out to be the kind of guy who'd start ignoring his kids when he got a new girlfriend, then he wouldn't be the kind of guy I wanted to be with.

As a lover, Kristof was everything I could have

wanted. Passionate and thoughtful—in bed and out of it. That was new for me. It was all new for me. I hadn't had a boyfriend since high school, and this was so far removed from that, I considered myself a relationship virgin. I think Kristof was, too. That sounds strange for a divorced guy, but everything I'd heard about his wife led me to believe that it had been a marriage of convenience, as Cabal ones often are. They select human wives from the upper echelons of society, where women are happy to marry into money and don't care to know the details.

Kristof had needed a wife and sons. She'd been suitable on both counts. He'd been fine with that, too—sex and emotion were as incompatible in his world as they'd been in mine. Together, we realized how wrong we'd been. You could have both. A friend and a lover—one person to share everything with, one person you could completely be yourself with.

We knew it wouldn't last. Couldn't. We didn't say that, of course. We just wrung as much from it as we could, while we could.

We'd been lovers for almost six months when Kristof got the rare vacation from both kids and work. His brother was taking the boys on a trip, and things were slow at the office, so Kristof took the week off. Then he booked a week in Acapulco for us.

It was an amazing week. Even as a couple, we didn't spend a lot of time together. That was mutual—we had our own lives and needed the room to live them separately, which made us appreciate those moments of intersection all the more. Having a whole week together was bliss.

We didn't spend every moment of it side by side, of course. I went into town and scoured the local underground spell shops. Kristof spent a few hours each day on the phone, taking care of business. But we were together more than we ever had been, and it was wonderful.

On our last night together, I was on the balcony, drinking beer and admiring the sunset. Kristof had gotten us a villa so private I could lounge on the deck, wearing only one of his shirts. I'm not the type to do that if there's any chance of being spotted. I value my privacy with a ferocity matched only by Kristof's.

He was inside, making his nightly call to his boys as he cooked dinner. When he came out, I had my feet on the railing, enjoying the last rays of sunshine. I opened my eyes to see him watching me, plates in hand.

"You look good," he said.

"Hold that thought, because right now, what looks *really* good is that steak."

He laughed and set the plates down on the patio table, then refilled his Scotch glass.

"How are the boys?" I asked.

"Good. Bryce is getting into trouble. Sean's holding down the fort. The usual." He took a long drink of his Scotch, then looked at me. "I'd like you to meet them, Eve."

"What?"

He frowned. "You don't want to?"

I set down my knife. "No. I definitely want to. I'd love to. Only I'm not sure how you plan to work that. Do you mean, *see* them? Like go to one of their games, watch from the stands? Or *meet* them? Introduce me as a friend, go out for ice cream."

"I mean introduce you as what you are. The woman I'm in love with."

My heart skipped a beat. I had to struggle for breath.

"Or maybe not," he said slowly. "Okay. If that's not what you want."

"Stop that," I snapped. "You just hit me with this out

of the blue. I think I'm entitled to be a bit thrown, okay?"

"And a bit upset, obviously."

"No, a *lot* upset, Kris." I pushed the plate away and stood, then waved at his Scotch. "I hope you've had a lot more of those than I think you have, because otherwise, I don't know what the hell is going through your head right now."

His lips tightened, eyes chilling. "What's going through my head is thinking that I love you, and I want to be with you, not just grabbing minutes when we can. I want to share my life with you."

"Tell your family, you mean. Everyone. Including your father."

"Of course."

"And how long of a life expectancy do you think I'd have after that?"

He stopped, glass halfway to his mouth, and went completely still and pale, and I knew he hadn't planned this, or even thought it through.

He put the tumbler down. "I'd never let anything happen to you, Eve. *Never.*" He straightened. "I want this. More than I've ever wanted anything, and my father will understand that. I'm more than just a son. I'm the future of his company. Most days, I *am* his company. I would like to think that my happiness would be enough for him to overlook his prejudice against witches, but I do know that I'm too valuable to lose."

"Yes, you are."

He knew what I meant. He was too valuable to lose to *me*. I wasn't just a witch. I was a dark witch with seriously questionable connections. I was, in my way, just as ambitious as Kristof. Cabal sorcerers didn't even marry supernaturals, and it was for this very reason—so no one would disturb the sanctity of the inner family. Not even a wife could jeopardize their hold on power.

I could sign a writ in blood saying I had no interest in the Cabal's business, and it wouldn't matter. I wasn't just unsuitable, I was a threat.

"I want to make this work, Eve," he said. There was a note in his voice that made my heart ache—a little boy who never got what he really wanted, not ever, and who knew that wasn't going to change now.

He looked up. "If I could make this work, would you . . . ?"

"Yes." I met his gaze. "I would. But not at any risk to you or your sons."

"And not at any risk to you." He nodded, straightening again, that imperious Nast ice seeping back into his eyes. "I'll find a way. It may take some time, but I will find a way."

It wasn't the same after that. A little something had been added into the mix that hadn't been there before—hope.

We'd both seen the possibility that this could be something real, something lasting, maybe even something forever. We'd seen it and we knew that the other wanted it, and that changed the timbre of the relationship.

But we both knew the problem was as close to insurmountable as they came. The Capulets and the Montagues had nothing on the five-hundred-year feud between witches and sorcerers, and that was only the most superficial problem. A Cabal heir could not be allowed to marry a powerful supernatural with a past as unsavory as mine.

We never actually discussed the problem. That would be depressing, and we still cherished our time together too much for that. But ideas would float into the conversation.

Was he set on marriage? Or would a common-law arrangement work? How about separate homes? It wouldn't make a difference, we realized. However we arranged it, I'd still have the same influence over him.

What if he wasn't heir? That idea came from him. His father would never allow it, though. If Kristof said he was stepping down, his father would eliminate the reason. Same if Kristof tried to leave the company.

There was only one possible solution. One so desperate we didn't discuss it, not even in the vaguest terms. Over the next couple of months, every now and then, when we made love, Kristof would forget to use protection. And I'd forget to remind him. It had happened before—we'd get caught up and "oh, shit" afterward. Only there weren't any "oh, shit" moments now.

As solutions went, this really was the last act of desperation. I wasn't sure I was ready for a child. I was pretty damned sure I wasn't. But Kristof was an amazing father, and I was determined to be just as good a mother.

It really did look like the answer we needed. Nothing meant more to the Nasts than family, and with one "whoops" I could join that family and give them the excuse they needed to accept me.

So it was no surprise that three months after our trip to Acapulco, I missed my period and when I tested, the results were clear. I was pregnant.

I called Kristof and left a message with his answering service. We'd started doing that months ago, working out a code that no one would question. I asked him to meet me for lunch at a place we sometimes went, outside L.A., where he stood no chance of running into anyone from the Cabal.

I'd agonized about how to do this. The news seemed better conveyed in private, but it also seemed like something to celebrate, something to "do right" the way he had with our first night together. I decided on the restaurant, but I'd meet him outside first and tell him before we went in.

I spent the rest of the morning waiting for Kristof to call back. I wasn't too worried when he didn't; it only meant that he couldn't make the call privately. Before heading out, I called the service and confirmed that he'd gotten the message. He had, so he'd be there.

Only he wasn't. I waited outside until it started to look like I was loitering. Then I went in. I started ordering a Coke, then changed it to a milk.

I was pregnant.

Oh God, I was pregnant.

The reality of that didn't hit until I ordered the milk. I was pregnant with Kristof Nast's child. What the hell had I been thinking?

I got a lot of deep breathing in while I was waiting. Good practice for eight months from now, I was sure.

It would be okay. Something must have come up. Or the answering service was mistaken and he hadn't gotten the message.

"Miss Levine."

I turned. A man in a suit approached. He had graying blond hair and blue eyes I'd know anywhere.

"Mr. Nast," I said, rising, extending a hand.

He ignored the hand and stopped in front of me. "My son isn't coming."

I slammed my expression into neutral and my brain into high gear. "So you figured out that I'm working for him? Or did he finally tell you?"

"I know you're doing a lot more than working for him, Miss Levine."

Before I could open my mouth, he slapped a photo onto the table. It was Kristof and me behind this very restaurant last month, tucked into a shadowy corner, kissing good-bye before he went back to work.

"Okay, we had a fling. A stupid move, but he's single, I'm single, we'd been working together awhile. It was bound to happen and we got it out of our system—"

"It's been going on for months. My son isn't nearly as good at hiding things as he thinks. Not from me. But I've confronted him with it and he's seen his mistake. That's why I'm here. He wants me to tell you it's over and he'd like you to leave Los Angeles—an inconvenience we'll compensate you for."

"Bullshit."

His eyes narrowed in a look I knew well. But there was a difference, too, in those frosty blue eyes. When I'd first met Kristof, as chilly as he'd been, I'd seen a spark of humanity there. Thomas Nast didn't have that spark.

"Kristof didn't send you to dump me," I said.

"You have a very high opinion of yourself, Miss Levine."

"No," I said, lowering my voice and sitting. "I have a very high opinion of your son. If he wanted out, he'd tell me himself. You found out about our relationship. You intercepted my message so you can bring one of your own: Leave my son alone. I'm going to suggest that's a conversation you have with him, not me."

"I don't think you want me to do that." He took a seat across from me. "I've done some digging into your past, Miss Levine, and while I'm sure you consider yourself a unique and interesting person, you are, to me, just another in a very boring stereotype—one my son has, until now, managed to avoid. You're a gold digger."

I laughed. I could tell he didn't like that, but I couldn't help it. "You really don't give your son enough credit, you know that? He's avoided gold diggers because he knows how to spot one, and he knows I'm as far from that as you can get. He offered me a job. When I did take it, I accepted a fair wage and nothing more. Whenever he's used his influence to help me, he's done it without my knowledge, because he knows I wouldn't accept that. Financially, I pay my own way, which I'm sure you'd know if you'd done a little more digging, but you didn't want to do that, because you might find out that I don't fit the little box you've prepared for me."

"And you can't be bought off."

"Nope. But feel free to try."

He did, of course. He offered me money. He offered me power. He offered me things that, a year ago, I would have jumped at so fast I'd have given the old man a heart attack. But today I didn't give them a second's thought.

"Do you have any idea what staying with you would do to my son's life?" he said finally.

"It's what he wants."

"What he wants." Nast gave a slow shake of his head, as if amazed that I was naïve enough to think that mattered. "That may be, but there's one thing he values more than you."

I lifted my chin. "I know that. His sons are the most important thing in Kristof's life, and I have no intention of threatening that."

Another shake of his head. "Pretty words, Miss Levine, but if you truly believed them, you'd leave this table and catch the next bus out of Los Angeles. Your very existence threatens them and their future. Stay with you, and their father will be ruined, and they'll be ruined with him. I won't let that happen. My son may be a grown man, able to make his own mistakes. His sons don't have that choice. They need someone to protect them. That someone will be me."

My hands clenched under the table. I knew what was coming. I told myself I was wrong—he wouldn't dare—but when he opened his mouth, I knew what would come out.

"If my son wants to be with you, so be it. He can leave. But he won't take his sons with him. Kristof will be given a choice. His sons or you."

"And to hell with what Kristof wants."

He met my gaze. "Yes, Miss Levine. To hell with what Kristof wants. I love my son. His happiness, though, must come second to the future of this company and of my family, and I will protect that, even if it costs me my son."

He stood. "If you're still in Los Angeles by the end of the week, I'll tell my son that I know about the affair. I'll give him his choice."

I wanted to fight. God, how I wanted to. I've spent my whole life fighting, yet the fire never burned as hot as it did that day. Fight for what I wanted. Fight for what I needed. Only I couldn't. Thomas Nast had cornered me.

I couldn't let Kristof make that choice. He'd pick his sons. He had to. That's the man I'd fallen in love with and I expected no less. But he wouldn't accept it. He *would* fight, with everything he had, but it wouldn't be enough, and eventually he'd lose, and all he could hope for then would be to salvage the very option he'd been given in the first place. Take his sons. Let me go.

He'd never forgive himself for losing that battle, so I couldn't let him wage it. I had to do the honorable thing.

Had I ever thought that running away could *be* the honorable choice? Yet it was. If there was one thing I admired about Kristof above everything else, it was his relationship with his sons. He was the kind of parent I'd dreamed of having, and I'd never take that from his boys.

I had to let Kristof keep his sons, his family, his job, everything that mattered to him and take away what he could most afford to lose. Me.

Don't let him know what his father did. Don't let him know there ever was a choice. And, above all, don't let him know I was carrying his child.

We'd thought this baby would be the solution. Now I realized just how blind we'd been. There was no way

Thomas Nast would accept a grandchild with a witch mother. If he found out, he'd make sure I suffered a fatal accident before I could give birth.

For Kristof's sake and for the sake of his children—all three of them—I had to go. Just go.

It wasn't that easy, of course. I had to let him know. I spent hours writing a note, over and over, saying everything I wanted to say. Telling him how much he meant to me. Telling him how much it was killing me to leave.

I wanted to thank him, too. For everything he'd done. I wasn't the same person he'd met a year ago. I was stronger, wiser, *deeper*, and I owed that to him.

But I couldn't say any of that, because then he'd know I hadn't left of my own will. He'd come after me and we'd be right back in this position, facing that choice. If I truly loved him, then I had to let him think I'd left because I wanted to. I had to be willing to let him hate me.

The only thing I could keep was the memories. No, that wasn't the only thing. I let my hand rest on my stomach. I'd been allowed to keep one small part of him, and I was grateful for that. More grateful than I ever could have imagined.

So I wrote my note. Only two words. *Thank you*. Then I folded the page, left it where he'd find it, picked up my bag, and walked out.

··BIRTHRIGHT··

Logan peered out the car window at the long wooded drive. Then he lifted the sheet of paper and double-checked the address. He didn't need to check. He'd already memorized the entire note. Easy enough—there were only ten words, including the address.

The first contact he'd ever had with his father, and this was all he got. Ten words.

Jeremy Danvers, 13876 Wilton Grove Lane, Bear Valley, New York

The note had arrived on Logan's eighteenth birthday, couriered to his college dorm room. He'd thought it was from his mother, a birthday check tucked inside a generic "for my son" card. He didn't mind the check—he always needed money—and it was better than the equally generic gifts she bought when she made the effort. Susanna Jonsen didn't know her children well enough to guess what they'd like. Some women just aren't cut out to be mothers, and unfortunately it had taken Susanna three kids to realize she was one of them.

Logan considered himself the luckiest of the three. When he was two, his mother had met his stepfather, who hadn't wanted a stepson of questionable parentage, so Logan had gone to live with his maternal grandparents. He'd grown up, if not with much money, with the kind of love and stability his mother couldn't offer.

He'd opened the envelope only to find another one inside. On it, written in barely legible black strokes: "For my son—important medical information." It wasn't his mother's spidery, precise writing, so it had to be from his father, a man Logan had never met. He only knew that he'd been dark-skinned—probably African American—and that only because it was obvious that Logan's brown skin didn't come from his Norwegian mother. As for details, his mother refused to elaborate.

"He wasn't nothing but a sperm donor," she'd say. "Took off the day I told him you were coming. Don't spend another minute thinking about him, because he doesn't deserve it."

Of course, Logan did think about his father, and for the past two years he'd had cause to think about him more and more. Something was wrong with him, medically wrong—something his doctor laughed off with a slap on the back, saying, "It's puberty, boy, you're supposed to be changing."

When Logan saw that envelope, he knew he'd been right. Whatever condition he had, it was the legacy of his long-vanished father.

Then he'd paused a moment, envelope in hand, as the implications hit. His father knew where he was. Not only remembered him, but knew his birthday, knew he was here, at college.

Logan had ripped open the envelope, reached inside, and plucked out a piece of notepaper. On it, a name and address. That's it—just someone's address.

This address.

He let the car roll forward and craned to peer through the thick evergreens, but if there was a house at the end of that winding laneway, he couldn't see it.

He knew this was the right place. Passing through the

town of Bear Valley, he'd stopped at the doughnut shop, ostensibly for coffee, but really to learn what he could about Jeremy Danvers.

They hadn't been able to tell him much, just that Danvers lived with his cousin and the two "kept to themselves," but that Danvers was "good folk," whatever that meant around here.

The only reason he was still in the car, at the end of the lane, was that he was stalling. He was afraid of what he'd find at the top of this drive—or what he wouldn't find. The most obvious answer was that this Jeremy Danvers *was* his father. Logan didn't know how he'd handle that. Worse, though, he didn't know how he'd handle the disappointment if it *wasn't* him.

He took a deep breath, then slammed the car into reverse and hit the gas. Dust billowed up as he zoomed backward on the dirt shoulder. One more deep breath, then he roared into the driveway.

The first thing Logan noticed as he stepped from the car was the smell of trees. A year ago, if anyone had told him trees had a smell, he'd have laughed and said, "I've never gotten close enough to sniff one."

He'd been raised in the city, with no interest in things like hiking, camping, or fishing. He'd never even gone to summer camp. Then, one day, he'd been cutting across campus and picked up a smell as alluring as Gramma's cinnamon rolls. He'd followed it and found himself in a stand of trees.

He'd stood there, drinking in the sharp tang of greenery and the loamy smell of damp earth, and he'd known this was what a forest smelled like. He recognized the scent from his dreams, the ones he'd started having almost two years ago. Dreams of the forest, of running.

Sometimes in the dreams he was being chased, heart

pounding, feet pounding, blood pounding as he ran, knowing he couldn't stop, if he did stop they'd—

That's where the dream always ended. He never knew who they were or what they'd do, only that he had to be prepared, he had to take shelter, and that shelter wasn't just a "where"—it was a "who." He chalked it up to anxiety. His last year of high school, then his first of college, of course he was stressed, and some days it felt like the whole world was against him, determined to keep his ambitions in check.

In the other forest dreams, the more common ones, he was just running. Barreling through the forest, wind in his hair, ground flying by in a blur under his feet, heart tripping with exhilaration. A strange feeling for a guy whose idea of strenuous exercise was a weekly game of basketball. Not only that, but he'd never been better at his weekly game. He could jump better, react better, move better, and even his friends had started to notice.

Now, as he walked to the front door, he had the sense of being watched, but when he listened and sniffed, no one was there. Yes, *sniffed*—something he'd never admit to doing. Forests weren't the only thing that had a scent, he'd learned. Sometimes he could smell his friends coming long before he saw them. His hearing had improved, too. So when he listened and smelled, and detected no one, he knew no one was there.

He stepped onto the front porch and lifted his hand. Then he stopped. Behind this door could be his father. Was he ready? What would he say?

"Looking for someone?" drawled a voice behind him.

Logan wheeled to see a young man step onto the porch. He was around Logan's age, maybe a couple of years older, well built, with curly blond hair and blue eyes, his strong jaw the only thing keeping him from tipping over into pretty-boy.

"You looking for someone?" the guy repeated.

Logan squared his shoulders.

"Jeremy Danvers."

The guy's eyes went from cool to icy. "Yeah?"

"Yes. Is he home?"

"You think this is a good idea?"

"Huh?"

"I'm asking if you want to reconsider. Maybe you made a mistake."

Logan met the guy's stare. "If Jeremy Danvers is here, I want to see him."

The guy gave a slow nod. Then his fist shot out, plowing into Logan's jaw. Logan slammed into the stone wall and everything went dark.

Logan's face sank into something soft and warm, and he inhaled the faintest scent of laundry detergent. He lifted his head. Pain throbbed through his skull and he let out a soft moan, then dropped back onto the pillow. A few more minutes of sleep, and then he'd—

His eyes snapped open as he remembered what had happened.

He lay on a twin bed covered with a clean bottom sheet, but no top sheet or blankets. In front of him was a bare wall. He picked up the slight scent of dampness. A basement. He rolled over and saw . . . He blinked. Bars.

Logan started jumping up, but the pain forced him down, and he bit back a wave of nausea. Jail? Oh, God, what had he gotten himself into?

He'd heard rumors of college kids venturing into a backwater town and winding up in jail. Well, if that was the case, these yokels would be in for a shock. He was a law student . . . well, prelaw anyway.

At the rustle of the page turning, Logan looked to see the guy who'd decked him. He sat on a folding chair outside the cell and was reading a textbook, with a pencil between his fingers. He jotted something in the margin, then continued reading.

A student? Logan looked around. He wasn't in jail; he was in someone's basement, with an older student standing guard. Now it made sense.

"It was a setup, wasn't it?" Logan said.

The guy lifted a finger, telling Logan to wait, as if he'd known he was awake.

"The letter, the address, it was all part of it," Logan continued.

A soft sound, almost like a growl, and the guy slapped his textbook shut.

"Part of what?" he said.

"The hazing."

"Hazing?"

"For Pi Kappa Beta. I told Mike I didn't want to join, but he signed me up as a pledge, didn't he?"

The guy met Logan's gaze with a steady stare. "Do I look like a frat brat?"

Logan sized him up. Blond, blue-eyed, ridiculously good-looking, athletic . . .

"Yeah, you do."

The guy snorted and shook his head. "You want to get out of this alive, you're going to need a better story than that."

"A—alive?"

"Dumb kid," he muttered. "You're lucky you *are* just a kid. Otherwise I'd be digging your grave out back, not babysitting you."

Logan lowered his eyelids so the guy wouldn't see the flash of fear. *Get a grip*, he told himself. *It's a hazing. Bury me in the backyard? Please. Couldn't Pi Kappa Beta come up with something more believable than that?*

"Did you really think you'd get away with it?" the guy continued. "Barely Changed, and you're going to challenge the Alpha? That first Change addle your brain?" He met Logan's eyes. "Or was it so bad that this seemed like an honorable way out? Suicide by Pack?"

Logan blinked, struggling to make sense of what the young man was saying, and fighting against the dawning possibility that he'd been taken captive by a madman.

A distant door clicked open. "Clayton?"

"Down here," the guy—Clayton—called. "We have a problem."

"So I smelled," a deep voice murmured as light footsteps sounded on the stairs.

A man rounded the corner. He was tall and slender, dark-haired with a close-trimmed beard and dark eyes. He couldn't have been much older than the other guy, and wore a polo shirt and trousers. Logan let out a soft breath of relief. Definitely a frat hazing.

The dark-haired man stopped short, nostrils flaring as he saw Logan. Dismay flickered in his eyes.

"New," he murmured.

"Very new," Clayton said. "And stupid. Walked right up to the door and asked for you."

"For—?" Logan began. "You're Jeremy Danvers?"

The dark-haired man gave a small twist of a smile. "Not quite what you expected?"

Logan told himself that didn't matter, that he already knew this was a prank and hadn't still hoped to find his father. And yet . . .

"What's your name?" Danvers asked.

Logan only glared at him.

"Logan Jonsen," Clayton said, lifting a driver's license. "Doesn't sound familiar."

"Jonsen?" Danvers said. "No."

"Hey," Logan said. "That's my wallet."

"Be glad that's all I took. I was thinking of taking fingerprints, too . . . with your fingers still attached." He looked at Danvers. "What do you want done?"

Danvers paused, then said, "I think we'll give Mr. Jonsen the chance to reconsider."

He stepped closer to the cell. Clayton tensed, as if Logan might grab Danvers through the bars.

Danvers continued, "I don't know what you thought you were doing, but if you ever do it again, it will be the last time. And if you share this story with any of the others, I will reconsider my decision. Is that clear?"

Logan met Danvers's eyes, and any argument dried up. He dropped his gaze and saw that his hands were shaking. He clenched his fists. Again, Clayton tensed, ready to lunge forward.

Danvers took a deeper breath and his chin jerked up. "You haven't Changed yet, have you?" he said.

Before Logan could answer, Danvers stepped closer and inhaled, then glanced at Clayton.

"I can tell he's new, but that's it," Clayton said. "If he hasn't Changed, he's damned close."

Danvers looked at Logan. "You *haven't* had your first Change yet, have you?" He studied Logan's eyes, then blinked. "Not only that, but you have no idea what I'm talking about . . ."

"Shit," Clayton muttered.

"How did you get here?" Danvers asked.

"Someone sent me the name and address," Logan said. "Supposedly my father, some bullshit about medical information, but obviously it was someone's idea of a joke." He looked up at Danvers, but couldn't meet his eyes, and shoved his hands into his pockets, unable to muster any kind of fight. "Can I go? I just want to go, okay?"

"I'm afraid I can't let you do that, Logan. Not just yet. Clayton? Bring him up to the study." Danvers turned and lowered his voice. "Nicely."

* * *

Logan looked longingly at the window. Beyond it, he could see a field and a forest, and in that forest, the promise of freedom. They'd left him alone in here, and he told himself he could open the window, climb out, and run, even if Clayton had warned he'd hear him.

In that forest, he'd find not only freedom, but the bliss of ignorance, where he could keep telling himself this had been an elaborate frat hazing . . . or a freak encounter with crazy people. If he stayed, he knew he'd discover the truth—that he was here for the very reason his father had sent him: to get medical information. And he knew that whatever condition he had, it wasn't anything normal.

He'd felt the strength in Clayton's punch and in his iron grip when he'd led Logan upstairs. He'd seen Danvers's nostrils flare when he'd first seen him, heard him say he'd already "smelled" the problem. And he knew, whatever they were about to tell him, he didn't want to hear it. But as alluring as ignorance was right now, if he left, he'd regret it. So he stayed, and strained to hear the distant conversation of the two men.

"—fucking irresponsible mutts," Clayton was grumbling. "What kind of father sends his kid to the Pack? If Dominic was still in charge, that boy would be dead."

"But Dominic isn't, and presumably Logan's father knows that. He must hope I'll be more sympathetic."

"Sympathetic?" Clayton snorted. "He's putting you in a hell of a situation. That's inconsiderate, irresponsible . . . and stupid. He wants to advise his kid to join the Pack? Fine. But do it after he knows what he is. This way, if the kid reacts badly, what are we supposed to do? Say 'oh well,' and let him leave?"

Logan didn't catch Danvers's response. He strained to hear more, but they'd stopped talking.

A moment later, the two men appeared in the doorway. Danvers took the recliner. Clayton sat beside him on the fireplace hearth.

Danvers began. "Do you have any idea what . . . condition your father was referring to?"

Logan shook his head. Danvers probed for more, asking how much he knew about his father, and the circumstances of his upbringing. Then he leaned forward and murmured something to Clayton. The younger man's jaw set, and he was obviously unhappy with what he was hearing. He didn't object, though. Just stood and glared at Logan, and in that glare, Logan read a warning, and he knew that the talk of cutting off fingers and burying bodies in the backyard wasn't just talk. He swallowed hard, but Clayton only stalked past him and out the door.

With Clayton gone, Danvers asked about symptoms now, probing for details, as if assessing the progress of Logan's "condition." Then he moved to less concrete areas, with questions about changes in behavior, urges and longings, emotions and dreams.

After about ten minutes, something clicked along the hallway floor. Danvers stopped, then glanced out the door and lifted a finger.

He turned to Logan. "I have no experience doing this, Logan, and I know that any way I do, it will be a shock." He paused. "It would be better if you'd figured it out on your own. Do you have any idea, however wild or preposterous it might seem, about what's happening to you?"

Logan shook his head.

"I think you do," Danvers murmured. "If you prefer it this way, though, I'll confirm your suspicions."

He turned to the doorway and motioned. A wolf walked in—a huge gold-colored wolf. Logan's brain screamed denials, though he had no idea, at least consciously, *what* it was denying.

The wolf walked to Logan. Its muzzle jerked, and it flipped something from its mouth onto Logan's lap. Logan looked down to see his wallet. Then he glanced up at the wolf, looked into its blue eyes—familiar blue eyes fixed in a familiar suspicious glare. Clayton's eyes.

It's a trick, his brain screamed. *Get out now. Fight! Run!*

He managed to hold himself still until the wolf turned away. Then he sprang at Danvers. Even as he did, some deeper part of his brain cried out in protest.

But it was too late. He was already in flight. Danvers easily dove out of the way, and even as that deep part of Logan's brain sighed in relief, he felt something hit his side. He heard Clayton's snarl. As he fell, Clayton's fangs flashed. Logan saw them slash down toward his throat, felt them close around it. And his final thought was that he'd made the biggest mistake of his life . . . and the last.

Logan buried his face in the pillow, now smelling more of himself than of laundry detergent. *This feels familiar,* he thought. This time, when he lifted his head and saw bars, his gut reaction was not fear but relief.

He should be dead. As crazy as that sounded—the thought that he could be killed just for lunging at a guy—it was true. And, in the strangest, most surreal way, he was neither shocked nor outraged, but only grateful to be alive.

He sat up. Blood rushed to his head, blurring his vision, and all he could see was an indistinct figure sitting outside the cell, reading.

"Clayton?"

A soft laugh. "No. Clay's not very happy with you right now. It seemed best if I stood guard for a while instead." Danvers laid his book on the floor. "If you're feeling up to it, Logan, we need to talk."

Logan could only nod.

Danvers continued. "I don't know your father, so I can't judge his intentions. I believe that he was somehow unable to tell you the truth about your birthright himself, and that he wanted you here, in the Pack. That's what it's called. The Pack—a werewolf Pack."

He paused, studying Logan's face for his reaction. While part of Logan's brain still dug in its heels and refused to believe, that deeper part was the stronger voice now, squelching logic and telling Logan with unshakable gut-level conviction that this was true.

When Logan didn't respond, Danvers continued. "As for why your father would send you here, the Pack offers things other werewolves don't have—security, training, companionship. Your father must have wanted that for you. But, in sending you here, without knowing what you are, he put us both in a difficult position. You know what we are, who we are, where we live—"

"I'm a threat," Logan said, his gut clenching. "You're going to kill me."

"I wouldn't have kept you alive just to explain why you can't remain that way."

"But Clayton—"

"Didn't try to kill you. You're young enough that he'll grant you a warning shot. But only one." Danvers met Logan's gaze. "If you ever attack me again, he *will* kill you. That is both his job and his nature. And I won't stop him. The same goes for Clayton himself or any other Pack member. An unprovoked attack warrants death. That is our Law. We face enough danger from without; we won't tolerate it within."

Logan rubbed his bandaged throat. "So if I promise not to tell anyone—"

"No. I can't take that risk. You cannot be given any opportunity to reveal what we are until you know, for certain, that doing so would risk your own safety as much as ours. You'll remain here until your first Change—when you become a full werewolf."

"But—but I have school—"

"This takes precedence for now. Even if you were to leave, when your Change does come—" He shook his head. "School would be the last thing on your mind. You'll be here, not just for our safety, but for yours, and you'll see that soon enough."

"So you're keeping me *here*? In a cage?"

A small laugh. "I'm afraid you aren't that great a threat yet, Logan. So long as you don't attempt to run, you'll be under what you might call house arrest, while we wait for your Change and I prepare you for it."

Danvers rose and walked to the cell door.

"So that's it?" Logan said. "I'm part of this Pack now?"

"That will be your decision, when you're better able to make it. For now, you have other things to worry about." He unlocked and opened the door. "Let's go find some dinner. You've had a long day, and I imagine you're hungry."

He headed for the stairs. Logan hesitated in the doorway, then shoved his hands into his pockets. There, at the bottom of one, his fingers grazed the wadded note.

So this was his birthright? Not the riches of an inheritance or the glory of a proud past. Not even a name. The blood of a werewolf; that's all his father had given him.

He touched the folded paper. No, maybe that wasn't all. An affliction, yes, maybe even a curse, but an involuntary one passed along with something every loving parent wants for his child: the chance of a better life.

Logan pulled his hands from his pockets and followed Danvers up the stairs. His life was changing. Here, with strangers, he might find what he needed to get through it. He might also find something his father never had—a place where he belonged.

··BEGINNINGS··

CHAPTER NINE

I

ELENA

Your hours will be four to eight Tuesdays, nine to five Saturdays, and the occasional Sunday afternoon." Ms. Milken looked up at me, watery blue eyes swimming behind her thick glasses. "I trust that won't be a problem."

"Twelve hours a week?" I said. "When you interviewed me, you said a minimum of twenty."

"Business needs change, Elena," she said, enunciating slowly as if I might be too dim to understand this concept. "I believe I said a *possibility* of twenty hours a week."

I clamped the tip of my tongue between my teeth. I knew she'd said a *minimum* of twenty, and damn it, I needed every one of them.

I pushed my chair back, hitting one of the two-foot drifts of paper that blanketed the floor. It didn't look like business was slow. And how the hell could her "business needs" have changed so much since she interviewed me two weeks ago?

As I composed myself, I glanced around the office. Blown-up copies of news articles covered the walls, struggling to convince the visitor that this was a real newspaper, instead of a weekly classified ad rag that scattered a few amateurish features among the advertisements.

When I saw those articles, so proudly displayed, I

knew what had happened. I'd walked in for that interview—a third-year journalism student applying for a minimum-wage job—and Ms. Milken had seen her chance to hire a trained reporter at a bargain-basement rate. I needed twenty to thirty hours a week? Well, what a coincidence; that's just what they had in mind. She'd flat-out lied, and I desperately wanted to call her on it, but I didn't dare. I needed this job . . . any job.

So I forced a shrug and said, "Maybe I misheard. But if you ever need someone to work extra hours, I can always use the money. I'll leave a copy of my schedule. I'm free anytime that I don't have classes. Even at the last minute. Just give me a call."

Ms. Milken pursed her lips, then reached over to a stack of paper, plucked a single sheet from the middle, and handed it to me.

"Tips for winterizing gardens," she said. "Turn it into an article. Ten inches. For this week's edition."

I took the sheet. An article on gardening tips? I smiled my keenest cub reporter smile. "I'll drop it off first thing in the morning."

"This week's edition goes to bed in two hours."

"Two—?" My smile collapsed. "I have a class at three."

"Is this going to be a problem, Elena? I've hired students before, and I was reluctant to do so again. I need to know that your priorities are here. Not with boys or parties or bar-hopping or sororities."

"I have my priorities straight," I said, slowly and—I hoped—calmly. "My job is second only to my classes."

"That won't do."

My fingernails bit into my palms, but I kept my voice even. "Maybe, after today, I can skip the occasional class, if it's for something critical." *Like a gardening-tip article.* "But this is the first week of classes, and it's my first time in this particular class, so I really can't miss it."

I met her gaze, and knew she was already mentally thumbing through her list of applicants. "But . . . well, maybe I could give it a shot. I still have an hour."

"There's a desk out front."

At 2:37, I handed the article to Ms. Milken. I'd worked on it for fifty-five minutes, but she'd informed me that the company paid in fifteen-minute increments, so I'd be reimbursed for forty-five.

Any other time, I'd have suddenly remembered that I'd forgotten to add something, and tinkered until I reached a full hour. But nothing makes a worse impression than being late for your first class . . . especially one you aren't officially registered in. So I accepted my loss and hurried out the door.

The office was on Grosvenor Street, within easy walking distance of the University of Toronto, which had been a major factor in my accepting the job. I'd been offered a proofreading position at a small press in Pickering, and it had paid better, but the round-trip on the Go train three times a week would have seriously cut into my earnings. And a job writing articles, however crappy, would look better on my résumé than proofreading.

Now, though, proofreading—as much as I hated it— didn't sound so bad. Nor did the coffee shop job or the clothing store job or any others that had phoned me back after I'd showered the city with my résumé.

Maybe I could call them, see whether any jobs were still open. Or I could do what I'd done last year—work two jobs. Oh yeah, and that had gone *so* well for me— stressing over scheduling, giving up all pretense of a social life, dropping off the running team, studying over breakfast, lunch, dinner . . . even reading while walking to class.

I'd nearly worked my way into a breakdown . . . and

almost lost my A average, which would have ended my partial scholarship and made it impossible to finish my degree.

That officious, conniving bitch. From "Of course you can expect twenty hours a week" to "Is this going to be a problem, Elena?" I should have complained. Hell, I should have told her where to stuff her gardening tips and her twelve-hour-a-week job and her ugly mauve suit and her condescending—

I took a deep breath and rubbed my hands over my face. Think of something else, like this next class.

I was looking forward to it, the only optional course on my schedule. Like last year, I'd chosen anthropology. It wouldn't help my future career one whit, but that was why I chose it, as a mental break in a life where everything was—and had to be—focused on the goal of a degree and a job.

In last year's anthro course, I'd had to do a paper on ancient religion. After some research, I'd decided to focus on animal symbolism in religious ritual, which sounded marginally more interesting than anything else. There I'd stumbled across a doctoral thesis by a guy whose specialty was gods that were part human and part animal.

He had some really fascinating ideas, and I'd based my paper on them. A few weeks later, I'd been writing a student paper article on staff changes when a name had jumped out at me. Clayton Danvers, the guy whose thesis I'd used. Seemed he'd participated in a lecture series the year before, and the school had invited him back to cover a partial term for a prof on sabbatical. I'd noted that in my planner so I could sign up for one of his courses. Then just before registration, my life had careened off course.

A former foster brother had tracked me down. After a lifetime of dealing with guys like Jason, I'd learned that most were cowards. Taking a firm stance usually scared them away. Jason was different.

Short of holding a gun to his head, there was nothing I could do to make him back off. After two weeks of darting between friends' apartments and cheap motel rooms, I'd finally persuaded the cops to enforce the damned restraining order.

Then I'd gone back to school, and registration had been the last thing on my mind. When I'd finally remembered, I'd discovered that Danvers's general-level anthropology course was full.

I was third on the waiting list, though, and in my two years at university, I'd learned a bit about waiting lists. Being third usually meant you were in, but sometimes it took a couple of weeks before a spot cleared, and by then you'd have missed those critical first classes. What you had to do was go to class anyway, on the assumption you'd eventually get a place. Most profs didn't mind. Hell, most profs didn't even notice. So that's what I planned to do: show up, sneak in, and start learning.

2

CLAYTON

AN EIGHT O'CLOCK CLASS," I SAID, GRIPping the phone as I dropped into my office chair. "I only asked for one thing: no classes before ten. Probably think they're doing me such a big favor, letting me teach at their damned school, that I shouldn't dare ask for anything special."

"Uh-huh," Nick said. "Well, at least—"

"What the hell am I doing here anyway? Oh, sure, I'd *love* to teach in Canada. It's only a few hundred miles from every goddamned person I know."

"Jeremy was right. You *are* in a pissy mood."

I swung my feet onto the desktop. "Bullshit. He'd never say that."

"No, he said you were in a foul mood. Not like I needed anyone to tell me that. I can even predict them now. Every fall, you're this way for at least a month. Like an annual round of PMS."

"What?"

"Never mind. Point is, I know what you need, and if you'd stop being so damned stubborn, we could fix this little problem. Why don't I come up this weekend, we'll hit the town—" He paused. "Do they have bars in Toronto?"

"How the fuck should I know? But if you mean what I think you mean—"

"Hey, you're going to need something—or someone— to keep you warm up there. How bad is it, anyway? Blizzards and stuff?"

"It's the second week of September."

"Yeah, so?"

"Was it snowing when you went with your dad to Minneapolis last week?"

"Course not."

"Well, Toronto is a few latitudes south of that."

He snorted. "Right. I might have failed geography, but I know where Canada is. North. Now, stop trying to change the subject."

A tentative rap at the door.

"You gonna answer that?" Nick said.

"No."

The door creaked open and a student popped her head in. "Professor Danvers?"

Nick's laugh echoed down the line. "Oooh, sounds cute. You—"

I dropped the phone, got to my feet, and turned on the intruder—a dark-haired girl in a skirt too short for any student who hoped to be taken seriously.

"Professor Danvers, sir? I was just wondering—"

"Was that door shut?"

"Uh, yes, but—"

"When you knock on a closed door, you're supposed to wait for it to be opened. Isn't that the point of knocking?"

The girl took a slow step back into the hall. "Y—yes, sir, but I wasn't sure you heard me. I just wanted to ask about your class this afternoon. I heard it's full—"

"It is."

"I was hoping maybe—"

"You want a spot? That's what waiting lists are for. If a place opens up, someone will call you."

"Is it okay if I just sit in—?"

"No."

I slammed the door. When I picked up the phone, Nick was laughing.

"Oh, Professor," he said. "Nasty boy. No wonder the little coeds line up for your classes, all hot for teacher."

"Yeah, you think it's funny? You wouldn't think it was funny if you were teaching classes full of those idiots, taking spots away from serious students—who might actually listen to my lecture instead of giggling with their girlfriends about me."

"Oh, you've got a rough life, buddy. If *I* was teaching your classes, and having your 'problem' . . . let's just say I'd be a very tired, but very happy, guy."

"Yeah? Well, thanks for taking my problems so seriously, *buddy*. Next time you get the urge to call and cheer me up? Don't bother."

I slammed the phone into the receiver. Ten seconds

later, it rang again. I ignored it. I'd call him back tonight. I knew Nick didn't mean anything by it, but we'd had the same damned discussion a million times, and you'd really think that by now he'd know how I felt—or didn't feel—about women.

In Nick's world, it wasn't possible for a guy not to want all the women he could get. Well, there *was* one logical explanation, and five years ago he'd tricked me into a gay bar, just to check. But when that didn't seem to be the answer, he'd returned to his quest, certain that if he just kept pushing, I'd "stop being so damned stubborn" and give in.

I slumped into my chair and stared out the window. Since the day Jeremy brought me home to Stonehaven, I'd never spent more than a week away from it or him, and balked at even being gone that long. Now here I was, voluntarily embarking on a two-month sojourn where I'd be lucky to get home every other weekend.

When the offer first came, I'd made the mistake of mentioning it to Jeremy, and the moment I'd seen his reaction, I'd known I was going to Toronto. He'd thought I was considering it, and he'd been so damned proud of me that there'd been no way I could back down without disappointing him.

This was what he'd once wanted for me—a life and a career that extended beyond the Pack. I'd kiboshed that plan before I'd even graduated from high school. Stonehaven was my home, Jeremy was my Alpha, and I wasn't going anywhere. He'd accepted that, but he still liked to see me make the occasional foray into the human world. As much as I loathed every minute away, I did it to please him. So I was here in Toronto until November. And I sure as hell hoped it would tide him over for at least the next decade.

I knew I was overreacting. I'd survive this, much like I'd survived having Jeremy pull out the odd batch of porcupine quills when I'd been a child—grit my teeth and suffer through it. But right now, I was, as Nick said, in one of my fall moods.

They'd started after my eighteenth birthday, but back then, they were mild enough that I'd passed them off as just another bout of moodiness. By my midtwenties, though, that annual dip had become a monthlong crater. Edgy all the time, snapping at everyone, haunted by the constant gnawing feeling that I was missing something, that I was supposed to be doing something, *looking* for something.

As I looked out the window, my gaze lifted to a distant line of treetops. That's where I wanted to be—in the woods, someplace deep and dark and silent, where I could lose myself for a few hours. A run wasn't the answer to whatever was bothering me, but if I ran far enough and fast enough, if I hunted and killed and fed, the blackness would lift for a day or so.

I'd do that tonight. Then, when I was feeling more myself, I'd call Nick back and make amends.

A good plan. If only I didn't need to get through the rest of my day to reach it. I scowled at the stack of notes for my next class. It was the general-level course, the one the girl had been trying to squeeze into. According to the clock, I had about five minutes before class began. Might as well get it over with.

I grabbed the notes, stuffed them into my satchel, and left.

3

ELENA

I CUT THROUGH QUEEN'S PARK. ONCE through the university gates, I veered toward Sidney Smith Hall, then stopped dead. I didn't have the classroom number. My timetable was in my knapsack, which I'd left in my dorm room, wanting to look professional for Ms. Milken. I'd assumed I'd have plenty of time to grab it. But my dorm was on the other side of the campus, and I only had a few minutes to get to class.

I hurried into University College, found a phone, dialed my room, and crossed my fingers. Penny, my roommate, picked up on the fourth ring. I directed her to my knapsack and my timetable.

You'd really think that someone who was in her third year would know how to read a timetable. But Penny's inability to decipher the paper probably explained why she was still in her dorm room half asleep. That and the fact that she'd told me on our first meeting that she was a night person, and would I mind not turning on any lights or opening the blinds before noon? Her parents wanted her at university, so she'd go, but damned if she was going to let it affect her social life.

If someone had been paying *my* tuition, I'd have been so happy—

I cut the thought short. With any luck, by the end of the term I'd have enough saved to move into the off-campus apartment two of my friends shared. Or so I'd thought, until Ms. Purple Polyester cut my hours.

Penny finally deciphered the schedule enough to give me the room number. I had three minutes to get there.

"Oh, and the bookstore called," she said. "About some job you applied for."

"Oh? That's great. Do they want—?"

"I told them you already had one. Oh, and tonight? Don't lock the door when you go to sleep, okay? I had a bitch of a time getting it open when I came in."

She hung up.

I let out a string of curses. Not out loud, of course. Too many people around for that.

I'd really wanted that campus bookstore job. It would have been perfect. And now I was stuck with—

Hold on. What if I called the bookstore back and said my roommate was mistaken, that I didn't already have a job? But that wasn't fair. I'd accepted this other position in good faith.

Yes, and she screwed you around! Cut your hours before you even started!

I rubbed my temples. Did everyone else have these mental battles? The two sides of my brain were at war, one telling me to stand up for myself, not to be afraid to get angry, the other side telling me to be nice and to be polite and everything else I'd been taught. The good-girl side usually won, much to my relief. It was easier that way.

This time, though, the fight wasn't so easily won. I didn't want to take the moral high road—I wanted a decent job that would give me enough money to free me from a full year of hell trapped with an inconsiderate party-girl roommate.

By the time I reached the classroom, I was seething, and more than prepared to let a little of that ire seep onto the next person who pushed the wrong button. I didn't need to wait long. I arrived at the lecture hall less than a minute late, and the TA was already closing the door.

The prof wasn't even there yet, just his teaching assistant, a blond grad student who had the audacity to glare at me as if I'd waltzed in midclass and did a cheerleading routine in front of the lectern. That did it. I might have to put up with a condescending new boss and a brain-dead new roomie, but I didn't need this shit from a damned assistant.

So when he glowered at me, mouth opening to make some sarcastic comment like "Glad you could join us," I cut him off with a glower of my own. Our eyes met. He blinked. And closed his mouth. I swept past him and stalked up the steps into the lecture hall.

"Elena!" someone hissed.

I turned to see a girl from my anthropology class last year. Tina . . . no, Trina. I vaguely recalled her saying she'd signed up for this class, too. She tugged her knapsack off the seat beside her and waved me into it.

"Thanks," I whispered as I sat down.

"Seemed like it was filling up fast, and I knew you were coming. Did you get off the waiting list?"

I shook my head. "Not yet."

"Did you check out the TA? Oh my God. I heard the prof was cute, but that TA is gorgeous. I'm already planning to have some trouble with this course." She grinned. "I'll need serious assistance."

I smiled and shook my head as dread settled in my gut. A TA might not wield as much power as a professor, but he had some clout. I'd just pissed off one of the people who would be grading me in this course. How could I be so stupid? I took a deep breath and told myself it wasn't that bad. After all, it *was* only a TA.

When I looked up from my fretting, the guy had closed the door and returned to the lectern. Where was the prof? Please don't tell me he was skipping the first class, after I busted my ass to get here on time.

The TA began. "If you're here for Anthropology 258, Ritual and Religion in the Americas, you're in the right place. If not, you have fifteen seconds to get out the door without disturbing those who know how to read a room number."

"Oh my God," Trina whispered as two kids snuck, shamefaced, out the door.

"Unbelievable, huh?" I said. "Nothing like a TA with an attitude."

"No, I mean his accent. That is the sexiest drawl I've ever heard. Where do you think he's from? Tennessee? Texas?"

I shrugged. The southern drawl definitely pegged him as American, if the rudeness didn't. Okay, that wasn't fair. I knew plenty of Americans, and most of them were great, but occasionally, you met an asshole like this who explained the stereotype. I took out my notepad as he continued talking.

"So, now that the rest of you know where you are . . . or think you do, let's get started. My name, in case you didn't read the syllabus, is Clayton Danvers. I'm your professor for this class."

My head whipped up so fast I nearly dropped my notebook. I looked down at the podium, and I swear he was looking straight at me.

Oh, shit.

4

CLAYTON

WHEN I ENDED THE LECTURE FIVE MIN-
utes late, half the class had already packed away their
notes, not even waiting to write down the reading assignment. As the last words left my mouth, students
vaulted from their chairs and flew for the door. And for
what? There were few, if any, five o'clock classes. They
just wanted to leave. I've never understood that mental-
ity, that school was a chore to get through. If you're not
there to learn, what the hell are your parents paying
thousands of dollars a year for? Babysitting?

As the students thundered from the lecture hall, a gaggle of girls enveloped me, questions flying.

"Is this the right textbook?"

"What are your office hours?"

"Is the final exam going to be multiple choice?"

Life-and-death questions, and every one right on the
goddamned sheet that I'd handed out at the beginning of
class. I slammed an extra sheaf of those sheets onto the
lectern, pointed at it, and strode toward the door.

I wasn't leaving. But someone else was . . . the blond
girl who'd glared at me coming in—and then hadn't re-
sponded to any of the names on my class list.

She'd ducked out the door without so much as a
glance my way. I swung into the hall to see her disappear
into a mob of students, her white-blond ponytail swinging. In a sea of brunettes and bottle-blondes, that pony-

tail was as easy to follow as deer prints through a maze of mouse tracks.

"You!" I called as I strode after her.

A few students turned. One girl pointed at herself, mouthing a hopeful "Me?" But my quarry kept moving, neither slowing nor speeding up.

I jogged right up behind her and called again, but she just continued weaving past the other students, giving them wide berth, careful not to jostle or even brush against anyone else. I found myself watching that, the subtle but clear buffer she kept around herself. Paid so much attention to it that I let her get a dozen steps ahead of me before I realized it.

She zipped around a corner and was gone. Damn it. I had to find out who she was, and why the hell she'd been in my class.

When I rounded the corner, I saw her ponytail bobbing through a small crowd. I called again, but it was clear that unless I used a name, she wouldn't respond. So I grabbed her arm. A last resort—as physical contact with strangers always was—and I would have let her go as soon as I had her attention, but she whirled, wrenching her arm away.

A flash of something crossed her face—pique mingled with wariness. I recognized that look as well as if I'd been standing in front of a mirror, the same reaction I'd have to a stranger grabbing me from behind.

The look vanished as she recognized me. Her shoulders slumped.

"Professor Danvers," she said, sliding backward out of the main thoroughfare.

"You know who I am? Good. Now maybe you'll extend me the same courtesy."

She tilted her head, nose scrunching. A smattering of freckles dotted that nose, invisible to anyone more than a few feet away. I don't know why I noticed that, just as

I don't know why I noticed that she was tall, only a couple of inches shorter than me, with a lean, athletic build; that she wore little or no makeup and smelled only of soap, a clean tang that I found myself committing to memory.

"Your name," I said finally. "You didn't answer roll call."

"Oh. Right. Elena. Elena Michaels."

In human society, an introduction is typically a jumping-off point for further conversation, at least followed by a handshake and an inane question or two. But she said it as a closing, her gaze sliding past me, hefting her bag to her shoulder, clearly hoping that answering my question would secure her release.

When I made no move to step back, she gave the softest sigh, inaudible to anyone with normal hearing, then backed against the wall, hugging her bag to her chest.

"I'm not in your class. I'm on the waiting list. Third."

"Classes are for registered students only."

One thin shoulder lifted in a shrug. "Sure, but I tried to register—"

"Not hard enough. The class didn't fill until near the end of the registration period, meaning you obviously couldn't be bothered—"

"Couldn't be bothered?" Her eyes flashed and she opened her mouth to say more, then snapped it shut, and looked away. "Fine."

"Fine? Fine what?"

Another blaze, doused just as quickly as the first, but lingering in a brittle clip to her words. "Fine, meaning I'll stay out of your class until I get a spot. *If* I get a spot."

This wasn't the answer I'd been aiming for, though I realized it only as the words left her mouth. I suppose I'd been digging for a reaction. Well, I got one. Just not the one I wanted.

"Excuse me," she murmured, jaw tight as she slipped around me.

She got two feet away before I swung into her path.

"Why?" I said.

"Why what?"

She snapped the reply, then tensed and winced, just barely, and I knew she was telling herself she shouldn't snap at me, shouldn't let me goad her. I've never been good at empathy, so to see someone—a human no less—react, and to understand, was a shock that knocked aside the last traces of my foul mood.

"The class," I said, softening my tone. "Why did you want to take the class? Is this your area in anthropology?"

She hesitated, eyes studying mine, wary. After a moment, she relaxed and leaned against the wall again. "No, I'm not in anthro. Sorry. Journalism."

"Journalism?"

The softest laugh. "Yes, people do choose to become reporters. Shocking, isn't it?" She shifted her bag to her shoulder. "I take anthropology as my annual extra. Last year I did my term paper on religion. I came across your thesis, read it, thought it was interesting, and used it. Then I saw you were teaching the first half of this course. I wanted to take it, but—" Another half-shrug, gaze disconnecting from mine. "Things came up. I registered late."

"You read my thesis?"

Her gaze met mine, and her smile dissolved. "You think I'm lying? It's published. There's a copy right here at—"

"Do you still have your paper?"

"You *do* think I'm lying."

"If you still have last term's paper, I want to see it. Then you can sit in while you wait for an opening."

Her eyes blazed again, and this time she had to struggle to put the fire out. I knew she wanted to tell me where to stuff my course, but she didn't want to cave either and walk away having me think she'd lied.

The battle raged in her eyes for longer than I'd expected. Had I made a misstep? I didn't doubt for a second that she'd read my thesis or that this was the reason she was in my class. No more than I doubted that I'd let her into that class. I'd just wanted to— I don't know. Maybe see whether I could rile her up. Maybe find an excuse to continue this conversation.

"Fine," she said. "I'll drop it by your office tomorrow—"

"What's wrong with now?"

Her jaw tightened, and I knew then that I had gone too far. When she told me, through clenched teeth, that she had a seven o'clock class and hoped to eat dinner, I agreed to let her drop it off tomorrow at ten, after my morning class.

5
ELENA

I STRODE DOWN THE QUIET HALL, LAST year's anthro paper in hand. Danvers's office was at the far end, probably a spare used for storage, then cleared out when the department had to find space for visiting lecturers.

For almost an hour last night, I'd sat in the computer lab, my paper on the screen, my fingers ready to strike the print sequence, but holding back. Finally I'd grabbed my floppy disk from the drive and left, getting all the way to the coffee kiosk in the next building.

Did I still want to take this course? My gut reaction was "no," that it was too much bother, that the prof was an arrogant jerk and I didn't need this.

And yet . . . well, the truth was that the more hurdles he made me jump to get into this class, the more I wanted in.

As for "proving" that I'd read his thesis, that just got my blood boiling all the more. Who did this guy think he was? There might be some girls who'd sneak into his class for the eye candy, but did that give him the right to assume that all female students were interested in *him* rather than his lectures?

I'd continued struggling until the lab was about to close, and I printed out the paper just in case. I'd only made up my mind that morning, after the campus bookstore called me back, and set up an interview for ten thirty. Since I was passing Sidney Smith Hall anyway, I might as well make that ten o'clock drop-off for Professor Danvers. Whether I still wanted to take the class didn't matter. At this point, it would be enough to prove I hadn't lied.

I brushed past two students trying to decipher a professor's handwritten office-hours chart. The next door was Danvers's. I didn't even get a chance to knock before he yanked it open. He must have been leaving. Five minutes later and I'd have had an excuse for leaving my paper with the department secretary instead. Damn.

"Just dropping this off," I said, stepping out of his way.

"Come in."

"That's okay. You were heading out, so I'll—"

He frowned. "I wasn't heading out. I was opening the door for you."

"How did you—?" I shook my head and held out my paper. "Here it is."

"Come in."

He turned and walked back in without waiting for an answer. The door shut behind him. Seemed like a good chance to escape. If only I wasn't still holding the damned term paper.

I opened the door. Danvers was taking his seat behind the desk. That desk, and two chairs, were the only furnishings in the cubbyhole office. On the bookcase sat two opened boxes of books. The desk was littered with papers, books, and professional journals.

"If you're busy unpacking . . ." I said.

"Unpacking?" He frowned.

"Never mind. Here's that paper." I started to lay it on the desk, then thought better of it and put it on an empty bookshelf instead. "My phone number is inside the cover. If I don't hear from you by Friday, I'll assume it's okay to show up in class."

"Sit."

"What?"

He waved at the chair across the desk. "Sit."

I resisted the urge to bark, and answered by not answering . . . and not sitting.

"Suit yourself," he said. "Pass me that paper."

I did. He opened it. I waited, expecting him to flip through. Instead he leaned back in his chair, put his feet on the desk, paper crumpling beneath his loafers, and began to read. I checked my watch.

"I have an appointment in twenty minutes."

He glanced at the clock. "I'll keep you for fifteen, then."

"It's way over in the Koffler Center. At the bookstore."

"You can buy your texts later."

"It's for a job interview."

He lowered the paper. "What the hell do you need a job for?"

"Excuse me?" As soon as I said it I regretted my tone. Well, kind of.

"College is for learning. If you work during school, sure, maybe you'll be able to afford a few extra drinks at the pub, but your grades will suffer."

I pried my jaws open enough to speak. "While I appreciate your concern, *sir,* I'm afraid I don't have much choice. If I don't work, I don't go to school."

"Your parents won't pay for it?"

"My parents are dead."

The moment the words left my mouth, I wished I could suck them back in. I braced for the inevitable "I'm sorry" or "That's too bad."

He just nodded. "Well, I guess you would need to work, then."

"So, may I leave?"

"Come back when you're done."

The interview did not go well. I couldn't even blame it on Professor Danvers. By the time I'd walked across campus, my initial outrage had worn off and I realized he probably didn't mean to be rude. Some people just say whatever comes to mind, bypassing the propriety filter.

The problem with the interview had nothing to do with my mood, but rather with my lack of experience. I knew my way around books, and I could be as courteous and helpful as any nervous first-year student could want, but when it came to sales and cash handling, my résumé boasted only a single summer job at a ballpark concession stand. I could tell that this wasn't enough.

So it was back to Ms. Purple Polyester and her gardening tips. Not for long, though. After calling back the bookstore yesterday, I'd felt rather silly for having struggled with the decision and resolved to work for that classified ad rag only until something better came along.

This time when I arrived at Danvers's office, I had a chance to knock. As my knuckles grazed the wood, the door creaked open. I called a hello, then peeked inside. The office was empty. Not very safe, leaving the door ajar, though I suppose there was nothing in the office worth stealing—not unless there was a black market in dog-eared, coffee-stained copies of *Anthropological Quarterly.*

From the door, I could see my paper on a stack of papers. There was a note on it. I slipped inside and picked it up.

Two words. *Elena* and *wait.*

"Woof," I said.

I looked at the note again. At the bottom was a letter. C. It took me a moment before I remembered his given name. Clayton.

Wasn't that an odd way to sign a note for a student? I reminded myself that, given his age, this was likely his first teaching gig. He probably wasn't used to calling himself "Professor Danvers" or "Dr. Danvers." And for a guy who considered a single-word command an appropriate mode of correspondence, signing with a letter was probably more a matter of economics than of familiarity.

The real question was: Would I do as he'd asked—or demanded? My first reaction was to get my back up. Yet when I thought it through, I simmered down. This wasn't a personal slight. Rude, yes. Condescending, maybe. Yet from what I'd seen in the classroom, no more rude or condescending than he'd be to anyone else.

My next class wasn't until after lunch. No reason why I couldn't pull out a textbook and study here for ten, fifteen minutes. If he didn't show up by then, I'd leave a note and go.

I'd only read two pages when the door banged open, hitting the wall so loudly I jumped.

"Good," he grunted, seeing me there. He tossed an armful of books onto the desk, sending an avalanche of paper to the floor. "You get the job?"

"It was just an interview."

He gave me a look, as if this didn't answer his question. Not much experience with the job market, I guess.

"I don't know yet," I said. "They'll call."

His eyes studied mine. "But you don't think you got it?"

I shrugged. "Probably not. Now, about—"

"Forget the bookstore," he said, thumping down into his desk chair. "I have a job for you."

I hesitated, not sure I'd heard right. "Uh, thank you, but—"

"I need a TA."

I stopped, mouth still open. A teaching assistant position had always been my dream job—good pay, work on campus, flexible hours. . . .

My brain slammed up a big stop sign. A teaching assistant? In anthropology? I was a journalism major. And an undergrad at that.

Maybe I'm too suspicious, but after years of dealing with abusive foster daddies and brothers, I've earned the right to be. When a guy offers me something that doesn't sound kosher, my brain automatically jumps to one conclusion: He wants sex.

In this case, I dismissed it, even felt a little silly for thinking it. Clayton Danvers didn't need to offer teaching positions to get sex. From the way he'd brushed off those girls yesterday, bedding coeds was *not* on his agenda. He probably had a girlfriend or fiancée at home—some gorgeous neurosurgeon or physicist who modeled for Victoria's Secret in her spare time. Might even have a picture of her for his desk . . . once he found it under that blanket of papers.

"I'm not an anthropology student," I said slowly, in case he'd forgotten.

"So?"

"I need to be in this discipline to be a teaching assistant. Isn't that a requirement?"

He brushed my words aside with a wave. "The school wouldn't be hiring you. I would. I'm a temp, so that's how it works. They hire me, and I hire an assistant if I need one."

I'd never heard that, but it sounded logical.

"What about grading papers?" I said. "I'm not qualified for that. And I sure can't teach your classes if you're off sick."

Another wave. "I never get sick. And you won't need to grade essays. I'll just give you the multiple-choice parts of tests. That and . . . uh, administrative work."

"What kind of administrative work?"

"You know . . . departmental . . . stuff. Whatever I need done."

I cast a pointed look at his desk. "Like filing?"

"Sure. Filing. More important, though, I need research—"

A tentative knock at the door cut him short. His nostrils flared, then his mouth set in a hard line. He made no move to stand. Another rap. I arched my brows. He shook his head. We stayed quiet until footsteps tapped away down the hall.

"That's another thing you can do," he said. "Handle my office hours. Talk to students."

"They probably want to speak to *you*. Especially if they're having problems with the course."

"Oh. Right."

He looked so disappointed that I felt a glimmer of empathy.

"I suppose I could screen student visits," I said. "If it's taking papers or answering easy questions, I can handle it. Otherwise, I could have them make appointments, maybe discourage the ones that don't seem too serious."

He smiled then, his eyes lighting up like a kid's. "That'd be great."

My cheeks heated. "Uh, and research. You were saying something—"

"Right. That's really what I need. I'm working on a paper, and I need someone to do the legwork for me, track down articles, print them up, maybe do some extra digging. You cover all that in journalism, right? Research?"

"Right up my alley."

"Good. We're all set, then. You can start—"

"Wait," I said. "Can I think about it? I should hear what the bookstore says first."

He rapped his pen against the edge of the desk, then leveled it at me.

"What's the pay?" he said.

"Huh?"

"The bookstore. What are they offering to pay you?"

"Uh, minimum . . . well, slightly above."

From his expression, that didn't answer his question.

"Five dollars an hour," I said.

"How the hell do you live on that? I'll pay you eight."

"That's very generous. But wages aren't the only thing I need to consider. Hours are another factor, and you might only need me for five, six hours a week—"

"Hours are negotiable. I need help with this paper, and I want to work on another one after that. How many hours would you need?"

I calculated quickly. "Fifteen, if you're paying eight dollars. That would leave me plenty of time to study."

"Fifteen it is, then. When you're busy with school, take less. When things are slow, take more. I'm not running a nine-to-five business. As long as the work gets done, I'm in no hurry."

That sounded damn close to the most perfect school job I could imagine, which had me wondering what the catch was. Well, I suppose the catch was that I had to work with *him,* but I could handle an abrasive boss.

Next question: Why me? He could hire a hundred students who were better qualified. Maybe part of that was just dumb luck. I'd mentioned that I needed work, and that had reminded him that he needed a TA, so he offered me the job.

As a future employee, I wasn't *that* bad of a choice. I clearly wanted to work—a quality that could be hard to come by in students. Plus, I wouldn't sit and moon over him, and I suspected that was a major qualification. I also knew his work better than most students.

Anyone could grade multiple-choice tests, file his papers, and shield him from students. And if he needed a researcher, a journalism student was a good fit. Why me? Why *not* me?

"Does this mean I get to sit in your class until I get a spot?"

"Huh?" He frowned. "Oh, right. The class. Hell, yeah. You're in."

I smiled. "Good. About the job, then . . . when can I start?"

6
CLAYTON

ELENA WAS DUE TO ARRIVE FOR WORK IN five minutes, and I still had no idea what *work* I was going to ask her to do. I didn't need a TA. Now, here I was, having volunteered not only to spend at least fifteen hours each week cooped up in this tiny office with a human, but paying her for the privilege.

I blamed temporary insanity, a new symptom of my fall moods. I could tell myself that I'd offered her a job because I'd been flattered that she'd picked my thesis for her term paper. Or that I'd been struck by a sudden wave of generosity, compelled to help a stranger in need. And if either of those explanations was right, then my fall moods weren't just making me moody, they were fucking up my entire personality.

I knew only that the moment she'd said her interview hadn't gone well, the idea had jumped into my brain and out my mouth before I could stop it. Every hurdle she'd raised had only made me more determined. When I'd succeeded, it felt like pulling down a buck single-handedly—a thrill of victory that had lasted right up until ten minutes ago, when I'd fully comprehended what I'd done.

Maybe I could tell her I'd made a mistake, that I'd reevaluated my workload and decided I didn't need a TA after all. Even as I considered that, a lick of shame ran through me. I pride myself on being fair in my dealings with humans. Sure, my idea of fairness and theirs may not always coincide, but I was never intentionally cruel to anyone who hadn't earned it. Elena had done nothing to earn it.

I'd hired her, so I'd have to find work for her to do . . . preferably someplace else. She could do research in the library or—

Footsteps sounded in the hall. The soft slap of sneakers. I inhaled and caught the faintest touch of her scent coming through the half-open door. My pulse revved up, as if I'd scented an intruder . . . and yet not like that at all.

She paused outside the door. Hesitating? Why was she hesitating? Had she changed—

A knock. A *tentative* knock, as if hoping it wouldn't be answered. She *had* changed her mind about the job.

Wait, that's what I wanted, wasn't it?

I yanked open the door to see her turning away.

"Elena!"

She spun. I mentally kicked myself for yelling at her. Was I *trying* to scare her off?

"Come in," I said. "We have a lot to do."

She stepped inside, shucked off her backpack, and looked around for a place to put it.

"Just toss it wherever," I said.

Another nod, and she tucked it into the corner, under the empty coatrack. My heart was galloping like a spooked stag. Something was wrong. She was *too* quiet. Not that she was usually noisy, but she was giving off palpable waves of distraction, as if she really didn't want to be here.

She was going to quit. The bookstore had called to give her the job, and she didn't quite trust my offer—

"Is this okay?" she said, tugging at her short-sleeved blouse to straighten it. "I wasn't sure if there was, you know, a dress code or something—"

"There isn't. Wear what you like."

She looked around. When her gaze skated past mine, I noticed purplish half-moons under her eyes. She'd slept poorly. Nightmares? Anxiety?

My gaze slid to a faint reddish blotch, the size of a fingerprint, on the side of her throat. A bruise? A lover's kiss?

Did she have a lover? My gut clenched. I shook it off. She was young, pretty. Why wouldn't she have a boyfriend?

"Do you, uh, want me to start filing?" she asked.

She turned toward the desk, and the light illuminated the mark on her throat. Not a bruise or a kiss, but a birthmark or an old, long-healed burn.

"Filing?" she said again. "Should I start—"

"No. Not today. Today we have to talk."

Her blue eyes clouded. "Is something wrong?"

"No, no. We just need to talk about—" *About you. Tell me about yourself. Do you have a boyfriend? What kept you up last night? Is something bothering you? Is it me?* "—your paper. We didn't get time to discuss that yesterday, so I wanted to spend a few minutes on it today."

"Sure." She moved the spare chair over to the desk, sat down, then looked up at me with a faint smile. "So, how badly did I mangle your theory?"

Elena had only been scheduled to work for two hours that day, and we spent the whole time talking, first about her paper, then shifting into the more general area of my work, my interests, theories, past and current projects. As happy as I'd have been to segue our next discussion into her own life, I knew I wouldn't get away with it.

Any other student would have been content to sit and chat with a prof. Well, she would if she was being paid eight bucks an hour to do it. But Elena expected to work. That was obvious when her shift ended and she thanked me, not for the stimulating conversation, but for the "background." That's how she saw it. That's what she was comfortable with. Still, it was a start . . . even if it did mean I'd have to find actual work for her to do.

When Elena came the next day, I let her file. Can't say I really understood why this seemed so important to her, but no one has ever accused me of being intolerant of other people's eccentricities. So I let her put my papers into neatly labeled folders. Since my handwriting was somewhat indecipherable, I had to stick close by and explain each page to her so she could file it properly.

When she finished, I had a file drawer every bit as beautifully organized as the file cabinet at Stonehaven. Not that I'd seen the inside of the one at Stonehaven lately—it'd been locked ever since Jeremy made the mistake of asking me to retrieve the property tax records, and spent nearly a week refiling the mess.

I'd be more careful with this one. First, though, I'd have to figure out where she'd put everything. Still, the desktop looked very neat and clean, with the pencils and pens in a mug, the stapler and desk calendar arranged just so. Jeremy would have been impressed. Well, actually, he'd probably have a heart attack, but he made it a rule never to visit me during one of my human-world sojourns, so I didn't need to worry about him seeing it.

After that, we had thirty minutes of Elena's shift left, so I spent it making a semipermanent schedule for her. I took into consideration her course load, extracurricular activities, and study habits, giving her a flexible schedule with short shifts, sometimes two per day to reach her goal of fifteen hours a week.

"Wow, that's great," she said, reading it over. "This will work out perfectly." She smiled up at me. "Thanks."

I'd have enjoyed that smile more if I hadn't known that I'd split her shifts to guarantee I'd see her at least once every weekday. And because it'd given me the excuse to ask her a ton of personal questions—what courses she was taking, what sports and activities she enjoyed, etcetera. Good enough, though. For now.

I soon discovered that my ingenious "teaching assistant job" plan was not as foolproof as I'd thought.

I was heading for the cafeteria to grab a second dinner, when a hand thudded onto my shoulder. I wheeled, jerking away.

"Professor Danvers." My assailant flashed a greasy smile. "Just the man I wanted to see."

When he sidled closer, I stepped back and crossed my arms. He moved closer still, checking over his shoulder for students, as if thinking I was getting out of their path. As body-language illiterate as most humans.

The man was middle-aged, dressed in corduroy pants and a tweed jacket that wouldn't have buttoned over his gut no matter how hard he sucked it in. A professor. Had I met him yet? Maybe, but obviously not someone I'd deemed important, or interesting, enough to remember.

"I hear you have a new teaching assistant," he said.

"What?" I hadn't told anyone on staff.

He laughed. "Rumors travel fast. One of my students went by your office yesterday to see whether you needed a TA and you told her you already had one." His fleshy features twisted into a mock frown. "Which seems odd, considering the department has no record of such a position being offered."

"It wasn't. I hired her myself. I'll be paying her myself."

"That's . . . generous of you, Dr.—may I call you Clayton?"

I settled for a shrug he could interpret as he liked.

He continued, "While we appreciate you funding your own TA, surely you can see where that might raise certain questions."

"Of what?"

He gave me a look, as if to say the answer should be obvious. I stood my ground and met his gaze with a level stare. He broke first, beads of sweat popping out across his broad forehead. I took a slow step forward, closing the narrow gap between us.

"Of what?" I said.

His gaze flicked to mine, then skittered away. Confusion fluttered behind his eyes, instinct warning him to back down, human reason wondering why.

"I hired her myself because she'll be working for me," I said. "As a research assistant for studies unconnected to the school. That seemed the only fair way to handle it."

"Yes, well . . ." The man blinked, struggling to recoup his composure. "That's all very sensible, I suppose, but there's another problem. She's taking one of your classes. If she graded papers for her own class—"

"She won't."

"Perhaps if she dropped out of your class—"

"That isn't necessary. She won't mark or grade papers or do any other teaching assistant duties for that class." Did that mean she couldn't cover my office hours? Shit.

A slow, reluctant nod. "I suppose that would be acceptable." His gaze rose to mine. "But, remember, we must always take care when dealing with students, particularly attractive young women."

"That won't be a problem."

He clapped me on the back. "Of course it won't. I just thought I should mention it. Eyes will be watching. Eyes are always watching. And minds are always thinking—usually the worst. Don't forget that."

The next day I told Elena about her job changes. When I finished, she busied herself hanging up her backpack.

"Okay," she said. "That makes sense. I guess I should have known that—"

"*I* should have known," I said, boosting myself onto the edge of my desk.

A brief smile, one that almost met her eyes. "Not your fault. You're as new at this as I am. So, uh, I guess we'll need to rework that schedule. How many fewer hours—?"

"That won't change. I'll just give you more research work."

The smile grew a quarter-inch, still hesitant. "Really? I mean, you don't need to—"

"More time for research means more research I can do. Publish or perish, that's the law of academics. We'll stick to the original schedule, and if you need more hours, just ask."

Her smile flashed full strength, so brilliant my breath caught.

"Thank you," she said, started to turn away, then stopped. "Oh, and what about your student drop-ins? That's more reception work than teaching assistance, right?"

"It is." *Whew.*

"We're all set then. So—"

Someone rapped at the door. I inhaled and scowled. Student. One who'd been here before, on business no more pressing than a sudden need to have me confirm, in person, the test schedule I'd handed out on the first day.

Elena pointed at herself, then the door. Did I want her to answer it? My nod was so emphatic she choked back a laugh. Then she arched her brows and pointed to a spot behind the door, mouthing "Wanna hide?" with lips twitching in a teasing grin. When I hopped off the desk and ducked behind the door, a small laugh finally escaped her. She tossed me one last breathtaking smile, then answered the door.

Over the next week, our working relationship hit a comfortable stride. When it came to any type of personal relationship, though, the ramparts stayed firmly in place. The moment I worked a conversation away from business, her body language cues were strong enough for a blind man to read, and they screamed "Back off." So I did.

But that left me with a quandary. I didn't just *want* to get to know her better, I needed to—a need that gnawed at my gut worse than hunger, that woke me up in the middle of the night.

As for why I wanted to know so much about her, I tried not to think about that. It made me nervous. A weak word, but there's no better way to describe it. Trying to understand my interest only brought on a strange feeling of apprehension. So I settled for accepting the situation at face value—I found her intriguing, and I was alone in Toronto, lonely, missing my Pack, and in need of companionship.

Yet it soon became obvious that she wasn't letting our relationship deepen until I'd earned her trust. And that, I suspected, would take a while—at least as long as it would take me to learn to trust a human stranger. But the need to know more was so overwhelming that within a week it took me to a place I'd rather not have gone. I started following her.

I'm not proud of that. Studying her when she was in my office or classroom was one thing, but I crossed a line when I started to follow her. I told myself it wasn't stalking. I didn't want to hurt her or scare her. I just wanted to learn more about her.

Despite my best justifications, I hated the way that following her made me feel, and after only a few evenings of it, I vowed to quit. Whether I would have been able to stick with that vow is debatable, but on that final night, fortune favored me with an alternative.

That evening, I spent an hour in the Laidlaw Library, sitting in a carrel, pretending to study a book I'd grabbed off the shelf. My real object of study sat at a table twenty feet away. Elena was working on an essay, driven from her dorm room yet again by her selfish roommate.

Her writing was going badly, a sentence stroked out for every two written, the strokes becoming harsher, angrier, each time. Any second now she'd give up and . . . And then what? I knew how I'd work off my frustration, but how would she?

I peeked over my book. She leaned back, pen in hand, staring at the paper. Then she shoved the pages into her backpack, threw it over her shoulder, and strode out of the study area. I counted to ten and followed.

When Elena returned to her dorm, I felt a trickle of disappointment. Was that how she resolved her frustration? Give up and go home? Maybe she'd gone upstairs to blast her roommate, tell the brat that this was her room, too, and she wasn't being run off. That's what I would have done, but I suspected Elena wasn't ready for that.

I'd just started back toward my apartment when I caught Elena's scent on the breeze. I turned to see her hurrying across the dorm lawn, backpack over her shoulder, but carried higher, as if she'd emptied out the load of books. She crossed to the sidewalk, jaw set, gaze forward, ponytail bouncing with each firm stride, moving fast into the gathering darkness. I waited until she vanished around a building, then followed.

Elena cut through the campus up to Bloor Street, then headed west. Although many of the small stores had closed, the nightlife was heating up as people spilled from restaurants and wandered the streets looking for entertainment.

Elena had already eaten. Was she heading to a bar? A date maybe? The question brought a now familiar tightening in my gut. Of all the questions I had about Elena, this topic obsessed me more than most.

I was pretty sure there was no steady boyfriend at school. I'd managed a few casual questions about Friday- and Saturday-night plans, and usually found that they entailed hanging out with friends.

I'd never smelled a man on her. Did that mean there wasn't one? Maybe he was going to school elsewhere or was working back at home . . . wherever Elena's home was.

The answer to *that* question had proved the most elusive. She had to have someone who'd raised her, someplace she called home. Whenever I broached the topic, though, she changed the subject.

Elena passed through the bar and restaurant district without slowing. As the crowds waned, I had to pull farther and farther back, until I was following her by scent, catching glimpses of her distant form only when she passed under a streetlight. Dusk had deepened to dark, yet she kept walking. At least two miles passed before she turned off. When I saw where she turned off, my heart did a double flip.

As I followed her trail into the park, I had to check my pace. I kept speeding up, anxious to see where she was going, hoping that I knew. I told myself I had to be wrong. Surely there was another good reason why she'd be here.

Like what? Nighttime lawn bowling league? Moonlight skinny-dipping? I knew where she was going.

When she ducked behind a building, I thought I was wrong. But then she stepped out again, the jeans and long-sleeved jersey gone, replaced by shorts and a T-shirt. She looked around the dark, empty park, then headed for the hiking path.

Near the head of the trail, she stopped. Another scan of her surroundings, more careful this time, head tilting to listen. She took something from her backpack, and tucked the bag beneath some undergrowth. When she straightened, she gave another long, careful look around. Then she held out the small cylinder she'd removed from the bag and pressed a button. A blade shot out. A nod of satisfaction, and she snapped it shut again, cupped it in her palm, walked to the head of the trail, and began her warm-up exercises.

When she finally stopped her stretches, she looked around one last time, then faced the trail, took a deep breath, and vaulted forward, off and running.

For a moment, I stood there, hidden in the trees, watching her. Only when she disappeared around a corner did I snap from my reverie and find a changing place of my own.

7
CLAYTON

I CHANGED IN A SMALL CLEARING, AS deep in the strip of woods as I could get. When I finished, I stretched, front paws sliding out as far as I could reach. My skin itched, like clothes kept in the closet too long, dusty and stale. More than any other, I hated this part of being away from home—Changing in the shadows, furtive, always on alert. A dangerous undertaking, meaning it couldn't be undertaken any more than necessary. Not like at Stonehaven, where I could Change anytime the urge struck.

I sprang to my feet and ran back to the path. I'd been gone long enough for Elena to get a good head start. Luckily, she was running upwind, meaning I could catch her scent on the breeze. I breathed it in, inhaling so deeply the cold air scorched my lungs.

When I was in human form, Elena's scent teased and intrigued me with unformed thoughts and vague urges. Now there was no vagueness or uncertainty. The smell of her cut through the night air like a drug, and I raced after it, as blind to my surroundings as if I'd been on a treadmill.

Finally, she was there, just ahead of me, ponytail bobbing in the darkness. I threw my front paws out, nails digging into the path, forcing the rest of my body to a skidding halt.

I should have slipped into the woods, then approached hidden along the side, but the tree cover was so far from the path's edge . . . so far from her. Just a little closer, then I'd cut to the shadows.

When I was close enough to hear the chuff of her breathing, I knew I should stop. But it was so dark, with only a sliver moon illuminating the path. She'd never see me. I could get closer.

She was sweating now, dripping scent. I drank in the smell, eyes narrowing to slits as I inhaled. I slipped off the path to run along the grassy edge, where I'd make less noise. Just a little closer, and then I'd—

Elena stopped, so fast she stumbled. I raced for the

tree cover, stopped just inside, and hunkered down, holding myself still.

After a moment, I peered out. She was still there, where she'd stopped, squinting to see in the near-darkness. She held her switchblade out, finger over the trigger, the blade still sheathed. Her gaze traveled over both sides of the path, searching the shadows. She cocked her head, listening. Then, with a soft sigh and a slow shake of her head, she tucked the knife back into her palm, checked her watch, then sighed again. After one longing look down the path, she turned around and started running back the way she'd come.

I stayed in the woods. As much as I wanted to be closer, I wouldn't risk spooking her again. So I ran alongside her, far enough away to keep silent, but close enough that I could hear the pound of her feet, and if I glanced over, see her pale form against the night.

Partway back, she slowed. I could tell from her breathing that she was far from exhausted. Had she heard me? I'd been running silently, skirting dead leaves and undergrowth.

Elena looked around, a casual sweep of the forest. She checked her watch. Her nose scrunched up, head tilted, as if considering something. A pause. Then she strode off the path, heading to my side. I stayed absolutely still. A few feet from the tree line, she lowered herself onto the ground beside a boulder.

I waited, then slunk closer and peered out. She sat on the grass, leaning back against the rock. After another minute, her eyelids began to flag. They closed halfway, then she sat there, relaxing in the quiet night.

I hunkered down to my belly and crept forward until my muzzle poked out into the clearing. Sweat trickled down her cheek. I watched it fall, wondered what it would taste like, imagined it, tangy and salty, imagined the feel of her cheek under my tongue. A shudder ran through me and I closed my eyes.

Something tickled my tail. My eyes flew open. A chipmunk scampered along my side. I stared, marveling at its stupidity. It must have figured I was a dog and stayed focused on its quarry, the human a few feet away. Around here, humans meant food, not danger. It'd probably smelled her and woken up, hoping to be given a late-night snack.

As the chipmunk raced toward Elena, I let out the softest growl. It just kept scampering along, determined to intrude on her solitude.

I slapped down my paw, pinning it. The chipmunk let out a tiny shriek and twisted in panic. I stretched forward, bringing my jaws a hairsbreadth from its head, and drew back my lips in a silent snarl. When I was sure it got the message, I lifted my paw. The chipmunk tore back into the woods.

I looked over at Elena. She was still resting, undisturbed. I stretched out, lowered my muzzle to my forelegs, and watched her.

The way to get to know Elena better was now obvious. She liked to run; I liked to run. Maybe not in the same way, but I could be flexible. The important thing was that this was a common interest that could get us out of that damned office and into an environment where I could be myself. Well, not really myself, but closer to it.

The problem was how to work the topic into conversation. Not only that, but how to formulate it into a request. I didn't have much experience with that—making requests. I told people what I wanted—whether they chose to give it to me was their concern.

I'd had friendships with humans before. Okay, maybe *friendships* is stretching it, but I'd had acquaintances. I never initiated the relationship, though. Even with something as inconsequential as partnering up for a school project, I'd always sat back and waited for someone to come to me, and eventually someone would, a classmate who'd learned to overlook my rudeness, or one who wanted my brains badly enough that he didn't care how unfriendly I was.

Even with Nick, I never said, "Hey, do you want to catch a movie tonight?" I told him I wanted to see a show, and he knew me well enough to understand that the matter was open for negotiation . . . at least in theory.

Yet I knew there was no way in hell I could go up to Elena and tell her to take me along on her next run. Even if I did manage to come up with a rational story to explain how I knew she ran, I suspected the demand-and-wait-for-results approach would leave me waiting for a very long time . . . probably on the opposite side of a slammed door.

This would take finesse. Finesse and patience. Had I possessed either, I'm sure things would have gone much smoother.

When Elena came to work the next day, it was obvious that her run had done its job, clearing her head and her mood. But if I'd hoped that somehow our shared experience had gone both ways, I was soon cured of that fantasy.

Elena came in and did her work, as pleasant as could be. But the moment I tried turning the conversation away from the paper she was researching for me, she steered it right back on track. Even a desperate "So, what did you do last night?" only earned me a murmured "Not much."

The next time she asked me a research question, I'd work conversation in the right direction . . . though I had no idea how I'd segue from prehistoric bear cults to jogging. So she continued skimming through the stack of books, making notes, while I graded quizzes. It went really well for the first ten minutes. Then I got tired of waiting and slapped the stack of quizzes down onto the desk.

"Do you run?" I said.

From the look she gave me, you'd think I'd asked whether she wore men's underwear.

"Do I what?" she asked after several long seconds of silence.

"Run. You know, jog, run, whatever."

She continued to stare at me. I probably should have worked it into the conversation better. Or started a conversation first, so I'd have one to work it into. So now I had to think up one on the fly, which would have been easier if she wasn't sitting there, nose scrunched, waiting for me to say something profound.

"Running is good," I said. "A good hobby—sport. A good sport. Good for you."

Her lips twitched. "Uh-huh."

"Well, it is, right? Gets you outside, in the fresh air, exercising. All good."

The phone rang—a sound I have never been so grateful to hear. As I lifted the receiver, she shook her head, smiling, and I knew my fumble hadn't been fatal—more of a pratfall, the kind of thing she was getting used to.

"Hello?" a woman's voice said on the other end of the line.

I started to hang up, but she spoke again, louder. Elena motioned at the phone, as if maybe I'd thought there was no one there. Damn.

I lifted the phone to my ear. "What?"

Elena sighed and rolled her eyes.

"Is Elena Michaels there?" the woman asked.

"No."

"Her roommate said she was there. She gave me this number and . . ."

The woman droned on, but I didn't hear. As tempting as it was to hang up, this could be urgent. I couldn't argue that talking to me about running was more important than a sick relative . . . not a close relative anyway.

So I passed the phone to Elena. She hesitated, brows knitting, then took it with a cautious "Hello?" No sooner did I hear the woman respond than Elena's eyes went wide with dismay, and I knew I'd made a mistake.

"This isn't—" Elena began. "No, I'm at work. I can't talk about this now. I—"

The woman's voice cut in. I caught a few words, none that made any sense out of context. But the next one required no context at all. And when I heard it, I reached over to slam down the plunger. Before I could, Elena caught my eye, and her cheeks went scarlet as she realized I was listening. She grabbed the phone from under my hand and twisted around, moving as far from the desk as the cord would allow.

"I can't—" she whispered. "Look, whatever he said, I didn't—"

The woman continued to rant. This time, though, when she called Elena a bitch, Elena's back went rigid.

"This is not my problem," Elena said, voice icing over. "No, *you* listen to *me*. I have never done anything—" The woman yelled something and Elena's back went so tight it looked ready to snap. "He's the one with the problem, not me, and I'm not going to—"

The line went dead. Elena stood there, fingers white around the receiver. After a moment she lowered her arm stiffly, and replaced the receiver in the cradle.

"I am so sorry," she said as she turned to me.

"Sorry? Don't be sorry. What the hell does that woman think—?"

"I'm sorry and it won't happen again."

Elena enunciated each word with care, and as her gaze met mine, my own words died in my throat. From her look, I knew if I continued, I'd cross a line that wasn't ready to be crossed.

"I don't know how she got this number," Elena said.

"Your roommate gave it to her."

Anger sparked in her eyes. "Then I'll have a talk with her."

She turned, still stiff, and looked around the room, as if trying to remember what she'd been doing before the phone rang. Her gaze lit on the stack of books. She reached for the open one.

"Running," I said.

She stopped, lips pursing in a frown, then cracking into a tiny smile. "Ah, right. Running. It's good."

I hoisted myself onto the desktop. "It is, and the reason I was asking is that I run, but I can't seem to find a decent track around here. So I thought, even if you don't run, you might be able to recommend a spot for me."

Elena took her seat. "Well, I do. Run, that is. There are a few good places around here. It depends on whether you like the street or the beach or—"

"Where do you run?"

"Uh, well, that depends. Usually in a park—"

"Good. I'll go with you, then."

She stared at me, as if replaying my words, making sure she'd heard right. Then she pulled back in her chair.

"I'm not sure that's such a . . ."

She let the sentence trail off and her gaze searched mine, wary, almost reluctant, as if looking for something she didn't really expect to find, but had to be sure.

"You like to run alone?" I said. "That's fine. Me, I like company. Back at home, no problem, but here . . . ?" I shrugged. "Not a lot of running buddies to pick from."

She smiled. "I'm sure I could find one for you. I'll make an announcement at the next class and—"

"I want someone to run with, not from."

She laughed.

I continued, "Now, this park you mentioned. Maybe you can show it to me sometime, or draw me a map."

She hesitated, then shrugged. "I don't mind company, I guess. Sure, I'll take you there, show you the trails. I usually run at night, but—"

"Night's fine."

"The park's actually closed after dark. That's one reason I go there. It's very quiet, and I usually have the whole place to myself. Technically, of course, I am trespassing."

"So if we hear sirens, we run faster."

She smiled. "Exactly."

"I'll go with you next time, then. So when's that? Tonight? This weekend?"

A laugh. "Eager to get back to it? Well, you should have plenty of running buddies this weekend."

"Huh?"

"You *are* going home this weekend, aren't you? That's what you said on Monday. Going home for Thanksgiving. Well, not *your* Thanksgiving—that's in November. For you, this is just a long weekend."

"Uh, right. That's right. I'm going home."

Any other time, it would have been a welcome reminder. Right then, though, I wondered whether there was some way I could get out of it.

"So we'll do it next week," she said. "And this weekend, you can run with your regular partners. Assuming you'll see them."

"I will. It's a Meet . . . ing. Meeting. Bunch of buddies coming over."

"Sounds like fun." She settled back into her seat. "You have trails near your place?"

"*At* our place."

Her brows went up.

"Big backyard," I said. "A few hundred acres."

"Oh, wow. Woods?"

I nodded. "Mostly forest, some field. Got a pond, a couple of streams. Lots of trails."

"Now that's the kind of place I'd like to have. Not that I've ever lived in the country. I'm probably one of those people who'd get out there and start missing the city life." She paused. "You're in New York, right? The state, not the city."

"We're up by Syracuse. Nearest neighbor is at least a half-mile . . ."

We spent the rest of Elena's shift talking. Okay, I did most of the talking, but she listened, and she was interested, and every now and then she'd let a little of herself slide into the conversation.

Early the next morning, I headed home. There wouldn't have been much use in staying behind. As Elena said, it was the Canadian Thanksgiving, so she'd be going home herself. I'd asked about her plans but, as usual, she'd ducked the question. I'd try again when I came back.

And, if I could, I'd broach the topic of that phone call again. That bugged me, someone tracking Elena down just to tell her off. I was sure Elena had done nothing to warrant that kind of treatment.

More on that later. In the meantime, I had a Meet to attend. And unlike the past few fall Meets, this time I was in the mood to enjoy it.

8
CLAYTON

By THE TIME THE PLANE TOUCHED DOWN in Syracuse, any urge to skip the Meet had passed, and I couldn't believe I'd ever considered it.

No one met me at the terminal, and I hadn't expected it. I'd come in on the red-eye flight, which I preferred, since it usually meant I didn't need to sit next to anyone. It made sense, then, for someone to drop off my car the day before, rather than get up at four A.M. to come and get me. Of course, it would have made even more sense for me to take a cab, but no one dared suggest that. Airplanes were bad enough.

At just past seven, I reached Stonehaven. As I drove down the long tree-lined drive, the road vanished behind me and the stone walls of the house appeared. The upper windows were black rectangles. Everyone was still in bed, probably sleeping off a late night. On the main floor, strips of light glowed around the drawn dining room blinds, borrowed illumination from another room, probably the study.

As I passed the cars flanking the drive, a light came on in the farthest upstairs room. Jeremy's bedroom. I hit the garage door opener, then pulled in beside his truck, left my bag on the seat, and bounded for the house.

Once inside, I saw that my earlier guess had been right. Someone was in the study. The door was ajar, light seeping out into the dark hall.

Logan sat in Jeremy's armchair. Being still fairly new to the Pack, Logan didn't fully understand the protocol, so he always chose the chair he liked best. His favorite just happened to be Jeremy's. He meant no disrespect, but still, whenever I saw him there, my hackles rose. No matter how many times I booted him out of it—with a snarl or a good-natured chair-tipping, depending on my mood—he kept doing it.

Logan was studying, hunched forward over his textbook, highlighter in hand, braids hanging in a short curtain around his face. No . . . not braids. What did they call them? Dreadlocks. A fitting name—they did look pretty damned dreadful.

Apparently, Logan wasn't over his new "search for cultural identity" phase. Made no sense to me. Who cared who your parents were, what their racial or cultural background was? I didn't give a shit about mine. As Jeremy explained, though—and explained often— my own attitude toward this, and most other things, was not the best ruler by which to measure others.

I should be supportive of Logan's identity quest, and if I couldn't be supportive, at least I could keep silent. And if I couldn't *voluntarily* keep silent, then I would do so under direct order. So I was forbidden to comment on the dreadlocks. Which was fine; Logan and I found enough to argue about as it was.

Logan had been with the Pack for three years. Although he was a hereditary werewolf, he'd grown up as a human—the product of an affair that ended after his conception. A few months before his first Change, when he'd been grappling with the initial physical and sensory changes, he'd received a letter from his father. It directed him to 13876 Wilton Grove Lane, near Bear Valley, New York, where he'd find answers to his questions. So he arrived on our doorstep.

To me, this was the height of parental neglect. First

you leave your kid with his human mother, who has no clue about her son's true nature, and therefore risk exposure with every childhood trip to the doctor. Then, you let him go crazy wondering what's wrong with him when his werewolf secondary powers kick in. And finally, when you *do* decide to intervene, you foist him off on strangers.

The identity of Logan's father was still a mystery. Logan assumed the guy was black. His mother refused to confirm it, but considering she came from a line of blond-haired, blue-eyed Norwegians, and Logan had deep brown eyes, brown skin, and brown hair, he figured it was a pretty good guess.

With that to go on, Jeremy had been helping to narrow down the paternal possibilities. His most recent theory was that Logan's father was Caribbean. Hence the dreadlocks. As for why Logan would even want to know his father—a mutt who'd abandoned him—that was beyond me. But, apparently, no one cared to hear my thoughts on the matter.

I snuck up behind Logan and loomed over the chair, casting a shadow on his book. He jumped, streaking highlighter across the page.

"Jesus fucking—!" He twisted and saw me. "Goddamn it, Clayton. Do you have to do that?"

"Honing your senses. A duty and a pleasure." I grabbed the text, swung over to the sofa, and dropped onto my back. "*Business Law: Ethical and Economic Considerations.* No wonder you were drifting off."

He stood. "There, I'm leaving the sacred chair. Now can I have my book back?"

"Sit down. Jeremy's shower's still running."

I flipped the page, keeping my finger in at his spot. When he didn't say anything, I lowered the book. He stood next to the chair, hovering like a dragonfly looking for a place to land.

"Well, sit down," I said, reaching out and kicking the chair.

"It's a test, right?"

"Huh?"

"If I sit down, you're going to pounce."

"That wasn't the plan, but if it's what you expect, I'd hate to disappoint you. Better yet, I could yank the chair out from under you." I looked up at him. "Let's test those reflexes. See if you can sit before I can pounce."

Logan snorted. "Yeah, like I'm stupid enough to—"

He dropped toward the chair, but not before I kicked it away from him. He hit the floor.

"Damn," he muttered, then peered up at me. "That was cheating. You said *yank*, not kick."

"Misdirection," I said. "A good try at it yourself, but you tipped your hand by glancing over to see how far back the chair was."

I helped him off the floor.

"Sit." I waved at Jeremy's chair.

He cautiously lowered himself onto it.

"So how's school going?" I said. "You get all your courses okay?"

"Most of them. I missed out on an elective I wanted, but squeezed it in next term. How about you?" He slid a sly smile my way. "Maybe Jeremy should send you away every fall. That seems to cure your moods. Torture you with teaching for a month, and you'll be so glad to come home you'll be bouncing off the walls."

I shrugged. "It's not that bad."

He arched his brows. "Come again?"

"The teaching." I tossed his book onto his lap. "I'm happy to come home and torment you and Nick for a couple of days, but it's going okay."

"Uh-huh." He studied me. "Did you have anything to drink on the plane?"

"Water."

"Did you leave it unattended? Close your eyes for a few minutes? 'Cause I'm pretty sure someone slipped something into it."

"Funny. I'm—"

At a noise from the hall, I shot off the couch and bounded to the door as Jeremy walked through. Behind me, Logan slid over to the sofa.

"Hey," I said. "I'm home."

Jeremy's lips curved in a half-smile. "So I heard. As did everyone else, I think. You seem to be in a good mood. I'm glad to see it."

I glanced over at Logan. "At least someone is."

"I'm glad to see it, too," Logan said. "Just exercising a healthy dose of caution. We've all been bracing for the storm, and I'm not quite ready to unlash myself from the mast."

Jeremy shook his head. "I told them you seemed better on the phone, and Nick agreed. A change of scenery was what you needed. I suspected that might be it. Seasonal restlessness."

"I was voting hormones," Logan said. "One of those weird wolf things you're so attuned to. Of course, that could still be it." He grinned at me. "Things getting a little steamy up in the frozen north? Taking Nick's advice when he's not around to gloat over it?"

"No, and if you want me to stay in a good mood, you'll leave Nick's advice where it belongs—with Nick."

"Speaking of whom, I believe I heard him stirring," Jeremy said. "And, if not, I'm sure you can fix that. I'll start breakfast—"

"Why don't we let Nick sleep in? I'll make breakfast." I turned to Logan. "Come and give me a hand."

He groaned.

"Fine, I'll go bug Nick then, and Jeremy can make breakfast—"

Logan leapt up. "I'll start the bacon."

"Good. I'll take the eggs and toast."

"And I'll try not to take it personally," Jeremy said.

"Nah, it's not about you," I said, grinning as I squeezed past him. "It's about me. I'm hungry and I want food I can eat."

I ducked his lethal glare and herded Logan toward the kitchen.

As the weekend slipped past, I found myself, for once, able to relax and enjoy it, not anxiously watching the clock, wishing I could stretch my time at home into infinity.

Nick, Logan, and I began Sunday afternoon with a workout. Within an hour, though, it was down to me pumping iron in the basement alone. Nick worked out to build muscles for girls, not fights. By the thirty-minute mark, he'd done all the body-polishing he wanted. He stuck around a little longer, lounging on the benches and talking to me before wandering off in search of more interesting diversions.

Logan was more dedicated to improving his fighting strength. As the newest and youngest Pack member, he was the one most likely to be targeted by mutts looking to challenge a Pack wolf. He went to Northwestern, in Illinois, which was outside Pack territory, so mutts considered him fair game. I'd tried to help with that, but he'd have none of it, and insisted on defending himself.

It was that streak of independence that usually had him fleeing the exercise room first. When Logan had joined the Pack, Jeremy put me in charge of his physical training. Logan had gone along with it, as he went along with everything Jeremy asked, but the moment he'd considered himself trained, he'd dumped his trainer.

Now, when we worked out together, I tried to give him tips and pointers, but he always acted as if I was criticizing him. It never took long before he was stomping back upstairs. That afternoon, though, he did a full workout, accepting what few tidbits of advice I offered with only the barest roll of his eyes.

I kept on for another half-hour after Logan left. At school, my workouts were barely adequate—I had to pick times when no one was around to see how much I was bench-pressing. I was wiping my eyes, getting ready to quit, when I lowered the towel to see Antonio in the doorway.

"You gonna work out?" I asked. "Let me wipe down the machines."

He shook his head and took a seat on the leg-press bench.

"What's up?" I said.

A half-shrug, but his eyes bored into mine as if they could see clear through to the other side.

"So . . . how are you doing?" he asked.

"Fine." I grinned. "Better than fine. Damned near perfect."

"I see that."

I whipped the towel at him. "Not you, too. Come on. Am I not allowed to be in a good mood without everyone wondering what's wrong? Logan's been joking about spiked drinks all weekend. Nick keeps giving me funny looks. Peter took me aside yesterday for a little heart-to-heart on how lonely it can be living away from the Pack, and how tempting it can be to start taking something to make things easier. The only person who seems happy to see me happy is Jeremy."

"I don't think there's anything *wrong*, Clay."

"Good."

He started to say something, then grabbed a dumbbell and began doing arm curls.

He smiled at me. "Still at ninety pounds?"

"Yeah, yeah. And I'm not going any higher for that one. I'm not built the same as you."

His smile grew. "Good excuse. So . . . I hear the teaching is going very well."

"*Very* well would be stretching it, but it's going fine."

He nodded, attention fixed on the weight. "Meeting new people, I suppose."

"Uh-huh."

He did a few more reps, then cleared his throat. "If there's ever anything you want to talk about, Clay, anything you don't feel you can discuss with Jeremy, anything you don't think he'd understand . . ." He met my gaze. "I'm always here. You know that. Just because Jeremy's my best friend doesn't mean I tell him everything. I know better than anyone that there are some things Jeremy doesn't understand. If you haven't experienced a thing, you don't know much about it. Like I wouldn't know how to paint a picture and he wouldn't know how to run a business."

After a moment's hesitation, I glanced at the door, then looked overhead.

"Jeremy's outside," Antonio said, laying down the weight. "He can't hear us."

"Well, there is something," I said.

"Yes?"

"It's not that I don't want to discuss it with Jeremy. I just— Like you said, he just doesn't *get* some things. I know he wants what's best for me, and I know he worries about me, but . . ."

Antonio shifted to the edge of his seat. "Go on."

"I need your advice. You have some experience in this area."

Something flashed behind his eyes. "Yes, I probably do."

"It's about motorcycles."

"Motor—" He blinked. "Motorcycles?"

"You had one, remember? Until you wiped out, and

Dominic didn't want you getting another one, went on and on about your responsibilities as a father—"

"I can still hear him every time I take my car up over a hundred."

I laughed and grabbed a fresh towel. "I've been thinking of getting a motorcycle for Toronto. I know Jeremy doesn't want me taking my car up there. He thinks using public transit is good for me, that the more I do it, the more comfortable I'll get with it." I looked at Antonio. "It's not working."

His lips twitched. "And exactly how many times have you taken public transit since you've been there?"

"Once or twice, but that's not the point. I need my freedom. My own transportation. I could afford a motorcycle. Buy it there, ride it until I'm done, then bring it home. Jeremy said no cars, but he never said no bikes."

The smile broke through. "If you think that's really what he meant, then why not just tell him—"

"Too complicated. Point is, a motorcycle would be perfect. Nick and I rode dirt bikes in Arizona last summer. Easy enough."

"You need a license and—"

I waved him off. "If I get pulled over, I'll play ignorant foreigner. But I'd need some help picking the right size bike, the right type, and all that. If I decide that's what I want to do, can I call you?"

He nodded. "A motorcycle might be just what you need. A car, well—" He looked over at me. "It's not as if you need room for more than one, right?"

I shrugged. "I can always buy an extra helmet, just in case, but—"

Nick barreled through the doorway. "You still down here?" He looked at his father. "Giving Clay workout tips? Hey, Logan! Come quick. Clay's getting told how to lift weights."

"Yeah, but is he listening?" Logan said as he walked

in. He paused and looked from me to Antonio. "I think we're interrupting something, Nick. How about we—"

"We're not interrupting," Nick said, dropping down beside me. "We're rescuing. Time to get Clay out of here before my father tells him all the things he's been doing wrong and shatters his delusions of perfection."

I snapped the towel at him and got to my feet. "We're done. So what's up? You guys ready for more?"

Nick snorted. "Not more of this. We have"—he made a show of checking his watch—"exactly six hours before we need to drive Logan to the airport. The question is, how to make the most of those hours. I say—"

"I say we let Clay pick something," Logan said.

"Like he's not going to do that anyway," Nick said.

"Yes, but letting him pick, and letting him bully us into letting him pick, are two different things." Logan looked at me. "We were thinking of heading into Syracuse. What'll it be? Dinner? A movie?"

"Dinner and a movie. Then dinner again."

Logan laughed. "Sure, why not? My last chance to pig out before school. Nick? Pick a movie."

"Are we actually going to see what I choose?" Nick said. "Or just pretend to consider it?"

"You pick the movie," I said. "I'll pick the first restaurant. Logan can pick the later one."

"Whoa," Logan said. "That sounds almost democratic. I'm switching my theory to alien possession. This has gone too far for spiked drinks."

I tried to smack him, but he dodged past me and we raced up the steps, leaving Antonio in the exercise room.

9

ELENA

As I walked through the doors of Sidney Smith Hall, I quickened my pace and surveyed the rapidly filling corridor. The chances of running into Clayton out here were next to nil, but I looked anyway. More significantly, I let myself look.

Part of me still rebelled, urged my legs to slow down, not to get to class early. But I wasn't giving in to that. Not today.

I spent too much of my life worrying about how things look, how they might be interpreted, never wanting to seem too enthusiastic, to let anyone know I gave a damn. It was hard work maintaining those defenses, and some days I wanted to tear them down, act as I pleased, and not care what anyone thought.

I'd begun to feel that maybe, with Clayton, I could. When it came to acting strangely, I was pretty sure I couldn't outdo him. He didn't care what anyone thought of him, so he wasn't likely to judge me. And, even if he did, he was leaving in another month or so, and I'd probably never see him again.

Was it only another month? Alarm raced through me, but I chased it back. I had other things to worry about.

At least the weekend was over. Any holiday that revolved around family saw me sitting in my dorm room alone, keenly aware of the empty halls, afraid to even turn on the television, knowing I'd be confronted with images of the holiday, even the commercials leaping out to remind me that normal people were home with their families.

I hated dwelling on this, but never seemed to be able to get past it. My one bit of "family" contact that weekend had been a former foster mother phoning, not to invite me to Thanksgiving dinner but to accuse me, yet again, of ruining her son's life. As if it was my fault—

"Elena!"

A dark-haired young woman pushed past a group loitering outside an open classroom door.

"Hey, Jody," I said, stopping.

"Hey, yourself. You didn't call when you got in last night. I was hoping we could grab coffee. So how was your weekend?"

"Good. And yours?"

"I survived." She stepped closer, moving out of the lane of foot traffic. "So, what'd you do? Visit lots of relatives? Eat lots of turkey? Pray you don't have to see either again until Christmas?"

I forced a smile. "Something like that. You joining us for dinner?"

"Of course. Share some holiday war stories before my night class. Get your best one ready, 'cause I think I've got everyone beat this time."

We chatted for another couple of minutes. I hated lying to my friends, but the alternative was worse. Admit you have no place to go for the holiday, and they'll do what any good friend would do—invite you to share their family celebrations. While I appreciated the gesture, the only thing worse than sitting alone in my dorm was sitting with strangers who were all trying very hard to make me feel like family, and only reminding me all the more that I wasn't.

* * *

After talking to Jody, I was no longer early for class. By the time I swung through the door, the room was nearly full. Clayton was at the front, sorting papers. I paused, expecting him to look up. He always did, with that weird sixth sense of his, seeming to know when someone was heading to the office even before I heard footsteps. He kept working, though. I swung past the desk. He lifted his head, but he didn't meet my gaze, let alone sneak me a smile.

I climbed to my seat, disappointment mingling with reproach. So he didn't notice me. Big deal. I was his TA. What did I expect? A hug?

As I took my seat, he began the lecture. He didn't look my way, and I tried not to worry about that. Of course, I *did* worry. Had he talked to someone at home who'd convinced him that a friendship with a female student wasn't such a good idea? Or, worse, convinced him that I might interpret his interest as more than friendship?

He began passing out papers, handing them down the rows. He gave me one, then passed the rest to the person beside me, his gaze never dropping within a foot of my head. Okay, something *had* happened.

I took my sheet. Instructions for an assignment . . . with a handwritten line, dark against the faded copy.

How was your weekend?

I looked up just as he was heading back down the middle row. As he passed me, he glanced over, brows lifting. I grinned, and his smile broke through before he turned away.

A second page followed the first, this one a list of possible topics. Again, mine came with an extra note.

Run tonight?

I laughed, startling my neighbor, then stuffed the pages into my binder. As Clayton stepped up to the lectern, his gaze shot my way, brows arched, expecting an answer. I bit back a smile and pretended not to notice . . . just as I pretended not to notice the glower that followed when he realized I wasn't going to respond.

When class ended, I took a few minutes to tidy my notes, waiting for the room to empty. By now students rarely lingered to ask more than a quick question, having learned that anything else only earned them a scowl.

As the last students filed out, I slipped from my seat. Clayton had his back to me, gathering his papers from the table.

"So?" he said, without turning.

"Passing notes in class? Isn't that a no-no?"

"Only for students."

"Still, you'd better be careful. Hand that to the wrong person and you'll get yourself in trouble."

"Which is why I passed it directly to you." He leaned against the lectern. "So? Can you run tonight?"

"Hmm, no. Sorry. But I could pencil you in for three weeks from Thursday."

"Watch it or you'll find yourself joining the ranks of the unemployed."

"There are laws against that."

"So?"

I swung my knapsack onto my shoulder. "Tonight is fine. I'm meeting friends for dinner, but I should be done by seven thirty. How about I meet you in front of the ROM at eight?"

He agreed, and I left.

It was a cold night for October, single-digit temperatures with a wicked north wind blowing in, reminding the unwary that it wasn't too soon for a blast of early snow. With daylight saving time over, the sun was long gone by eight, taking any hope of heat with it. When I arrived at the museum, I was ready to head back to my dorm and dig up my winter coat, but once we started the long walk, talking as we went, I forgot the cold.

"Change facilities are a problem," I said as we entered the park. "The washrooms are locked, so I usually slip into the woods. Hardly decorous but—"

"Whatever works. I never see what the big deal is anyway. Someone sees a flash of bare skin, what are they going to do, run away screaming?"

I laughed. "I'd hope not. But if the flashing involves certain sections of skin, they'll run screaming to the nearest cop. On a night like tonight, though, I'd be more worried about frostbite than unintentional flashing."

"You want me to break into a bathroom for you?"

I glanced over, wondering whether he was joking, but pretty sure he wasn't. When he just looked back at me expectantly, I shook my head.

"Thanks but no. I run year-round, so I've learned the art of speed-changing. If we head around that pavilion, we should be out of the wind."

So we did, each finding a place in the woods to change into our running clothes. Had I been with anyone else, this is the point where I would have gotten nervous, undressing in the forest a few feet from a near-stranger. But one advantage to being with a guy as good-looking as Clayton is that I was sure he didn't need to lure girls into the forest to get them out of their clothes.

When I stepped out of the woods, he was already there, and I quickly realized one *disadvantage* to being with a guy as good-looking as Clayton. The gape factor. In the last few weeks, I'd become less aware of his looks. As Shaw said, "Beauty is all very well at first sight; but whoever looks at it when it has been in the house three days?"

So far I'd only seen him in his professorial clothes—usually a jersey or pullover and loose-fitting casual pants. As he stepped out in a tank top and shorts, I became keenly aware that, as nice as the picture had been with those baggy clothes, I'd been missing half of it. It was obvious Clayton wasn't the kind of guy whose only exercise was the occasional jog around the block. I tried not to look. Failing that, I tried not to stare.

As much as I like the solitude of running alone, there's something to be said for having company of the right sort. Preferably someone who can keep up a light chatter and keep up the pace. Clayton managed both easily, and we were back where we started before I knew it.

"—hadn't seen it, so we ended up watching *Die Hard* again," he said as we slowed to a walk.

"Is that the kind of movie you like?" I asked.

"Pretty much. Action and adventure flicks, mostly, though comedy's fine, sometimes horror. A few months ago, we went to see the new *Crocodile Dundee* one, but it was sold out, so we saw . . . now what was it? Something about a baby. *We're Having a Baby*, I think. Now, that *wasn't* my kind of movie."

"A chick flick."

"Huh?"

"A film aimed at the female portion of the moviegoing public."

"Oh." He peered over at me. "You like those kind of movies?"

"No, I'm saying that's who they're *made* for. Not that every woman likes them, no more than every guy likes movies where stuff blows up."

"What kind do you like?"

I grinned. "The ones where stuff blows up."

"We should go to a movie, then."

I glanced over at him, but already knew what I'd see. No hint that this was anything other than a friendly suggestion. Like the invitation to run together, he blurted out such things with a guileless innocence that couldn't help but put me at ease.

"Sure," I said. "We should do that someday."

"How about Friday?"

I laughed. "I said *someday*." A pause, then I glanced over at him. "Maybe Saturday."

"Saturday, then. Any idea what's play—"

He stopped. As I took another step, his fingertips brushed my arm, and I looked back to see him still standing there. He motioned for me to stop and scanned the grassy hill leading to the pavilion.

"Someone's here," he murmured.

"Oh?" I squinted into the darkness. "Where?"

"Over by the parking lot. You go get changed. I'll wait."

When I came out, he was standing by the pavilion, watching the distant parking lot.

"Still there?" I asked.

"There *again*. He left a couple times, but keeps coming back. Like he's waiting for someone."

"Probably is. Get dressed, then. I'll stay here."

After about a minute of squinting at the parking lot, I saw a figure. Male, it looked like. A cold night for a tryst, but I suppose that never stops anyone who's determined enough. I ducked behind the pavilion wall. No need to advertise my presence.

A moment later, a man appeared, walking along the path beside the pavilion. He didn't see me, and I only caught a glimpse of his back as he passed. Something in his stride made my heart jump into my throat, but I shook it off. Couldn't be. Not out here.

He reached the end of the path, then headed back. As he turned, I stiffened. No one knew I was here . . . no one except my roommate. Damn it! I quickstepped back into the shadows, but not before he saw me.

"Elena!" he called, grinning as he broke into a jog. "There you are. You're a hard girl to find."

Apparently not hard enough.

10

ELENA

WHAT ARE YOU DOING HERE, JASON?" I asked, shooting a quick look over my shoulder and praying Clayton didn't pick that moment to step from the shadows.

"I should be asking you that." He walked over to me. "What are you thinking? Jogging in a park at night? When your roommate told me where you were, I thought she was putting me on. Who the hell does crazy stuff like this? It's not—"

"Normal?" I said.

"I didn't mean it like that." He stepped forward, hand rising to brush a stray wisp of hair off my cheek. "You know I didn't."

I backpedaled out of his reach. His gaze dropped in that wounded look, as if he was the victim here, the poor besotted guy under the spell of the evil ice bitch.

"I'm not canceling the restraining order," I said. "So you can tell your mother to stop calling me."

"Ah, shit. Is she—?" He smacked his palm against the

pavilion wall. "Goddamn her! Why does she always do this to me? You were right to get that."

"Don't."

"No, I deserved it. I got carried away. I couldn't help myself. You weren't returning my calls. You wouldn't see me. I got confused—"

"Confused?" I said, nails biting into my palms. "What the hell is confusing about the word *no*?"

The wounded look again. "You don't have to swear, baby."

"I am not your *baby*." I dug my nails in harder. "I have never been your *baby*. I have never been your *anything*. No, wait . . . I was your something. Your foster sister."

"I know that. But I couldn't help it. You were so—"

"Available? Trapped? I couldn't slam the door in your face and walk away, because there was no place for me to walk to. You were there, all the time, and there wasn't a damn thing I could do about it. Complain to your mother, and she tells me I'm overreacting. You're a seventeen-year-old boy; I'm a seventeen-year-old girl. What do I expect? I should be flattered. Well, I'm not seventeen anymore. I wasn't flattered then. I'm not flattered now. And I want you to get the hell out of my life before I do something that is really *not normal*."

"You're upset, baby. I understand that. My mother pisses me off, too, so I don't blame you one bit."

At that moment, I wanted nothing more than to haul off and deck him.

But it wouldn't help. I could knock Jason off his feet and he'd just look up at me with those hurt eyes and say, "I understand why you did that, baby."

I spun on my heel and strode away. Got about ten feet before his hand closed on my shoulder.

"Let me go," I said, voice low, back still to him.

"No, Elena. Not until you've calmed down."

I jerked forward, but his grip only tightened, fingers digging into my shoulder. I flung his hand off. His jaw set. I stood my ground. He stepped forward, closing the gap between us.

"You don't want to do that," drawled a voice to our left.

I looked to see Clayton in the shadow of a pine tree, arms crossed, as if he'd been there for a while.

"I can handle this," I said.

My words came out sharper than I intended. I glanced over at him and lifted a finger. He nodded, and stayed where he was.

"Go home, Jason," I said, "or I'm walking to the nearest phone booth, dialing 911, and seeing how well that restraining order works."

The perfect threat—calm yet clear—and I'd have been very proud of myself . . . had Jason heard a single word of it. Before I was half finished, he was striding toward Clayton.

"Who the hell are you?" Jason said.

"An interested party."

"Interested in what?" Jason swung to face me. "Is this guy with you, Elena?"

"Could be," Clayton answered before I could. "Or I could be just a fellow jogger, heard the ruckus, and came over to see if I could help. Or maybe I'm not a jogger at all. Maybe I just like hanging out in empty parks, see what kind of sludge crawls out of the pond after dark—" He grinned, teeth flashing. "See what kind of trouble I can get into."

"What the hell is that supposed to mean?"

"Not a damn thing. Now, I think Elena was talking to you, and I think you'd better start listening."

Jason stalked over to Clayton and pulled himself up, eye to eye. "Or what?"

Clayton only shrugged. "You'd have to ask her that."

Jason looked from Clayton to me, face scrunched up in confusion. "Who is this guy?"

"An interested party," Clayton said.

Jason's finger shot up, pointing in Clayton's face. "Don't you start—"

Clayton grabbed his finger. I tensed, but he only held Jason's finger, then pushed it slowly down.

"Lift that hand to me again, and you'd better be prepared to use it. Now go on back to Elena. This is her fight, and I'm not making it mine unless you insist."

Jason looked from me to Clayton. He paused, then stalked off, calling over his shoulder a promise that he'd talk to me later. I wanted to run after him, grab him by the shoulder, the way he'd done to me, swing him around, and set him straight—tell him he *wasn't* going to talk to me later and why. But I was just happy to see him go. Happy and relieved, and dead-set against doing anything that might interfere with his leaving.

"You want to go get something?"

I wheeled to see Clayton at my shoulder. I hadn't seen him move from his place by the trees.

"Hmm?" I said.

"You want to go get something? I'm sure I can find a place on the way back."

I shook my head. "No. Thanks, but I'm really not . . ." I shrugged.

"Not hungry?"

"Eat? Oh. I thought you meant a drink."

I should have known he didn't mean the obvious. He never did.

"We could get a drink, if that's what you'd like," he said.

"Definitely not. Doesn't do a thing for me except put me to sleep. But something to eat would be good." I forced a smile. "Vent my frustration on a hapless burger."

"Good. Grab your knapsack and we'll go."

* * *

We walked down out of the park in silence. Comfortable silence, not that dead-weight quiet that comes from waiting for me to talk about what had happened. He didn't mention it, and I appreciated that. Like I appreciated the invitation to a late-night snack—something, anything, to keep my mind off Jason and to give me an excuse not to head back to my dorm room, where he could be lying in wait.

Clayton found an all-night diner. We couldn't see it from Bloor Street—not even the sign—so I assumed he'd been there before, but when we got inside, he looked around, orienting himself the same as I did.

He started toward a table in the back corner, then glanced over his shoulder.

"There okay?" he said, jerking his chin toward the table.

"Perfect."

We settled into our seats.

"Burgers page three," he said after a glance through the menu.

"On second thought, I may change my mind. They serve all-day breakfast." I skimmed through the grease-spattered menu. "I think I might go for pancakes. Weird, I know, but—"

"Have what you like."

"Comfort food. Does the trick better than alcohol."

He started to say something, but the server arrived, coffeepot in hand.

"No, thanks," I said, covering my cup. "Too late for caffeine. I think I'll have . . ." I flipped to the back of the menu, then smiled. "Root beer floats. Haven't had those in years. I'll take one. And the pancakes and ham steak."

The server peered over her half-glasses. "With a root beer float?"

I hesitated. Kicked myself for letting a server make me rethink the "appropriateness" of my order, but I did it nonetheless.

"Same here," Clayton said, smacking down his menu. "Pancakes, ham, and a root beer float."

The server rolled her eyes and left mumbling about college kids.

"You like root beer floats?" I asked.

"Never had one."

I stifled a laugh. "Well, I'm not sure how well it'll go with maple syrup, but we're about to find out." I glanced around the diner. The few other customers were all across the room. "I should have said it earlier, but thanks for trying to help back there. At the park. I didn't mean to snap at you."

"You wanted to handle it yourself. Nothing wrong with that."

"Hmm, well, as you saw, handling it myself doesn't seem to be—" I bit off the sentence and looked away. "Anyway, thanks." I glanced back at him. "You confused him, and that's probably the best way to get rid of Jason."

"Not too bright, is he?"

I laughed and eased back in the booth. "No, not too bright, though I'm pretty sure he can't be as dense as he acts. It's just an excuse: Pretend he honestly misinterpreted our relationship—or lack of one."

"So you and he never . . ."

"Absolutely not. When you're a foster kid, you can't get into that."

I paused, realizing I'd let slip something I preferred to keep to myself. But if he'd overheard any of my conversation with Jason, he already knew I'd been in foster care. So I continued.

"Any relationship Jason thinks we had took place only in his head."

"But he keeps following you? What's it been now? Three, four years?"

"Three. And two since I turned eighteen and got the hell away from him and his screwed-up family. As for Jason, I don't know what his problem is. He doesn't have a problem getting dates with willing girls. So why me?"

"Because you're not willing. Buddy of mine is like that. Not like *that*—stalking and shit. But if you put him at a party with ten girls, and nine of them are falling over him, he'll make a beeline for number ten, spend the night trying to charm her."

"The thrill of the hunt."

"I guess so. He likes the challenge. 'Course, if she tells him to get lost, he does."

"Most guys do. A chase is fine, but if she fights when cornered, they back off."

Our floats arrived. Clayton waited until the server left.

"Has he ever hurt you?" he asked.

I shrugged. "Not really. He sometimes grabs me, like he did in the park. Leaves bruises, but not the 'fear for my life' kind of hurting."

Clayton's jaw worked, and he dropped his gaze, but not before I saw a flash of rage there, so intense it startled me. It should have scared me—I know that. But it didn't.

"That's bad enough," he said. "You can't let him do that or it'll only get worse."

My head jerked up. "You think I'm *letting* him—"

"No." He reached out and, for a second, I thought he was going to put his hand on mine. At the last moment, he plucked a napkin from the dispenser. "I didn't mean it like that. The problem is, the harder you fight, the harder he's going to pursue. You can't give in, and you can't fight back, so you're stuck."

"So I've noticed."

He crumpled the napkin. Then he looked at me. "I could fix this for you. Make sure he doesn't come back. Not kill him—if he isn't threatening *your* life, then that isn't necessary. But I could make damn sure he never wants to see your face again."

Again, I should have been shocked. Again, I wasn't. I knew he wasn't just offering to give Jason a stern talking-to. And the casual mention of killing him, as if this was an option I should keep in mind? That should have sent me bolting for the door.

Instead, I only shook my head. "Thanks, but I still want to try handling it on my own."

"If you change your mind, you let me know."

"I will."

Clayton walked me back to my dorm. Luckily Jason wasn't there. Nor did he make good on his "promise" to talk to me later. Maybe he was still trying to figure out what Clayton had been threatening in the park. Or maybe he'd seen something in Clayton's eyes, the same thing I'd seen later at the restaurant, and decided he didn't want to find out what he'd been threatening. Either way, I was glad for the respite.

Clayton and I did go to see a movie that weekend. Had a good time, too, though by now I'd come to expect that. Over the next few weeks, we saw a couple more movies, went out for a few meals, and jogged together almost every other day. I knew I should have been concerned about getting him in trouble—socializing with a student—but he was careful and I was careful, and the selfish truth was that I didn't want to worry about it, didn't want *him* worrying about it, not if it meant we'd spend less time together.

After that night in the diner, I started opening up. Not

that I poured out my guts at his feet; I just didn't change the topic when conversation turned personal.

He gave as good as he got. Before that night in the diner ended, I'd found out that Clayton understood my situation better than I could have imagined, having been orphaned himself when he was only a couple of years older than I'd been.

Like me, Clayton had no biological family . . . or none that he knew of. Unlike me, though, he'd found a home, with a guardian that sounded like everything I'd ever dreamed a foster parent could be, plus a close extended family. I suppose I could have felt jealous about that, but instead it reaffirmed my own hopes that just because you didn't have blood relatives didn't mean you couldn't, someday, have a normal life with a family of your own.

As October drew to a close, I became increasingly aware of Clayton's imminent return to New York. We hadn't discussed that. Maybe there was nothing to discuss. His term would come to an end, he'd hand me my final paycheck with a "Nice to know you," and that'd be it. Maybe if I expected otherwise, that was my mistake.

I held out as long as I could, until exactly two weeks before he was due to leave. Then I asked whether I could use his office computer to rework my résumé. He mumbled something, but when I tried to get an intelligible answer, he changed the topic.

Two days later, I showed up at work to find the office empty. With no note. For a few seconds, I stood by the desk in shock, wondering if he was already gone. Silly, I know, but he was always there when I arrived for my shift. If he couldn't be, he left a note, telling me he was gone—as if I couldn't see that for myself—and telling me to wait—as if I might take his absence as an opportunity to snag a day off.

So when there was no note, I kind of panicked. Then I saw that his books were still on the shelf. He might leave papers and old journals scattered all over the office when he finally did vacate it, but he'd never abandon his books.

I sat down and started to work. Less than ten minutes later, the door banged open.

"I hope that's not your résumé you're typing," he said as he tossed a file folder onto the desk.

"Not without your permission."

"Good, 'cause I don't give it. You may not revise your résumé."

"I meant I'd need your permission to use your computer and printer, not to write the résumé. That I don't need."

"And you need it to use my printer? Why? I might complain about you using up the ribbon? Hell, I have a box of them." He dropped into his chair and spun it to face me. "But, back to the original subject, you do not have my permission to revise your résumé. I expressly forbid it."

"Uh-huh. Well, that's great, but I do need a job—"

"You have one."

"*After* you leave."

"Not leaving."

"What?"

"Is that disappointment I hear?" He bounced off the chair and scooted his rear onto the desk, looming over me. "Too bad, 'cause I'm not leaving. The university likes the research paper we're working on, and they want me to finish it here, so they can slap their name on it. Plus Dr. Fromme wants me to keep teaching his fourth-year class. Meaning you're stuck with me until the end of the term."

"Damn."

"Damn?"

"Well, see, there's this other job. Better working conditions. Less demanding boss—"

"You'd better be kidding, because I just went through a helluva lot of work to make sure you kept your job."

"Oh, so you did it for *me*."

"Of course. You need a job." He jumped off the desk and headed for the door. "So get back to work and earn your keep. I have to meet with Fromme. It might take a while, but I'll be back by lunch, so wait for me." He threw a grin over his shoulder. "You're buying, too. A token of appreciation for your continued employment."

He zipped out the door before I could answer. I sat there, smiling, then turned back to the keyboard.

At ten, I decided to go grab a coffee. I was pushing the office door when it flew open, nearly sending me into the wall.

"Thanks a helluva—" I began, then stopped, cheeks heating.

In the doorway stood, not Clay, but one of his students. A guy about my age with short dreadlocks and an easy grin.

"Sorry about that," he said. "Is Clay—Professor Danvers here? This is his office, right?" A glance over at the paper-littered desk and the grin returned. "Oh, yeah. This is definitely his office."

"You must be in his fourth-year class," I said. "I'm Elena, his TA."

His brows arched. "TA?"

"Well, TA, receptionist, typist, research assistant. All-round girl Friday, pretty much." I waved at the office. "Housekeeping not included."

As he laughed, I unearthed a pen.

"Professor Danvers has office hours tomorrow, but you can leave a note for him, or I can pencil you in for an appointment."

"Sure, you can pencil me in for an appointment, but will he *keep* the appointment? That is the question."

I smiled. "Yes, he *does* keep them. I make sure of that. So can I schedule—?"

"Actually, I'm not a student. I'm a friend of his."

"Oh?"

"Yes, Clayton has friends. Shocking, isn't it?"

"I didn't mean—"

"No?" He met my gaze, grinning. "Oh, come on. Admit it. *Friends* and *Clay* are not words that go together."

"Okay, I was a little surprised. Not that I didn't know he had friends. I just haven't met any of them. And, now that you mention it, I'm going to hazard a guess that you're Logan."

The grin fell away. "Uh, yeah. He's mentioned me?"

"Now you're the one who sounds surprised."

"I am. Not that I'm not perfectly mentionable, but Clay doesn't usually talk about his personal life. Huh. Well—" He looked around. "So what kind of— Oh, wait, you were going somewhere when I rudely barged in, weren't you?"

"Just to grab a coffee."

"Perfect. I could use one . . . and I have no clue where to find it here. Mind if I tag along?"

"Sure. Or I could bring you back one—"

"I've just spent six hours in the car. Please don't ask me to sit and wait."

I smiled. "I won't, then. Come on."

After we got our coffees, Logan persuaded me to sit in the cafeteria. Normally, I would have pulled the "Gee, I'd love to, but I really have to get back to work" routine. I'm not antisocial, but neither do I go out of my way to have coffee with strangers. Yet Logan was one of those people with the gift for making you feel, almost from the first word, that you've known him for years. So we sat and talked, mostly about school. He was also in his third year, at Northwestern, which gave us plenty of common ground.

"You live on campus or off?" he asked halfway through our coffees.

"On. Though I'm hoping to change that next term."

"Same here. And I bet I know the reason. DMFH, right?"

"Hmm?"

"DMFH. Dorm mate from hell. There's gotta be a better acronym, but that's the best I could come up with on the fly. So how bad's yours?"

"Not too bad . . ."

"She has to be bad," he said, "because that's the rule."

"The rule?"

"You're a serious student, right? Obviously, if you're a TA. You work your ass off because that's what college is for—learning and getting a job, not an all-expense-paid party tour."

"Sometimes I wish it was."

"But it isn't. Especially if you're paying your own way. You are, I'll bet. Otherwise, you sure as hell wouldn't take a job with Clay."

I smiled. "Yes, I'm paying my way."

"Me, too. Well, someone's helping me, but I have every intention of paying him back. Point is that we've paid for this education, and we're damned well going to get the most out of it. So we're guaranteed to get dorm mates who don't give a shit, who stay up all night, expect us to get up quietly in the morning, blast music while we're trying to study, give their friends the room key. . . . Happens to me every year."

"Same here."

"It can't be by accident. I think it's a baby-boomer conspiracy."

I sputtered a laugh. "Baby boomers?"

"We're studying to take their jobs, right? What better way to keep us out of the workforce than to make sure we have a rough time at college? They pair us up with the worst party animals and hope we fold."

A flash of motion across the cafeteria caught my eye. I looked to see Clayton barreling toward us, eyes blazing, mouth set in a grim line.

"Looks like Clay got my note," I said. "But I don't think his meeting went very well."

Logan glanced over and grimaced. "No, I do believe that scowl is intended for me." He looked around. "Think it's too late for a speedy escape?"

" 'Fraid so."

"Damn. Hold on, then. I'm about to get blasted."

11
CLAYTON

I STOOD AT THE BACK OF THE CAFETERIA and watched Logan with Elena. He'd pulled his chair as close to the table as it could get, and was leaning forward. My hands clenched. There was a rule about Pack brothers visiting me when I was here. A rule *against* it. Jeremy's rule. It was bad enough that Logan didn't respect my authority. But to disobey Jeremy? That went too far.

Elena laughed at something Logan said and replied,

hands moving. Her back was to me, but I could imagine her face, eyes sparkling with animation, her full attention on him. How long had it taken for me to see that spark, to get her to look me in the face every time? She'd known Logan for an hour. Probably less.

I started toward them, looping around the cafeteria. The moment I passed into Elena's field of vision, she looked up, almost instinctively. I braced myself, expecting to see consternation. Instead, she grinned and lifted her hand in a wave.

My stride caught. I tried to smile back, but my lips didn't move fast enough, and she saw my scowl. Her smile faded, eyes clouding. She turned and said something to Logan. He glanced up at me, eyes widening in feigned horror. My fury returned. It was bad enough he was here; I was damned if he was going to mock me, too.

I strode to the table.

"Clayton," Logan said, smiling up at me. "About time you—"

"I want to talk to you."

"Well, then, you're in luck, because that's what we were doing. Talking." With his foot, he pushed out a chair—the one on the far side of the table. "Elena and I were just about to swap roommate horror stories. Did you ever get a bad one?"

Elena grinned up at me. "Or were you the bad one?"

My anger started to fizzle under the blaze of that smile. A glance at Logan, and I rallied it back.

"I want to talk to you," I said. "In private."

Elena pushed her chair back. "You guys don't need me hanging around. I should get back to work—"

"No," I said, touching her elbow as she started standing. "You stay. Finish your coffee. I just want to talk to Logan for a minute."

She hesitated. Logan shot me a "don't be a jerk"

look—one I'd seen often enough to recognize. As much as I wanted to snarl something back at him, I couldn't help noticing Elena's discomfort.

"Stay," I said. "I can talk to Logan later."

She hesitated another moment, studying my face, then sat down, and pulled out the chair beside hers. I took it.

We spent the next hour talking. Logan did most of it. Typical. More than once, I got the impression he was steering the discussion in directions he hoped I couldn't follow. Yet Elena always managed to bring it back to a three-way conversation.

When Elena talked to Logan, I watched her expression. She seemed less guarded than she was with strangers, but not nearly as open as I'd envisioned, and I was pretty sure there was extra wattage in the smiles she tossed my way.

As for Logan, I knew him well enough to pick up his signs of interest. When Nick, Logan, and I went out, Nick never made the return trip home with me. Put him in a bar with more than one woman, and he could always find someone suitable. It took a lot more looking for Logan to find someone he liked, but when he did, it was obvious—and sitting at that table, watching him with Elena, I saw all the signs. I told myself it was just Logan being Logan, always finding a way under my skin, always challenging me. But I wasn't sure that was it.

After the first half-hour, I started watching the clock. At 11:45, I cut Logan short.

"Elena? We have to get lunch or you'll be late for your next class. Logan? There's food here, food out on Bloor Street just north of campus, and food back in my apartment. I'll meet up with you at my office later." I took my keys from my pocket. "You want these?"

Elena looked at me, brows knitting, and I knew I'd

committed some social misdemeanor. I glanced at Logan for a clue, but he rubbed at a smile and avoided my gaze.

"I'm sure you want to eat with Logan," Elena said.

"Not really."

Logan choked on a laugh. "And you wonder why you've never met any of his friends before?"

I glared over at him. "If you'd called or otherwise told me you were coming, I'd have left lunch free. But I have plans. I'm buying Elena lunch to celebrate her continued employment."

"I thought I had to buy lunch," she said.

"I was kidding."

"Good," Logan said. " 'Cause you'd put the poor girl in hock. Have you seen how much he eats?"

"I have," she said. "Which is why I'd planned to take him to McDonald's."

"Well, consider yourself saved from that fate, 'cause I'm buying," Logan said. "You're the townie, Elena, so you pick the place. My mom sent me a check this week, which is how I could afford the gas money to get up here. Every few months she remembers she has a son and sends guilt money, some of which I promptly blow on the most frivolous, unnecessary expenses I can find. That way, neither of us feels guilty about it."

Elena laughed. I shook my head. I never knew how Logan did that, tossing out the most private tidbits of his life as if they were nothing more intimate than his name.

"Shall we go?" he said, grabbing Elena's empty coffee cup. "What time's your class?"

"One thirty."

"Lots of time, then. Is it journalism?"

She nodded. "Advanced interviewing techniques."

"Oooh, could use some of those in my prelaw course. I'll sit in on it with you."

"You can't do that," I said. "It's against the rules."

"Words we never thought we'd hear Clayton Danvers say," Logan said. "Profs don't care if you sit in—not if you ask them first and ask nicely. If I get in shit, I promise not to mention your name. Now come on. I have fifty bucks burning a hole in my pocket, and I intend to have it gone by one thirty."

After her class, Elena returned to finish her shift. Not that she got much work done, between answering Logan's endless questions about our project and arguing with me over the interpretation of data. This was an ongoing debate—a spirited disagreement over two ways to interpret our research findings. Her interpretation was wrong, of course, but I liked challenging her about it, if only to see her temper flash.

I had no interest in renewing a personal debate in front of Logan, yet when she got to that part of the explanation, there was no way around mentioning our disagreement, if only in passing. Logan jumped on it and had to hear both our arguments. Then he promptly declared that Elena's interpretation made more sense. This from a guy who has never taken an anthropology course in his life, has never read any of the articles we cited, and hadn't even heard 10 percent of the facts.

I told myself he was only baiting me, but I couldn't shake the suspicion he was trying to impress her. It didn't work . . . or at least I didn't think it did.

At five thirty, Elena left for dinner. Logan tried to persuade her to join us, but she insisted she had enough homework to last her into the night, and besides, we must want time alone together. From the look on Logan's face, this was the last thing he wanted.

He closed the door behind her, then slowly turned to me.

"Okay," he said. "Blast away."

I leaned back against my desk, crossed my arms, and said nothing.

After a minute, he sighed. "Okay, I know I shouldn't be here. Jeremy—"

"Jeremy forbade it. This is a direct violation of his authority."

Logan lifted a finger. "Uh-uh. He said he doesn't think we should visit while you're here. He never said we couldn't."

"You knew what he meant."

"But it's what he actually *says* that counts as law, not our interpretation of it."

"Who the hell told you that?"

"You."

I pushed off the desk. "I never said—"

"Not in words, maybe, but certainly by example."

I growled and leaned back again. "The point is—"

"The point is that I came because I was concerned. Obviously something was up, and I wanted to know what it was. One Pack brother looking out for another."

I met his gaze and held it. After a moment, he sighed again.

"Okay, more curiosity than concern, but only because I know you're capable of looking after yourself. As a friend, I wanted to know what was going on. Now I do."

"And what are you going to do about it?"

"Do?" He laughed. "You like a girl. Hardly cause for emergency intervention. If you don't want to tell the Pack, that's your choice and, frankly, I don't blame you. That 'no long-term relationships' rule?" He shook his head. "Most Laws I can understand, but that one goes way overboard. Couples keep secrets from one another all the time. What's the big deal? Hell, there's no reason a werewolf couldn't *marry* if he was careful."

I stared at him.

"What?" he said.

"How could you keep a secret that—?" I bit the words off, turned, and grabbed my jacket. "I'm hungry."

"After that lunch? Shit, I couldn't even look at food."

"Well, I'm going to, so if you want to come, get your coat."

He slid a look my way. "I was right then?"

"About what?"

He rolled his eyes.

"If you mean the Pack Law, no, you're not right."

"I didn't mean that."

"Well, what then?"

He searched my face, then shook his head. "If you didn't dispute it that must mean there's nothing to dispute. You like her."

I threw him his jacket.

"More than like, I suppose," he continued. "If Nick's right and you haven't shown a passing interest in a woman since puberty, you're not going to start now with just a passing interest. You're serious."

"I'm hungry."

"Oh, so you're not interested? Good, then you won't mind me asking her out—"

I turned on him.

"Down, boy," he said, lifting his hands. "I was kidding. Well, not that I wouldn't mind asking her out, but I know I'd get turned down. Doesn't matter how many other guys are in the room; that girl only sees you."

I grabbed my keys from the desk. "Elena isn't like that. I don't even think she notices what I look like. She sure as hell doesn't care about it."

"I don't mean that. I mean you're the only guy she's—" He caught my blank look and waved his hand. "Never mind. You'll figure it out eventually."

* * *

Logan left after dinner the next night. He accompanied Elena to both her classes, including mine. I tried not to read anything into it, but couldn't help being relieved when he finally left.

That night, Elena and I went for a run. Afterward, we found a grassy spot overlooking the water and ate the subs and sodas we'd brought along.

"So you like Logan?" I asked finally.

"Sure. He's a nice guy." She smiled. "Easy to get along with, you know? I envy that in people."

"So you like him."

"Didn't I just say—?" She caught my expression and choked on a mouthful of sandwich. "Not like *that*. Is that what it seemed like? I hope he didn't think—"

"He didn't."

"Good." She leaned back against a tree trunk. "That's the problem sometimes. You meet a guy, and think he's nice, but you need to worry about how that will be interpreted. Sometimes I'm interested because I'm, well, interested. Most times, though, it's just because I think he's nice."

I looked across the water, then over at her. "And what about me?"

I heard the thought coming from my mouth, and tried to bite back the words, but it was too late.

"Do I think *you're* nice?" she said.

Her lips twitched, then her gaze met mine. She blushed and, in her eyes, I saw what Logan had been talking about.

"Yes," she said softly. "In your own way, I think you're pretty nice."

I leaned over, and my mouth found hers before I even realized what I was doing. The moment our lips touched, I finally got it, and even if my brain still didn't quite understand what "it" was, my body did. My lips parted hers. I shivered at the feel of her, the smell and taste of her, and my hormones kicked into overdrive, like when I'd been sixteen, finally hitting puberty, feeling everything and not having a damned clue what to do about it. Now I knew. I'd found—

Shit. Was she kissing me back? I could feel her lips moving. Or was I moving them with mine? An image shot into my brain: Elena's face, frozen in horror, too shocked to push me away.

What if she wasn't kissing me? It was Logan's fault. Damn him! He'd tricked—

Was I still kissing her?

I pulled back. "Shit, I'm sorry."

She blinked, eyes sleepy, as if waking up. "S—sorry?"

"I didn't mean— If this isn't what you want—"

She leaned over and kissed me, her arms going around my neck. For a second, I just sat there, stunned. Then I kissed her back.

A few minutes later, she eased out of my arms and smiled. "And that, I hope, clears up any confusion."

"It does."

Another smile. "It does, doesn't it? I wasn't sure myself, but—" She looked up at me. "I think I've figured it out."

Someone laughed and we both jumped. I inhaled and caught the scents of perfume and booze.

"Kids coming," I said. "You wanna go head back to my apartment?"

Panic darted behind her eyes. Why? She'd come to my apartment before, to eat or study. As I replayed my words, I heard an interpretation that wouldn't have been there ten minutes ago.

"No, not for sex. I just want—" I shrugged. "You know, to spend more time with you."

"Me, too. I mean with you, not with me. I like spending time— I'd like to spend more time—" She pulled a face. "Blah. I think my tongue's gone on vacation."

"Is that a yes, then? Head back to my apartment and hang out there awhile? No strings attached. I'd tell you if there were."

"Like 'Hey, do you want to go back to my apartment for sex?' "

"Exactly."

She laughed. "You probably would, too."

For a moment, she just looked at me, then she broke my gaze, her face reddening. She pushed to her feet and brushed herself off. I followed her to the path.

12

ELENA

And again our relationship changed— a sudden veer that didn't seem sudden at all, as if we'd been curving in this direction from the start, but only saw the signposts when they were upon us. From teacher to employer to friend to boyfriend, the signs drifted past, evoking no more reaction than a raised eyebrow and a halfhearted "Hmm, wonder how that happened?"

Eventually there might be another sign: lover—but I wasn't going to crane my neck over the horizon trying to see it. Like the others, it would come when it was time. Or it wouldn't. I'd never reached that stage with a guy. One could say, I suppose, that technically I'm not a virgin, but I don't—won't—see it like that. I've never made love, so when it does happen, it'll be my first time.

I do date, but sporadically, never letting it amount to

much. I wasn't ready for that. Not after what I went through as a foster kid. I'm not afraid of an intimate relationship—it'll just take a lot of trust building to get me there and so far no guy had made it. Whether Clay would remained to be seen.

The next month spun past like a carousel ride. New emotions, new sensations, new thoughts, everything so blindingly new, a merry-go-round of first love, all bright colors and laughter and music and, occasionally, a slightly queasy feeling, as if it was all just a little too much to take.

It wasn't perfect, but the flaws kept it real. Of course, that didn't keep me from worrying about them.

First, Clay was possessive. Maybe that's not the right word. More like he was jealous of my time. He liked being together. A lot. If I wasn't in class or in my dorm sleeping, he wanted to be with me. Not that he clung to me or demanded my attention. He was content to be in the same room, each doing our own thing, sometimes a whole afternoon passing with scarcely a word exchanged.

There was a sense of comfort in having him there, reading across the room as I did my homework. But I felt like I *should* mind. Such behavior was one of the four danger signs of an unhealthy relationship—a list that had been drilled into my head in a twelfth-grade health class.

Another sign was not wanting you to spend time with your friends. While Clay didn't complain about me hanging around with others, I could tell he was biting his tongue. But I suspected that was just part of his desire to spend time together, so that would make it only one danger sign, not two. One quarter of the list, not half. Or maybe I was rationalizing away something I didn't want to see.

Equally troubling was that Clay kept our relationship a secret from his family and friends. Again, maybe I'm overstating the matter, but that was the impression I got. He called his guardian, Jeremy, daily and yet, no matter how much time we spent together, I was never around when he made that call. I couldn't help feeling that was deliberate.

At least once a week, I was at Clay's apartment when his friend Nick called, and Clay would always make a quick promise to call back. When I'd tell him to go ahead, take the call, he always refused, saying he had plenty of time to talk to Nick later, that this was his time with me.

And yet . . . well, it was almost enough to make me wonder whether he had a girlfriend at home. My gut told me it was unlikely to the point of impossible, yet the only thing that kept my brain from overruling it on this was Logan. He'd come up to Toronto again a few weeks after his first visit, and whenever he called Clay, and I was around, he and I did more talking than him and Clay.

From Logan, I knew there was no other girl. He'd laughed when I'd tiptoed past the subject. Laughed his head off, and assured me there was no one else in Clay's life—no girlfriend, no boyfriend, no past lover he was still pining for, absolutely no cause for concern on that front.

So why the secrecy? When I broached that subject with Logan, he brushed it off with a crack about Clay's eccentricities, and a quick change of subject. So the answer, I assumed, was "no." So what, right? Clay was a grown man, not a boy who needed his parent's approval. Maybe he just didn't think this was a "meet the parent" kind of relationship yet.

It didn't help matters that our first rough spot hit right after his next trip home. He'd called me five times that weekend. The first time, from the airport in Syracuse, he'd sounded fine, bitching about the flight, normal Clay stuff. The next two calls had been furtive and short. I could picture him in some back room, whispering for fear of being overheard, and I'd started getting angry, wondering why he'd bothered calling at all.

The next call was clipped, almost angry, as if I'd done something to piss him off. I'd blasted him for that. I told him he was under no obligation to call me when he was away and if this was how he was going to act when he did call, I'd rather he didn't. Then I hung up.

Two hours later he'd called back—from a pay phone, judging by the background street noise. He'd talked then, talked and talked, as if desperate to keep me on the line.

None of it made any sense and by the time he returned, my gut was twisting, my brain feeding me all those little warnings I tried so hard not to hear, telling me something was wrong, wrong with us and wrong with him, and why the hell wasn't I taking the hint?

I didn't sleep much Sunday night, and barely heard a word the prof said in my first class Monday. I spent the whole period glancing at my watch. When class ended, I was the first one out the door.

I zipped over to Clay's office. Only when I could see his door did I slow down. It was cracked open, as it always was when he was expecting me. See? Nothing had changed. A bad weekend, that was all. Everyone has them. Going home can be stressful . . . or so my friends always told me.

Everything would be back to normal now. He'd hear me coming, as he always did, and he'd be there, sitting on the edge of the desk or lurking behind the door waiting to pounce. He'd grab me and kiss me, one of his deep, hungry kisses that would drive away every worry—

I stepped inside and he was across the room, leaning over the printer, fiddling with the buttons. Even when I closed the door with a loud click, he didn't turn.

"Jamming on you again?" I said, forcing the disappointment from my voice. "Here, let me—"

"I got in last night," he said, still bent over the machine.

I stopped. "Well, that's good. That's when you were supposed to get in, wasn't it?"

"I thought you'd come to see me."

"When? Your flight didn't arrive until two."

He said nothing, just kept playing with the printer. I gripped my backpack, knuckles whitening as the trepidation in my gut hardened into anger.

"I had an eight o'clock class," I said. "You expected me to meet your plane at two A.M.?"

He turned and rubbed his mouth. "Yeah, I guess not. I'm sor—"

"And even if I didn't have an early class, how the hell would I get to the airport? Pay twenty bucks for a cab? I can't afford—"

"I wasn't thinking. I'm sorry."

He stepped toward me, but I backpedaled, lifting my backpack to my chest. He looked down at it, then up at me.

"I didn't expect you to meet me at the airport," he said. "I just— I wanted to see you. If I didn't make plans, like meeting you for breakfast, then that's my fault."

I let the backpack slide down. He crossed the few feet between us, arms going around me.

"I missed you," he said.

I lifted my mouth to his. The moment our lips touched, it was like a dam breaking and he grabbed me, kissing me hard, pushing me back against the bookcase. When I tensed, he pulled back, breathing ragged, gaze searching mine.

"I missed you, too," I said.

I lifted my hands to the back of his head and kissed him. This time when he grabbed me, I let his kiss shove back all my doubts. There was an air of desperation in his passion, like when he'd talked to me on the phone the day before. After a minute or two, that frenzy ebbed and, after another couple of minutes, we pulled back to catch our breath.

"I'm sorry," he said. "This weekend. It was just . . . I don't know."

"Did something happen?" I asked.

"No. It's . . . I had a rough time. I wanted to be there, but I wanted to be here, too."

I took his hand and walked to the desk, and backed my rear onto it. He did the same, then shifted against me, forearm resting on my leg, hand on my knee.

"You've never been away this long, have you?" I said. "From home, I mean."

"I guess that's part of it. I'm happy here, but when I go back, I'm reminded that I miss being there, and at the same time I miss you." He shook his head. "It'll work out. I'm doing okay. Better than usual. When I was away at college, I hated it. Loved the education part, the classes and all that, but once my day was over, I'd just pace in my dorm room, going nuts, wishing I was home."

I smiled. "See? You *were* the dorm mate from hell."

"Nah, I never had roommates. Not for very long, anyway."

I laughed and leaned against his shoulder. "Did you go home every weekend? Or is that a stupid question?"

"Left the minute my last class ended and didn't come back until my first one. It was better in my undergrad years, when I was still living at home and I could pick my optional courses according to scheduling. I could usually wrangle an extra day or two at home each week if I did it right."

"So you took whatever courses gave you days off? No matter what they were?"

"Well, within reason. Usually I could get something I wanted. In my last year, though, the only thing I could find to fit my schedule was a course in women's studies."

I sputtered a laugh. "So what'd you do?"

"Took it. Nothing wrong with women's studies. I think I got off on the wrong foot with the prof the first day, though, when I asked why there weren't any men's studies courses."

"What'd she say?"

"Nothing. Just gave me a look, like I shouldn't even be asking. But we got along okay after that. She even mailed me a congratulations card when I got my doctorate, said I was still the only guy who'd ever earned an A in her course and she hoped that I'd live by the lessons I learned there."

"What lessons were those?"

"I have no idea."

I laughed, and hopped off the desk. "We should get to work. Mind if I go grab something to eat first? I skipped breakfast."

"I'll go with you." He glanced over at me. "So we're okay, then?"

I smiled. "We're fine."

We were "fine" for another couple of weeks. Then we hit our next rough patch and, again, it blindsided me. Everything was great, and then, things just started getting . . . strange.

Clay had to make a presentation to the department on his paper, and he was stressed. I'd never imagined he *could* be stressed, but he was, working at it relentlessly and driving me almost as hard, snapping over details, getting frustrated over every setback.

When the printer jammed for the umpteenth time, he threw it against the wall. Smashed it to pieces. I could only stand there and stare. He snapped out of it right away, and apologized for losing his temper, but still . . . well, it knocked me off balance. When you're trying very hard to pretend you don't see things in someone, it never helps to have them thrown in your face . . . or at the wall near your face.

I could understand a young academic worrying about the initial presentation of his first big paper. Or I would if that young academic was anyone but Clay. His attitude toward his career was laissez-faire at best, that arrogant, casual air of someone who knows he's brilliant and doesn't give a shit if anyone else agrees. To see him flipping out over this made no sense.

The presentation seemed to go fine. So I wanted to surprise him with a celebratory night. I made reservations for dinner in the theater district. Then I'd try to scoop half-priced last-minute tickets to a show. And then . . . well, I wasn't sure about the rest of the night, but if things went well, maybe, just maybe, we'd be passing that next sign on the road. I didn't quite feel ready to take that step yet, but I really wanted this to be a big night, to shift our relationship back on track.

I bought a new outfit. A black wool dress. I never wore dresses, or even skirts, and I wasn't sure whether Clay would like me in one, but I was willing to give it a shot.

So I left a note on his desk telling him I'd come around to his apartment with dinner. Then I hurried to my dorm, showered, dressed, put on makeup, fussed with my hair, strapped on a new pair of heels, and walked the two blocks to his apartment, trying hard not to fall in the heels.

I used my key, went up to his apartment, and knocked. Then I waited. Knocked again. Waited some more. I had a key for this door, too, but I wanted that moment when he opened it and saw me dressed up for the first time.

Finally, after five minutes of waiting, I let myself in.

"Clay?"

"Here."

I went into the bedroom, where he was pulling on a sweatshirt. I waited. He straightened and ran his hands through his curls, his back to me.

"I gotta go," he said, grabbing his motorcycle keys from the nightstand. "Wait here for me."

"Clay?"

"What?"

He snapped the word, his back still to me. I stood there, teetering on my heels, my stomach lurching and twisting. He snatched his motorcycle helmet from beside the bed and brushed past me without even looking.

"I gotta go," he mumbled. "Wait here. I'll be back in an hour."

Three long strides, and he was out the door. I stood there for at least five minutes, too stunned and hurt to think. Then I brushed back the first prick of tears, whipped his keys across the room, and marched out the door.

I lay on my dorm bed, staring up at the dirt-speckled ceiling. I wasn't the perfect girlfriend. I had my moods, too. But I'd been nothing but cheerful and supportive these last few days—nauseatingly cheerful and support-ive, which was undeserved considering how he'd been acting. He should have been the one taking me out for a special night, a reward for putting up with him.

The roar of a motorcycle sounded outside my window. My heart skipped. I rolled over, trying hard not to listen for the next sign, but straining just the same, then exhaling a small puff of relief when it came: the tinkle of stones at my second-floor window.

I forced myself to wait for the third pebble shower before I deigned to respond. Even then I just walked to my window, not opening it. He was probably just here to give me shit for not "waiting" like he commanded. At the thought, I clenched my fists. I shouldn't have thrown away his keys. I should have kept them, so I could throw them at him now, see his reaction.

I stood at the window and looked down. He was there, between the back hedge and the wall, blond hair pale in the moonlight. He lifted something white. A Styrofoam box. He opened it and pointed inside, mouthing something. I shaded my eyes to see better. It was a takeout box stuffed full of pancakes. He mouthed something again. This time I could make it out: "Please." I hesitated, then lifted a finger and pulled the curtains to dress.

13
CLAYTON

WHEN I WAS YOUNGER, I OFTEN TRIED to figure out the thought processes of animals—both predator and prey—convinced that if I knew what was going on in their heads, I'd be a better hunter and a better fighter. Same with humans. If I knew how their brains worked, I could alter my behavior just enough to fit in, and not one iota more.

What eluded me most was the mental lives of prey animals. They consistently fell for the same tricks that wolves had been using for eons. At first, I thought that this was because they never got the opportunity to learn from their mistakes or to pass that knowledge on to the next generation.

I'd tested this theory. I persuaded Jeremy to chase a young deer into my ambush position, then I pounced, and let it escape with only a torn flank. A few weeks later, we found the same yearling, and did the same thing. Again he fell for it—and this time paid with his life.

So I asked myself, what was going through that deer's head when he saw the same scenario playing out? He couldn't have forgotten the first time; his wound had barely healed. Did he think, "What stupid wolves, trying this again." Or did he see what was happening, and not know how to stop it? When Jeremy jumped out behind him, and he started to run, did his heart start thumping with blind panic, knowing what was coming but seeing no way to avoid his fate?

Now I was that deer. I was racing headlong into danger with both Elena and the Pack. I saw it. And I seemed unable to do anything about it.

I was breaking Pack Law. Having an affair was fine, having a casual girlfriend was fine, but long-term relationships were forbidden. Six weeks was hardly longterm, but I knew there wasn't anything casual about what I felt for Elena.

When I'd hit puberty, my wolf brain had made itself very clear: I needed a mate. A lifelong mate. Now that part of my brain was finally at rest, having found what it wanted . . . and abandoning the rest of me to flounder about trying to figure out how to make it happen.

Logan had said he saw no reason why we couldn't have wives, and just never tell them our secret. The thought of that—well, it baffled me. Of course, Elena eventually needed to know I was a werewolf. Even now I felt sick every time I had to lie or misdirect her.

I saw no reason why any human mate couldn't know. Sure, there was a risk that if the relationship broke down, she might betray him. But what sane woman would reveal such a thing, knowing that the Pack would be forced to kill her to protect itself?

Yet none of that applied to Elena. No matter how angry she might get with me, betrayal wasn't in her nature. With Elena, the true danger was that she would hear what I was and run the other way, never to return. What I had to do, then, was bide my time. Wait until she loved me enough, and trusted me enough, to hear the words and stay.

Now if I could only get that far before I scared her off for good. That was proving increasingly difficult. Like the deer, I was already hurtling toward peril, sealing my fate with every stride.

First, the catastrophic trip to Stonehaven. Talking to Jeremy by phone was one thing. Having him there, delighted by my happiness and clueless about the cause, made me miserable. Then there was Nick. He knew something was up, and he'd be hurt when he learned the truth, especially when he discovered that Logan had known.

Even just being at Stonehaven, out for runs and hunts, had been painful, reminding me that this double life was betraying two more people: Elena, by not telling her that this was what I was, and myself, by pretending that this wasn't what I was. For the first time in my life, there were moments when I wished I was human. They didn't last long, but the fact of them shamed me.

In Toronto, runs were no longer the highlight of my

week—they were a chore to be squeezed in quickly so I could get back to Elena. I was Changing only as often as I had to, pushing it off as much as possible. Then, in the last week, I'd pushed too hard.

I needed to stay in Toronto. That was a given; our relationship wasn't strong enough yet for me to head back to Stonehaven after Christmas. To stay, I needed an excuse. As I'd been scrambling to create one, a fresh opportunity landed in my lap. A new professor who was supposed to start in the winter term had accepted a job offer from a more prestigious American college, and the department had to find someone to take over his classes next term. This time there was another interested party, a semiretired prof, and the department had made it clear that there was only one way I was getting the job: with my research paper. They wanted a presentation . . . in four days.

For those four days I worked my ass off, and worked Elena's off, too. I couldn't tell her why this was so important. My need to be with her was already making her nervous.

So we'd worked on the paper, and I'd put off Changing. By that time, I was already due for one, but I thought I was strong enough to hold out. I wasn't. My temper frayed, and by the end of it, I could feel my skin pulsing, the wolf clawing at my insides.

When Elena told me she was bringing dinner over that night, I should have said no. But I needed to make up for all the crap I'd put her through that week. So I told myself I'd leave her a note, hurry out to the ravine, Change, and get back to her. Then she showed up before I could get away.

I hadn't dared look at her, fearing she'd see something, a twitch of my skin, a look in my eye. Better to get the hell out of there, hurry back, and make it up to her then. Only when I got back, pancakes in hand, I found my apartment empty, the keys thrown across the room, and I knew I'd gone too far.

When Elena came out from the dorm that night, I'd planned to take her back to my apartment, where we could eat and talk in private, out of the bitter November wind. But the moment I saw her face, I knew I'd be lucky if I could get her out of the parking lot. I settled for a secluded spot behind a wall that blocked the worst of the wind.

She let me lead her there without a word. I snuck looks at her, trying to read her body language, but she kept her gaze down and her body still.

As she looked around for a place to sit, I tugged off my jacket, but she sat on the grass before I could offer it. When I tried to hand it to her anyway, she fussed with her own coat, adjusting the zipper and pretending not to see me holding out mine for her.

"I found your shoes," I said.

She stopped fidgeting. "My shoes?"

"The ones you left in the parking lot at my building. Beside the trash bin."

"How'd you know they were mine?"

"They aren't? I thought— They weren't there when I left, and they were there when I got back, and I just figured . . . Well, if they aren't yours, I'll put them back."

"They're mine. New shoes. They were pinching my feet, so I took them off by the bin. I guess I was distracted and just left them there."

Her gaze shifted from mine, confirming what I already knew, that she'd thrown them away, probably as hard as she could, like she'd whipped the keys across my apartment.

If I hadn't smelled her scent on the shoes, I'd never have guessed they were hers. They didn't look like anything Elena wore, which had made my mind flip back to the scent lingering in my apartment, the one I'd been too busy to notice when she'd first come in: the smell of soap and shampoo, with the faintest touch of perfume. There was no reason for Elena to shower before coming over with a take-out dinner, and certainly no reason to wear new perfume and new dress shoes . . . which told me I'd made a bigger mistake than I'd thought.

"You had something planned," I said. "For tonight. Something special."

A shrug. "I knew you were worried about the presentation and, now that it's over, I wanted to . . . I don't know, celebrate, kick back and relax, something. But when you plan a surprise, you take a risk. The other person might have different plans. I accept that." She looked up, her gaze meeting mine. "What I don't accept is how you reacted."

"I—"

"I asked if I could bring over dinner, so you knew I was coming. I didn't barge into your apartment without warning. I knocked. You've told me a hundred times just to use my keys and come in. I didn't ask for keys. I wasn't even sure I wanted them. But you insisted so I could use the apartment to study when you're not there. It was your idea, not mine."

Logan had exploded when he'd found out I'd given Elena keys to my apartment, but I knew what I was doing. There was nothing in there that Elena couldn't see. I had to keep one secret from her, but the rest of my life was open for her inspection, and I needed her to know that.

"And that still stands, right?" she said. "You didn't change the key-ownership rules in the last twenty-four hours and neglect to inform me?"

"Of course not."

"Well, you sure as hell acted like you had. I put up with your shit all week, Clay, your moods, your temper, your demands. And when it was over, I felt like I should treat you to an evening out, 'cause god knows, you deserved it. I told you I was coming over, I knocked, I let myself in. You snarled and stalked out without a word of explanation."

"It wasn't your fault."

"I know."

Her eyes bore into mine. Fury blazed just below the surface. Her face was taut as she struggled to keep it under control. A tendril of that heat licked through me, sharp and white-hot, and my hands gripped the cold ground as I fought the urge to reach for her. I wanted to kiss her, to taste that anger, feel it release as she—

"I owe you an explanation," I said quickly.

"No, you don't. You never owe me an explanation for anything you do, Clay. If I haven't made that clear already, let me state it, for the record, right now. I only demand two things of you. One, that you treat me with respect. Two, that you're honest with me—that you be yourself. If you're doing that, then I don't need to know what you're doing, where you're going, where you've been, and I'll never demand to know."

"Like me, you mean. Like I do."

She blinked. "That wasn't a jab."

"I don't demand those things from you, Elena. I ask because I like to know what happened in your day. If I can't be there, I want to hear about it. If you don't want to tell me, you can just say so."

"And sound like I have something to hide." She opened her mouth to continue then, again, shook it off. She picked up the box of pancakes and opened it. "They're cold, but I can pop them in the toaster oven. Just hold on and I'll—"

I grabbed her arm as she jumped up. When she stiffened, I let go fast.

"Just a sec, okay?" I said. "I *do* want to explain."

She hesitated, then lowered herself back to the grass.

Of course, I couldn't explain; not really. Maybe it would have been better to keep my mouth shut. But, like giving her the keys to my apartment, I needed for her to know as much as I could tell her.

"You're right, about the presentation. I kept thinking, when it was over I'd be fine, but then it ended, and I still wasn't sure how well it had gone. I came back to the apartment, and I was just . . . frustrated. Restless. More than restless. Ready to jump out of my skin. I wanted to work it off before you came over. I didn't want you seeing me like that."

I shifted, stretching my legs, but careful not to get closer to her, knowing I hadn't earned that right back yet. "I already screwed things up this week. And I knew that if I even stopped to give a proper explanation, I'd snap. I shouldn't have let things build up that way in the first place."

She glanced up at me, eyes hooded. "And now you're going to tell me that it was a mistake and it'll never happen again."

I wished, really wished, I could tell her that. But my conscience wouldn't let my lips form the words.

"I can tell you that I'll *try* not to let it build up like that," I said finally. "I can tell you that I'll warn you if it does. I can ask you to tell me if you see it starting. But I can't promise that it'll never happen again."

She pushed up onto her knees and I knew I'd blown it, that she was leaving. Why hadn't I just told her what she wanted to hear and—?

She leaned over and kissed me.

"Thank you," she said. "For being honest. That's all I ask."

Her lips went to mine again. For a moment, I sat there and let her kiss me, knowing I didn't deserve this. I wanted to be honest with her.

And so you will, whispered a voice in the back of my brain. *When she's ready, you'll tell her, and everything will be fine. You can't rush it or you'll lose her.*

My arms went around her and I kissed her hard enough to make a laugh ripple through her. I eased down onto my back and pulled her along with me. In the beginning, she'd tensed every time I moved her into any position approaching horizontal, but she'd soon learned it meant nothing.

I'd told her from the start that I'd let her set the pace, and I'd meant that. Patience was never one of my virtues, but in this case, it wasn't an issue. I'd waited more than ten years to find a lover, and there was no rush to get to the finish line.

As Elena stretched out on top of me, her hands slid under my shirt, fingers tugging it out of my jeans, palms running over my stomach, skin hot against the rising chill of the night air. She pulled back, kissing me more lightly as her fingers tickled over my sides, pushing my shirt up. Then she paused.

"Too cold?" she whispered.

"Never."

I pushed my shirt off over my head and tossed it into a nearby bush. Elena laughed. As I lifted my head to kiss her, I unzipped her coat. Then I pulled her shirt out from her waistband and unbuttoned it. She wasn't wearing a bra. My hands slid up to her breasts, covering them, nipples squeezed between my thumbs and forefingers.

"Too cold?" I asked.

She grinned. "Never."

Her tongue peeked between her lips as my mouth moved to her breast. She wriggled up to meet me, her bare stomach pressed against mine. Her knees slid down over my thighs, and she straddled me. She wriggled again, up then down, sliding until she found just the right spot, then she moaned softly as she pressed into me. I moved my hips up, rubbing against her, and felt her heart race as her fingers dug into my sides.

I teased her nipple with my teeth, then moved my hands down to her waistband, undid her jeans, eased one hand inside, and squeezed it between us. I slid my middle finger into her. She gasped, head arching back. As my finger moved in her, the back of my hand rubbed over my crotch and I pushed against it, swallowing a growl.

I could feel the wet heat of her, smell it, and the scent permeated my brain, scattering every other thought. I moved my mouth up to hers and kissed her hard. She returned the kiss full force, arms going around my neck. I ground against my hand and imagined that I was inside her.

When I thrust up, she nipped my lip, just hard enough to draw blood. I felt her tense as she tasted the damage, but I only kissed her harder, tongue flicking against hers. She started to relax, then tensed again, this time the muscles around my finger tensing with them.

I pushed into her, thrusting my hips against her, and her breathing accelerated, my own racing to meet it. Her fingers dug into my shoulders and I pulled back from the kiss to watch her as she climaxed. Her lips parted, eyes rolling up. A soft growl rolled up from her throat, and I lost it, thrusting against her, barely able to see her through the haze of my own climax.

A few moments later, her grip on my shoulders relaxed, and she pulled back, exhaling in a long sigh. Then she paused and wiped something from my shoulder. I caught the scent of blood on her fingers.

"Sorry," she murmured. "I didn't mean to—"

"Hear me complaining?"

A soft laugh. "No."

"Then don't apologize."

She rolled off me, shivered, then slid her hands to my waistband. "Now, your turn."

"I'm good."

"Hmm?" She looked into my eyes, then blushed. "Ah, okay, then." Another chuckle. "I'll get you next time."

I reached up and pulled her onto me again. She started to lie down with me, then stopped and looked around.

"What's wrong?" I asked through a yawn.

"Uh, just realizing that we're lying on the ground, half naked, about twenty feet from my dorm building."

"See anyone around?"

"No."

"Then don't worry about it. If I sm—see anyone, I'll tell you." I yawned, gulping fresh air to wake my brain before I slipped again. "And you're not half naked. Just me." I straightened her coat over her shoulders. "There. Lie down on me again, and no one will see anything."

"Except me lying on the ground in the middle of November, on top of a professor."

"Stop worrying. I won't let anyone see you."

She grinned down at me. "You'll protect me?"

"Always."

As she looked into my eyes, her cheeks reddened slightly, and she ducked her gaze, almost shyly. Then she kissed my chin, snuggled up, and relaxed against me.

November turned to December before the university told me I had the teaching position. By then, though, I'd already come up with an alternate plan. I'd stay and work on that second proposed paper, whether the university chose to support me in it or not.

Two days before my monthly trip home, when I'd planned to tell Jeremy I was staying, the department gave me the news. If my decision to accept surprised Jeremy, he gave no sign of it, just told me he was proud of me. That made me feel just about as good as when Elena had thanked me for my honesty. I reminded myself that I was on the road to truth. I'd just have to earn forgiveness once I got there.

The next week, as Elena and I headed to High Park for a run, a light snow started to fall and we decided to forgo jogging and enjoy the mild winter night. We'd been out for about an hour when we passed a huge evergreen on a corner. As we walked by, the tree suddenly lit up in a blaze of colored lights.

Elena jumped back, then shook her head. "Must be on a timer."

I walked a couple more steps before I realized she was no longer beside me. I looked back to see her still in front of the evergreen, looking up at it. When she glanced my way, her eyes shone brighter than the tree lights.

"Do you like Christmas?" she asked.

I blinked. "Um, sure. I guess."

She laughed. "Not big on the holidays, huh?" She caught up with me and resumed walking. "Christmas can be stressful. All that pressure—buy the right gifts, spend too much money, hang out with relatives . . . not that I ever—well, I've *heard* it can be stressful."

"It isn't. Not for me, anyway. We're pretty laid back about the holidays. And I do like Christmas, I just never considered it before. How about you?"

I asked on reflex, then wished I hadn't. From the look she'd given the tree, I knew Christmas meant something special to her. Yet I also knew that if it brought back any happy memories, they'd be bittersweet, the vague remembrances of those few years before her parents had died. Since then she'd have spent the holidays alone, maybe with foster families, but still alone in every way that counted.

She turned to look out at the street and let the shadows swallow her expression. Before I could say anything, she looked back at me, eyes bright again.

"When do you go home?" she asked.

"Go—?"

"For the holidays. I was just thinking, maybe we could do a little Christmas of our own, before you leave. Nothing big, maybe presents and a nice dinner. Just . . . something. If that's okay with you."

I looked at her, then made a decision. "I'm not going home."

"But—"

"I need to have that paper done by the end of the year, remember? So I'll stay here, have Christmas with you, and go home for the first week of the new year."

"You're almost done with the paper. You should spend Christmas with—"

"They'll wait. Everyone usually comes down for a couple of weeks anyway, and they don't care exactly when we celebrate it. If someone can't make it, everyone else waits."

Her smile turned wistful. "That must be nice." She looked at me. "If it's really okay—"

"It is."

I put my arm around her waist and we started walking again.

I'd call Jeremy tomorrow. We'd rescheduled Christmas for others before, and the holidays weren't really a big deal for the Pack, just another excuse to get together. For Elena, though, Christmas obviously *was* a big deal. Or it would be this year. I'd make sure of that.

14
CLAYTON

Wʜᴀᴛ ɪ ᴋɴᴇᴡ ᴀʙᴏᴜᴛ ᴄʜʀɪsᴛᴍᴀs ᴄᴏᴜʟᴅ be summed up in three words: holiday, presents, and food. For the Pack, that's what it was—an excuse to take two weeks off work, hang out together, and eat. The gift exchange was the only thing that differentiated it from an extended summer Meet.

As for the customs, traditions, and spiritual significance of Christmas, I understood the last best, having studied the religious aspects of Christmas in relation to non-Christian midwinter celebrations. Yet I doubted that Elena's idea of a perfect Christmas meant listening to me expound on Christianity's adaptations of Mithraic and winter solstice celebrations . . . though I could always fall back on that if things went wrong.

What Elena wanted was something closer to the Pack's interpretation of the holiday: a celebration of family. To her, though, that meant more than food and gifts and time together. As I'd seen in her face when she'd looked at that tree, she wanted trappings, all the things that meant Christmas. And I'd give them to her. As soon as I figured out what they all were.

"First we need a tree," I said.

Elena stopped drying a plate and looked at me, nose scrunching. We were in my tiny apartment kitchen, doing the dinner dishes.

"A tree . . ." she said slowly.

"That's where I thought we'd start."

"With a . . . tree . . . ?"

"Right. Or should we buy the decorations first?"

"Decor—" She laughed. "Oh, you mean a *Christmas* tree. Context, Clay. You must learn the fine art of conversational context." She slid the plate onto the shelf. "A tree would be nice. Is it too soon?" She leaned over the counter to squint at the dining room calendar. Her lips moved as she counted. "Just over three weeks—it should last that long. When do you want to get it?"

"Tomorrow. We'll stop by the hardware store for an axe, then head out to the ravines."

"The ravines?"

"Right. That's where the trees are."

"So we'll just go chop one down." Her cheeks twitched as she bit back a laugh. "Highly illegal, but perfectly sensible, and that's what matters in Clay's world."

Before I could answer, she leaned toward me, chest brushing mine, thumbs hooking my belt loops. Her lips moved to my ear.

"Did you notice the trees in the grocery store lot? Hint: They didn't grow there overnight. That's where we get Christmas trees from in our world."

"Yeah, half-dead ones, cut down in October. Damn things would be naked by Christmas."

"True."

She started to move away, but I put my hand against the small of her back, keeping her close.

"I suppose that's what you do at home, isn't it?" she said. "Grab an axe, walk out to the back forty, and chop down a tree. That'd be nice."

A wistful look, then she brightened. "Oh, wait a sec. There are tree farms, outside the city, where you can cut your own—"

She stopped, gaze skipping to the side. "On second thought, maybe not. They'll be packed with people—crying kids, crowded wagons—definitely not your idea of a good time."

"I'd survive."

"No, we can—"

"Find a place and we'll go tomorrow."

The tree-cutting trip did hit an obstacle, but it wasn't the one Elena had anticipated. Yes, the farm was packed, and the hay wagon trip from the parking lot to the bush was hellish—crammed onto a trailer full of grumpy adults, overtired kids, straw that smelled like it'd been recycled from a horse barn, and two lapdogs dressed in knitted pink sweaters, which spent the whole trip yapping at me.

But I survived. Better than that—aside from the wagon ride—I had a great time. We stayed on the trailer until the last stop, when everyone else had impatiently tumbled out right at the start. So we found ourselves alone in the bush, tramping along the rows of trees as dusk turned to moonlight, our footsteps crackling across the frozen ground, the silence broken only by the distant shouts and laughs of children and Elena's equally excited chirps of "Oh, this one . . . No, wait, there's one over there."

We were in no rush, so we wandered, bickered, and teased, all the while pretending to search for the perfect tree, but really just enjoying the clear winter night. When we did choose one, I chopped it down. Then we celebrated the victorious hunt with powdered dough-nuts and a thermos of hot chocolate, and when that didn't warm Elena up enough, I moved on to other heat-producing activities.

We caught the last wagon back, paid for our tree . . . and hit the roadblock. You can't strap a Christmas tree to a motorcycle. We had debated taking the bike, but only because we knew how cold it would get when we left the insulation of the city. We'd decided that with no fresh snow on the road in days, riding the motorcycle would be cold, but better than the hassle of taking a cab. The motorcycle's limitations as a method of tree transport had somehow failed to occur to either of us.

So we had to arrange delivery after explaining our oversight to the tree farmer who, on hearing my accent, took twenty minutes to kindly explain to the young southerner that Canada really didn't have a winter climate suitable for motorcycles, and to recommend places where I could pick up a cheap winter beater. Then Elena's stifled wheezes of laughter got the farmer's wife scrambling for cough drops and we spent another ten minutes waiting while Elena dutifully copied down her herbal cold remedy recipes. Finally, we escaped, and headed home, with our tree to follow.

The next day we put up the tree and decorated it. Only one thing was missing: the presents to go underneath. At home, I did most of my shopping by catalogue, as did Jeremy. We suffered through an annual New York gift-buying excursion with Nick and Antonio, but always scheduled it for early November, to beat that Thanksgiving-to-Christmas rush.

Just picking out decorations at the department store had been enough seasonal shopping for me, but it was getting late for catalogue ordering, so I resigned myself to a Saturday in shopping mall hell. And if I was going to put myself through that torture, I might as well get a second duty over with, and please Elena by inviting Logan to join us.

For a few weeks now, Logan had been making noises about paying a visit. Had it been just me, I'd have welcomed the company. But I knew I wasn't the one he wanted to see.

His growing friendship with Elena baffled me. It worried me, too. I couldn't help but think he had an ulterior motive. The most obvious answer was that he didn't want me to forget that he knew my secret. A blackmail card he could use against me at any time. Yet I didn't get the impression that's what he was doing.

Logan's interest in Elena seemed genuine. Too genuine for my liking. I pictured him circling over our relationship like a vulture, waiting for it to die so he could swoop in and take my leavings.

Only Elena, and my concern for her happiness, kept me from thwarting their relationship. That and the knowledge that she saw him only as a friend. So, as much as his attentions rankled, I bit my tongue and invited him up for a Christmas shopping weekend.

I stood in a store corner, wedged behind a rack of clothes, the only place I could stand without being jostled and bumped. I breathed through my mouth. I could still smell the mall, though, and my brain spun, trying to sort out and categorize all the scents despite my best efforts to ignore them.

My breath came in short, shallow gasps, almost hyperventilating. My heart raced, gaze darting about the store, trying to map escape routes as my brain kept trying to organize the scents, sorting them into predator and prey, threats and food.

I squeezed my eyes shut and choked back a growl of frustration. I should be able to control my instincts better than this. Most times I could, but when the stimuli became overwhelming, my brain dropped into survival mode, knowing only that I was trapped in an enclosed space with potential enemies at every turn.

Logan shifted the rack to slide in beside me. "Really don't like humans, do you?"

I said nothing. My feelings about humans, like my feelings about other werewolves, could never be summed up under the simplistic umbrella emotion of like versus dislike. Yet I'd rather my Pack brothers interpreted my hatred of crowds as a dislike of humans than as the panicked fear of a trapped animal.

Elena walked around a corner. My gaze followed her, grateful for something to cling to, something comforting and distracting.

"Have you asked her what she wants?" Logan asked.

"Don't need to."

She caught my eye, smiled, and started searching for an open path through the crowd. Partway to me, she stopped, gaze snagged on a rack of sweaters.

"Word of advice, Clayton," Logan murmured. "Save yourself a world of grief and ask for a list."

Elena's fingers flipped through the jewel-bright colors, frown deepening, then lightening. She paused on a dark burgundy, then shook her head. As she looked away, she stopped, and tugged out the arm of a deep royal-blue sweater. A smile. A glance at the price tag. The smile faded and she dropped it fast then resumed her course to me. I glanced around at the store, committing it and the location of the sweater rack to memory, along with the other items that had caught her eye.

"You want me to ask her what she wants?" Logan said. "Then at least she won't be expecting them from you. I'll make up a list—"

"Don't need it."

He sighed. "You'll pay the price, my friend. Don't say I didn't warn you." He turned to Elena as she approached. "I don't know about you, but I'm ready for lunch. How about that food court we passed on the first level?"

Elena's gaze darted my way, then back again too fast for Logan to follow.

"One more stop and my list is done," she said. "Maybe we can grab a muffin or something, finish up, then swing through Chinatown on the way back, find someplace less crowded. And more appetizing."

"Works for me," Logan said.

"So who do you guys have left?" she asked.

"Jeremy." Logan looked at me. "And, I'm guessing, Jeremy."

I nodded.

Elena laughed. "There's always one, isn't there?"

"Is there an art store here?" Logan said. "That's the usual standby for Jeremy."

Elena pulled a face. "And I'm sure when he picks up a gift from his pile, he's going, 'Hmm, paintbrush or paper?' Let's show some originality this year, guys. There's a huge sports store in here. We'll head there."

Logan looked my way. "Uh, Jeremy's not really the sports type . . ."

"Clay said he likes marksmanship, right?"

"Uh, sure. But—"

"Come on, then."

On the way to the sports store, Logan kept shooting looks my way, clearly worried about what Elena had in mind, but not wanting to denigrate her efforts. I was trying just as hard to think up a way out of this potential minefield. Jeremy . . . well, it was tough enough for us to pick something for him. I couldn't imagine someone who had never met him being able to do it.

Elena led us to a row of locked glass cabinets near the back of the sports store. Inside were tournament bows, BB guns, camping knives, and all the other sports paraphernalia that couldn't be put out on the shelves.

Logan pretended to survey the cabinets. "Umm, you

know, this would be a great idea . . . if Clay or I knew a damned thing about what kind of equipment Jeremy uses. I know, we should pay attention, but, well, it's Jeremy's thing." He shrugged. "Bullets, sights, arrows, they all look the same to me."

"Which is why I'm not suggesting that," she said. "Bullets and arrows are as bad as paintbrushes and paper. Supplies, not presents. A gift should be something different, something he doesn't already own." She moved down the row and stopped at a bow display. "Does he have a crossbow?"

I shook my head.

"Has he ever said he *doesn't* want one? Tried one and didn't like it?"

"Nope." I bent to look at the crossbows. "That's what I'll get him, then."

"You don't have to. It's just a thought—"

"It's a great thought. He likes trying new stuff. Thanks."

Her lips curved in a shy half-smile. "You're welcome. Oh, but make sure you save the receipt. And pick out something not too expensive, so he won't feel bad if he doesn't use it."

Logan bent beside me. "You know, that *is* a good idea." He slanted a look my way. "Clay must have told you a lot about Jeremy, huh?"

Elena shrugged. "This and that. He sounds . . . well, I look forward to meeting him." She blinked fast. "Assuming, I mean, that I will meet him. I'd like to, of course . . ."

"You will," I murmured.

"Someday, right?" She hesitated, as if considering something, then said quickly, "Maybe you can set it up when you're home for the holidays."

"I . . . sure, I could . . ." I glanced at Logan for help, but he'd busied himself with a racquetball display.

"Not a weekend visit or anything big like that," Elena hurried on. "We could meet halfway, like in Buffalo for dinner."

"That would be a good idea." I turned. "Hey, Logan. Help me pick out one of these, will you? I'll buy the bow, you can pitch in with the arrows and stuff. Make it a joint gift, then get the hell out of here and track down lunch."

Logan looked over at Elena, then nodded and walked back to help me.

That night, when I returned after walking Elena to her dorm, Logan was in the living room, flipping television channels. I stopped in the doorway.

"I gotta get one of these," he said without turning.

"A TV?"

He gave an exasperated sigh and waved the remote over his head. "This. Mine is still one of those old 'get off your ass and do it yourself' jobs."

"Speaking of getting off your ass, you can do that right now. Time for a run."

He still didn't turn. "You have to tell Jeremy."

I wanted to say "About what?" but I knew.

"I will," I said. "As soon—"

"I know, all along I've been telling you there's no rush. No need to worry Jeremy over a fling. But obviously that's not what this is."

"I told you—"

"That you were serious. I know. But what the hell do you know? It's your first time, and it always seems serious the first time. Then there's Elena. She might not—" He paused, lifted the remote again. "But she does. So that's that."

He turned to another channel. Canned laughter filled the room. A quick flip and the evening news came on.

Logan continued. "Jeremy was right. All that stuff

about how your moods were about searching for a mate. It sounded like bullshit to me—Jeremy taking the wolf stuff too seriously again. You're a man, not a wolf. A little fucked-up sometimes, but still a man."

Another channel change. A cooking host exhorted her audience to use only whole peppercorns, freshly ground. Logan turned the television off. Then he looked over at me.

"I'm getting worried," he said.

"I'm fine."

"It's not you I'm worried about."

I flexed my hands against the door frame. "I'd never hurt her."

"Are you sure?"

I met his eyes. "Absolutely."

He locked gazes with me. "Good, because if you ever . . ." His eyes sparked with anger, then he jerked his gaze away and got to his feet. "You have to tell him. Soon."

"I will."

15
ELENA

ARMS LOADED WITH WRAPPED GIFTS, I twisted sideways to push open my dorm room door. I held the door with my foot, then managed to swing around and get out of the way before it hit me. Penny sat on my desk and watched me struggle.

I lowered my load to the bed. The stack looked impressive, until you realized this was every gift I was giving this year. They were all for friends, stored and wrapped at Clay's apartment because I knew if I'd kept them here, one or two would be missing by wrapping time.

Not that Penny would covet any of my friends' presents—they weren't her style and certainly not her quality—but she'd likely have scooped a couple and passed them along as duty gifts, to cousins, aunts, and the like, because, god knows, Christmas shopping can really take a toll on your social life.

I'd hoped she'd be gone by now; she'd said she was leaving for home this morning, but for Penny, I guess morning was anytime before dark. I could only hope she wasn't desperate enough to snag a prewrapped gift, in hopes it contained something suitable for Aunt Milly.

"He called five times," she said. "I'm not your freaking answering service, Elena."

Normally, "he" meant Clay, but even he wouldn't have called five times in the twenty minutes it would take me to walk from his apartment.

"*Who* called?" I said, unwrapping my purse from my arm.

"Your ex."

I swore under my breath. "Jason, you mean. He's not my ex."

"Whatever. Just tell him to stop phoning. Other people have to use this line, too, you know."

"If he calls back, you have my permission to hang up on him."

She was about to answer when the phone rang. I busied myself rearranging the parcels. Penny grabbed the receiver and passed it out to me without answering.

"Hello?" I said.

"Hey, gorgeous," slurred a male voice. "Why'd ya take off so early this mornin'? I wasn't done—"

I held the phone out to Penny. "It's for you."

* * *

So Jason was back. Not unexpected timing, considering that for the past three years, he'd used the holidays as an excuse to get in touch. He'd say he had a present for me. No strings attached. He just wanted to give it to me and say hello, maybe have a coffee. The first year I'd fallen for it.

I'd ended up getting groped in a dark parking lot behind the coffee shop, until he'd ended up with a knee to the crotch. I should have kicked harder. As it was, that little jab wasn't enough to deter him from trying again.

I didn't return Jason's call. Even phoning to tell him off only encouraged him. In a few hours, I'd be lunching with friends before they went home. From there I'd head straight to Clay's for Christmas Eve. If I could make it through the next few days without a Jason encounter, his "Christmas gift" excuse would expire.

I wrapped the gift I'd bought for Clay. One gift. Not even a very big one. I turned it over in my hands, wondering whether there was still time to race out and buy something else.

I did have another present for Clay. Something I couldn't wrap in a box. But the more I thought about it, the more I was convinced it wasn't just the lamest gift idea ever, but inappropriate.

A gift implies something you selflessly give to another person, with no expectation of deriving anything from it yourself. To apply that concept to the gift I had in mind was hideously old-fashioned. And just plain wrong. But couples gave each other mutual gifts all the time, things they could both use, like a new stereo or a romantic getaway. So I was giving him this in that spirit, and could only pray he didn't say, "Hmm, thanks, but I was really hoping for a new pair of socks."

* * *

"Just one," Clay said, sliding his foot under the tree and nudging the stack of gifts. "Look, lots there. Opening one early won't hurt."

We were stretched out on his living room carpet, surrounded by shortbread and gingerbread cookie crumbs, two mugs of hot chocolate leaning precariously on the deep carpet pile. I'd made the drink from scratch, with baking chocolate and milk, spiked with a dollop of crème de cacao and topped with real whipped cream. I'd even grated extra chocolate on the whipped cream. Turned out pretty good, which was more than I could say for the gingerbread men. They tasted fine but looked like circus freaks—one drawback to having two non-artistically-inclined people fashion cookie men without cutters.

Clay waved his cookie toward the tree, scattering more crumbs. "Go on. Open one. You've been eyeing them all night."

"Have not."

"Have too." He hooked one with his foot and punted it out. "There. It fell off the pile. Don't make me put it back. Open it."

"But if I open one, then you should open one, and I only brought—"

"I don't need gifts. I already told you that. And I'm *far* more patient than you."

I snorted a laugh. "Who burned his tongue on the hot chocolate after I told him it was still too hot?"

"That's different. That was food."

He twisted and stretched over to the end table, reached up, and grabbed a tissue. Then he took two cookies from the plate and wrapped them.

"There, a gift for me," he said.

"But you already know what it is."

"Doesn't matter. If it's edible, I'm not complaining."

He unwrapped the tissue. "Oh, look, a hunchback cookie. Thank you."

He bit off the head.

"There," he mumbled around the mouthful of cookie. "I've opened and accepted my gift. Now your turn."

I laughed. He grabbed me around the waist and pulled me to him. He kissed me and I tasted gingerbread. The kiss deepened and I pressed against him, feeling the first lick of heat. My mind tripped to what I had in mind for tonight, and the heat spread, confirming what I already knew—that I was ready to pass that last signpost, and had been for a while. I was glad I'd slipped into the bathroom a few minutes ago to prepare. I only hoped I'd put the damned thing in right.

After a few minutes of kissing, Clay pulled back and twisted as he reached behind him.

"Now for your gift," he said.

"You mean *that* wasn't it?"

"Nah, I don't reserve that for special occasions, darling, or I'd have to make up a whole lot of them. Two-month anniversary; two-month-and-one-hour anniversary; two-month, one-hour, and twenty-three-minute anniversary . . ."

He lifted the gift and rolled back to see me staring down at him.

"What did you say?" I said.

"I said I don't reserve that for special occasions, or I'd—"

"No, what did you call me?"

"Call you?"

"Maybe I misheard. I hope so, because if you have to call me something—" I shook my head. "Never mind. Just give me the gift."

"So we've gone from 'Oh no, I don't really want one early' to 'Hand it over'?"

I sighed and snatched the gift from his hand. It was

rectangular, about half the size of a shoe box, with something inside that jangled.

"It's a present, not a psychic test," he said. "Just open it already."

I ripped off the paper, opened the box, reached inside, and pulled out a key. Two keys, actually, looking remarkably similar to the set I had in my purse.

"They're for the apartment," Clay said.

"That's what I thought." I lifted them from the box. "Oh, wait, it's a new keychain. No, that's the free one they give you at the key-cutting place."

"The keys are the gift, not the chain."

"A set of keys to match the set I already have?"

"Right."

I looked at him.

"Backup keys," he said. "If I piss you off, and you get the urge to throw my keys away, go ahead. You now have replacements."

"Doesn't that defeat the purpose?"

"Only if the purpose is really to break up with me. If you just want to tell me I'm being a jerk and I'd better shape up, then this works fine. Symbolic key whipping without the risk of keyless inconvenience."

"Uh-huh."

"I could get you a nicer keychain."

I laughed and flicked cookie crumbs off the carpet at him. As I took another swig of hot chocolate, I glanced at the tree again.

"What, eyeing the pile, hoping there's something better in there?"

"No, I was just—" I leaned toward the presents. "What happened to that one? Looks like you used a whole roll of tape on it."

"I ran out of paper, so I covered the hole with tape."

I inched toward the tree. "Meaning, if I look closely, I can probably see right through it?"

"Don't you dare."

As I lunged for the present, Clay scissored his legs around my waist. I squirmed, and almost got free before he grabbed my arm. I knew better than to struggle. Clay had a vise grip—once he got hold of me, I wasn't getting away.

I let him tug me away from the tree. When he let go of my arm, I shot back toward the gift pile. My foot accidentally struck his jaw. He let out an oath and I turned to see him wincing as he ran a finger along his front teeth.

"Shit," he muttered. "It's loose."

I scrambled back to him. "I'm so sorry. Which one—"

He grabbed me around the waist and yanked me off my feet. His hold slipped as my shirt pulled from my jeans, and I managed to twist almost out of his grip, but he moved fast, tugging me down as he rolled on top of me.

We tussled for a few minutes, laughing and cursing, depending on who had the upper hand. Soon his mouth found mine and he pinned me, arms over my head, grip slack, letting me know I could get away anytime.

I caught his lip between my teeth. He growled, the sound sending shivers through me. I slid the tip of my tongue between his teeth and he let go of my hands, his fingers sliding to the back of my head to kiss me deeper.

I counted to three, then pushed out from under him, scuttling to my feet. He grabbed for me, but I danced out of the way. He rose up on one knee, then crouched there, body tight, tensing for the pounce.

His gaze lifted to mine and his lips curved in a tiny smile. The look in his eyes sent my pulse racing, and I could hear my breath coming in pants. I took a slow step backward, smiling a challenge. His eyes sparked and he let out a rough chuckle, almost a growl.

He pushed to his feet. I stepped back again. He matched me, step for step, keeping a small gap between us. When I feinted to the left, he quickstepped right, gaze locked with mine. Another feint left. He started to match it with a step right, then lunged left and wheeled around me so fast he was behind me before I knew it.

I twisted and leapt out of his way. He followed. I backed up . . . and hit the wall. He gave another chuckling growl and took a slow step forward, stopping close enough for me to smell the cookies and chocolate on his breath.

"Clay . . ."

"Hmm?"

"I want to stay the night."

He tilted his head. Then his lips curved in a slow grin that licked fresh heat through me.

"You sure?" he murmured.

"Very."

A flash of a grin, then he leapt, grabbing me around the waist and whirling me around. His mouth went to mine and we crashed over the ottoman, hitting the floor hard, still kissing. I seized the sides of his shirt and yanked. He lifted his hands and wriggled out as I pulled. Then he grabbed the back of my shirt. When it caught, twisted around my torso, he wrenched, and the fabric ripped. He froze.

"I'll slow down."

My fingers slid to his waistband and I popped the button on his jeans. "I don't want you to slow down."

A sharp intake of breath. He grabbed for my shirt again, then stopped, tensed, as if holding himself back. "I'll be careful."

I looked him in the eyes. "I don't want you to be careful."

When he hesitated, I lifted my mouth to his. Only a split-second pause, then with a growl, he pulled me to him in a crushing kiss, mouth hard and insistent, hands ripping away the rest of my shirt. Our pants followed, off so fast I didn't even notice until I felt his bare legs against mine. Underwear followed, just as quickly.

I felt him between my legs and my brain fogged. I wriggled into position, felt the tip of him brush me, closed my eyes, held my breath, and—

"Are you sure?"

My eyes flew open. His face was over mine, so close I could see only his eyes.

"Are you sure?" he said again, words coming in raspy gasps.

I pressed my lips to his and arched my hips up, pushing against him, feeling him slide into me. A moment's . . . something, maybe pain, though my brain refused to interpret it as such. He threw back his head and inhaled sharply.

Then his head whipped forward, lips slamming into mine, kissing me hard. Only a few thrusts, and my nails were digging into his shoulders as the waves of climax rocked through me. I heard him growl deep in his throat, the sound hard and dangerous, and I gasped as he shuddered, arms tightening around me.

A moment later, he looked down at me. "It's supposed to last longer than that, isn't it?"

"How would I know?"

We collapsed into a fit of laughter, limbs still entwined. Then he rolled over, pulling me on top of him.

"So was that my gift?" he asked.

My cheeks heated. "Uh, no. Of course not. I just thought . . ."

He grinned. "It *was* my gift, wasn't it?"

"Yes," I said. "And you only get it on special occasions. Valentine's Day is next. Maybe Groundhog Day, but I'm not making any promises."

He laughed and tugged me down in a kiss. Then, lips still close enough to feel them tickle mine, he said, "You know this is it for me, right? *You're* it. First and last."

I looked up and met his gaze. "Same for me. First and last."

16
CLAYTON

I ARRIVED AT STONEHAVEN EARLY ON the twenty-seventh. I sailed through those first few days, riding the high from my Christmas with Elena, finally reassured that we were heading in the same direction. Christmas Eve had proven that. Sex might mean little to Nick and the rest of the Pack, but to me it signified a life commitment, and I knew it was the same for Elena. One lover, one partner, one mate for life; that's how we were made.

For three days, I coasted on that high, enjoying my visit, playing with Nick, hanging out with Jeremy, hunting with the Pack, calling Elena when I could, for once feeling no guilt, no warring loyalties. Whatever came, we'd work through it.

Not having Logan at Stonehaven helped with the guilt. Since I'd planned to come home late, he'd decided to spend Christmas at his half-sister's place. They weren't a tight-knit family—never had been—but they liked to maintain the illusion of closeness at Christmas, and if he skipped out, he'd feel the cold front all year.

While I was in a great mood, Nick seemed off, one minute bouncing along on whatever adventure I suggested, talking nonstop, then next minute reflective and quiet. I'd catch him studying me with an odd look on his face, or turn and see him hovering in the doorway, as if waiting for me to acknowledge him before he'd enter. I asked him if anything was wrong—trouble with his human friends, problems with women, tension with his father—but he'd just give me that piercing look, then mutter something and walk away.

On the second night, as I waited for Nick in the sunroom, I watched the snow falling outside the window. It reminded me of Christmas night, when Elena and I had gone out after dinner. We'd hoped the long trek to High Park would give time for our turkey dinner to settle so we could run, but when we got there, Elena was still stuffed, so we'd walked through the ravine instead.

When it had started to snow, I'd pulled her to the side for a warm-up. As we'd kissed, I'd slid my hand under her shirt and she'd jumped, laughing at my cold fingers. When I'd asked if I should stop, she'd smiled, unzipped her jacket, unbuttoned her shirt, and let it fall open, bra-less underneath. I'd grabbed her under the armpits and lifted her up, mouth going to her breast, her nipple cold and hard against the heat of my tongue—

"There you are!"

I jumped as Nick swung through the sunroom doorway.

"Ready for that run?" he said.

"In a minute," I said, brushing past him.

"What?" He followed me into the hall. "Where are you going now?"

"Shower."

"Shower? It's ten o'clock at night. What the hell do you need—?"

I bounded up the stairs to my room, cutting him short as I closed the door behind me.

* * *

When I came out, I found Nick in the guest room, snappish, almost sullen, declaring he didn't want to go for a run anymore. After ten minutes of teasing and cajoling, he gave in, but grudgingly, as if he was doing me a favor. As I ushered him from the room, I decided I'd talk to Antonio in the morning, see if anything was wrong at home.

We finished our run in the early hours of the morning. Still in wolf form, we stretched out in the snow and dozed. Jeremy, Antonio, and Peter weren't back from their evening in Syracuse, and probably wouldn't be for an hour or more.

When the car sounded in the drive, we roused ourselves to Change. The rousing part came harder for me—I'd been in the midst of a sleepy daydream about Elena, and was reluctant to leave it. So by the time I was pulling on my pants, Nick was already done. I was buttoning up when I noticed him standing, uncharacteristically silent, behind me.

"Trying to sneak up?" I said without turning. "Thought you knew better by now."

"What's on your back, Clay?"

"Huh?"

I reached over my shoulder, and found healing nail-tracks from Elena. I grabbed my shirt and twisted around.

"Did I lie in the mud again?" I said. "Never fails. Spring, summer, winter, fall, if there's mud back here, I'll find it."

"There are scratches on your back, Clay."

"Yeah? Figures. The ravines up in Toronto? They're in the middle of the damned city. Only safe way to run is through forest so thick I get covered in scratches."

He said nothing as I pulled on my shirt. Then he looked at me.

"You aren't going to tell me, are you?" he said quietly.

"I'll tell you I'm starving—if you can't hear my stomach growling already." I headed for the path. "Jeremy better not have forgotten the takeout this time. And it better not be curry. Last time he brought curry . . ."

I kept talking, filling the space as fast as I could. I was almost at the house before I realized Nick wasn't behind me.

The next day, Nick and I picked Logan up at the airport, and the pressure started almost the moment he got off the plane. We went to collect his luggage, and as soon as Nick got separated from us by the crowd, Logan glanced around, then asked, "Have you told them yet?"

I shook my head.

"Are you going to tell them? And I don't mean someday. You have to tell at least Jeremy, before he figures it out." He grabbed his suitcase from the conveyor belt. "Christ, I can't believe they haven't *all* figured it out by now. Every time they start floating theories about your good mood, it's all I can do to keep from groaning. Guess when it's the last thing you expect, it's the last thing you see, no matter how obvious it is."

I snagged his other bag and hefted it onto my shoulder.

"They're going to figure it out, Clay. Remember what Plato said: 'Once you eliminate the impossible, whatever remains, no matter how improbable, must be the truth.' " He pulled a face. "Or was that Sherlock Holmes? Damn, I need a break. Two weeks after my last exam and I'm still reeling. But the point is—"

"Nick!" I called, lifting my hand.

A dark head in the crowd turned. Nick threw up his hands and hurried over to us.

* * *

I'd been hoping that once Logan arrived, it would be easier to phone Elena. Nick didn't follow at my heels all day, but at any given moment he was liable to drop whatever he was doing and seek me out for a change of activity. If I announced I was going into town, he'd want to join me. And if I didn't announce it, he'd know something was up—I never left Stonehaven without asking whether he wanted to come along. So I'd been getting by on short, furtive calls when he was busy.

With Logan around, Nick would have someone else to hang out with. Or so I thought. Yet I'd wait for the two of them to get talking, then sneak from the room . . . only to hear Nick's footsteps in the hall before I could even finish dialing Elena's number.

"You want some help?" Logan asked, after my third attempt of the day was thwarted.

"In return for what?"

His eyes widened in feigned outrage. "Geez, maybe a thank-you, if it wouldn't be too much to ask."

"Yeah, okay. I'd appreciate it. Thanks."

"Good. After dinner, then, I'll tell Nick I'm calling a friend. Let me talk to Elena for a bit—"

"A bit?"

He shrugged. "Fifteen, twenty minutes . . ."

"And it's *me* you're helping by making this call, right?"

"So I'll chat, make it look good, then you slip in and take over, and I'll keep Nick occupied for a few minutes."

"A *few* minutes?"

"Hey, I'm doing my best here. You in?"

I paused. "You have to call collect. Then I pay Elena back."

"Will do." He paused, expectantly, then looked at me. " . . . and where's the 'Gee, thank you, Logan, you're such a pal'?"

I snorted and headed for the kitchen to start dinner.

*　*　*

After we ate, Logan told us he was going to call a friend, and left us in the weight room. I gave him fifteen minutes with Elena, then headed upstairs. When I got there, though, he took another ten minutes "saying good-bye," meaning I got to talk to her for exactly sixty-five seconds before I heard a creak in the hall.

Logan stalled Nick while I signed off. When I got in the hall, Nick was standing there with a look on his face that I hadn't seen since we were teens, and I'd gotten into a scrap at his friend's party.

"I want to talk to you, Clayton," he said, barely unlocking his jaw enough to get the words out.

"Sure," Logan said. "Let's all talk. Better yet, let's go into town, get a drink—"

"I want to talk to Clay."

Logan laughed. "Why the hell would you want to do that? *I* am, by far, the more engaging conversationalist. Come on, let's grab our coats. Hey, did I tell you about my Christmas Eve? Had all-star wrestling, right in my sister's living room. Her husband and my brother were absolutely wasted, started bickering about—"

"Who's Elena?" Nick cut in.

"The girl I just called," Logan said. "Friend of mine from school. We went out a few times, didn't really go anywhere, you know how it is. Stayed friends, though, which is—"

"It's okay," I said. "I've got this."

Logan shot me a "You sure?" look. I nodded and waved Nick to my room.

"Why didn't you tell me?" Nick said before I could start.

"I was going to, but—"

"Twenty years, Clay. We've been pals for twenty years and I have never—*never*—kept anything from you."

"Yeah, I know, but—"

"For fifteen years, I've been trying to get you a girl. Fifteen years of worrying about why you didn't want one, feeling bad for you, wondering what I could do. 'Cause I'm your friend, and I feel like I should do something about it. I give you advice. I set you up. I take you to gay bars. Hell, I even bought you a hooker for your birthday. But nope, you aren't interested. And when you finally are, I have to find out about it by listening at the door."

I pulled the chair over from my desk. "It just happened."

"And you 'just happened' to tell Logan about it first?"

"I didn't tell Logan anything. He showed up in Toronto and found out for himself. Otherwise, I sure as hell wouldn't have told him. Anyway, I wasn't looking. I met someone and it just . . . happened."

He struggled to keep his scowl, but a tiny smile broke through. "About time."

"Guess it took the right girl. Even then, it was a while before I figured it out, but we've been going out for a while, so—"

"Going out?"

"Yeah."

"How long?"

I shrugged. "Couple months now."

"Couple—" Nick groaned and thumped backward onto my bed. "Damn it, Clay, *this* is why you should have talked to me. I always said, you get interested in a girl, talk to me."

"I'm doing fine."

He lifted his head. "You've been seeing the same girl for months. You don't have to do that. Yeah, sure, that's what they might like. And sometimes, it's what they expect. That's why you have to be careful. You have to let them know, right up front, what you're looking for—a little fun, no strings attached. Be honest, that's what my dad always said. Don't ever let them think it's going to turn into something else, and if they do, apologize for the misunderstanding and cut out. Be nice, be respectful, but most of all, be honest."

This was why I hadn't been looking forward to telling Nick about Elena. "This is what I want. Elena and I— It's not—"

"You're in love," he said.

"What?"

"You're in love. She's the most amazing girl you've ever met and you want to spend the rest of your life with her."

"Uh, yeah."

"And that's why you didn't tell me. Because of the whole 'no long-term relationships' rule. You didn't want to tell me something that could get me into trouble with the Pack."

"Yeah . . ."

He leaned forward and thumped me on the back. "I'm still pissed, but I understand."

"You do . . . ?"

"Your secret is safe with me. No need for the others to find out. So when does your term end?"

"April."

A small, almost superior smile. "Should be just about right. For now, though, it's my turn to educate you. I've been waiting a long time for this. Make up for all those days you left me in the woods to help me get better at tracking. I know tricks you wouldn't believe—make your girlfriend so happy she'll never let you out of bed."

"Thanks, but I think I'm doing pretty good—"

"Sure you are." That smile again. "Now, the first thing you need to remember is that girls aren't like us. They need foreplay—the more the better. It's like exercise. If you want to get the most out of it, you can't skip the warm-up. Takes time and it can be frustrating, but it's worth the effort . . ."

I considered telling him that Elena didn't seem to need much warming up, but he looked so happy at finally having the chance to advise me that I couldn't bring myself to interrupt.

My last night at Stonehaven I had a dream. I don't have them often, and when I do, it's usually a mishmash of images. This one came as clear as a daydream.

I was at Stonehaven with Elena. We were out back. Running—only I'd changed to wolf form and was play-chasing her, the sound of her laughter leading me. Finally, I saw her hiding in the bushes, naked, peering out and trying not to laugh. I snuck up behind her and dropped into a crouch. When I pounced, I was careful, making sure I hit her only with my body weight, keeping my fangs and claws clear of her bare skin. When I pinned her, I resisted the urge to put my mouth around her throat, even in play.

She laughed and crawled out from under me, and I Changed back right there beside her as she waited, patient and unperturbed. When I finished catching my breath, she jumped up and ran again, and I chased her, catching her easily this time. We fell, laughing and rolling, then kissing and groping, working each other to a fever pitch before I slid inside her.

We started rolling again, mock wrestling as we made love. Her teeth nipped at my upper arm, her nails dug into my back, each dart of pain only adding to the pleasure. My mouth went to her shoulder. I felt her skin there, under my teeth, but held back, knowing I couldn't. One last thrust and I came, and as I did, my teeth closed on her shoulder, chomping down in a hard bite. I pulled back, but it was too late.

I wiped the blood from her shoulder.

"I'm sorry," I murmured.

Only I didn't feel sorry. I felt relieved.

I woke up streaming sweat. I pressed my palms to my eyes and tried to push back the images. But it wasn't the images that were making my heart pound—it was that overwhelming sense of relief.

As I gulped air, my door eased open. Jeremy looked around the edge.

"You cried out," he said.

"Me?" I took a deep breath and shoved the covers off me. They were soaked with sweat. "Nightmare, I think. Can't remember." A pause, heart thudding, then I forced myself to look up at him. "Did I . . . say anything?"

He shook his head. "Just a shout."

I mopped my face on the sheet, then kicked it off the bed and lay down, hoping he'd leave. All went quiet, but I could still hear his breathing.

After another couple of minutes, he said, "If you ever want to move out, Clayton, you can. Things change. I know that. Most kids grow up saying they never want to leave home." A small laugh. "You were never *most* kids, but I still didn't expect you to stay forever. If you're staying because you think I need you—the company, the protection—then, as much as I appreciate that, it isn't necessary. I'd be fine."

"I'm not leaving. Not until you kick me out."

Another soft laugh. "I'd never do that, no matter how badly you tempt me sometimes. This is your home and you can stay as long as you like. But . . ." A pause. "Being away these last few months, it obviously—well, you certainly don't seem to be suffering. Maybe that means something, even if you don't want it to."

I mumbled something and feigned a yawn. I doubt Jeremy bought it, but he took the hint and, with a quiet good night, closed my door.

I stayed awake, thinking about the dream. That initial rush of emotion past, I could analyze it logically. Did I want Elena to become a werewolf? Sure I did. Had I thought about it? Of course I had. Did I plan to give her that option when I told her the truth about myself? Absolutely.

The process would be difficult, but not dangerous. Yes, most people didn't survive a werewolf's bite, but that was because they were bitten and abandoned, as I'd been, left to deal with the physical changes unaided and unprepared. Elena wouldn't have that problem. She was young, physically fit, and strong willed, and she'd have Jeremy to guide her through it, as he had for Nick and Logan. Like them, she'd know what was happening, and what to expect, which is why it had to be her choice, an informed, unequivocal personal choice. Anything else . . . well, nothing else would do.

17

ELENA

THE DAY CLAY LEFT, JASON CALLED. HE'D probably been phoning since Christmas Eve, but I hadn't been back to my dorm since then. Had I been thinking, avoiding Jason would have been the perfect excuse to take Clay up on his offer to spend the week in his apartment. Instead, I was stuck in my crappy little dorm room, answering the phone every time it rang in case it was Clay. Half the time it was Jason.

For two days, I fielded his calls with excuses, demurrals, and, when that failed, hang-ups. Then, on my way to the gym, I walked out the side door and saw Jason heading in the front.

My first thought was "Whew, I missed him." Then, on the verge of making a run for it, I turned around and strode to the front of the building.

"Jason!" I called.

He stopped and squinted my way, shielding his eyes against the sun. As I drew closer, confusion passed behind his eyes, but he flashed a wide smile.

"Merry Christmas, baby." He lifted a garish metallic bag. "Thought I'd better deliver this in person, or you'd never get it."

"Thanks."

When I reached for it, he didn't move, just clutched the bag and stared at my outstretched hand. Then, almost reluctantly, he passed it over.

"I—uh—hope you'll like it." As he regrouped, his gaze shifted past me and fixed on the path leading into the bushes. "How about we grab a coffee? We can cut right through there and head up to Bloor."

"That doesn't lead to Bloor. Or to any coffee shops. But I'm sure we could find a nice shadowy parking lot somewhere."

His gaze went blank.

"I'm sorry, Jason, but I don't have time for coffee. I was just heading out to meet my boyfriend. So thank you for the gift, and please, give my regards to your mother—"

"Boyfriend?"

"Right. You've met him, remember? A few months ago? In the park?"

A flash of recognition with a chaser of fear. "Is that a threat, Elena?"

"No, it's a hint. I'm with someone else and never was, or will be, with you."

The hurt look fell again. "Aww, baby, I know we've had some problems—"

"But if you choose not to take that hint, then yes, it will become a threat. Not that I'll sic my boyfriend on you. He has nothing to do with you and me. I'm talking about the restraining order. I'm tired of doing this the nice way, Jason. If you phone me again or visit me again, I will go to the police. Is that clear?"

"You don't need to get mad, baby—"

I stepped toward him and lowered my voice. "It had better be clear, Jason, because I'm serious, and a hundred nasty phone calls from your mommy won't change my mind. Understood?"

I gave him a moment to answer. When he didn't, I walked away.

Jason didn't call again or stop by again or "accidentally" bump into me again. With any luck, my outburst had solved the problem. And if it hadn't? Well, it had felt damned good, so I didn't regret it.

Clay came home in as good a mood as he'd left, proof that things were finally hitting an even stride. Better yet, those strides were advancing in the direction I wanted, because almost the first words out of his mouth were "When do you want to meet Nick?"

Nick's visit didn't happen as soon as either of us hoped. Clay kept inviting him, but Nick was always busy. Work commitments, he said, which made sense to me, but only seemed to infuriate Clay. I didn't care. The point was that Clay wanted me to meet his best friend. It was only a matter of time before he introduced me to everyone else in his life. Then I could stop worrying.

Clay's next big relationship move was quite possibly the last I would have expected. The night before Valentine's

Day, we went to a movie, and Clay insisted on cutting through the mall instead of heading out the theater's rear exit, which was the first sign that something was afoot.

When he steered me into a jewelry store, my heart sank. I knew what was coming: He'd want me to pick out a gift for myself. Very sweet, but I'd been hoping he'd follow up on hints about my fraying backpack instead.

Clay had never been the roses, candy, and jewelry kind of boyfriend, and I liked it that way. But I guess Valentine's Day brings out a certain set of expectations in even the least conventionally romantic lover. So I slapped on a smile and let him lead me to the jewelry counter.

A salesperson flitted over, her smile as wide and fake as my own.

"Can I help you, sir?" she trilled.

Clay waved her away. She didn't leave, but he acted as if she had, turning sideways to face me.

"How about one of these?" he said, tapping his fingers on the glass.

Inside the case were rings. Diamond engagement rings.

I bit back a laugh. "Uh, wrong type. I think what you want is over there." I pointed at the regular ring display on the other side. "Offer me one of these and you'll find yourself forced to make good on that first and last thing."

"That's the idea, isn't it?"

My heart skipped. For a minute, I stared, certain I'd misheard. When I finally opened my mouth, Clay's gaze slid to the hovering clerk. He tugged me aside and lowered his voice.

"That is what you want, isn't it?" he said. "Marriage? Doesn't matter to me. I said first and last, and I don't need a piece of paper to hold me to it. But it's important to you, right?"

"I, uh, well—" *Oh God, were we really having this discussion in a shopping mall?* "I don't *need* it. Not now, that's for sure. I'm only twenty. But someday, of course, well, that *is* where I'd like to end up . . ."

"It's important, then. Getting married."

I nodded. "Yes, it's important to me."

"Then that's what we'll do. Whenever you want it. But even if you don't want that"—he jerked his thumb at a bridal photo—"just yet, you should have *that*." He nodded at the ring display case. "Make things clear."

"You mean, if we're engaged maybe I'll stop being so damned stubborn and move in with you?"

"Makes sense. That roommate of yours—"

I lifted my hand. "I've heard all the arguments, and I'm not going to promise that an engagement ring would change my mind. I'm funny about that, I guess. Old-fashioned."

"You want to do it right. So do I." He nudged me back toward the counter. "If I'm going to do it right, I want to make sure I get something you like." He pointed at the biggest rock in the display. "How about that?"

I laughed. "You can't afford that."

"Don't be so sure."

The clerk sidled back again.

"Even if you could, I wouldn't want it," I said. "Definitely not my style."

"So pick your style. Anything you'd like."

I surveyed the selection. "I don't know. Something simpler, I guess. Any ring can be an engagement ring, right?"

The clerk cleared her throat. "The diamond ring is the traditional choice, and you have lovely long fingers, perfect for showing off a large solitaire—" At a look from Clay she swallowed the rest of the sentence. "Or, if you'd like something nontraditional, it is, of course, your choice."

I moved to the standard rings, frowning as I looked them over.

"I want something simple," I said. "But . . . I don't know. It should still *look* like an engagement ring, I suppose."

"How about this?"

Clay pulled a box from his pocket. Now it was the clerk's turn to glare, arms crossing over her chest. Clay opened the box. Inside was what looked like two rings, one crossed over the other. When I looked closer, I could see that the thin bands were fused in the middle. The outside one was white gold with diamond chips across the front. The other was yellow gold, inscribed with a delicate pattern. Very simple . . . and yet not simple at all.

"Wow," I said.

"You like that?"

"It's— Wow." I stared at the ring, speechless, then blinked hard. "Can I try it on?"

"Nope." He snapped the box shut and shoved it back into his pocket. "Haven't proposed yet."

"What—? Didn't you just ask—?"

"No. I was just checking. Even I know better than to propose in a shopping mall."

"So when are you—?"

"Eventually. No rush, remember?"

"I didn't mean—"

He headed out of the store, leaving me sputtering. The salesclerk rolled her eyes. I ignored her, laughed to myself, and hurried after Clay.

I woke up early the next morning to make a surprise Valentine's Day breakfast for Clay. The night before, I'd cracked open the blind so the sunlight would wake me.

From the way Clay was snoring, though, I could have set the alarm without disturbing him.

I rolled over. Strange, seeing someone lying beside me. Not that I'd never awoken to find someone in my bed, but when it had happened, it hadn't been by invitation. Those first few times with Clay—well, waking to the sight of a person beside me had brought back a rush of memories, and I'd scrambled back so fast I'd fallen out of bed. Now the neural pathways of my brain were changing course, coming to accept that this wasn't a cause for panic.

Clay was sleeping on his stomach, his head half buried under the pillow. I reached out to run my finger down a thin scar on his back. When I closed my eyes, I could trace it by memory. I loved that—the sense of knowing someone's body so well that you could close your eyes and still see every freckle, every mole, every scar. Someday, when I was feeling brave, I'd learn the story behind each of those scars. I'd memorized the map; now I wanted to know what it meant.

When I reached the end of the scar, I opened my eyes. And I blinked, seeing something on my finger. The engagement ring.

"Fits?" he said, voice muffled by the pillow.

"When did—?"

"Last night while you were sleeping. Happy Valentine's Day, darling."

I said nothing. He flipped onto his back, face clouding.

"What's wrong?" he said.

I took the ring off. "I can't wear this."

"What?"

"I didn't accept."

"Wha—? Sure you did. In the jewelry store."

"But that wasn't a real proposal, remember? Therefore my answer couldn't have been real either." Struggling to keep a straight face, I dropped the ring on his chest. "Sorry. Maybe next time."

He growled and grabbed for me. I tried to scramble off the bed, but he caught me and pulled me down, then showed me—once again—the best part about not waking up alone.

Afterward, I curled up against him, drowsy again, thoughts of my special breakfast giving way to plans for a special brunch instead. His arms tightened around me, and his mouth moved to my ear.

"Marry me, Elena," he whispered.

I put my hand out, and he slid the ring on.

By late March, those two nights a week at Clay's apartment had increased to five, sometimes six. I still refused to formalize the move, but I kept so much of my stuff there that the point was moot.

Late one afternoon, when I swung by Clay's office to grab my jacket, I found a note.

Got a surprise for you.
Wait here.
Be back soon.
C.

I waited for forty minutes. By then, I'd run out of homework, and really needed to start working on the essay I'd left at the apartment. So I wrote an addendum on Clay's note, telling him I'd meet him there.

When I got to the apartment, I found the door unlocked.

"Hey," I said as I stepped inside. "I thought you wanted me to wait at the office."

I tossed my backpack into the hall closet and followed the sounds of movement from the bedroom.

"If you're hiding that surprise you mentioned, you'd better hurry," I said.

When I stepped into the bedroom, the first thing I saw was a sweater in a man's hands, and I was about to backpedal and give Clay time to hide it. But then I recognized the sweater as the blue one he'd bought me for Christmas. My gaze traveled up to the man's face . . . and I didn't recognize *that*.

Before I could hightail it out of the room, I realized I *did* recognize the guy staring at me. I saw a teenage version of him every day, in a small watercolor Clay had pinned on his bedroom wall.

Something about the face was different, but all the pieces added up—dark, wavy hair, olive skin, and heart-stopping big brown eyes in a classically handsome face. I realized what was missing. The smile. In the picture, he had a wide, easy grin that lit up his face. There was no trace of that on the man holding my sweater by the edges, as if he'd picked it out of the trash.

"You must be Nick," I said. "I'm Elena."

I smiled and stepped forward, hand extended. He didn't take it. Didn't return the smile. Just stared at me with a look not unlike the one he'd given my sweater.

My gut clenched and I stood there, feeling like an idiot, hand still out, smile still pasted on. His gaze dropped to my other hand.

"You have keys," he said.

"Uh, yeah." I lifted my hand and tried to smile brighter. "Two sets, actually. Long story."

He blinked, shock darting across his face. I followed his gaze, not to the keys, but to the ring on my finger. He opened his mouth, but before he could say anything, Clay barreled through the bedroom door and grabbed me from behind.

"Hey, darling. Didn't I say wait?" He swung me off

the floor, then kissed me before plunking me back on my feet.

"Yes, and you also said you'd be back soon."

"Yeah, I know. I got tied up in the dean's office. So I see you've found your surprise."

He turned to Nick, who was staring at us with that same look of shock he'd given my ring.

Clay walked over and slapped his back. "About time he showed up, huh?" He bared his teeth in something that could be passed off as a smile. "For a guy who doesn't believe in working, you've been doing an awful lot of it lately, buddy."

Nick didn't seem to hear him.

"What?" Clay said, smile turning brittle. "At a loss for words? That'll be the day. Come on. I bought some steaks—"

"I need to talk to you," Nick said. A glance my way, one that didn't even bother to meet my eyes. "Alone."

"Anything you have to say to me, you can say in front of Elena."

"No, that's okay," I said. "You guys obviously have a lot of catching up to do."

Clay grabbed my elbow as I backed up. I hesitated. Then I looked at Nick, saw that gut-twisting expression on his face, the one I'd feared seeing when I finally did meet Clay's friends and family, that look of bewilderment that said "What the hell are you doing with *her*?"

So this was why Clay had taken so long to start introducing me. Because he knew I'd be a disappointment. Exactly what I'd felt every time a new foster family had taken me in. That I didn't measure up.

Dimly, I heard Clay say something, but the blood pounding in my ears drowned it out. I tugged free of Clay's grasp, and hurried out the door.

18
CLAYTON

I FOLLOWED ELENA INTO THE HALL AND tried to talk to her. The moment someone stepped off the elevator and looked our way, though, she brushed me off with assurances that everything was okay. I wanted to pursue it, but I was seething at Nick and knew that every sharp word I said, Elena would take personally. She promised to meet me for breakfast, and I watched her leave, then stormed back into my apartment.

Nick was in the living room.

"What the hell were you doing?" I said as I strode toward him.

He stood his ground. "What the hell are *you* doing? There's a ring—an engagement ring—on that girl's finger. If you're screwing around with some guy's fiancée—"

"That's my ring."

He winced, as if that was the answer he'd been dreading. He slumped into the nearest chair. "How could you—?"

"I told you I was in love."

"With the first girl you've slept with. Of course you think you're in love! Do you have any idea how many Pack rules you're breaking?" A harsh laugh. "Sure you do. You're the rule expert. And you make damned sure that *we* follow each and every one of them."

"This is different."

"Right. Because you're different and the rules don't apply to you."

"Yes, they do. I know I'm disobeying—"

"*Betraying*, Clay. Not disobeying. Jeremy trusted you up here. You lied to him and you lied to me and to everyone in the Pack. The only person you told the truth to was Logan, and only because he found out your secret."

"I never lied—"

"Bullshit! You lied every time we asked you what was going on and you said 'Nothing.' "

"I was waiting for the right—"

"And what about this girl? She's in love with you, and she thinks you're going to marry her."

"I am."

"You—" He stared at me, unblinking, then leaned back into the chair and shook his head. "You can't keep this a secret, Clay. My father tried it."

When I looked over sharply, he continued. "Yes, I know about that. I pretend I don't because he doesn't want me to know, and bringing it up would only hurt him. That's important to me—not hurting people."

"And you think it isn't important to *me*? Since when have I—"

"Lied to everyone you're supposed to care about?" He shook it off. "It doesn't matter. It won't work. It didn't with my father and it won't for you. This isn't a secret you can keep from someone you're supposed to love."

"I'm not going to. I plan to tell her."

"Tell—?" His mouth worked, but nothing more came out. After a moment, he rubbed his hand over his lips. "Jeremy won't let you. He can't. It would break Pack Law and he cannot do it, even for you. You know that."

"He'll understand."

Nick threw up his hands and stood. "Oh, right. Stu-

pid me. He'll understand. And I suppose she'll understand, too. Whoops, did I forget to mention I'm a werewolf? Hey, you understand, don't you?"

"She will."

"In what universe—?" He stared at me, then gave a
slow shake of his head. "Yesterday, if someone had
asked me who I know better than anyone in the world,
I'd have said you. But now?" He met my gaze, then
dropped his. "I don't know who you are. Maybe I never
did."

He walked to the door, then stopped, his back still to
me. "You have to tell Jeremy."

"I will. Just as soon as—"

"You're going home next week for Easter, right?"

"Yes, but—"

"You'll tell him then," he said, his voice taking on a
tone I'd never heard from him before. "And if you don't,
I will."

"Nick, you—"

"I won't let you fuck up your life, Clay, and I won't let
you fuck up that girl's. When my father did this, he was
just a kid. He didn't know better. You do."

He opened the door and walked out.

I stood in the middle of the room, blood roaring in my
ears. I hadn't betrayed anyone. I would never do that.
Never.

Nick didn't understand. Jeremy would. He'd know I
never intended to hurt anyone, that I would never hurt
anyone I loved. I couldn't. If my best friend didn't know
that—

I don't know who you are. Maybe I never did.

My hands clenched and my skin started to pulse.
Change—I had to— No, I couldn't. Elena could come
back. I couldn't let her see me like this.

Can't let her see you like what? *Like you really are?*

Can't let her see the truth? Can't let her see that every-thing you've told her is a lie?

"It's not a lie!" I said aloud. "She knows me."

Like Nick knows you? Like Jeremy knows you? What is she going to say? What is Jeremy going to say?

"He'll understand," I muttered. "They both will."

The voice started again, but I clenched my teeth and willed it to silence. I had to Change—no, I had to see Elena. Yes, Elena. When I saw her, everything would make sense, as it always did. I'd see her, and I'd see a solution, a way to make it right.

I took deep breaths and watched the hairs retract from my arms. Then I straightened, grabbed my coat, and walked out.

As I left the parking lot, I saw Elena at the side door. At first I blinked, sure I was mistaken. Then I caught the unmistakable sound of her voice.

"—test my threat, Jason, you've made a very big mistake. I said I'd go to the police, and that's what I'm doing. Right now."

She took three steps, then the figure beside her shot forward and grabbed her arm.

"Let go of me or—"

He twisted her arm. She yelped. I charged.

I got to them just as Elena kicked Jason's shins. As he stumbled, I grabbed him by the collar. Through the blood pounding in my ears, I heard her shout for me to stop, that she had things under control. But it wasn't under control. Nothing in my life was under control. I'd broken Pack Law. I'd lied to my Pack brothers, my Alpha, my mate. I hadn't even been able to protect Elena from this bastard.

I slammed Jason into the wall. His head crunched against the brick, eyes going wide, the irises sliding up as he lost consciousness.

"Clay!" Elena ran up behind him. "Don't—!"

I loosened my hold and Jason slumped forward.

"Oh, my god," she whispered. "You—you killed him."

"Not yet."

I drove my fist into his jaw. Bone crunched. Elena screamed, her voice filled with panic and rage as she shouted at me to let him go. I heard footsteps coming toward the corner. I grabbed Jason, dragged him behind the building, and was about to throw him to the ground when a hand clamped around my arm. I wheeled, fist in flight, saw Elena and checked my swing, blowing past her face so close my knuckles grazed her cheek. Her eyes went wide. For a second, we just stared at each other. Then she turned and ran.

It took me a moment to recover enough to go after her. I tracked her to the subway station, but she'd already boarded the train, so I went back to her dorm to wait. There was an ambulance there. I ignored it. Yes, maybe someone had seen me earlier. Maybe they'd recognize me now and point the police in my direction. I couldn't have cared less. I plunked myself onto a bench behind the dorm. I waited all night, and she didn't come back.

I split the rest of the weekend between waiting outside her dorm and checking places she might take refuge— the library, the museum, the student lounges. When Monday came, I waited outside her first class, and both other classes she had that day. She didn't show up.

On Wednesday, I walked into my office to find her sitting there, face pale, dark circles under reddened eyes.

"I can't do this, Clay," she said as I walked in.

She put her hand out over the desk and let the ring drop. It rolled, hit a pile of papers, and fell still. I stared at it.

"I've tried," she said quietly. "I kept telling myself—I

kept *lying* to myself, saying everything was okay, but it isn't, and I can't do this."

She stood and stepped toward the door. I jumped into her path. Panic flashed behind her eyes. I quickly moved aside.

"I can explain," I said.

"Explain *what*?"

"Everything. Everything that worries you about me— scares you."

"I don't think any explanation could—"

"Come home with me."

A slow shake of her head. "If you have something to say, say it here. I'm not going back to your apartment again."

"Not the apartment. Home. Stonehaven. Come with me to Stonehaven this weekend, and you'll understand everything."

She met my gaze. "Understanding doesn't always mean accepting, Clay."

The knot in my stomach tightened, but I pushed on. "I know. But just—just come with me, and then you can make up your mind."

A hesitation that seemed to go on forever. Then she nodded.

19
ELENA

THIS WAY." CLAY TOOK MY HAND AND led me off the driveway onto the lawn.

It was past ten at night and the yard was dark, with a half-moon lighting the way. Clay's eyes glowed, like a boy returning home after his first summer camp. Still holding my hand, he ducked through the evergreens, following a faint path. I could picture him as a child taking this same route, his secret trail home.

Home. *His* home. I swore I could feel him, embedded in this place like the well-trodden pathway etched on the lawn.

We turned a corner and he swung behind me, grabbed me around the waist, and held me still. I could feel his breath against my hair, the pound of his heart. Then he eased us to the left, past the trees . . . and there it was. Stonehaven.

A house with a name. I'd only ever heard of such things in books. An ancestral home. A place you grew up in and died in, as had your family before you and as would your family to come. A place so important, such an integral part of your family, that it needed its own name.

If anyone had asked me to picture a house called Stonehaven, the one before me would have been exactly what I would have imagined. A stone house over two stories tall, as plain and sturdy as the material it was made of. A haven of stone, like some residential fortress tucked away from the world, surrounded by its cushion of lawn and trees.

"You like it?"

When I looked at him, I saw how important it was that I liked it. This was where he wanted us to live after we were married. Here, with Jeremy. As much as I loved the concept of a family home, when it came to the reality . . . well, I hadn't been so sure. I knew how close Clay was to his guardian, but to set up married life in your father's home . . . ? As I looked up at this house, though, and looked over at Clay, my gut ached with longing.

"I love it," I said.

He smiled, a smile so wide that it cast my doubts into exile. I smiled back, and he grabbed my hand and led me to the front door.

Those doubts resurfaced as we stood on the front step, doorbell rung, awaiting a response. Clay's reason for ringing the bell was the same he'd given for taking a cab on the long and expensive ride from the airport.

"I want to surprise him," he'd said.

"He doesn't know we're coming?"

"It's Easter. Of course he knows I'm coming home. It's *when* that's the question."

Of course, he knows *I'm* coming home. I hadn't missed that. Yet Clay was the one who'd be expected each Easter, not Clay and his fiancée, so the phrasing wasn't inappropriate.

I could have squelched my doubts with a single question: Does Jeremy know you're bringing me? But I told myself that was ridiculous. Clay wouldn't bring me home without telling Jeremy. This visit was so important that he'd never risk screwing it up like that.

Clay was lifting his hand to knock again when the door swung open. I braced myself, then relaxed. This wasn't Jeremy. I hadn't seen pictures of Clay's guardian—Clay kept only sketches Jeremy had done of their friends, and there were no self-portraits. Yet I knew this wasn't him.

As Clay's surrogate father, Jeremy had to be at least in his late forties and this man, without a wrinkle on his lean, angular face, or a strand of gray in his black hair, couldn't have been more than thirty. I mentally flipped through the portraits on Clay's wall. Jorge? The friend who'd moved to Europe a few years ago? The coloring was right, but the face—

"Hey, Jer," Clay said, his voice tight with strain. "Aren't you going to let us in?"

I blinked and looked at the man again. It couldn't be . . . But as I saw the look on his face, his shock double my own, I knew the truth. This *was* Jeremy. And not only hadn't he known I was coming . . . he hadn't known I existed.

Those next few minutes were a blur. Jeremy backed up to let us in and Clay performed introductions, both Jeremy and me struggling to overcome our shock and give some appropriately polite response. Then Clay grabbed our bags, mumbled something about seeing Jeremy in the morning, and rushed us up the stairs.

He ushered me into the first bedroom on the left. I'd often wondered what his room here would look like— he kept his apartment and office so utilitarian—but now that I was there, the room could have been empty for all I noticed. The moment the door closed, I turned on him.

"How could you?" I whispered.

He reached for me, but I backed away.

"How could you?" I said again, rage turning the whisper to a hiss. "To bring me here—show up on his doorstep—without a word of warning to him—to *me* . . ."

Clay said nothing. In his eyes, I saw desperation and shame. And fear—fear that he was losing me. He looked so lost that I had an overwhelming urge to hug him and tell him everything would be okay. He loved me. Sincerely and deeply, and I so desperately wanted that to be enough.

How many times had I seen women in destructive relationships? Friends, classmates, foster mothers. I'd seen women battered by abuse—physical, sexual, and psychological—and when asked why they stayed, so often their only defense was "I know he loves me." Until now, I'd never understood how you could cling to those words, that belief, and use it to wash away every misgiving.

I had other talismans, too. He doesn't drink. Doesn't use drugs. Doesn't gamble. Doesn't even smoke. He's never cheated on me. Never even looks at other women. He's never insulted me, degraded me, pushed me to do something I didn't want to do. He's never hit me. Never threatened to ... except for last weekend, when he'd turned on me, hand raised, eyes blind with rage, knuckles brushing my cheek. But that had been a mistake. A mistake ...

So many excuses. Talismans to ward off the fear and doubt.

"So ..." I said. "We're here. You said you'd give me something when we got here."

"Hmm?"

"An explanation."

"Right. I will. Just as soon as—" Doubt flickered over his face. Then he shook his head. "No, I'll do it now. We'll—"

A rap at the door. Clay tensed. His gaze cut to me. A pause, then another knock, louder. I motioned for him to answer it. He paused, then called, "Come in."

Jeremy eased the door partly open, but stayed in the hall. He nodded my way, before turning to Clay.

"I'd like to speak to you."

"We were just—"

"It's getting late and I'm sure Elena is tired from the trip. I'll keep it short."

Clay hesitated for at least thirty seconds. Then he swallowed, murmured something to me, and left, closing the door behind him.

2 0

CLAYTON

JEREMY LED ME INTO THE STUDY. THEN he sat in his recliner and stared at the fire.

"I'm sorry," I said after a few minutes.

"Sorry?" The word came slow, hesitant, as if spoken in a language he didn't recognize. "I don't even know what to say, Clay."

Neither did I, so we sat in silence for at least ten minutes.

"I should have seen this coming," he said finally. "I knew what you were looking for and when you came home, excited and happy, the obvious reason should have been that you'd found it. But the thought never crossed my mind because I thought you could never find what you wanted, because there were no female werewolves. A human mate? That never occurred to me. The way you feel about humans—"

"Elena's different."

"Different?" Again, that careful, confused enunciation. "How long have you—? No, I guess I already know that. Since fall. But all those months . . . And you never . . . Not a word. I can't—" He let the sentence fall away.

"I knew I had to be sure—to be able to prove to you that I was sure."

"Sure of what?"

"Of us. Elena and me. That we could make it work."

"Make it work?" Enunciated even slower this time. He paused. Then his gaze swung to mine. "And how do you intend to make it work, Clay? By turning that poor girl into a werewolf?"

"No. Never. Not unless she—" I saw his look and backpedaled. "*Never.* I meant that we could be together without that."

"With that secret between you?"

"There wouldn't be any secrets."

Jeremy's hands clenched the chair arms so tight his knuckles went white. "You haven't told—"

"Not yet. I'm telling her tonight."

"No, you will not." His gaze locked on mine. "You will not tell her, Clayton. That is an order."

"You don't understand. She—"

"No, *you* don't understand. Maybe that's my fault. All your life I've made allowances for you. Yes, maybe you need a mate, but do you think none of us ever feels that urge? If I've led you to believe that this is another concession to your nature that I'll make, then that is my fault. But the misunderstanding is about to be corrected."

He met my gaze, held it, and said, "The girl must go."

"*Never.*"

The word came out as a snarl. Jeremy blinked, genuine fear flashing behind his eyes. Then he pulled himself up straight, face going as hard as his eyes.

"Don't you ever challenge my word, Clayton." His voice was low and sharp. "You have a choice to make and, as Alpha, it is my duty to insist that you make it. Either you end it with this girl or you take her and walk out that door—for good."

I jerked back as if punched. I stared at him, unable to think, let alone speak.

Jeremy blinked, and in that tiny reaction, I knew that he hadn't understood at all. He'd thought that if he put it that way, I'd capitulate. I might rage, throw a tantrum, break furniture, but there would be no question about which I would choose.

"Don't make me. It would—" I swallowed hard. "*Please* don't make me."

An awkward moment of silence. I could feel his gaze on me, confused. Finally, he sighed, head falling forward, exhaustion etched on his face.

"Let me . . ." he began. "Give me some time to think about it. I'll look after this for you."

With that, he pushed to his feet and left the study.

As I climbed the stairs to my room, one refrain looped through my head: Jeremy will help. I repeated it over and over, not because I believed it, but because I so desperately needed to believe it.

Jeremy was more than my Alpha, more than my father. He was my savior. He'd rescued me from the bayou and he'd rescued me from every pitfall I'd stumbled into in the twenty years since. There had been nothing he wouldn't do for me, no battle he wouldn't fight for my sake, no obstacle he wouldn't find a way to overcome. And so he would again.

Yet I knew I had found the one battle he couldn't fight on my behalf. I'd broken Pack Law. The only way he could avoid punishing me, by death or exile, was to eliminate the threat. To clean up the mess I'd made.

He wouldn't kill Elena. As long as there was another way, he wouldn't take that step. But if I pushed him into a corner—

No, he still wouldn't do it. Never.

As much as I told myself that he'd find some convoluted way around the Law, I knew that wouldn't be it. He would solve my problem by making the choice for me. He'd convince Elena to leave me. And, as I walked into the bedroom and saw her in bed, gaze shuttered and cool, I knew he wouldn't have to work very hard to do it.

For a long minute, we just stared at each other. Then she crossed her arms, fighting to keep her expression hard, to hide the tremble of her lips.

"You aren't going to tell me, are you?" she said.

Goddamn it, why *hadn't* I told her? Told her yesterday, in the office, when I'd promised an explanation. Told her tonight, on the front yard, her eyes bright as she stared at the house.

I gritted my teeth and tried to force my brain past Jeremy's command, but it wouldn't budge. He'd expressly forbidden me to tell her, and I could find no loophole to slip through.

"I—I can't."

She lifted her hands to her face, shoulders crumpling. I hurried to the bed and sat beside her.

"I can't tell you tonight, Elena. But I will tell you before this weekend is over. I swear it. If I don't . . ." I took a deep breath. "I'll lose you if I don't. I know that. Believe me, I know it."

She nodded, gaze down, her face as exhausted as Jeremy's had been. Exhausted from worry and doubt and disappointment. Nick was right. I'd let everyone down. Betrayed them all.

My gut clenched and I reached for her, but she shook her head and moved to the other side of the bed and curled up with her back to me. A moment later, I heard a muffled sob. When I touched her shoulder, she shrank from my fingers, and all I could do was lie beside her, listening to her struggling not to cry.

More than once that endless night, I thought of waking her, begging her to pack her things and come away with me. To leave here. Get someplace safe, where we could sort all this out. But each time I reached to wake her, Jeremy's words stopped my hand.

If I left, would he think I'd chosen exile? If he did, could I ever come back? Banishment would destroy me, just as sure as losing Elena would. My Pack and my mate—two equal commitments, an impossible choice. I had to find another way.

The next morning, when I woke, Elena was gone. I jumped up so fast I tumbled out of bed. Then I saw her coming out of the bathroom, showered and dressed.

"Wait," I said, scrambling up. "I'll be ready in a second, and I'll make you breakfast."

She nodded and, without a word, sat down to wait.

Jeremy had already eaten. When we finished, he took me aside as Elena cleared the table.

"Last night you said you wanted me to understand," he murmured, too low for her to hear from the kitchen. "You're right. I need to understand, and the only way I can do that is to spend some time with this girl, talk to her, get to know her."

A day ago, I'd have jumped at those words. But now I knew the truth. Jeremy would never understand. Like the rest of the Pack, he obeyed the Law by avoiding temptation and drawing a firm line between sex and emotional involvement.

While others had a string of casual girlfriends, Jeremy never even did that. He had no idea what I felt for Elena, and I'd been deluded to ever think otherwise. As he stood there, telling me he wanted to get to know her better, I knew he only wanted to learn more about her so he could figure out the best way to get rid of her. Still, I held out hope—

"I can't talk to her with you hovering. I want to speak to her alone."

"I'll keep quiet—"

"No, you won't. You can't. I'm going to speak to her, and you will stay away while I do. Then I'll figure out a solution for your problem."

My gut dropped. I opened my mouth to argue, but knew it would do no good. I had to find another way. So I nodded, and went to tell Elena.

I left them in the study. Then I went into the kitchen and filled the sink, as if I was going to wash dishes. There was only one thing I could do to stop Jeremy from sending Elena away—something that would make sure he couldn't let her go. She had to know what I was. Then she would understand and Jeremy would see that she wasn't a threat, that she loved me too much to ever betray us.

I'd found the loophole to Jeremy's command. He'd forbidden me to tell her what I was. So I wouldn't tell her. I'd show her.

I eased open the back door, slid into the sunroom, undressed, and began my Change.

As I padded down the hall, I heard Jeremy talking. I concentrated to understand the words, still clinging to the hope that he really was just trying to get to know her better and all this could be avoided. He was talking about Elena's schooling, and how she expected to continue after we were married, and did she understand what she'd be giving up. Searching for the weakness, the way to make her leave me.

I eased open the door with my muzzle and slipped in, head low. Jeremy had his back to the window. As I crept forward, Elena saw me and gasped. I paused in midstep. Then she smiled. Smiled right at me and in that second I was sure she recognized me. After all those months of worrying about how she'd react, now she finally knew, and she wasn't angry, wasn't even surprised. Maybe she'd known all along—

"She's . . . gorgeous," Elena said. "Or is it a he?"

She kept smiling, fingers out, coaxing me forward, and I knew she didn't see me at all. She saw a dog.

As she spoke, Jeremy turned and saw me for the first time. He said my name and again, for that brief second, I thought I'd succeeded—surely now she'd make the connection. But she only said something about me letting the dog out, and I knew then that she would never see—that it was too far outside her realm of possibility.

I crept forward, drawn by her smile and her dangling fingers, calling me closer. Jeremy tensed, as if not knowing what to do. But I knew, and even as my brain screamed for me to stop, instinct took control and I grabbed her hand, my teeth sinking in, breaking the skin. As she let out a yelp of surprise, I ran my tongue over the wound, working in the saliva.

And it was done.

EPILOGUE
CLAYTON

ELENA PASSED OUT AFTER I BIT HER. Hours later, she was still unconscious, fevered and delirious. That wasn't what I expected. I don't know what I did expect. Even when I realized what I'd done, I told myself she'd be fine. I'd been bitten and I was fine.

Elena was not fine.

Elena would not be fine for a very long time.

Would I have done things differently if I'd known how much she'd suffer? Yes. Without question.

I can try to justify what happened. I panicked. I was in wolf form, not thinking rationally. Excuses that can never excuse what I did.

I was the only person Elena had ever allowed herself to trust, and I'd broken that trust. When Jeremy banished me that night, I left determined to make it up to her . . . and knowing I never could.

·· EXPECTATIONS ··

As I listened to Victor Tucci's story, a single refrain ran through my head.

And what do you expect me to do about it?

I wouldn't say such a thing, of course. Perhaps some politer variation, without the inherent connotations of indifference. Yet the gist would be the same. What did he expect me to do about it?

A rhetorical question. I knew precisely what he expected and that when he made clear that expectation, we'd both be disappointed. Perhaps I even more than he, for I was about to receive yet another glimpse into my future, where my value would forever be measured by my parentage and what it could do for men like Victor Tucci.

I was Lucas Cortez, son of Benicio Cortez, CEO of the most powerful American Cabal. Heir to the throne, despite being the youngest of his four sons. I'm sure my father has a very shrewd political reason for this farce, but until he tires of it, I'm forced to deal with the expectations it engenders.

I thought of stopping Tucci. I suppose I should have, to save us both the bother. It was two A.M., I had an exam at eight, and when it came to sleep, I was well below my quota—a combination of a busy exam study schedule and a stressful visit from my father two days ago.

Yet my father taught me to hear people out, whether it was a VP with a new marketing concept or a junior custodian complaining about a switch in toilet paper brands. Cutting people short demonstrated a basic lack of courtesy, and suggested that their thoughts and opinions weren't worthy of your attention. Ironic, isn't it, that as fast as I run from my father's influence, it's still his words I hear and his words I follow.

I swallowed a yawn and blinked hard.

Maintain eye contact. Don't fidget. Don't check your watch. Don't glance at the clock. Don't do anything that might make it seem you have better things to do. Don't just try to appear *interested; try to* be *interested.*

That last part was easy. I *was* interested in what Tucci had to say. Any conversation involving the words *rare, black market,* and *spellbook* were guaranteed to get my attention. Of course, I could have informed him that the proper term for what he was describing was *grimoire,* but it's never polite to correct someone when you know perfectly well what he means.

From the sound of it, though, this book didn't contain the sort of spells I'd care to add to my repertoire. I have no aversion to dark magic, not in principle nor in practice, provided that the principle and the practice are guided by ethical standards. All martial forms of magic are considered dark magic. Dark, not evil. The morality depends on the application. One cannot argue that using an energy-bolt spell to kill a business competitor is moral (unless you happen to be my father, in which case morality is a clay that can be molded to suit the requirements of circumstance), but nor would most people argue that using that same spell to foil an assassination attempt is equally immoral.

Still, there is a limit to how many such spells one needs. A nonsupernatural who foresees the need for self-defense may acquire different weapons for different circumstances. Yet the only person who requires a dozen varieties of guns is one who is not fending off assassination, but carrying it out.

Given the type of spells Tucci was describing, a more accurate analogy would not be guns, but instruments of torture—to put out an eye or disfigure a face or create a wound that causes untold agony. That is one form of weapon I have no use for—proof that I have not absorbed *all* of my father's teachings.

"So you can see why I'm concerned," Tucci said as he finished.

"Naturally. Such spells should not be in the public domain, and yet . . ."

I paused, about to ask some variation on "What do you expect me to do about it?" when a thought struck. Perhaps what he wanted was . . .

"You'd like me to retrieve this grimoire," I said, straightening, the drowsiness I'd been fighting finally falling away. "To remove it from circulation."

A blank look. I was about to rephrase myself, substituting *spellbook* for *grimoire,* when Tucci nodded.

"Yes, yes, that's it exactly, Mr. . . . ." He faltered on the word, as if he couldn't bring himself to use the formal mode of address for someone half his age. "Cortez."

"Lucas. Please." I snatched my notepad and pen from the side table. "Now, first, let me be very clear that I'm not certain I could undertake a task of this magnitude. My work thus far has been limited primarily to simple legal advice. Yet that is not to say I have no experience with more *active* work, including surveillance. The removal of property not my own would entail slightly more expertise than I currently possess, but one cannot gain experience without taking that first step."

Tucci stared at me, uncomprehending. A not-uncommon reaction when I open my mouth.

I propped the notepad on my knee. "Why don't you

tell me some more about where this grimoire is being held, and by whom?"

He continued to stare. I mentally replayed the last sentence, but it seemed straightforward and simply worded enough. So I waited, presuming he needed more time to organize his thoughts.

"You're going to . . . get it . . . yourself?" he said finally.

"Preferably. Although, if necessary, I do have a few contacts with experience in this sort of . . ." I let the sentence drop away as I saw the look in his eyes. "You wanted me to take this to my father."

"Well, yes," he said, as if that should have been obvious. And it was. I'd been misled only by my own misguided surge of optimism.

Tucci continued, "I'm sure your father would let you help. As you said, it would be good experience for you, getting to know the business from the bottom up, so to speak. Can't learn everything sitting behind a desk, can you, son? At your age, I'm sure you don't want to either."

I waited, to be sure none of my disappointment leaked into my words. "True, I'm certain, for any young man who intends to follow the path into the family business. However, as you are doubtless aware, I have disavowed all connections to the Cortez Cabal."

"Yes, yes. That tiff with your father—"

"It isn't a—" I swallowed the word. "I realize that my alienation from my father and the Cabal is widely considered an adolescent act of rebellion, but I should think that having outlasted my teens, it is apparent that this is more."

From his look, I knew that the only thing apparent to him was that I was proof that some young men didn't outgrow teenage rebellion. To him, I was a resentful, ungrateful brat, someone he'd rather not deal with at all, but he stood no chance of an audience with my father or brothers, so I was as close as he could get to the Cortez Cabal inner family.

"I'm sorry," I said, rising to my feet. "If you wish to bring this to the Cabal's attention, I would recommend you notify—"

I stopped. Did I want him bringing this grimoire to the Cabal's attention? Granted, my father probably had a copy hidden somewhere. If he didn't, though, did I want to hand it over to him? And possibly get the current owner killed?

I forced the worry back with logic. My father wouldn't order the owner killed as long as he could get the grimoire without resorting to such drastic and potentially untidy measures.

"Notify who?" Tucci said, his gaze impatient. "See here, I don't think you're understanding the seriousness of this, young man. This is a very important spellbook, and it's in the hands of a witch."

My head jerked up. "A witch?"

"I said that, didn't I?"

"You said Evan Levy."

"Who the hell is Evan Levy? I said—" His jaw shut with a clack, reminding himself that, inattentive brat or not, I was still a Cortez. "I'm sorry, but you must have misheard. I said Eve Levy."

"Eve Levy?" I frowned. The name sounded familiar.

"Levy, Levi, some—" Tucci's hands fluttered. "Some Jewish name."

"Levine," I said slowly. "Eve Levine."

I sat down. Tucci rambled on, but my father's lessons flew out of my head, and I made no effort to pretend I was still listening. Victor Tucci wasn't bringing this to my attention because it was a dangerous spellbook, but because it was in the hands of a witch.

While my father's attitude toward witches was pragmatic—he'd try to buy the book from her and, failing that, intimidate her into handing it over—my brothers and the board of directors would not be so willing to treat Eve fairly.

Eve Levine made her living instructing sorcerers in magic they weren't skilled enough to use properly. She gave them the power to torture and kill. An executable offense? I don't know. What I do know, though, is that my brothers and the Cabal board of directors would not kill her for this. They would kill her for the indignity of a mere witch presuming to teach sorcerers, and an indictment on those grounds was as despicable as a lynching.

"A witch," I said, adjusting my glasses as I pretended to ponder this. "That does make a difference. You're quite correct. She needs to be stopped, and anything I can do to help, I will."

Tucci tried not to smirk. "Glad you feel that way."

I picked up my notepad. "If you can provide me with the particulars, I will pass them along to my father immediately."

My motorcycle idled at the curb as I looked up at Eve Levine's apartment building. A modest high-rise in a good neighborhood. One might expect something more luxurious for a world-class teacher of the dark arts. If you're going to sell your soul, you might as well put a decent price tag on it. Teaching, though, isn't the most lucrative way to make a living.

As with my law professors, Eve would see people pass through her classes destined for jobs that netted triple her income. Yet the old adage about "Those who can, do, and those who can't, teach" failed in this instance. For Eve Levine was widely known as an expert practitioner of her art.

I will admit to some optimistic bent in my nature that

made me hope she refrained from acts of evil out of a basic core of good. Yet if it was possible to rate such things on a continuum, teaching magic to maim and kill must be seen as *more* wrong than carrying out such acts oneself.

It's a matter of scale. By teaching, you give lethal power to countless others. One could argue, and rightly so, that most of Eve's students didn't have the spellcasting wherewithal to maim a cockroach, but the fact remains that her lessons exist to give people that power.

It is possible that Eve taught out of a misguided sense of morality that let her conscience rest easy. Yet I suspected it was prompted by the same impulse that compelled her to rent a modest apartment in a good neighborhood, rather than a good apartment in a seedier section of town. That reason showed itself ten minutes later, when the front door opened, and out strode a slender woman with dark hair to her waist, wearing boots that added another inch or two to her already formidable height. Eve Levine. And that "reason"? It was at her far side, almost hidden behind her—only sneakers, a backpack, dark hair, and gesticulating hands visible. Eve's preadolescent daughter, Savannah.

A cab waited at the curb, as it did every weekday morning. Eve opened the door and waved her daughter in. The girl paused, hands still moving, relating some story that couldn't be interrupted. Her mother playfully shoved her into the taxi and climbed in after her.

The school was less than a mile away, not an unreasonable distance for a child to walk, but they always took a cab and Eve always went along, then walked back and picked up a coffee on the way. It was an unwavering routine that I'd been following long enough to reassure me that I now had close to an hour to break into Eve's apartment.

I waited for a break in traffic, then swung out. At the

light, I stopped beside two young women in a sports car, who tried to get my attention. This, however, was one case where I could, without guilt, pretend I didn't notice them. The driver rolled down the window, calling to me, and I considered employing my surefire method of deflecting unwanted female attention while riding my motorcycle: removing my helmet.

The safety gear necessary for proper use of a motorcycle—a full helmet with tinted visor, bulky leather jacket, gloves, and boots—renders one's features and physique invisible, and even the most unlikely male suddenly becomes attractive: a mysterious figure astride a vehicle that symbolizes rebellion and freedom from cultural mores. To destroy that image, I merely needed to remove the helmet and endure the looks of surprise, disappointment, and even, occasionally, anger—as if I'd committed the unforgivable sin of false advertising.

Once about a year ago, a young woman had, after a few moments' hesitation, asked me out to dinner. I'd accepted—out of surprise, I think, and perhaps a healthy dose of optimism. We hadn't even made it through the appetizers before she'd started making suggestions. Had I considered contact lenses? Perhaps a less generic hairstyle, preferably longer. Highlights might be nice. And while I appeared to be in reasonably good physical condition, she knew a friend who swore by protein shakes for bulking up. In short, if I wasn't what she'd hoped I'd be when I removed that helmet, perhaps she could rectify that. After dinner I'd begged off with a lie about an overdue paper, walked her to her car, and beat a fast retreat.

The light changed, sending the memory skittering away.

I let the sports car get two car lengths ahead of me before zipping into that lane and turning the corner beside Eve Levine's apartment. I'd park a block over. I'd mapped out my route—indeed, every step of this expedition—days ago. Then, yesterday, I'd carried it through right to the point of opening her front door, then walking through my escape. Overkill, I'm sure, but having never undertaken a break-and-enter before, I was leaving nothing to chance.

I hid my jacket, helmet, and boots, and changed into flat shoes, then walked to the nearby strip mall, from which I purchased an oversized floral arrangement and affixed a large card with *Congrats!* scrawled across the front. Then I walked to the edge of Eve's apartment building. When I saw a man striding through the lobby, I hurried to the front doors and began struggling, trying to open them while holding the flowers. The man took one look at me—a clean-cut young Latino carrying flowers—and held the door for me with only a laughing comment about dropping them off at apartment 318 for his wife.

Next, Eve's front door. She didn't even bother spell-locking it. Perhaps that also bespoke an overreaching confidence, arrogance even, assuming that anyone who knew she kept valuables like rare grimoires would also know her reputation enough not to attempt to steal them. Within a few minutes, I was inside Eve's apartment, ready to begin my hunt for her grimoires.

As I expected, Eve's confidence didn't extend to leaving her grimoires in plain sight. She'd placed a false back in the bedroom walk-in closet. It was only upon searching her closet that I realized the trick. I cast a trap-detection spell, but found none—not surprising, considering she had a child.

After I got what I came for, I should have made my escape. However, when confronted with a wall of grimoires, most of which I had never seen, I couldn't resist lingering. The temptation to fill my bag was overwhelming. Was it not my obligation to remove them? The impulse shamed me—using the excuse of "doing right" so I might have these spells for myself. Still, I permitted myself a glance through several.

I was poring over a spell, wondering if I had time to jot it in my notebook, when I heard a floorboard squeak behind me. I'd cast a perimeter spell at the front door, which was the only viable entry point. Yet perimeter spells were witch magic, which I was not yet proficient in. I realized this just in time to slap shut the grimoire in my hands. When I heard a sound from the doorway, I shoved the book into my bag, and whirled to see an energy bolt coming straight for me.

I dove to the side, hands rising in a knockback spell. She anticipated my move and leapt aside. Her next energy bolt hit me like a high-voltage blast to the gut. Everything went black—a split-second loss of consciousness that ended as I crashed to the floor and jolted awake.

I tried to leap up, but I was frozen in a binding spell. Eve advanced on me, then stopped a few feet away.

"My God, they're right; you do look like your father." She tilted her head for a closer look. "The eyes at least."

She took a step back. "So, Lucas Cortez. When my neighbors described the young man at my door yesterday, I wondered if it could be a Cortez employee. But a Cortez himself? That I *didn't* expect."

I cursed myself for my carelessness. So that was why Eve hadn't employed traditional security methods.

"So what is Lucas Cortez doing stealing one of my grimoires?" she continued.

She scooped out the book she'd seen me shove in my bag. I wiggled my fingers. They moved, but only barely and with effort, proving that she'd let her binding spell weaken so I could speak.

"I'm sorry," I said, affecting the guise of a sheepish schoolboy. "It was an initiation prank for my Cabal fraternity. I didn't want to do it, but . . ." A shrug. "Being a

Cortez, I don't get off easy on stuff like that. I know it was stupid, and I'm sorry—"

"You lie almost as well as your father."

"I *do* apologize—"

"Only Ivy League schools have Cabal fraternities, and unless the rumors are wrong, you don't attend one of those. So what could you possibly want with this grimoire?" She leafed through it. "This magic is far too advanced for a twenty-year-old sorcerer."

I waggled my fingers again. The spell was fading as her attention wandered. One good wrench, and I'd break it.

"I—I need the money," I said, dropping my gaze as if embarrassed. "You've probably heard, I've cut ties with my father. Someone told me you had more books than you could possibly use, so I thought you wouldn't miss one—"

She cut me off with a laugh as she tossed the book onto the bed. "My God, you *are* good. But as entertaining as it is to watch a budding master of the art of bullshit, I'm going to insist—"

I hit her with a hard knockback spell and jumped to my feet.

Something hit me in the shoulder, harder even than the energy bolt. As I flew back toward the bookcase, I reached out to catch myself, but her spell was so strong that I still slammed into the bookcase, my arm cracking, pain ripping through it. I slid to the floor, cradling my broken forearm.

"Shit!" Eve said.

She moved forward as if to drop to her knees beside me. Then she backed off, cursing. When she wheeled on me, her eyes were hard and cold.

"That changes things, doesn't it?" she said. "Do you think I don't know why you're here, Lucas Cortez? You fancy yourself some kind of crusader against injustice.

Well, you should stick to giving legal advice, boy, because you're in way over your head. What would happen to me if Papa Cortez found out I broke your arm? Smartest thing I could do right now? Safest thing?" Her eyes went colder as they met mine. "Finish the job. Dispose of the body."

I pitched to my feet and made a headlong run, zigzagging to avoid her spells. I sheered past the bed to grab the grimoire. When she lunged for it, I changed course and ran for the door instead. As she snatched up the book from the bed, I slammed the door, casting a lock spell even as it closed.

Eve wrenched the doorknob, then let out a bark of a laugh.

"Witch magic? You really are your father's son. Pragmatic to the core. It'll take me twenty seconds to get out this door, so you'd better have your running shoes on. And I swear, if I ever hear a peep of this from anyone . . ."

I didn't hear the rest of the threat. I threw open the door and raced down the hall. She didn't follow.

I paced my dormitory room, trying to contain my impatience as I placed the unavoidable call to Victor Tucci.

"Yes," I said. "I have removed the grimoire from her possession, and have surrendered it to my father, who will deal with Ms. Levine."

"And he knows who gave you the tip?"

"Absolutely. He's grateful to you and will not forget your assistance in this matter."

As Eve pointed out, I have a facility for falsehoods—a talent both natural and learned. There was little chance of Victor Tucci ever discovering my lie. A man like that only wanted to think that he had earned some credit with my father. If he tried to redeem it, any request to speak to the Cabal CEO would be denied out of hand.

With regards to my injury, Eve Levine had nothing to fear. Even had I been inclined to exact revenge for my arm—which I wasn't—I retained enough of my family pride not to admit that I had been bested by a witch.

I also had no fear that Eve would come after me. Had she ever intended to "finish the job and dispose of the body," she'd hardly have told me her plans. Ever the teacher, she'd been imparting a valuable lesson. I was ill prepared for such endeavors. Before I ever attempted such a thing again, I needed to vastly improve my criminal skill sets.

So the exercise had been valuable—in more ways than one. After I hung up with Tucci, I sat on the edge of the bed, my broken arm in a makeshift sling, and fumbled with my pant leg, tugging it up with my good arm, then holding my leg aloft while I removed the elastics from my calf and let the thin volume fall to the floor.

I reached over and picked up the grimoire—a slender tome containing no more than a dozen spells. As I flipped through, I couldn't decipher what more than a few of them did. That explained why Eve had stashed it on a high shelf, amid dusty grimoires—those with magic too difficult even for her advanced skills. Future volumes of study, put aside until she had the time and skill to revisit them. By the time she noticed this one missing, she'd never connect it with my visit.

I closed the book and tapped it against my legs. What to do with the thing? Considering what sort of magic it was purported to contain, I suppose I should have destroyed it. Yet that seemed sacrilegious and presumptive, burning a book so rare, a piece of history, because I feared what it could do. My ancestors had been guilty of a similar crime, setting fire to a form of power they feared: witches.

Yes, the analogy was a poor one, but could I pass judgment on this book? Should I? It was a matter that would require more consideration. For now, I had other things to do. First, call a local shaman physician to get my arm set. Then take a three-hour bus ride to retrieve my bike, presuming I could ride it with my arm in a cast. Once that was done, I had a week's worth of missed classes to catch up on.

I found a good hiding spot for the grimoire, put it out of my mind, and reached for my phone book.

··GHOSTS··

I SAT IN THE STUDY, LISTENING TO THE silence of the empty house. Antonio and Nick were right outside the window, on the patio, but even their muted whispers didn't disturb the hush. Clayton and Elena had only been gone a few hours, but the house had already settled into hibernation, waiting for their return.

Every now and then, I'd catch echoes of a voice raised in anger, joy, frustration, laughter—always raised. Every footstep was a pound or a stomp, as they barreled through doorways, sprawled across sofas and carpets, their presence so loud I could hear it in the walls when they were gone.

Gone.

Temporarily, I told myself. I should think of it as a respite—a few days to rest and plan before their return invasion. God, let there be a return—

There would be. And as hard as this was, it was for the best. Daniel Santos—the former Pack werewolf who led the fight against us—had now set his sights on Elena. After this threat had been annihilated, and our dead vindicated, they would return and every corner of the house would boom with those shouts and footsteps until I retreated to my studio and wonder why I hadn't enjoyed the peace while it lasted.

I hated the silence.

I had loved it once, during those blessedly short years

between my grandfather's death and Clayton's arrival. Silence then truly did mean peace—that my father was gone again and I could relax. But then Clayton came, and Elena . . . and it was never quiet again.

I turned from the window and, for a second, time stuttered and I was standing here, in this same spot, ten years ago. Elena was on the couch, giving the first genuine smile I'd seen from the quiet, confused young woman who'd appeared on my doorstep with Clay.

She was smiling at something. I turned to see a golden wolf slinking into the room. The pieces didn't connect and it took a moment to realize it was Clay, and by then, it was too late. He'd bitten her, and one thought had filled my brain: This is my fault.

I know it wasn't entirely my fault, though I do share some of the blame, as we all do. I should have seen it coming, should have understood months earlier what was happening in his life.

But I'd been too busy worrying about what his change in mood portended. I'd seen him drifting away, and specters of a silent, ghost-filled house had risen. I'd told myself that I was happy for him, and hated the selfish pit of grief in my gut every time I thought of him leaving.

"Jer?" Antonio called from outside the window.

He was waiting for me to come out. It was time to plot an end to this threat. Yet I wasn't ready. Not ready to get down to business, and not ready to face him.

I'd suggested sending Nick to Toronto with Clay and Elena. Antonio refused. We needed him here. So I hadn't pushed. I should have. My family, my "children," were gone, tucked out of harm's way . . . and his son remained.

He'd refused my suggestion. That was the logical thing, and Antonio put logic first, emotion second. He hadn't always been like that. A self-taught life lesson, and a harsh one. As much as he wanted to send Nick away from this, his brain had said no; we'd need the extra fighter. I should have insisted.

"I'll be out in a moment," I called. "I'll just switch the laundry over and bring out some lunch."

He called that the laundry could wait, but I was already out of the room.

I headed down to the basement. As I passed the cage, soft crying followed me. I turned, but of course there was no one inside. Just ghosts. The crying stopped, muffled by a snuffle, hands swiping away tears, throat unclogging in a cough.

"Jer—Jeremy." My name came awkwardly from Elena's lips, as if she'd prefer not to use it, to call me something more formal, keep that distance between us: captor and captive. "Can I come out, please?"

I walked faster. Ten years ago I hadn't walked away. I'd stayed and tried to reason with her, knowing how ludicrous that was—insisting on applying the dictates of reason to what must have been, for her, sheer madness. She'd come to meet her fiancé's family, and ended up locked in a basement cage, changing into a wolf every few nights—her lover banished, the keys to her dungeon held by a stranger who insisted she be *reasonable,* of all things.

I made it as far as the laundry room before the next ghost called out to me, still from that damnable cage.

"Jer?" It was Clay now. "Jeremy, please. Let me go with her. I'll find her. I'll make it up to her. She'll understand. Just let me talk to her."

That time, I *had* turned away. I'd bolted up the stairs two at a time, hearing Clayton's pleas turn to shouts as he begged me to let him help find Elena. Upstairs, I'd packed a bag and left before I turned around, marched down those stairs, and screamed back at him, venting all my frustration and rage and helplessness.

I'd itched to say the words—to shout them—to make

as much noise as he did for once. Why had he opened the cage door and let Elena out? Did he think me a monster, locking her up? I'd had no choice. He'd left me no choice.

He'd bitten this girl, and I was the one who had to listen to her sob, rage, scream until she had no voice left and, worst of all, cry quietly in the corner, calling his name when she thought no one was listening. I had to restrain her during her Changes, fight her, bear her bites and scratches, none of them more painful than that look of utter terror on her face as her body changed forms.

Still, that wasn't why she was in the cage. I could deal with the rages and the fits. But she wasn't weak or foolish enough to simply lie down and let the madness envelop her. Every time she thought I wasn't watching, she tried to escape.

That's why I locked her up: because I knew if she made it away from this place, she'd find true hell. Bitten werewolves rarely survived. Clay had, but only because he was a child—a bright, resourceful, and, most important, accepting child. He'd accepted what he was and dealt with it. Elena could not accept it. Who could blame her? Turned into something that, in her world, existed only in nightmares and horror films. And made that way by the man she'd entrusted her life and future to.

While I'd been out, Clay had snuck back, hoping to explain—as if such a thing could ever be explained—and hoping to make amends. He'd opened the door. She'd knocked him out, locked him in, and ran . . . only to discover that this nightmare wasn't one you woke up from, nor one you could leave behind by simply fleeing the madhouse.

I'd never considered taking Clayton with me to find Elena. Just as I hadn't considered forcing him to stay and help mend what he'd broken. After the bite, I'd been so furious, I'd inflicted the worst punishment I could imagine on him: banishment. Later, when Antonio suggested I let him come back so he could see the damage he'd wrought, I refused. By then, any thoughts of punishing him had passed, and I cared only about healing Elena. Having him around would only remind her of his betrayal.

So when he begged to come with me, I'd refused.

It took a few days to find Elena. She'd returned to Toronto. As for how she made the trek with no money—I hadn't wanted to think about that. Once I arrived in the city, tracking her down had been a matter more of patience than of skill. I'd returned to her school, found her old dorm, even located a couple of friends, all to no avail.

After a few days of tail chasing, I was eating dinner, having skipped lunch. I was so hungry that for a few minutes, I'd stopped worrying about Elena. That's when I realized that I knew where she was. Just *knew,* as if picking up a beacon.

Holding on to that beacon wasn't easy—it wavered and faded, and seemed to slip away a few times. I tried too hard, as I always do. The strange connection I have to my Pack is a fragile thing, rarely coming when I need it, and always threatening to leave before I'm done with it. It was like being given a complex piece of equipment with no manual—I fumbled and experimented, and sometimes it worked.

Eventually, I found Elena.

When I did, I wished I'd brought Clay along. He should have seen her there, cowering in the shadows, driven half mad by her Changes and the horror of what she'd done under their influence, starving and brain-fevered. Then he would have truly seen what *he* had done.

In that moment, I wanted him there. But later, I'm not

sure I could have made that choice. Would it have forced him to understand? Or would it have broken him?

I pulled myself from my memories, filled the laundry, and headed back upstairs, hurrying past the cage, now as silent as the rest of the house.

Had I been right to send them away? I could have used their help. Yet how much help would Clay be, knowing Elena was a target? And how much help was she, still burning to avenge Logan, our first casualty? Passion can inflame a warrior to greatness, but if the flames burn too hot, they consume common sense. Plus, there were greater things to consider.

Choice can be an impossible thing. A leader must be decisive. Yet how can anyone with foresight, hindsight, and the ability to link the two ever truly be decisive? You see the mistakes of the past, and the possible outcomes of your decision on the future, and no choice can ever be absolutely right.

Even decisions that seem blatantly obvious can have ramifications you never imagined.

As a young man I'd seen problems with the Pack, particularly in the way they treated non-Pack werewolves, right down to the derogatory term they used for them: mutts. To a modern, Westernized human, our class system and rules would seem abhorrent. Yet even I realized we could never live by human standards of equality. A class system is hardwired in our brains. We understand wolf ways best—living in a hierarchical society based on power, territory, and survival of the fittest.

Yet it had made sense to stop indiscriminately killing non-Pack werewolves and target only those who posed a threat. It made sense to open a dialogue with them through a delegate who'd speak on the Alpha's behalf. It made sense to treat them as fellow beings worthy of our notice and even our protection.

But had my simple and sensible changes been interpreted as weakness? Were my choices responsible for the situation we now found ourselves in? Would Daniel have found outside werewolves willing to rise up against the Pack if Dominic was still Alpha?

Now I had to prove that despite the changes there was no weakness. I had to end this threat with all the force and finality Dominic would have used. And if that failed? A good leader always has a backup plan, and in sending Clayton and Elena away, I'd launched mine.

I walked into the kitchen and found Antonio and Nick making sandwiches.

"Five minutes, and we'll be eating," Antonio said.

Nick glanced at the microwave clock. "Their plane should have landed by now."

"Elena will call," I said.

I wiped a trail of mustard Antonio had splattered. He made a face, telling me he would have gotten it, but I just kept cleaning. It gave me something to do.

"You sent them to Elena's apartment, right?" Nick asked. "Where she was living with that guy." He meant Philip, the man Elena had met while trying to live as a human again.

I nodded. "Perhaps not the wisest—"

"No, it's good." Nick managed a laugh. "*I* wouldn't want to be there, but maybe it'll help. Give Elena a chance to see her choices better. And show Clay she's really thinking of moving on—not just screwing around to piss him off. He has to shape up."

Antonio and I nodded, though I'm sure we were both thinking the same thing, that Clay might not be able to "shape up"—at least not in any way significant enough to overcome what he'd done.

"They'll work it out," Nick said as his father handed him a tray of sandwiches. "Just watch. Imagine how much mileage I'll get out of this one—reminding them of the time I helped put down the mutt revolt, risking my life to save theirs, while they were holed up in Canada."

Antonio waved him from the kitchen. I watched him leave. When the door closed, I turned to Antonio.

"Nick should go after them. If Elena's a target, she needs protect—"

"That's why Clay's with her." He took the dishrag from my hand and pitched it into the sink. "If you really thought there was a risk of them following Elena, you wouldn't have sent her away."

"It's a possibility—"

"So is a plane crash. Or a nuclear attack. When Daniel and his gang realize Clay and Elena are missing, they'll smell an ambush. While they're watching their backs, we strike from the front."

I nodded.

"Good plan, right?" he said. "Of course it is. It's yours. Remember that."

As I took a pitcher of water from the fridge, I noticed something on the floor. One of Elena's hair bands. I picked it up.

Antonio shook his head. "I don't even want to ask why that's there. Let's just hope they wiped off the counter afterward."

I turned the elastic over in my hand. Long hairs still clung to it, as if it had been yanked out and tossed aside.

"They're coming back, Jer."

"I know."

He walked over, took the band, and met my gaze. "And we're going to be here when they do."

I looked into his eyes. He knew. Of course he did. Yes, I'd had good reasons to send Elena and Clay away. Very good reasons. But there was one added advantage that had made me quick to decide when the question arose.

An Alpha must put the well-being of the Pack first. At all times. At all costs. Each individual member within that Pack must be protected, but an Alpha's priority is the Pack itself, as an entity, as a construct. If no members of the Pack remain, the Pack ceases to exist. I cannot allow that. Ever.

"They're coming back," Antonio said again, "and we'll be here to see it. That's the plan."

I gave a small smile. "It's a good plan."

"Of course it is." He slapped my back. "Now get outside and make it work."

··WEDDING BELL HELL··

Countdown: three weeks

CROSS-LEGGED ON THE BED, I STARED at the white blanket of papers around us, another stack in my hand.

"Roses, carnations, or orchids? Chicken, fish, or beef? Music playlist, guest requests, or a mix of both? Photos inside, out, or off-site? Rent a limo, car, or use our own?"

I sighed. I was usually very good at dealing with adversity. I was Paige Winterbourne, daughter of the Coven leader. Witches knew all about adversity, and I did better than most. At the age of twenty-two, I'd found myself with custody of Savannah Levine, twelve-year-old daughter of a dark witch—her mother dead, her father to follow soon after. Flash forward a couple of years and I'd been kicked out of the Coven, watched my house burn, and been driven from town. I still had Savannah, though. And, as a bonus, I got an amazing guy who wanted to spend the rest of his life with me . . . which was where the current problem started.

I flourished the papers. "We rented the hall, reserved the chapel, picked caterers and florists and photographers and DJs . . . and still the work never stops. Isn't that what we hired all these people for?" I looked over at the page Lucas was studying. "What's that one for?"

"Matchbooks."

"What for? To light the centerpieces?"

"No, as I recall, we have yet to reach the critical 'table arrangement' decision."

"Candles. Or maybe the goldfish bowls Savannah wants. Or your mom's disposable camera idea, to get candid shots—" I slapped my palms to my temples and thumped back onto the bed. "Ack, more choices."

Lucas rubbed my bare feet. After a moment, I peeked through my fingers.

"Do I even want to know about the matchbooks?" I asked.

"Probably not."

"Procrastinate, and we'll only have more work later. Let's get it over with."

"Well, it appears that commemorative matchbooks were included in the cost of our wedding invitation package."

"Bonus. Okay, then, that's settled. On to the next order of—"

"Not so quickly, I'm afraid. We need to decide what we want the matchbooks to say."

"Oh, I don't care. Paige and Lucas. Lucas and Paige. Whichever. Then the date. There, on to—"

"Color."

"Color of—?"

"The matchbook and the text. We also need to select a typeface. And artwork. Plus, they'd like to know if, for an extra hundred dollars—"

"—we can cancel the damned matchbooks altogether?"

He chuckled and resumed my foot massage. I let myself enjoy it before pushing onto my elbows.

"You realize there's only one answer."

"To which question?"

"All of them."

He arched his brows.

"Elopement," I said.

He shifted closer to me, carefully moving the papers aside as he did. "If you really want that . . ."

I sighed. "We can't. Your mother—"

"Has already said it's our choice. Yes, she'd like a church wedding, but considering that I found someone actually willing to marry me, she's not about to quibble over the specifics."

"But she'd be disappointed. And your father wouldn't forgive us."

"Which, one could argue, is all the more reason to elope."

I play-punched his leg. "Things are going well with your dad—far better than I dared hope. If a church wedding makes him happy, it's a small price to pay." I lifted the ledger. "Well, not a *small* price, but worthwhile."

I glanced over at Lucas. "He's still letting us run the show, right? Hasn't insisted on paying again?"

Lucas shook his head. "Just general 'if the costs get to be too much' reminders that his checkbook is available."

"Nothing else, right? No advice, no suggestions . . . ?"

"None."

"Which worries you."

"Terrifies me. But perhaps he realizes this is one area where his interference wouldn't be welcome." He paused. "And, in the more likely event that he's simply lying low, plotting his mode of attack, we have the backup plan."

"We do, indeed. Now, on to the next life-or-death matter." I flourished a page. "Rubber chicken, dried-out beef, or fish that hasn't seen water in a week . . ."

Countdown: one week

Savannah and I were out front planting mums. I wasn't much of a gardener, but I figured that as a new homeowner in a neighborhood with magazine-ready gardens, I should at least make an effort.

"I wouldn't," Savannah said. "If you can't compete, don't join the race, my mom always said. Better a spectator than a loser."

"Dig," I said.

"Like you have time for this crap. What's more important, saving the world from evil or having a pretty garden? It's stupid."

"No, it's 'fitting in.' Now dig."

A horn honked, and I looked up to see a sporty little black car pulling to the curb, passenger window sliding down. Leaning over from the driver's seat was a tall woman in her late forties, her dark hair short and stylishly tousled, broad grin lighting up an unexceptional face.

"You girls look busy," she called.

I smiled and stripped off my dirty gloves. Savannah tossed her trowel onto the sidewalk and bounded over to Lucas's mom, her arms wide.

"Grand—" she began.

"Don't you dare," Maria said, raising a warning finger.

"One more week," Savannah said as she got in the passenger side. "Do you prefer Gran or Granny?"

As Maria eased the car into the driveway, I grabbed my trowel and gloves and followed. When Savannah jumped out and headed for the back door, I stepped into her path.

"Maria's suitcases are still in the car," I said.

Savannah sighed and gestured for Maria to pop the trunk.

Maria hesitated, key fob raised. "Are you sure about this, Paige? I can stay at a hotel. Just drive in to help and—"

"And waste precious time traveling? We have a lot to do. Stay here. Please."

As we headed inside, Savannah was still razzing Maria about becoming a grandmother. It was a dubious connection, but Maria never pointed that out. Just emphatically declared that she was far too young to be the grandmother of a teenager.

"But I've never had a grandmother," Savannah said, making puppy eyes at Maria as we cut through the kitchen. "You wouldn't deprive me of that, would you?"

"Tell you what. If you call Benicio Grandpa, we have a deal."

"Okay."

Maria laughed as we walked into the living room. "Now, *that* I have to see. Of course it means you also have to start calling our son Dad."

"Certainly not," Lucas said from the couch, not lifting his gaze from his notebook. "I intend to insist on Father, spoken with the proper degree of respect."

Maria bent to kiss Lucas's cheek, then glanced at his notes. "What are you working on?"

"A list," Savannah and I said in unison.

Lucas lifted his gaze, fixing us with a baleful glare. "I'm making note of everything we still need to do for the wedding, organized by date, priority, and probability of enlisting help to complete it."

"It's a list," I said, sliding onto the sofa beside him.

"Watch it or you'll find your name beside every item." He looked up at Maria. "How was your trip, Mamá?"

Maria sat down and regaled us with tales of late-summer construction horror, as crews worked feverishly to finish before winter blew in. She'd driven down from Seattle. When Lucas and I bought the house, deciding to settle in Portland, Maria had moved from Illinois to Washington State, declaring it was "close enough to pester her son, but not close enough to drive him crazy."

It was a joke, of course—few mothers meddled less in their child's life than Maria. She and Lucas were close, but she had her own life—her career as a high-school teacher, boyfriends, a wide social circle, and a string of causes that she championed.

Lucas was telling her about damage my car had sustained in a crater-deep pothole when the doorbell rang.

"Probably the neighborhood beautification council," Savannah muttered. "Come to complain because we left gardening tools unattended on the lawn for ten minutes."

"If so, they're *your* tools," I said, getting up. "Practice your hostess skills on Maria while I answer the door."

While I doubted it was the beautification council at my door, it wasn't impossible. When I'd first seen our house, I'd fallen in love with the neighborhood, which had reminded me of the one where I'd grown up in Boston—quiet streets of modest, immaculately tended older homes. As I'd learned, most of the residents were either retirees or urban professional couples, one with the spare time to landscape and the other with the cash to hire someone. We had neither.

When I swung open the door and saw a fortyish woman in a suit, designer clipboard at the ready, I thought my time had come.

"Miss Winterbourne?" She forced a smile. "You won't be hearing that much longer, will you? By next week, it'll be Mrs. Cortez. Or will that be Winterbourne-Cortez?"

"It will be Winterbourne," Lucas said from behind me. "May I ask—?"

"Winterbourne-Cortez," the woman murmured, marking it onto her pad. "Lovely." She proffered her hand in a shake as brief and light as an air kiss. "Margory Mills, wedding planner, at your service."

"Wedding planner . . . ?" I glanced over my shoulder at Lucas, who winced, pushing his glasses up the bridge of his nose. "My father hired you, I presume?"

"He did indeed. A very generous man."

"Yes, well, while we appreciate the gesture, and apologize for any inconvenience the misunderstanding might cause—"

"You want to plan your own wedding," she said, stepping inside and brushing past us. "I understand, as does your father. But you already *have* planned it. All that's left is coordinating the affair so your special day is as perfect as you imagined it."

"Yes, but—" Lucas began.

I caught his attention and cast a privacy spell, so we could speak without Ms. Mills overhearing. "If it makes your dad happy, it's not such a bad idea. There *is* a lot of work still."

We turned to accept Ms. Mills's proposition, but she was already in the living room, introducing herself to Maria and Savannah.

"The troops are rallying, I see," she said. "Splendid. Many hands make light work. Now let's see these wedding plans."

I retrieved the overstuffed file folder while Savannah—after two meaningful looks and a nudge—offered refreshments. Once the coffee and the cookie tray were delivered, Savannah retreated to her room while we went over the plans.

"Amazing," Maria said when we finished. "I don't know how you kids did it. All that work. Makes me glad

I'd never—" She stopped with a sidelong glance at Ms. Mills. "*Planned* a wedding. This certainly will be lovely, though."

"Of course it will," Ms. Mills said. "First, though, you'll need to complete the wedding party list. I don't see a maid of honor or a best man."

"We're just having bridesmaids and ushers," I said.

"Oh . . ." She looked ready to comment, then snapped her mouth shut. "Well, I presume you have a third usher, to even out the party."

I shook my head. "Savannah's more of a junior bridesmaid and flower girl combined. We wanted to keep the wedding party small."

"I see. Well, on to the dinner then." She perused the menu. "Red wine. I don't believe I've ever heard of that brand . . ."

"It's a local winery. They also have a great nonalcoholic sparkling wine."

"What about white?"

"Well, we're serving beef, to support the beef farmers."

"Some people will still prefer white, and you must cater to all your guests. I'll add a case of that—at Mr. Cortez's expense, of course."

Lucas glanced my way, ready to argue, but I gave a small shake of my head.

"Now, about dinner." She pored over the menu, frowning. "I only see beef . . ."

"That's the primary option, but we also have vegetarian."

"What about kosher? Lactose-free? Gluten-free? Nut-free?"

Lucas shook his head. "There is one lactose-intolerant guest, but he simply avoids dairy products. While we would love to offer meals for every conceivable personal choice and food allergy, it isn't feasible with a guest list of only forty. We've hired a women's shelter to cater and, while they will provide ingredient lists for concerned guests, the menu must understandably be limited."

"Women's shelter? Oh, dear." A brisk note in her book. "No matter. I know an excellent four-star restaurant in Portland that will cater on short notice. We'll have a choice of beef medallions, sea scallops—"

"We've already hired the shelter group," I said.

"And Mr. Cortez will compensate them with a sizable donation, I'm sure. Now, about the DJ. Your father would prefer a live band, and he's told me you both like jazz, so we're flying a lovely quartet from—"

Lucas held up a finger, asking her to wait. Then he took out his phone and dialed.

"Papá? It's Lucas. Your wedding planner is here." Pause. "Yes, the gesture was—" Pause. "Yes, we *are* quite busy—" Pause. "Yes, it was very thoughtful of you. However . . ."

Countdown: three days

"Okay," I said, rounding the bottom of the stairs, cordless phone still in hand. "I've straightened out the hotel. Seems the desk clerk was looking at next month's reservations. The block we reserved for our guests *is* still booked. Crisis twenty-nine averted. Oh, and twenty-seven, too. I've spoken to Petulia's Petunias and convinced them that having lived for three years without a Web site feedback form, they don't absolutely need one done this week."

Lucas nodded and put his cell phone into his satchel. "And I believe potential crisis twenty-eight is resolved as well. I've cleared up the misunderstanding with that necromancer, assuring him that while I'm happy to investigate his legal case, I cannot represent him, not being a member of the bar in Utah . . . and I cannot begin *any* investigation in the next ten days."

"Good." I collapsed against him. "All bullets dodged so far."

Savannah walked around the corner, shaking her head. "You guys don't need wedding planners; you need life planners."

"Are you volunteering?"

She snorted and headed past us for the stairs.

"While you're up there, get changed for dinner, assuming you're joining us . . ." I backed away from Lucas. "Elena's plane. It's after five, and they said they'd phone when—"

"She called your cell," Savannah yelled back. "The house line and Lucas's line were busy. They're on their way. Oh, and they invited Maria to dinner as well. And yes, I reminded them that means no supernatural talk at the table."

"Thank y—"

"Hey, someone's here," Savannah called from upstairs. "It's a big black SUV."

I stiffened, and Lucas's arm tightened around me, chin jerking up.

"Just kidding," Savannah said, grinning as she hurried past us down the stairs. "It's only Adam."

"Ask him—"

Too late. She was already in the kitchen, making a beeline for the back door.

Countdown: two days

Lucas had asked Benicio to come no sooner than Thursday, which we'd figured was too close to the wedding for him to interfere, yet early enough that he didn't feel like "just another guest."

He was there right after breakfast.

Lucas had said that his parents got along fine, but I'd still been nervous, wondering if—like many estranged couples—they only put on a good show for their child. If that was the case, though, Benicio and Maria were both excellent actors. They exchanged hugs and "How's teaching?" and "How are your grandsons?" chatter . . . and seemed genuinely interested in the answers.

While they were talking, I sent Savannah out to the SUV to offer refreshments to Troy and Griffin, Benicio's bodyguards. Benicio hadn't brought them inside—according to Lucas, that would be rude, suggesting Benicio thought he needed protection in our house. I wanted to invite them in, but wasn't sure that was allowed. Emily Post doesn't cover etiquette for dealing with a guest's bodyguards.

"They'll take coffee," Savannah said as she came back in. "And muffins."

"You're becoming quite the little hostess," Maria said as Savannah set about preparing the tray.

"I feel like I'm stuck in a Jane Austen novel," Savannah grumbled.

"The lowly ward," I said. "Consigned to servitude. When you're done with that, you can report to Maria for your next orders. We'll be showing Benicio the house."

"And this bedroom we turned into an office," I said, walking from the master bedroom into the adjoining area. "It's too small for a second desk, so we're thinking of finishing the basement for a large office, making this room a sitting area or library."

"There's only the three bedrooms?" Benicio said.

"Yes, Papá." Lucas kept his voice soft but words emphatic. "We don't need any more. Not for quite some time."

Benicio smiled. "So you think now, but things may

change once you're married." He stepped into the hall. "I noticed a lovely new subdivision going up just outside the city. It has estate-sized lots, and the builder assured me their zoning would allow a second, smaller residence on the property for hired help." He lifted his hands against our protests. "I know you don't want a battalion of employees, but you're both very busy. I'm sure a housekeeper—"

"We have a woman who comes in every week," I said.

"Perhaps, but that must hardly make a dent in your workload, Paige. A housekeeper could do the laundry, cooking, day-to-day tidying." He looked at Lucas. "I'm sure it isn't easy for Paige, especially with you gone so much."

"We do fine," I said.

"Perhaps, but I have someone in mind. A young witch, recently emigrated and in a rather difficult position."

"Father," Lucas said sharply. "That is—"

"I—I'll be downstairs," I said quickly. "Helping Maria and Sav—"

Benicio caught my arm. "My apologies, Paige. That was underhanded of me. Yes, there is a witch, but I'll find her other work. I simply want to make things easier for both of you. Your time is so much better spent on the work you love. We'll speak no more of housekeepers, though."

"Or new houses," Lucas said.

Benicio nodded and let us lead him down the hall toward Savannah's room.

"I did want to ask about your honeymoon, though. How are you getting there? The last thing you need is airport delays. I'm not using the jet this week—"

"No, Papá."

"Have you decided how you're getting to the reception? I hope it's not a limousine. Weddings should be special. Romantic. Perhaps a horse-drawn coach—"

"Benicio?" Maria looked up as she climbed the stairs. "If you want to help, I have something you could do. I know Paige and Lucas wouldn't want to impose by asking . . ."

"Anything," Benicio said.

"It's the reception favors. Savannah and I are making them—putting the candies into the little pillows and tying on the ribbons. Could you give us a hand?"

"Er, yes, I suppose—"

Maria put her hand on Benicio's arm and led him away. "And could you ask the boys to come in and join us? Yes, hardly bodyguard duties, but I know they'll be good sports. We can make a production line of it . . ."

Countdown: nineteen hours

"Black and white," I said, staring down at the brandy snifters stuffed with matchbooks. "Black and white. Could it be any simpler?"

Savannah plucked out a fuchsia matchbook. "Maybe they thought they were doing you a favor. Livening up a seriously boring wedding color scheme."

Elena took a book and turned it over. "Maybe we could bleach them. The matches won't work, but it's a nonsmoking reception anyway. Who'll notice?"

"I'll buy some flowers to match," Jaime said. "Just a few scattered in with the white ones, so it'll look like an intentional accent color."

"It's not that bad. At least everything else is—" Elena stopped and crammed the matchbook back into the snifter. "Savannah? Jaime? Grab a couple glasses and we'll set them out for the rehearsal party."

I snatched a matchbook before they could whisk the

glasses away. "Lucas with a K? Who spells Lucas with a K? Where's my phone? Maybe a rush order—"

"I thought you didn't even want matchbooks," Savannah said.

"Well, no, but—" I took a deep breath. "Oh God, I can't believe I'm panicking over the matchbooks."

Jaime grabbed my arm and motioned for Elena to take the other one. "Savannah, hon? See if you can scare up a bottle of champagne. If anyone complains, tell them it's an emergency."

Countdown: fifteen hours

After three glasses of champagne, the matchbooks could have spontaneously combusted and burned down the reception hall and I wouldn't have cared.

We held the rehearsal party in the hotel meeting lounge. Just finger foods and drinks, decompressing and enjoying the company of friends before the insanity to come.

"—walking around the corner," I was saying. "And Lucas is madly waving me back, but, nope, I'm not retreating because I have this spell."

"Which she'd only mastered the week before," Lucas said, quickly glancing around to make sure his mother wasn't nearby. "But, naturally, she's eager to use it."

Elena grinned. "Naturally."

"Understandable," Lucas said. "Though, perhaps, in hindsight, testing it against a Ferratus half-demon may not have been the most . . . judicious choice."

"So he's barreling around the corner, and I'm standing there, as calmly as can be, reciting my spell. I cast it and— Pfft. Nothing. Here comes this half-demon, high on god knows what, and me planted in his path like a moron going, 'Hmm, that's odd. The spell should have worked . . .' "

Someone tapped Lucas's shoulder. I turned to see Troy.

"Fair warning," Troy murmured to Lucas. "Your dad's making his way over here. He wants to talk to you about the wedding."

"Wedding's tomorrow," Clay said. "Tell him it's too late to bug you about it. Better yet, I can."

Jeremy laid his hand on Clay's shoulder and shook his head. "Let me run interference this time. He wanted to speak to me on another matter."

As Jeremy slipped away, Jaime shook her head. "Is it just a control thing with Benicio?"

"I think he honestly wants to be involved," I said. "Problem is, his idea of involvement *is* control. But if it gets worse, we have a backup plan."

"In the meantime, why don't you guys call it a night," Elena said. "It's getting late. Slip out now and get a good night's sleep. I'll call you a cab."

"Better yet, take your dad's ride." Troy grinned. "He can't complain about that . . . and he can't follow you without his wheels. Come on. I'll talk to the driver."

"Here," Troy said as we crawled into the SUV's leather rear seat. He handed us a bottle of champagne and two glasses. "I've told the driver to take the scenic route. Oh, and—"

He leaned in and pressed the button to raise the black glass divider between the front and rear seats.

"How, uh, private is that?" I asked.

He grinned. "One-way glass and completely sound-proof. Enjoy."

Countdown: eight hours

Lucas reached over and brushed a curl off my cheek. I slid across the six inches of mattress between us, and snuggled under his arm, head on his chest.

"How long have you been awake?" he asked.

"Awhile."

"Worrying?"

"A bit."

He adjusted his arm under me, hand dropping to my bare hip. "About the wedding particulars . . . or the generality?"

I tilted back my head to look up at him. "The particulars. You know that. I'm definitely getting married today, and I've been practicing my binding spell, so don't even think of running."

A soft chuckle. "I won't. So I presume, then, that a wedding gift, given now, would not be unreasonably premature?"

I jumped up and swung over him, crouching on all fours and grinning down. "A gift? For me?"

He blew strands of my hair off his face. "No, for my other wife-to-be."

I scrambled off him and hopped from the bed.

"It's in—" he began.

I grabbed a bag from under the bed and handed it to him. "Yours first."

His brows arched, then he pulled himself up until he was sitting, his back against the headboard. He reached into the bag and pulled out an old leather-bound grimoire.

His brows arched higher. "I've been looking for this for—"

"Years," I said, plunking down beside him. "But you didn't have Robert Vasic to dig it up for you. Now, where's mine?"

He opened the book and began leafing through it.

"My gift, Cortez," I said, reaching for the book.

He snatched it away at the last second. As I fell forward, he grabbed me and pulled me to him in a laughing kiss that turned slow and delicious, and all thoughts of my gift slid from my brain until I felt something poke my shoulder.

I turned to see him nudging my back with a manila envelope. I took it, opened it, and pulled out . . .

"A list?" I said, staring down at the handwritten page.

"A to-do list." As I frowned, he plucked it from my fingers. "Step one: Pick a suitable date. Step two: Confirm with all parties. Step three: Select a destination from the choices provided." Still reading, he took three glossy brochures from the envelope and passed them to me. "Step four: Book flights. Step five: Plan itinerary. Step six: Enjoy seven days of hell chaperoning five teenage girls." He laid the paper down. "I thought it was time the Sabrina School had a class outing."

"You mean—" My throat dried up. "A get-together? With the girls? That'd be amazing. Some of them might not be able to afford it, but if I can scrape together—"

"Would I give you a gift you need to pay for yourself? It's been scraped. Or, I should say, reallocated from the fund formerly designated for a suitably ostentatious engagement ring, which the recipient refused to allow her fiancé to purchase."

I kissed him so hard he pulled back, laughing and gasping for breath. Then he lowered me onto the bed and we kissed, bodies entwining—

The alarm sounded.

Lucas glanced over at it. "When is your first appointment?"

"Eleven."

He shut off the alarm, then leaned over me again. "Then I propose we take advantage of the respite—and the empty house—and allow ourselves a well-earned lazy morning." He tickled his fingers up my side. "I'll finish what I began. Then, when you're properly woken, I'll whisk you away to a leisurely breakfast at Angelo's."

"I think I'm going to like being married."

His mouth lowered to mine. I slid my hands down to his—

The doorbell rang.

"Didn't hear it," I murmured against his lips.

"Hear what?" he said, resuming the kiss.

It rang again. I let out a curse. Lucas lifted his head, hesitated, then motioned for me to wait. He crawled from bed, pulled on pants, grabbed a shirt, and padded into the hall as the bell rang again.

I waited two minutes, then pulled on my robe and crept in the hall to hear him arguing with someone at the door, his civility quickly fraying. Yes, the breakfast tray was a thoughtful gesture, and please, thank his father for that. Yes, while the morning at a spa sounded quite nice, we'd already booked our appointments. No, Lucas did not need to consult with his wife-to-be on that. No, we did not need lunch catered for the wedding party. No, we had not changed our mind about the jazz quartet. . . .

Finally, after physically edging his father's messenger out, Lucas sighed, forehead resting against the closed door. I crept up behind him and put my arms around his waist.

"Time to enact the backup plan?" I murmured.

"I believe so."

Now that Lucas *wanted* to meet with his father, though, Benicio was nowhere to be found. So we enjoyed our breakfast at Angelo's, then headed to the hotel to gather our respective halves of the wedding party and get ready.

Before we parted, I squeezed Lucas's hand. "So I guess the next time I see you will be at the altar."

He leaned down to kiss my forehead. "It's a date."

Countdown: five hours, thirty minutes

I found Savannah with Elena, Jaime, and Talia—Adam's mother—in a corner table at the hotel restaurant.

Talia pulled out a seat for me. "I was just telling Savannah how much I loved the invitations. She did such a great job with them."

"The invitations?" I laughed. "Believe me, Savannah didn't pick those. She said they were the most boring things she'd ever—"

I stopped, gaze crossing over three confused faces and settling on Savannah, who was studiously picking apart a chocolate croissant. I turned to Talia, who had her wedding invitation in hand.

"May I see that?" I said, taking it before she could answer.

On the front of my invitation—my very formal, very simple wedding invitation—someone had sketched a cartoon of Samantha from *Bewitched* and Harry Potter. I stared at it, then burst out laughing.

"Did you do that on all of them?" I looked at her and sobered. "Please tell me you didn't—"

"Only ours," Savannah said. "The humans got the boring plain ones. Well, except Talia."

Talia's brows arched. "Humans? Is that what we are to you? *Humans?*"

"Okay, supernaturally challenged." Savannah ducked Talia's swat, then looked over at me. "So I'm not in trouble?"

"Only if you don't make us one for our keepsake box. Now, we have hair appointments—"

My cell phone rang. It was Lucas, still looking for Benicio.

"Is my mother there?" he asked.

"Not yet. We were just going to swing by and grab her for the salon."

A pause. "Ah. Well, if you see my father . . . anywhere, could you please tell him I'm looking for him?"

Maria was up, but not quite ready. She popped into the bathroom. I could hear low voices from inside, like she'd turned on a radio. As I turned, my gaze snagged on a pair of leather loafers half hidden under the bed. Men's leather loafers, brand new and very expensive.

The bathroom door opened and Maria hurried out, closing it behind her.

"Oh," I said. "Lucas is looking for Benicio. He wants to speak to him. If you see him . . . anywhere, could you relay the message? I'll just wait in the hall. Let you finish getting ready."

I called Lucas back from the hotel.

"Found him, I presume?" he said.

"Umm-hmm."

A soft sigh, then he started to say something, but stopped mid-syllable. "Ah, he's calling me now. That was prompt."

Countdown: fifteen minutes

I watched my reflection in the mirror, tugging a curl over my shoulder, then brushing it back. Over, back. Over, back. The noise from the tiny chapel was a distant rumble, like the far-off roar of the ocean. I had asked for a few minutes to practice my vows, but I didn't need it. I knew them by heart. Felt them by heart.

The door creaked open and a face appeared above mine in the mirror. For a second, Adam just stood there, staring.

"Now that is a sight I never thought I'd see," he said finally. "Paige Winterbourne in a wedding gown."

I turned and grinned, and he faltered.

"Looks that bad?" I said.

"Awful. Doesn't suit you at all. Take it off and burn it while you still can." He walked over and handed me my bouquet. "You left this in the front room. Lucas found it, and I think the poor guy had visions of a runaway bride, dropping her bouquet and bolting."

"How is he?"

"Happy." Adam swung around me, getting a full view of my dress. "His dad's pretty pleased, too. That was a smart idea Lucas had."

"It was my idea."

Adam rolled his eyes. "Of course."

The door swung open. Savannah popped her head in, then let out a dramatic sigh.

"There you are. You're supposed to be at the front of the church, loser."

"Yeah," Adam said. "Move it, Paige."

"Not her." Savannah grabbed Adam's arm and dragged him out. At the door, she looked at me. "I'll be back for you in a minute."

I walked into the church to the tune of popping flashes. Elena and Talia led the procession. Savannah was ahead of me, her "bridesmaid" role having been upgraded to maid of honor. You need a maid of honor if you have a best man. And we now had one, standing beside Adam and Clay at the front of the room. Benicio, beaming brighter than any of the flashbulbs.

And to Benicio's right, Lucas. My destination.

"I think I have rice in my bra," Savannah hissed as we posed on the front step for pictures.

"Join the club," I murmured, teeth clenched in a jaw-aching smile.

Lucas leaned into my ear. "I'll help you with that in the car."

"I bet you will."

Another blinding round of flashes. Then the crowd parted, path opening to the limousine that would whisk us to the reception hall.

As the last of the people moved out of the way, and the opening cleared, I stopped in my tracks.

"Oh my God," Lucas murmured.

Savannah started to snicker.

"That's very . . . fancy," Elena said.

"Not my idea," I muttered between my teeth.

"Oh, I didn't think it was."

Talia let out a small laugh. "Last time I saw something like that was on TV. Lady Di's wedding, I think."

Lucas and I both turned to see Benicio smiling.

"You never did actually say no to *that* idea," he said.

I looked at Lucas. He shrugged, then swooped me up and carried me down the red carpet to the coach and four waiting at the end.

··THE CASE OF
EL CHUPACABRA··

SOMETIMES THERE'S A THIN LINE BE-
tween cowardice and common sense. Sean had made the
mistake often enough to recognize when he'd made it
again. Recognizing it *before* he made it would be nice
but, it seemed, too much to ask for.

He looked around the small, crowded bar. The patrons were over 90 percent male, which was the only
sign it catered to a specific clientele. A typically under-
stated small-city gay bar. Or so he'd heard. His only
other visit to one had been in New York City where,
drunk and in a rare rebellious mood, he'd gone into a
popular one ... only to walk out again five minutes
later.

Common sense, he told himself. If you're a Nast
Cabal prince who is desperately trying to hide his sexual
orientation, you don't go to gay bars. Yet that little voice
had always gnawed at him, telling him his decision was
cowardice.

"You look like you could use some company."

Sean looked up into the slightly bloodshot eyes of
a man standing by his shoulder. Midthirties. Decent
enough looking in a bland, pleasant way. A nice smile.
Overall, about a seven. Sean liked sevens. Easy on the
eyes, but not high maintenance. Yet buried in that "nice
smile" was a nervousness that, combined with the
bloodshot eyes, told a story Sean had heard too often

and never wanted to hear again. So he said he was waiting for someone, and the man retreated to his seat across the bar.

Sean sipped his Scotch and looked around. More than a few men caught his eye, trying to get his attention, but they were all brethren to the one who'd approached him: over thirty, in town on business, and hoping to score before driving home to the wife and kids.

Sean shuddered and stared down into his glass. He wasn't getting what he wanted tonight; that much was obvious.

Any of the guys *he* was eyeing—the ones his age and here for a good time—were giving him wide berth. It wasn't his looks—he was twenty-three, blond, physically fit, and attractive. The problem was what his last visitor had said: that he looked like he needed company. Not "a wild night of anonymous sex" company, but a shoulder to cry on. The former was exactly what he *did* need, but he wasn't going to get it by staring morosely into his drink like a jilted lover on the rebound.

Sean straightened and slugged back his Scotch, wincing at the icy burn.

Not jilted, he reminded himself. He'd ended it.

Atta boy, Sean. After being lied to, betrayed, and humiliated, you ended it. Takes courage.

He slammed back the rest of his drink and motioned to the server for a refill.

He'd been a fool. He saw that now, the realization made all the harsher by knowing that if he'd had a female friend in the same situation, he'd have seen the truth right away.

He'd met Chris at his health club, almost two years ago now. It had started with a locker room conversation, Chris noticing Sean's racket and lamenting the shortage of racquetball partners. Sean had offered to play with him. It took a few weeks to get going, both uncertain, but when it did start, everything had happened very fast. Like a slow fuse on a keg of dynamite, Chris always said, grinning in that way that—

Sean took his fresh drink from the server and downed most of it.

Chris. High school science teacher. Thirty-two years old. New to New York City. Lived with his in-laws. Yes, in-laws. Normally, Sean avoided married men, but he'd understood Chris's predicament better than most.

Chris had been raised in a small conservative town, growing up as the son of an evangelical minister. Being gay wasn't an option. So Chris had done what he was supposed to do. Dated a cheerleader. Married her. Had two kids.

Living up to expectations.

Sean knew all about that.

But now Chris was in love, and he was tired of hiding. He wanted to leave his wife for Sean. He just needed some time before he took the plunge.

How many married men say that to their mistresses? Everyone around them knows it's bullshit. Everyone thinks the women are fools for buying it.

Yet Sean *had* bought it. The situation wasn't the same, and he couldn't fault Chris for not coming out of the closet when he was still in it himself. So Sean made a decision. If Chris was willing to risk his family for Sean, then Sean would take the same chance.

Chris had been all for it. But he wanted to wait until after the holidays, so he'd have one last family Christmas with his kids. Then his son had chicken pox, and that wasn't a good time. Then his wife had plans for a spring break getaway, and he couldn't tell her then. . . .

Sean considered coming out first, both to prod Chris and to prove his commitment to the relationship. When Chris had suggested he wait, and he'd agreed, his conscience had called him a coward.

Cowardice? Or common sense?

As Easter had approached and Chris had continued to stall, Sean's bullshit radar finally switched on. He'd hired an investigator to check a few things. To quell his suspicions.

The investigator had only needed a week to make his report. That small midwestern town Chris had grown up in? Chicago. The evangelical minister father? A United Church minister who preached acceptance of all diversity, including sexual orientation. Chris even had an openly gay uncle.

So all Chris's "excuses" for maintaining his hetero-sexual life were just that: excuses. For him, Sean was the equivalent of a hot young mistress—someone who could scratch the itch his wife couldn't, add a little excitement to his life, and be strung along indefinitely with prom-ises.

The server brought over a fresh glass of Scotch. Sean's stomach churned at the sight of it.

He lifted a hand. "Had my fill."

"It's from the gentleman at the bar."

The server's lips twitched, as if to say: "Can you be-lieve this guy, sending over drinks like you're some pretty girl in the corner?"

"Shall I send it back, sir?" the server asked, mock-formal.

"Please."

"Don't blame you," the server muttered under his breath.

Sean glanced at the man who'd sent the drink, and saw his reaction when it was refused—the confusion and dismay and embarrassment. Another thirtysome-thing businessman, thinking Sean looked like a tempt-ing morsel. A pretty boy, yet respectable; someone he wouldn't be ashamed to be seen walking down the street with.

Better take a good look, Sean, because in ten years, that will be you. Wife and kids at home, sneaking into small-town bars on business trips, looking for pretty boys.

Sean's gut twisted, too much Scotch drunk too quickly threatening to come back up the way it'd gone down.

He pushed to his feet, tottered, and grabbed the chair for support. The room spun, suddenly too hot, and his stomach lurched.

Toilet.

A sign over the back hall pointed in the right direction. He headed toward it, as fast as he could without staggering.

The restrooms were occupied. It was a small bar, and they only had two single-occupancy bathrooms, though Sean suspected they weren't always used for single occupants. In a town that courted business conventions, most of the people here weren't the type who'd even walk out the front door with their date, let alone take him back to their hotel.

One couple waiting for a bathroom looked like they'd be finished needing it before one was free. Sean averted his gaze as he passed them. Farther down were two guys, separate, on cell phones, getting away from the noise of the bar. One, around Sean's age, pulled his phone from his ear and said, "If you need to take a piss, better head out back."

He jerked his thumb down the hall. As Sean passed, he felt the guy's gaze on him, appraising. He considered looking back but, faced with the possibility that he might get what he came here for, he realized he no longer wanted it, and it had nothing to do with his churning stomach.

When he avoided gay bars, that little voice called him

a coward. Maybe there was some cowardice in the decision, but there was a bigger dose of common sense. Why take the risk to do something he didn't really want to do? If he'd been straight, he wouldn't be in a bar picking up women. It just wasn't him.

His younger brother, Bryce, called him a homebody. *You can always count on Sean,* he said, with that mixture of envy, pride, and derision that was pure Bryce. But it was true. Sean had never held wild parties when their dad had been away on business. Never skipped class to smoke up with his friends. Never came home puking drunk.

Making up for it now, aren't you?

His stomach lurched, and he steadied himself with one hand on the wall as he walked.

How much longer was this hall? There was an unmarked door to the left. He didn't want to throw up in a storage room. Maybe the exit was around that corner—

Another stomach revolt, telling him he wasn't going to make it. He grabbed the nearest doorknob. The door was ajar, and flew open. He stumbled, then righted himself, and blinked in the darkness. A storage closet, but there was a sink across the way. He started toward it.

Always the good boy, aren't you, Sean? Can't puke on the floor if there's a sink. Wouldn't be right.

His foot hit something, and he pitched forward. He grabbed a pile of boxes. His gorge rose at the sudden movement. Then he saw what he'd tripped on. An arm, stretched out in front of him.

He followed the arm to a body. It was a man, lying on his back, eyes wide and lifeless, face unnaturally pale. On his neck were two ragged gashes. Bite marks.

2

LUCAS

Paige was on the telephone. Not unusual at three o'clock on a weekday afternoon. Though she encouraged her business and volunteer contacts to communicate via e-mail, when something went wrong, her name was at the top of their call list. What *was* unusual was that she'd been on the phone for—I checked my watch—eleven minutes.

When it came to business, Paige was nothing if not efficient, and for even the most convoluted problem, she could take the details in minutes and end the call to begin working on the solution. A lengthy conversation meant it was a problem of another sort: personal. One of her friends or witch students or fellow council members with some crisis that needed a sympathetic ear more than a quick solution. I admired Paige's ability to empathize, yet it was at this moment somewhat inconvenient.

I'd come home a day early, eager to see her, and had slipped into the house unnoticed. Now I was stuck waiting. Rather awkward, like crouching behind the sofa at a surprise party while the guest of honor chatted with a neighbor at the door.

As the call reached the fifteen-minute mark, I checked the display on the kitchen telephone and felt the odd twist of pleasure and consternation I always had on seeing Adam's name.

While I was certain that Paige's feelings for Adam were platonic, and probably always had been, I'd never been as positive with him. I had the sense that my relationship with Paige had come as an unwelcome shock. I suspected he'd harbored, not a great unrequited love for her, but some romantic interest and the complacent confidence that should he decide to act on those feelings, she would always be there to receive them.

I slipped across the kitchen to a chair, having realized my hopes of a quick end to the conversation were futile. When I drew close enough to pick up the conversation, I tried ignoring it . . . until I heard my name.

"I have to tell Lucas," she was saying. "I know I have to. But . . ." A moment's silence, then her voice dropped, barely audible. "I don't know how I'm going to break it to him. He's going to . . ." She inhaled sharply. "Oh God, I don't want to be the one to tell him."

My mind threw up a dozen explanations, none of them remotely related to our relationship. Of all the uncertainties in my life, our marriage was the thing I was sure of.

"No, it's not your—" Pause. "No, you were right to tell me. If you hadn't, and I found out you knew, there'd have been hell to pay."

They bantered over Paige's threat, then she said, "I guess I have twenty-four hours to figure a way to tell him."

While Paige signed off with Adam, I laid a gift box on our tiny kitchen table. As gifts went, it was hardly worth the fancy box and bow. New spells were the exchange of choice in our marriage, but I'd been unable to find one, as often happened on shorter business trips.

My backup gift was candy or pastries, something small and rich from a specialty shop. Paige struggled, not with a serious weight issue, but with the issue of self-perception, vacillating between "I really should lose a few pounds" and "I'm healthy and comfortable, so I'm okay with it." The candies and pastries were my way of saying "I'm more than okay with it."

Today's gift was a quartet of handmade truffles. I was adjusting the bow when she hung up. I darted into the back hall.

Her soft footfalls entered the kitchen, then stopped.

"Lucas?"

I glanced around the corner. Seeing me, her face lit up—so radiant that, as always, I faltered, caught in that split second of "Is this really my wife?" shock.

"When did you get in?" she asked, crossing the floor to meet me.

"Just now. It became clear that my presence at the trial—"

Her arms went around my neck.

"—while welcome, was in no way a necessity—"

Her face turned up to mine.

"—so I decided that any further consultation could be conducted—"

She pulled me down, her lips going to mine, stopping the end of my explanation, which, I suppose, had already been sufficient.

Her kiss swallowed all thought, and I lost myself in the faintly spicy taste of her mouth, flavored by herbal tea with notes of lemon and chamomile—

Her tongue slid into my mouth, light and teasing, as the kiss deepened. As her body pressed into mine, I lifted her and set her on the edge of the table. Our kiss broke as we shifted, and when I moved in to recapture it, she pulled back, face tilting up to mine, hands moving to the sides of my face.

She gave a slight smile—half happy, half wistful—and I read her sentiments as surely as if she spoke the words. Yet she *wouldn't* speak them. She used to. After my first few business trips, she'd met me at the airport or at the door with a passionate kiss and an equally fervent "I missed you." And I'd stumbled into apologies, promising I'd be home longer, wouldn't be gone for as long next time, would find more local work soon. Three years later, those local jobs had yet to materialize.

Portland didn't have a Cabal office. That meant it was a city that I felt was safe for Paige and Savannah, and a place where I could escape my family name. But no Cabals meant few supernaturals, and that meant no work for a twentysomething self-employed lawyer with a spotty formal employment record. After passing the Oregon bar exam, I'd managed to secure only a few human clients. Most of my work remained in the few states, like Illinois, where I'd passed the bar *and* had supernatural clients.

Soon, seeing how much it pained me to be gone, Paige had stopped saying she'd missed me. But that didn't resolve the underlying issue, which was that I *was* away too much and, as much as we struggled to pretend otherwise, we keenly felt the separation.

"I believe I may be able to forgo the Cleveland trip next week," I said. "I can, instead, provide long-distance consultation with the local lawyer my client has retained to represent her in court."

"That would be nice," she said. "But if you can't, we'll work it out."

Her lips touched mine. I held back, wanting to promise that whatever arose in the Cleveland case, I would remain firm, and refuse to fly out and solve it myself. But I could make no such promise. There were always complications—emergencies and contingencies—and my cases were so specialized that there was never anyone else to handle them.

So I lost myself in her kiss again, pushing aside other thoughts as she was clearly doing herself, endeavoring to forget whatever crisis Adam had mentioned.

As the kiss deepened and she pulled me closer, I snuck a look at the microwave clock.

"Savannah's going to a friend's after school," Paige murmured.

"Ah." I pulled back and smiled. "In that case, I declare a change of venue unnecessary."

She pulled me back into a kiss and I started unbuttoning her blouse.

Two hours later, leaving Savannah with her homework and a delivered pizza, Paige and I went out for dinner. Now sixteen, Savannah could be left on her own for an evening—a milestone that had seemed a long time coming. I'll admit that falling for a young woman with a teenaged ward hadn't been what I'd consider an ideal situation. I suppose, though, that if I said I'd been overjoyed to find that my life partner came with a thirteen-year-old girl in tow, that would reflect most suspiciously on *me*.

But I'd always known that Paige and Savannah were a package deal. Were it not for her guardianship of Savannah, we would never have met.

Four years ago, Savannah had been kidnapped, her mother killed. Before her death, Eve had told Savannah to take refuge with Ruth Winterbourne, the Coven leader. Only Ruth had died, leaving Paige to take Savannah . . . and fight Kristof Nast for custody.

At the time, no one, even Savannah herself, had believed Kristof was her father, so Paige had taken up the battle. I'd offered my services. Paige lost everything in that fight, but in the end, we'd won, more by default than anything—Kristof had died, and his family didn't pursue the claim.

Tonight I'd taken Paige to her favorite bistro in Portland, a tiny place where the view was as exquisite as the food. Sitting there, watching her nibble a slice of duck confit, her eyes closed for that first bite, I heard my father's voice, telling me that this was how she should be treated every day—not as a special occasion when I had a little extra money.

I *had* money, he'd remind me, and even if I refused to touch my trust fund for myself, I shouldn't deprive Paige of the luxuries it could bring. Vying with my father's voice, though, was Paige's, telling me that if I ever dipped into that hated trust fund for something as frivolous as buying her fancy dinners, she'd—well, she never specified the threat, but the message was clear enough.

"That's the first smile I've seen from you all evening, Cortez," she said. "And you've hardly said a word."

"I could say the same for you on both counts."

Her smile faltered, and I upbraided myself for reminding her of Adam's call. Now it sat on the table between us, ruining a rare private meal. Would I spoil it more by pushing the matter to a resolution? Was it not crueler to watch her suffer and feign ignorance?

I sliced through my stuffed pork tenderloin. "When I professed earlier to having 'just' arrived home when you entered the kitchen, I was being somewhat fallacious. I had in fact arrived sooner, when you were in conversation with Adam."

"Oh."

"And while I didn't intend to eavesdrop, I did inadvertently overhear a portion of the conversation—one pertaining to myself and a problem Adam had brought to your attention."

She sipped her wine, her fingers tight around the glass as she tried to figure out a way to salvage our peaceful meal without lying.

I forced a smile and ducked to catch her eye. "Were it not for Adam being the one bearing the news, I'd be convinced that my father was behind this problem. As that cannot be the case—" My smile turned genuine. "Well, then, it can't be that bad, can it?"

She looked up at me, and my smile froze.

"It is my father, isn't it? But what would Adam have to say about my—" I winced. "Graduation. Adam is preparing for graduation and seeking employment. My father has offered it to him."

Paige nodded, and took a long drink of wine.

"Well . . ." I said slowly. "An Exustio half-demon is a rare prize for any Cabal. While I had hoped he'd stopped mentioning Cabal employment possibilities after Adam expressed disinterest, we all feared he was simply waiting for Adam to graduate. Disappointing and frustrating but, I'm afraid, not unexpected. Is he pushing the matter? Or is that, I suppose, a silly question?"

"He isn't pushing yet. The problem—" Paige inhaled. "He *has* offered Adam a post. As head of security for a new Cabal satellite office."

I stopped, my fork partway to my mouth. "Security? I don't blame Adam for being upset, then. Though it's a prestigious position, it's hardly what Adam envisioned when he returned to college."

"That's not it. The problem is the location of the new office."

I took my bite of tenderloin and chewed as I thought. Had my father decided to go ahead with the satellite office in Anchorage? Or a new one overseas?

But if Adam wasn't interested in the position, what difference did the location make?

"He's putting it here," Paige said. "In Portland."

My head jerked up so fast the meat slid into my throat, and I started to choke.

3

SEAN

SEAN BACKED OUT OF THE CLOSET, HIS gaze glued to the bloodless corpse. A vampire kill? It looked like one, but *here*? With no serious attempt to even hide the body?

Don't analyze it. Just get out.

He turned and smacked into the dark-haired young man with the cell phone.

"Hey," the guy said. "I was just coming to tell you *that's* not the exit—"

He looked over Sean's shoulder. And Sean froze, brain screaming advice—close the door, stall, run—none of it useful unless he cared to be a murder suspect.

"Holy shit! Is that—?"

He pushed past Sean and crouched beside the body.

"He's dead," Sean said. "I was just going to call the police, but . . . I have to take off. I can't— I can't be found here."

The guy glanced up.

"Door's down there," he said, pointing.

Sean blanched, seeing the same contemptuous look he'd given the businessmen who had tried picking him up, and he knew he wasn't in danger of ending up like them—he already had. Maybe he didn't have a wife or girlfriend at home, but was he any different otherwise? Sneaking in here on a business trip? Running from a crime scene to avoid being caught at a gay bar?

Epiphanies for another time. Right now he *did* need to get out of here. A Cabal son at the site of a vampire kill? Not the time to take a stand.

As the dark-haired guy reported the death, Sean turned and almost smacked into a trio of men, two older business types and a kid younger than Bryce.

"Hey, bud," the kid said, his eyes glazed. He hooked his thumb in the direction of the storage room. "That free?"

And Sean Nast—scion of the Nast Cabal, descended from a line of men who could talk or bully their way out of any situation—stood there, mouth open, brain blank.

Sean wished his father were still alive. There were many reasons he wished that, but what he missed most often was his father's guidance. Of all the lessons not yet imparted, this was chief among them: how to act like a Cabal son.

If Kristof Nast had been here, no one would have gotten into that storage room. He'd have bluffed and intimidated his way out of this dilemma. Then there was Sean . . .

"The, uh, room—? No, it, uh, it's not free . . ."

One of the businessmen had already brushed past, too eager to wait for Sean's reply. Sean reacted on instinct, reaching deep into his genetic pool, throwing up his chin, steeling his gaze, and stepping into the man's path.

"You'll have to move back, sir," Sean said. "This is a crime scene."

Even as the words left his mouth, Sean realized his error, and cringed as the cry went up.

Crime scene.

Sean wheeled, seeing the hall stretch before him, the exit somewhere at the end. But his chance had passed. Run now and he'd be chased down as a suspect.

People crowded into the storage room doorway. Gasps and cries of "Is he dead?" rose from all sides.

"Back away," Sean heard the dark-haired young man inside say. "You heard the guy. This is a crime scene."

Sean came to life then, mustering that air of authority to move the bystanders back. Not the way to keep a low profile, but it was the right thing to do.

"Yes, he's dead," Sean said, waving people back as he moved into the doorway to block it. "The police are on the way."

"What's wrong with him?" someone asked.

"He's all pale," another answered.

"Everyone, please—" Sean began.

"I saw bite marks. Fang marks, in his neck."

"Oh my God," the kid with the glazed eyes said. "Blood drained. Fang marks. It's gotta be—"

Sean cut in quickly. "The cause of death has yet to be—"

"It's El Chupacabra!" someone shouted.

El Chupacabra.

Sean had no idea what the hell that meant, but in his language, it translated into trouble.

He'd given his statement to the Middleton police. Even used his real ID, as he'd been taught. When other kids were being told how to behave if pulled over for speeding, Cabal boys were drilled on how to handle criminal investigations. If you're not involved and the crime isn't Cabal related, never risk using fake ID.

He'd cooperated fully, and asked that his privacy be respected. He was sure that many patrons had asked the same thing, but that didn't make the look the officer gave him go down any easier. Just another closeted businessman on the make. Pathetic.

Sean stepped from the room the police were using for interviews. Those still awaiting their turns glanced up with equal parts curiosity and trepidation. If they were checking his expression to see how well he'd fared, they found no clues there. Sean's attention had moved on to the media gauntlet waiting outside.

He tried to remember how much money he had in his wallet. A few hundred. Would it get him out the back door? No, it would only call more attention to himself.

He picked up his pace, heading for the exit.

"—cause of death is clearly exsanguination," boomed a voice behind him.

"You mean he bled to death," replied a woman.

"That, my dear detective, is the definition of *exsanguination*."

Sean glanced over his shoulder. A sixtyish man with gray whiskers and a potbelly was striding through the bar, a pinch-faced brunette struggling to keep up.

An officer stepped into their path.

"Detective," he said, nodding to the woman. He turned to the man. "Doc? You might want to go out the back. What with this chubawumpa business . . ."

"Chupacabra," the doctor corrected, giving the word a Spanish lilt. "And it's not 'business,' young man. It is nonsense. Superstitious nonsense."

"Okay, but you still might want to—"

"I do not fear the media," the doctor boomed, like a general about to take on the Mongolian hordes.

Sean let the doctor and detective pass, then slid out in their wake, staying a few yards back so he wouldn't be mistaken for one of their party.

As soon as the doors opened, the flashes and shouts began.

"Dr. Bailey! Are you aware this is the first recorded instance of a chupacabra killing a human?"

The doctor answered with a derisive snort.

"Detective, over here!"

"Doc, is it true that—"

"Detective MacLeod! Could this be the Middleton Chupacabra?"

The detective turned to the young woman who'd yelled the last question. "Sandy, you know I'm not even going to dignify that with an answer. Chupacabras? Next thing you know, you'll be telling me it was a vampire."

A wave of laughter rolled out.

As the crowd pelted the coroner and detective with questions, Sean slid away.

The next morning, Sean sat on his hotel bed in Tacoma, and stared down at the newspaper. Even here, twenty miles from Middleton, the chupacabra story had made the front section. It was near the back, and written as tongue-in-cheek monster speculation, but it was there nonetheless.

Even after reading the article, Sean still didn't know exactly what a chupacabra was. Obviously a beast of folklore that some people around here believed in. That was a problem. Unlike a vampire story, which no self-respecting journalist would touch, the chupacabra was news in this region, having apparently been "terrorizing" Middleton for months now.

The Cabals would find this. They'd been vigilant about vampire activity for two years now, ever since a vampire had gone on a killing spree, murdering Cabal youths. One of Sean's cousins had been among the victims.

The Cabals would find this and they'd find Sean's name attached, and discover where he'd been. Part of him wanted to say "Oh, well" and accept the consequences. But he wasn't ready for that.

A rap at the door.

It was his executive assistant, Mary. Now nearing retirement, Mary had been with the Nast Cabal since Sean's father had been a boy. When Sean had selected her from the secretarial pool, his grandfather had praised him for choosing experience over attractiveness. Truth was, Sean didn't dare pick one of the nubile twentysomethings or there'd be office cooler talk when he didn't at least flirt with her.

"Mr. Nast, sir?" Mary eyed his jeans and sweatshirt with disapproval. It might be Saturday, but that was no way for an executive to dress. "Shall I send the porter up for your bags?"

"No, I'm not taking the jet back. I'm driving to Portland for the weekend."

Her disapproval solidified with a hardening of her lips. Everyone knew what Portland held for Sean—his half sister, Savannah, lived there with her guardians, Paige Winterbourne and Lucas Cortez. His family refused to acknowledge Savannah. Her name couldn't even be mentioned in his grandfather's hearing.

"If you're quite certain, sir . . ." Mary said.

"I am," he said firmly, then nodded a dismissal, waited for her to step back, and shut the door.

He stood there a moment, behind the closed door.

Portland. Savannah. Lucas. The solution to his dilemma had just landed in his lap.

4

LUCAS

A CORTEZ CABAL SATELLITE OFFICE IN Portland.

I stared down at the untouched legal papers on my

desk. I didn't know who I was more angry with: my father for doing this or myself for not seeing it coming.

Paige had tried to convince me that this decision might be simply part of an overall expansion plan. According to Adam, my father had asked him to keep quiet only because the proposed office was still that: a proposal.

Perfectly valid explanations. And patently false.

I sighed, lifted my glasses, and pinched the bridge of my nose, struggling to focus on my work. Paige had gone shopping in preparation for a weekend visit by Savannah's half brother Sean. I wanted to get through this work before he arrived. I didn't want to spoil our weekend by retreating to do paperwork, particularly when we had a guest.

I picked up the top sheet. Real estate law. Closing a purchase. As dull as legal work got, but it paid well enough.

Speaking of real estate, where was my father planning to build—?

I slapped the stray thought aside and concentrated on the papers. The business property in question had sold for an astounding price, considering the neighborhood. Portland was doing well. Very well. Perhaps that was why my father—

No. I knew better. Five years ago, the Cortez board of directors had debated northwestern expansion, but they'd rejected the idea. There was no solid supernatural community in Portland. The market, while good, didn't suit Cortez Corporation interests. And they already had a tiny office in Seattle, which had staffing problems, being so far from the Miami headquarters that employees saw it as an exile.

"Hey, Lucas," Savannah said, walking in. "Is there a stapler in here?"

I held out mine, but she ignored it, plunked down in

Paige's chair, and started looking through the desk drawers.

At sixteen, Savannah was almost as tall as me, finally outgrowing her awkward coltish stage and maturing into a willowy young woman. She was also growing into her strong features, and starting to turn heads. But boys had yet to begin banging down our door. There was something about Savannah—an edge, a forthrightness— that I suspected frightened off many a would-be admirer. I'd heard the same said about her mother—that men had admired from afar . . . preferably out of spellcasting range. Having met Eve both before and after her death, I didn't blame them.

"So," Savannah said, continuing her drawer search. "Are you still brooding about the satellite office thing?"

"I'm not—" I stopped. Argue with Savannah and she'd only needle all the more—sharp and deep enough to draw the blood of truths more comfortably left hidden.

"Is it really such a bad idea?" She lifted her hand to ward off my argument. "Hear me out, okay? Yeah, going to Adam—especially behind your back—was a dirty trick, even for Benicio. Setting up in Portland without warning you? Really nasty, especially since you're too settled here to move easily. I'm sure he's counting on that. And he's definitely going to use this to advance the whole 'get Lucas to run the company' master plan. It's going to cause problems, but . . ." She met my gaze. "It could actually *solve* one big problem. A Cabal office here means more supernaturals here and more Cabal wrongs for you to right. Without ever leaving home. And Paige can help. That's what you guys want, isn't it? Pool your resources more often, combining your—" A dismissive hand wave. "Crusades."

I sighed. "Our work is not a cru—"

"Whatever. Point is, it won't be all good, but maybe it won't be all bad either."

"True, but the bad, I'm afraid, will significantly out-weigh the good. Do you know what made us choose Portland?"

She started listing reasons on her fingers. "Escape the Cabal stuff. Give you a break from your dad's Cabal heir crap. Keep me away from Grandpa Dearest. Protect Paige from anyone wanting to get at you. Protect Paige from anyone wanting to help the Cortezes rid them-selves of a witch daughter-in-law." She stopped. "Shit. Paige."

"My father would try to ensure that a Cabal office here would not increase the danger Paige faces," I said. "However, her comfort with living here, and her con-cerns over *our* comfort and safety, would grow."

"She worries more than enough already."

"And, in this case, it would be justifiable. An in-creased supernatural presence *would* mean increased risk—for all of us—from those outside my father's sphere of influence. He should have considered that."

"But then he'd have to admit there are supernaturals who aren't afraid of Benicio Cortez."

Paige's car sounded in the drive.

"Go help her unpack the groceries," I said. "And tell her I'll be right down."

Sean arrived just before lunch. He was the only Nast who'd formed any sort of relationship with Savannah. According to their grandfather, Thomas, Savannah was not his son's child—it was all part of a beyond-the-grave scheme by a notorious black witch to secure a share of Nast wealth for her daughter. As for the fact that Kristof—not Eve—had been the one to proclaim his pa-ternity, that apparently was a minor and inconsequential detail.

When Savannah came of age, the choice to pursue her birthright or let the matter lie would be hers. For now she enjoyed a growing relationship with Sean, who had also set up a trust fund for her using part of his inheritance.

During lunch, Sean alternated between distracted and rushed, as if the meal was something merely to get through. So I was not surprised when, as Savannah served dessert, Sean said, "I need to talk to you about something, Lucas." He paused, then turned Paige's way. "And you, too, Paige, since it's something the interracial council might want to look into."

He related the story of how the night before, in a bar, he'd stumbled upon an exsanguinated corpse with fang marks on his neck.

"Some vampire's getting sloppy," Savannah said. "Bet it's Cass. Getting senile in her old age and forgetting where she left her dinner."

"The chance of it being a real vampire's annual kill is slight," I said. "However, given the Cabal's current attitude toward vampires—"

"Exactly what I was thinking," Sean cut in, leaning forward. He stopped and eased back. "Sorry. I didn't mean to interrupt, but it's true. Granddad still . . . well, he hasn't forgotten what happened to my cousin."

"Forgotten or forgiven," Paige murmured.

I nodded. "The perpetrators may be dead, but the murders only served to exacerbate an already tense situation, giving the Cabals reason to intensify their suspicion of all vampires. However, a single case in a small city will likely pass unnoticed."

"There's more," Sean said.

He explained.

When he finished, Savannah screwed up her face. "They think it's a what?"

"Chupacabra," Sean said.

"A cockroach?"

Paige stifled a laugh. "Better brush up on your Spanish. That'd be *cucaracha*. Though a giant vampiric cockroach could be interesting."

"Fine, Little Miss Can't Be Wrong. What's a chupa-whatever?"

"I have no idea. The literal translation would be something like *goat-sucker*."

"Goat-sucker?" Savannah chortled. "Now who's in need of remedial Spanish?"

"Paige's translation is correct," I said. "The nature of the creature is, at the moment, unimportant. Sean is right. If this is making statewide news, it's unlikely to pass unnoticed. Cassandra must be notified and ready for a Cabal investigation into any vampires living near—"

"Uh, actually," Sean said, "I was hoping it could be solved *before* the Cabals get involved. If you aren't too busy, I'd be willing to hire you—both of you—to investigate."

"Well, that's one idea," Paige said. "But I'm not sure it would be worth—"

"There's something else," Sean said. "This bar. I went there with a coworker, for him, and . . . well, if anyone found out what kind of bar it is . . . they'd jump to the wrong conclusion and . . . it could be embarrassing."

"What was it?" Savannah said. "A fetish club?"

We all looked at her.

"What? He said it'd be embarrassing."

"It was a gay bar," Sean said.

Savannah made a rude noise. "Is that it? Geez. Big deal."

"I'd really like to hire you," Sean said.

I glanced at Paige. "Let us check our schedules and discuss it."

* * *

"Well," I said as Paige poured tea later that afternoon. "I suppose that answered *that* question."

"And you owe me a spell, Cortez."

I arched my brows. "No, you suggested the bet, but if you recall, I failed to formally accept."

"Oh-ho, so you need to *formally accept* bets now? And I suppose you wouldn't have claimed your prize if it turned out *you* were right about why Sean never mentions girlfriends."

"Dating a married woman would have been a perfectly reasonable explanation."

"He says, adroitly avoiding an answer."

She sat across from me at the kitchen table and sipped her tea. Sean and Savannah had gone trail riding. She'd started horseback riding after we'd come to Portland, and fallen in love with the sport. When Sean began visiting, riding with Savannah had been an easy excuse to spend some time together, and it had grown into something for them to share.

Horseback riding seemed an odd choice for someone as restless and impatient as Savannah, but Paige thought Savannah simply liked having control over something bigger and stronger than herself. It *was* teaching Savannah patience, and her spellcasting had improved. Too much, as Paige often pointed out. Savannah was powerful enough as it was.

"I'd like to—"

"We should—"

We spoke in unison, then laughed. I waved for Paige to go first.

"I'm all for it, taking Sean's case," she said. "Sure, I'd like to help him. And anything vampire-related *is* a concern. But, being totally selfish—"

"It would be a welcome opportunity to work together."

She smiled. "Exactly. Close enough to home to commute. Unless your schedule's changed, you're home next week . . ."

"I am."

"Then I'll clear some time from mine. Besides, you could use a break from thinking about this satellite office problem."

"It's agreed, then. Nothing stands in our way."

"Well, I wouldn't say that. There is one obstacle. A less-than-pleasant aspect to the case that may have us both regretting our decision."

"And that is . . . ?"

"We'll have to work with Cassandra."

5

LUCAS

IF THERE WAS A HEAD VAMPIRE IN NORTH America, Cassandra DuCharme would be it. Had she not been the oldest, she could have laid claim to the position by attitude alone. Cassandra could teach Cabal CEOs lessons in imperiousness.

Because she was the senior council delegate for the vampire community, anything affecting that community should be brought to her attention. Yet as Cassandra neared the end of her life, she found it increasingly difficult to care about the rest of her community—a condition made worse, I suspect, by a preexisting lack of natural empathy.

This alone would be an excellent excuse to bypass Cassandra and go straight to her codelegate Aaron, who was far more likely to know—and care—about vampires in the Pacific Northwest. But as Paige pointed out, Cassandra was trying to overcome her disconnection and involve herself more fully in vampire affairs. To go directly to Aaron would not only be rude, it would undermine and denigrate her efforts.

So off to Cassandra it was. And we did need to go *to* her. Flying across the country was ridiculous in an age of telephones and e-mail, but one doesn't tell a 350-year-old vampire that one doesn't believe she's worth the effort of a personal visit.

We couldn't even claim want of funds. As soon as we'd agreed to take the case, Sean had whipped off a check for ten thousand dollars as a retainer. An exorbitant amount, and both Paige and I had protested, but Savannah had snatched up the check with a thanks. As for Sean, he couldn't write it out fast enough. Come Sunday morning, he was heading back to Los Angeles, and we were off to see Cassandra.

On the plane, we read through the pages Paige had printed off the Internet, on chupacabras in general and the Middleton incidents in particular. Savannah was with us, having told Sean how important it was for her to be involved in interracial council business from a young age. He'd bought it, and insisted we include expenses for Savannah's participation. After he'd left, Paige had tried to persuade Savannah to stay behind, but an opportunity to bedevil Cassandra was not one Savannah could pass up.

So we were seated on a small commuter flight, Paige and me on one side of the aisle, and Savannah on the other. This part of an investigation—researching a mythological beast—she was interested in . . . particularly if it provided support for her theory that your average human was a gullible fool.

As for the indiscretion of discussing such matters on a public flight, it wasn't a concern. Those hearing Savannah passing us tidbits like "Oooh, look, this one has bat wings" merely glanced at her with amused tolerance. Even Paige, leaning over to see, only earned the occasional "Should you really be encouraging her?" look.

According to the most reliable sources we found, chupacabras were a relatively recent addition to the pantheon of paranormal beasts. First reported in Puerto Rico in 1975, they'd been blamed for attacks on farm animals. Livestock had been found with neck incisions, their corpses drained of blood. Sporadic Puerto Rican reports continued for twenty years, then like many Puerto Ricans, the creature decided to investigate opportunities on the mainland.

Over the last ten years, chupacabra attacks had been reported in Mexico, Chile, Central America, and the southern United States. It was when they reached Chile that another requisite component of any decent supernatural legend was added—some of the creatures had been caught by U.S. government officials who were, of course, denying all allegations.

As for exactly *what* a chupacabra was, the most common representation looked like the flying monkeys from *The Wizard of Oz*. The creature was said to be about four feet tall, with leathery gray skin, coarse hair, fangs, and glowing eyes.

As for how one arrived in Washington State, none of the local papers speculated. One article mentioned a Michigan report of a chupacabra attacking a cat, so perhaps that was supposed to be proof that a northern precedent had already been set.

The Middleton case had begun just over a month ago, when a couple that ran an organic sheep farm found one of their animals dead, drained of blood with throat incisions. The death was blamed on local youths. Then, when a pig was found with the same marks, the rumors of El Chupacabra hit Middleton, and from that first whisper, a local legend was born.

A few chickens and an aging goat had followed, along with a sighting of the beast itself, making off with a cat. From the tone of the articles, though, no one in Middleton seemed particularly worried about having a demonic beast ravaging their livestock. The outbreaks were contained, few animals were affected, and on the whole it seemed to be viewed as a welcome break of frivolous speculation after a long, dull winter.

Then Billy Arnell died with puncture wounds in his neck, and everything changed.

Paige rang the bell on Cassandra's condo. We waited two minutes, then Paige turned and started down the steps.

"We called, we came, we made every effort—" she began.

The door opened.

"Damn," she muttered. "So close."

"Paige, Lucas, finally," Cassandra said, opening the door. Her gaze turned left and her polite smile faltered. "Savannah. Don't you have school?"

"Not on Sunday," Savannah said, brushing past and walking inside. "And you got my name right. That's the third time in a row. You *can* still remember people. You just don't bother."

Cassandra turned to Paige. "Still working on her manners, I see."

"They gave up," Savannah said. "They kept thinking I'd grow out of my rudeness, but then they'd look at you and . . ." She shrugged. "Proof that it doesn't always happen."

Cassandra shook her head and opened the closet so we could hang our jackets.

"Did I mention I'm considering going to college near here?" Savannah said. "I thought maybe I'd room with you. That'd be okay, right?"

"Certainly. So long as you abide by the house rules." Cassandra smiled, flashing her fangs. "Boarders have to provide dinner for the host."

Savannah only laughed and strode into the living room. "Any new paintings?"

"In the sitting room. It's a—"

"Don't tell me. Let's see if I can figure it out."

Cassandra's green eyes glittered. "Twenty dollars if you do. Artist and period. It's a difficult one."

Savannah accepted the bet and strode off.

We walked into the living room. Large, airy, and modern, it was hardly what one would expect from a vampire, particularly with the sunlight streaming through the three large windows. We sat on the sofa—a modern designer piece that I was sure was worth more than our entire living room suite. All the furnishings in the room were modern, including the paintings. It seemed odd for someone who made a living dealing in antiques and historical art. But as Paige says, trying to determine Cassandra's motivation for anything is an exercise in futility.

"Savannah is joking, isn't she?" Cassandra said as she sat down. "About college. She can't possibly be old enough."

"One more year of high school," Paige said. "Though she's kidding about coming here. She's thinking of taking a year at a local college first. She'd move out, live on campus or close to it, but still be in Portland. I'd like that."

"Yes, I imagine you're eager to get her out of the house."

"I meant the 'living close for a year' part, not the 'moving out' part."

I cut in. "In regards to this potential vampire problem . . ."

Paige told Cassandra the story.

"Oh, that is preposterous," she said when Paige finished. "I can't believe someone is wasting their money and your time to prove the obvious. It's clearly not a vampire."

"Yes," I said, "but do you know of any living in the Washington area?"

"Am I talking to myself? This is *not* a vampire and, while I can forgive you for not knowing better, Paige should. Vampires do not leave their annual kills just lying about—"

"May 1979," Paige said. "The council investigated reports of a corpse found in New Orleans—"

"Oh, that's New Orleans. It doesn't count."

"September 1963. Philadelphia."

"That was a mistake. An untrained new vampire. There are no new vampires in North America right now."

"Recent immigrants?"

"Not that I've heard of."

Paige looked at Cassandra. She said nothing, but they both understood what her look imparted—the reminder that Cassandra wasn't always up to date on vampire activity. Cassandra conceded the point with a dip of her head.

"But still, to leave gaping neck wounds? Unnecessary, which you know, Paige. That alone should rule out vampires—"

"New York, 1985."

Cassandra let out an exasperated sigh. "Do you memorize the council records?"

"No, I just came prepared."

"Then you know that New York case was special. The vampire was interrupted and the body was discovered before she could finish and dispose of it."

A moment of silence, then Paige said, "Do you want to call Aaron? You're right. This almost certainly isn't a vampire, so there's no reason for you to get involved. We just want to warn any vampires living in the area, in case the Cabals get wind of this and give them a hard time. Aaron can answer our questions and leave you out of it."

Cassandra looked out the front window, and I could see she was struggling not to give in to what must have been an overwhelming urge to say: "Yes, give it to Aaron."

"Aaron could use the experience . . ." she mused.

"Okay, then, we'll call."

Cassandra continued, as if not hearing Paige, her gaze still on the window. "But if the Cabals do get involved, they've been looking for an excuse for retaliation, after Edward and Natasha. Though it seems obvious a vampire is not responsible, the outward appearance of a vampire kill may be enough to provide that excuse . . ."

"That's our fear," I said.

"*Are* there any vampires living in Washington, Cassandra?" Paige asked.

"I believe there is one. Let me call Aaron."

6

LUCAS

AARON DARNELL WAS CASSANDRA'S CO-
delegate on the interracial council. Their relationship
went back further than that—much further, as is often
the case with vampires. While I had the impression it
ended with a betrayal, I knew none of the details,
though I would presume Cassandra had done the betraying. It was in her character as much as it was *not* in
Aaron's.

I did not know any vampires well. Like werewolves,
they play no role in Cabals, and while I always say, half-
jokingly, that's because Cabals are loath to employ anyone who might mistake them for lunch, the antipathy
goes far deeper than that. It's fear of the other. That's
what werewolves and vampires are, even to supernaturals. The other. Too different. Too foreign.

Sorcerers and witches can harness the power of
magic, necromancers can speak to the dead, half-
demons can influence weather or create fire, and shamans can project their spirits from their bodies, but we
are all essentially human. We look human. We share a
human anatomy. We live a human life, with human vul-
nerabilities, and die a human death. Should we choose
to deny our powers, we can pass for human.

While it's true that werewolves and vampires can live
undetected among humans, they cannot deny their essential selves. Werewolves must change into wolves reg-

ularly. Vampires must feed from humans and take one life per year. Werewolves are long-lived and slow-aging. Vampires live for hundreds of years without aging, and are invulnerable to injury.

Centuries ago, when the sorcerer families began building Cabals, they looked at the potential workforce and made their choices. Sorcerers, half-demons, shamans, necromancers, and minor races? Yes. Witches . . . if necessary. Vampires and werewolves? No. Too much "the other." And, perhaps, at some level, too much a threat. Too uncontrollable. Too . . . predatory.

I grew up with that prejudice, though I work to overcome it. It doesn't help that the vampire and werewolf communities are so small that I rarely encounter one. Paige's ties with the werewolf Pack immersed me in that culture by necessity, and I can now count werewolves among my friends. Vampires, though? I can work with them. But comfortably? I still struggled with that.

Those prejudices ran a dozen times deeper within the Cabals, which meant that it was critically important to solve Sean's case before the Cabals heard of it.

"Spencer Geddes," Aaron's voice crackled over the speakerphone after Cassandra finished explaining what we needed. "Lives outside Seattle. Or he did last I heard. Geddes isn't the type to provide a forwarding address."

"A loner," Cassandra said. "Even for a vampire."

"Christ, that echo's bad. You got me on speakerphone, Cass? Lots of great inventions in the last century, but that's not one of them."

"Do you have a last known address for Mr. Geddes?" I asked.

"Sure do. And they're forecasting rain tomorrow, so no bricklaying. I'll swing out to Portland, meet up with you guys—"

"I have this, Aaron," Cassandra said.

A static-filled pause. "You sure? I can catch up and we'll both go."

Cassandra hesitated long enough for Aaron to whistle.

"Still there?" he said.

"Yes, and while I appreciate the offer, he doesn't need both of us showing up on his doorstep. If you have an address and a physical description—"

"You've never met him?" Paige said.

"Neither have I," Aaron said. "When Cass said he's a loner, she wasn't kidding. He emigrated from Europe in the late nineties. Josie apparently went to extend a welcome shortly after he arrived—"

"I'm sure she did," Cassandra murmured.

"Her welcome *wasn't* welcome," Aaron said. "Maybe you'll be more his type."

We finished getting everything Aaron knew about Geddes. It was remarkably little, considering how well connected Aaron was within his community. After we signed off, I suggested Paige, Savannah, and I return to Portland. Cassandra could fly into Seattle the next morning, where we could meet and escort her to Geddes—

"You have a guest room, do you not?" she said.

Paige shook her head. "Just a pullout sofa. And Sean used that last night, so I haven't cleaned—"

"I don't sleep very much these days anyway. What time is our plane?"

Paige looked at me, begging for a way out of this.

"Six o'clock," Savannah said.

"I'll go pack then."

On the flight back, Paige had Savannah sit with Cassandra. As she reasoned, if anything would persuade Cassandra to find a hotel for the night, that would be it.

The ploy failed. On some level, I think Cassandra was genuinely fond of Paige, whom she's known from birth. It was not, however, a grandmotherly sort of relationship. More like a mother-in-law, Paige always said.

It's difficult for me to watch Cassandra badger Paige, second-guessing her decisions, giving her unwanted—and almost always critical—advice. The discomfort was magnified by the knowledge that I could not interfere. I'd once tried to defend Paige against Cassandra's tongue, only to have Paige ask me not to do so. She was right. Arguing with Cassandra only made things worse.

I know, too, that to Cassandra my silence spoke ill of me. To put it bluntly, I looked like a wimp, standing by silent as my wife was harangued. If I stepped in to defend her, I might feel better about myself, but I'd insult Paige. Yet concern over my image is hardly sufficient grounds for insulting my wife.

So I would do as Paige wished and keep my mouth shut. Cassandra already thought poorly enough of me on other counts that clearing up this misconception wouldn't make a difference.

Once back in Portland, Paige and I wanted to drop Cassandra and Savannah off at the house and head out on the case. Cassandra stared at us as if we'd gone mad. Or more accurately, stared at me as if this was clearly my idea and I should be ashamed of myself, dragging Paige to Washington so late.

"Surely this can wait until morning," she said. "I can't imagine what you hope to accomplish at this hour."

"Checking on Geddes, of course," Paige said.

"You're hoping to secure this man's trust and assistance by arriving on his doorstep at two in the morning?"

"No, we're hoping to make sure he hasn't bolted. Or gone looking for a fresh victim."

"And if he's not there? You can hardly speak to his neighbors or employer after midnight. Better to rest tonight and get an early start in the morning."

Paige looked at me. I knew she was eager to get to work, but Cassandra did have a point. The Cabal wouldn't learn about the case until today as they reviewed the weekend news. If they decided to pursue it, it would take time to assemble an investigation team. While they were capable of moving faster, the dead man was human and Cabal interests were not in danger, so there was no need for haste.

When we arrived home, Cassandra insisted on a proper tour. She'd been to our home once, for a Christmas party, but now she wanted the opportunity to explore— and evaluate—it fully.

Our house was in one of the older but less prestigious neighborhoods of Portland. A street of narrow two-story homes, most of which had been allowed to "age gracefully" for many years—neither neglected nor regularly renovated, but owned by middle-class families that'd lived there most of their lives.

As the owners died and the homes went up for sale, the area underwent a "revitalization." Gentrification, one could say, though not to the extent of boutiques and cafés popping up on the corner. A strictly residential neighborhood, with homes that ranged from high-end to . . . ours.

Our house had been one of the last holdouts, standing firm in the face of real estate suitors who'd stuffed the mailbox with offers. When the owner died, his grandson—a particularly danger-prone half-demon whom I'd helped several times—had seen the opportunity to repay me by offering us the house at a fair market price, uninflated by demand in this particular neighborhood. So we had bought it.

Or, I should say, *Paige* had bought it. She'd argue the point—marriage means shared property—and my "contribution" had been the reduced price.

At the time, it had seemed a deal my pride could live with. She had money from her inheritance and insurance, so it made sense for her to buy it, but soon I'd be contributing my full share to our living expenses.

Almost three years later, that had yet to happen. If anything, I contributed less—most of my income going to expenses incurred in taking on out-of-state clients. I told myself I was building credibility and it would pay off . . . but I'd been building it since college with little change in income.

Now, as we led Cassandra around the house, I was keenly aware of her roving gaze, picking out a repair I had yet to complete or a project Paige was undertaking in my absence—and keenly aware, too, of her language, which attributed the house and all it encompassed to Paige.

While others would focus instead on the good I was doing in my work, Cassandra gave me no such allowances. She had come to accept, albeit grudgingly, that I did love Paige, but persisted in seeing me as an idealistic gadabout, so intent on saving the world that he doesn't tend to his own corner of it. Like so many of Cassandra's criticisms, as unfairly critical as it seemed on the surface, there was, underneath, that harsh kernel of truth that made it all the more uncomfortable.

On her tour, Cassandra lingered longest in the office.

"We're still working on plans to move this to the basement," Paige said. "We keep meaning to, but we haven't had a chance yet."

Cassandra's gaze cut to mine, telling me she knew full well who "hadn't had a chance yet." She surveyed the room.

"I hope you aren't clearing it out for a nursery," she

said. "Once Savannah finally leaves, you should take time for yourselves, not pop out babies—"

"No nurseries in the foreseeable future. We just need"—Paige waved around—"a bigger office."

"Why don't you use Savannah's room? It'll be empty soon enough."

"Excuse me?" Savannah said as she passed on the way to her room. "I'm going to college, not Siberia. I'll be back on weekends and holidays."

"I'm sure you'll find the sofa bed quite serviceable."

Savannah snorted and disappeared into her room.

"I hope you're getting that twenty you owe me," Cassandra called.

"Like you need it," Savannah called back. "And I only owe you ten—I got the artist right, just not the period."

"Well, I should hope you got the artist right, considering he signed his name." Cassandra turned back to the office, gaze going to the oversized wipe-off calendar. "Is that *your* schedule, Paige? My God, how do you find a moment's time for yourself? You really have to learn to say no to people—particularly with your volunteer efforts, however just the cause."

She waved at the blinking answering machine. "And five new messages on a Sunday? I hope those aren't for work. If you let clients get away with calling you at all hours—"

"Lucas?" Paige cut in. "Could you check those? I want to show Cassandra the bed." She turned to Cassandra. "It's an antique. Needs some work, but I picked it up cheap—"

"I should hope so, if it needs work. You must watch antique dealers, Paige—"

"—and I was hoping you could give us some advice on how to find someone suitable to repair it."

Paige waved Cassandra into the bedroom and pan-
tomimed throttling her from behind as she passed.

"Wouldn't do any good," I murmured.

"I know," she whispered with a grin. "But that's okay.
All the pleasure. None of the guilt."

In the next room, Cassandra returned to her diatribe
about Paige's workload. I knew Paige had already tuned
her out. Yet it was one subject on which I wish she'd listen. Like Cassandra's quiet insinuations about my free-
loading, there was some truth in this. Paige did work too
hard.

If someone needed help, Paige was always there.
While I understood that urge better than anyone, I saw
the toll it took and knew that the real solution was not
to reduce her volunteer efforts, but to focus them in the
direction she loved: her work for the council.

Yet how could she jet off to Indiana or South Car-
olina, chasing a council investigation, when she had Savannah to look after, a household to run, and a full-time
job to attend to? She had to refocus that altruistic urge
on local charities, concentrate on her Web site business,
and let me pursue cases of injustice involving supernaturals. Let me live her dream while she paid our bills.

That would change. When Savannah left for college,
Paige would have more freedom to travel, either on her
own cases or accompanying me, taking her programming work with her. And yet . . .

Perhaps it's pride speaking again, but I didn't want
Paige to have to wait for Savannah to leave. More important, I didn't want Savannah's leaving to resolve
the problem for me. I wanted to prove to Paige that I
recognized and regretted the injustice of our financial
arrangements and was willing to make sacrifices to see
her dreams realized. But I had yet to find a way to accomplish my goal, and had begun to suspect with each

passing year that Savannah's leave-taking would solve it before I did, however much I wished otherwise.

I lowered the volume on the answering machine. Three messages were indeed work-related for Paige—two clients and a coworker from a volunteer group. The fourth was also for her. It was Adam, asking how "that, uh, thing went." Then came the fifth.

"Lucas, it's Papá. I'll be in Portland later this week. I have business in the area and I'm looking forward to seeing you and Paige. Give me a call—"

I hit the stop button and went to join Paige in the bedroom.

I could have pretended not to have received my father's message. Four years ago, I would have . . . then suffered the self-disgust that would accompany so blatantly immature an avoidance tactic. When I first contemplated a relationship with Paige, I'd assumed it would further damage my fractious relationship with my father. I know others have speculated that I began seeing her for that very reason—to upset him. Nothing could be further from the truth.

I had no desire to hurt my father. I rebelled against his way of life by retreating, not by lashing out. With my father, my defensive strategy had always been to ignore him. Engaging him, by dating someone who would cause embarrassment to the Cabal and the family, would hardly have achieved that goal.

And yet to everyone's surprise, perhaps my own most of all, my relationship with my father has improved since I began seeing Paige. Greatly improved. Ignoring him had always been difficult for me. Whatever our ethical differences, I wanted a relationship with him. Even though I'd grown up with my mother, I'd been closer to him than most children who live with their fathers.

Paige taught me that it took more strength to stand firm in my opposing philosophical beliefs than to run and hide them from his influence.

It was a far from easy situation. Lately, though, he'd eased back in his manipulations and his attempts to return me to the Cabal fold. I thought we'd been making progress. Now I saw my error. He'd simply been letting me relax my guard before a strategic strike—the Portland satellite office.

I wanted to call him back and demand answers. Yet I knew that even if I caught him off-guard, there was no guarantee I could elicit the truth. The telephone also placed the matter in his favor, giving me no body language cues or facial expressions with which to judge the veracity of his claims. Better to wait until he was here and get my answers face-to-face.

In the meantime, I had other things to occupy my attention. So I called and left a message explaining that I was on a case, but if he let me know when he'd be in town I'd set aside time to meet him.

7

LUCAS

THE NEXT MORNING, PAIGE DROPPED me off in Tacoma. She and Cassandra would continue on to Geddes's house while I'd rent a car and drive back to Middleton to investigate the murder. I understood this was an efficient division of labor—one that I'd suggested—yet I couldn't help wishing I could fully share this investigation with Paige . . . preferably without Cassandra.

Before we left, Paige had joked about sending Cassandra to Middleton in my place. Let her sweep through town, demanding answers, and they might give up the killer willingly, just to get rid of her. The alternative would be to send Cassandra to Seattle alone to deal with Geddes. But, again, while tempting, she was liable to stride up to Geddes's door, ring the bell a few times, and if he didn't answer, leave and declare her duty done.

I arrived in Middleton at ten and proceeded to the police station. I did not, however, go inside, but instead found the nearest coffee shop. It was the sort one could expect to find in any town—heavy on linoleum and vinyl, the faint smell of burnt coffee ingrained in every surface.

I picked up an abandoned newspaper from a booth, then perched on a stool at the counter. After ordering a black coffee, I opened the paper, not so much to read it as to persuade the two police officers sitting beside me that I wasn't interested in their conversation.

One glance at the newspaper heading told me the murder had not been solved. It took only a few minutes more of eavesdropping to know it wasn't even close to being solved.

The chupacabra attacks had not been a high priority for the local authorities. They'd been playing hot potato with the state police. The town side argued that livestock attacks were a rural concern and therefore state jurisdiction. The state side argued that the first had fallen within town boundaries and the perpetrators were almost certainly town residents. Both sides argued that they had neither the budget nor the manpower to invest in isolated attacks on livestock. Now that a murder had been committed, the town police had taken control but were practically starting from scratch.

When the officers left, so did I, pausing only long enough that I wouldn't appear to be following them. They headed back to the station, the one place I *couldn't* follow them, so I stopped to check my phone. Paige had sent a text message, to avoid interrupting me.

"House yes. Occp'd no. Will check records."

In other words, the address Aaron provided appeared to be correct, but Geddes was not at home. They'd take some time checking public records while awaiting his return.

If he was home and hiding, I hoped Paige didn't realize it. She was not above taking risks in pursuit of a suspect she deemed a danger to others.

I reopened my phone, then stopped. Paige could handle this.

I took a deep breath, then closed the phone, pocketed it, and continued walking.

I pushed open the front door to the *Middleton Herald* and stood in line behind a woman dropping off a classified ad for a washer and dryer, and debating with the receptionist the merits of "good working condition" over merely "working condition."

I assessed my surroundings. A small reception area with offices to the rear and stairs to the left, presumably leading up to more offices.

"Can I help you?" asked a voice to my right.

A middle-aged, heavyset man stood in a doorway, eyeing me, likely trying to figure out what I was selling. While I'd forgone my suit that day, I was well aware that my definition of casual—a dress shirt and slacks—didn't coincide with most people's.

I extended a hand. "Luis Cortez, *Miami Standard.* I was wondering whether someone might have a moment to discuss the chupacabra case."

I flashed my press pass. The *Miami Standard* was a

tiny Spanish newspaper in Miami, owned by a half-demon I'd helped years ago. In return, he'd provided me with press credentials for his paper and was always ready to verify my employment.

"Miami, huh?" The reporter waved me toward a flight of stairs. "Guess that makes sense. Case like this would probably interest your readership down there. I suppose you people know more about this chupacabra stuff than we do."

I suspected that by "you people" he didn't mean Floridians, but I only said, "Yes, sir," as I followed him upstairs.

At the top, he ushered me into a small room with a table and a few cheap chairs.

"So, where you from?" he asked as I sat.

"Miami."

A laugh. Then, "Before that, I mean."

I resisted the urge to say "Miami." My father's family had come from Spain nearly two hundred years ago. My closest immigrant relative was my maternal grandfather, whose parents had arrived from Cuba when he was an infant. We must pick our battles, and this wasn't one I'd chosen for my life. So I lied and said my family was from Mexico, and listened while he waxed eloquent about a winter trip to Acapulco.

"I believe there were reports of chupacabra activity in that region in the early nineties," I said, not because I knew any such thing, but because it provided a polite segue back to the topic. "And I do appreciate you taking the time to speak to me this morning, Mr. . . ."

"Sullivan. Call me Sully."

I told him what I knew so far about the case.

"Yeah, cops dropped the ball on this one," he said. "Can't say I blame them, though. I think this whole chupacabra nonsense made them—" He stopped. "I mean, not to offend anyone's beliefs or mythology . . ."

"The chupacabra is considered a modern myth, unconnected to any religious or cultural beliefs. It's merely a legend that people enjoy propagating, but one that most do not believe in. Similar to, let's say, werewolves."

Sullivan grinned. "Good, then, we're speaking the same language. The lingua franca of superstitious bullshit. That's why the cops were giving those animal mutilations low priority."

"Not wanting to lend credence to what is presumably a hoax."

"You got it."

From Sullivan, I received the names and addresses of people involved, from the farmers originally targeted by the mutilations to the dead man's widow. It was rarely so simple, but in Sullivan I'd landed a fortunate break. He'd lived in Middleton all his life and had likely been the paper's lead reporter in his day. As he'd neared retirement, though, he'd been moved to an editorial desk and appreciated the distraction and ego boost of talking to a young reporter.

"So the question is, how does Billy Arnell's death tie in with these livestock killings?" he finished.

"Does it?" I asked.

Sullivan frowned. "You think the murder is separate? Seems to me there has to be a link, and I'll bet it has something to do with that bar."

"Was Arnell gay?"

"That's the million-dollar question, isn't it? He had a wife—ex-wife, too—and four kids, but . . ." Sullivan shrugged. "Maybe someplace like Miami, a young man such as yourself might go into a gay bar with some friends, and it doesn't mean anything. But here? A guy like Arnell? Thirty-eight, blue-collar worker, never lived anywhere but Middleton? He doesn't just walk into a place like that for a beer."

* * *

As soon as I left the office, I tried calling Paige, telling myself I only wanted to provide an update. If I'd had any doubts as to my true intentions, they evaporated when Paige's voice mail clicked on and my stomach clenched. I disconnected and called again. Still no answer.

Here then was my excuse to go to her and reassure myself that she was safe, join her hunt for Geddes. Yet logically I knew that the chance that she needed rescue was minimal. Whatever scrapes Paige got herself into, she always managed to find a way out. Most likely, it was simply an inconvenient time to answer her phone.

If I dropped my investigation to run to her aid, only to discover that she'd been busy chatting up a city hall records clerk when I'd called, it would be awkward. Serious backpedaling and prevarication would be required.

No, I had to leave a message, and phone back when I could.

Next, I stopped at the bar. The owner was in, doing paperwork. Pictures of his wife and kids plastered the office walls, competing for space with centerfold pinups and girlie calendars. A man who wanted everyone to know he ran a gay bar purely for the profit.

He agreed to answer my questions, thrilled that his establishment might be mentioned in a Miami newspaper. His answers added little to my current knowledge. He knew Arnell, but swore he'd never been a patron or had any reason to be in the bar—deliveries, odd jobs, and such. I was, however, welcome to take a look around.

The police had finished processing the scene, and the bar had returned to business as usual. On a Monday afternoon, though, it was closed and empty, so I could investigate freely, arousing the interest only of a lone cleaner.

The storage room was located in the bathroom hall, which Sean said had been occupied by several people when he'd found the corpse. Difficult then for someone to drag Arnell's body in during business hours. It could be done, though, if executed early enough in the evening.

Contrary to Sullivan's suspicions, I doubted Arnell had been a patron. Sean had come here because he deemed it safe—a place far enough from home and his colleagues in Tacoma that he wouldn't risk encountering anyone he knew. A gay Middleton man attempting to hide his sexual orientation wouldn't set foot in here.

I checked the storage room. The lock was broken. Sean said the door had been left ajar. Someone had wanted the body found.

I walked to the rear exit. It opened only from the inside. From outside, it required a key. Unless . . .

I found the cleaner and asked whether she ever arrived to find the back door propped open.

"At least once a week," she said. "They use it to sneak outside and do . . . whatever, then come back in. I tell Neil—that's the bartender—to check it before he leaves, but he never remembers. I tell you, one of these days, he's going to come in and find me dead, killed by some punk cleaning out the liquor."

While I was in the bar, Paige had text-messaged. I phoned the moment I got outside. She was fine and had been questioning someone when I'd called. They were making the rounds, gathering information on Geddes while regularly swinging past to check his house.

"No sign of Geddes yet, but I think he's only out for the day. There were wet tire tracks in his driveway earlier, suggesting he left this morning. He's a financial advisor, self-employed, but a neighbor said he's often gone for the day, so he probably conducts his business through house calls. His home is a single-family detached bungalow in a suburb, which makes a stakeout tough, but we found a church parking lot about a half-block down and we can see his driveway from here. When we've exhausted our sources, that's where we can hole up and wait for him."

"Sounds as if you have everything under control."

A husky laugh. "Not really, but I'm trying. All those years on the council, thinking I knew how to conduct an investigation . . . then finding out how little I *did* know."

But it was under control. Meaning there was no excuse for me to join them. I swallowed my disappointment and offered a few suggestions.

As we discussed the possible necessity of a postdark break-in, I'll admit that prospect helped alleviate my disappointment. Standard investigative work, such as I'd been doing all day, while necessary, is somewhat less than exhilarating. And while I understand and accept the need for the monotony, I'm more than happy to alleviate it with the occasional bout of "less than legal" adventuring.

I continued my rounds of the places and people involved in the chupacabra "appearances." While I maintained the guise of a Miami reporter, the subterfuge was hardly necessary. Half of those I approached took one look at me and guessed I was there about the chupacabra. Even when I thought it prudent not to mention my supposed newspaper affiliation, they still talked to me, seeming to assume I was on some sort of cultural pilgrimage.

Speaking to the farmers, I got the distinct impression that the attacks brought more benefit than harm. Rather like crop circles. As annoyed as they may have been to lose their livestock, the loss was relatively minor and their subsequent fame more than adequately compensated for it.

The first "victims"—a young couple running an organic sheep farm—had used the interest to promote their struggling enterprise. One farmer, a widower, now had a freezer stocked with sympathy cakes and casseroles. Another family's refrigerator was covered in articles, their names highlighted in each. The fourth's enterprising preteen children had preserved their goat's corpse as a science fair project, and charged area youths a dollar to see it.

As one farmer put it, "To be honest, son, this chupacabra is the most exciting thing to hit Middleton since the kids won the state football championship in '99."

One person who would doubtless disagree was Billy Arnell.

I didn't get the opportunity to speak to the widow herself. I was met at the door and told she was tired of talking to reporters and asked to be left alone to grieve. I couldn't say I blamed her.

Arnell's coworkers were more inclined to talk. According to everyone I spoke to, Billy Arnell was an "all-round great guy." A fine epigraph, but not terribly useful in a murder investigation.

8

SEAN

I'LL BE DONE WITH EXAMS ON THE SIX-teenth," Bryce said. "Then I'll fly home the next day. You guys haven't given away my office yet, I hope."

Sean laughed and leaned back in his office chair. "Never. You know how Granddad is. We get our name on an office door at sixteen and it's ours for life, whether we want it or not."

Silence. Sean wondered whether he'd injected more frustration into that statement than he meant to.

"Not even going to ask how my exams are going, are you?" Bryce said. "You don't dare."

Sean winced. There was no right way to handle Bryce's school situation. Ask how it was going, and Bryce would get short-tempered and defensive. Don't ask, and it sounded as if Sean knew he wasn't doing well and didn't expect that to change. Bryce was a smart enough kid, but he had no head for, or interest in, political science. His chances of getting into law school dimmed with each passing semester.

"Sorry," Sean said. "I've been preoccupied. Some internal problems here."

"Nothing you can't handle, though, right? You're the golden boy. Going to make VP by Christmas. I'd lay bets on it."

Again Sean hesitated, replaying Bryce's voice, assessing his tone. Were the sentiments spoken with brotherly pride? Sibling envy? Or simply a statement of fact? Any of the three were equally possible.

Bryce had always been a difficult one. No, Sean thought with a smile; the "challenging" one, as Dad always said. Since their father's death, Bryce's moods had grown more volatile, fueled by the frustration of failing at a career path Bryce was convinced their father would have wanted for him.

They talked for a few more minutes, making plans for Bryce's summer at home. When Sean hung up, he heard Bryce's words again. The golden boy. Already on the path to VP. Did he want either distinction? Not particularly. He worked hard because that's how he'd been raised—to do a job to the best of your ability. But if he didn't care about making VP anytime soon, if at all, wasn't that all the more reason to come out? To show Bryce that he was far from the perfect CEO son?

But how could he help Bryce find his place in the Cabal if *he* no longer had one?

Oh, come on. Do you really think they'll kick you out for being gay? Lose their golden boy?

Honestly, he had no idea what would happen. The few Cabal sons he'd heard of who had declared their homosexuality had been disowned.

His grandfather doted on him, but the old man had immovable views on right and wrong. His treatment of Savannah proved that. He'd lost his eldest son, yet refused to take any solace in the discovery of a new grandchild. He would even allow her to be raised by his rival's son. All because she was a witch.

The thought of Savannah, and by extension, Lucas, made Sean's gut twist. There was no disguising *that* act as common sense. He had been a coward. Pawning off his problem on someone else, pulling out his checkbook to solve it, preying on his target's sense of moral decency and need of money.

Worse, he'd done it to someone he liked. He didn't fully understand what drove Lucas. The Cabals could be corrupt, but wasn't corruption best fought from within? Without leaving the family? Whatever his feelings about Lucas's life choices, though, he'd had no right to take advantage of them.

A lousy thing to do.

A cowardly thing to do.

Was this what living a lie would mean? Not just deflecting questions about his love life and avoiding blind dates, but turning into the kind of man who had to sneak into gay bars on business trips, then pay off friends to cover it up when things went wrong?

A tap at the door. Without waiting for a response, his Uncle Josef popped his head in.

"Sean? We need you in the boardroom."

"Come in, Sean," his grandfather said, waving to the empty seat to his left.

Sean stepped inside and closed the door as his uncle returned to his chair at his grandfather's right—Sean's father's old seat.

Sean surreptitiously scanned the table as he crossed the room, seeing his grandfather, both of his uncles, the head of security, and his second-in-command, plus the AVP of special accounting. It must be a security issue, then, something requiring budget considerations.

"We're hoping you can help us with something, Sean," his grandfather said. "You were in Tacoma last Friday, meeting with the investors for the Domtar project."

"Yes, sir."

"Then perhaps you can tell us more about this."

His grandfather opened a folder and passed it over. It was a file of newspaper clippings. The top one was from a Seattle tabloid. Sean read it.

"Chupacabra Attack in Middleton?"

9
LUCAS

THERE WASN'T A TRUE CORONER'S OF-fice, per se, simply Dr. Bailey's regular office in the county hospital. When I asked to speak to him, I expected to be told that he, like Ms. Arnell, had done enough press conferences. The nurse *did* give me a "not another one" look, but told me to go downstairs to the morgue, speak to the attendant there, and Dr. Bailey would be with me momentarily.

I found the morgue attendant—Greg Regis, according to his name tag—sitting at his desk reading a medical journal.

When I announced myself, he pushed reluctantly from his seat.

"I expect you've seen more than your share of journalists these past few days," I said as he led me down the hall.

"Oh, yeah. Doc's in his glory. Biggest case of his career."

He ushered me into what looked like the actual morgue. An odd place to entertain reporters, and uncomfortably chilly, but if the coroner was enjoying the attention, I supposed he liked some theatrics to go with it.

"Guess you want to see the photos," Regis said.

"If I can. I'd love to see the body itself, but I imagine that's out of the question."

Regis shrugged. "Me, I wouldn't care, but the widow's already claimed it."

He pulled out a folder and opened it to the photos. I examined them, comparing the corpse's condition with the research I'd done into exsanguination. As a cause of death, exsanguination simply means that enough blood was lost to cause death. What I saw supported that conclusion.

Close-ups of Arnell's throat showed two holes. Both in the jugular. Both more like tears than a vampire's precise fang pierces. Yet, on closer examination, the tops of the holes appeared neatly made, with the tears at the bottom, as if fangs—or some instrument—had perforated the jugular, then ripped down to make the tears.

There were any number of explanations. A vampire disturbed from his feeding, ripping and accidentally leaving his meal to die. A vampire covering up a victim, making it look like an animal or chupacabra attack. Someone with little knowledge of true vampires staging an attack.

"Cops are trying to say some guy did it." Regis gave a derisive snort. "Those look like anything a person could do? They're clearly animal bites."

"And Dr. Bailey agrees?"

"Said they look like animal bites to him. Took molds and shipped them off to a lab."

I considered how to best phrase my next question, without sounding either incredulous or mocking. Finally, I went with the simple, emotionless "Chupacabra?"

Regis shrugged. "Why not?" His gaze met mine, defiant and defensive. "Maybe it's just a real animal, something that lived deep in the jungles and only came out when they started clear-cutting, taking away its habitat. I've heard of things like that happening."

"That would make sense."

Regis relaxed. "It would, wouldn't it? These things originate in Latin America, then catch a ride on the rails. Happens all the time with other animals. Why not these?"

I could point out that no rendering of the chupacabra gave it opposable thumbs, therefore making it impossible for any such beast to open two doors and dump Billy Arnell in a storage room. But if Regis thought he had a convert for his theory, then I had a valuable contact in the coroner's office.

Dr. Bailey arrived soon after. As Regis had said, the man was clearly "in his glory," puffed up with self-importance, spelling his name three times to make sure I got it right. On the subject of Billy Arnell, he was far less helpful—though, I suspected, not for lack of enthusiasm.

Death by exsanguination. Presumably caused by the neck injuries. The exact cause of those injuries was still under investigation. He wasn't ruling out an animal attack, but neither was he ruling out murder, suicide, or even accident. In other words, while Dr. Bailey liked having his name in the paper, he had enough pride and common sense not to make himself look a fool by speculating.

Unable to provide very much medical information made him quite willing to answer questions about evidence that a more experienced coroner would have told me to get from the investigators and crime scene. The drained blood had not been found at or near the crime scene. No spilled blood had been found, and evidence indicated that Arnell had been moved postmortem. No defensive wounds. That could suggest a sedative. Toxicology screens were being run. Time of death indicated he'd been killed the same evening he'd been discovered. The wounds were similar to those found on the animals, but that was also pending laboratory confirmation.

Before I left, he offered me a photograph of himself. I accepted it and slid it into my briefcase, alongside the picture of Arnell's wounds I'd pilfered from the file.

When I left the coroner's office, it was nearing five. I called Paige. She answered on the second ring, slightly breathless.

"Done yet?" she asked, before I could say a word.

"No, I believe I have a few more hours' work here, which was why I was phoning. I will attempt to arrive before midnight, to conduct the break-in if required, but you should make plans for a lengthy stakeout with Cassandra."

She let out a curse. Then, after a moment of silence, she said, "That's not funny."

"I couldn't resist."

"So are you on your way?"

"Do you want me to be?"

"What do you think?"

"Hmm, it's difficult to tell. Perhaps we should discuss this further, discover exactly *how* much you want me there, what you're willing to do to get me there . . ."

"Three hours until dark, Cortez. Then I'm breaking in, with or without you."

"Ah, in that case . . ."

"You're on your way?"

"I am."

I stopped in the local copy shop first and faxed Arnell's autopsy photograph to a contact—a former Cabal forensics expert whom I'd helped leave the organization after a dispute with his employers. A common case, the sort I handle with disturbing frequency. When a Cabal employee balks at doing something that violates his professional code of ethics, he's reminded that his job is at stake. Then if he decides to quit, he discovers that's not as easy as it might seem. For someone like me, who knows the inner workings of Cabal structure better than any employee, it's an easy enough matter to resolve, but it earns me enough gratitude to have a contact for life.

Minutes before I arrived, Paige phoned back to say Geddes had come home.

"Do you want us to wait for you?" she asked.

"Yes, but only as backup. Having me accompany—"

I stopped as I heard Cassandra's voice in the background.

"Cassandra thinks you should come with us," Paige said. "Geddes isn't likely to know who you are, so that isn't a problem. With the older vampires, sometimes they'll take a message more seriously if a man delivers it."

"I'll be right there."

Paige and I stood on Geddes's porch, Cassandra behind us. I rang the bell. The door opened. A man stood there. Early forties, with dark hair graying at the temples. He wore slacks and a dress shirt, tie discarded, top buttons open, brandy snifter in one hand, looking like any other businessman after a long day.

With the storm door still shut, he surveyed us. His gaze fell to our hands, looking there for an explanation—a briefcase, sales folder, charity envelope, or petition.

"We should've brought our Bibles again," Paige murmured.

"Mr. Geddes?" I said, raising my voice to be heard through the screen door. "Spencer Geddes?"

"Yeah."

"We'd like to speak to you."

"Not interested."

He started closing the door.

"We aren't selling—" I began.

"Actually, we are," Paige said, flashing her most winning smile.

Geddes stopped, door half closed, gaze on her, wary but curious.

"We're offering anti-Cabal insurance," she continued. "We believe you may be in need of it, and we're here to offer it at no cost or obligation to you."

Geddes's gaze turned cold. "Not interested."

"I think you will be, if you'll just hear us out—"

"I don't care what the fuck you're selling, little girl. Get off my goddamn porch."

I bristled, but Paige's fingers wrapped around my forearm.

Cassandra stepped in front of us, her gaze out-freezing Geddes's. "My name is Cassandra DuCharme. I am your interracial council delegate—"

"I don't care if you're fucking queen of Sheba. I said, get off my porch."

"As your delegate, it is my responsibility—"

Geddes leaned into the storm door, nose touching the screen. "You are not my delegate for anything, Ms. DuCharme. I didn't elect you. I don't want any part of your 'responsibilities' or your protection or your goddamn community barbecues. Is that clear?"

"So you wish to be left alone?"

"Got that impression, did you?"

"I'm simply clarifying, for the record, that you do not wish any information we may have regarding a potential problem, or any warning—"

Geddes slammed the door.

Cassandra turned to Paige. "And you thought *I* was difficult."

"Yeah," Aaron said, after Cassandra passed me her cell phone. "As much as I think this asshole is making a very big mistake, I gotta go with Cass on this one. He doesn't want our help? Fuck him."

"That would be my sentiment as well," I said. "However, what Paige and I need at this point is your and Cassandra's blessing, in light of Geddes's behavior, to pursue him as a possible suspect. If he's responsible for this death, then it's a matter for the council."

"Hell, yes. Vamps want an ombudsman? I'm here. They want someone to hide behind when they screw up and leave bodies lying around? They got the wrong guy. If it turns out he's your killer, Cass and I will take over through the council."

* * *

Twenty minutes later, Cassandra was driving back to Portland. She'd offered to stay with Savannah overnight while Paige and I staked out Geddes's house. Our visit may have been just the impetus he needed to run, fleeing justice, fleeing persecution . . . or stepping out to hide the evidence.

It was almost midnight and Geddes hadn't left his house. Paige and I had spent the evening talking about the case. Even just lobbing ideas back and forth was gratifying in a way I would never have imagined before I met Paige.

I'd always been a loner. Even in childhood, while I always had playmates, I'd had few true friends. I wasn't antisocial or unfriendly, but I'd never been comfortable allowing anyone more intimate access to my life. Then I met Paige and found myself not only willing to open up and share my life, but eager to.

I didn't need her at my side every waking moment—we were both too independent for that. But having someone I could talk to about a case, bounce around theories, debate motivations and courses of action? Having that person be just as passionate about it as I was? It was something I'd never dared hope for.

As we talked, she was more animated than she ever was talking about Web site programming, however much she enjoyed her job. It was like legal work with me. I enjoy it well enough, but it is a means to an end—for me, access to the cases I love and the legal know-how often needed to resolve them. But a life of nothing but law? I couldn't imagine it. Paige knew that. When I'd suggested significantly increasing my legal work, even taking a job with a firm, she'd vetoed the idea. Yet she too needed more, and being here on this case together, seeing her excitement, only proved that.

By midnight, we were running out of steam and Paige was doing more yawning than talking.

"Crawl into the back," I said. "We can take turns napping."

"Let's give it another hour first. This might be just the time he'll leave, when the neighborhood quiets down for the night."

As she rolled down her window more to get some cool air, I said, "Shall we play a game to pass the time?"

"Such as . . . ?"

"I was thinking Hangman. Unoriginal, I know, but with only a paper and pen, I'm at a loss for anything more interesting. However, I'm certain we could overcome that problem by laying wagers on the outcome."

She grinned. "Like the winner gets the last bottle of water?"

"That's one possibility, though I was hoping you might be amenable to satisfying something other than thirst."

"Winner's choice?"

I considered the possibilities. "The stakes, I believe, should be implicit in the solution of the puzzle, though not necessarily explicitly so. The winner, then, receives the appropriate prize."

"You're on."

She grabbed a pen and paper from the back.

Paige created the first puzzle.

I won it.

Five minutes after my victory, as I was relishing my reward, I noticed a movement near Geddes's house, a dark shadow moving against the darker backdrop. Not being particularly eager to interrupt Paige for what might well be a neighbor's pet, I squinted to watch it. Even when I saw a flicker of light—a flashlight beam swiftly doused—I told myself the matter was not urgent and could wait a few minutes . . . perhaps longer.

I must have conveyed my mild distraction to Paige, though, and she lifted her head from my lap with a murmured "See something?"

When I hesitated, she sat up and peered out my window.

"It looks like Geddes is sneaking out."

"Unfortunately," I sighed.

"Guess that wasn't the wisest idea," she said as she zipped my pants. "Too distracting a distraction."

"Rendering me somewhat disinclined to react promptly to an outside concern."

"Somewhat?"

"My apologies. The correct word choice would be *significantly*."

"*Somewhat* is fine," she said, smiling, as she slid out of the car. "It only means I'll need to practice more to perfect my technique."

While I could argue most vehemently that her diagnosis was incorrect, it would be foolish of me to dissuade her from pursuing her solution. As she walked around the front of the car, I gave myself a moment to refocus on the task at hand. She motioned that she'd start heading over to Geddes's, and I watched her go, her hips swaying, sweater tight around the generous curve of her breasts . . . which wasn't helping me refocus at all.

I allowed myself a moment longer to watch her, while reminding myself that we'd be able to pick up where we'd left off, in the more spacious and comfortable surroundings of a hotel room. Then I tore my gaze away and opened my door.

The houses were on large lots made private by wooden fences and fast-growing evergreens. The fences made sneaking through backyards impossible, so we settled for the road, affecting the only disguise we could: a couple out for a late-night walk. When we drew close enough to Geddes's house to be spotted, we slipped into the shadow of an SUV parked at the side of the road.

"His car is still there," Paige whispered. "And there's no sign of anyone in the yard."

I motioned for her to stay down as I peered out. A faint, flickering glow shone from between Geddes's drawn curtains. A television.

A movement alongside his car caught my attention. A figure was huddled there, watching the house, hands and face dark. Camouflaged. As he lifted something to his lips, I pulled back.

"Cabal SWAT team," I whispered.

Paige let out a curse.

"Our options are limited," I said. "It's too late to get to the house and warn him—"

She lifted her cell phone. I nodded and she crept up the front yard of the neighboring house. I covered her retreat, then followed.

She'd found a spot behind a cedar and was already dialing as I approached.

"Mr. Geddes," she said, keeping her voice low. "This is Paige Winterbourne. I came by today with Cassandra DuCharme—"

Even three feet away, I heard the line disconnect. Paige looked at me, eyes fuming. I reached for her phone and pressed redial.

The answering machine picked up on the first ring.

"Mr. Geddes," I said. "Evidently either you believe we're lying or the Cabals don't frighten you. If it's the latter, then all I can say—most respectfully—is that you are a fool. If it's the former, I'd suggest you confirm the situation by looking out your window, to the right of your vehicle, where you will see an armed Cabal security officer approaching your home. You may be aware of a death Friday night in Middleton, where a man was found drained of blood with bite marks in his neck."

A click. Then a cold "I didn't do that."

"Perhaps, but—"

"And I'm not going to run and look as if I'm guilty."

"Under normal circumstances, that might be judicious. But the Cabal most likely to be staking out your house is the Nasts. Their CEO, Thomas Nast, lost a teenage grandson to a vampire two years ago. Edward Hagen. Perhaps you heard of the case?"

Geddes let out a string of curses, many in languages other than English.

"I don't want to run," he repeated.

"And you won't—for long. Our primary objective at this moment is to transfer control of your defense—"

"Defense? I haven't done anything."

"And the best people to prove that are the delegates of the interracial council. First, though, we need you out of the house."

I instructed him to slip out the back, make his way out of the suburbs, then call us. As soon as I finished, he hung up.

"Was that a yes?" Paige whispered.

"I hope so."

Once we'd given Geddes the opportunity to escape, it was time for me to do what, according to many, I did best: interfere.

I told Paige to stay behind. A simple matter of safety, which she understood. My immunity did not extend to her.

As I crossed the road, it would appear that my stride was determined, my chin high, my confidence unwavering. A necessary facade for pulling off such a delicate act of faith. Striding into the midst of a Cabal takedown operation, I could be shot by any new Cabal employee who didn't recognize me. I could even be shot by an employee who *did*, but decided that the darkness would excuse accidentally killing me . . . and claiming the quiet gratitude of his employers. The surest way to stay a Cabal security officer's hand on his weapon was to look and act as if I had every right to be there, and had every confidence that if any harm came to me, my father's retaliation would be swift and merciless.

As I walked toward the dark figure crouched by the side door, the man turned, tensing. Then he straightened, like a soldier snapping to attention. Still walking, I dropped my gaze to his outfit. It bore no insignia—a secret ops team is hardly going to announce its affiliation—but I knew Cabal uniforms well enough to identify the design. This wasn't the Nast Cabal's SWAT team. It was my father's.

10

LUCAS

I ENTERED THE HOUSE THROUGH THE rear door, which the team had already discovered unlocked and had used to infiltrate the house. As I canvassed the rooms to ensure Geddes had left, I gave more than one prowling team member a start. All must have been wondering what I was doing there. Yet not one asked, and I didn't enlighten them.

I was in Geddes's living room, thumbing through his address book, when footsteps sounded in the hall—not the heavy clomp of boots, but the slap of dress shoes. A man snapped an order. At the sound of the voice, the hairs on the back of my neck rose. But I kept my gaze on the book, perusing the endless client numbers. The doorway darkened as a figure filled it. He walked into the middle of the room, the heat of his rage palpable.

"Hello, Hector," I said.

My oldest half brother, twenty years my senior and the only one of the three whom I can say with honesty that I fear. The youngest, Carlos, had inherited his mother's cruel streak, but none of our father's intelligence. The middle one, William, sadly received neither, and little to compensate for the lack. Only in Hector did both traits coincide—venom plus the mental capacity to use it to its fullest advantage.

Hector called to a SWAT team member in the hall. "Get Stanton in here."

"The team leader is Gus Reichs," I said mildly. Then I looked at the security officer. "I believe you'll find him on the upper level."

"Yes, sir."

Moments later, the young officer returned with Reichs, who paused in the doorway, his gaze going from Hector to me, uncertain whom to address.

I greeted him, then said, "Hector wished to speak to you."

"We've searched the house, sir," Reichs began. "But there's no sign of—"

"Of course there isn't," Hector snapped. "If *he's* here—" A thumb jerked my way "—then the vampire isn't. Lucas is stalling us, giving his client time to escape."

"Spencer Geddes is not my client." I picked up Geddes's Day-Timer. "However, as the actions for which he is being investigated in no way affect Cabal business, they are a matter for the interracial council, not the Cabal."

"He murdered—"

"Not a Cabal employee or even a supernatural. And if it was his required annual kill, it does not, according to the statutes, constitute murder, however much we may argue the point. Instead this would be considered improper body disposal, which is a council concern."

As I spoke, I leafed through Geddes's planner. Distancing myself from the argument. My usual approach to dealing with Hector.

"Find the vampire," Hector said to Reichs, "and place him in Cortez Cabal custody."

Reichs glanced my way, waiting. Hector's eyes glittered, his blood pressure rising.

"Hector has given the order," I said, "but please exercise restraint in the capture. I was the one who told Mr. Geddes to run."

"Since when do you approve my orders, Lucas?" Hector said as Reichs left.

"I didn't. I was merely clarifying the situation, so the team doesn't blame Geddes for fleeing."

I returned my attention to the planner. Hector strode over and plucked it from my hands.

"Don't you *ever* give an order to my employees after I've already done so."

"I apologize. I assure you, my intention was not—"

"Your intention was to make a fool of me. Don't make it worse with your pompous apologies."

I hoped I didn't flush, but turned my face away, just in case. "If that officer looked to me for verification of the order, that is not my fault. I wish you'd place the blame where it belongs—on the man who created the situation."

"You're pathetic. You manipulate Father into making you his heir, then blame him for it."

"If you'll excuse me—"

Hector wrapped his fingers around my forearm. "No,

I don't excuse you. For anything. But speaking of excuses, you've set up a nice one for me here. Barging in on a takedown. The perfect excuse for a tragic accident."

I caught a flicker and looked past Hector to see Paige in the doorway, lips moving in a binding spell. I gave a small shake of my head. She stopped casting, but hovered there, watching Hector.

I took out my cell phone.

"Let me guess," Hector said. "Time to call Father. Tell him you're being bullied again."

Even from the earliest threats in childhood, I'd never complained to my father about any of my half brothers. But there was no sense pointing that out. Hector had created his own version of reality to explain why our father favored the son who was arguably least worthy of the honor. Nothing I could ever say would change Hector's mind.

My father answered his cell phone and I explained the situation as succinctly as I could.

"And, as such," I concluded, "it does not fall within Cabal judicial jurisdiction, which is why I'm here to assist Paige in investigating the matter for the interracial council."

At that moment, an officer hurried in to tell us that Geddes had been apprehended.

"This is a matter for the council," I repeated.

My father agreed that there was some "possible" basis for the claim, and that it would be "considered." I didn't push the matter. Even Paige, stepping from her hiding spot, gave me a reluctant nod when I looked her way.

The council had abdicated its rights in such matters, if not in theory, at least in practice. For decades they had bowed to Cabal claims, however spurious. Knowing they lacked the numbers to fight, they'd concentrated their efforts elsewhere. Paige, Adam, and the other delegates were trying to change that now, but it was not a battle that could be won in this moment.

"I'll meet with you and Paige as soon as you arrive in Miami," my father said. "The jet is—"

"Paige and I would prefer to remain close to the scene of the investigation, and I'm sure Mr. Geddes does not wish to serve his incarceration on the opposite side of the country."

"Understood, but the Seattle satellite office isn't equipped to hold a prisoner. The nearest one that has a proper cell is in Chicago."

"Oh? There's nothing . . . closer?"

My father paused. "Well, there is the office in Phoenix—"

"What about Portland? Or are the security cells there still undergoing construction?"

A longer pause. Then, "I can explain—"

"I'm quite certain you can, and very convincingly. However, it's growing late and we have a long drive ahead of us. If there are cells in that office, that is where I'd like Mr. Geddes to be taken. Please have someone e-mail directions to me, and Paige and I will meet the team at the office."

I hung up before he could answer.

"Maybe this isn't the place," Paige said.

We stood in front of a small warehouse that appeared to be in the last stages of a renovation. From the exterior, it was difficult to tell what it was being converted into—there were no signs, not even one advertising the construction company. Yet I knew once we passed through those main doors that we'd find ourselves in a Cabal satellite office. There was no mistaking the structure.

"I don't get it," Paige continued. "Construction has obviously progressed far enough to have a holding cell ready, but your father told Adam they hadn't even decided whether they were going forward."

"A useful fiction. If Adam knew the offices were almost complete, and my father still didn't want me to know . . ."

"He'd smell trouble and tell us."

"Mr. Cortez!"

I turned to see a small, balding man hurrying down the sidewalk. Hector and his bodyguard followed at a distance.

"I'm sorry, sir," the man said. "I hope you weren't waiting long."

"Not at all. And I apologize for getting you from bed to let us in." I extended my hand. "Chris Ibsen, isn't it? I believe we met a couple of years ago. In New York, when you were supervising the renovations to the offices there."

Ibsen beamed, as if I paid him an enormous compliment simply by remembering who he was.

"And this is my wife," I began. "Paige—"

"Mrs. Cortez," he said, taking her hand between his. "A pleasure to meet you."

"She is *not* a Cortez," Hector said as he rounded the street corner.

"Hector is correct," I said. "My wife kept her maiden name, Winterbourne."

"Paige is fine," she said with a wide smile. Then she turned to Hector. "Has Mr. Geddes arrived yet?"

For a moment, Hector said nothing. Paige rolled her eyes at me.

"He's being brought in through the rear," Hector said finally, though he addressed his answer to me.

Ibsen unlocked the door and escorted us inside. As he walked through the lobby, he explained the layout and the progress of construction. Paige hung back a few paces while she phoned Cassandra, to tell her that Geddes had arrived in case she wanted to join us.

I slowed, ensuring she didn't fall too far behind, and kept an eye on Hector as he drifted to the side with his bodyguard. Harming Paige in front of witnesses would be too bold a move for Hector, but that didn't keep me from watching.

As we walked, Ibsen sought my input and approval on everything, as if this was vitally important. When I'd first taken Paige to the Cabal head office in Miami, I'd watched her reaction, that mix of amazement and amusement as everyone in my path tripped over themselves to greet me.

"Sure, you're the boss's son," she'd said to me later. "And they *think* you'll be the next boss, but come on—it's an employer, not a king. I don't even think kings get that treatment anymore . . . not outside of tiny despot kingdoms." And that, I told her, was quite possibly the best analogy for a Cabal—a tiny despot kingdom.

Unlike modern companies, where employees were loyal only as long as it behooved them to be so, Cabals were, in most cases, life employment. Certainly that was the goal—to work for the Cabal all your life, the same one your father worked for, the same one your children would work for.

Most employees were an integral part of the entire Cortez Cabal community. Some, particularly half-demons, had weaker ties—lacking that hereditary link—and they would move from Cabal to Cabal chasing better opportunities. But a man like Ibsen had grown up in the organization. From the earliest age, he'd socialized with other supernatural Cabal children—went to the same schools, joined the company ball team, used the company's private doctors, dentists, hospitals. He'd married within the organization. His children were now growing up in that same community.

For Ibsen, being a supernatural had never been a disadvantage. Every complication was resolved simply by being part of the tiny despot kingdom that was the Cortez Cabal.

In return, the Cabal had his complete loyalty. Why wouldn't they? He didn't know how to survive in the human world; he'd be lost the moment his child needed a doctor who could treat supernaturals.

Can one blame him, then, for kowtowing to the man he believed would be the next ruler of his kingdom? I might hate the lie—and the reminder of the power Cabals wielded—but I could not blame him, so I had to accept his obeisance with grace.

As we approached the elevator, I motioned for Ibsen to wait until Paige joined us. Once she did, he pushed the button.

"The day-care facilities are on the second floor with the executive offices," Ibsen said. "We debated that. Would it create too much disturbance? Or would it be an advantage, having one's children close enough to visit? Your father and I decided good soundproofing would resolve any noise issues. I was hoping to have your input, but your father didn't want you bothered. If you'd prefer to move the day-care, we can still do that."

Paige gave me a quizzical look, wondering why my input mattered, but I was accustomed to this. My father often found ways to "consult" me on office renovations, doing so under the guise of simply valuing my opinion.

When I'd met Ibsen working on the New York offices, Paige and I had supposedly been enjoying a mini–New York vacation, courtesy of my father. Then he just happened to be in New York at the same time and, after softening me up by treating us to box seats at a Broadway show Paige had wanted to see, he'd "had to make a stop" at the office renovation on the way back to our hotel.

While there, naturally, he'd had to take us on a tour, then take me aside to meet Ibsen and discuss the design. My father had no plans to retire anytime soon—this was just his way of reminding everyone that they'd be answering to me someday. "Someday" as in "when hell freezes over," but if I said so, I'm sure he'd find a way to accomplish that as well.

"The security cell is in the basement," Ibsen said as he ushered us into the elevator. Hector and his bodyguard headed to the stairs. "It's just a single cell, but that seemed adequate, under the circumstances."

He pressed the button, not for the basement, but for the second floor.

"While you're here, I want to ask a few questions about the executive suites."

"We really should see to Mr. Geddes," I began.

"It'll only take a moment, sir."

Once off the elevator, he led us to the main office at the end. It was still under construction and we had to pick our way through the debris.

As I stepped inside, Paige murmured, "This is an office? It's huge."

Ibsen chuckled. "As befits the top executive. Or, I should say, executives. That brings up my main question. According to the plans, it's a single office with a partial divider severing the space into two equal areas. Conjoined offices, so to speak. Is that what you want? Or would you prefer completely separate spaces, perhaps with a joint sitting room?"

"Conjoined offices?" I said. "I'm afraid I don't follow, Chris. My father hasn't briefed me on the management arrangements."

Now it was Ibsen's turn to look perplexed. "Perhaps you want to think about it, then, sir? Discuss it with your wife." He nodded to Paige. "Mr. Cortez *did* say you two like to work together, but this might be closer than you want."

"Closer . . . ?" Paige looked around, then asked with trepidation, "Whose office is this?"

Ibsen laughed. "Yours, of course. For the two of you. It is your operation, after all. A new division for the Cortez Corporation, and I can't tell you how excited I am to be a part of it."

II
LUCAS

As we headed to the elevator, leaving Ibsen behind, I struggled to forget what he'd said. More of my father's manipulation and delusions, thinking he could tempt me with my own satellite office . . . comanaged with my wife.

"We should hurry," Paige murmured. "I don't like leaving Hector alone down there with our vampire."

Her words started me out of my thoughts and that, I knew, was their purpose. But I played along. Anything to steer my mind onto another course.

"There's little danger," I said. "Yes, killing Geddes would be a nose-thumbing 'screw you' in the face of my efforts to protect him. If it was Carlos down there, I'd be worried. But Hector would never lower himself to such a crude ploy. He'll want to battle me on this matter through the appropriate channels."

As I reached for the elevator button, Paige shook her

head. "Your dad won't allow it. I'd be surprised if he hasn't recalled Hector to Miami already."

I glanced at her.

"Do you think he sent Hector to Seattle knowing you were on this case?" she asked as we stepped onto the elevator. "Never. Whatever set him onto Geddes, his motivation wasn't to head you off at the pass. If that was the case, Hector wouldn't have been there."

She was right. While I'd learned not to commit the cardinal sin of underestimating my father's gift for manipulation, that did not extend to putting his eldest and youngest son at odds to see who would triumph. When Paige and I had been chasing Edward in Miami, Hector had been ordered to stay in New York on business. My father wouldn't send Hector to Seattle knowing I was also pursuing Geddes. It was an error that would be rectified with a speedy recall to Miami. I won't say I wasn't relieved.

Cassandra arrived before we made it downstairs. We introduced her simply as "a council member" and no one inquired further. Hector was in an office, taking a call from my father, but had left orders with Kepler—the young officer I'd first met at Geddes's house. Kepler was to escort us downstairs.

"We didn't try to sedate him, sir," Kepler said as we reached the basement. "We weren't sure that would work when, you know . . ." A faint shudder. "The guy's already dead."

"He's not dead," Cassandra said.

"Undead, then."

"Vampirism is simply another state of consciousness," she said. "You will find that vampires do not appreciate being called—" Her lips twisted. "Undead."

"Aaron doesn't mind," Paige murmured. "He uses it himself."

We stopped before a steel door. The security pad wasn't connected yet, but Reichs—the team leader— seemed to be working on changing that.

"How is Mr. Geddes?" I asked.

Reichs grunted and pulled at a wire. "Behaving himself, sir. He's an arrogant SOB, but he hasn't fought. And hasn't tried to eat anyone yet."

"Feed," Cassandra said. "Vampires do not eat anyone, they feed off their blood."

"Like giant mosquitoes," Reichs said. "Parasites."

He wiped sweat from his brow as he pulled back to look at the panel wiring. "No offense to the council"— a nod to Paige—"but after that business with those psycho vamps killing kids? You gotta start thinking the St. Clouds' proposal might not be such a bad idea." He jerked his thumb toward the security ward. "We can start with this one."

"St. Cloud—?" Cassandra began.

"One of the Cabals," I said, quickly ushering her past. "The second smallest one."

"I know *who* the St. Clouds are—"

"Is he in there?" I asked Kepler, pointing to a steel door with a small window.

"Yes, sir. It's not locked—we're still working on that—but he's in a cell inside. Would you like me to go with you?"

"No, thank you."

As I pushed open the door, Cassandra passed Paige to get up beside me.

"*What* is the St. Cloud proposal, Lucas?" she demanded.

"I have no idea. But I suspect we'll find out soon."

"You!" Geddes roared the moment we stepped inside. He gripped the bars of his cell, glaring at me like a Rikers Island lifer. "You double-crossing—"

"I double-crossed no one," I said calmly. "I'd hoped you'd be able to outrun them—"

"Bullshit! You're not some pesky council do-gooder. You're a Cortez. Benicio Cortez's heir, no less, they tell me."

"I'm a Cortez, yes. And Benicio's son. But as for his heir . . . I fear that's a misunderstanding between my father and myself. I can assure you that I do not work for any Cabal—"

"Bullshit. You're a Cabal brat—"

Cassandra cut in. "And *that* is the reason you are here, Spencer. Incarcerated, but relatively safe, and speaking to council representatives instead of a Cabal interrogator. The only way you're getting out of that cell with your head attached to your shoulders is if Lucas and Paige solve this crime before the Cabals invent evidence against you."

"I didn't—"

"Before you disavow the crime, consider that if you did leave that body there, you might want to admit it and be turned over to the council for a reprimand. Better that than to deny it and see what other charges the Cabals can bring against you."

"I didn't—"

"Perhaps it was simply an error in timing or judgment. In making your annual kill, you were surprised before you could dispose of the body."

Geddes crossed the cell and sat on the cot. He rubbed his hands over his face as if taking a moment to rein in his temper. "No. My rebirth date is in January and this year I took a homeless person in Seattle, as I have since I emigrated."

"How long have you been a vampire?"

"Almost fifty years."

Her brows arched. "Young, then. Perhaps this was a

feeding accident. You took too much. It happens, particularly with new vampires—"

"I'm not *that* new. I know how to feed."

"Another sort of feeding accident, then. He had an affliction, anemia or—"

"I only hunt in Seattle. I've never even been to . . ."

"Middleton," I said.

"Wherever."

Cassandra walked along the front of the cell, her hand sliding across the bars. "Then perhaps not a mistake at all. You didn't want to speak to us earlier. You didn't want to run when Lucas warned you. Could that have been more than common stubbornness?"

"What are you driving at, woman? Suicide by Cabal?"

She pursed her lips. "I hadn't considered that."

"Well, don't. I'd find a sharp wire and decapitate myself before I'd let a Cabal do the job for me."

"Given this some thought, I see," she said.

He met her gaze. "Haven't we all?"

"No," she murmured. "However, what I was thinking was perhaps that in killing this man you were hoping to force the Cabals to react. To bring to a boil what has been simmering for two years now."

Geddes barked a laugh. "Offer myself up to the Cabals to force their hand on behalf of the vampire community? You want political statements, you've got the wrong guy."

"That," I said, "I suspect is true. As for whether the Cabals will realize it is another matter."

It was almost dawn by the time we returned upstairs. Cassandra had stayed behind with Geddes, hoping he might be more forthcoming in the company of his own race. I doubted it, but appreciated the effort. Cassandra had clearly resolved to put her full efforts into acting as Geddes's council advocate. I knew this pleased Paige.

As for Hector, he was already at the airport, awaiting my father's jet so he could return to Miami. We learned of his leave-taking only upon inquiring. The official reason for his departure was that in light of our father's imminent arrival here, Hector was needed to head operations in Miami.

We left the Cabal office before my father arrived. Had we stayed to demand an explanation about the offices, I suspected neither Paige nor I would later be in any mood to concentrate on an investigation.

When Cassandra finished with Geddes, she would return to our house to see Savannah off to school. Then she would meet with my father later to discuss Spencer Geddes. They'd worked together before, negotiating an uneasy truce between the Cabals and the vampires after the Edward and Natasha case. I had few qualms about leaving them together. They were evenly matched, and would, I was certain, come to an agreement regarding Geddes's incarceration with a minimum of bloodshed.

An hour after we left, Paige roused herself from a nap, stretching in the passenger seat.

"Pull over at the next off-ramp," she said through a yawn. "I'll drive for a while."

"No need. I wouldn't sleep anyway."

I felt her gaze on me and turned to see her twisted sideways, her cheek against the seat as she watched me.

"You okay?" She shook her head. "I know you're not, but . . ."

"I'm just trying not to think about it until I have the time to get a proper explanation."

"A good idea. Let's go back to where we left off then. Theorizing—about the case, that is. Before Billy Arnell, this creature wasn't really causing any grief. Well, I'm sure those dead animals would object, but you know what I mean. Those who lost livestock gained back value-plus in publicity and temporary fame. Who was first hit again?"

"The organic sheep farmers."

"Probably not the sort to kill an animal to promote their business. Maybe one of the others then."

"Striking first at sheep farmers to deflect initial scrutiny?"

"Right. We have preteens in one family. Plus the teenager who claims he saw his cat attacked. That's where I'd look."

I nodded. "Teenagers take the greatest interest in supernatural phenomena, and are most likely to undertake such acts to gain attention and shock adults."

"And prove their theory that all grown-ups are gullible fools. So we'll start with young people attached to the case."

We stopped at a diner just off the Middleton exit and dallied over breakfast. We had time; we couldn't begin our investigation so early in the day.

While we lingered over coffee, my father called. I'd left a message at the Portland office, explaining that we'd returned to the investigation, but he still seemed put out that we hadn't stayed until he'd arrived. Barring unforeseen problems, we'd be home for the night, and could speak with him then. In the meantime, he'd have Cassandra to keep him busy.

Ten minutes later I received a second call, one that suggested we might be back in Portland sooner than I thought.

"That was my contact at the *Middleton Herald*," I said as I hung up.

"A break in the case?"

"Better. They've arrested a suspect and called a press conference for nine."

* * *

I used my press pass to gain entrance to the conference. When Paige accompanied me into the room, no one tried to stop her.

The conference began promptly at nine with the police announcing the capture of the culprits believed responsible for the chupacabra attacks. It was a quartet of teenage boys, including the neighbor of the organic sheep farmers and the son of Billy Arnell.

"They have been charged and have confessed to the livestock attacks," announced the detective—a woman named MacLeod. "As for the murder of William Arnell, we are continuing our investigation, but expect to lay those charges soon."

"Against the boys?" someone asked.

"They remain our primary suspects."

The detective steered questions back to the chupacabra attacks. Though she remained evasive on motive, a picture emerged from the pointed questions of the reporters and the detective's responses.

Four teenage boys, all friends, bored and restless as the school year dragged on toward the tantalizing freedom of summer. One completes a school project on modern monster legends and shares it with his friends. They fantasize about how much fun it would be to stage an outbreak in Middleton.

Fantasy soon turned to challenge. Could they pull it off? They decided on the chupacabra. The first target? The neighbors who'd been involved in a groundwater dispute with one boy's father. Sheep weren't goats— the chupacabra's favorite prey—but they were close enough.

"But about Billy . . ." said a young woman from the *Middleton Herald.* "Peter Arnell, one of the suspects, lived with his mother, and Billy had a history of child support payment defaults there. Is that the assumed motivation for Billy's death? A son striking out on be-half of his mother?"

"Peter Arnell has not been charged with his father's murder," the detective reiterated.

Her denial didn't matter. Throughout the room, re-porters were madly scratching down the young journal-ist's words. With the possibility of patricide, this case had taken a turn as exciting as the chupacabra claims.

"I don't buy it," Paige said as we took a booth in the coffee shop. "Sure, I'd like to believe no son would mur-der his father, but I'm not that naïve. If Peter lived with his mom and was constantly hearing what an SOB his dad was—and that every new pair of Nikes he couldn't buy was because his father wouldn't pay up—he might consider murder to collect child support back pay through the estate. He might even be able to pull it off . . . with a gun or a knife. But exsanguination?"

"The animals were fairly simple to kill in that manner. Certainly easy enough for four boys with a rudimentary knowledge of anatomy. From the photographs, the job was a messy one, suggesting the perpetrators possessed no medical finesse."

"Not so with Billy Arnell."

I nodded. "Whoever inflicted those wounds knew what he was doing. Also, he had to subdue Arnell, who was a big man and would hardly allow himself to bleed out, even if he was being held down by three teenage boys."

"Sedated."

"Most likely."

"Did the coroner find anything?"

"He submitted the tests. They should be back by now."

"Time to visit again?"

"I believe so."

* * *

We obtained a copy of the coroner's report from Dr. Bailey's assistant, Greg Regis. He might have provided it willingly, but we didn't ask. If there's any doubt as to whether someone will part with an item, there is an advantage to not requesting it. It's easier to steal something when no one knows you want it.

So Paige went down to the morgue alone, posing as a reporter, and charmed Regis away from his desk. Then I slipped in, found the report, and slid a copy into my briefcase.

"Pentobarbital," Paige said. "Used in veterinary work as an anesthetic and in hospitals to reduce intracranial pressure and induce comas. Also used in euthanasia. Serious stuff."

We were in the car, pulled off along a residential street. Paige was on her laptop, using someone's wireless Internet connection. Less than ethical, but we'd been unable to find a wireless-ready coffee shop in Middleton. So I'd driven along this road until Paige found a signal that wasn't password-protected.

She continued. "The drug is probably available in hospitals or veterinary clinics, but it's not something the average person could pick up in the drugstore."

My cell phone rang and I glanced at the display.

"My father," I said. I let it ring one more time, then answered.

"Lucas? I know you're busy with the murder investigation, but you need to come back to Portland. We have a situation."

My father's news, while troubling, was not unexpected. Nor did it require our immediate return. I told him we'd finish a few things and be back by midafternoon.

Paige and I had a lead we wished to pursue before

leaving. While there was always the possibility Billy Arnell had been a random victim, statistics show that such things are rare. People kill because their target blocks them from achieving a goal. The goals are equally predictable: satisfaction of the major drives—money, sex, power, and survival.

The most obvious suspect was Arnell's first wife—Peter Arnell's mother. It was unlikely that Peter would realize that his mother could recoup her lost child support payments through Arnell's estate. But she would.

She could also know that her son was involved in the chupacabra attacks. It's my experience that parental ignorance is often merely an excuse. Parents suspect what their children are doing—be it drugs, unsafe sexual behavior, or criminal acts. Whether they choose to pursue their suspicions to a conclusion is another matter. If Ms. Arnell *did* investigate her son's activities, perhaps she saw in them an opportunity to get away with murder.

Paige and I split up again. When I returned to the car just over an hour later, she was already there. We began the trip to Portland before sharing what we'd learned.

"Well, I didn't need an hour," Paige began. "Took me ten minutes to find out whether Maggie Arnell could have had access to pentobarbital. According to your initial research, she worked as a home-care worker with the elderly, right?"

"Yes, but that wouldn't provide easy access to drugs."

"No, but she's also a registered nurse. Looks like a case of burnout after the divorce, but she still temps as a public health nurse. She's known at the hospital. No one would question her hanging around, and she'd know where to find what she needs."

Paige ratcheted her chair back, getting comfortable. "Access to pentobarbital, plus the medical know-how to use it and to make those cuts. I think we might have struck it lucky with our first shot." She glanced at me, studying my expression. "Or not . . . What did you find?"

"That Ms. Arnell's claim of child-support negligence appears to have been exaggerated. In the five years since their divorce, Billy Arnell has only defaulted on payments once. In January of this year, his factory unexpectedly shut down due to a supply problem. It was closed for almost a month. Arnell, already struggling with postholiday bills, could only make partial payments for the next two months. He has, however, been repaying the loss willingly. Currently, he owes his exwife less than a thousand dollars."

"Not worth killing for, though I guess it wouldn't clear Peter Arnell's name. They could claim he heard his mother badmouthing his dad about support—and denying him things because of it—so he assumed his dad owed more." She paused, thinking. "I still like Maggie Arnell, though. What about other sources of money? Life insurance, maybe, if he hadn't remembered to remove her as beneficiary. Or if his kids were the beneficiaries, would she get control of their funds?"

"I have a call in to an insurance contact who's looking for the policy details."

She smiled. "One step ahead of me, then. So now our next move is . . ."

Her smile faded as she realized there was no "next move." We'd finished what we'd come to accomplish and couldn't tarry any longer, not when a complication had arisen in Geddes's case.

It was time to go back to Portland.

12

SEAN

Sean." BENICIO CORTEZ STRODE FOR-
ward and clasped his hand. "Good to see you, son. And
belated congratulations on your graduation last year. I
hear you're doing an excellent job already. Your uncles
must be looking over their shoulders."

As they waited for Sean's grandfather in the lobby of
the new Cortez Portland office, Benicio peppered Sean
with questions. How was Bryce? Was he enjoying political science? Did Sean miss New York? Was he settled
into his new condo in L.A. yet? Was he looking forward
to having Bryce home for the summer?

The questions revealed a thorough knowledge of
Sean's public life, and suggested a keen interest in his
well-being. It was flattering, of course, to think that such
an important man took notice of you. That was the
point.

Of all four Cabal CEOs, Benicio Cortez was the most
popular in the purest sense of the word—that he was
well liked by the general Cabal populace. When Sean's
grandfather entered a few minutes later, Benicio greeted
him, then his bodyguards—by name, asking after their
families, even mentioning the names of their children.
And the bodyguards—though they'd met Benicio many
times before—never failed to give the desired response.
They were flattered.

It was a lot of work knowing the details of his rivals'

organizations, and the lives of those people important in the organizations. But as Lucas had told Sean once, it all came down to one principle: Know thy enemy.

While his grandfather and Benicio feigned pleasant small talk, Sean wondered yet again if he'd done the right thing, volunteering to come along so he could help Lucas.

Help Lucas? Help yourself, you mean. The only reason you're here is to protect your ass. You're making sure the identity of Lucas's "client" doesn't get leaked.

No. For once, Sean could be fairly certain the nagging voice of his conscience was wrong. While he didn't think Lucas and Paige would turn him in, one uneasy glance in his direction when asked about their "client" might be enough.

Or is that what you're hoping for, Sean? Outed by someone else, someone you can blame if you get disowned?

No, if he was revealed to be Lucas's client, he wouldn't wait to see whether his grandfather followed that information to the logical conclusion—that Sean was gay. If his client-hood came out, so would he. Voluntarily.

"There's a meeting room upstairs," Benicio said. "But the elevator isn't working reliably yet. I can have my men bring the furniture to a room down here, if that's easier for you, Thomas."

His grandfather glared over the poke at his age and growing infirmity. Benicio was almost twenty years Thomas's junior and as hale and vigorous as a man half that age, and Thomas Nast never appreciated the reminder. Yet when Benicio put it that way, as a considerate suggestion, Thomas couldn't argue without sounding petty. He *could* come back with a clever rejoinder . . . but that would require thinking of one first, and verbal jousting wasn't one of his grandfather's battle skills. Instead, he said he'd try the elevator and, if it failed, the stairs would be fine.

As they headed for the elevator, Sean noticed a young woman just outside the main doors. She was walking past the window, scrutinizing the building.

Tall and slender, she wore a midriff-baring black T-shirt, red slim-fitting jeans, and knee-high boots. Her dark hair was gathered back in a hastily tied knot. Oversized shades partially obscured her face but showed a strong, fine bone structure, worthy of a runway model.

The young woman walked to the glass and put her face against it, like a kid peering through a store window. With a jolt, Sean realized who she was.

Leaving the men still talking, he hurried across the lobby and pushed open the door.

"Savannah."

Her face lit up in a grin. "Hey, what are you doing here?"

"I should ask you the same thing."

As she walked in, Sean struggled to get over the shock of momentarily not recognizing his sister. He'd seen her just a few days ago and yet, meeting her out of context, seen at a distance in her dark glasses . . . He shook his head, thinking, "My God, when did this happen?" as if she'd grown from child to woman overnight.

When he turned to his grandfather, he saw he wasn't the only one caught off guard. Benicio was smiling, clearly recognizing Savannah, but their grandfather, who hadn't seen her in more than two years, shot Sean a look as if to say, "Who is this girl and why are you letting her into a Cabal office?"

Savannah strode past Thomas's bodyguards, who stared after her with looks Sean didn't like seeing directed at his sixteen-year-old sister.

A few feet from Benicio and their grandfather, Savannah whipped off her sunglasses with a dramatic flourish and a blinding smile.

"Grandpa!"

Recognition hit Sean's grandfather, first in a slack-jawed look of shock, then in a glower.

"I am not your grandfather, Savannah," he said.

"Oh." Her blue eyes widened. "I didn't mean *you*, Mr. Nast."

She crossed to Benicio, who embraced her.

"Shouldn't you be in school?" Benicio asked.

"I have a late lunch today, then a spare period, so I thought I'd swing by and see if Cassandra was still here, maybe talk her into taking me out to eat. Someplace nice. Cass might not eat, but she has great taste in restaurants." A wicked grin. "Expensive tastes."

"Well, I'm afraid Ms. DuCharme left a little while ago, but if you wait, Lucas and Paige will be here shortly. I'll take the three of you out for an early dinner." He smiled. "Someplace suitably trendy, I promise. First, though, we have some business to attend to."

"No problem." She glanced across the lobby. "So this is the new office, huh? Mind if I poke around? Make a nuisance of myself?"

Benicio gave her an indulgent smile. "Have fun."

A moment later, as they stepped onto the elevator, Thomas turned to Benicio.

"You're just going to let her 'poke around'? Unsupervised?"

"Of course. Savannah has free run of all the Cortez offices. She's my son's adopted daughter. That makes her family."

A guileless smile at Thomas, then Benicio stepped aside as his bodyguard pushed the second-floor button and the elevator doors closed.

* * *

Lucas and Paige arrived shortly after, and the meeting became a three-way struggle for control of the case, and Spencer Geddes with it.

Thomas argued that the West Coast was considered Nast territory, and this vampire's brutal public attack while Sean and his colleagues were in nearby Tacoma was clearly a slap in the face of the Nast Cabal. Quite possibly, it might even be a taunt, or a declaration of war.

Benicio dismissed both possibilities, but claimed that a problem in Middleton fell under the jurisdiction of the Cortez Cabal, which had the closest offices—in Seattle and now here in Portland.

Lucas and Paige declared that it didn't matter whose territory it was. The case might involve a vampire and *didn't* involve a Cabal, so it fell to the interracial council for resolution.

Lucas said, "Cassandra and my father agreed earlier that the council—as represented by Paige and Cassandra DuCharme—will allow Spencer Geddes to remain here, in custody, as long as we are permitted unhampered access and he is not mistreated."

Benicio's brows rose at the word *mistreated,* but when Lucas looked his way, as if challenging him to comment, he didn't.

"If this is council business," Thomas said, "then what are you doing here, Lucas? Interfering on their behalf?"

"I was hired—"

"Oh, that's right. The mysterious client, the one you won't allow anyone to contact, to confirm his existence."

Sean tensed, but neither Lucas's nor Paige's gazes flickered his way.

"All my clients are assured of complete confidentiality," Lucas said evenly. "I cannot break that confidence."

Not even if it meant losing control of the case. Losing control of Spencer Geddes. All to protect Sean's privacy.

Sean took a deep breath. "What if this client was asked to come forward?" He met Lucas's gaze. "If he understands that remaining quiet might hinder the case, he'd probably give up that right to confidentiality."

"And that would be his decision. But at this point I don't feel it would resolve this particular matter." Lucas turned to Thomas. "Am I correct, sir, in assuming you would not release your claim on Spencer Geddes if I produced my client?"

Thomas's expression answered for him. Whatever Sean might say, his grandfather wasn't going to drop the matter.

"I wasn't bluffing or trying to divert their attention," Sean said afterward, when they'd left the two older men alone and gone searching for Savannah.

"I know," Lucas said. "Your offer was sincere, as was my response. Revealing yourself to be my client will eliminate one excuse for them, but they will only find another to take its place. If you wish to tell them, I can't stop you, but I would ask that you ensure that no one thinks I encouraged you to come forward. That would make supernaturals wary of hiring me. If you have your own reason for wanting this information to be revealed, please consider attaining that end in another way. It will not help this case."

Sean felt his cheeks heat. Lucas kept walking, his gaze forward. Paige glanced his way with a small, sympathetic smile.

They knew.

With that, he lost any hope that discovering his presence in a gay bar might not make his family jump to the obvious conclusion. As soon as they had cause to wonder, they'd look at his dating history for reassurance—and they wouldn't find it.

He'd never been good at "playing straight." Rather than date women, he'd simply kept his romantic life private. Easy enough to do at college. Harder now that he was working full time in the Cabal. By their standards, it was time for him to marry and produce heirs. Before long, he'd need to make a decision.

He glanced at Lucas. Here was maybe the only person who could understand his situation. Lucas was a Cabal son himself, but—being outside the life—he would have no personal stake in any decision Sean might make. He longed to ask Lucas's opinion on the matter. Yet before he could work up the courage, they rounded the basement corner, heading toward the security cell, and heard Savannah's voice ahead.

13
LUCAS

SAVANNAH WAS TALKING TO KEPLER, THE young officer guarding Geddes. While nothing in her body language suggested blatant flirtation, she was giving Kepler her undivided attention and that, it seemed, was encouragement enough.

Kepler was no more than Sean's age and Savannah could—when she so desired—act mature enough to pass for eighteen. So Kepler's attentions were not inappropriate. That didn't mean I was eager to encourage them, though.

"I see you've met Savannah," I said as we drew up beside the pair. "My ward."

"And my sister," Sean said, injecting the words with the warning mine had lacked.

Kepler colored slightly. "I was just telling Miss, uh, Nast, er, Cortez."

"Levine," Paige said. "And yes, it's horribly confusing. Better just stick to first names." A smile for Kepler, then she turned to Savannah. "Shouldn't you be at school?"

Kepler's eyes widened. Flirting with a Cabal "daughter" might have an illicit allure, but he clearly didn't feel the same about a high school student.

"I had lunch, then a spare," Savannah said.

Paige made a show of checking her watch. "Can't have lasted this long."

"No, but Benicio told me to stick around and go for an early dinner with you guys. Can't argue with Benicio Cortez, right?"

"You can try that explanation on your teachers." She handed Savannah her keys. "The car's out back. Put your knapsack in. We'll head out to eat when Benicio and Mr. Nast are done."

Plans for an "early dinner" quickly became promises of a late one. We left word with my father that we'd be at home, and he could pick us up whenever he was ready.

The negotiations over Spencer Geddes and the case were not going well. Thomas Nast refused to cede authority to my father. Even with the most mundane of cases, this would not have surprised me.

The Nast and Cortez Cabals had been rivals for centuries. In the past few decades, that competition had hit its peak, with the title of "victor" in constant flux. The Cortez Cabal was the most powerful on the continent, which left the Nasts to accept "largest" as a consolation prize. To surrender their claim over Spencer Geddes would be to acknowledge the Cortezes as their superiors, which Thomas Nast was understandably loath to do.

Such things could usually be handled diplomatically, one side or the other surrendering control without loss of face. Here, though, the vampire angle added a dimension that ensured Thomas Nast would not back down willingly. So, by protocol, they had to consult the CEOs of the other two North American Cabals to attempt a resolution. If that failed, they'd call on the impartial inter-Cabal judges for full mediation.

Paige could have joined the fray, pressing her claim on behalf of the council. But as she put it: "Let 'em fight. Hopefully we'll have the case solved before they decide who it belongs to." Which was further proof that I'd married a very smart woman.

We'd just arrived in our driveway when my insurance contact called back.

"Billy Arnell had a quarter-of-a-million-dollar life-insurance policy," I said as we settled into the living room, where Cassandra had been reading the newspaper.

"Who's Billy Arnell?" Cassandra asked.

"The dead guy," Savannah said, sitting beside Cassandra. "Pay attention."

"Two hundred and fifty thousand isn't too shabby," Paige said. "Not suspiciously high for a guy that age with a wife, an ex-wife, and four kids. But it would be a nice chunk of change. So who gets it?"

"His current wife is the sole beneficiary."

"Ah, the grieving widow . . . who was in quite a hurry to get her dearly departed into the ground." She paused. "She works in retail, doesn't she?"

"A grocery store clerk."

"Probably not much hope of a hidden medical background there, but let's go see what we can find."

I left Paige to her Internet research. After about thirty minutes, she called me upstairs.

"I'm on a roll for lucky breaks today," she said as I walked in.

"Terri Arnell has a medical background?"

"No, but Middleton High has an incredible alumni site and grads with way too much free time."

She pointed at the screen as I sat down. "Meet Teresa—Terri—Arnell, nee Regis. We have her parents' names, her date of birth, educational highlights, careers past and present, husband's name—with a convenient link to *his* alumnus page—plus the name, birth dates, and pictures of their daughter, their current address . . ."

Paige shook her head. "An identity thief's wet dream. For our purposes, though, the information only rules out leads. Terri doesn't have any medical background. She graduated from high school and married Billy the next year—she was nineteen, he was thirty." She shuddered. "I really hope she wasn't his kids' babysitter. Anyway, all her regular jobs have been in retail, and her only listed volunteer activity is helping Billy's softball team."

"Hmm."

"My sentiments exactly. Far from promising. However—" She flipped to a page of graduate photos. "You saw a man at Terri's house. The one who stopped you from speaking to her. Did he give you a name?"

"No. I barely had a chance to give mine. It was a rather abrupt dismissal."

"Care to take a shot at finding him?"

I moved closer and started looking through the years surrounding Terri's graduation. No one seemed familiar. Then, in the graduating class two years before hers, I saw someone who did—the morgue assistant. But he wasn't the man who'd kept me from seeing Terri, so I was about to flip to the next year when I stopped.

"What was Terri's maiden name again?"

Paige clicked on the bookmark. Siblings: one sister and one brother. I clicked the link for her brother, and it took me to Greg Regis—the morgue assistant. According to his profile, Regis had been enrolled in medical school, but hadn't graduated. Now he worked in the hospital "with plans to resume his medical training."

"That explains how Terri got Billy's body released so quickly," Paige said.

"And it might explain why Regis was so eager to show me the photos 'proving' an animal attack, and to espouse an honest belief in the existence of the chupacabra."

We told Cassandra what we'd found.

"Good," she said. "So now you'll return to Middleton and prove this theory."

"That, I fear, would be difficult and likely dangerous. We have no right to be solving the case. That's the province of the Middleton police. All we can do is bring these links to their attention."

"Which you have?"

"Through my contact at the *Middleton Herald*. I explained my findings and asked his opinion. He was very intrigued by my discoveries, which he's going to pass along to his contact at the police station."

"And that will be enough?" Cassandra asked.

"I hope so."

When my father finally *did* take us out to dinner, only Paige and I joined him. Paige had persuaded Savannah to eat earlier. I appreciated that. Having Savannah around when my father explained about the Portland office would have been awkward. In her presence, I must be careful of the example I make, and I had a feeling that tonight it wouldn't be a good one.

My father knew Paige liked small, intimate bistros, so he'd selected the most exclusive one in Portland. Years ago, he'd learned that this favored political strategy—blatantly catering to a target's tastes and desires—didn't work on me. Yet when I fell in love with Paige, he'd found a way around that. I might refuse a trip to New York, but if he offered it *for Paige,* knowing how much she'd enjoy the break, how could I refuse?

Paige had been flattered, as most people were, thrilled that he'd taken pains to get to know her, proof that my father was working toward a better relationship with me. I'd known better.

I'd decided to let Paige figure it out for herself. While my decision had been rooted in my confidence in her intelligence, my silence had been a *betrayal* of trust only fully apparent after she found out. It did not, as I expected, take long. After the New York trip, she'd confessed her suspicions. When I'd been unsurprised by her conclusions, she'd realized I'd seen through my father's ploy all along.

Paige and I rarely argue. We might passionately debate outside matters—the progress of an investigation, the interpretation of facts, or some aspect of ethics—but on a personal level, we rarely squabble or fight. It is as if, recognizing that we both have enough external conflict to deal with, we wish to keep this one arena of our lives free from petty arguments. But when Paige found out that she'd been, as she put it, "played for a fool" as I'd "stood by and watched," I'd learned that trust truly is the cornerstone of a relationship and even the strongest one can be tested if you deliver a hard enough blow.

So in taking us out to a restaurant Paige would love,

my father committed a serious tactical error. He realized this when she ordered bisque and mineral water, and refused any wine or entrée, declaring she'd lost her appetite.

My father then switched strategies and began asking about Savannah—had she decided to pursue art postsecondary and if so, did she have any schools in mind? Safe conversation, designed to reduce any building antagonism. Paige was having none of it and deflected all queries to me. Then, when the entrées arrived, she said, "You put Adam—and me—in a very awkward position, Benicio."

My father opened his mouth.

She continued. "You gave Adam information he knew Lucas should have, and asked him not to pass it on. His only option was to ignore that. And my only option was to tell Lucas what he should have heard from you."

"That wasn't my intention."

"No, I'm sure it wasn't. You thought Adam was gullible enough to buy your story and keep his mouth shut. Your intention was to use him to sweeten the package before you presented it to Lucas—the same reason you designed those 'conjoined' offices for us."

My father blinked.

"Yes, we know who's supposed to occupy that main office. Next time you have a secret, make sure everyone working on it *realizes* it's a secret. But the point of those offices, like hiring Adam, was all part of your strategy. You knew Lucas would never accept a Cabal satellite office of his own. But one that offers employment for a newly graduated friend? Plus the chance to work with his wife?"

My father's gaze shot to me. "That wasn't—"

"Your intention," I finished. "It never is."

"I realize I may have handled this poorly, Lucas."

"There is no way such a thing could be handled well."

I cut into my salmon. "You have built a satellite office near my home. I can mitigate the damage by managing it myself, which ethically I'd never do. Yet if I refuse, then I accept—on behalf of my family—the danger of having the Cabal so close."

"That's not—" My father caught my gaze. "I wouldn't do that to you. This is merely a proposal—"

I arched my eyebrows. "A proposal? I believe that is the step that precedes construction, not follows it."

My father didn't miss a beat. "True, but in today's market, I could easily refit and resell the offices at a profit, which is exactly what I'll do if you don't wish to accept my offer."

"Then I'd suggest you call your real estate agent."

"I'm not asking you to manage a Cabal satellite office, Lucas. This is something altogether different."

"A new division for Cortez Corporation," Paige murmured, remembering Ibsen's earlier words.

My father nodded. "Yes, and that new division would be internal security. A Cabal watchdog. You'd continue to do exactly what you're doing now, except from within the organization, where you'd have complete access to Cabal resources and our full cooperation."

"That wouldn't work," I said.

"Why not? Law enforcement does it—policing their own. I recognize the capacity for abuse that is intrinsic in the Cabal structure. With power comes the temptation of abuse. I want to stop the worst offenders. The Cabals *must* do that to be the kind of organization the supernatural community needs. And you're the best person to help us reach that goal."

I suppose he expected me to thrill to those words. Knowing that made the knife dig in all the deeper, breaking through the scabs of old wounds, and I was a teenager again, accidentally discovering that Cabals weren't what he raised me to believe—a utopian communal organization for supernaturals, with the Cortez family as its beneficent leaders.

I could hear my father's voice again, dictating execution writs as casually as if he'd been ordering office supplies. Later, when we attempted reconciliation, I'd heard that same voice, lamenting the "abuses" within his organization, vowing to clean them up, as if they were a cancer that others had planted.

Today those abuses continued unabated. But now he was telling me *I* could change that. No longer a naïve child or an idealistic youth, I was a young man with delusions of knighthood—a condition best handled by satisfying those delusions.

Gotham is corrupt, son, and you're the only one who can save it.

"Paige?" I said, barely trusting myself to speak. "I think we should leave."

"I agree."

I led her out, my hand against her back. We had just stepped onto the sidewalk when my father strode up behind us, his bodyguards staying discreetly inside the glass doors.

"Lucas."

I kept walking, Paige beside me. My father fell into step on my other side.

"I know you're upset, but I hope you'll reconsider. Think what this office would mean for you. A steady income, less travel, and a chance to work with Paige, pursuing a goal you both believe in." He stepped in my path, then turned to face me. "This *is* what you want, isn't it?"

I stood there, gaping, unable to believe he'd so blatantly exploit my dreams and fears to satisfy his own agenda. I wanted to say something, but there was no calm or measured response that wouldn't sound like the tantrum of a hurt child.

Paige's warm fingers enveloped mine and she tugged my hand.

"Lucas? Please. Can we go? It's cold."

With that, she saved me from having to make any response. I could turn away from my father and busy myself taking off my coat and putting it around her shoulders, then lead her away.

My father didn't follow.

Once around the first corner, Paige tried to pass back my coat, but I refused. My blood was running too hot to need it.

We walked for three blocks in silence. Paige didn't try to get me to talk about it. She never did, knowing I would if and when I was ready. Nor was there any danger of her trying to downplay the situation by convincing me that my father hadn't meant to manipulate me or, worse, that I was overreacting.

Paige was the one person whom I could trust to understand my father's actions and how they would affect me. So we walked in silence, and it was enough to know she was there for me, as she always was. I don't think she'll ever know how much that means to me.

As we passed a small park, we took the path leading inside. I don't know if I led or she did. Perhaps neither, the choice being made by mutual understanding.

Back from the road, we found a gazebo sheltered by trees. Paige cast a questioning glance toward it, and I changed direction. Once inside, she led me to the most secluded spot on the benches.

I sat, and she eased onto my lap, her skirt hiked up as she straddled me. Her lips moved to mine and we kissed, her usual playfulness replaced by a sharper edge, an urgency I desperately needed.

Her hands soon slid down my shirt and undid my pants. She stroked me, her grip firm, bordering on rough, and everything else—every thought, every worry—fell away. When my fingers moved under her skirt to her panties, she worked them off. Then, after one last glance around, she lifted her skirt and arranged it to hide us, then slid down on me.

When we arrived home, via taxi, Savannah was asleep. Cassandra was still awake, which was to be expected. She slept little these days, a symptom of the condition she refused to acknowledge—her impending death.

She wanted to know whether I'd heard back from Sullivan at the *Middleton Herald*. I remembered then that I'd turned off my cell phone for dinner. When I checked, I found Sullivan had indeed called. The police had acted on his tip and must have already found the evidence they needed to support our theory, because as of midnight, Teresa Arnell, Greg Regis, and a second man had been arrested.

I phoned my father. He must have already been on a call because his voice mail came on immediately. I left a message and said if he needed more information to contact me tonight. Otherwise I'd be at the office by eight to oversee the vampire's release.

Cassandra was satisfied with this, so Paige and I headed upstairs. We engaged in more "physical therapy" before bed. By the time we finished, I could view the events of the evening calmly, too drained and sated to work up any emotional response.

"He's right," I said, lying in the dark. "That *is* what I want. What I dream of. Not within a Cabal, of course. But working together, in an office, here in Portland . . ."

Her fingers clasped mine.

I turned. "Do you know what I was thinking when I saw that office? I couldn't have designed it better myself."

"You know what I was thinking?" She looked over at

me. "With a shared office that big, we could fit in a futon and screen. Maybe even a bed."

I laughed, and her hand tightened on mine.

"That's the plan," she said softly. "We've always said so. Our 'someday' goal. What we're working toward. And we *will* get there. When we can. We have plenty of time."

I was fortunate enough to fall straight to sleep . . . only to be awoken thirty minutes later by my cell phone. As I checked it, Paige stirred beside me.

"Sorry. It's my father. Probably returning my call." I felt on the nightstand for my glasses. "I'll take it in the office."

"Stay," she said through a yawn, snuggling back down into her pillow.

I answered with "You got my message, I presume."

"I did, but that's not why I'm calling. Spencer Geddes escaped tonight. I need you down here."

I sat up. "I certainly hope you don't expect me to help look for him. In fact, in light of the arrests, I hope you *aren't* going to look for him. Perhaps this isn't the way you'd like his incarceration to end, and I'm sure you'll suffer some embarrassment with the Nasts because of it, but Spencer Geddes is an innocent man."

"No, Lucas, he isn't. He killed—"

"Unless you have substantial evidence to disprove the Middleton police's theory—"

"I don't mean that man in Middleton. In his escape, Geddes killed one of the guards. Gus Reichs."

14

SEAN

SEAN PAUSED OUTSIDE HIS UNCLE'S hotel room door. It was almost one, but they'd all been downstairs in the lounge until past midnight, so it was unlikely his uncle had retired yet. Still, Sean moved closer to the door, listening for sounds of activity.

And hoping you won't hear any, right? If he's sleeping, you can go back to bed and forget this whole thing.

But he didn't want to forget it. He'd spent the evening working up the nerve, and downing more Scotch than usual to find it.

Drinking "more than usual" a lot these days, aren't we?

Sean ignored the voice. If alcohol would get him through this, he'd take it.

He'd chosen to break the news first to Uncle Josef. This was the person least likely to judge and most likely to help him. He'd lost his own son to the vampire, Edward, and they'd grown closer since then—a son without a father and a father without a son.

Sean could hear no sounds from within, but he knocked anyway, lightly at first. When his uncle didn't answer, he swallowed and assessed his reaction. Relief mixed with disappointment, but heavier on the disappointment. So he knocked again, louder.

The door opened.

"Sean." His uncle smiled. "I was just in the washroom. Come in."

"I'm sorry to come by so late."

"No, no. I still have some work to do before I can even think about sleep." He walked toward the minibar, waving Sean to a chair in the sitting area. "Can I get you a drink?"

"Yes. I mean, no. I'm fine, thanks. I—" Deep breath. "I came by to tell you that I know who hired Lucas Cortez to investigate the Middleton murder."

He paused, waiting for his uncle to ask *how* he knew. Instead, his uncle smiled, then walked over and thumped him on the back before taking a seat.

"I knew it. I told your grandfather. He *wanted* to believe it, but I don't think he dared."

"Wanted to believe . . . ?"

"The reason you've been getting cozy with your half—sorry, *alleged* half sister. I told your grandfather that you're a clever lad. What better way to keep an eye on Lucas Cortez than to befriend his ward?"

"You think I spend time with Savannah to spy on Lucas?"

His uncle raised his glass in a dismissive wave. "*Spy* is a harsh word. Keep tabs on him. And it paid off this time. I'm not sure whether knowing the name of his client will help, but it certainly can't hurt."

"I'm the client, Uncle Josef."

His uncle stopped, glass in midair. Then he swore and smacked it down on the table. For a moment, his uncle said nothing, and Sean held his breath, watching his uncle's face for his reaction.

"We can work with this," his uncle said after a moment. "Your grandfather doesn't need to know the truth—"

"I think he does."

His uncle met his gaze, expression hard. "No, Sean,

he doesn't. Your father had a sentimental streak when he was younger. He had . . . ideas. About the treatment of witches, vampires, werewolves. He wasn't a bleeding heart like Lucas Cortez, but he argued for some changes. Your grandfather cured him of those ideas quickly enough."

Sean flushed. "My father has nothing to do with my choices. It isn't even a choice. I didn't wake up one morning and think—"

"Of course you didn't. You came by it honestly, that's all I'm saying. You read about this chupacabra attack when we were in Tacoma, and you knew we'd see it. So you hired Lucas to investigate, to ensure this vampire got a fair trial."

Sean eased back in his chair. "You think I hired Lucas because I read—?"

"A problem easily solved. We'll admit to your grand-father that you're responsible for Lucas's investigation only because you read that article and, in stopping by to check on Savannah, you mentioned it to them. Casually. But Lucas, always looking for a battle to fight, saddled up and rode out to save the vampires. Not your fault."

And here, Sean realized, was a solution to his di-lemma. He could declare himself the cause of the inves-tigation without coming out. A few days ago, he'd have seized the chance. But now? It wasn't an option now. The end was close, and he was determined to get there.

"I hired Lucas because I was there, at the scene of the crime. I found the body, and I didn't want anyone to know it."

His uncle nodded. "Because you didn't want to get in-volved?"

"No, because of where the body was found. In a gay bar." Sean paused, then pushed on, forcing the words out. "I'm gay."

His uncle lifted his glass and took a long drink. His

expression was somewhat guarded, but mainly just thoughtful.

"So it's true, then," he murmured after a long moment of silence.

"You knew?"

His uncle laid the glass down. "There have been rumors for years, Sean. Even when you were young, when your cousins were ogling girls at the beach, you barely bothered to look. How old were you when you stopped dating altogether? Sixteen, seventeen? Do you think no one noticed?"

Sean felt his hands trembling on the chair arms. Trembling with relief. All this time, they'd known, and nothing had changed. He'd been a fool to hide it.

"So Granddad knows?" he said.

"Of course not. Nor will he."

"But— I can't—"

His uncle leaned forward. His blue eyes went ice cold, like his father's when he'd give a subordinate an order he didn't want questioned. "What you do in your personal life is your own business, Sean. You will not make it the family's business. You will do what every Nast son is expected to do. You will marry, and you will produce heirs. This is your responsibility to your family."

"My responsibility? To trick some woman into marrying me?"

"No woman needs to be 'tricked' into marrying a Nast. You have wealth and power. I'm sure you'll have no problem finding a wife, even if you tell her the truth."

"But I— I'm not attracted to women. I can't—"

"We all have to do things we don't like."

Sean could only stare, unable to believe what he was hearing.

His uncle patted him awkwardly on the shoulder. "I'll get you that drink now."

As Sean sat there, stunned into silence, someone knocked. It was his grandfather's executive assistant.

"Sir?" She saw Sean across the room. "Oh, good, you're both here. You're both needed in Mr. Nast's room as soon as possible. Something's happened at the Cortez office."

His uncle promised they'd be there. As he closed the door, Sean's shock finally faded, and he stood.

"I'm sorry if you don't agree with my choices, Uncle Josef, but—"

His uncle lifted a hand. "Before you continue, Sean, I'd like you to remember that you aren't the only one affected by your 'choices.' Imagine what your grandfather will think if he learns you found this victim in Middleton. A Cabal son, tripping over a vampire kill? Hardly a coincidence, I'm sure."

"Yes, it was, because it *wasn't* a vampire kill."

"According to who?" His uncle's face hardened. "Vampires are a threat to us all, Sean. I know that better than anyone. Give me the excuse, and I'll have your grandfather believing he almost lost another grandson to the beasts."

"That's not—"

"Fair? Let's talk about fair, Sean. Would it be fair for you to do this to your family? To rob your grandfather of another grandson? How will Bryce cope without you to guide him? He doesn't have what it takes to be in business. Without you, he'll fail. You'd do that to them for the sake of personal gratification?"

"Personal grat—?"

"Enough." His uncle strode across the room. "We have business to attend to." At the door, he glanced over his shoulder and met Sean's gaze. "This conversation is over, and I never want to resume it. Is that understood?"

His uncle left before Sean could answer.

15

LUCAS

WHEN WE ARRIVED IN THE PARKING lot, a dark-haired man the size of a linebacker stood in the delivery door alcove, waiting for us.

"Hey, Troy," Paige said. "How are you doing?"

"Shocked. I used to work with Reichs when I was back in general security. Good guy." He glanced at me. "Your dad's inside. Gotta go around. The back door's part of the crime scene."

"Care to fill us in?" I said as we circled to the front.

While my father would reiterate the story, Troy could be counted on to provide the least biased version.

According to Troy, he and his partner, Griffin, had accompanied my father here after dinner last night so my father could make a few calls from the secured landline. Before leaving, my father went downstairs to check with the guards. They'd discovered Reichs dead in Geddes's empty cell and found the other guard, Kepler, regaining consciousness by the back door. Geddes was gone.

"What does Kepler say?" I asked as we reached the front door.

"Not much. He's pretty confused. Banged up his leg, too. Your dad has him resting on a cot upstairs while he flies in a Cabal doctor."

My father met us just inside the door. As he retold the story, Troy fell back to give us privacy.

"While this is a tragedy, it's a tragedy of the Cabal's

making," I said when my father finished. "You confined a vampire for a crime, with absolutely no proof that he had committed it. You failed to release him when others were charged with that crime. You've given vampires no reason to trust Cabals, so when Geddes saw a chance to escape, he seized it. I'd suggest time allocated to hunting him could be better spent on an internal review of the situation."

"Right now, finding Spencer Geddes isn't at the top of anyone's agenda," my father said. "In fact, the Nasts would rather we didn't look at all. The first thing they did on hearing the news was to call an emergency Cabal conference to vote on the St. Cloud proposal."

Paige looked over sharply. "Reichs mentioned that. What is it?"

"The St. Clouds have proposed declaring all vampires dangerous offenders. Those living on American soil would be given thirty days to evacuate. Then—" He paused. "Those who remain would be executed."

I would like to say that the details of the St. Cloud proposal came as a shock. They didn't.

I'd heard rumblings of similar ideas even before Edward's rampage. Afterward, the rumbles had surged to roars, but only temporarily, before my father and others managed to stifle them and deflect attention to other matters.

To the council and the vampire community, such talk had been temporary fear mongering, too ludicrous to take seriously. Yes, Edward had killed innocent supernaturals, but others had done the same many times. Three years ago, a disgruntled Cabal employee had set fire to a Cabal satellite office and killed eight coworkers. Afterward, no one had suggested exiling and executing all half-demons.

Yet vampires were different. Like werewolves, they

were inherently dangerous. Like werewolves, there were so few of them that an exile could be enforced. But rarely did anyone suggest that werewolves be exiled or exterminated.

The excuse for the different treatment was that one *needed* to kill and the other didn't. Vampires had to take a life a year to prolong their own existence. For werewolves, bloodlust was merely an extension of their predatory nature, and could be controlled. The werewolf Pack did not condone man-eating, and promptly punished offenders, so while the Cabals might fear werewolves, they had little reason to act against them.

The deeper reason for the prejudice, though, was that vampires posed a theoretical threat to Cabal power. Unlike werewolves, vampires resented being kept out of Cabal life. They had an innate sense of entitlement, reinforced by their semi-immortality and invulnerability. Shouldn't they, not sorcerers, stand at the apex of the supernatural world?

Most prominent vampires, like Cassandra and Aaron, had no interest in running a supernatural corporation, so the threat of a vampire uprising remained unrealized. Yet a threat it remained. Here was the perfect opportunity to dispel it . . . and few supernaturals would complain.

The other two Cabals were expected in Portland by dawn. That meant Paige and I had only those few hours to investigate before they swept us aside. While we had little hope of exonerating Spencer Geddes, we might at least be able to reconstruct the events before the Cabals did their own creative reconstruction.

My father gave us full access to Kepler and the crime scene, along with the services of the crime-scene technician he was flying in with the doctor. He didn't support the St. Cloud proposal, so he had little reason to block me.

The doctor and crime-scene technician arrived shortly thereafter. The technician was a shaman named Simon—a man I'd worked with before, which smoothed the process.

Reichs's body had been found inside Spencer Geddes's cell. He'd been bitten, but that wasn't the cause of death. It takes time to drain a man's blood, and Geddes could hardly afford to do that with Kepler presumably nearby. Geddes would have only bitten Reichs to render him unconscious and kill him. Then Geddes had gone upstairs, encountered Kepler, disabled him with a bite, then fled.

All the evidence Simon found supported this theory, including the bite marks in Reichs's neck. This was no repeat of the chupacabra killing—a "bloodthirsty monster" blamed for a human attack. Spencer Geddes had bitten these men. But there were still questions.

How had Geddes managed to get Reichs into the cell in the first place? If the bite disabled Reichs, why strangle him? If he felt the need to kill Reichs, why not Kepler? Was there an element of self-defense? Of provocation? If there was anything to be said in Geddes's defense, I needed to find it—quickly.

The doctor had examined Kepler and confirmed the bite on his neck did, like Reichs's, come from a vampire. Kepler's leg, while badly bruised, did not appear to be broken, so there was no need to fly him to Miami for further examination. We were then free to interview him.

We started with inquiries into Kepler's health and condolences on the death of his superior officer. Paige had brought coffee and a pastry assortment from down the road, and by the time we launched into our questions, Kepler's initial nervousness had vanished.

"This is what I was doing when Geddes escaped," he said, lifting his coffee cup. "Caffeine run, probably from the same place. Mr. Cortez lets us do that, as long as one person stays with the prisoner and stays away from the cell."

"Was there a scheduled time for your coffee runs?" I asked.

"Nah, just whenever we needed the boost or the break."

"You say you were warned to stay away from Spencer Geddes when the other was gone."

"Uh-huh. To avoid being hypnotized . . . or whatever it is vamps do."

"Do you know why Reichs would break that rule?"

Kepler dropped his gaze. "No, sir."

A lie, but I pushed onward. "And then you returned . . ."

"I came in through the back door. The vampire was right there, like he'd heard me. I went for him, but he pushed me over a pile of boxes and that must be how I hurt my leg. I don't remember. Next thing I knew, I was waking up in the back hall when you guys found me."

"Do you have any idea why Geddes would kill Reichs? He'd disabled him and could have simply taken his gun for self-defense."

"Well, sir, he is a vampire. They don't like us. He probably killed Reichs just because he could. Maybe revenge for getting locked up."

"Then why not kill you, too?"

As I held Kepler's gaze, he reddened. "I—I don't like to speak ill of the dead, sir. Reichs was a great guy. He taught me a lot. He just . . . He didn't like vampires. A lot of us don't."

"But Reichs didn't bother to hide it," Paige murmured, remembering his comments the night they captured Geddes.

"Did Reichs make his feelings known to Geddes?" I asked.

Gaze down again, Kepler nodded. "He liked to taunt him. He told him about the St. Cloud proposal. Told him it didn't matter what you guys found, the Cabals planned to execute him. Geddes would get so mad. . . . It scared me, sir. I wondered if I should tell anyone, but I didn't want to get Reichs in trouble."

Kepler went silent and I let him.

After a moment, he said, "I think that's why Reichs was near the cell. He knew it made me uncomfortable— teasing the vampire like that—so he was doing it while I wasn't there. That's probably why Geddes killed him, too. Reichs pushed him too far."

A few minutes later, my father came in to tell us the St. Clouds' plane had landed. The meeting would begin in an hour. Now it was time to take a step we both dreaded: telling Cassandra.

Paige phoned and told her about the St. Cloud proposal. If Cassandra was surprised, she gave no sign. Cassandra was adroit enough to know such a threat had always been possible. She wanted to be at the meeting, of course, which we'd foreseen, and my father had agreed to.

Before Paige signed off, she said, "Quick question. We're trying to figure out how Spencer Geddes's cell got opened. We know Reichs was alone with him at the time and may have approached the cell. Could Geddes have charmed him into opening it?"

Paige listened to Cassandra's answer, interjecting a few "uh-huh" and "I see" responses.

When she hung up, she turned to me. "Short answer? No."

I nodded. "Because vampires charm not by hypnotizing their prey, but by inducing a highly suggestible state. Meaning if Reichs had no desire to open that door, Geddes couldn't make him do it."

"Begging the question: What would ever possess a guy to open the door for a pissed-off vampire?"

16
SEAN

SEAN SAT AT THE MEETING TABLE BEtween his uncle and his grandfather and, at that moment, it was the last place he wanted to be.

His uncle's words still burned. *Suck it in and do your duty to the family.* As incredibly insensitive as that was, his uncle had made one valid point. If Sean left the Cabal, he'd hurt the two people he cared about most: Bryce and his grandfather.

With his uncle's words, any fantasy of being accepted by his family had evaporated. They *did* accept it . . . as long as he didn't let his sexual orientation stand in the way of his duties to marry and have children. The need to provide heirs was just an excuse—any gay man could still have children via surrogacy. But Nasts had to uphold the Cabal culture of machismo. Being gay wasn't an option.

So Sean was trapped between two impossible choices: abandoning his family or living a lie. This wasn't a choice to be made today, or even this month; perhaps not for years. Yet he knew one thing. He wouldn't play the hypocrite. He wouldn't flaunt it, but neither would he date women and marry.

Things would eventually come to a head. But for now, he'd start carving his own path, making the decisions that were right for him rather than the ones that would make the fewest waves. In some ways, he'd already been doing that—as with his relationship with Savannah— but he'd no longer feel guilty or torn.

The meeting got off to an explosive start a few minutes later when Lucas and Paige joined them. The grumbles rose to ill-concealed gasps of surprise and grunts of outrage when Cassandra DuCharme followed them in. The few who hadn't met her after the Edward and Natasha problem were promptly educated by their neighbors, and a fresh round of shock and outrage surged.

Cassandra's gaze lighted on Sean's with a faint frown. He'd met her several times, and always got the same look, as if she wasn't sure whether she should know him. He smiled and she nodded, favoring him with a faint, regal smile.

Frank Boyd pushed to his feet. "This is most inappropriate—"

"I know," Cassandra said. "It's rude of me, and I apologize. It's much simpler to condemn a race when one of them isn't sitting in the room."

Benicio rose and pulled out a chair on his left as he gestured for Lucas and Paige to sit at his right. Cassandra took her place and removed a leather-bound notebook from her purse, then a gold pen. When she looked up to see everyone watching her, she smiled.

"Please, proceed. Consider me merely an observer. I'm most interested to hear what you have to say on this matter."

And so the discussion began, not flowing and rising to the fever pitch of impassioned debate, but limping along. It was indeed harder to condemn all vampires when one was sitting there listening. Especially when that vampire wasn't a belligerent asshole like Spencer Geddes, but the sort of attractive, well-mannered woman you could imagine gracing the halls of your own organization.

When Lionel St. Cloud's nephew, Phil, began reading his prepared notes on vampire behavior, his gaze kept shooting to Cassandra, clearly not as confident in his facts as he'd been when he wrote them.

"May I?" Cassandra said. "I believe I'm something of an expert on the subject."

Phil nodded and Cassandra began a thorough, dispassionate explanation of vampire life: their powers, their feeding habits, and their required annual kill. Even the last she explained with no apology or emotion, as if it was a simple fact of their life. When asked how they chose their victims, her answer was equally honest and neutral. Vampires ranged from those who used their annual kill to stop criminals, to those who selected the elderly and ill, to those who just picked random strangers.

Vampires killed people. An indisputable fact. Move along. So they did.

Discussion then swung back to known cases of vampire attacks on Cabal members. The St. Clouds and Sean's uncle trotted out every suspected case in the last two hundred years. A few weeks ago, Sean would have stayed silent. Not today.

Sean signaled for the floor. When his request was granted, he stood.

"And how does that compare, per capita, to half-demon attacks? Or sorcerer attacks? Maybe we can break it down further, save ourselves having to punish all vampires. Is it the women? The whites? The middle-aged?"

"Sean," his uncle warned under his breath.

"No, this is silly. It's prejudice and fear and we all know it. Even if we knew that fifty percent of white, middle-aged female vampires will kill a Cabal employee in their lifetimes, how does that justify punishing all of them?"

"And there is another point to consider," Benicio said, his voice soft but carrying through the room. "While Sean makes a valid case from a humanitarian stand-point, we must also consider the political ramifications of exiling all vampires. First, it will damage our relations with Cabals in other countries. We don't want vampires here, so we send them there. Beyond that, let's think this through." Benicio eased back in his chair. "So we exile all vampires. If I'm a werewolf, that would make me nervous. While a vampire has the advantage of invul-nerability, their physical threat is minimal compared to that of a werewolf fearful of losing his territory. So we'll need to exterminate them, too. Now who is a danger? Witches? Powerful sorcerers living outside the Cabal? With each step, we anger a larger group and reduce the overall supernatural population. Hardly good business sense."

The debate continued. While Sean would love to believe his speech had some effect, he knew Benicio Cortez's argument—the coldly political one—would carry more weight.

"One thing we're forgetting," his uncle said, "is the need for decisive action. If we hesitate, these vampires will—"

A discreet rap at the door. One of Benicio Cortez's bodyguards poked his head in.

"Sorry, Mr. Cortez, but—"

Savannah slipped past the guard, who made only a token attempt to stop her. The sophisticated young woman Sean had seen the day before had vanished, re-placed by the Savannah he knew better—wearing sneakers and jeans, her hair in a ponytail, no makeup. Her face was flushed, eyes anxious. Sean pushed his chair back.

"Sorry," she said, "but I have to talk to Paige. It's about the murder."

Sean, closest to her, started to rise. His uncle laid a hand on his arm, a clear warning that while Sean could privately acknowledge Savannah, he should not do so here.

Sean slipped from his uncle's grasp and went to his sister. Paige and Lucas were right behind him.

"I think I know why that guard went into Geddes's cell," Savannah whispered, too low for the others to hear. "And I think it's my fault."

17

LUCAS

Cassandra stayed in the meeting room, not giving the Cabal heads a chance to debate behind her back.

Paige led Savannah past the bodyguards assembled in the hall. Troy leaned over to murmur something as they passed, then pointed, directing her to a room where we could speak in private.

As Sean closed the office door behind us, Savannah said to Paige, "I heard you and Cassandra talking on the phone about whether Geddes could have charmed the guard. After she left, I remembered something. When I was talking to the younger guard, he was going on about vampires, trying to impress me with what he knew." She rolled her eyes. "Most of it was the kind of stuff you'd find in pulp novels. A supernatural—even a half-demon—should know better."

"So you set him straight," Paige said, crossing her arms. She gave Savannah a look that said she knew Savannah had done no such thing.

"Hey, if someone's that ignorant, it's not my job to straighten him out."

"You played along."

"Right, then he started going on about how he'd heard vampire saliva was a really strong aphrodisiac, that vampires used it to seduce their victim. Stupidest thing I've ever heard. So I . . . you know . . ."

"Played along. And played it up. Playing him for a fool."

"Yeah. I told him he was right. We got to talking about how you could collect the saliva, waiting until the vampire was asleep and using a swab." She looked at Paige. "It was a stupid thing to do. I just got carried away."

"Seeing how far you could take it."

Her cheeks colored. "Yeah. But I never figured he'd actually do it. He was terrified of Geddes—of all vampires. I guess he must've told the other guard."

"The one who wasn't nearly as frightened of them," Paige said. "And who decided to collect some himself."

We split up again. Aaron was arriving from Atlanta in an hour, so I'd meet him at the airport, then we'd head to Seattle and see whether we could find Geddes or some sign of where he'd gone. His story would answer our remaining questions . . . if we could persuade him to give it. Sean offered to help, so we'd take him along.

Meanwhile, Paige would escort Savannah to school by taxi, then return to the house where she and Cassandra would review our notes, looking for any missed leads.

They left immediately. Sean had to speak to his grandfather first. While I waited, I wandered the second floor and ended up, not surprisingly, in the office meant for Paige and me.

Last night, Paige had said we were working toward this. I was certain that if I delved into her financial records, I'd find a "Cortez Winterbourne Investigations" fund. And my "Cortez Winterbourne Investigations" fund? It existed solely in my head, at the top of the list of "things I'll do when I get ahead."

In law school, I'd seen this—husbands and wives toiling at substandard jobs to put their spouses through school. Then it would be their turn. I was like the floundering D student who'd never passed the bar, but just kept plugging along, blinded and selfish, letting my spouse support my dreams.

How much longer would Paige wait for her turn?

I wanted to give her this office. This building.

Oh, it's too big, she'd say. *Too fancy.* But even as she was figuring out what rooms could be rented, she'd be dreaming of the day when we'd need all this space.

I could see her walking through our office, pointing out what would go where, talking about how we'd divide the cases, about what staff and supplies we'd need. Overwhelmed by the work to come, but absolutely in her element.

At a sound behind me, I spun, certain it was Paige coming back. I flushed with guilt at being caught here, daydreaming.

"I was just—" I began, then saw it was my father. "I was looking for Sean. Have you seen him?"

"No, but—"

"I should find him. We have work to do."

"A moment, Lucas, please." He laid his hand on my

arm. "I know you think I'm trying to trap you with this—" A wave around the office. "But I'm not. I'm honestly trying to help."

"I'm sorry, Father, but I need to—"

His grip tightened. "Things aren't working out as you'd hoped with Paige. You're married to a strong, independent young woman who can take care of herself. Which is fine . . . except you're just as independent and don't want her taking care of *you*."

"It's a temporary problem, which I intend to resolve—"

"How? Take a full-time job at a law firm? You'd be miserable . . . and Paige wouldn't allow it. Refusing clients who can't pay? Whatever drives you to do this, I planted the seed. I want to help. This is my solution."

"Join the Cabal? Become part of the problem?"

"No, become the solution. You'd be an independent division—"

"But still within the Cabal structure."

"Only financially, and with no obligations placed on your allotted budget. You'd have full power to prosecute offenders—"

"*From within* the Cabal. Almost all my clients come from outside Cabals."

"And that's how you will subsidize your operating budget—by taking on paying clients. You'll have the facilities and the staff to pursue and attract new clients."

"How many supernaturals in trouble with a Cabal will hire a company with Cortez Cabal on the letterhead?"

"We'll be more discreet than that, of course."

"Which will only look like deception when they find out who's underwriting the firm."

My father didn't even blink. "Your reputation will overcome that, Lucas. And you'll have the option to buy the business from me whenever you wish."

There it was. The carrot on the stick. The antidote to the pain of delayed gratification. Have what I wanted—this office—today and make no payments until . . . whenever.

I didn't need a crystal ball to foretell the future of this deal. I'd take the office with every intention of buying it in a few years. But then I'd see my paying clientele dwindle, frightened off by the specter of my Cabal association. My outside work would be primarily pro bono, meaning we'd see no profit . . . and the cost of the business would continue to escalate, flying beyond reach.

"No, Papá," I said. "I understand that you're trying to help, but this is a problem that I need to resolve myself."

I found Sean looking for me. On the drive to the airport, we discussed Cabal life or perhaps more "non-Cabal" life—what it was like to be a Cabal son living outside the organization. I suspected he was trying to get a sense of what it might be like for him, should he be forced into that situation, but I didn't pry, just answered his questions as honestly as I could.

As we arrived, my cell phone rang. It was Sullivan from the *Middleton Herald*. Terri Arnell's boyfriend had cut a deal, implicating the others and providing evidence. So the case was officially solved . . . and it was disheartening to realize how little that mattered now, how far things had escalated beyond the murder of a factory worker in Middleton, Washington.

Aaron's plane was delayed. As Sean went to buy us coffees, I was left alone with my thoughts and, as hard as I tried to turn them to the questions surrounding Reichs's death, they kept sliding back into forbidden territory: the Portland satellite office.

Was there any way Paige and I could manage this

without becoming employees of the Cortez Cabal? Had Paige put aside enough to make a down payment on the business? Would he sell it, as he'd claimed? Or would he set the price so high we'd never afford a down payment? But even if we *could* make it, Paige would have to cover the monthly payments while the business struggled to its feet.

No, this time the sacrifices had to be mine. Could we rent the building? Agree to provide internal security investigation work to ensure the steady income needed to pay the rent? This would be a slippery slope but if it was the only solution . . .

The answer came to me so fast I inhaled sharply. There *was* a solution—one I'd trained myself never to consider. Yet under the circumstances, it was a compromise of ideals I was ready to make, if my father would agree.

As Sean returned with the coffees, I called home. Cassandra answered.

"Cassandra, it's Lucas. Aaron's flight has been delayed. Is Paige there?"

"You just missed her. She headed back to the Cabal office to check something about the case."

I frowned. "Is she hoping to meet Simon there? He isn't. But she should know that—they were planning to all go to breakfast after we left."

"Well, she certainly didn't share her plans with me. Something about discrepancies and coffee cups and taunting. You know how Paige is. She gets going and no one can understand her, let alone stop her."

"Coffee cups and . . . ?"

"Taunts. Apparently the young guard said Mr. Reichs was taunting Spencer Geddes, and Paige asked me if Spencer complained about it."

"Did he?"

"No, and he was hardly the type to play silent stoic."

"Meaning, Kepler lied. And Kepler said he'd gone for coffee, but I'll wager Paige couldn't find any mention of coffee cups in Simon's crime scene report."

"She tried to call you, but couldn't get through."

"And now she's heading to the office knowing the only person there is Kepler himself."

"Going to confront him? Surely Paige wouldn't be so—" Cassandra stopped. "How far are you from that office?"

"I'm on my way."

18
LUCAS

I LEFT SEAN TO AWAIT AARON. I PHONED Paige's cell, but only got Cassandra again. Paige had been in such a rush to get a cab that she'd left her phone behind.

I would like to believe that Paige would never do anything as foolhardy as confront a potential killer in an empty building, but I wasn't so sure. She would see Kepler as a handicapped opponent, still weak and injured. Perhaps she hadn't jumped to the conclusion that he could be the killer, but merely viewed him as an unreliable witness.

I didn't know what had happened in that cell, but I was reasonably certain now that it hadn't been Reichs who'd gone in to collect that vampire saliva. I also suspected it hadn't been Geddes who killed Reichs. He'd simply rendered his captives unconscious with bites.

Kepler must have recovered first and killed Reichs. But why? The possibilities were endless—a personal vendetta, paving the way for promotion, starting a Cabal-vampire war. . . .

I reached the Cabal office in record time. My father had promised to leave the rear door open for us, should we need to return to investigate. I slipped inside and eased it shut behind me.

I used a light spell to guide me through the back halls to the stairs. On the second floor, they exited near the main office. A few doors down was the room where Kepler had been recuperating.

That door was open. And the bed was empty. I paused there a moment, heart hammering. Then I heard the faint sound of Paige's voice, sharp with irritation, coming from down the hall.

I recast my blur spell and slid along the wall to a closed door. It was the room we'd earlier used for the meeting. Paige's voice came from within.

I cracked the door open. Then I started a binding spell, ready to kick the door open and cast it—

A second voice sounded . . . but not the one I expected. It was my father answering, his words indistinct through the heavily soundproofed walls.

Something hard and cold pressed against the back of my neck.

"Don't move," Kepler whispered. "Say one more word of that spell, and I swear to God I'll pull this trigger. Don't think I won't."

Kepler's voice was pitched high, as if trying to convince himself. The gun barrel trembled against my neck. The only thing more dangerous than a determined gunman is a nervous one. I swallowed the spell and closed my mouth.

"We're going to turn around and head for the stairs."

I didn't question. Better to play along and let him lower his guard.

"Don't think I won't kill you," Kepler said as we reached the stairwell. "In for a penny, in for a pound."

He gave a high, shaky laugh and pushed open the door with his foot, guiding me through with the gun.

"You mean that having killed Reichs, you're quite prepared to take another life," I said as we started down the stairs.

An obvious ploy to get him talking and distract him, but few criminals can resist the urge to explain. It's as if they're waiting for the opportunity to unburden themselves, impressing me with their cleverness or winning my sympathy with their excuse.

"It was Reichs's fault," he said. "He was supposed to be out getting coffee. The vampire was asleep, and I'd slipped in to get something from him. But then Reichs came back early, and he saw me and started shouting."

"And woke up Geddes."

"Right. And then . . . Goddamn it, Reichs got me all confused. He was yelling at me to get out of the way so he could take a shot, and then the vampire shoved me into the chair and I hurt my leg, and I was there on the floor when he attacked Reichs."

I could envision it. Kepler, on the ground, armed but doing nothing to help his comrade. Intent on saving himself. Training forgotten. Survival taking over. An inexcusable mistake for a security officer.

"Then he came after me," Kepler continued. "He bit me and I passed out."

"But you woke first."

Kepler gave me a shove to the bottom landing. "I didn't mean to kill Reichs." He pushed open the door and prodded me out. "I was just so mad, thinking it was all his fault, that I was going to lose my job, probably even be charged, all because he had to play cowboy, rescuing me from a vampire."

"A vampire who hadn't touched you," said a voice behind us. "And probably wasn't planning to."

Kepler whirled, hand still on my arm, whipping me around with him, gun still to my neck. Cassandra advanced on us.

"S—stay back, lady," Kepler said. "This is none of your business. I've got a gun."

"So I see," she said, still walking.

I started to cast, but Kepler swung the gun from me and fired at Cassandra. The bullet hit her in the chest. She staggered, grimaced, shook it off, and continued her advance. Kepler's finger tightened on the trigger, then stopped, caught in a binding spell. I followed it with an energy bolt that knocked him off his feet. Then I leapt onto his back, grabbing for the gun first, wrenching it from his fingers and sending it skating over the floor. Kepler reared, trying to fight, but I pinned him with his hands behind his back.

The stairwell door opened and my father and Paige flew through.

"The situation, I believe, is under control," I said.

Ten minutes later, Paige and I were in a closed office, Troy and Griffin having taken custody of Kepler and placed him in the cell he'd once guarded while my father contacted the other Cabals with the news.

Paige had come to the office to see my father and discuss her findings with him, having called and found he was still there.

"You thought I came to confront Kepler?" she said. "By myself? Please. Give me a little credit."

"Well, you can be somewhat impetuous . . ."

"That's not impetuous. It's stupid." She put her arms around my neck. "I was being very careful, which is more than I can say for the guy who came rushing in here to rescue me without backup, without even checking to make sure the building was *empty*. Troy and Griffin were right downstairs in the lobby, if you'd bothered to check."

"I was concerned for your safety."

She rolled her eyes, face tilted to mine. "Ah, so when I act without thinking, I'm impetuous. If you do it, you're chivalrous. Well, Cortez, your chivalry could have gotten you killed."

"Hardly. I had the situation under control."

"Uh-huh."

"I did. As Kepler was talking, I was compiling a list of escape possibilities, starting with—"

She pressed her mouth to mine, cutting off my explanation and, after a moment, I realized it wasn't really that important.

19
LUCAS

Two days later, the dust had settled. The Cabals had still voted on the St. Cloud proposal but only the Nasts had supported it. The matter would not rest forever. For now, though, all was quiet.

That night, after we'd retired, I told Paige about my own proposal.

She listened quietly, taking it all in, then said, "Are you okay with that?"

"I am."

She sat up in bed. "Are you sure? Because I know this is something you've said you'd never do . . ."

"Does it disappoint you that I am?"

She shook her head. "If you're ever going to do it, this is definitely the right reason. I just want to be sure you aren't feeling pressured into it. We can wait, get something in a few years—"

"I want to do this."

"Then I guess the next step is finding out whether your dad will go for it."

And that, indeed, was likely the biggest sticking point.

I'd invited my father to breakfast. I went alone.

Halfway through the meal, I said, "I'd like to discuss the office situation."

"You've come to a decision."

"We have. You said that if I took this office now, I could someday buy it from you. Would that offer stand now?"

"You mean, would I sell it to you now?" He leaned back, sighing softly. "I hope you aren't thinking of taking out a loan. The operating costs alone could equal or outweigh loan payments, and I don't want to see you and Paige saddled with that—"

"I mean buying it outright." I met his gaze. "With my trust fund."

He blinked. To me, my trust fund has always been off-limits. It was an unwanted inheritance from a corporation I wanted no part of. But, as Paige said, if I was ever to use it, this was the right way—Cabal money to build a firm to defend supernaturals, investigate Cabal injustices, and rebuild the power of the interracial council.

"Do you have enough?" he said. "Not just to buy the building, which I'm sure you can afford, but operating costs *will* be heavy in the early years, Lucas, and I know your brothers were badly hit when stocks sank a few years back. If you don't have at least half of your original five million . . ."

"I invested rather conservatively," I said. "A choice that saw me through the dips with minimal impact and, in subsequent years, paid off quite well. I have just over seven million."

He smiled. "I should have known. Well, then, as finances are not a concern, let me make a few calls and we'll see what we can do."

We agreed on a figure. It was not a bargain—my father knew I'd balk at any hint of getting a deal and therefore being indebted to him. But neither did he attempt to overprice it and frighten me off. It was a fair deal.

Any custom work needed would be finished by my father's crew, and was included in the price. Then Paige and I would complete construction, and save money by slowing the pace and choosing modest fittings and furnishings. The frugal choice, as always, which suited us both.

Later that same day, I brought Paige over and took her up to our "conjoined" office. As I sat on a pile of lumber, she wandered around, checking everything out, eyes glowing.

"So the divider goes here, I presume," she said. "Equal windows, separate doors, a shared bathroom . . . I think we can fit a sitting area here, beside the divider, to further separate the spaces. Get a couple of chairs . . ." She grinned my way. "A comfortable futon . . . Oh, and locking doors. We definitely need locking doors."

She walked to the plans. "We should consider renting out the offices on the first floor. We certainly won't need them. But we'll need to make sure access to the other floors is strictly secured, maybe use a key or code for the elevator. We wouldn't want tenants wandering, especially into the basement with that cell."

She lifted the plans. "The meeting room is perfect, big enough that we can start holding council meetings here. We'll install teleconferencing abilities—that's something we always wanted. We'll move the receptionist's office up here, with one executive assistant to cover reception and secretarial." A sly grin. "Think we can talk Adam into it?"

"That, I believe, would be even less welcome than head of security."

"I didn't get the impression he was all that offended by head of security. Not when he realized it included detective work and SWAT detail. I was thinking . . . well, I'm not sure he'd take it . . ."

"You can always try. He'd be a welcome addition."

She searched my gaze. "Really?"

I smiled. "Really."

"Maybe security plus research, then. For executive assistant, maybe Savannah to start. It's important for her to get some job experience. I know I've never pushed because she struggles with school, but it's time. And working for us, we can make sure she's free when homework heats up. So a security-officer-slash-researcher if Adam agrees, plus an executive assistant. I think that'll be it for staff, at least for a few years."

She continued to the windows. "These are gorgeous, huge windows, but being on the second floor, we'll need blackout blinds for security when we're out. I'm not sure how big a concern that is, but you'll be a better judge of such things. Speaking of security, we'll want a computer network with a server. A small one that can be expanded . . ."

And so she continued, happily making plans, barely stopping for breath. I added little, just sat in my spot and watched her. That was enough.

CPSIA information can be obtained at www.ICGtesting.com
Printed in the USA
LVOW02s2015230915

455473LV00005B/18/P

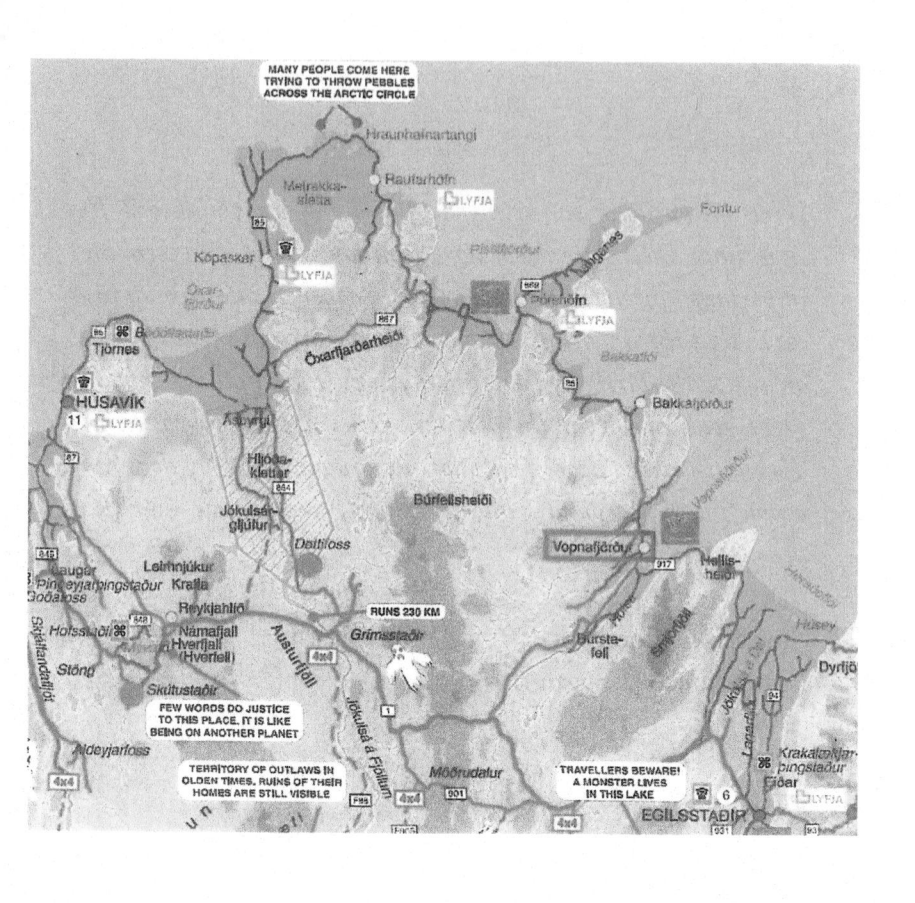

What memories do we bring with us out of our childhood? The significant ones? I think we do, even though they often seem unimportant, unrelated to one another. Sooner or later we all discover that the important moments in life are not the advertised ones, not the birthdays, the graduations, the weddings, not the great goals achieved. The real milestones are less prepossessing. They come to the door of memory unannounced, stray dogs that amble in, sniff around a bit, and simply never leave. Our lives are measured by these.

Susan B. Anthony.
(Grandniece of Susan B.)

CHAPTER 1
TRAVELING THE FJORDS
TO VOPNAFJÖRÐUR.

June 1935

THEY'D FOUND ME! I could feel the ground tremble as they stomped their giant feet and coming closer, and closer. I shot out of the cave where I'd been hiding and started running in total panic, faster - faster - faster... but then my legs began to feel like lead, I could barely move. Clenching my fists, I grit my teeth and desperately tried to run, but I was going slower and slower. My heart felt like it was pounding clear out of my chest. Then the ground shook again and I sensed horrible, bony fingers reaching inside the cave, ready to grab me...

Startled, I jumped upright in bed, what a nightmare! Just then a jolt shook the bed. I waited a moment, all was quiet, just a small aftershock from the earthquake couple of days ago, I thought, as I laid back down.

Suddenly I remembered; *today is the day!* For a moment I lay still, feeling the anticipation tingling from my head to

my curled-up toes. Then, carefully, I untangled my legs from my siblings'. Rubbing my eyes I looked at the sleeping kids. Búddi was tucked up into a tight ball, his nose scrunched up against the wall. Sísí was on her back, with her hands clasped under her head, dark hair spread out like raven wings. Lilla, sleeping next to me, had her knees pulled up to her chin. Her, curly, blonde hair was in damp ringlets at the back of her neck. I rubbed the spot where her heels had been digging into my back. The four of us older kids slept in the same bed, packed end to end like sardines in a tin can, while Frankel, my baby brother, slept in Mother's small bedroom.

A sliver of murky daylight showed through a small slit in the dark-brown curtain hanging at the window. I swung my skinny legs out and eased from between the, cozy and warm, top and bottom duvets. The floor was cold and I shivered as my bare toes hunted for my wooly socks, not bothering to see if I got mine or my siblings'.

Quietly, I tip-toed into the dusky, grey-lit living room. The quake had caused the large oil-painting of Gullfoss to hang slightly crooked on the green-painted wall. The copper pendulum on our large Grandfather clock swung with soft, clicking precision, side to side, *tick-tock, tick-tock*. Nanny Gróa's loud snore came rumbling from the corner, where she slept on our divan. The white duvet rose and fell as she breathed slowly and deeply.

Stealthily, I slid my feet across the wood planks. A small *crack* from a loose board on the floor sounded like a shot-gun blast had gone off in the quiet night! I froze. My heart did rapid flip-flops... the snoring stopped. I held my breath. Then the quivering, snoring rumble started up again, a notch louder.

Nanny Gróa was married to Sigurður [Siggi], a fisherman shipmate of Father's. When both he and Father were out at sea, Gróa helped Mother with housework and us kids. She was a big woman. Not fat, just big; big hands, big feet, big nose, and a very big voice. She kept us kids in line with just her voice. None of us were ever spanked, but oh THE LOOK, and THE VOICE.

I grabbed a black, knit, shawl thrown over the back of the rocker and wrapped it tightly around my bony shoulders as I crept up to the window. Lifting a corner of the ecru-colored, crocheted curtain, I peered out through the dusty pane. The ragged clouds in the pale-blue sky above Mount Esja were streaked and edged with golden-red sunrays above her snow-white top. Grey, eerie shadows floated in and out of her crags and crevasses and gave the rocks a haunted look.

The long, gloomy, dark days of winter were ending; the four-hour, grey, day-lights were beginning to give way to nights that were getting lighter and lighter. Soon we'd have twenty-four hours of daylight that would last until mid-August, and then the cycle would start again.

I looked at the ticking clock: four-thirty. I had a long wait!

Glancing down, I spotted the small blob of quicksilver in the corner of the window-sill. We kids, frustrated ourselves for hours with trying to pick up the elusive blob. Father had poured the silver onto the sill after Gróa had accidentally broken a thermometer.

Yawning, I pondered the slithery lump then tried to pinch it between my fingers. But it broke into pieces and scattered across the sill in several tiny, silvery balls.

I gave up. Curling up on the floor I went back to sleep.

I was ten, and school was finally over. My two, travel-worn, scratched-up, brown suitcases, and a bag full of books, sat by the back door as Mother and Nanny Gróa bustled about with breakfast. After last-minute checking of everything and everybody, Mother crammed our pockets with kleinurs (twist-shaped donuts).

"Time to leave." Mother said, as she picked up little Frankel.

Gróa grabbed the two suitcases while Sisi picked up my bag of books. Then we hurried out the door that was never locked. Sísí dragged Búddi by the hand as Lilla and I exuberantly ran ahead. We all thumped down the stairs and came out at the back of the house. Running through the dark passage that separated our house from the one next door we sped down the street to catch the rickety Strætó that would take us to Lækjartorg center in downtown Reykjavik.

Several people were on the bus and few seats were available, except the backseat; adults didn't care for the jostling and bouncing of the ancient, dilapidated vehicle and shunned the back of the bus, to the delight of us kids.

"Head for the back seat!" Búddi hollered. Sísí, with book-bag clunking against the seats, Lilla and I rambunctiously followed him while Gróa managed my suitcases. Mother carried Frankel.

After a bumpy, twenty-minute, stop-and-go ride down to the square, we got off and headed for the dock where the passenger ship, *Goðafoss II*, was anchored.

I was literally skipping down the pier to the gangplank of the ship. The harbor was crammed with a mixture of fishing

vessels of all sizes, both foreign and domestic. Their masts reached to the sky like slender trees in a forest while a variety of national flags snapped crisply in the stiff breeze. Raucous noise and the steady roar of ships' crane-engines filled the air as bustling crews loaded cargo, shouting directions. Swarms of seabirds swooped and screeched overhead. Their abundant, gross, droppings, splattered and white-streaked the pier.

Breathing the salty, tangy air, and smelling gasoline and hot diesel oil, added to my expectation of adventure. I was on my way to Vopnafjörður, and I was going by myself. After much hugging, kissing and admonitions from Mother and Gróa I worked my way up the gangplank among the boarding passengers.

Shivering with excitement and a little chill, I tucked my lopi scarf tighter around my neck. Yanking up my creeping wool stockings and smoothing down my homemade, brown cotton skirt, I leaned over the ship's rail, and searched for my family among the crowd clustered on the dock.

My two sisters had traveled with me before; Lilla, now almost nine had gone with me just once, last year, when she was not quite eight. And Sisi, twelve, who had gone almost every summer was now old enough to help in the grocery store owned by our aunt Þrúður, and would be staying in Reykjavík.

As usual, I could hardly wait to see my father's family. Aunt Þórbjörg, my Grandpa Björn, and, of course, my favorite uncle, Uncle Bjössi, whose given name was Eldjárn, my father's half-brother.

The morning sun was hidden in a sky that was now overcast, pewter-grey, with occasional patches of ice-blue

showing through streaky, low-hanging, clouds. Snow-capped Mount Esja was barely visible from across Reykjavík harbor. The island Víðey, sitting in the middle of the bay between Reykjavík and Mount Esja, had snow patches on the ground, and the black slate roof of the lone farm-house was streaked with white, powdery rime.

With good weather it would take four nights and five days to get to Vopnafjörður. I was sharing a cabin with a young woman who was going to Akureyri, a town in north Iceland. My sisters and I had always traveled by ourselves. However, a passenger or crew-member was aware and available if we needed help.

A nippy, northern gale rippled the dark-blue water of the bay. The sea-water sloshed up against the black barnacle-covered pilings, sending freezing-cold sprays over the folks waiting to see the *Goðafoss II* off. I spotted my family who were huddled together to wish me good journey.

I giggled as I saw my two sisters running for cover shrieking in surprise when they got showered with the water. Yanking their lopi sweaters over their head they tried to keep their hair covered and wave to me at the same time.

As the ship blasted the horn in preparation for departure, five-year old Frankel screamed and covered both of his ears with his hands. Mother picked him up as Búddi, my mischievous seven-year old brother, stomped both feet in the puddles. His shoes, socks, and pants were getting soaked as he wildly jumped, laughed and waved.

I covered my face when I saw him stumble. I was sure he'd go face-first into the bird-droppings grimy water. Then I saw Gróa grab him before disaster happened. It didn't faze

my brother a bit as he squirmed and tried to wriggle out of her tight grip.

Another blast and the ship began slowly to move away from the pier. I was waving both hands and hopping up and down as my family waved back, Mother smiling. Her reddish, light-brown hair, wet from the unexpected shower, fell in long curls to the shoulder of her brown and white knit sweater.

The kids were jumping and shouting at a fever pitch as were other folks gathered to see their loved ones sail away. The yelling and the hollering noises were deafening;

"Bless, bless.!"

"Have a good trip!"

"See you in a few months!"

It seemed like everyone was shouting at the same time, adding to the commotion.

Frankel had buried his head in mother's neck and I could just make out his chubby fingers doing a little wiggle, no doubt Mother coaching him. My half-brother, Kalli, who was 14, wasn't there with my siblings. He was being raised by my Mother's sister, Aunt Þrúður and her husband, Jón. I didn't see Kalli often.

Mother had been married to a fisherman, Karl Ágúst Kristjánsson, who drowned at sea when Kalli [Karl Ottó Karlsson] was two years old.

Kalli was very much like Mother in looks and temperament. He had light brown hair, sky-blue twinkling eyes, easy nature as Frankel and Lilla [Herdís, named after Mother's mother]. But Búddi [Björn], Sísí [Sigríður, named after Father's Mother] and I took after our father, Jónas. We had

dark-brown hair, brown or hazel, somber eyes, but each of us quite different. Sísí, was quiet, but at the same time could be quite fun-loving. Búddi was outgoing and lively, and I was a sprinkling of each, but probably more daring or fool-hardy than any of them.

As the *Goðafoss II* headed out of the sheltered harbor, past the two lighthouses, out of the calm bay and into the open, rough, Atlantic Ocean, I watched as Reykjavik got smaller and smaller in the distance. How the Capital of Iceland got its name is part of Nordic History; Norwegian, Ingólfur Árnasson, had heard about an island in the Atlantic Ocean. After a bloody fight in Norway he left and sailed for this land. When Ingólfur saw mountains on the horizon and got closer to the land, he threw carved, wooden, pillars overboard and vowed to settle where his gods washed them on shore. The pillars were found in a bay where steam from hot geysers billowed into the air. Ingólfur mistakenly thought the mist was smoke and named the place Smoke Bay [Reykja-smoke, Vik-bay] the town is now 80% heated by natural, geothermal, hot water piped into the city, and is virtually smog free.

Although others, like Garðar Svavarsson and Flóki Vilgerðarson had found Iceland before Ingólfur, he is recognized as the country's first settler, building his homestead in Reykjavik in 874.

As we sailed past Garðarskagi, the Garður lighthouse and headed toward Vestmannaeyjar, our first stop, the greenblue sea became choppy, and the ship began a roller-coaster move in the waves. The ocean fanned out wing-like on each side of the bow sending streams of foamy, salty water into the air. I loved to stand at the front rail and pretend I was

a figurehead like on the ships of old, stretching my neck, pointing my nose into the air and let misty spray soak my face. I licked my lips, savoring the taste of brine. [Nine years later, on November 10, 1944, this same ship I was sailing on was torpedoed just west of Garðarskagi. A German U-300 submarine hit the British tanker, *Shirvan*, setting it on fire. When the *Goðafoss II* stopped, against the Nazy orders, to pick up survivors from the tanker, she also was torpedoed, and sank.]

Vestmannaeyjar is a cluster of blue-black lava isles rising out of the water about nine miles from the southern coast of Iceland. All but one isle were formed eons ago by volcanic eruptions from the bottom of the Atlantic Ocean. The latest addition to this group erupted out of the ocean in 1963 just west of Heimaey. The new isle, Surtsey, is named after the fire-giant of Norse mythology, Surtur, whose mission is to destroy the earth by fire at the end of time.

Heimaey is the only inhabited isle in this cluster. As we sailed closer, I could see white, frothy sprays shoot high up into the air as the ocean crashed fiercely against the sheer, massive, grey-black, cliffs. Then it swirled back into eddies of receding waves only to send another booming surge against the rocks.

Thousands of seagulls, krias, gannets, puffins, and other seabirds soared in the cloud-covered sky. Some of the birds seemingly hung in the air by an invisible string. Others would suddenly dive straight down like a falling star, totally disappear into the tumultuous waves, then come flying up with a wriggling trophy in their beaks. *How can they do that?* I was quite intrigued and wondered why they didn't drown.

On this tiny island, only about three miles wide and four-and-half miles long, ancient volcano Helgafell rises 741 feet, among strangely distorted, eerie formations of lava boulders, scattered about from her own long-ago eruption. Another volcano erupted in January, 1973. It was named Eldfell. It rose 721 feet.

At the foothills of these two volcanoes sits the village, and like the isle, is named Heimaey. Half of the village was buried in lava flow from the eruption of Eldfell, which also threatened to ruin the harbor. The villagers took the unusual step of spraying ocean water on the flow, stopping it and thereby saving some of the homes and the harbor. Two volcanoes live on this small remote rock of an island!

CHAPTER 2
VESTMANNAEYJAR
AND THE TRÖLLS AT VÍK

THE MOURNFUL-SOUNDING BLAST from the horn of *Goðafoss II* announced our entry into the fjord, echoing and bouncing off the towering cliffs that sheltered the harbor in a horse-shoe shape, sending gazillions of birds into the air screeching manically in fluttering frenzies. Starchy puffins, with their huge red-and-yellow, gaudy-colored beaks sat on the edges of the cliffs, sitting on numerous ledges and on the steep rock walls. There were puffins fishing in the ocean and puffins flying over the ship, baby eels in their beak. There were puffins everywhere!

I gazed at the knot of people who were gathered on the pier, suitcases grasped in their hands and boxes at their feet. As the ship slowly navigated the harbor, a few stragglers, mostly kids, were running down the unpaved, lava-cinder covered, street. Fine black dust flew up and swirled in the not-yet-bright sunlight. I watched as those kids carefully grabbed a few wayward pufflings on the wharf and dropped

the baby birds back into the ocean to be reunited with their mammas, who were anxiously swimming in circles.

Excitement escalated and folks began to shout and wave as we eased up to the dock. Passengers gathered at the portside of the ship as the gangplank was being lowered for those that were leaving and others to come aboard. All the while, there was the grunting and the hustle of the crew as they loaded and unloaded freight. It was a lively, noisy scene; the droning of the engine of the ship's crane, directions shouted as cargo was moved, and the clamor as folks shouted to one another.

This dockside activity was repeated, with various intensity at every fjord we stopped; women, men, and children were greeting the arrivals, others kissing and hugging goodbye; curious kids pushing and shoving to get a closer look. The large ship was a once-a-month anticipation, when stores would replenish their goods.

With much waving and hollering of "Bless, bless" we again headed out to the open sea and toward the south-east tip of Iceland, the harbor of Höfn.

With a book in hand I found my favorite place, the bow of the ship. The air was chilly, and most folks preferred the comfort of being inside drinking hot coffee and Brennivin [fire wine], also called Black Death because of its potency. The story goes that when an old, drink-hardened sailor from another country took a swig, he had to run six kilometers to get his breath back!

Drowsily, I dropped the book to my lap to gaze idly at the coast and dreamily ponder the mountains and the glaciers on the mainland as we sailed by. I watched with quickened

interest as Eyjafjallajökull and Mýrdalsjökull came into view. Both glaciers had volcanoes hiding beneath their ice-caps. It was just a matter of time until they would blow their tops. Hopefully not as wickedly as old Hekla, who lurked menacingly a few miles inland, her perpetual cloud obscuring her top. In the old Sagas, she was called the Gateway to Hell. I shuddered.

Suddenly, the hairs on the back of my neck stood straight up, I could feel my skin crawl… I bolted upright staring at the sea-stacks out in the ocean between the ship and land. *Two of those stacks were from Grýla's family, the worst tröll of all the Icelandic trölls, that tried to snatch a three-mast ship that was sailing in these waters! I'd heard how they tried to drag the ship ashore to Vík. Then the sun came up and the two trolls turned into those stone-stacks!*

Puffing out a deep sigh I relaxed as the *Goðafoss II* steamed full speed ahead toward Höfn and the 'trölls' were swallowed in a shroud of grey, foggy mist. I shivered in relief as they disappeared from my sight.

The coast of the mainland was hazy but I could still see the majestic, panoramic view of the largest glacier in Iceland [and Europe], *Vatnajökull.* The glacier rose dramatically into the air, top barely visible in wispy shreds of fog. An ice boulder the size of a house had broken from the glacier, and came tumbling down Jökulsár. Hurling into the Atlantic the boulder broke into smaller chunks.

Mesmerized, I watched the back and forth fight as ocean waves pushed the ice back into the mouth of the river, only to have the river push the ice back out. The river won; I saw the chunks of ice being tossed about in the sea, then thrown up

against the rocky headlands as the relentless waves showered the black lava rocks.

Drawing my knees to my chest and hugging myself, I stared in fascination as Humpback whales' powerful spouts exploded like miniature Geysers, white dotting the Atlantic. Seals lolled about on small volcanic skerries and dolphins shot up in graceful arch, wet backs glistening, as a flock of screeching gulls hovered over them. A gaggle of honking geese added to the melee. I found it very entertaining.

In traveling the fjords around Iceland, this was one of the longer stretches without a stop so I thought this diversion was perfect.

The village of Höfn was small. Numerous fish-racks were scattered at the edge of the pier with cod hung out to dry, the fishy smell saturated the air. Krias [arctic tern] and seagulls clustered and circled above the racks diving down and pecking at the fish.

Children were so heavily bundled up in bulky sweaters, I couldn't tell boys from girls. They scrambled on the brownish, algae-slippery rocks, yelling and chasing the screeching birds that would fly up in the air, then come back down, fluttering their wings and hopping onto the racks.

Small rowboats and larger fishing boats were anchored in a seemingly hap-hazardous manner. The small boats smacked the sea as they bounced up and down in the incoming waves.

A small group of men from the village had gathered to watch the activity on the dock. Some were mending their nets that were draped among the numerous, strong smelling fish barrels. Puffing on their pipes, they occasionally glanced at the horizon and murmured among themselves. Their pipes,

clamped between their teeth, bobbed up and down as they spoke. Tobacco smoke floated in the air, the whiff blended with the salty smell of the ocean and the rank odor of haddock, herring and other fish.

One woman passenger came aboard and none disembarked. It didn't take long for the energetic and experienced crew to unload cargo. We left Höfn and headed back out.

So far the sea had been moderately calm, most of the time. But as the *Goðafoss II* made its way past the peninsula and headed north, past the island of Papey and toward Djúpivogur, our next stop, the wind became northeasterly.

On the horizon appeared swiftly rolling, dark-gray, ominous looking clouds.

CHAPTER 3
THE EAST FJORDS AND ÍNGI'S BOAT.

SUDDENLY THE ICY, north-east, wind came barreling across the ocean, and the *Goðafoss* began serious pitching and rolling as the heaving waves became more boisterous. Some of the passengers started to get seasick and threw up over the side of the ship, before dashing down to their rooms below deck. But once we entered the sheltered fjord of Djúpivogur the sea calmed, the plunging lessened and folks cheered up, even though the air was quite chilly for June.

Djúpivogur was typical of the eastern fjords; picturesque fishing villages surrounded by tall, ruggedly-eerie lava mountains that plunged straight into the deep fjords. Numerous brightly-painted fishing boats were anchored everywhere, by the dock, near the dock, away from the dock. Red and black painted boats, white and black, green and black, some were peeling, and badly in need of paint. Others were freshly painted.

The air was filled with hovering, screeching seagulls and

the even more raucous, aggressive, seabird kria. As always, they were greedily fighting over any morsel that passengers tossed overboard.

The usual loading and unloading of the ship took place, and new passengers came aboard. I became interested in watching one of them, he looked about twenty years of age, with a cheerful round, ruddy face. A navy-blue knit stocking cap was pulled over long, reddish-blonde, hair that curled over the collar of his black jacket. His grey sack was tied up with black rope and slung over his left shoulder. In his right hand he carried a brown, beat-up, square shaped case, secured with rope, badly frayed from being tied and re-tied. I was thinking it might contain an accordion. Bjössi's accordion case was very similar. *Maybe we'll have a rollicking polka dance. Wouldn't it be hilarious to watch people try to dance while the ship tossed them around like puppets on a string?* I laughed to myself as I imagined the riotous scene.

Easing away from the pier, the *Goðafoss* headed out of the fjord toward the open East Atlantic. Turning north and stopping at smaller villages along the way, we arrived at Reyðarfjörður. Men and boys were in couple of small fishing boats, and a row-boat, their fishing lines trailed along-side of the boats. The men and boys waved in cheerful greeting. Some of us waved back. After the *Goðafoss* had docked, a couple of passengers got off. One older man took his time ambling down, no one was there to greet him, and a woman who, firmly, walked down the gangplank. Her black hair was pulled into a tight bun at the back of her head, a off-white hat, (I thought it looked like a straw-hat) perched precariously on the top of her crown. Black ribbon on the hat flopped up

and down as she walked with deliberate steps. She carried a brown leather valise in her left hand as she steadied herself at the handrail with her right hand, and stepped onto the pier. She was quickly surrounded by an enthusiastic, young-looking, group.

"She looks so prim. I bet she's a school teacher." I thought, as I watched the group walk toward the village.

As we left Reyðarfjörður, we sailed out of the fjord and skirted the eastern-most point of land in Iceland, a huge out-crop named Gerpir. Great hulking masses of volcanic cliffs reared up. Heaving waves broke furiously on their sides. Powerful waters swirled up crags then hurled back down into the sea. Wide-eyed I gaped at the fantastic lava formations of turrets and spirals, poking tröll-like fingers into low lying clouds. In school I'd been taught that Gerpir had some of the oldest rock formation in the country, believed to be around 12 million years old. A chilling flutter crawled up my spine as I gazed at the grim black rock and thought of the massive eruption that must have taken place. I hadn't realized what I'd missed on previous trips, as this part of the fjords had then been traveled during the night.

A strong gale, again, was whipping up as we headed towards Seyðisfjörður, after which we had two small fjords to stop at. I was getting anxious. We had been in and out of numerous fjords for four days and three nights and should be on time, if nothing slowed the ship.

The *Goðafoss* rolled and plunged entering the fjord, that was sheltered by the enormous, towering sea-cliffs. The sea calmed some, and the ship arrived at the pier. Soon the disembarking and embarking, the kissing, shouting and hugging

began. The crew was working furiously to unload and load cargo. As I watched the haste, I wondered just how bad the weather report was. I felt anxiety creep into my stomach; I didn't want any delay. We were so close.

Sólveig, who was "looking after me" on this trip, suggested we take a stroll along the pier. I agreed, glad to exercise my land-legs for a while. Avoiding dogs, fighting with the ever-present greedy, noisy gulls, we walked on the ocean-washed planks and made our way to an old, orange-painted corrugated lean-to. A red-enamel, chipped coffeepot, with a hearty steam billowing from the spout, sat on a rough semblance of a counter, made from pieces of driftwood. Several tin mugs and a bowl of sugar cubes were at one end. A smiling couple greeted us and introduced themselves as Ketill and wife Sturla, owners of the small Kaffihús[Coffee-house]. They offered us harðfiskur [air-dried fish] to munch on, hot coffee for Sólveig and a mug of hot milk with sugar cubes for me.

Wrapping my fingers around the cup, I carefully sipped and blew on my hot milk, wishing it was coffee. I didn't ask for any, knowing that some folks thought I was to young. Looking out the grimy window, I watched as four men and a young boy were working on a small fishing boat. It looked to me like they were preparing to sail.

"Hey Íngi, I hear the weather report isn't so good." Our host had stepped out the door and bellowed, as he buttoned up his heavy yellow slicker. "Not planning to go fishing, are you?"

"Yah, but it won't be a winter-storm this time of the year, snuff and coffee on me when we get back, Ketill." Íngi

grinned and touched his black cap smartly as he entered his pilot house.

Ketill grimaced, scratched his scraggly beard, and squinted hard as he stared at the grey-black clouds, rolling even more aggressively across the horizon.

"I have a bad feeling," he muttered.

Sturla, standing behind her husband, pushed windblown strands of auburn hair from her face as her left hand nervously twisted a corner of her long, black apron.

"I can't believe my sister would let her youngest go on that boat today; Ragnar is only ten!" Her brown eyes were shiny with unshed tears - I felt sorry for her. But children started working at a very young age, and most were self-reliant and independent. We knew fishing had to be done to put food on the table and the ocean is good to Icelanders. But we also knew that it can be their cold-hearted, merciless enemy. My family knew that as well, as several of our forefathers lie at the bottom of various fjords around the country.

We thanked the couple for the refreshment and followed other passengers who had started back to the ship. My eyes followed the little fishing-boat that seemed swallowed up at times in the roiling ocean.

The *Goðafoss* was at the mouth of the fjord when Sólveig pointed to Ingi's boat. We watched as the waves pitched the boat high on top of a crest, pausing for a moment then taking a slow, steep descent into a swell and disappearing, only to rise so high we could see the red-painted bottom of the boat and enormous hills of water streaming off the deck. Again the boat disappeared. Sólveig tightened her grip on my shoulder. I don't think I have ever had such a sinking,

horrible tension. I held my breath. Then slowly, like rising out of a watery grave, Íngi's boat appeared. I blew out a deep breath of relief, releasing the white-knuckled grip I had on the rail. The *Goðafoss* turned north and we didn't see the boat again.

CHAPTER 4
THE LAGARSFLJÓTORMURINN
[THE MONSTER WORM]

THE MENACING, LOW clouds, scudding on the northeast horizon blended with the surface of the leaden, heaving ocean. The *Goðafoss* began to seriously pitch and roll, sending a heavy mist of spray over the deck. Sólveig and I ran for shelter by one of the lifeboats.

"Let's go inside" she said, tugging my arm. I just shook my head, my eyes riveted on the huge waves. "I'll go and get us something hot to drink." Sólveig looked into my face, smiled and left.

I was so glad that my mother had picked this woman to be my "look-out". She watched out for me but at the same time respected my independence. Her neat, wispy, mouse-brown hair, and slightly squinty, faded-blue, eyes made her look very plain, but when she smiled with that extra-wide mouth of hers she had the sunniest expression. I liked her and knew I'd miss her as she continued on to Akureyri where she had a governess job lined up.

I grabbed at a rope as a sudden pitch tilted the ship and I began toppling sideways. My heart flopped crazily. With a spine tingling sensation my mind went to my father. Last winter he had been a crew member on a fishing trawler that was on its way to Liverpool, England. They had just passed the Isle of Man when a winter storm caught them. The ship sank. Seven members of the crew perished.

That night my mother dreamed that father came to her bedside, dripping water and covered with slimy-brown seaweeds. "The ship is down, I tried to save Siggi... " Then she woke up. Later, I overheard as a spokesperson for the Icelandic Fisheries came and confirmed her dream. Father was safe. He had helped a crew member into a life-boat and tried to save Siggi, Gróa's husband, but Siggi wouldn't let go of the death-grip he had on the rail. He went down with the ship and drowned. I had nightmares of perils and shipwrecks for several nights but kept my feelings and fears to myself. I was a quiet, somber girl, very independent and, at times, quite impetuous.

Mother had quite a few dreams of this sort and was somewhat sought after to interpret dreams. Women would come to visit and drink coffee. Then they would turn their cups upside down and wave them three times over their head, and let the coffee form various designs on the inside of the cup as it dried. Then Mother would interpret the designs and swirls to "read" their future!

Six years later, when I was sixteen, she "read" my coffee cup and said she could see that I was going to travel far away, across a very wide ocean. I had dreamed of going on a safari in Africa. *"Doctor Livingstone, I presume"* was one of my favorite lines. I could just see it; deep in the jungle there I am

fanning myself with a huge palm leaf and someone comes up to me and says "*Doctor Jónasdóttir I presume.*"

"Hot milk" Sólveig's voice startled me out of my daydreaming. I let go of the rope that I had been holding onto and reached for the cup, just as a fierce Nor'easter struck. A raw, numbing drizzle, a mixture of sleet and rain right out of the arctic stung our cheeks and chins, forcing us passengers who had been watching the raw display of an angry ocean, to take one last look then, shivering, scuttle inside, shaking our drenched coats.

The captain and the crew were now battling the elements in earnest. We could barely hear the yelling of the crew over the screeching cables and howling gale that blew high and low.

I ran, spilling my milk when running, but when I got inside the steward filled my cup again, and gave me skyr [yogurt] and pönnukökur [pancakes filled with jam and whip cream]. Suddenly, the plunging and pitching of the ship threw a metal coffeepot clanking to the floor, sending splatters of coffee on the walls, ceiling and floor. Glasses slid across tables while people were frantically trying to grab them. Flying forks, knives and spoons were clattering every which way. My skyr slathered a stool, but I held onto my pönnukökur, squeezing them into a gooey mess between my fingers.

Sólveig grabbed me as we all were being thrown about like rag-dolls. Men were uttering swear words under their breath, others bellowing and grumbling "It's first week of June and we're in the middle of a winter snowstorm; only in Iceland do you go through four seasons in one day!"

The shrieking of the wild, north wind, and the shouting of

the crew was getting un-nerving when, Svenni, the passenger from Seyðisfjörður, reached for his case, and opened it up ... *it was an accordion!* In no time, his fingers were flying over the keys and pounding out a rollicking polka. There wasn't enough room for us to get up and dance, we probably would have ended up flopping on the floor anyway! But we stomped our feet and thumped our hands in beat with the music as we crashed into one another with every roll of the ship. It was a real neck-snapping time! Then we started belting out our favorite folksongs, if not forgetting the ferocious weather, at least ignoring it for the time being. This bedlam went on for hours and we were getting hoarse from all the singing.

All of a sudden, in mid-song, Svenni stopped, cocked his head. "Listen..."

It was almost eerily quiet. I heard the creaking of the ship, still rolling and pitching, but not quite as violently. The booming of the foghorn blasted out! *FOGHORN!* That had to mean the wind had changed directions, warmer air brought fog!

The men scrambled out the door, we women clambered right behind, holding onto whatever we could as the *Goðafoss* plunged thru another billowing wave. We had sailed past Húsey, Borgarfjörður and were slowly skirting Héraðsflói. Ice-floes of various sizes tumbled and swayed in the churning ocean. The top of Mount Smörfjöll was hidden in fog, but I knew that on the other side was the fjord, and the village of Vopnafjörður.

I was getting very excited until I saw the ice ahead of us and heard one crewman say that fishing boats were stranded in ice in the fjord. *What if one of them is Grandpa's boat? No,*

I'm not going to think of that!

I began to pester Sólveig "Do you think we'll get in there? Do you think there's too much ice?" I was very near tears. I moved away from the passengers that were milling around, some glaring at the sea in frustration. I found a spot where I could be by myself. Staring at the constantly heaving waves, I wondered if the monster-worm, Lagarfljótsormurinn, had lost his way, and was in the ocean wrathfully trying to find his way back to Lake Lagarfljót where he had lived for centuries. We were not very far from where the Lagarfljót River emptied into the bay. Fearful, I peered into the tumultuous waves, wanting to, and not wanting to spot this awful monster that was known to bode ill tidings if it reared its back out of the water!

"EEEK!" I screamed and must have jumped up a foot. My hands flew up in the air. "You scared the daylights out of me!" I was so absorbed in my imagination that I didn't know that Sólveig was by me until she grabbed my hand.

"You're gripping the rail so hard your knuckles are white," she said. "What's the matter? Your mother said you've traveled the fjords since you were six. You must be used to all kinds of weather and we're past the worse. What is it?" Sólveig asked softly.

I started to tell her about the worm, but then realized she had answers for everything, even the unexplainable. I knew she was not a believer in trölls, elves, and hidden people, but *I believed in them!*

"The weather has been so awful, I just wondered if the little fishing boat at Seyðisfjörður made it home safely." My lips trembled, I was also thinking of Grandpa and those

boats stranded in the ice.

"Yes, dear, all we can do is hope and pray that they're alright." Sólveig patted my shoulder. "Goodness, look at that soupy fog roll in!" She exclaimed.

The *Goðafoss* had slowed to a stop. I could now see Mount Smjörfjöll's peaks covered with snow. Fingers of fog were swirling thickly, reaching into clefts and crevasses of the lunar-like landscape. I could barely make out a few white sheep grazing on the incredibly difficult, steep mountainside.

The thickening fog shrouded the ship. Crew and passengers looked like ghostly spooks as they moved about. The heavy mist gave me a feeling of being wrapped in wet, grey gauze. Staring into the thick fog, I could see eerie faces; hollow black holes for eyes, long curvy noses, and creepy bony fingers curled for the grab. My imagination was in high gear as I backed into Sólveig, who promptly claimed I was soaking wet and would get my death from cold. I looked at her, disgusted. She had absolutely no imagination!

Changing my lopi sweater and putting on a dry skirt and dry, black wooly-socks, I watched for a moment as the clothes swung and swayed with every roll of the sea, then went back out. Breezy gusts had lifted the fog quite a bit. It was still very cold. Ice-floes the size of grown sheep were bumping up against the sides of the ship causing scary, creaking-grinding, scraping sounds.

Uneasy, I watched as the tide and movements of the ocean caused the ice to sway, bounce and head away from land. Hearing the engines start up again and feeling the vibration, I hugged myself in anticipation. Maybe only three more hours and I would see my family again.

CHAPTER 5
THE FJORD IS ALIVE WITH SEALS AND ICE

THE *GOÐAFOSS* SNAKED its way slowly along the coast to avoid icepacks. As we rounded Hellisheið cliff and entered the fjord of Vopnafjörður, exclamations of unbelief rumbled up and down at the rails of the ship as passengers gathered in awe. *The fjord was alive with tumbling, rolling, bobbing ice-chunks and floes.*

"Oh look, the seals are going for a ride on the ice, isn't that cute!" Some of the women cooed.

"Wonder if there are any polar bears; wouldn't that be something!" One man muttered. The ship, or perhaps the noise of the folks, must have bothered the seals; they began to scoot off the ice and flop into the sea, their large, shiny eyes looked at us curiously as they swam away.

The combination of ebb-tide and flowing of the ocean was moving the ice pack to the mouth of the fjord. I followed one large mass with my eyes... would that one reach Færeyjar Islands? Maybe it'll get to Norway, and by then be

melted into an itsy-bitsy piece? How long would it take for a chunk like that to melt? Would the seals get back onto the ice and take a long ride? Would the ice just disappear from under them?

I was mulling this over when I spotted a wrecked fishing vessel lying on its side and half-submerged in the ocean. My stomach lurched, and I felt icy cold as I saw the exposed, black painted stern, waves washing over it in great sloshing gushes. Then I noticed the Norwegian flag painted on the side. I felt guilt at the feeling of relief that warmed my body. This wasn't Grandpa's boat.

I was ecstatic when we arrived at the dock. Aunt Þórbjörg gave me a tight bear hug as I got off the ship, pushed me back, took another look, then grabbed me again, rocking side to side. I always felt special when I was with them. She and Ólafur didn't have children, they treated me more as a daughter.

Þórbjörg was wearing her blue and white striped nurses' dress. She had taken off her white apron and stiff cap. Her short, black hair had a two-inch wide patch of white hair above her left eyebrow and went back to just above her left ear. Like Grandma Sigríður's mother [grand-Amma], Þórbjörg's right eye was brown and the left one blue. She had easy laughter and great patience. She also was a very good nurse, and the only one in the village.

Ólafur was the caretaker of the sjúkrahús [hospital]. He was a quiet, rather powerfully built man that could, and did, handle any difficult patient at the infirmary. His grayish-blond hair was thin and receding although he wasn't old. They both were in their mid-thirties. His large, brown lopi

sweater drooped unevenly below his waist, giving him a be-draggled but comfortable look.

Sólveig had been standing by, and now the introductions took place as we ambled to a small building where coffee was being served. When Ólafur heard that she was on her way to Akureyri to be a governess, he wanted to know the name of the family she was going to. It turned out he knew the family quite well. Akureyri had been his home town when he was growing up.

Sólveig's face was flushed with delight. Until then I hadn't had an inkling of her unsure feelings about this post. After visiting awhile we walked back to the ship to see Sólveig off, she glanced over to the wreck of the Norwegian boat, then looked at Þórbjörg with a questioning look. My aunt nodded. "I have three of them at the infirmary. The rest we weren't able to save." She looked away, but I saw the single tear that trickled down her left cheek. Sólveig reached out and gave her a sympathetic hug as the whistle for departure rang through the air.

Grabbing me tightly she laughed "Bless, bless, elska mín [my love]." Then giving me a droll wink she chuckled again. "And don't daydream too much!"

After embracing Þórbjörg then Ólafur she swiftly walked up the gangplank. As she stepped on deck she turned, waved, and blew us a kiss. I was going to miss her.

Ólafur reached down and picked up my two suitcases as Þórbjörg was inquiring about medical supplies she was ex-pecting. She was told that her box was already unloaded and at the warehouse. We walked past a couple of empty corru-gated sheds so weather-beaten that it was impossible to tell

the original paint. The warehouse was in better shape. The wood front was freshly painted white. A window and the extra-wide door were red-trimmed matching the red corrugated roof. Several people were milling around inside as we entered the door. Many started to ask about the survivors.

"Þórbjörg, over here I have your supplies." The roar came from a bear of a man who towered over everyone. His huge, red beard drooped down his chin and his fiery red hair stuck out from his head as if he'd stuck a finger into a electric socket. "How are the Norwegians doing? It's too bad, we couldn't get to all of them, but..." His voice was rough as it boomed from his massive chest. I cringed and snuck behind Ólafur.

"Scared the little one," he said. "Sorry. Anyway here's your box, Þórbjörg. Not very heavy."

"Thank you, Halldór." Then she turned and looked at the folks that had been asking about her patients. "All but one is doing well, but I'm sure they'll all recover soon and be able to rejoin their families." My aunt smiled as she and Ólafur walked out the door. Little one, hmmp! I was big enough to travel by myself for five days and four nights. Well, almost by myself. I was no little one! Þórbjörg glanced at my kicking feet raising the dust.

"I need to have coffee roasted and ground when we get home. I'm almost out." She said that to Ólafur. I cooled off. I knew she meant that for me, knowing that my absolute favorite job was to grind coffee beans!

We walked past the white church where old Snorri, the bell ringer, rang the bell every Sunday morning; winter, snow, sleet or summer, he was there without fail. Every Sunday that I was with Aunt Þórbjörg and Ólafur we attended that

little Lutheran church. Christianity was first started in the year 1000 in Iceland, introduced by the Viking, Leif "The Lucky" Eriksson.

As we walked towards the infirmary I glanced to my left. The wide inlet of the fjord was still heaving and splashing against the rugged coast. Huge columns of powerful sprays shot up into the air, making the seabirds, especially the gulls, screech like crazy. Through the mist I could see Smjörfjöll reach grandly up to the sky. There was less snow on her peaks than the other side where we had sailed past few hours before.

The steep, rugged, basalt-black rock wall rose high on our right side as we walked toward the house. Several rjúpa [Ptarmigans] sat on ledges in the crevasses, their white winter feathers beginning to turn a summer speckled-brown. Walking by didn't disturb them at all.

Kristján, the shoemaker, had a small house and shoemaking shack on top of that cliff. Finna, his eleven-year old daughter, ran out to holler and wave at me, her high-pitched voice echoing in the crags. I waved back and had to grab my aunt's skirt to keep from falling as I stumbled. My eyes were everywhere except on the road!

When Finna and I would go to see one another we didn't bother to use the road, but climbed up and down the sheer lava cliff by finding a gritty ledge in which to stick our toes, or grip with our fingers. At times the brittle shale would break off with heart-stopping suddenness that sent our adrenalin racing, and momentarily scaring us half to death, but it was never enough to stop us from using the precarious mode of visiting one another, and perchance picking a few bird eggs.

I was getting more anxious as we got closer to the

house-hospital, I couldn't wait to look around. I wanted to be sure nothing had changed.

The two corrugated sheds were askew from the earthquake last year, but still standing. I could still jump from one shed to the other! My mind went back to the earthquake...

CHAPTER 6
THE YEAR BEFORE, WITH MY TWO SISTERS.

"HEY LOOK, LILLA, if we put flour sacks over our arms we could fly just like the gulls up there." I squinted my eyes to watch one bird standing on a large lava rock. I stomped my foot to see how he'd take off; spreading his wings wide, he glided up into the air, feet tucked under his body. Gracefully swooping in a curve, he came for a landing on another rock a stone-throw away. I could see his webbed, yellow feet come down straight and watched as he hopped a bit before settling down.

"Did you see that? We can do that!" I hollered. "See? When we get up on top of the shed, we'll put the sacks on our arms, spread them out like wings and when we jump, pull up our knees and fly from one roof to the other. Come on, Lilla. Grandpa and Sisí will be here later. Let's show them how we do this!"

I was already climbing on top of one of the sheds.

"No, no, come on down. The roof is shaking!" Lilla

shrieked as small rocks began to rain down the cliff at the back of the sheds. I could feel the shed swaying and hear the clattering noise as the rocks pelted the corrugated sides. Frantically, I scrambled back down yelling, "Run Lilla,run, it's an earthquake, the trölls will be coming!" Then both of us were running oddly, like we were on the deck of a ship in a stormy gale. Reeling and weaving, we screamed hysterically *"The trölls are coming, the trölls are coming!"*

Both Ólafur and Aunty came running out of the house, each one grabbed one of us and tried to calm us down, even as it felt like a giant worm was crawling under our feet.

"This is just a little tremor, and the center of the quake is miles away!" Ólafur said as he tried to calm us down.

"What on earth do you mean 'the trölls are coming'?" Aunt Þórbjörg asked as we hurried into the house. A few pictures were hanging crookedly on the walls. A spoon, two forks and a cup had bounced off the table and were quivering on the floor. A small rivulet of coffee meandered across the wood planks, from the upside-down, black-enamel coffeepot.

"What was that? What's happening?" The gravelly, querulous voice was that of old, blind, Olga, who had been in the infirmary as long as I could remember. Þórbjörg went into the sick-room and we could hear the soothing voice of our aunt as she told the old woman about the earth tremor. When she came back out, she straightened a couple of the pictures. Ólafur had given us some bread and milk and we were settling down. After awhile, she stopped fiddling with stuff, turning, as she fixed a sharp stare on me, black eyebrows in a tight frown, not on Lilla, mind you; but *me* and said,

"I want to know about this nonsense of the trölls." Her

voice sounded grim.

"Íeda has told me about the trölls and I'm scared they'll get me" Lilla said, whimpering.

Crossing her arms across her chest she frowned at me. "Alright, out with it. Why have you been scaring your sister?" She didn't even call me "Diddamín." I'd thought I was the favored child! I opened my mouth and then yelped and jumped toward my aunt who opened her arms to catch me. "It's just a little after-shock Diddamín. Let's sit down." The house gave a little shudder and a couple of cooking-pots clattered on the stove. A few glasses clinked shrilly in the cabinet. Then, everything quieted down. Aunt Þórbjörg evidently forgot to be angry; she hugged me and rocked from side to side as Ólafur comforted Lilla.

"Tell me what you've heard about this silly superstition" Aunty squeezed my shoulders.

"Uncle Bjössi said trölls live in those big, black rocks in Vopnafjörður." I shivered. "He said it was a recorded history in the *Heimskringlan* that the trölls first started here; the volcanoes opened fire and spewed them out. The trölls come out when earthquakes split openings in the cliffs. The trölls snatch children, especially the naughty ones" I shuddered as I buried my face in Aunties white sweater. I knew I was naughty at times, a little stubborn and did things I shouldn't. I was sure I'd be the first one to be snatched! I felt a little shake go through her body. Was she laughing? Anxiously, I peeked at her face. Sure enough, her face was all puckered up in a silent chuckle.

"My brother, Bjössi. I should have known!" She said. "This is quite a story! Honey, don't you know any better than

to believe his tall tales? But you really shouldn't scare your little sister with these stories, and I know all about your outrageous imagination!" Aunty chuckled again.

"You don't believe the trölls are real?" I asked, shocked.

"No trölls? The trölls aren't real?" Lilla asked in a squeaky, trembling voice.

"Definitely not real." Ólafur's voice was firm.

I got off Auntie's lap. With my hands on my hips, I planted my feet apart, and with a pugnacious stare at her, then at my uncle, I demanded, "You don't think trölls are real?"

I was sure such heresy would bring the wrath of the trölls upon us! "What about the *Monster-worm*? Everybody knows he's real and lives in the lake not far from Smjörfjöll over there." I pointed to the mountain range across the fjord. "He is just as bad as the trölls in causing bad things to happen. I've heard people whisper about that one, Aunt Þórbjörg!" My voice rose with indignation.

Uncle Ólafur tried to hide a smile in Lilla's hair, as my Aunt snorted.

"You silly goose, of course he's not real either." My aunt was unable to control her laughter. I didn't like this one bit. I bent forward and looked her straight in the eyes, wrinkling my nose, scrunching my face...

"Well, what about the ´Hidden People´?" I didn't stamp my foot, but I sure felt like it. I'd rather enjoyed the delicious thrill of fear that crawled up my spine as Bjössi would drop his voice to a whisper;

"Hush, listen, don't you hear moaning and wailing?" Then, curling his fingers into claws, he'd suddenly grab me and make me screech with fright.

Then he'd get serious. "Don't wander too far away from the ruts the horses and cows have made, Diddamín. They know their way, but it's easy for folks to get lost out there. When a thick fog comes up suddenly, I let Thunder take over and guide me home. Always remember, if ever you find yourself lost, let your horse, the dog, or even the old cow Rauða guide you. Take a hold of a tail and don't let go!" Bjössi was eighteen and, in between unmerciful teasing, he did teach me quite a bit about being careful in our remote, and strangely eerie, country.

Þórbjörg quit laughing. Looking sideways at Ólafur, she gnawed at her lower lip as she reached for me.

"I'm sorry Diddamín. I shouldn't laugh. You're right. There are some things one can't explain, but you can be sure that trölls and monsters aren't real. And you don't have to be afraid of them. People that believe in 'Hidden Folks' say that they are the kind, and helpful. There are many tales about these beings, how they have guided folks to safety after they had lost their way on fog-shrouded tundra." Aunty paused a moment, then with a serious look on her face she continued.

"I have no personal experience, but I do believe in being kind to strangers. What story did you tell Lilla that scared her so?"

"If I tell the story won't Lilla start screaming? She *always* screams!" I bumped into the stove as I backed away from Aunty.

Lilla let out a blood-curdling howl as a big kettle careened off the stove and noisily crashed to the floor, the lid banging away as it rolled into a corner of the kitchen and came to a quivering stop. We hadn't noticed how precariously close the

pot was to the edge. Fortunately, it was empty. Aunt Þórbjörg picked up the pot and lid and placed them back on top of the stove. There were no more tremors and no aftershocks.

"Let's sit outside for awhile and you can tell me the stories your uncle has been telling you while Ólafur and Lilla take some coffee to Olga."

We walked down a short lane and seated ourselves on a flat lava rock. The northern breeze blowing across the ocean was chilly, even though it was June. We both had on our warm lopi sweaters.

Taking my right hand, she rubbed it with both of hers. "I'm not mad at you, Diddamín. Well, maybe a little bit at first. It's just that I don't want you and Lilla to be scared of these folk-tales, and that's all they are!"

"But I've read many stories up in Grandpa's attic, and I asked Bjössi about them." I argued. " He said they were all true!" I wasn't willing to give up my favorite daydreams!

"So what makes Lilla so very scared?" Aunty narrowed her left, blue, eye almost shut.

Rubbing the toe of my right sheep-skin shoe into the dirt, I drew little circles, giving Aunty a sideways, sheepish look.

"The trölls are full of tricks, and always cause trouble." I explained. "The 'Hidden Folks' are kind and try to help when the trölls have been mean. The scary thing is that the trölls snatch naughty little kids, so I told Lilla since she was the littlest of us girls, she'd be the easiest one to catch. And better be good or she'd be snatched for sure!"

Aunt Þórbjörg got up, brushing her skirt. "Well it's not nice of you to scare her like that. You should be taking care

of your pretty little sister."

Ah, there it was. Lilla was the 'pretty' little girl. Which meant; she's 'lady-like'. Sísí had a 'head on her shoulders.' Which meant; she's 'the smart' one. And I was the tomboy, which meant; 'one of these days she's going to break her foolhardy neck'! I loved my two sisters, but I didn't like to be in the middle; not the younger one, not the older one, just there.

"I only told her that if we stare hard into the fog, or clouds, or the cliffs, we could see the faces of trölls and ghosts!" The loose scoria from the tremor rolled, and crunched, under my feet as I walked over to the cliff that sheltered the house.

"Can't you see this face over here?" Timidly I pointed to two black holes in a crag of the lava-rock wall. "See? Two eyes, a long, curvy nose and an open mouth with long whiskers on a huge chin. And why is it that so often we hear awful wailing and moaning all around us if it's not the naughty children the trölls have taken?"

"Now you've added ghosts? You are hopeless!" Aunty plunked back down shaking her head.

"First of all, that's not a face, just a formation from an old lava flow. Fog and clouds will do similar formations. Some people say they see a man's face on a full moon. It's all in the imagination, and you've got more than your share of that!" She chuckled. "As far as the moaning noise, that's the wind. We have the wind constantly blowing through all the crooks and cranny's of the volcanic cliffs. They do make odd sounds, especially when it's the Northern wind."

I wasn't finished. "Why do all the places have names? The farms, the waterfalls, the mountains?"

Þórbjörg turned abruptly and stared at me for a second,

shaking her head again in an 'I give up' gesture. After a moment she said.

"Folks have been giving names to places forever, something that has meaning for them or a description."

"Well then." I argued. " If there are no trölls, why name a waterfall Tröllafoss, or a lake Tröll Lake, or the Tröll Peninsula, or..." " My aunt gave me a scorching look that told me I had gone a bit too far. I clamped my mouth, but inside I felt giddy with triumph. There were trölls, I knew it!

Abruptly, Þórbjörg stood up, smoothing her hand over her backside, she started for the house. Her skirt swished and billowed, as her long legs strode firmly up the walk.

I followed with somewhat subdued elation. I wanted the trölls to be real, and at the same time I didn't. I wasn't too terribly afraid they'd catch me if only I saw them first. I could tell from the drawings of the trölls that Bjössi had shown me, that their faces were extremely ugly, their bodies warty and lumpy. But many were only about the size of a medium pig with very, very short legs. I was sure I could easily outrun them any time. After all I was always chosen to be on the relay team at school. I might not be able to outrun a giant tröll like Grýla and her ilk, but they lived near Vík, on the south side of the country.

As I entered the house, Aunty turned and gave me "that look". I knew I'd better drop the subject. She and Mother had this similarity in correcting a misbehavior; no angry words, no spanking, just what Sísí, Lilla and I called "That look". Frankly, many times I'd rather had the spanking than the guilty feeling I got from "that look."

Ólafur and Lilla had been busy. Soup-bowls and coffee

cups were on the table and a couple of glasses of milk for us girls. I knew I'd get coffee later, so I thanked my uncle and took a sip.

The lively music from old Olga's harmonica drifted into the kitchen. She might be old and blind, and at times exceedingly cranky, but she could sure belt out the music! I envied her ability and tried to imitate her style when Björssi tried to teach me. I did better playing the accordion, but wasn't very good at that either.

The music stopped, and Olga came into the kitchen scooting her feet across the floor, guided by Ólafur. Her white hair was tucked up into a green nightcap that folded over the left side of her face. The long, white tassel on the end flopped across her face as she sank heavily into her chair. Wiggling and sighing she tucked her ample skirt under her thick thighs.

"Your Grandfather will be here pretty soon to pick you up, Diddamín." Aunty was dipping up mouth-watering mutton soup as she spoke. "He'll want to load up his supplies and head home so he won't miss the out-going tide." Turning, she looked at me and asked:

"Do you have your bags ready?"

I nodded, knowing that if we missed the tide it would add hours to our travel time to Hámundarstaðir, since we'd have to skirt around the inlet instead of across it to get over to the other side. Lilla and I had been in Vopnafjörður for three weeks while Sísí had gone directly to Grandpa's farm. It was planned that Lilla and I would be with Aunty for awhile, then I would join Sísí. I was now old enough to help with the hay.

The sounds of trotting, snorting horses, jangling of harnesses, and the barking of old Snati brought us out of the house on a dead run. I leaped into Grandpa's arms as Lilla wrapped her arms around his right leg. Sísí was being hugged by Aunty and Ólafur, all of us talking and laughing at the same time. We secured the four horses to the weather-beaten wood posts, then arm in arm went inside. Ólafur walked across the kitchen and took down several cups and saucers. Lining them up on the table he poured coffee into each cup then sat down. Each of us reached over and helped ourselves. Aunt Þórbjörg dipped up soup for Sísí and Grandpa.

"Did the tremor do any damage at the farm, Dad?" Þórbjörg asked handing him a brimming bowl.

"No. Not at our place," he said. "The livestock in the sheepcote got a little nervous but then enjoyed the unexpected shower of hay that tumbled down from the loft." Grandpa held his beard back with his left hand as he blew on his hot soup. "I did see where snow slithered down in the clefts between the high crags further inland. We don't have anything to worry about." His eyes twinkled as he looked at us girls. "Just a little greeting from our peculiar country." The adults chuckled at Grandpa's wit.

Aunt Þórbjörg turned and looked at me as if to say "See, I told you so!"

CHAPTER 7
ON MY WAY TO GRANDPA'S FARM

AS WE CAME to the top of the moss and lichen-covered lava ridge we could see the tide was way out. Grandpa's timing was perfect. He guided his horse, Blési, the lead horse, into the deep hoof-ruts carved out by many years of use. The three packhorses followed. Two of them were loaded down with 50 pound bags of flour, sugar and various other supplies grandpa had stocked up. Plus each horse carried me on one and Sísí on the other. The third horse was a young colt that carried my suitcase and a food satchel. Grandpa allowed only light weight on the young horse while training him.

The sure-footed Icelandic horses trod down the lava-rock-riddled hill with ease, even though the two of them carried the extra weight of Sísí and me. We sat squarely in the middle, legs spread apart over the bags, our hands tightly gripping the two pack-saddle pommels. The load was well balanced, and the easy gait of the horses was like sitting in a rocking chair, but gently swaying side to side instead of back

and forth.

We stopped at the edge of the ocean inlet. Blési snorted and pulled toward a small, gurgling creek that tumbled down the hillside and into the shallow, salty bay.

With one easy movement Grandpa was out of the saddle and leading his horse to the water. Digging into his pocket he pulled out a handsome cow-horn snuff holder, intricately carved, and silver adorned. Removing the ornate cap, he made a deep hollow in back of his left hand by curving his forefinger and thumb, then poured in a generous amount of snuff. Sniffing deeply, and with a loud "Ahh" he started checking the girths, harnesses and baggage, giving extra yank on the oilskin covering the flour and sugar.

I loosened the reins of Stjarna and stared across the bay. The horses were enjoying the short break and started nibbling on the sparse, pale-green, grass. Sísí's horse, Sokkur, and the colt, Töfri, were slurping noisily in the ice-cold creek. A flock of geese darted off in a flutter of feathers, while the gannets haughtily stuck their long, pointy bills into the air, flew up and then came after us, angry at being disturbed. By beating the air with our horse-whips, and yelling back at their screeching, we fought them off.

"Grandpa, why didn't you use your boat this time?" I asked. I'd thought that he preferred to use his fishing boat to travel across the bay to the village.

"The motor has been acting up. I've got it apart to clean. I'll have it ready for the next trip in." Grandpa shaded his eyes against the misty sun, dimly glimmering through low-lying clouds over the dark, distant hills.

Rubbing his grey-whiskered chin, his eyes scoured the

sea-shore across the bay. Then chuckling, he pointed to the mouth of the inlet; the surface quivered and rippled. Sisi and I held our breath as five little brown heads popped up and large, shining black eyes inspected us with curiosity. The baby seals were totally unafraid. I guess they sensed we were not hunters. We watched as they playfully swam and dived up and down barking noisily, until older seals showed up and shooed them out to the open ocean.

"Those Harbor seals know the tide is about to turn. We'd better go across now." Grandpa swung into the stirrup of his saddle and whistled for Snati. Patting the rump of his horse, he motioned to his dog. "Come up here, old man." The stirrups skimmed the top of the sea as Grandpa urged Blési into the water that came up to the horses' knees.

Icelandic horses are small, only about 12.2 to 14.1 hands high and weigh 600 - 900 pounds. Some Polar bears are bigger than that. People in other countries often refer to them as "ponies" but they are a true Icelandic horse, having been brought to the country by Vikings in the mid-800s AD. My first ancestors arrived in 840 AD and may have brought some of them.

Icelanders are very protective of the purity of the breed, and foreign horses are not allowed into the country. If an Icelandic horse is sold and transported overseas, it is not allowed to come back.

Turning in his saddle Grandpa looked at us.

"Hold the pommels with both hands but give the horse a free rein," he said. "Our horses are quite used to this path, but the ocean floor can change with every earth tremor, even a small one like we just had, and leave pockets of holes. If

Sokkur and Stjarna stop, don't urge them on. Just wait and let them decide if it's safe to go on. I'll be watching."

Sísí and I somberly nodded. I peered into the water, while my sister warily eyed me with Aunt Þórbjörg's don't-you-dare look. I grinned at her impishly and whispered:

"If you look real close Sísí, there's some kind of gruesome, greenish tail right by Sokkur's right foot!" I made a big show of squinting my eyes as I looked down.

"If there is, Sokkur would stop!" She hissed. "You can scare Lilla, but not me!"

I would have been better off paying attention to my horse. She kept swishing and lifting her tail, her rump giving out loud rumbling noises. Then Stjarna stopped, and the others kept going. Slowly I became aware that I wasn't sitting upright. I was leaning precariously to the left, my body slowly inching down until my long braids brushed the water. Just as I opened my mouth to yell, Stjarna shifted her body, my head went under and I ended up with a mouth full of salty water that went down my throat the wrong way.

"Grandpa! Stjarna's girth is loose! Íeda is drowning!" I heard Sísí shrieking at the top of her lungs. The next thing I knew Grandpa's strong arms were lifting me up and putting me onto Töfri's back. He then handed me his, reeking of tobacco, red-bandana to dry my face as I gagged and spit. I felt chastened, I should know better than to joke about the water monsters!

"What's the matter, old girl?" Grandpa ran his hand over Stjarna's flank. "Ah, gas!" Tightening the girth again, he lifted me off Töfri.

"You'll be alright now on Stjarna, Diddamín, Töfri has

all he can carry." I nodded. Grandpa was very protective of his horses and took exceeding good care of them. Although Icelandic horses can carry one third of their weight he liked to wait until the colts were four to five years old before breaking them to saddle. He was very aware of the weight he put on his colts.

Halfway across the inlet the first wave rolled in, almost imperceptibly, and water was now up to the belly of our horses. Reaching the shore, they quickly scrambled up the black volcanic sand that was littered with slimy kelp and brown seaweed. Their hoofs slid as they worked their way between wet, barnacle-riddled, lava rocks until we reached the mossy bank. Following the ruts we reached a slight hill where we dismounted.

Snati took off like an arrow shot from a bow. A riotous sound of squawks and whirring of feathers shattered the quiet countryside as a flock of rjúpa flew from the hollows of the moss-covered basalt rocks. Snati came back with a self-satisfied look on his old face. His mouth was open, long tongue flopping as he mightily shook his body. He looked like he was laughing his head off.

I had asked how old the dog was. No one could agree on his exact age, but I thought he might be as old as Grandpa. They both had grey whiskers.

Snati was a superb livestock herder. No dog, in any of the nearby farms, was as good as he was in herding the sheep during réttir - roundup - a festive Fall celebration among farmers as they separated, and claimed, their sheep according to their markings. He was relentless and didn't care how far up into the mountains he had to go. Grandpa truly had

bragging rights when it came to his dog, a powerfully built animal with a thick, shiny coat, mostly black in color. His four paws were brown-tipped as were his long straight ears. He had a tuft of brown on the very tip of his tail.

While Snati was lapping at a small pond, fed by a short, tumbling waterfall, and the horses nibbled at grass tufts, Sísí and I sat cross-legged on the soft, grey moss while Grandpa perched on a large lava boulder. I ran my hand over a small berry-patch, but it was too early in the season. The blueberries were green, rock-hard nubs, just barely starting to grow. It will be August before I get to taste them! I sighed.

Then I saw Grandpa opening a brown burlap sack. Digging into the bag, he handed us dark, rye-bread sandwiches with thick slices of cheese and heavily smeared with butter. Pulling out a long piece of dried cod, he peeled off strips and handed them to us. Then each of us got two twist cookies as dessert. We ate contently for awhile, watching the inlet fill up as the tide swept in. The silvery bodies of salmon and trout shot up into the air and dropped back into the water with soft, plopping sounds. Rings formed on the water and floated to the shores in ever widening, diminishing circles.

A seagull winged her way down and landed on a small patch of gravel, cocking her head first to one side then the other. She eyed me for a moment with her beady eyes, then swiftly took off toward me. I could just read her tiny mind. She was after my cookies! I jumped up and shooed her away amid the screaming of other greedy gulls that had now gathered to grab their share. One headed for Sísí and I yelled;

"Get her Sísí, get her!"

"How do you know it's a *'her'*?" Grandpa roared with

laughter as he too was fighting off the crazy birds.

"Well, this bird just looked smaller than the others and just *looked* like a 'lady-bird,' but she sure didn't act like one!" I huffed, out of breath.

As we gathered up what food was left over, a thick band of fog was rolling in from the mouth of the fjord. We heard the motors of a couple of fishing boats start up and watched as they headed toward Vopnafjörður harbor.

"Well," Grandpa drawled, "looks like we got across just in time. From the looks of that fog we may be in for a soupy time. We'd better get a move on."

After washing down our food from the little waterfall, we remounted. With Blési leading, we continued in the hoof-ruts that were so deep in places that grandpa's feet were literally dragging on the ground. He lifted his feet and spread them out wide as he came to higher mounds of moss and grass-covered rocks. My mare, Stjarna, was at the end of the 'caravan'.

The days were getting longer and we would have no real darkness from now until fall. The nights would get lighter and lighter until the sun would dangle on the horizon all night. Now, only a dusky, grey sky gave an eerie look to the black, craggy cliffs. A small farmstead sat far back in the hills, barely discernable in the gravelly background. Streams wandered and gurgled down in small waterfalls then disappeared into gravel beds. The countryside was bleak and sparse. Meager grass tufts were sprinkled with small patches of purple wildflowers, which somehow were able to find roots among the moss and lichen. The huge waves of white fog were now wallowing in like a slow-moving avalanche.

CHAPTER 8
THE FOG

GRANDPA HELD HIS right hand up, indicating we should stop. He then took a rope from his saddlebag and rode in front of Sokkur. Tying the rope to the pommel in front of Sísí he then proceeded to tie Töfri. Stjarna was next. He guided Blési to the back holding the rope loosely in his hand as he motioned to my sister.

"Sísí, Sokkur will now lead," he said. "The fog may get so thick we'll not be able to see one another. I want to be sure we don't get separated." Sísí nodded.

Well, for once I was very happy to be in the middle. I thought the oozing, slithery fog in Vopnafjörður was absolutely the creepiest thing. It always seemed to me that the whole countryside became a completely different world, filled with ghostly cities and 'hidden people' constantly moving and changing shapes At the same time I was fascinated by the strangeness of the grey-white, rolling mist that never looked the same.

Our sure-footed horses plodded along, staying in the

deep path. They didn't hesitate or stumble, even when the fog caught up with us and the rut totally disappeared from sight. In no time it was as if we'd been covered with a huge, silver-grey, downy duvet. The swirling damp fog was tangible, filling my mouth and nose. I felt I could take a handful and wad it up like a snowball. I could no longer see Sísí, and Töfri was a moving grey blur. I turned and looked behind me. Grandpa was a hunched-down shadowy shroud, rocking side to side.

Then came the welcoming sounds of hoofs clomping on the wooden bridge that spanned a small glacial-fed creek which swiftly rushed by Hámundarstaðir.

Suddenly, there was a small rift in the fog, as if someone had flung back gauzy curtains. A slight wind had come up, and slowly the fog dissipated in twists, swirls and spirals. The path widened, flattened and became more visible.

"We are here, we made it!" Sísí yelled eagerly.

She had spotted the open gate with the metal arch proclaimin 'HÁMUNDARSTAÐIR' etched in bold letters. The loaded-down horses picked up their pace and trotted up to the front door as it was flung open by Björsi, Grandma Sigríður and Grand-amma following close at his heels.

Grandpa's farmhouse was a complex of three wood gable fronts, built side-by-side and divided by two short walls of rock and turf. The roof and each end of the gables was covered with turf that grew thick, green grass where we, constantly, had to chase off the sheep. This type of farmhouse was called burstabær (gable farm). In the middle gable was the main entrance to the hall, the passage way to the kitchen, and the stairs to Grandpa's attic room.

The left-side wall of the dark, hard-packed dirt floor was

finished with rough, wooden boards. Several wood pegs were placed at various heights for men's, women's, and children's coats. Also there were pegs for the horsewhips everyone owned; light-weight, heavy-weight, short, long. Some plain and some very elegantly silver adorned, handsomely carved with initials of the owner. An assortment of bridles were hung on heavy, higher-up pegs. The right side of the hall had a wall of various size stone and daubed with solidly packed dirt, and a door leading to the cow-house, very convenient for milking in the winter.

A narrow dung-trough went across the entire width and to the opposite wall. About a foot up this wall was a two foot square opening with a hinged door. On the other side was a huge hole where Bjössi pitched the manure, which in time seeped and disappeared in the porous volcanic ground.

This was also the bathroom when it was too cold to go outside to the outhouse. When I had to squat over the dung-trough to use the 'facility,' I had to be sure to hold a cow's tail or I'd get a whopping of a slap!

Just outside the front door was the hitching rock where we, or guests, would tie the horses' reins. A weathervane sat on top of the central gable. The small outhouse nearby was also covered with turf, except for the front where the wood door with the half-moon was.

Bjössi lifted Sísí off the packsaddle as Grandpa dismounted and came to Stjarna. Swinging me down and holding me in his arms as if I were a baby, he handed me to Grandma, who promptly started kissing and hugging me. Sísí stood by, grinning ear to ear. I could tell by the gleeful look on her face that she was just dying to tell Grandma how

she'd saved my life. She'd probably tell that I was teasing her about the monster-worm. I glanced at her sideways. She looked like she'd swallowed the whole bird. Hmm, how can I stop her? I'd have to come up with something mighty quick!

"It's wonderful to see you, Diddamín!" Grand-Amma got up from her rocking chair shooing the plump black cat off her lap. Grýla yowled and took off, swishing her tail with displeasure, then ran over and rubbed against my ankles as Grand-Amma gave me a tight hug. With her arm resting on my shoulder she turned to Sísí.

"Pour us some coffee, my love, and tell me all about Þórbjörg, and the trip," she said. "I was really concerned when the fog rolled in so quickly." Grand-Amma sat back down with a deep sigh. She was rather heavy set and quickly got short of breath.

I helped Sísí get the cups and saucers off the wood shelf. We settled ourselves in the kitchen where boiling coffee and soup blended in a delicious aroma, permeating the air. My stomach growled so loud that Grandma Sigríður exclaimed, "Are you starving? Didn't that man feed you?" She glared at Grandpa who was coming in the door, slapping and rubbing his cold hands together.

"Oh yes, Grandma. He fed us!" Sísí and I spoke up at the same time.

"It just smells so good in here that my stomach got greedy!" I jumped up and grabbed Grandma around her neck. "I'm so very happy to be here. I liked it at Auntie's house too, but I really missed all of you and missed doing things with Sísí." I sneaked a look at her. Maybe she'd go easy on me!

"Oh, it'll be fun to have you here. We'll go egg hunting

and berry-picking, milking old Rauða...," she said, then stopped and gave me a big grin. Was my sister being her nice self, or was there a wicked gleam in her eye as she mentioned the milking? I was sure that Grandpa's "Old Rauða" was the meanest tempered cow in all of Iceland!

CHAPTER 9
GAMLA RAUÐA (OLD RED)

AS SÍSÍ AND I entered the cow-house, the chickens, and especially the threatening, vicious, rooster, cackled and fussed. Each time I stuck my hand into a nest to gather eggs he'd spread out his red-gold wings, screech, and glare at me with his glittering, tiger-yellow eyes. One of these days Grandma will get tired you attacking her and us. She'll wring your scrawny neck and you'll end up in the stew-pot, I thought to myself, glaring back, then followed Sisi as she went to the cow-stall.

She carried the milk-bucket in her right hand while holding onto me with her left. I tiptoed alongside her, carefully side-stepping Rauða's droppings. Clutching a three-legged wooden milk-stool with both hands I tried not to breathe the potent dung smell.

"Now hold tight onto Rauða's tail, don't let her whack me!" Sísí swept a squawking chicken off another cow's back and took the stool out of my hands, then stomped ahead of me to Rauða's stall.

Sisi detested milking the cows, detested going into the reeking stall, and detested Rauða, who either slapped you with her gross tail or sent gross, slimy yuck with her long tongue. The nasty tempered cow would kick your leg, or milk-bucket at every opportunity, and she was forever butting her horns into the wall where she had dug out a huge hole. I thought for sure that one day she'd gore an opening right through the thick, dirt wall.

Rauða was one crabby old cow.

"Why don't you tie the tail to her leg?" I grumbled. "That's what Grandma does." I didn't like this chore either.

Sisi glared at me. "No, just hold the tail!"

I did my best. My arms flew side to side as the cow tried to loosen my grip. I gritted my teeth and held on; *I would've tied the yucky thing!*

Sísí did a good job. The spurts of milk made pinging sounds as they hit the inside of the tin pail, the milky froth piling up. Rauða was a mean-spirited cow but she gave lots of good milk, with very thick cream. Her udder was full and tight with milk and must have been quite uncomfortable; she seemed rather subdued for a change. I should have been suspicious.

After the milking, Sísí stood up and placed the pail in the corner by the door. I let go of the tail and Rauða, predictably, relieved of the weight on her udder, promptly kicked back and sent the stool flying into the side of Freyja, the heifer in the next stall. The ensuing out-of-control bedlam that followed was stupefying; cows bellowing - chickens loudly squawking - Sísí and I wildly screaming and jumping, trying to get out of the way of madly flailing tails. There wasn't a

whole lot of room for us to duck.

"Stupid, dumb cow!" I yelled as I got swatted across the back.

"What in heavens name is going on?" Grandma Sigríður came running into the cow-house.

"Old Rauða got mad at me for holding her tail." I was steamed.

"Well, she's used to her tail being tied, try *that* the next time." Grandma shook her head as she picked up the milk bucket and went to the kitchen. Glancing at Sísí I tried to give her the Aunty Þórbjörg's "I told you so" look. It didn't do me any good. My sister completely ignored me.

We followed grandma into the kitchen where she poured the milk into the two-spout separator. Grand-Amma, was sitting on a stool, her left hand on the handle ready to crank the machine. Pretty soon the thick cream came out of one spout while thinner milk gushed out of the other. Grandma poured the cream into a wooden churn. Sísí and I took turns in sloshing the butter-paddle up and down, until we heard the solid mass of butter plopping in the bottom. Grandma reached down into the churn and took out the big blob of butter and salted it.

The mouth-watering aroma of baking bread permeated the kitchen, along with the constantly-cooking mutton soup that cooked away all day. Grand-Amma pulled the bread out of the oven and set it beside the always-brewing coffeepot. I sniffed deeply, devouring the delicious bouquet mix.

Slicing the hot bread, Grandma Sigríður put on a thick slab of butter before handing us each a slice. The melting butter ran between our fingers and we licked as fast as we

could, Sísí ever-so-daintily. I slurped mine "'cause it was slur-py-licking good!"

Grandma picked up the pail containing the thinner [skimmed] milk, and walked over to the storage area of the kitchen and poured the milk into a short wood tub. Next to it sat the pickled herring, pickled whale blubber and the singed-and-pickled sheep heads, with eyeballs intact, all preserved and stored in wooden barrels. There was also a barrel of pickled ram testicles. We girls gagged at the thought and refused to eat it. There also was a barrel pickled blood-pudding.

From a rack above the barrels hung a side of smoked mutton and dried cod, which we liked very much and could nibble on all day! There was also fermented shark, though not our favorite food.

Grandma added a small clump of skyr [yogurt] from a previous batch and dumped it into the skimmed-milk tub. This clump would start the 'setting' process for a new batch. She would then save a handful from this batch to be added to the next. This method of making skyr started with the Vikings. For centuries a small batch has always been saved to continue the fermenting process.

The next day we would have more yummy skyr. We ate the scrumptious yogurt for breakfast, with cream and sugar sprinkled on top. Later in the summer, we would top it with blueberries when the berries were ripe.

CHAPTER 10
HAYING TIME

"I'LL HAVE LUNCH ready in a little while. Both of you will need to go out to the field and take the food to your grandpa and the workers." Grandma said as she turned to me. "Diddamín, Sokkur and Stjarna are just outside the fence. Go and get them while Sísí helps me to finish up here."

Grand-Amma, who had been watching Grandma as she bustled about, arose from her chair with a deep sigh and followed me out of the kitchen.

"I guess you both are riding bareback as usual?" She asked in somewhat disapproving tone. "The way you two gallivant on those horses isn't very lady-like." Shaking her head she reaching a blue-veined hand to one of the higher pegs and took down two bridles.

I grinned as I took the harnesses out of her hands. Sísí and I knew that Grand-Amma thought the only way for ladies to ride a horse was side-saddle, in a culottes-style split skirt.

"Thanks, Grand-Amma. You are right, Sísí and I won't

be bothering with saddles." I gave her a quick peck on the cheek and darted out the door.

I jogged across the lumpy field. The bridles clunked on my shoulder as I leaped between moss-covered lava rocks. At the noise, Stjarna and Sokkur lifted their heads from nibbling the meager, pale-green tufts of grass. Neighing and snorting they ambled toward me.

Töfri came running and nuzzled against me. I liked him. He was growing up to be very special. He had a shiny, silver-grey coat and coal-black mane and tail. His eyes were large, bright and intelligent. I rubbed behind his left ear. He seemed to sense my affection and whinnied softly.

"Sorry, Boy. You stay put." I patted his black, velvety-soft nose.

Stjarna and Sokkur trotted up as I rattled the reins. I got the bit in their mouths, gave Töfri a couple of sugar cubes then swatted him on the rump and watched as he scampered away.

Stjarna [Star] was a reliable, grey mare, with a long, white mane and tail. Sokkur [Socks] was glistening-black, with a white, narrow stripe from his eyes down to his nostrils, and white 'socks' on all four feet. They all held their head proudly, a sure sign of loved and well-tended horses.

Stepping up on top of one of the rocks, I jumped on Stjarna's back, and holding Sokkur's rein, we went at a gallop back to the farm-house.

Grand-Amma, Grandma and Sísí were all outside waiting. I didn't dismount since the food was all packed and ready. My sister put her left foot on the hitching-rock, swung her right foot over Sokkur's back and wiggled a bit as she settled

herself. Each of us had food satchels and milk pails in front of us. We waved as we headed for the valley where Grandpa, uncle Bjössi, and their summer help, Helgi, Guðrún, and Dísa were cutting and drying hay. Grass grew sparsely around the farm and Grandpa had to go way up into the foothills of the mountains to find enough to cut, and store away for the winter.

We went at an easy canter past the stable, down the lane, and over the bridge. As soon as we crossed the bridge the horses went swiftly into rack, and then into flying pace, a five-gait that's unique to Icelandic horses. Bjössi liked to show off the smooth gait by carrying a glass of water and riding at break-neck speed on his horse, Thunder, not spilling a single drop.

Sokkur and Stjarna kept up the galloping run across the outer field, until we reached the start of the foothills. We heard the whinnying of Blési before seeing him. Our horses neighed back. Biting at their bits, they eagerly plunged up the hill that led to an incredible volcanic cliff formation pointing to the sky with mystic shapes and deep crevasses. If that isn't the perfect place for trölls, I don't know what is, I thought to myself. Suddenly, a couple of ptarmigans scrambled away from the hooves of Stjarna, startling me but not my calm horse.

"Hey Sísí, you know there are trölls living up there, don't you?" My hands were gripping the reins. The mare sensed my tension, she shook her head and grunted, both in displeasure with me and exertion with going uphill.

Sísí turned, dark brows knit tightly over the bridge of her nose. "Stop it, Íeda. Iceland is weird, and weird things

happen, but there are NO TRÖLLS!"

She shouted the last words. Why is she shouting? I wondered. And how did she get to be so grown up and sound like Aunty? She's is just eleven years old, and I'm nine and a half. I stared at the high crags where few, long fingers of wispy fog were curling over the edges. The cool sun was playing hide and seek in fluffy, cottony clouds, sending eerie, grey shadows stealthily moving across the mountain.

I turned and looked down toward the ocean. Hámundarstaðir was hard to see unless you knew where to look; the turf roof blended with the ground. The farm looked like a toy house in the distance, sitting precipitously at the very edge on the cliff that skirted the long fjord.

The horses clambered over the last hill, and there were the workers.

Grandpa's scythe was swinging up and down, Helgi was a few feet behind him and Björn a few feet behind Helgi. Each man had a firm grip on the two knobby handles on the long pole, swinging their scythes in perfect rhythm; *up-down-swish-up-down-swish...* the curve of the sharp blades smoothly cutting the grass. The two women followed behind raking the newly cut, green leaves into rows of long, narrow piles. Four bales of hay were tied up and ready to be taken to the farm.

"Lunch time!" Sísí and I hollered unnecessarily as the workers were already laying down their tools. The rare sun had made all of them work up a sweat, their lopi sweaters were piled up on a large lava rock.

The men pulled out their fancy tobacco-horns. Grandpa's was by far the most ornate. He and Björn poured snuff on

the back of their left hand while Helgi poured his on the back of his right hand. Snuffing mightily, each sat down on a moss-covered rock.

Guðrún handed the bags to Dísa who started passing the food around. The two women, both in their twenties, were as different as night and day. Blond-haired Guðrún was short and slim with sky-blue twinkled eyes. Merry, easy-going and given to teasing, she and Bjössi got along extremely well. She was also a whirlwind of a worker that Grandpa really appreciated. Dísa had red hair and a temper to go with it. Striking, almost-green eyes, tall and graceful, she also pulled no punches when it came to work.

Helgi was a quiet, thirty-something, brown-haired, square-built man, well-known for his strength. He was an undefeated arm-wrestler in the area. Even though there was such an age difference, he and Bjössi complemented each other. Eighteen year-old Bjössi was outgoing in nature, very popular with the young folks as he played his accordion at many country-dances in the village.

After lunch was finished we put everything away and went back to work. We hustled for several hours, the men cutting grass steadily, occasionally stopping to sharpen their scythes. They'd pull out a pumice stone from their back pocket, spit on the scythe blades, then swish the stone back and forth, starting at the pole and following the curve of the blade to the end of the point. Periodically they'd check the blade with a thumb until satisfied with its sharpness.

Guðrún and Dísa followed, raking and turning the rows of grass, it smelled faintly of thyme and crow-berry leaves. Sísí and I did our best to keep up. My sister was getting

pretty good. She seemed to be able to just go ahead and work, whereas I tended to stop and breathe the aroma of the grass, look around, and frequently inspect the odd-looking, black lava cliff.

I leaned on my rake and wiped the sweat off my face with the back of my hand, staring for a minute at the rocky crags then went back to raking. After awhile I looked where we had been working. None of the rows were straight for any length. Several outcrops of rocks were scattered about and we had to work around them. I hope we aren't disturbing the 'Hidden Folks' that live in those rocks, I thought. At least we aren't moving any of them like some farmers have done and grief came upon them and their household!

Lost in my day-dreaming I accidentally dropped my rake. It clattered noisily against one of the boulders. Shivering and mumbling an apology I started raking like one possessed! Sísí turned at the noise.

"Wow, you sure got pumped all of a sudden!" She grinned. She sure has a way of reading my mind, I glared at her as I chewed on my bottom lip. Turning away from my sister I concentrated on my raking.

The dangling sun in the northern sky was hidden in the crimson-streaked clouds that brushed the tips of the cliffs. To the east, the clouds on the horizon touched the mouth of the fjord. Sky and sea were turning dark-grey, and, as so often in the fjords, it was hard to tell where one started and he other ended.

The wind was picking up and it was getting chilly. We put our lopi sweaters back on and prepared to quit for the day and head back to the farm.

Grandpa got one of the horses and fastened a packsaddle on its back. He hoisted one of the bales of hay and hooked it on the right side peg. Then he motioned for me to do my job. I knew what to do, bending over I backed my butt up against the flank of the horse and under the bale, holding it up while Grandpa went around and lifted another bale onto the left side peg. Bjössi put a packsaddle on another horse and lifted up a bale of hay. Sísí held it up in the same manner as I had for Grandpa as the other bale was put into place.

Helgi, Guðrún, and Dísa got the rest of our horses and our "caravan" started for home.

I could never figure out how Grandpa could get those bales so perfectly balanced. He had no scales to weigh them.

Grandpa was a very smart man!

CHAPTER 11
EIDER BIRD EGG·HUNTING

SITTING ON THE soft, grey, moss-covered volcanic cliff, Sísí and I dangled our legs over the edge, watching the white-crested ocean waves roll in. Two screeching seagulls circled, then dove at our heads. They flew off as we stood up, waving our hands, shooing them away.

We could feel the shaking of the ground as powerful ocean waves crashed against the rocks, and sent up columns of, shooting, ocean spray into the air. Fine, salty mist clung to our wooly caps and moistened our faces. Not a hint of fog anywhere for a change. Tall, white waterfalls cascaded down Smjörfell Mountain in the distance. The rivers meandered in curvy ribbons down the valley and emptied into the fjord. The ice-blue sky was filled with big bales of white, cottony clouds that sailed along in the cool, brisk, steady breeze.

Tucking our hair tighter under our lopi-knit caps, we scanned the eider ducks flying about, then coming down and waddling to a nest, we hoped, among the rocks on the damp lava sand.

"There are hundreds of ducks. We should be able to get tons of eggs and Down!" I whispered, although we were a good twenty feet above the ocean beach. The insane noise of the gulls and krias, and the pounding of the sea, would have made it virtually impossible for the ducks to hear me.

"Some of them went to the moss patch behind the big boulder where that seal is, he'll leave when he sees us come down. Let's go." Sísí said as she started scrambling like a fly down the, almost-sheer, rock wall. I followed close behind. With tiny toeholds and small ledges for our fingers to grip, we crept down, causing loose shale and lava rocks to roll. The clatter disturbed some haughty-gaudy puffins that pompously waddled away.

We had two flour sacks tied to our waist; one for the Down and one for the eggs. I looked forward to eating those scrumptious eggs. They tasted stronger than chicken eggs and were about three times as big, with huge, reddish-yellow yolk.

The last few feet were loose pebbles and sand. We skidded down on our bottoms until we reached the beach. Catching our breath for a moment, we sat still as two groups of grey geese spanned their wings wide, flapped and squawked raucously, then went at each other. I saw what they were fighting over; a large, dead trout lay on the ground half-way between the two. They separated and flew off as we got up and started to walk toward them. I was glad it wasn't gannets, they would have attacked us in a heartbeat' with their saber-like pointy beaks.

Sísí was right. The seal belly-flopped off the rock, then, awkwardly, flip-flopped on the pebbly beach to the ocean

and smoothly swam away.

We found some nests and gathered two dozen eggs, always leaving one or two in the down-filled nest to hatch, since Eider ducks rarely lay more than five eggs. We divided our eggs in two bags and carefully tucked some Down all around them, then filled the other bags with the soft, downy, feathers.

"Grandma will be happy to know there are so many nests here." Sisi said, as she tightened the string on her sack and fastened it back to her waist. "She was wanting to make more bed-pillows. If it doesn't rain tomorrow, we'll have to get a group of us together and come back." She started to walk back toward the cliff.

"Wait a minute, Sísí. Let's wade for awhile." I said. "Look, there is a small cave over there! The ocean is so clear, I see some pretty neat seashells on the bottom." I sat down on a rock and started to take off my shoes, then jumped up howling:

"Oh gross! A fulmar has spit his yellow gook here. The rock smells of rotten fish!"

Sísí was doubled over with laughter as she unfastened her bags. Turning, she pointed to where we had clawed our way down.

"There are a lot of them nesting in the hollows of the seacliff; we're lucky we didn't touch their mess. We'd be stinking to high heaven for days!" She gave an exaggerated shudder.

Taking off our shoes and socks we tip-toed among the shells and pebbles. I stuck my foot into the pool.

"Wow, the water is ice-cold" I yelped, yanking my foot back, shivering.

Looking down I saw little fish darting about. Large, silvery, trout swam gracefully in the pond-like water in the shallow cave that had been carved out by the unceasing surging of the ocean waves.

Hollering "EE-OW" at the top of our lungs, we waded in the freezing sea waves hopping backward as a wave would roll in and slosh white froth up our legs. The hems on our skirts were getting soaked, it was time for us to go home. We fastened our bags to our waists and headed back up. As Sísí and I clambered up on all fours the sandy shale caused our feet to slide one foot back for every two feet upward. Our soggy sheep-skin shoes and wool socks were soon caked with powdery, black volcanic sand.

Although the wind was nippy we had beads of sweat on our foreheads by the time we reached the top. We jammed our hats tighter on our heads. The ends of our lopi-scarfs whipped across our shoulders and flapped behind us as we, puffing and breathing hard, walked and skipped back to the farmhouse.

This had been a wonderful day. I looked at Sísí and grinned. I hadn't said anything about the trölls, the awful Grýla, and Leppalúður (well, actually that's really a Christmas thing, I'll wait!) And I hadn't breathed a *word* about the 'Hidden Folks' who were in abundance in this region.

For a change, I'd been VERY good!

CHAPTER 12
SÍSÍ AND I GO BERRY PICKING.

"THE BLUEBERRIES SHOULD be ripe about now, and I'd like to have some to make jam, and top our skyr," Grandma said as she walked into the kitchen. "How about you two go and pick some, and don't bother with picking any crowberries." Reaching under the bench she pulled out two tin buckets. Each had a folded, white flour sack. "The weather looks good and your grandfather and Bjössi have already taken the boat over to Vopnafjörður. Dísa and Guðrún are hoeing the garden and cutting the Rabarbarinn [Rhubarb]," she continued as she handed us two bulging lunch satchels.

"We love to go berry picking!" Both of us cried enthusiastically, jumping up from our stools. We smiled gleefully at each other at the same thought: Riding into the valley the berry hunting and picking would take most of the day. We'd be gone at milking time and wouldn't have to put up with mean Rauða!

"Shall we go back to the foothills where we are haying?" Sísí asked casually, as she reached around door-post and got

couple of rope-bridles.

"The cows meandered over that way, look for them and bring them back with you after you've filled your buckets." Grandma said grinning. She knew exactly what we'd been thinking! I squirmed, a guilty blush warming my cheeks. Sísí turned with a shrug, wrinkling her nose.

"We'll do that Grandma." She said. Slinging one halter over her shoulder and handing me the other one, Sísí reached down and picked up her pail and satchel as I picked up mine. We kissed Grandma on the cheek, then went out the door and headed for the field. We waved to Dísa and Guðrún. They had paused working to wipe the sweat off their foreheads with white handkerchiefs. Leaning on the handles of their hoes they waved back.

Snati and Goldie got to their feet, stretching. The dainty Goldie lifted up her right paw, grooming it with long strokes by her tongue. Snati sat up, his dark-brown eyes glittering as he cocked his head.

"Yes you may go with us." I said patting his head. His body quivered with excitement. He was probably ten years older than Goldie, but still acted and worked like a much younger dog, and he was *ten* times smarter than she!

Sísí whistled for the horses as we sauntered past the sheepcote. The horses were in the outer field and came trotting toward us. As usual I got Stjarna while Sísí put the bridle on Sokkur. We didn't use saddles unless we were visiting a neighboring farm, or on a trip to the village of Vopnafjörður or north to Bakkafjörður.

After a brisk, one-hour ride, we got close to where we'd been haying. The fearsome, grotesquely-shaped lava rock

wall loomed forebodingly before us. I would never be able to understand how Sísí could be so calm, almost serene, in these eerie surroundings. I loved my rugged, bleak country, full of mysteries and adventure but I also saw ghosts and gremlins in every crack and crevasse!

We went past piles of blue-grey lava chunks spaced few meters apart. Travelers from centuries ago had stacked up these landmarks - tall ones and squatty ones - as guideposts.

Dotting the valley were towering, skinny, lava-formed pillars with grey-black trunks. Their tops were covered with the grey velvety moss that was everywhere. Small, white and purple flowers were somehow able to grab roots in non-existing soil.

After another hour of riding farther into the ravine, we spotted the cows ambling away, munching at the meager grass. A tall waterfall cascaded down the craggy, basalt-formed hill, and the wide, shallow river meandered our way. One cow was standing in mid-stream slurping away. This was a good place to stop. We led the horses down for a drink then tethered them and went to look for berry-patches. Both dogs lapped the water then scampered off to chase birds.

"Kónguló, kónguló, vísaðu mér á berjamó," [Spider, spider show me the berry-land] we chanted as we searched for ripe, juicy blueberries. We believed the old folks' stories; the spiders always led the way to the best berry-spots, and we were very careful not to squash those long-legged, helpful creatures.

Sure enough, we came upon a nice area thick with berries. It was getting close to lunch- time so we decided to eat before we started picking the fruit. Grandma had fixed

enough for a small army; strips of dried cod, slices of smoked mutton, and twist-cookies. We drank fresh water from the river and then started gathering the berries. At first, I could hear them clunk into our pails, but as they accumulated, the only sound was a soft *plop*. The narrow valley was quiet. Every now and then a ptarmigan would cluck and dart out from under a small bush, wings whirring. The horses occasionally snorted softly, and the cows chewed contently. The air was calm. A faint, salty, smell from the ocean mingled with thyme and berries. A few fluffy clouds wandered across the sharp-blue sky.

Sísí had crawled up the hillside and was furiously picking away, left hand bending down the berry-bush, while her right hand busily picked off the berries. My bucket was over half-full, but the way she was going, I was sure she had hers almost full. I sat back on my heels and glanced at the craggy mountain. Then did a double-take! Thick fog was gathering on top and oozing down it's slopes!

"Sísí, look." I stood up, but she kept going. I raised my voice.

"Sísí look at the mountain." Rubbing her berry-stained hands on the moss she got up slowly.

"I've my pail full. What about the mountain?" Then turning her head, she followed where I was pointing. "Oh no," she whispered.

"Maybe it'll move north." I said. We watched and gauged the move of the fog. Looking at each other, we wordlessly agreed it was coming our way, and by the looks of it, we were in for 'a soupy one' as Grandpa would say. Putting a pail into each flour sack, we tied the top tight to keep the berries from

falling out.

Getting back on our horses, we yelled at the dogs to start the cows moving. Old Rauða mooed in protest then reluctantly led the way. The bell on her neck clanged as she started to walk in the hoof-path. Freyja didn't want to move, but Snati knew what to do; yipping from side to side he threatening to nip her legs. The heifer decided to fall in line with Rauða. The third cow, Hilda, followed. Cow-poke-slowly the parade started.

Sísí kept Sokkur close behind Hilda. I followed on Stjarna and kept twisting and looking back keeping an eye on the fog as it swirled down the crags. I, of course, was expecting to see one or more, of the 'Hidden Folks' that materialized in any good, proper fog.

Icy fingers were already playing up and down my spine when I heard an awful sound; *baagh, baagh, baagh!*

My blood ran cold and the hair on the back of my neck curled up!

With my heart thumping a mile a minute I whacked Stjarna on the rump, moving her out of the rut and up on the bank. Catching up with Sísí I poked her arm with my horse-whip. She looked at me startled.

"What's the matter with you?" She asked, a little irritated. "The fog is still behind us, I think we'll beat it if we can get these cows to move a little faster!"

"No Sísí listen. Can't you hear it?" I asked.

Sísí stopped her horse and cocked her head just as another *baagh, baagh, baagh* resounded in the cliffs.

"It doesn't sound scary. I can't quite make it out. Wait. Look at that sheep up there, by that boulder." Sisi pointed.

"She's just standing there '*baaing*'. The other ones around her are eating. Something isn't quite right." She squinted her eyes intently at the sheep.

For a moment I stared at the ground by the boulder, then kind of recognized the sound and said to my sister. "I bet her lamb fell into a hole and is crying down in there. That's what makes it sound so weird." I turned Stjarna and had her take a few steps toward the hillside and the sheep, she watched me, but didn't move. Then I heard the sound again '*baagh,*' and now I could tell that it was a lamb in distress. My fears were replaced with anxiety.

"Come on Sísí, we've got to get the lamb out or it'll die."

"Let's hurry then! The dogs will get the cows home, and if we get caught in the fog our horses will take us to the farm."

Quickly, Sisi turned Sokkur out of the rut and joined me on top of the bank. We went across the river and up the gravelly side of the mountain toward the large rock. The ewe warily eyed us as she backed away a few steps, then stopped.

When we came around the boulder, we could see an opening in the ground where the yammering was coming from. As we dismounted, I looked with unease at the thick fog that had now drifted into the bottom of the valley, slowly obliterating everything in it's path.

We got down on our stomachs and looked into the narrow chasm. The young lamb had left numerous marks where it had tried, in a futile attempt, to climb out. From the way it was moving around, it didn't look to have any broken limbs, but was exceedingly nervous.

"It's too deep to jump into." Sisi said as she sat back on

her haunches and stared sadly at the pathetic little ewe.

"We could slide down, but we wouldn't be able to get out of there. The walls are extremely smooth. There are hardly any toeholds."

We sat for a moment contemplating our dilemma. The lamb cried piteously. From the droppings in the hole, I surmised that the lamb had been there overnight and was very hungry.

"Well, tell you what, I'm taking the bridle off of Stjarna. She won't leave," I said handing the harness to Sisi. "I'll go down, and you hand me the rope. I'll catch the lamb and strap it down then lift it up to you. Since I'm littler than you, it'll be easier for you to pull me up than for me to pull you."

Sisi gnawed her bottom lip, looking dubious. "Are you sure we should do this, Íedamin?"

"We've been in volcanic crevasses before, Sisi. No-one will be able to get here in time to save the lamb; it'll starve to death." A shudder ran down my sister's back, biting her quivering lower lip she nodded. I slid down into the hole as Sisi dropped the harness after me holding the loop end tightly in her hands.

The lamb frantically tried scramble away as I grabbed it, but I desperately held on. Wrapping my arms around it, I held the weakly-kicking feet and worked the rope around the white, wooly body. I saw the two VV cuts in the left ear, Grandpa's mark. Holding tight, I lifted the small lamb to Sisi, who was on her stomach, her hands reaching down.

"Got her," she exulted, working the small ewe from the bridle. Then I heard a soft, "Oh, she headed straight for mamma." Sisi's head came back in view. She was giggling.

"Her stubby tail is a blur, she's wagging it so fast. She must have been absolutely starving. She's suckling like there's no tomorrow!"

I was happy to hear that, but I was more than ready to get out of this tröll-hole.

"Here it comes, I have my feet braced against a rock." Sisi said as the rope slithered down. I held on to the loop of the harness and pulled myself up hand-over-hand as Sisi, grunting loudly, pulled and held on.

We sat on the rim of the fissure for a moment catching our breath, watching the ewe and her lamb. We were grinning from ear to ear as we clapped our hands in joy..

We just barely beat the fog. By the time I'd put the bridle back on Stjarna, the grey, soggy mist wrapped around us. We remembered the admonition from the family:

"If you're ever caught in a fog, loosen your hold on the reins and let the horses take over; they'll know the way." They sure enough did!

This was the last time we sisters were together at Vopnafjörður. For the next four years, I traveled by myself.

CHAPTER 13
VOPNAFJÖRÐUR

1935

THE TWO CORRUGATED sheds where I had tried to get Lilla to jump, were askew from the earthquake last year, but still standing. I could still jump from one to the other! I ran ahead of Aunty and Ólafur and entered the house. A low moaning-groan greeted me. I skidded to a stop, my heart thumping wildly. Then the moaning faded to a grunt, and I heard a soft voice.

"I'm sorry, just one more bandage and I'll be through." A woman said gently.

A man's gruff voice said something. I didn't understand the words, but I understood the groaning. I assumed it must be the Norwegian patient. He must be hurting bad! My heart stopped pounding as I realized what the moaning was. I turned as Aunty dropped the box on the table and went into the sickroom.

Although I didn't speak Norwegian, I'd been around

sailor-fishermen often enough to recognize the language. I could hear Aunty speaking, sounded to me like she'd asked a question. The man's voice answered in a loud voice that, I thought, sounded belligerent. She returned shortly, with a wide grin on her face.

"Hans wants to get up and walk around!" she, gleefully, told Ólafur. "He is getting much better."

"He sure groaned a lot for someone who's getting better. He scared the wits out of me!" I said looking around the room, still feeling a little freaked out.

A tall, rawboned, very capable-looking woman came into the kitchen. Her abundant, orange-red, hair stuck out in all directions. It reminded me of Halldór's hair, the big man down at the warehouse.

"Halló there, and you must be the visitor from Reykjavik." Cocking her head, she measured me up from my shoes to the top of my head with her piercing green eyes.

"You're one spunky girl, aren't you? I'm Sigga." She stuck out her right hand and I stuck out mine. Her, very large, calloused hand totally made mine disappear. I winced a bit as she gave a hearty squeeze.. We shook hands like two adults. She didn't call me a little one, not a little girl, but spunky. I liked the sound of it; it wasn't wimpy.

"I'm pleased to meet you. My name is Íeda." I said politely as I'd been taught. "Þórbjörg is my aunt and Ólafur is my uncle." I added primly.

"Íeda. That's an unusual name. I like it." Sigga smiled broadly.

"I don't like my name at all!" I grumbled. My dark eyebrows were pulled together in a tight knot. "Some say its

Ýta, others say Íta, another Ída, still another Æda. No matter what it is, the kids at school like to make fun of it and rhyme it with bad words." I frowned, gnawing the inside of my mouth. "Grandpa said I was supposed to be named after Aunt Þórbjörg; he said my name was 'outlandish'. He calls me Didda or Diddamín. No one ever heard of my *real* name, whatever it is." I stared at the floor. My eyes felt hot. I'm not going to be a cry-baby! Grandpa always said that Viking children never cried; they howled, screamed, bellowed - but did not cry! I clenched my jaw and rubbed the floor with my toe.

"Your name must be hidden" Sigga mused, rubbing her left thumb across her lower lip.

Auntie's chair scraped loudly on the floor as she shoved away from the table, clearing her throat.

"What?" Startled, I lifted my head and looked into Sigga's face. She had her head cocked, her left eye scrunched shut, looking first at Auntie, and then at me. Leaning close, her wild hair shook like birds shaking bush-leaves as she lowered her voice;

"No one has heard of your name, right?" She asked

I nodded. "That's right."

"No one seems to spell it correctly, right?" Her nose was just inches away from mine.

Puzzled, I nodded again. Auntie cleared her throat again, this time quite loudly.

"So you're not named after anyone in the family?"

Pursing my lips, I shook my head vigorously.

Sigga stared Auntie right in the eye as she leaned back and made herself comfortable in the rocker. Lifting me up

onto her lap, she softly brushed a strand of hair from my face. Rocking gently for a moment she got a 'Far Away' look on her face, then said; "Once upon a time, eons ago, in the kingdom of the misty 'Thule the Hidden' realm, the first Monarch ever, had a gorgeous newborn. Her rainbow-hue hair was in tight curly ringlets and sat on her head like a coronet. She had four-color freckles all over her opaque body; an extremely unique looking baby." Sigga stopped, then continued…

"The King and Queen decided that they must choose an exceptional name for their child but they had been warned by the elf Queen, Borghildur of Álaborg, that a certain tröll was planning to do a 'changeling' attack, that is, sneak into the palace and switch the King's baby with a tröll baby and this way take over their land. She suggested a secret name and the King heeded her advice and named their baby a secret name. No one knew that name except the baby's Guardian Angel. The name would be kept secret until the end of days. But the name that she was known by was Snotra. This was an elf name that would be a charm and protect the child all through her life."

She stopped again for a moment, took a deep breath and with a piercing look at me said; "Perhaps your mother heard of this and gave you an unusual name, for a charm and good luck."

"Sigga!" Auntie started. The chair legs tottered and clattered as she abruptly stood up. She stopped when Sigga glared at her.

"And the kids at school? What do they know? Pouf, to their opinion and name calling, and give it to the trölls!" She waved her hand and snapped her fingers.

Wow, I loved this woman! Hah, when I get back to school, and they start the teasing, I'll just say, "I give your opinions to the trölls!" I bet that'll scare them witless!

Simply delicious, I could hardly wait! In just a few moments this woman I'd just met took care of my name-dilemma just like that! [I tried to snap my fingers... I'll have to learn to do that!]

I scooted off Sigga's lap and ran for the door. I had to share this with Finna! Then I turned and gave Sigga a fierce hug until she grunted, then laughed.

"Diddamín, remember not to take this story seriously." Aunt Þórbjörg called after me, looking very concerned.

"Oh, but it's very good, and the kids don't know if it's true or not, we have so many stories like this, but this one is simply the best!" I giggled as I sped out the door.

My grin stayed plastered on my face as I clambered all the way up the cliff. Wadding my skirt around my knees I raced to Finna's house.

I liked Finna. She had lots of shiny, auburn, hair. Her blue-green eyes sparkled with merriment. We were the same age, but she was three inches taller and somewhat heavier than I. Her mother had died when she was very small, she didn't remember her at all. Her father was a good shoemaker but a stern, taciturn and opinionated man. He had not married again. About Ólafur's age, he had none of his tact, or gentleness, especially when it came to talking politics. Kristján was of the opinion that the "government should see to it that everyone has the same in life."

I remember a community meeting where Kristján started his usual "the government isn't taking care of people

like they should" rant. Things got heated as men took sides. Ólafur tried to soothe the tempers. But Kristján got purple-faced and belligerent. Finally, Grandpa, just as belligerent as Kristján, stood up and shouted that one should work hard and *earn* their way, not just be handed *stuff* on a "silver platter." This was like waving a red flag in the face of an angry bull, and brought on a free-for-all, as they got into fierce arguments over this.

Then Grandpa threw up his hand and told Kristán "I suppose if some people are born more beautiful than others, you'll want to cut off their noses to 'even up everyone's looks'!" Then he stomped out of the meeting.

Finna listened to me with as much glee as I had with Sigga. Dancing around the room, she chanted, "I kept telling you your mother gave you a name that is unique!"

Then she stopped, a pensive look came on her face as she murmured, "I miss not having a mother. I want to go to the country-dance that's coming up, but I have outgrown my dresses. I have fabric but I can't cut it out on myself. Dad can't do it." She paused, then cocked her head at me and asked, " Will you cut it for me?"

I had made quite a few doll clothes for sock-dolls, and at ten years of age was rather adept with the sewing-needle. I wasn't sure I could do this, but looking into the wistful face of my friend I knew I had to try.

I contoured the fabric on her body and pinned it in place, then cut all around her. Scraps fell to the floor as I re-fitted and re-pinned and snipped away. After the cutting we sewed the whole dress by hand, we didn't have a sewing-machine.

The dress turned out quite pretty, and we attended the dance where we had a great time taking turns dancing with old men, young men, women and girls. The old wood floor buckled and popped under our energetic, polka-stomping, feet.

Sitting down for a spell to catch my breath, my head swiveled side to side as I watched the twirling dancers, and Bjössi's flying fingers on the accordion. My cousin Nonni, from Hámundarstaðir, was trying to keep up on drums Bjössi had fashioned out of seal-skin, tightened over a wood barrel. Keeping fair time with a couple of sticks, he was making plenty of thumping noises until he decided to join the ring of dancers.

Clapping my hands in rhythm with the music, I thought back to last year when Lilla, Sísí and I were here on this dance floor. A man, about Ólafur's age, had come over and asked Lilla for a dance. She was too shy. Ducking her head, she'd turned away. Later the man came back and, with a big grin, handed her a twine-twisted ring and told her it was a called a 'bashful ring.'

Shyly, she put it on then twisted her hand this way and that, proudly admiring the ring when Sísí told her she should dance at least one dance with the man. She looked up at the guy, still standing by, and slowly nodded her head. The next thing we knew she was clear across the floor hopping like crazy in a riotous polka, his five kids circling and dancing around them. We knew the man's eleven year-old son, Grímur had been wanting to meet Lilla, but he too, was also very shy. We joked about this for the longest time, but we

also thought it was a clever way of giving Grímur a chance to dance with my little sister.

I got up, smoothed down my skirt and grabbed Nonni's hand as he came flying by me. We all went twirling faster and faster until everyone was out of breath. Mercifully the music stopped.

"Coffee-time!" Laughing and hooting we gathered around the table piled high with cheese, dried cod, smoked mutton, and more. Vienna tort, pancakes, twist-cookies, and, of course, coffee and fire-wine [for the adult males.]

Finna came up behind me, smiling, cheeks beet-red, grabbing my waist she whispered,

"Thanks for helping with my dress, Teitur sure likes it." He was a boy that Finna had liked forever.

We danced almost through the whole night. None of us wanted to waste the day-bright nights of the short summer.

What a wonderful time we had. We were ten and life was good.

CHAPTER 14

HÁMUNDARSTAÐIR
GRANDPA'S FARM

SQUINTING AND SHADING my eyes, I searched the white-capped ocean waves for Grandpa's small, black and white fishing boat. Cocking my head I tried to hear the *chug-chug* of the motor over the screeching of seagulls, and the slapping of the ocean swells against the rocks. I watched as patches of gray fog twirled over the choppy waves in the formidable northern Fjord. Leaning forward, I scrunched my eyes almost shut, but I saw no sign of his boat. After the dance the night before, I'd slept late and Grandpa had gone back to Vopnafjörður.

Standing on the edge of the distorted, odd shaped lava cliff, I felt the grounds tremble and heard the powerful ocean crashing and rumbling up the gorge. Swooshing, sucking sounds came from deep within the cave the ocean waves had carved eons past.

Scrambling down a gravelly crevasse, I dug in my heels and my fingers gripped the gritty, sharp lava ledges. Scattered

clumps of heather bravely tried to find roots in small beds of smooth, volcanic ash, the small pink and white flowers contrasting oddly with the blue-grey surrealistic surrounding. The racket of rolling stones alarmed the nesting puffins, warily they pointed toward me with their red, yellow and black striped, huge beaks. Shaking their short wings and portly bodies, they waddled off on their fiery-red feet.

I touched a moss-lined seagull's nest, which promptly came alive with necks stretching and twitching, hungry mouths wide open. I jerked my hand back as the angry mama bird streaked down like a meteorite, yellow beak wide open, screaming fiercely.

Carefully avoiding white streaks of yucky bird droppings and inching my way to the bottom of the cliff I started running on the narrow strip of gray-black volcanic sand. My sheepskin shoes made squishy, slushy sounds as small waves wet my feet. Gross smells arose when I kicked against slimy patches of algae and hopped around carcasses of birds, crabs, brittle fish bones and blue seashells.

Stopping for a moment I leaned against a half-buried relic of a rowboat. Pulling at the coarse brown fish-net that hung over the rotted bulwark, I disturbed five napping Harbors seals. They looked at me with their brown, marble-shiny eyes, then moaning, groaning and grumbling they closed their eyes.

Tugging the seaman's yellow rain-hat tight over my hair I tried to avoid bird droppings, as a gazillion seagulls swept overhead.

The wispy shreds of fog across the water were slowly dissipating as the sun broke through the clouds. A brilliant

gold, red and blue colored rainbow curved over a tall misty waterfall. Rivers and brooks cascaded down the jagged, immense, snow-capped mountain sheltering the fjord.

I climbed to my favorite place, the top of a barnacle-crusted lava rock accessible on one side in the outgoing tide. Waves caused spray to slosh on my face and sting my cheeks. Licking my lips I tasted the salt water.

A fog-shrouded steamship made its way across the mouth of the fjord. The warning blast of the ship's fog horn boomed mournfully between the basalt-black towering cliffs.

Powerful spouts from Humpback whales dotted the sea. They slapped their long flippers, roiled the water and made it difficult to spot Grandpa's small boat.

Gray seals shot up out of the ocean, grabbing squirming fish from the beaks of diving gulls. The seals' bodies glistened and shone like well-polished whale bone as they leaped up and then dove back into the waves. For awhile I watched, mesmerized, then searched the fjord again, my stomach churned. I knew well the deadly perils of the sea. I'd heard that Íngi and his crew had drowned in Seyðisfjörður, shortly after our ship had turned north. I shuddered at the thought of how close we were to seeing that happen.

Dragging my feet I turned back. A virtual blizzard of seagulls and puffins floated below the fluffy clouds in the gray-blue sky above my head. Slowly I climbed back up the bird-filled lava cliff.

"Come on everybody. Down to the dock!" I heard Uncle Bjössi shout.

Reaching the top, I spotted the boat a little way out. White froth sprayed out like wings at the bow as the boat

swooped up and down in the choppy water. Leaping to my feet I ran to catch up with my uncle, grandma, and her summer help, Þóra. All of us whooping and running as we headed down to the dilapidated dock.

The pilings were old, barnacle-covered, and rotting in places, but still strong enough to hold us as we ran. The wet uneven planks bounced up and down by our clomping feet and made small bait-bucket rattle. A tattered old fishnet shook as Bjössi ran then tossed to Grandpa the end of a coiled up rope fastened to an old rusty motor.

Catching the rope with his right hand, Grandpa's gnarled left hand held tight on the wheel as he brought the rocking fishing boat to the dock with experienced ease. We started to unload the large, heavy bags of flour, sugar and other supplies, and as always, fighting off the screeching, greedy, diving seagulls.

Grandpa was safe.

CHAPTER 15
COWS GO CRAZY
IN THE SPRING

IT WAS A sunny day for a change. A rare, warm, breeze was blowing in from the ocean, causing the salty air to bring faint smell of musty algae and spring weeds.

Björssi was ready to let the cows out for the first time this Spring. Old Rauða, Hilda, and the heifer, Freyja, were restlessly two-stepping in their stalls.

I stood outside with my cousins from the farm, Hámundarstaðir II. Nonni (his name was Jónas, but there were so many Jónases already in the family that he was nicknamed Nonni), who was twelve. He had sky-blue eyes, sparkling with mischief, adventurous and outgoing; his sister Dóra, cautious and timid, while the younger sister, Sigga, was a bit of both: cautious and spontaneous.

Grandpa called them *The Three Golden Gremlins*, because all had almost identical hair- color, golden-yellow, and where you saw one, you saw the other two.

"Alright, come in and get ready," Bjossi hollered from

inside the cow-house.

I got ready to tiptoe around the cow's manure, but Bjössi had cleaned the dung-trench.

"I...I don't want to do this, I...I just want to watch." Dóra stuttered, cringing.

"Ok, Nonni, you can have Hilda. Sigga you take Freyja, and Diddamín, you take old Rauða, you know her and her mean ways!" Bjössi chuckled.

Just outside the front door, Grand-amma was sitting on a three-legged stool. Grandma Sigríður was perched on the hitching rock. Þóra stood by, arms akimbo, eyebrows knit in a heavy frown.

The show was about to begin. The one who held their cow's tail the longest was the winner!

Nonni, Sigga and I had stationed ourselves behind our respective cow, firmly grabbing a tail. The cows mooed and twisted their heads to look at us, at the same time trying to swish their tails.

Old Rauða was getting riled, her hind feet started stomping from side to side.

"Hurry, open the door!" I jumped away from a hoof aimed at my legs.

"I have to untie them. Dad will open the door when I yell," Bjössi was scrambling at the hay-trough lifting the ropes off the cows' heads.

"Ok, Dad!" Bjössi hollered. The door opened with a screechy-creaking noise, not having been opened all winter.

Suddenly it was as if a fox had jumped into the cow-house. The cows backed out every which way trying to get

outside and at the same time feeling the pull we kids had on their tails.

Freyja started out first. The heifer stopped and stared, wild-eyed. Sigga was tugging the tail, screaming and urging the heifer to move. Nonni was next with Hilda dragging him on a fast run, his long, skinny legs were wildly pumping up and down. His hollering and yelling startled the heifer, which scrambled outside and yanked Sigga off her feet. She let go of the tail and Freyja took off jumping and bucking.

Old Rauða rolled her eyes at me then viciously kicked back. Turning like she was a teen-cow she took off out of the cow-house at a clumsy, kick-hopping clop.

I could hear the adults laughing and egging us on. Bjössi was whooping like a cowboy herding cattle. I glanced sideways and saw that Sigga had let go and the heifer was clomping into the field. I could hear Nonni almost catching up. Then I tripped and fell on my stomach, I bit into gritty dust but still held on while Rauða dragged me on the ground. She was kicking and bucking like an ill-mannered horse. My mouth was getting full of dirt and grass, mixed with blood from my slit lip, but I was not about to let go!

"Stop, you've won! LET GO! LET GO!" Everyone was screaming at the same time. Gritting my teeth, my fingers were frozen in a stubborn death grip as sharp, lava pebbles stung my cheeks. Rauða did a turn-around, and I swung in a big arch, let go of the tail and tumbled into the creek where we did our laundry, and washed the wool after the sheep were shorn.

I sat in the ice-cold water, steaming-hot temper at a full

boil. I was a bloody, dirty mess and old Rauða had gotten the best of me. She stopped and looked at me. I swear she smirked as she rolled her big, brown, cow-eyes at me again. Mumbling a soft *'Moo'* she nonchalantly ambled after the other cows, stopping now and then to curl her long tongue around little tufts of fresh grass.

I was infuriated. I didn't mind a horse dumping me, but a *cow…!?!*

The whole family came running, hysterically laughing, although my two grandmas were concerned. Bjössi jumped into the creek with a rag in his hand and proceeded to mop off the blood on my face as he pulled me up to my feet.

"She's fine, just madder than a wet hen." Bjössi chortled, as I spit out a sliver of lava-shale.

"You'd be mad too if a *cow* dumped *you* into the creek!" I spit out the words and glared at my uncle, who kept dabbing at my face, grinning.

"You should have let go!" Nonni wiped tears from his eyes with the back of his left hand, while still doubled up with laughter.

"Yeah, why didn't you just let go?" Sigga and Dóra giggled.

I started shivering, then mumbled, "Just get me outta here!"

"Here Bjössi, wrap her up in my shawl." Grandma Sigríður handed him her black lopi-wrap. As we walked up to the farm, my sheepskin shoes made slushy, squeaky sound in harmony with the *slop-slop* of Bjössi's water-filled, seal-skin boots. I turned and looked grimly at Rauða. She was totally oblivious of me, contently chewing her cud.

With much merriment, we all got to the farm where Þóra suddenly jumped out of the door. Looking at my scratched-up face, she exclaimed "Good heavens girl, don't you EVER learn?!" She softened her words by giving me a soft thump on the shoulder. Quickly she dabbed her eyes with the corner of her shawl. "Come on, Diddamín, let's get some hot drink into your tummy." I was touched by her obvious concern and patted her hand.

After a cup of hot coffee and a batch of twist-cookies, I got my humor back. I laughed along with the others as each one took a turn in describing the event, each one trying to outdo the other, laughing and slapping their knees.

"I think you all are just plum crazy." Muttered Dora. "I thought you all were going to get killed! That old cow, Rauða, with her sharp, pointy horns and mean eyes, is the most wicked- looking thing!"

"Well, the old 'thing' doesn't have the best temper in the ruminant world, but her horns sure are beauties." Grandpa had a dreamy look on his face. I wondered if he was think-ing of a new snuff-horn! I realized that her horns *did* have striking markings: black-brown streaks on ivory bone. Those horns would make a very handsome tobacco-holder; very likely could be the envy of the local farmers who competed for the most colorful and ornate "snuffy".

"Tomorrow we'll start shearing the sheep before turning them out." Grandpa rubbed his chin, twirled his mustache and squinted at my three cousins. "You Gremlins want to come over for some fun and work? We'll have eighteen ewes and four rams to shear and a few lambs to earmark."

"Don't forget we'll also be washing the wool in the creek."

Grandma motioned to the kids with her cup of coffee.

"We'd love to help!" Nonni, enthusiastically, spoke for his two sisters as they nodded. "We'll be back in the morning then!" They headed out the door, waving and hollering.

"Bless, bless!"

CHAPTER 16
SHEARING TIME

WE WERE GATHERED by the fast-running, gurgling creek where I'd been dumped the day before. The sun was shining, although not very bright or warm, it *was* lurking in the thin, raggedy clouds. I hoped, for the sheep's sake, that it would warm up. They were sure to feel cold when shorn of their wooly coats.

The fire was roaring, devouring the dry peat-and-cow chips. Steam from the iron kettle curled up into the cool air, and grey-white mist swirled over the bubbles rolling in the water. Þóra dropped in a handful of green, homemade, lye soap. The effect was like the gushing of Little Geyser, shooting up into the air.

Þóra and Grandma were sitting on lava rocks that were softly cushioned by thick, silver-grey moss. Grand-Amma and Dóra were sitting on wood stools just outside the sheepcote, carefully situated out of the way when the door would swing open and Bjössi, Grandpa, and Nonni would come out with a sheep, hands firmly holding the horns. Sigga and I stood by

with the shears in our hands, like nurses in an operating room; *knife-scalpel-scissors.* The men came out, each one straddling a sheep. When Grandpa stumbled and let go of the ewe, Sigga managed to grab a handful of stringy, dirty wool, slowing the sheep down enough for me to grab the horns and frantically hold on. Swinging my leg over her squirming back, I squeezed her between my knees and dug my heels into the ground. Sigga let go as Grandpa grabbed the shears from her hand and took over the horns, twisting the sheep's head to one side and forcing her to lie down. I sat down by her head and held her tight, she kicked her feet a bit and let out a plaintive "bah." Grandpa was quick and the sheep was speedily shorn. As I let her up, she vigorously shook her head and body. I wondered if she felt as ridiculous as she looked!

Grandpa went in for the next one. Nonni was done shearing, and Sigga let go of the sheep she was holding for him.

"Yow! Get the ram!" I heard Bjössi yell in a weird voice.

The ludicrous, half-shorn ram was wriggling, and clumsily waddling down the field, his feet tangling up in the wool dragging on the ground. Bjössi was crouched on the ground grabbing his crotch trying to get his breath back. The rest of us ran and formed a circle, slowly forcing the ram to get closer to the sheepcote. Bjössi was staggering to his feet, slaughter in his eyes. He was okay. I didn't dare ask: *Who is madder than a wet hen now?*

The shearing was done swiftly. Now it was time to mark the lambs. I felt sorry for them as Grandpa cut his two V-marks in the left ear. I noticed Sigga and Dóra averted their eyes as the bright-red blood dribbled down, and stained the lambs' curly wool. I knew farmers had to mark their

sheep, but wished there was an easier way of doing that.

When the hot water was ready, we gathered some of the sheared, dirty wool and pitched it into the boiling water. Using long-handled wood poles, Grandpa and Björssi stirred and then lifted the heavy, wet fleece out of the black kettle and into the, sparkling, clear creek. My cousins and I jumped into the ice cold water and rinsed out any residue of soap. Then the women spread the wool on the ground to dry.

Later we gathered the wool and brought it inside. We kept it in a corner of the kitchen, where Grandma had her spinning wheel. A skein of spun brown yarn was looped over the spindle. Above the spinning wheel was a wood shelf with a clutter of books, and a collection of snuff-horns displayed among the volumes. An oil lamp sat in the middle of the table with its chimney clean and shiny from Þóra's obsessive washing.

Grand-Amma took the skein off the spinning wheel and draped the loop across my hands, I spread them apart so the skein wouldn't droop as she started to wind the yarn into a ball. As days went by, Grandma Sigríður, Þóra and I would comb the new wool, while grand-Amma would spin it into desired yarn thickness.

Icelandic sheep wool has an inner, fine undercoat and a coarser outer-coat. We knitted the soft Lopi sweaters from the soft inner fleece that grand-Amma just barely spun, this was called "*lopi.*" The outer wool she spun into tight, strong yarn from which we knitted mittens, socks and *leppar*, which were inner-soles for our sheepskin shoes, and usually children's first knitting project.

Spinning wheels, wool-cards (combs) and looms were a necessary part of Grandma's household equipments.

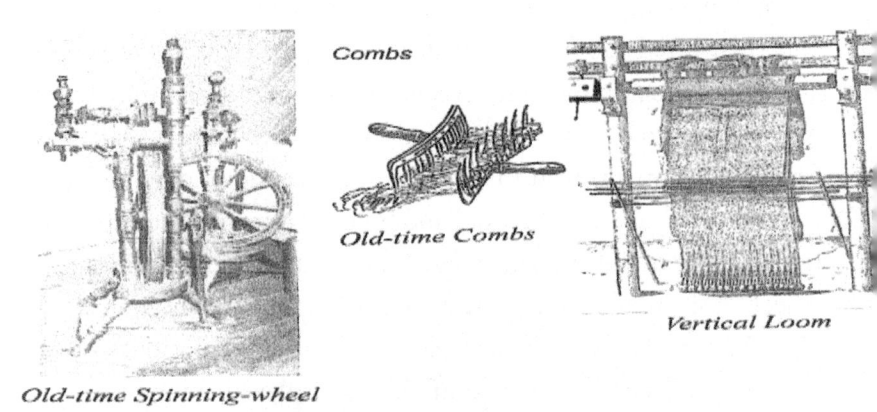

Combs

Old-time Combs

Vertical Loom

Old-time Spinning-wheel

Old-time Butter-churn

CHAPTER 17
GRANDPA HIRES SUMMER HELP

THE HUSTLE AND the bustle on the day Grandpa got ready to hire summer help was nothing short of amazing. I was shooed from one corner to another while Grandma and Þóra swept, scrubbed and cleaned.

Strong aroma of green coffee beans browning in a black kettle that hung over the fireplace permeated the kitchen. I loved the smell of coffee, and one of my favorite chores was to grind the coffee in the wooden coffee mill. Every so often, I'd pull out the boxy drawer at the bottom of the mill and sniff deeply, blissfully, as the ground coffee accumulated.

I watched as Grandma filled the blue and white speckled, chipped, coffee-pot with boiling water. When she dropped in a handful of coffee and a pinch of chicory, the water in the pot erupted hissing and steaming like a miniature volcano.

A large, black, kettle was on the back burner of the kitchen stove. Delicious whiffs of the mutton soup that was simmering in it made my mouth water. All day, bits of mutton-meat,

potato, carrots and rutabaga were added. Coffee and soup simmering away, all day, was a tradition with Grandma.

"Diddamín, we are almost out of sand to scrub the floor." Grandma handed me a grey, beat-up, metal bucket. "Run down and get some. And get Snati and Goldie to chase the sheep off the roof."

I looked at the floor that, to me, was clean enough to eat off of. The boards were white as could be from numerous, down-on-our-knees, scrubbing with rough scoria. But if Grandma said it needed scrubbing, it needed scrubbing!

Running across the rock-scattered field, I scrambled down the lava cliff, deliberately making scraping racket with the bucket just to startle the starchy, important acting puffins. They seemed so unflappable. I wondered how it would feel to be a puffin, or seagull, or a kría, just floating ever so smoothly up in the air, without a care. And here I came messing up their lives. I felt a small twinge of remorse; I didn't like to have *my* life messed up every Spring and every Fall.

I'd been shipped from Reykjavik to Vopnafjörður and back again as long as I could remember. I loved the fjord, and didn't like to have to go back to the city. *I can go to school here just as well*, I thought, slamming the bucket on the rocks, driving hundreds of seagulls into the air, screaming fiercely. They dove at me in a fit of temper before settling back on the lichen- and moss-covered lava ledges.

Filling the bucket with the volcanic sand, I stood for a moment watching the hypnotic slow-moving, blue-green, waves slapping the shiny-wet black rocks. Long strings of yellow-brownish algae floated slowly. Up and down, up and down, up and down.

The fjord was calm today.

"Halló child. What's keeping you?" Þóra leaned precariously over the edge, her shrill voice echoed and bounced off the cliffs causing the seagulls again to fly off into the air, screeching manically.

"I'm coming, I'm coming" I hollered back.

"I declare, you're the most day-dreaming child I've ever met!" She yelled in an aggravated voice.

After I scrambled back up the cliff, Þóra grabbed the bucket from my hand and ran toward the house. "Don't forget the sheep, your Grandma wants them off the roof before company arrives."

I got Snati and Goldie to chase the protesting sheep off the turf-roof and then ran inside. Quietly slipping past the busy women, I sped up the rickety stairs to my favorite place in the whole wide world, *Grandpa's attic*. This area had an aroma all of its own, musty papers, old leather, and tobacco. Even the salty, tangy smell of the ocean found its way into the attic room.

Grandpa had literally hundreds of books lined floor to ceiling, wall to wall, heaped on a table, on top of his massive desk, and even stacked on the window sill. I couldn't walk a straight line in the room, but had to meander around books and old, yellowing, newspapers with curled edges and piled up on the floor in a haphazard manner.

Those papers were something else! I once asked Grandpa why he had saved all these old papers, many written in English. I knew he was uncomfortable speaking the language, but read it with ease.

"I read about families, like your Grandma's sister,

Guðríður, who emigrated to Manitoba, Canada. She, her family, and many others left after the world's worse volcano eruption happened here in Iceland. The Laki eruption in 1784 ruined much of the countryside and for years made living extremely difficult." As Grandpa picked up a paper, fine dust flittered to the floor.

"This here is called The Heimskringlan, printed in Winnipeg. It's written in Icelandic and tells where some of the Icelanders settled, many on an island called Gimli, Manitoba. All of these books and papers are like good friends. I read and enjoy them again and again, I wouldn't part with any of them." He fondly patted the stack of papers.

I don't remember any "children's" books but all the stories of the Vikings came to life in that attic. This was pure heaven for the bookworm that I was. I loved reading the *SAGAS* and *EDDA*, written by one of our ancestors, Snorri Sturluson (1178-1241). Our country was so isolated from the rest of the world that our language had not changed much. I was able to read the old writings with ease.

Grandpa and I were alike in reading more Icelandic history than anything else. We had some lively discussions about the Vikings, their travels, discoveries, and so-called murderous blood-thirsty ways. Many Vikings were farmers. They also were skilled navigators and sailors. Of course I was *ALWAYS* taught that Leifur Eirikursson [another well-known ancestor, this one on mother's side according to her] discovered America 500 years before Columbus!

"Child come down here!" Þóra's thunderous voice shattered my solitude. I should have known that she'd seen me slip upstairs. I was sure she had eyes in the back of her head!

"I have to brush your hair before company arrives!" She thumped the wood ceiling for emphasis.

I'm ten, as if I couldn't brush and braid my own hair! Fuming I scrambled to my feet. The books on the floor bounced as she thumped again, harder this time. I didn't mess around but flew down stairs and jumped on the three-legged wooden stool she'd set out for me. Undoing my long black braids, my hazel eyes watered as she firmly brushed out the tangles. Grimacing and pursing her lips she gave me her no-nonsense look as her ample bosom bobbed up and down with each stroke.

Grandma Sigríður, who was short and slim, sat on a stool that Grandpa had built just for her. She sat with the butter churn firmly held in place by her skinny knees. Her black skirt and long white apron hiked up revealed black, woolen stockings. She had both hands clamped on the wooden butter-pole, hand over hand. The churn slurped and sloshed as Grandma, energetically, pumped up and down, making the sleeves on her blouse flop and flounce.

Great-Grandma sat in the corner rocking back and forth and knitting so fast I couldn't see the points of the four, clicking, needles. The metal needles made fascinating click-clack rhythm sounds as the sock she was knitting took shape.

"Why are you knitting so fast Grand-Amma?" My eyes followed the fast-moving needles with fascination.

Finishing a row, she pulled out one needle, and pushed an escaped tuft of white hair back under the black cap she always wore. The cap had a long tassel, reaching from her left ear down past her shoulder, a carved three-inch silver cylinder placed close to the cap kept the strands from separating.

Like Grandma and Þóra, she wore a long skirt and an apron tied at the waist.

She had on a black vest intricately embroidered with silver thread, and laced up at the front with a silver chain that hung over her bosom. The vest was similar to the other women's Sunday clothes but great-Grandma wore "dress-ups" every day, except during haying time when the men worked close to the farm, at which time she would not wear the ornate vest, but a brown and white knitted *lopi* sweater. She'd kind of waddle out to help rake and turn the rows of hay.

Scratching her head with the needle she quizzically looked at me. She had a habit of cocking her head to one side and closing her left blue eye, while wide-opening her right, brown eye.

"I want to get this sock done before I run out of yarn." Grinning she held up a slowly disappearing ball of yarn, then looked up into the faces of chuckling Grandma and Þóra.

"But Grand-Amma... " She was teasing me, it was the same amount of yarn used whether she knitted fast or slow. Þóra was finished and I got off the stool in a huff and went to look for Grandpa. I could hear him in the guest room, blowing his nose. A rake was lying on the floor, across the doorway. I picked it up and leaned it against the wall.

"You're hired!" Grandpa's voice boomed.

I jumped "What? Oh, Grandpa, I bet you could be heard all the way outside!"

"Diddamín, I've taught you right!" Grandpa gleefully slapped and rubbed wrinkled, red hands on his knees. "I'm getting ready to hire summer workers and I laid the rake there as a test. If a person steps over it, I will not hire them.

The same goes if they kick it aside, but if they do what you just did, it's an indication of a good worker. I learned that from my Father who learned it from his father. It has worked well for us for generations!" He chuckled and blew his nose again.

"Grandpa, you're funny." I loved both my grandparents, but I 'took after' Grandpa more than Grandma, just as I 'took after' my somber, brown-eyed, black haired Father more than my Mother.

Grandpa had very thick black hair now peppered with gray. Bushy eyebrows over keen dark brown eyes and a handlebar, graying mustache that he had a habit of twirling when meditating, or working on endless math problems. Besides reading, he had a passion for math. Papers, scribbled with fraction problems, were scattered about wherever he rested for a bit. I thought that was strange, I didn't like math at all!

"I heard the butter-churn sloshing, and now I smell newly baked bread." Grandpa scrunched his nose, sniffed, tilted his head back and roared.

"How about some coffee and fresh bread, Þóra!"

Grandma's blue figurine-painted china was already on the table that was handsomely covered with a white tablecloth that she had embroidered in an intricate "cut-out" design. Grandma *always* put out her best for company; after all, they were few and far between in this rugged, remote fjord, situated in the north-east coast of Iceland, not far from the artic circle.

Þóra brought in the coffee, scrumptious hot bread and a bowl of butter. Grandpa poured part of his coffee into the cup's saucer, then he held the small dish between his hands

and blew on the drink to cool, then he took a sip. I watched him for moment, then imitated him. Grandpa chuckled as he reached over and tore off two thick pieces of the hot bread and smeared on big slabs of butter that melted, and ran down the sides and onto the dish.

We sat by the window and looked at the mountain bathed in rare rays of golden-red light, and made the blue-green ocean glimmer and shimmer. I saw our reflections in the glass. So did Grandpa. His eyes crinkled at the corners as he smiled at me and nodding his head, reading my mind.

"Diddamín, there is no place like this." He said, softly.

Contently sipping my coffee from the china cup and looking at our reflections in the window glass, I whole-heartedly agreed. I wanted to stay here, like this, forever!

We heard the yipping of the dogs, neighing of horses, and cheery greetings.

Company had arrived.

CHAPTER 18
HANNA

I RAN OUTSIDE in time to see Helgi, whom I'd met last year, dismount and grab Björssi in a bear hug.

"Good to see you, Helgi." Björssi suddenly stopped. Staring at Helgi's companion the, normally, glib Uncle of mine seemed at a loss for words. Then, somewhat haltingly, he asked,

"Is this your cousin you said wanted to work for Dad this summer?" Björssi eyes were glued on the young lady that swung her slim legs gracefully off of her horse, a lazy looking, cross-eyed roan. The young woman looked about eighteen to twenty, and was very attractive. She wore loose fitting long trousers that looked more like a split skirt. Her white sweater was knit in the usual intricate Icelandic pattern. In her hand, she held a whip with an elaborately designed silver handle.

Her beautiful blond hair was in braids that wound around on top of her head like a golden crown that almost gave her an ethereal demeanor. She had wide open, violet-blue, eyes that didn't miss much, like the admiring looks from Uncle

Bjössi, who was about the same age. She gave me a slow, right-eye wink which reminded me of Sólveig. I loved her right away and tried to figure how I could give her a hint about grandpa's test. I couldn't think of anything; I just fervently hoped she would pick up the rake before she entered the room.

"Welcome Jóhanna Jóhannessdóttir, come on in," Grandpa called.

"Blessings on your home. Glad to meet you, Björn Jónasson. Please call me Hanna, my mother is Jóhanna." She smiled as she started to step inside. Stopping, she reached down and picked up the rake and leaned it carefully against the wall. Grinning from ear to ear I peeked around her and caught Grandpa's face. I *knew* we had new help.

Turning around, I almost tripped over Bjössi's feet. He and Helgi had followed close behind me and Bjössi couldn't take his eyes off the new girl. I saw Helgi look at Bjössi. An oddly sad, small, smile curved his lips. I thought about that for a moment then shook my head; I'm letting my silly imagination run wild again! Grandpa stood up and shook Hanna's hand motioning for her and Helgi to sit down.

"Diddamín, ask Þóra to bring us some more bread and coffee." Grandpa said with a humorous glint in his eyes as he observed Bjössi's reaction to the girl. I thought Grandpa himself was acting a little strange. He usually tilted his head back in his chair and bellowed for his coffee. Now he was being quite the gentleman! I went to speak with Þóra.

As the adults visited, I watched Helgi´s cousin with curiosity, especially because of Bjössi´s obvious interest. Uncle Bjössi was an accomplished accordion player, and was much

sought after to play at weddings and country-dance in nearby villages, and outdoor gatherings like the Fall sheep-roundup. With his quick mischievous smile, bright blue eyes, auburn hair and broad shoulders, he was very popular with the young ladies, but hadn't been particularly interested in any one of them. I had always thought of him as an adult, but now he became just as goofy as the boys at school who liked to yank on my braids. Hanna didn't seem interested in Björssi. Her soft, serene glance was the same for all of us.

Grandpa told Hanna that she was hired, and after a short visit Helgi took off for their family farm. Þóra showed Hanna where she would be staying while working on the farm.

I was old enough to help the adults with the haying but had a hard time keeping up with Hanna who was a whirl-wind of a worker, like Guðrún was last year. Furiously raking the rows of hay, Hanna caused the dry grass to whirl up in the air as in a strong, northern, gale. I thought she worked too hard. Every so often she'd lean over and take a strange gulping breath. I wanted to say something to Grandpa, but she gave me a warning look as she shook her head and put a finger to her lip then went back to raking with intense deter-mination. I don't know if Helgi knew of Grandpa's test and told Hanna.

But Grandpa's test was good anyway.

CHAPTER 19
DO HORSES AND DOGS HAVE 'ESP' ?

"AREN'T WE READY to go? They are here, we'll miss the tide if we don't hurry!" I shouted to Hanna who was still inside the house. I was outside, watching my three girlfriends from the nearby farmsteads arrive. Gréta, who was ten, Unnur, eleven, and her ten-year old sister, Sína, were grinning from ear to ear in anticipation as the horses came, pell-mell, across the field.

"Hi, shall we dismount?" Unnur asked, as her horse came to a rearing stop.

"Hi. I don't think you need to." I greeted the girls. "I just hollered for Hanna, she should be right out." I finished adjusted the stirrups on my saddle, then turned to the house, a little puzzled, wondering what Hanna was doing.

Their horses snorted, impatiently chewed at the bits and pranced around. My horse, Stjarna, the oldest and laziest of them all, danced about, eager to take off. But Bjössi's horse, Thunder, was almost subdued. I'd never seen him like this.

Thunder was well known for his competitive nature, and couldn't stand to have another horse in front of him. He was the fastest runner in our county, and Bjössi proudly displayed several of their racing awards in his room. We were going swimming in a geothermal-warm swim hole on the other side of the fjord's inlet and Hanna was planning to ride Thunder for the trip. Her cross-eyed horse was getting old and stayed pretty much out in the pasture until needed at haying time.

I sure hoped Bjössi's horse wasn't sick, not just for his sake, but the other horses were way out in the outer field, and I was afraid we'd miss the outgoing tide if we had to go and get another horse, which would mean riding the long way around instead of crossing the inlet. And that could mean losing what little sun we might have for our swim.

Darting inside I called for Bjössi. He and grandpa were at the kitchen table drinking coffee.

"Would you both come out and look at Thunder? He isn't acting like himself!" I said, as a flutter of unease churned in my stomach.

Bjössi shot up out of his seat. The chair teetered for a moment before tumbling over and skittering on the wood floor. Both he and Grandpa dashed outside. Carefully they ran their hands over the horse, looked into his eyes, and checked his mouth. Grandpa carefully examined Hanna's saddle. Thunder tossed his head at the close inspection. Now swishing his tail, he nuzzled Bjössi then started his usual prancing around eager for a run; he sure seemed to have recovered mighty quickly!

Hanna stepped out of the door and walked up to Thunder,

who nervously shied away from her. Her hair was in two long braids and hung almost down to her waist; she looked so pretty. Swinging her right braid over her shoulder, she cocked her head, puzzled.

"This is the first time Thunder has acted like he didn't like my saddle, or even me!" she murmured, sadly.

"I'll just take him for a quick run and see how he does" Bjössi jumped into Hanna's saddle. The stirrups were too short, but he managed to scrunch up his legs and off they went at a brisk gallop across the grassy field. Then Thunder went into his famous tölt and from there into flying pace; a pace unique to Icelandic horses, where the horse moves both legs of one side at the same time. Bjössi and his horse became as one in a spectacular flying form. Thunder's bronze coat with the black mane, glistened in the sun, black tail plumed out behind him and his four black socks were a blur.

"Not a thing wrong with that horse." Grandpa proclaimed proudly. Thunder was born on Grandpa's farm when Bjössi was twelve. His dad had given him the colt with the understanding that my uncle would have complete charge in taking care of him and train him. Bjössi had done an outstanding job and Grandpa was justifiably proud of both his son and horse.

"Thunder is fine, Hanna, just a little temperamental when I'm not the one in the saddle. I guess I have him a little spoiled. It'll do him good to get used to you."

All the way to the inlet Thunder stayed behind the other horses. This was so unusual I couldn't help but keep looking back. Thunder behind Stjarna? Unbelievable. Strange foreboding crept down my spine. The three girls had already

entered the inlet, giggling as the cold water sprayed over their legs. Stjarna was just going in when I heard Hanna's voice.

"Jump up here, old boy." She patted the back of her saddle as Grandpa and Bjössi had often done before. But Snati whimpered and stuck his tail between his legs. To my astonishment, the old dog took a flying leap and landed on Stjarna, right behind me!

I looked at Hanna, her face was ashen. She looked like she'd seen a ghost.

"What's the matter, Hanna?" I whispered, looking around, scared. The three girls' horses were plodding ahead, sloshing a great deal of water as they went across the bay.

"It's nothing, I just felt funny for a minute. I think Thunder and Snati have me spooked!" Her laugh seemed a little forced.

"Maybe we should wait to go swimming, Hanna." I thought she looked really ill.

All of a sudden Thunder decided it was time to move. Wading in, he took off more like his old self and almost galloped in the water! Stjarna followed at a more sedate pace. I could hear the girls' laughter and the pounding hoofs of the horses as they got out of the water and onto the ground, then took off at a brisk canter. Our horses sloshed across the inlet, and we reached the other side, where both horses acted like it was time to race, Stjarna a sure loser.

I didn't get it, this was so unusual.

The sun was shining between puffy clouds that were lazily floating in the pale-blue sky. Racing to the pool, tearing off our clothes down to our underwear, we flung ourselves in. There was a big splash, and we shrieked gleefully as we

jumped up and down in the naturally warm waterhole, which was the only geothermal heated hole in the area.

Hanna, being the adult, tried to slow us down without much success. The water was just right, and the four of us were having a glorious time. We'd been swimming for a good half an hour when the wind picked up, making us cringe every time we stuck our heads up out of the warm water.

Shivering, Unnur and Sína got out and wrapped themselves in towels. Gréta and I started to pull ourselves out when Unnur pointed to the water.

"Hanna is on the bottom, something is wrong with her!" She shrieked as she pointed.

I saw Hanna, face down, in the water. The way she looked I knew she wasn't pulling a prank, that wasn't like her anyway. Gréta and I dove down and got Hanna to the surface. She was deathly white and her wide-open eyes were totally blank. The braids had come loose and her golden hair floated about her face.

I screamed.

As in a nightmare, I heard Gréta yell.

"Sína, quick, ride up to the farm and get Jón! Unnur help us lift Hanna out!" But the dead weight was more than we could manage. We all were crying and sobbing, as we tried to keep Hanna's head out of the water until help arrived.

"I should have known something was wrong. It's my fault!" I wailed. "Thunder and Snati knew something was wrong. I should have known." My teeth chattered as I rocked back and forth, rubbing my eyes with my fists

"No, it wasn't anyone's fault." Jón, the farmer tried to comfort me. "I know Hanna's family and we've known she

had heart problems since she was a baby. She didn't want to be treated differently than other kids. She wasn't expected to live much past her thirteenth birthday. This is very sad, but she lived her life the way she wanted to." He patted me on the shoulder.

The family came and took over. They tried to console us, but there was just too much to do. They asked Jón and his wife to take us to our respective homes. We got on our horses. Burying my face in Stjarna's mane I sobbed my heart out. Unnur stared, dry-eyed, straight ahead. Sína and Gréta wept, tears streaming down their cheeks.

Jón and his wife rode back with us. At each farm, the couple quietly spoke with the families of the girls. Grandpa's farm was the last stop and Jón's horse galloped ahead. In one motion he swung off of his horse and dashed inside. Grandpa came running out and grabbed me off Stjarna and held me tight and whispered, "Hush now, it's going to be alright."

I stopped sobbing. I felt numb.

Bjössi was standing by the door, stone-faced, as we came in. He looked into my face. Suddenly he came to me and hugged me in a fierce hug before he bolted out the door. I heard Thunder's hoofs as he galloped away. [I didn't see Bjössi again. He'd moved away when I came back the following year. He married six years after this happened.]

"If we'd just not gone swimming, or if I'd listened to Thunder, maybe this wouldn't have happened. I knew something was wrong and I didn't do anything. It's my fault!" I stuttered.

"Come here, Diddamín" Grandma Sigríður wrapped her arms around me and led me to Grand-Amma who was in

her rocking chair, lifting me up onto her lap.

"She was too young and pretty to die. I should have been able to save her." I started wailing again.

"Hush now, child. You heard what Jón said about her having heart problems since she was born. None of you, none of us, could have done anything to save her life. She's in Heaven now." Grand-Amma rubbed and patted my back, as she dabbed at her eyes with her hankie, then continued softly, "Hanna was doing what she wanted to do, be like all the other girls, as long as she could. You know she worked as hard, or harder, than many others, just to prove to herself she could. She'd like for you to remember how she enjoyed her life. She was a very happy, God-loving person. Remember how she had you put your hands together and had you repeat the prayer we taught you and your sisters 'Now I lay me down to sleep'..." I stopped her, putting my finger on her lip.

"Please, Grand-Amma, I don't want to hear the rest of it now." I whimpered.

The soothing rocking and her sing-song murmuring relaxed me so that I began to think of Hanna. The more I thought, the more I remembered the way Hanna had lived and the numerous times she had mentioned God and His angels, even *guardian* angels, which I thought might be a very good thing to have.

I'd been so absorbed with my own life I'd not paid enough attention. I decided I'd like to be more like Hanna. I didn't know if I could do it. She was so good and I was... well...

For a change, for late August, it was almost warm outside. The four of us, Nonni, his two sisters, Sigga and Dóra and

I were sitting halfway up on the turf-roof of the sheepcote.

"I'm going to miss you when you go back to Reykjavik next week" Dóra said, squinting at me with moist eyes.

"I'd like to go to school in the city." Nonni muttered, as he chewed on a blade of grass he'd stuck between his teeth.

Sigga didn't say a word. Her head was bent as she worked her fingers around a small tuft of grass.

"Well, I don't want to go. I like it here. I'd like to stay forever." I said, grumpily.

We sat for awhile without speaking. I gazed over the farm, the ocean. On the horizon a ship was making its way north across the fjord, a plume of black smoke trailed in the air. It looked like a trawler and wasn't stopping at Vopnafjörður.

"I hope they had enough pins to protect Hanna." Nonni sat up, abruptly. "She was too nice to turn into a ghost."

I looked at him, stunned. Both girls turned their heads, mouths open, staring bug-eyed at their brother.

Nonni turned beet-red at our reaction.

"You all have heard the story, how you have to put pins into a dead person's shoes to help them from turning into ghosts." Nonni said defensively.

"Grand-Amma said that Hanna was in Heaven so she *couldn't* have turned into a ghost." I pointed my finger into his face so menacingly that he jerked his head back. "She also had a guardian angel to protect her. She didn't need pins. When I get older I'm going to ask God for one of those angels. Maybe Hanna was so good because those angels kept her out of trouble!"

The girls nodded their heads agreeing with me, but Nonni looked troubled.

"Boys are supposed to be strong. I guess angels are alright to help girls, but I can take care of myself!" He looked at us defiantly as he stood up and brushed his pants.

I was going to miss my cousins.

CHAPTER 20
THE NORTH FJORDS

LIKE AN OVER-ENDOWED, elderly, dowager elbowing herself through a crowd, the Gullfoss plowed through the ocean waves at a full roll toward Bakkaflói. The sky was lead-grey and the abominable stiff breeze bit my cheeks and the gusts watered my eyes. The tip of my nose was red and ice cold.

Summer was over, and I was on my way back to Reykjavik.

I tucked my chin deep into the thick collar of my lopi sweater as I sat, hunched up, in the fo'castle amid coiled up brown rope and wood crates. I wrapped my arms tight around my chest as I rocked back and forth. Just a few hours of sailing and already I missed everyone at Vopnafjörður. I didn't want to leave. I didn't want to go back to Reykjavik.

A whiff of tobacco-smoke caused me to look up. Two men were standing by the rail. One of the men was round and short. The top of his head was covered with a black, limp hat. He had a curled-down, shiny black pipe clenched between his teeth. The pipe bobbed up and down as he spoke

rapidly, both hands jammed into the pockets of his overcoat. The other was a taller, lanky, bareheaded younger man. With his heavy coat unbuttoned, he'd reached inside and looped his left thumb under one strip of his frayed, black suspenders, yanking and snapping as he used his straight pipe as a pointer. He would remove the pipe from his mouth with his right hand and jab it into the air as he made comments. The smoke odor reminded me of Grandpa and his attic. I squeezed my eyes hard.

"Are you alright?" I lifted my head at the concerned voice and felt a hand gently grip my shoulder. I looked up into the dark-brown eyes of Einar. He'd graduated from Iceland's Navigation School with my Father so I was quite comfortable with him "looking out" for me.

At age forty, he was two years older than my dad. His hair seemed to be of no particular color but he had lots of it; it stuck out from under his cap above his ears and curled at the neck of his black turtleneck sweater. Whereas Father was a stocky, short, solidly built man, Einar was tall, stoop shouldered and wiry. Both men had the strong, weather-beaten face of the seafaring man. Einar was a father of twins who were a year older than I.

But right now I was wanting to talk to Sólveig, who had been so understanding as we traveled the fjords last Spring. Maybe she had answers for the questions that were churning inside of me. I knew she was going to meet the ship when we docked in Akureyri, and she just might be going back to Reykjavik. I was looking forward to that.

"Yes, thank you." I answered politely as Mother had repeatedly taught me.

"You're getting pretty wet from the spray. You look like a lamb that's fallen into a creek!" He chuckled as he brushed the water off my sweater.

Oh good grief, I thought. He sounds just like Sólveig!

"Why don't you go down below and dry off a bit? We'll be at the village of Bakkafjörður pretty soon." Looking up into his kind face I nodded. Giving me a soft pat on the shoulder, he went back to work.

Clambering down the metal steps, I saw the back of a woman who slipped into a cabin. Something about the jet-black hair pulled into a tight bun looked familiar. I couldn't remember where I might have seen her before. I hadn't seen many passengers topside and wondered if they'd gone to bed already, or if it was because this ship was like a cork in a puddle. It rolled and wallowed in the smallest of waves.

The *Gullfoss*, built in 1915, was older than the *Goðafoss II* by six years. It was also somewhat smaller. The newer ship was 1,542 tons, whereas the *Gullfoss* was 1,414 tons. The ships were named after our better known waterfalls.

I shared a cabin with three older, very quiet women. A top berth had rope webbing in front to keep me from rolling out of it when the ship tilted in a wave. The ladies took little notice of me which suited me just fine. They seemed overly sensitive to the motion of the ship and had 'taken to their beds'. It got pretty raunchy-smelling in there at times, and I stayed topside as much as possible.

After changing into a dry sweater and pulling off my damp socks, I hung my wet clothes on a couple of pegs so they would dry out for another wear. By the time I came back up on deck, we were well into the bay of Bakkaflói. We

did not go the dock, instead, a tugboat met us and loaded and unloaded what little cargo there was. No one got off. I thought he small wharf looked dilapidated. The pilings were rotted in several places, high out of the water on one side and sagging low to the water on the other. I wasn't sure if the tugboat was running back and forth because the pier was unsafe or because of low tide. From the deck of the ship the village of Bakkafjörður didn't look particularly interesting. Maybe the awesomeness of previous fjords had made me blasé.

Across the bay was the totally different Long Point. Stretching 40km northeast into the Atlantic Ocean, it ended in a pointy place called Fontur. As we sailed around the peninsula and looking at the forbidding faces of cliffs called Skóruvík my mouth dropped open, veritable millions and millions of seabirds filled the over-crowded sheer crags. It was mind-boggling. I couldn't imagine any birds left in the world. They must all be here on this rock-face! Stórikarl [Big Man], a rock column standing by itself in the ocean, was so teeming with Gannets it didn't seem possible to squeeze in another feather, let alone a whole bird!

The everlasting wind had become fairly calm but felt bitter cold when I moved from a shelter. We were getting closer to the Arctic Circle. Sailing past these treacherous, amazing, sea cliffs, we came to another village named Þórshöfn, an old trading center. Þórshöfn means "Thor'sHarbor." According to Norse legend Þór was the thunder god and the son of Óðin, the most powerful of Viking gods. One night, Þór rode his eight-legged horse, Sleipnir, through the sky, at a flying pace. Sleipner touched one of his eight hoofs down

on the ground, just west of Þórshöfn. To this day his hoof print can be seen in an awesome rock-form as a giant horse-shoe. My mind went to Grandpa's attic and the Sagas. How I missed them.

I wrapped my sweater tighter and stared at the un-ending ocean as we sailed across the bay of Þistilfjörður and to the village of Raufarhöfn. While we were unloading the cargo, the town and the wharf became engulfed in a dense wall of fog, we had to stay moored longer than anticipated for fear of our ship ramming into another. But as often happened, stiff gusts moved over the restless sea and whipped away the fog. The *Gullfoss* was able and continued north.

At Hraunarhafnatángi, Iceland's northernmost tip, we started going west. The ship was sailing right along the Arctic Circle, less than a mile north of the peninsula.

On the north horizon, where open sea should have been, there appeared to be a huge land mass. In reality, it was massive, towering icebergs floating east and south in the North-Atlantic Ocean. It was far enough away to be of no danger to our ship, but the air got noticeably colder. As we continued west we encountered several ice-floes.

On one of the ice-slabs was a large Polar bear and another smaller one. This caused a terrific excitement and some fears among the passengers. I'd always thought that Polar bears were snow-white. But the larger bear was more straw-yellow than white. The fur looked bedraggled.

"They look sad and pitiful with their heads hanging down like that." One of the passengers remarked.

"They've probably traveled on that floe broken from those icebergs on the horizon." Einar said coming alongside

where the group of us was gathered at the rail, watching the bears. "It'd be a shame if they try to swim to land. They'd be hunted down immediately." He shook his head, sadly.

"Why would anyone do that?" I exclaimed, appalled.

"There aren't any bears in our country and we want to keep it that way." Einar said, his voice husky. "A few, like those two, have drifted on ice close enough to swim ashore, but they were quickly disposed of. Folks here are extremely afraid of them and with good cause. Polar bears are very dangerous, especially when hungry." I was glad to see them float out of sight and hoped they'd find a place where they could be safe.

CHAPTER 21
GUNNAR AND THE POLAR BEAR

IN DOCKING AT Kópaskér, we were greeted by much excitement. Not just the kind as at previous villages; a hunt was on for a Polar bear sighted near the town. Folks were running and yelling. They were unable to agree as to where this animal was or even if there was one. A thirteen-year old boy named Gunnar Haldórsson had taken his rowboat out into the fjord to do some fishing. He had to navigate around an ice-floe stuck half on shore and half in sea.

As he rowed his boat to the other side of the floe he saw something move on the ice, then watched in horror as a bear, "bigger than my horse," jumped across the ice and loped up the countryside. With the hairs on the back of his neck standing straight up, he frantically rowed his boat back to the pier of Kópaskér, hollering and screaming at the top of his voice.

"Polar bear on land, I saw a Polar bear on land!"

Some men scoffed and made fun of him yelling for him to stop his nonsense.

"You probably saw a chunk of ice break off and imagined the rest." They hooted and took a swig of their fire-wine. But others took it seriously enough to follow Gunnar who showed them the bear tracks. That sobered up the doubters, and now many were arming themselves with any available weapons. Women and children were warned to stay indoors until the bear could be found.

On board the *Gullfoss* it was business as usual, but amid the loading and unloading, seamen were glancing over their shoulders checking out the activity of the villagers. The loud whooping of a group of men brought everyone to the rail. Some of us went off the ship and walked up to the knot of people that had gathered, jabbering and pointing.

"I'm not sure you should see this. It might be gruesome." Einar said as he and I followed the folks from the ship. Someone moved, and I saw what they were looking at. The huge bear was sprawled on the flat wagon, all four paws hanging over the edges. Bright red blood dripped from a hole in the middle of his broad chest. The small eyes were open, looking at me, lifeless.

All the agony of Hanna's death surged through my being. Trembling violently from head to toe I turned and ran toward the ship, nausea snaking through my stomach. I didn't make it. Halfway on the pier I had to run to the edge where I hung onto a reeking fish barrel. Sobbing and heaving, I vomited into the ocean, totally miserable.

Then I felt a cold, wet cloth on my face. Turning, I saw Einar's troubled face through my tear-blurred eyes.

"That was a magnificent bear, but very dangerous," he said. " It was obviously half starved and would have attacked

livestock, or even people. The villagers had to kill him." Einar brushed my hair with his rough hands.

"I know," I gulped. "But it still doesn't seem right. None of this 'dying' stuff is right." I said, angrily. He looked at me puzzled. Reaching with his right hand he pulled me up to my feet, just as the whistle blew, preparing the ship for departure.

Dragging my feet, I went below to my cubbyhole of a bed. Tucking my knees up to my chin, I completely covered my head, twisting the blanket around me into a tight shroud. Why do people have to drown? Why kill the poor bear? Then I remembered; I wanted Grandma to wring the roosters neck, that would have killed him! Confused, I fell asleep.

Loud clamor, running feet and hollering jarred me awake. Peeking out the porthole, I jerked back as an enormous splash of seawater pummeled the glass. As I clambered up the metal steps, I heard thrilled voices of passengers squealing;

"There's another one! At least a dozen of them. Look!"

The astounding sight that met my eyes wiped out, for the time being, all my previous misery. The magnificent whales that breached gracefully, even playfully, up and down in the ocean were breathtaking. Their powerful spouts shot up like the Humpback whales south of Iceland, but these were much larger whales and their blowing were more forceful. Like the difference between Geyser and little Geyser their noise swooshed explosively into the air. I watched with breath-holding interest as we sailed across the wide bay of Öxarfjörður and into the bay of Skjálfandi where our next village-stop was.

Húsavik was an intriguing, picturesque fishing-whaling station. But I trembled at the thought of stopping here. I'd

heard stories about men being shanghaied from this boisterous hamlet; rumor had it that captains from foreign whaling ships would ply Icelandic men with fire-wine and get them intoxicated. Then their sailors carried the unconscious men aboard their ships, thus replacing men lost due to illness, or having been thrown overboard for any perceived insubordination! I have no knowledge of this being true, but those telling it sounded believable.

Shuddering, and thinking this was one town I was not interested in exploring, I stayed on board and kept my eyes furtively glued on the comings and goings of foreign boats and their men. I saw nothing suspicious, and glad of it.

As we continued our journey the sea was teeming with whales and seals. A killer whale shot up out of the ocean and seemed to do a slow twirl in the air. Its beautiful black and white body shone like it was dressed in a slinky, satin tuxedo. I was mesmerized and watched until most of the whales had swum north and out of sight. It was a good therapeutic feeling. I was back to enjoying the magnificence of the ocean and gazing at the hypnotic, and at times bizarre, coast line.

After we sailed past Flat Island I got real anxious and decided to go back below and check my clothes to see what I had to wear, wanting to look my best when I would see Sólveig again.

CHAPTER 22
AKUREYRI

WE NOW ENTERED the fjord of Eyjafjörður. As we sailed along the east coast I could see the west side, as this is a very narrow firth. The mouth, where we entered, is the widest part of it being approximately 8 miles, but mostly, in its 20 miles length, the fjord is about 2-4 miles in width. On each side are towering mountains with steep hills that roll directly into the sea.

As we passed the island of Hrísey, I remembered reading the diary of Sveinn Þórarinsson "Hard Times in Eyjafjörður"*, an account of the dreadful times people had in May and June of 1869. The fjord was totally filled with ice and people were starving because the ships couldn't enter with supplies. At the end of this long fjord sits Akureyri, second largest town in Iceland. Hearing the *Gullfoss* announce our arrival with the usual blasts, I quickly finished changing my clothes and rushed back up. I found a place at the rail and leaned over staring hypnotically down at the seawatching the ships' wake. I'll never get tired of watching moving water, I thought.

More and more passengers were now gathered topside. Suitcases and boxes were piled close to the gate where the gangplank would be lowered. It was interesting to see how people dressed for the unpredictable weather. The older folks had only a sweater thrown casually over their shoulder or clutched in their hands. A few young men wore heavy coats, and had caps set at a rakish angle, while most of the girls were bareheaded, their hair blowing freely in the ever-present wind, and colorful lopi scarves wound casually around the neck.

Rain-grey clouds hung over the mountain tops, but the dock was dry. A sizable crowd had gathered to meet the *Gullfoss*. My eyes searched the group as they milled about. Then I spotted her standing to one side, shielding her eyes with her right hand as she watched the ship ease up to the pier.

She had thrown a large black shawl over her head. With her left hand she bundled the scarf tightly under her chin. It made her look much older than she was and a little dowdy. But then she saw me waving and jumping up and down, and that wondrous smile of hers lit up her face and lifted my gloomy spirit.

"Have you seen this woman, Sólveig, your aunt told me about?" Einar had stopped. He carried a thick stack of papers in his left hand that he used to motion at the people on the dock.

"Yes, she's over there. See the lady right in front with the black shawl?" I pointed and waved, she waved back. Einar gave her a crisp salute.

"You'll have about three hours," he cautioned me." I'll

check and make sure you get back, or your father will have my head!" His brown eyes twinkled, as he chuckled and walked away with the measured, purposeful steps so like my Dad's. I had a momentary sense of loss, I hadn't seen Father for many months. He'd been out to sea when I left last spring. I didn't see him very often.

I followed the folks that were now disembarking. Amid much shouting and greetings of the families meeting one another I worked my way to Sólveig. She had to take a few steps back as I exuberantly threw myself into her open arms. After hugging and laughing a bit we walked into town.

We seated ourselves in a small ocean-front café, a fancy word for the ramshackle, red-rusted corrugated shack that had five round scarred wood tables. A few chairs were scattered about in uneven numbers at the tables, as if people had indiscriminately used them and then not bothered to put them back properly.

In one corner two men were playing chess oblivious to all but each other and the game. Four oil lamps were hanging from the rough, unfinished rafters, their chimney streaked with black soot. The place reeked of an odd mixture of fish, coffee, tobacco and kerosene.

We sipped on our coffee and nibbled at our cookies. Sólveig had already told me she wouldn't be going to Reykjavik at this time.

"The family needs me a little longer." She said patting my hand and looking into my gloomy face.

"The girls that I take care of are about your age," she continued. "I enjoy them very much. By the way, they are in Girl Scouts and last weekend I went with their group to Dettifoss

and stopped at Lake Mývatn where they baked bread in the hot ground!" She rummaged a bit in the large black bag she'd carried. Then she pulled out a tin can and handed it to me. "I told them about our travel together so they baked this just for you."

"Tell them "thanks," I said. "I wish I could have been with them."

Baking bread in the boiling, geothermal mud holes at Mývatn how cool was that!

Pinching off a piece of the bread I put it into my mouth rolling it around my tongue, tasting its sweetness. It was very good. Unconsciously crumbling a piece between my fingers, I dropped my head, staring at the crumbs on the table.

Feeling Sólveig watching me I looked up. Her eyes crinkled at the corners as she squinted at me with her eyebrows tightly knit, and eyes dark with concern. Her coffee forgotten, she leaned forward and reached out, laying her hands on top of mine she squeezed tight.

"This sad face of yours doesn't have much to do with me not going to Reykjavik, does it?" She asked.

I shook my head. "No. Well, maybe a little bit." My hands trembled in hers.

Sólveig nodded, waiting.

"Do you remember Íngi, at Seyðisfjörður and his ten-year old son, Ragnar, and the real bad storm we had?" I asked, pulling my hand away and rubbing my face.

"That's something I'll never forget." Sólveig shivered.

"Did you know they all drowned?" From the shock on her face I knew she hadn't heard. Then I just spilled everything out about Hanna and ended up with the awful killing

of the bear.

"So why did Ragnar, and his dad and uncles have to drown? Why did Hanna have to die? Even the bear hadn't hurt anybody. He was just hungry. It all seems so unfair!" I put my forehead down on Sólveig's hands. My eyes were dry. I couldn't cry anymore. I just wanted to understand. I'd been unable to talk about the things that lay so heavy on my heart. Events had moved too fast at Grandpa's and Aunt Þórbjörg's. The last Norwegian left the infirmary two days before I left Vopnafjörður. There seemed to be no time to sit down and really talk. I'm not sure I could have anyway so soon after the tragedy.

"I never saw such a girl for asking questions!" Sólveig shook her head, with a small smile.

Then she leaned forward, a serious look on her face.

"Listen, Íedamín, we know Íngi wasn't wise. Other fishermen had quit and sailed into the harbor for safety. Íngi had the same information on the weather as they had, but he chose not to heed the warning. Some people think they are invincible and nothing will happen to them. Many have lost their lives because of their own stubbornness. But also storms can come up suddenly and cause rogue waves and, through no fault of the fishermen, their lives may be lost."

She was silent for a moment, then she bowed her head. When she looked up her eyes were misty with unshed tears.

"I met Hanna when she was thirteen." Sólveig said softly.

"I stared at her, startled. "You knew Hanna?"

"I met her at the hospital in Reykjavik, where my younger sister was a patient. They both had been born with heart problems and were not expected to live past twelve years of

age. My sister died at age twelve. I was so glad to know that Hanna had several, wonderful, years. Her family writes me, and I knew how much she loved being with you and your family. Kind of funny. I didn't know the connection with you until just a week ago." She smiled at me.

Sólveig's story just completely lifted my spirit. It was really true, I couldn't have saved Hanna, no matter what I would have tried to do! I got off my chair and went to her, slipping my arms around her neck. All the guilty feeling rolled off of me. I felt light as a downy feather!

"Thank you Sólveig," I said. "I'm sorry about your sister, but she's in Heaven with Hanna. Isn't that just wonderful to think about?!" I kissed her cheek as she squeezed me tight, nodding her head. "And I really understood why the bear had to be killed. It would have been horrible if he'd gotten to a farm and killed people. I just overreacted... So will we meet in Reykjavik sometime?" I cocked my head giving her a big grin.

"Absolutely, elskamin!" She got up, grabbed me and whirled me right out the door.

The timing was perfect. The blast of the *Gullfoss* let us know my time was up.

Elskamin, my mind sang over and over as I ran up the gangplank and boarded the ship. We'd already said our good-byes, and Sólveig was walking away. I turned, just as she turned, and blew me a kiss. I felt on top of the world as I returned the kiss. I looked to the rest of my trip with eagerness instead of dread.

Clutching the bread tin tightly in my hand, I meandered to the bow of the ship. Scrunching down I wiggled until I

was comfortable among coiled up ropes and some pieces of canvas. There always seemed to be plenty of thick rope, the size of my skinny arms, rolled up, fore and aft, making either place a cozy hide-away.

Opening the tin, I pinched off a lump of the dark rye bread and stuck it into my mouth. Contently chewing, I leaned back and stared up into the sky watching the clouds rolling and tumbling along. I loved clouds, and like the moving of water, they were an endless fascination for me.

Thinking about Sólveig's trip to Dettifoss - the most powerful waterfall in Europe - and the waterfall itself, I pinched off another piece of the bread and chomped away. It is not a pretty waterfall like so many others in our country, this one being fed from melting, inland glaciers which always made it's river muddy-grey looking. Grandpa had explained this when a group of us had gone there for a weekend. We had also stopped at the Krafla caldera, and the Víti crater. The Icelandic word "Víti" means "Hell." People often believed hell to be under volcanoes.

The bread was mouthwatering and I pinched off some more, rolling it in my mouth, I pondered the volcanic hotspots at Mývatn where the girls had been baking. I'd read how in the old days some folks had cooked their fish and mutton in the boiling hot water that bubbled out of the ground in various places on the island.

I wondered about other countries. Were they like Iceland? Fire and ice side by side? Eerie looking lava-rock formations, deep crevasses slashed into the countryside? Boiling mud pools and steaming fumaroles? Volcanic eruptions and earthquakes every few years?

When I grow up I want to explore what is beyond the endless horizon and find out, I thought to myself.

In 1965 and '67, American moon-landing astronauts used the Krafla and Askja area to study the geology for their lunar mission, as this barren lava field is one of the more moonlike places on earth. Krafla last erupted in 1984.

CHAPTER 23
THE HERRING ARE RUNNING!

AS WE SAILED from Akureyri, we headed north in the fjord toward Siglufjörður. I thought about the tremor we'd had last year in Vopnafjörður that scared Lilla and me half to death. I knew the earthquake had originated near Dalvik which is on the west side of this fjord and about halfway between Akureyri and Siglufjörður. I'd heard there was some damage in this area.* I craned my neck this way and that way, but wasn't able see any evidence from aboard the ship. The cliffs and rocks were just as high, just as formidable and bizarre as I remembered from previous journeys.

The grounds are always shifting in Iceland anyway. A volcano decides to explode and change the landscape. Some folks may go to bed at night then look out their window the next morning to see a new island forming practically under their nose, like Surtsey.

The island of Hrísey,* which is Iceland's second largest island - Heimaey being the largest, - sits in the middle of this long fjord, across from the Village of Dalvík.

As the *Gullfoss* plowed her way through the waves and past the island a cloud of seabirds clamored in the air. I watched ducks fly up from the water and disappear among the clouds. The powerful ocean waves crashed and roared up the sides of the weird cliffs. I could, and did, spend hours upon hours watching the move of the restless sea.

As the ship eased up to the pier at Dalvík we passed a couple of boys sitting in their rowboat, fishing. They looked about my age. The boys waved and I waved back.

After the gangplank was lowered I disembarked and picked my way along the dock, around the, now familiar, coils of rope, barrels, and tubs of smelly fish. Men, both onboard ship and on the dock, talked loudly and shouted to one another as they worked at unloading and loading cargo.

Einar hollered something. I turned slowly and walked backward a step, then stumbled. Swinging my arm out I connected with a soft hand steadying me.

"Oops, careful there!" A woman chuckled. "I've got her Einar!" She hollered toward the *Gullfoss* where Einar stood by the rail. I lifted my hand in a wave to let him know I was alright.

"Well now, I guess introductions are in order." She smiled. " My name is Kristín Flósadóttir and I'm from Einar's hometown, Stykkishólmur." She was the small woman I'd seen disembark at Reyðarfjörður last Spring!

I wasn't surprised when she told me that she was a school teacher. I recalled that back then, when I first saw her, I had thought she looked like one. As we walked along on the pier, she proceeded to tell me that she was traveling back home, and back to teaching, after hiking and exploring Gerpir.

"Nice meeting you, and thanks for catching me." I smiled, and politely stuck out my right hand. She grasped mine with a very small hand that was surprisingly strong. She had a big smile on her friendly face, and her dark, hazel eyes were fringed with the longest eyelashes I'd ever seen on a person. She wasn't pretty, but looked quite striking.

We walked about the village as did most of the passengers. It felt good to walk on a surface that wasn't constantly moving under our feet. Several of us would thankfully stop for that ever-offered coffee and enjoy a moment of sitting at a table that sat on solid ground.

When I saw a couple of half-collapsed houses, I asked Kristín if she had heard about last year's earthquake here in Dalvík.

"We didn't hear much in Stykkishólmur. But captains and fishermen talk amongst themselves and I heard stories about how the quake caused gigantic waves to rise here in the fjord. A ship was tossed about in waves that men said were as 'tall as those mountains'."

Both of us gazed at the towering crags. I tried to imagine a wave of such monstrous proportion, but it was too mind-boggling. I couldn't wrap my head around it.

As we started ambling back to the ship, I saw the two boys still fishing. My mind went back to the story of the waves. Where were those boys last year when the monster-wave happened? I bet they were as scared as Lilla and I, even more so, being right here!

We sailed out of Dalvík and past a rock face scarred with great gullies. Cliffs with hues of grey, black, and slate-blue gave a spooky atmosphere to scatterings of stark, and lonely,

farmhouses. They sat in tiny patches of sparse green grass in the barren mountainside that sheltered the 'picture perfect' harbor of Siglufjörður, one of the northern-most, and busiest [in 1935] fishing villages in Iceland.

Over a hundred fishing boats from numerous nations crowded the mountain-sheltered harbor. I tried to recognize the countries the flags represented but was able to name only ten or so. Kristín, the teacher, knew many more, but even she didn't know all of them.

The *Gullfoss* was still being unloaded when a great cry went up:

"The herring are running, the herring are running."

The effect was electric. Boats were scrambling to race out, each one trying to out-maneuver the other to get out as fast as they could and be the first to reach the enormous, silver-blanket of fish.

Way out in the mouth of the bay, we saw the wide band of silvery sloshing of herring stretching out into infinity. The heads of huge whales bobbed up, mouths wide open to gobble up millions of baby fish, while frantic seabirds screeched overhead and boats raced pell-mell into the melee.

Poor herring. Between man, whales and birds, they don't have a chance, I thought.

A sudden squall of rain caused Kristín and me to run for the ship. Passengers that were walking on the pier were getting dripping wet from the unexpected shower. The rain pinged noisily against the metal steps, rail, and smokestack of the ship. Then, just as quickly as it came, it quit. But the sky and ocean were turning an ugly, dark color.

The light was fading into gloomy grey by the time the

crew had finished the loading of the cargo and we were back on our journey. The grey-black mass of clouds was dropping toward the sea with amazing speed. I could no longer see the activity of the fishing boats that, in so much excitement, had set out earlier. Lights bobbing up and down among the deep, dark waves was the only indication of boats in the area.

Suddenly, it seemed we were in a totally different world. The weather became horrible. Rain started pelting down hard, and at times, almost sideways. We'd sailed into the teeth of a gale coming from the direction of Greenland. The waves became huge. The hills of water towered higher and higher, then rushed to meet us. The ship was lifted high into the air, then went down, down, down, then up, up, up again. I wondered if it would just roll over and go down to the bottom of the sea. I thought of Ingi's boat and for a moment knew genuine stomach-gripping fear. What a terrible night to be out on the ocean.

Kristin had bid me goodnight and gone below. I was cowering under the steps that led to the pilot house, out of the rain, as the wind rose to an unnerving shriek. I covered my ears with both hands as I followed the seamen with terrified eyes. Water streamed down their rain-hats and ran into their faces dripping into their beards. I watched them as they steadied themselves, firmly gripping cables and rail. Some were even grinning and just went about their usual activity. They are like my father, I thought, they love the sea, even as brutal as it can get. If they aren't scared I guess I don't have to be. But I really was. Dreadfully so.

I couldn't help but think of the "unsinkable" Titanic. Seamen still talked about the historic shipwreck that

happened in April 1912. More than 1500 people drowned when the ship collided with an ocean-floating iceberg, now feared more than ever. I leaned forward, both hands clenched fiercely on my knees. Clamping my teeth I muttered again and again, I won't be afraid, I won't be afraid!

I think I jumped a foot in the air when I felt a tap on my shoulder. I hadn't heard anyone coming. The noise from the howling wind and the smashing of the ocean against the ship drowned out everything else. The young man tapped my shoulder again and motioned up to the pilot's house where Einar was waving at me to come up. Swaying, and scrambling up the steps, the young man and I were drenched by the time we reached the door. The wind almost tore the door out of Einar's hand as he reached for me. I was glad to be with him, but the view from here was even more fierce than below.

At times the ship was on top of waves that kind of eased out from under us, and the ship just dropped and came down with teeth jarring thump. The *Gullfoss* wallowed, plunged, and slopped seemingly in all direction but actually was making a sluggish, steady gain toward Hornbjarg peninsula. As the saying goes in Iceland, "Just wait a bit, this will change!" By morning the weather did change.

We had sailed past Skagafjörður and Húnaflói while I slept through the night where Einar had securely tied me into a large chair. I was still snoozing in the warm pilot-house when the weather broke. He woke me up to see a magnificent sight; the sea cliffs rose steeply, dramatically, straight out of the ocean. A towering waterfall cascaded down the black lava cliff and plunged into the rocks and the seething,

white-frothing ocean below. A few icebergs glittered on the horizon, while straggling calves bounced on the waves; heading wherever the wind would take them.

The captain, skillfully, steered the *Gullfoss*, skirting around treacherous the shore. We left the North Fjords behind and entered into the West Fjord of Ísafjarðardjúp and to the Village of Ísafjörður, our next stop.

---

* Hard Times in Eyjafjörður, appendix B

* Earthquake in Dalvík, appendix C

CHAPTER 24
THE WEST FJORDS

THE NORTHWEST STORM had pushed such massive ice from Greenland that all the fjords between Ísafjörður and Látrabjarg were packed with ice-floes. Ísafjarðardjúp, through a quirky pattern of wind and waves, was spared this colossal intrusion. I was glad our ship had brought us safe through the, long, wicked storm.

What seemed like one hundred boats had taken shelter and were anchored about in the fjord. Two wooden piers ran out from the shore, the restless sea sending heavy waves sloshing up against its pilings. A, black and yellow painted, trawler and a small, red, fishing boat were moored to one pier, bouncing up and down with every billow.

The *Gullfoss* eased up to the other dock. Several people were gathered to greet us with the news that Dýrafjörður, Árnarfjörður, and Patreksfjörður, were packed with ice, and the passengers headed for those fjords would have to make a choice; either stay here and hope for the ice to break up soon, or to continue to Stykkishólmur and find a way back to their

various destinations.

The crew had been unloading the cargo meant for this village. Upon learning that some passengers were staying (kind folks were coming down to the dock and offering places for them to stay), the crew then unloaded both personal belongings and cargo meant for the ice-blocked villages.

"Do you think that there'll be ice problems in Breiðarfjörður?" I asked, turning to Kristín.

"I really don't think so. At Stykkishólmur we don't get near the ice these north fjords do." Kristín answered as she rubbed her chin and squinted her right eye, intently watching the animated knot of people gathered at the end of the pier. Motioning to the mountain across the bay, fingers were pointing, hands were wildly swinging. Women came and grabbed kids that were staring open-mouthed at the excited men. Voices were getting really loud and more men came running, yelling;

"WE'VE GOT TO GET THEM, NOW!"

Already, word was spreading like wildfire: A polar bear had come ashore. The men were acting like the so-called blood-thirsty Vikings of old, and the hunt was on…!

I, for one, was glad we were leaving. I had no desire to see more pandemonium over a bear. We were on our way out of the fjord when a young passenger, who looked to be about eighteen, came by the rail and stared intently toward the eastern shore.

"I thought I saw a polar bear going up toward Drángajökull." He muttered, as he removed his cap and scratched his head.

"Well, Bjarni. Why didn't you say something?" One of

his friends exclaimed, disgusted. "We could've had some real fun watching the locals go berserk!"

Watching for awhile, as we sailed past the mountains, we didn't see any sign of a bear. Kristin went below deck to do some reading and I was back in my favorite spot, crouching among the usual crates and large piles of coiled-up damp rope. A couple of old, yellow, life-rings with faded letters that spelled *Gullfoss* on them were propped up by the crates. I stuck my feet into the hole of one of them, and as my eyes scoured the horizon, my mind was back on the shipwreck of the *Titanic*. Seamen and passengers still talked about the "unsinkable" ship, even though it had been 23 years since the unthinkable tragedy took place.

I was looking out for icebergs and had every intention of shouting; *Icebergs ahead!* And thereby save the ship, and all the passengers!

We sailed out of the mouth of the fjord and turned west. As I looked north and west, the sea became a hazy undulating plain with no beginning and no end. I couldn't even see the faint outlines of Greenland.

When I grow up I'm going to see what's on the other side, I mused. Surely women can be explorers. Many Viking women were written about in the Saga as being as brave and ferocious as the men. The problem was I was neither brave nor ferocious. I couldn't even stand up to the bullies at school!

The ship now turned south, and we sailed along the west coast of Iceland.

Jaw dropping, inky-black rock faces rose steeply out of the sea, meeting the stares of passengers that were gathered at the rail of the ship. Incredulous, I gaped at the home of

millions of seabirds that were rarely disturbed, and left free to multiply into an chaotic horde. Now and then, a few hardy men would climb the spectacular sea-cliffs and gather eggs, or save seamen who had shipwrecked at the base of these perilous, hostile crags.

As we made our way around massive Látrabjarg, the western most land of Europe, I thought of the similarity of these cliffs, and the Skóruvik cliffs at Lánganes: One far east, one far west, both fascinating, fierce and menacing. Both peninsulas were notoriously treacherous to seamen. We made our way past these rugged coast and entered Breiðafjörður, heading to Stykkishólmur, which is situated on the north side of a long peninsula called Snæfellsnes. This long arm reaches almost as far west in the Atlantic as Látrabjarg, but was far more hospitable.

The Gullfosswas now moving in soft rolls in an much quieter ocean; A nice change from the wicked weather we'd been through.

Although this was my fourth time to travel around Iceland, I had previously been either too young or too busy playing with my sisters, who had traveled with me, to pay much attention. Now, at the age of ten, and traveling by myself I was intrigued by this fjord. I was full of questions, curiosity and wild imagination!

Squirming, and making myself comfortable, I gazed across the bay, then turned over on my back and dreamily stared up into the cloudy sky and watched my favorite wild characters take shapes in the clouds as they moved and changed. A loud slap of an ocean swell against the hull startled me from my daydreaming. I sat up, stretched, and

looked around. We were sailing slowly across the middle of this, very wide, fjord. I started thinking about the many tales I'd heard; how the, horribly greedy, ocean had claimed so many of mother's fishermen relatives in these waters.

I peered over the rail of the ship, down into the blue-green ocean waves slapping against the ship, as we moved across the fjord. I could imagine we were sailing over the bones of my forefathers. It was a gruesome thought.

My mother, Dagbjört Oktavía Bjarnadóttir, was born at Frakkanes and raised in Skorravík. Both are located on an inner peninsula in this fjord, across from Stykkishólmur.

Leifur Eiríkursson was born about four miles south of this area, at Eiríkurssaðir, the home that his father, Eirikur the Red, built and named.

According to Mother, Leifur is in our genealogy of ancestors.

The Saga records this story of the family; Eirikur had killed a man in Norway and was banished from the country, so he sailed for Iceland to cool off. Obviously, it didn't work; when Leifur was about twelve, his father, Eirikur, took him to Þingvellir, which is about 30 miles east of Reykjavík and was the place of the first parliament in the world. There, at *The Law Rock*, the chieftains and the people met annually. At the assembly Eirikur got into a fight with a neighbor he'd been feuding with. He killed the man, and the Þing [Parliament] banished him from Iceland for three years.

He took his Long Boat, filled it with family and provisions, and crossed the Atlantic where he discovered an ice covered island. In 982, when his banishment time was up, he sailed back to Iceland to tell people about this 'Greenland'

he'd found. No doubt he named it so, to entice people to go with him and start a colony there. Surely Greenland sounds more appealing than Iceland, he must have reasoned.

Iceland has had several names. First one was Thule, or Ultima Thule, given by Pytheas, a Greek explorer in 330 B.C. The second name, Snæland (Snowland) was given by a Norseman Viking named Noddoddur, in 850.

The third name was given by Garðar Svavarsson, a humble Swede who named it after himself; Garðarshólmur [Garðar's little Island]!

Then came another Norwegian Viking, Flóki Vilgerðarson, who chose the name of Iceland, for the fjords were filled with ice, and the mountains covered with snow. He went back to Norway and bad-mouthed this inhospitable place. Later he changed his mind and came back and lived here for many years [12ᵗʰ Century Landnámabók; Book of Settlers]. The name 'Iceland' stuck. *

As the ship arrived at Stykkishólmur and maneuvered up to the dock, the passengers began to gather in little groups. Some were checking their bags and making plans on how to get to their various destinations. Others were loudly discussing the bears.

"Man, that bear I saw loping up the country side towards Drángajökull was huge! I thought at first that it was a white horse!" Said Bjarni, the young man, I'd seen back at Ísafjörður. He scratched his left ear and adjusted his brown stocking cap, pulling it down to his dark eyebrows.

"Maybe it *was* just a horse, Bjarni!" One of the guys howled in merriment, slapping his thighs.

"But a horse doesn't lope. I saw a *bear!*" Bjarni's voice was now adamant. The young men began to holler over the side of the ship to a group of young women that were calling and waving. "You should have seen...! Really, humongous Polar bears...!" Bjarni and his friend were whooping and shouting. The bear story was getting bigger and bigger. Kristín and I grinned at each other, as we listened to the young men trying to outdo the other. It was getting pretty outrageous by the time the gangplank was down and the guys ran down to the pier to the group of girls. I can only imagine how many bears the story ended up having!

I didn't look around for Einar's family. He had told me that they were at their summer cabin at Kirkjufell for a few days, before school started. He gave Kristín a wave then went back to work.

I gave her a kiss on the cheek, and we hugged before she disembarked. She walked away with a firm step down to the end of the pier, where she called out to a group of young children teasing seagulls. When they saw her they started running and shouting, exuberantly throwing their arms around her. Two boys took her suitcases while other kids clung to her skirt. I wondered who they were. I'd somehow got the idea that she taught older students. I'll have to remember to ask her the next time we meet, I mused, as the group disappeared around a brown-rusted metal building.

And again the *Gullfoss* sailed on and went past the Snæfellsnes Peninsula where the glacier, Snæfelljökull, rose grandly to the sky. It is well known for being the setting for the novel "Journey to the Center of the Earth." A

story written by the French author, Jules Verne, where he describes how a professor and his nephew hire an Icelander to be their guide in a daring exploration of the center of the earth, by entering a volcanic opening in Snæfell. The "Snorre Tarleson" in the story is based on Snorri Sturluson, author of Heimskringla, mentioned in the story by Verne.

As we continued sailing around Snæfellsnes Peninsula, toward Faxaflói, a wide bay we would cross to get to Reykjavik, I saw the tip of the glacier in the distance bathed in an orange glow from the just-below-the-horizon midnight sun. The sky was bathed in brilliant reds orange and golden glows making the clouds look like a fairy land.

Elves and 'Hidden Folks' are considered abundant in this area, and many farmers do not cut hay or disturb the ground around certain boulders. This was a well-known practice among farmers all over Iceland and not just here on Snæfellsnes.

A little over halfway in this fjord is Borgarfjörður. I mention that because one of our more famous ancestors Snorri Sturluson*, who lived from 1172-1241, had his home there called Reykholt. Snorri is also the author of Egils Saga one of the best known of the Icelandic Sagas. Grandma Sigríður is a direct descendant.

The sun was dangling a little higher on the horizon when we sailed between two urgently flashing lighthouses, and pulled into the harbor of Reykjavik.

Even though I hadn't wanted to leave Vopnafjörður, I was getting excited at the thought of seeing my mother and siblings. Father was probably out at sea.

* I would like to mention again, that although the Vikings had a terrible reputation, cruel - blood-thirsty, etc. the truth is they were excellent sailors, ship-builders, craftsmen, daring explorers and great navigators who navigated by the sun and stars. They were also superb storytellers, rich in tradition that lives on in the Saga. And, for their times, they had a very open and democratic society.

* This is the same Snorri Sturluson mentioned in Verne's novel.

CHAPTER 25
BACK HOME IN REYKJAVÍK

EINAR WAS NOW very busy. I'd thanked him already and said my goodbye. The hustle and bustle of the crew seemed to take much longer than usual. I guess that was not surprising, I thought; all the passengers would be getting off. It would be several hours before the ship would be scheduled to sail back out so the groups on the pier were folks waiting for the arrivals.

I was leaning at the rail with my two suitcases at my feet as I scanned the people, huddled in groups. I didn't see Mother, but then I spotted my Father. What a wonderful surprise. I was the first one to jump on the plank when it had been lowered. I flew down toward the pier and exuberantly flung myself into his arms.

Father gave a low chuckle as he tottered back and swung me around, then put me down. "You have grown a little taller Íedamín, but still skinny as a rail!" Father grinned as he inspected me head to toe. "Trust you had a good trip. I heard from Einar that you had a few encounters with icebergs, and

Polar bears." He brushed hair from my face and kissed me on the tip of my nose. Quite unusual, I felt a little apprehension.

"It's great to see you, Father. I was expecting Mother to meet the ship. Is she alright?" I tried to be casual, like this was nothing out of the ordinary. I turned as I heard a soft clearing of a throat behind me.

"Oh, thank you, Jón." Father took my suitcases out of the hands of the young seaman I'd seen working aboard the ship. I'd completely forgotten about them in my excitement at seeing Father.

"Your Mother is fine, so are your brothers and sisters." Father's voice was reassuring. "I'm meeting you because the *Gullfoss* arrived so early this morning, and my ship is docked just a couple of piers over." He pointed where an orange and black painted trawler was anchored. I knew Father was on another ship since the trawler he'd been on had shipwrecked last winter.

Derricks and cranes cluttered the wharf to the delight of the seagulls, and other seabirds that perched up high, their screeching piercing the quiet morning. Ships and fishing boats were moored at the pier. Another fifty or so were anchored in the bay, their various national flags hanging limply in the still air. A tugboat idly smoked near the entry of the harbor. I turned back and looked at the *Gullfoss*, mentally thanking her for bringing me safe through the awful storms.

The old tub did better than the fancy *Titanic!* Funny how one can get attached to ships that bring you safely home. *

We ambled toward the trawler. My Father, the ultimate seaman, was not tall in stature, he stood only 5'8" in his stocking feet. But he had an air of solid authority about him.

His round, weather-beaten face was usually serious. Hooded dark-brown eyes, under dark heavy eyebrows made him look mysterious, I thought. He was wearing his dark-blue captain jacket and a white cap on his dark-brown hair. A tough, square-built man, without an ounce of fat, his body shaped and hardened by a hard taskmaster, the sea.

Father started walking with the slow-rolling gait of a sailor I always tried to imitate. I'd take a long step, then sway from side-to-side as if I were walking on a ship that was being pummeled on a high sea. This sent my two sisters into gales of laughter as they tried to imitate me, which usually ended in a squabble. I'd get fighting mad, run into a room and hide there with a book.

We walked along the base of one pier and passed a grey, weather-beaten, corrugated metal shed. The sea below was moving gently. In the rare stillness of the morning, I heard ducks murmuring. I peaked over the edge and saw them dipping their heads and paddling in formation under the wharf. An old skiff, broken and rotted-out, lay on the rocks of the shore, a perfect perch for the thousands of seabirds fluttering around.

We reached the second pier and turned to go toward the ship. A boy who looked about my age was sitting with his bare feet hanging over the rim of the dock, the legs of his trousers rolled up and over his bony knees.

A fishing-line, with a hook without bait, dangled from his hands. Three fish, a good two- feet-long each, wriggled in the hemp-bag lying by his side. His wrinkled red shirt was partly tucked into the waist of his pants. He'd pulled his black wool cap down to his almost-white eyebrows, and

completely covered his hair.

"Good morning. Fish looks good." Father remarked as he touched the bag with his right toe. The boy turned, nodded his head and motioned for us to come closer. He pointed down to the ocean. We leaned over. It was unbelievable; all I saw were fish and more fish. They were in thick layers, flopping and sloshing over each other in the sea. The boy had literally dropped his fish line into the chaotic mess and pulled up his catch without bait!

Looking up, the boy grinned, his grey-blue eyes gleeful. "You know the saying, Cap'n, 'fish is food on the table and gold in the pocket.'" He said, chuckling.

"How right you are, son. How right you are." Father tipped his right hand to his cap and I waved at the boy when we heard a shout:

"Halló, Captain Jónas, breakfast is ready!" My Father was very well liked, and respected. Men addressed my Father as 'Captain', long before he was one.

"That's our cook, Juan. Are you hungry?" Father asked. I nodded as my stomach growled.

We walked up to the ship and I read the name *Max Pemberton**. An odd-looking, short man was leaning at the rail of the trawler, his black Kong-Fu mustache draped the lower half of his swarthy face. His black eyebrows went from the left of his brow, dipped over his nose, then continued to the right of his forehead. I was reminded of a black raven in flight. His dark eyes were piercing. Frankly, he scared the daylights out of me; he looked just like I imagined a pirate or a shanghier would look. But boy, could he cook! The table was loaded with cheese, boiled eggs, fish balls, dark bread,

and hot coffee. He made coffee like no other; two dollops of export (chicory). My fears melted like ice in hot lava flow.

* Five years later, in 1940, during WWII, the *Gullfoss* was seized by Germans occupying Copenhagen, Denmark. Einar was not among the captives. By then he was on another ship.

* Father was with the skipper, Captain Pétur Maack, for several years then got his own ship. In 1944 the *Max Pemberton* disappeared in the Atlantic, never to be seen or heard from again. [Maritime Museum in Reykjavik, Iceland.]

CHAPTER 26
THE "LOOK"

IT WAS NOW the first week of September. Father had gone back out to sea, and it would be close to Christmas before we'd see him again.

We were all packed and ready to catch the old bus in the morning. Mother had planned for us to spend the week at our summer house and enjoy vacation time before school started next week. I wasn't to sure I'd be able to stand up to the bullies at school, but I knew I had to try Sigga's suggestion; to give their opinions to the trölls.

Our friends, Ása and Gógó (her name was Góa, but she stuttered and when she said her name it came out " Gó-Gó-Gó") had gone home after spending most of the day playing "hide and seek". It was late afternoon and Sisi, Lilla and I started to play hopscotch.

"Sísímín, I need for you to run down to the store and get milk to take with us in the morning." Mother stood in the doorway with the shiny, tin, milk-pail in her hand.

"Íeda, you go, I'm in the middle of this play," Sísí said and

kept hopping. Tripping, she caught herself, barely touching the ground with her fingertips. "That doesn't count. I didn't put my whole hand down!" she yelled.

"Does too!" I screeched. "You go, Lilla. That's cheating, Sísí!"

"I don't want to. My turn is coming up!" Lilla hollered.

Mother gave each of us a searching look for a few seconds then, without a word, turned and went back inside.

"You know that's cheating, Sísí. You're not supposed to touch the ground. You lose your turn." I argued.

"My turn my turn..." Lilla started to hop at the beginning square. Sísí gave her a shove and my little sister promptly howled at the top of her lungs.

"That's not fair." We were all arguing and yelling at each other when Mother came out, purse in one hand and the pail in the other. She never said a word. I could hear Búddi and Frankel playing with their friends at the back of the house.

Sísí looked up as Mother started down the road. "I'll go." Mother didn't look at her.

My stomach churned. "No, I'll go." Terrible guilt built up inside of me.

"Mother, I'll go, I'll go." Lilla grabbed Mother's skirt. Mother kept walking, didn't look at any of us. She didn't look to the right or to the left but kept her eyes fixed on the road ahead of her. Her steps were long, solid and purposeful as she plodded down the street toward the milk-store. Mother was a small woman who now tromped her feet like someone twice her size. My guilt felt like a heavy rock in my stomach.

Sísí started crying, reaching out for the pail and pleading with Mother to let her go to the store.

"I'm sorry." She whimpered.

"Me, too." I sobbed as I scrambled after Sísí.

Lilla was crying and wiping her tears on Mother's skirt, barely able to keep her feet on the ground as she tried to keep up with Mother.

Mother kept clomping all the way to the store, totally silent.

Garður, the store owner, looked up as we entered the shop, our faces dirty and streaked with tears, still begging. He inspected each of us, curiously. Then smiled into the calm face of my Mother who acted like she didn't know any of us. She didn't seem to be aware that we were around.

"Good evening, Dagbjört, what can I get you?"

"I need milk, Garður. I'm heading for the summer house in the morning."

"This is fresh milk and you have that ice-cold creek running close by your cabin to store the pail. That will keep the milk good for several days."

"I expect so." Mother nodded as she handed him the bucket. Garður took it from her hand and carefully filled the pail. Fastening the lid, he wiped off a small streak of milk dripping down on the side of the bucket, then handed it back to Mother who had taken money from her purse and laid it on the counter

"Do you need anything else, Dagbjört?" He glanced at us, standing by the door in a miserable heap, shuffling our feet and sniffling.

"No, thank you, Garður. The milk is all I need at this time. I'll see you when we get back."

"Thank you, Dagbjört. You have a good evening." Garður

looked at us, opened his mouth to say something, but when he saw Mother's set face, he clamped his teeth and eyed us soberly.

Quietly reaching over Lilla's head, mother pushed the door open and stepped out. She didn't look at us but started walking the same way, all the way back home.

Mother was a very easy-going good natured mother who never yelled at us. We were never spanked, but there were times (like this time) when I'd rather have the spanking than the "*look*" and the silent treatment.

We sniveled all the way home. The three of us never forgot.

I must have driven my mother to the edge of her patience with my insatiable reading. One day she came into our bedroom where I was curled up on the floor beneath the window, totally absorbed in a book. Taking it out of my hands and gently, but firmly she said; "It's your turn to clean your kids' room. Sísí did it the last time. I'll give you the book back when you're through." With my book in her hand she turned at the door and gave me "*that look*" then walked out of the room and closed the door.

Half-heartedly, I started picking up clothes and putting them away. I glanced around and saw a corner of a book sticking out from under a pile of socks. Now, mind you, I wasn't going to read it; just see which one it was, just the title you know…

"I thought I removed all the books!" Mother's voice was inches away from my ear. I must have jumped a foot high into the air. It was getting to be a habit! I'd get so engrossed in day-dreaming or reading I'd forget where I was or even

what day it was.

I watched sheepishly as mother hunted for more books that might be hidden. Turning to me with a deep frown between her normally-twinkling blue eyes, "Couple of women are coming over and I want you to have these clothes folded up and put away by the time they arrive. That will give you one hour. Is that clear?" Mother's firm voice was very clear. I nodded.

I did quite well once I got going. The clothes were put away and the top of the duvet was smooth. I finished by dusting the top of our chest of drawers and then sweeping the floor. Putting the broom by the door I sat back down on the floor by the window, the best light for reading. Looking around I made sure I hadn't missed anything. Twisting my fingers and twiddling my thumbs I sighed. No books.

Scratching my head I straightened out my leg and wiggled the bottom duvet with my toe, a smidgen of paper slithered out. Eagerly I picked it up. It was one page that was missing from one of the books mother had removed from the room. I was totally in another world when I heard the explosive laughter from mother and her friends as one of them exclaimed, "Just one piece of paper, she is hopeless, Dagbjört!"

But the room was as neat as when Sísí cleaned, and I got my books back!

CHAPTER 27
MOTHER FALLS INTO VOLCANIC CREVASSE

WE WERE AT the summer-house enjoying our vacation; fishing, splashing in the creek, and skipping stones, when the wind died down enough for the water to be still. It was quite a competition among us to see how many times a rock would skip and hop before sinking.

Other times we'd find small lava rocks that would float. This fascinated Frankel the most, he looked under the pumice to see what made it move.

"There should be a motor." He fussed. We showed him how to throw pebbles to cause waves in the water so he could see his little 'boat' wobble and bobble . I picked up a stick and stirred the water some more.

"See, that's how the Vikings looked at the current," I said. "They didn't have a motor on their longboats, only oars. They studied the waves to see which way to go for their discoveries." This made Frankel very content, he liked to hear the stories about the Vikings, as we all did. He could lay on his

stomach for hours and watch the 'Viking boat' move.

The widest part of the creek that ran across the field in front of the little house was pond-like, and shone like a mirror on this particular afternoon. The fish plopped up and down, pink and silver scales shining in the elusive sun. Wispy, raggedy clouds hung in the grey-blue sky. A group of seagulls hip-hopped on the rail of the wood bridge that spanned the creek. Cocking their heads and puffing up their wings, they watched the fish jump in and out of the water.

This, our last day, was unusually still and mild. The mountain range was hidden in soft, lazily floating, grey-white fog.

Iceland's most wicked volcano, Hekla, sat quietly in the distance, her usual, perpetual, white fluff hanging over her in the sky.

Mother's summer house was in the country at a place called Laugberg a short drive from Reykjavik. The only other house, barely in sight, was a farm across the creek, sitting a way up in the countryside. We kids called them "the rich people" because their farm was so large. The farmer there raised pigs and was looked down on with much disdain by the sheep farmers.

Our cabin was a small two-room place, divided crosswise in the middle. Two bedrooms were in the back part. Built-in beds lined two walls in each room. Each bed had its top and bottom down-duvets. The bottom duvet was the only kind of 'mattress' we had.

The sitting, dining and cooking area was in the front part of the cabin. Pots and pans were stacked on open shelves by the black, peat-burning stove. Dishes, cups and saucers were on shelves built on each side of the center-placed bare

window. The dishes would clatter and dance noisily at the smallest earth-tremor. A wood table with six chairs placed two to a side and one at each end sat in front of this window.

On the table were four wood cylinders ornately carved with old-time scroll-pattern, and the words; *Hnífar-Gafflar-Matskeiðar-Teskeiðar (Knives-Forks- Soupspoons-Teaspoons)* each one filled with the appropriate utensil.

A roughly built, long bench served as a sofa, where plump, eider-down-filled pillows of various sizes in red, brown and white and a few fur ones, were propped haphazardly up against the wall. A rough, wooden ladder was in one corner, it lead to a crawl-around-only attic. The three of us girls would sleep up there when, Gróa, or a visitor came to stay overnight.

Lilla and I were sitting outside on the top step. We were finishing a long necklace that we were making from the dandelions we'd picked. Snipping off the yellow blooms, we made a circle out of the stems by threading the ends together then looping each one to make a chain. We'd made a bracelet, a coronet and a necklace that now decorated Lilla. We were working on more necklaces for Sisi and me, and hoping we'd have enough to finish, as the weed was getting scarce.

"Do you have the scissors?" Lilla asked, running her hand under the pile of dandelion heads.

"No, I don't have them. Maybe you're sitting on them, or maybe the 'Hidden Folks' needed to borrow them." I searched half-heartedly around me. "If they borrowed them, you know the scissors will turn up. The 'Folks' always return stuff."

Scowling, Lilla stood up.

All of a sudden horrendous screaming and crying echoed

through the air. As we jumped up and ran down the steps, we saw Sísí coming across the lava field. She had her skirt hiked high up with both hands so she could run faster.

She stumbled and cried when we reached her. I couldn't make anything out of her stuttering, but I saw Frankel sitting on the ground mouth wide open crying, "Mamma, mamma!" Búddi was on his stomach, both arms flailing, feet kicking in the air. He was looking into what seemed to be a narrow split in the moss-covered ground.

"What happened to Mamma!" Lilla cried.

"She fell into a crack in the ground. I thought I heard her cry, but now she's awful quiet." Sísí finally gulped, tear streaming down her cheeks.

"We'll have to get help from the pig-farmer!" I turned to Sisi, who was wiping her face with her skirt.

"I'll get him. Sisi, you're the oldest you have to stay with Mamma, and the kids." I started running for the creek.

"Don't you dare!" Both of my sisters screamed.

I stopped, turned, and stared at them.

"What else can we do? They are the only people close by. We've got to get help!" My stomach was in knots. I had no idea how badly Mother might be hurt, but I knew I couldn't waste time. The lava rocks are sharp and can cut deep, and Sísí had indicated that Mother was unconscious. I turned and ran towards the distant farm and started to cross the ice-cold creek. Wadding my skirt into a knot I stomped into the rushing water that came up to my knees.

I saw the young roan just on the other side of the bank.

"You're gonna get killed." Lilla shrieked. "Remember the last time!"

Oh yes, I remembered the last time. I had disobeyed and gone across this same creek and jumped on this same colt. He had promptly bucked me off his back and knocked me out cold. I had promised, "cross my heart" never to go over that creek again! But this was an emergency I assured myself.

Carefully, I crawled up the bank on the other side. This time I wasn't going to surprise the horse. I talked to him, my teeth chattering.

I took a running leap and jumped onto his back. Snorting fiercely and shaking his head, he took off like he'd been whacked on the rump. I was ready. I fastened my legs tightly to his smooth back and clenched both of my fists into his air-tossing mane as he galloped toward the farmhouse.

As we neared the huge pig-pen, the farmer came running toward us, purple-faced, and both fists angrily pounding the air. Then, leaping, he grabbed his horse by the neck and quickly brought him to a halt as he growled at me;

"I told you the last time if you ever... !" He stopped as he saw my terrified, tear-streaked face.

"All right, girl. Don't look so scared. I'm not going to hurt you, but you really . .." He scowled.

"It's Ma…ma" I stammered as I slid to the ground, tears pouring down my face.

It was surprising how gentle this 'horrible, bad-tempered pig farmer' became. I was terribly afraid of him. He was known to have a short fuse because people gave him a hard time over raising pigs, nasty animals that looked gross and smelled worse. The sheep farmers around here argued 'No one that had any sense would eat such meat! They were as unclean as chickens, that no one eats. But at least chickens

laid eggs and had useful feathers!'

Patting my head he turned, whistled for his older horse which promptly came running, then he roared. "Helga, come here!"

"Coming, Árni." The woman turned from the clothes line where she'd been pinning snow-white sheets. The snapping sound of wet cloths followed her as she slowly plodded closer to us. Then she stopped.

Furious, she knit her black heavy brows, and grimly fastened her gimlet eyes on me. She was large of bone and feature, and looked very strong. I was scared to death of her, too, even when she didn't look so grim. Firmly, she placed her hands on her ample hips and glared.

"You really are in trouble now. I've got a good mind to... "

"Hold it, Helga." Árni waved his right hand. "We have an emergency. Her mother is hurt. Get your first-aid kit and come on over. I'll go now and take the child with me. I'm amazed she was able to hold onto this unbroken colt." Árni was putting the reins on his horse as he talked. Swinging his right foot over the horse's back, riding bare-back, he moved and made room for me in front of him. Then he reached down as I lifted up my hands.

Árni gave his horse a smart whack and we went at a brisk gallop across the lava-field, sloshed across the creek where Lilla and Búddi were waiting, faces wet and streaky from tears. Sísí was holding Frankel, rocking and crooning.

She looked up as we rode up. Árni lifted me off after he had dismounted, and I ran to Sísí. All of the kids were trying to talk at the same time;

"Mother is alright. She can talk, but she hurts." They

babbled, as Árni knelt down and looked into the crevasse.

"Halló, Dagbjört. Talk to me." He said." How are you hurt? Can you move at all?"

There was noticeable relief in Mother's voice as she gasped "I'm alright, Árni, but I can't move my right ankle without hurting pretty bad."

"Helga is riding up now. She'll come down and look at your foot. We'll get you out of there pretty soon." Árni's voice was reassuring.

Helga was riding up at a flying pace. She had tied her skirt up between her legs so she appeared to be wearing black, billowy, bloomers making for easier bareback riding. Interesting design I thought. I was impressed. In one surprisingly fluid motion she was off the horse and kneeling down by her husband.

Lilla and I had climbed on top of a boulder so we'd be out of the way. Búddi and Frankel sat on the moss below our feet, while Sísí stood by Árni, ready to help.

Helga carefully scrambled down into the hole. We could hear the murmur of her voice as she spoke to Mother.

"No broken bones, Árni." She called, " I'll wrap her ankle so we can move her. But first, hand me your bottle. We'd better give her a stiff drink." As he handed her the bottle we heard the two women giggling like a couple of young girls. Then her hand came up, something seemed to be wadded up in it.

"Look here, Árni, our little Kisa was down here, I didn't know she had wandered off!" She lifted a small, coal-black, mewling fur ball to her husband. He gently stroked the small head with his big hands then handed it to Frankel

who seemed in awe of the purring creature. We never owned pets.

After careful lifting and pulling, the couple were able to get Mother out. The fissure was only about six feet long, three feet wide and five feet deep but had sharp, jagged cinder rocks on the bottom. Mother had landed on the side of her right foot, hitting her head on the edge of the rift as she fell in. She had a large bump on the back of her head.

Helga had wrapped Mother's right foot from toe to knee. I couldn't imagine how anyone could jam so much bandage into such a small emergency kit.

"I feel like a silly sheep, falling in like that. I thought I heard a child cry, but it was the kitten. I could feel the brittle shale giving way at the edge, but I couldn't stop my falling." Mother shook her head, then groaned and grabbed her head in her hands, then, looking up she saw Lilla and me sitting on top of the rock.

"Sísímín, get the girls off of there. They know better." She murmured.

Lilla and I looked at each as we scurried down. Yes indeed, we knew better. She had told us numerous times not to climb on that particular rock.

"Remember your cousin who limps? She got that way because she climbed a huge rock that was known to be a castle of the elves. They don't take kindly to kids who climb on top of their buildings." She had warned us.

Fearful, I looked behind me as we followed Sísí, who had Frankel and Búddi by a hand. Frankel had the kitten wrapped up in his sweater, protecting the bundle with his free hand. I didn't see the angry elves, but I walked a little

faster, dragging Lilla with me.

Árni and Helga crossed their hands together and formed a seat for Mother to sit. She wrapped her arms over the neck of each of them, and we all walked slowly toward the cabin to wait for Gróa. The farm couple had offered to stay with us, but Mother assured them that we'd be alright. Nanny Gróa would be on the evening bus as planned, as she was coming to help close up the cabin for the winter.

Mother thanked them for their kindness and we kids stepped outside to wave as they rode off.

I thought of the kind way they treated Mother, and even me, although I had caused them trouble. I hoped I'd never listen to other people's opinion about folks.

Frankel's lower lip quivered as he watched the kitten curl up in front of Árni. Mother had told the kind couple that we couldn't own a pet, when they offered to give it to Frankel. He was a quiet boy who liked to play by himself. He loved trucks, machines of all kinds fascinated him. He would use sticks and rocks for his imaginary trucks and make roaring noises as he 'drove' his machines up and down the plank-walls of the cabin. He'd grown rather independent during the summer I'd been gone, which was a good thing since Búddi was so rambunctious!

Sísí herded us back inside and got us started on packing our own stuff.

Later, Búddi, Lilla and I stood by the side of the road and watched the rattling bus lumber up the volcanic-cinder, one-lane road. Gróa got off, and immediately we all started talking at the same time.

"Mother fell into a crevasse..." I started.

"She hurt her head and foot... " Lilla hopped around Gróa.

"The pig-farmer and his wife came... " Búddi said, excitedly.

"Whoa, hold it. One at a time." Gróa stopped. "Your Mother is all right?"

We all vigorously nodded and followed Gróa inside.

The next morning the weather had changed. Hard, north-east gale was blowing across the lava field. Dark-gray clouds scudded across the somber sky.

We kids, and Nanny Gróa were bundled up in lopi sweaters and knit caps as we sat by the road, suitcases by our feet. We heard the rattling old bus drive up the ash covered road. All of us jumped up as it swung up to our lane and stopped.

Gróa talked to Skúli, the bus driver, for a minute. Then both of them walked up to the cabin and went inside. Pretty soon they came out carrying a bundled-up Mother the same way as Árni and Helga had done; clasping their hands to form a seat, as Mother wrapped an arm around each one's neck.

Walking down the lane and over the wood bridge was a good distance and both Gróa and Skúli were puffing hard, as they reached the bus. By the time Mother was settled in, and the pillows we'd brought out were cushioned under her foot, she looked very pale.

Just three days and we'd be back in school. I dreaded it.

CHAPTER 28
ÓLI THE BULLY

GÓGÓ AND I stomped grumpily down the crowded, blue-painted hallway that smelled strongly of green lye-soap. Neither one of us were happy to be back in school where both of us were teased unmercifully, I, because of my name and Gógó because she stuttered.

We entered the classroom where Óli and his two friends were already seated. My heart sank. I was destined to put up with those hooligans forever. And to make matters worse, my desk was in front of Óli's, giving him perfect opportunity to annoy me, yank my hair, and whisper taunts, without being detected by the teacher. Gnawing at my lower lip my face felt red-hot as my temper rose ten degrees.

"Good morning, children. My name is Ínga and I'll be your teacher this year." The teacher was disgustingly cheerful as she swung a blue and white-checkered towel over her shoulder. On her left arm hung a small tin bucket, and in the hand she had a bottle full of a shimmering, sickly-yellow, oily liquid. She had a large tablespoon in her right hand that she

jabbed in the air as she spoke.

"You know the routine of first things first." She chuckled as if she were enjoying a huge joke.

I brushed strands of hair from my face and looked at Gógó who was sitting at the desk in front of me. I could see the red flush creep across the back of her neck, blending with her red hair. Slowly she turned, we rolled our eyes at each other; the cod-liver oil! My mouth went dry. Desperately I tried to think of some way to get out of having to take the oil...

"Hold your nose and open wide, Góa." Teacher's voice was positively chirping!

How can she be so chipper? She knows we all hate this stuff. I was sure I was going to throw up in front of all these kids. Óli and his friends would never let up on the teasing and name-calling. I'd never be able to come back, or maybe I'd be lucky and just choke on the stuff and die on the spot! I grit my teeth.

Then I thought, if I keep gritting my teeth it'll be my luck to be toothless, like old Olga. Unconsciously I snapped my fingers like I'd been practicing for so long. All of a sudden, I relaxed. I bit the inside of my lip to keep from giggling. I'd forgotten Sigga's advice on the bullies! I sat up straight in my seat as Ínga stood by my desk and happily sang out;

"Hold your nose and open wide, Íeda."

"Íeda..." I heard Óli snicker behind me.

I turned to him and hissed "I gave your name calling to the trölls." I smiled sweetly at the teacher, who was looking at Óli, her smile replaced by a tight frown knit between her green eyes.

I pinched my nose with the thumb and fingers of my right hand and opened my mouth wide, for the teacher to pour in a spoonful of the stomach-churning stuff. With heroic effort I managed to nonchalantly swallow. She nodded her head a couple of times then turned to Óli.

"Your turn, Óli. Hold your..."

"That's girl stuff. I don't need to hold my nose." Óli boasted.

The spoon clicked against his teeth as Ínga poured the yellow liquid into his mouth.

"Swallow!" The teacher was firm, no longer cheerful.

I heard Óli's strangled gulp and turned just in time to see him turn grey-green, gag violently, and then throw up into the bucket Ínga was holding. With a wicked smirk on my face, I leered into the red face of my tormentor and snapped my fingers. My antagonists eyes glared at me.

The first day was always the hardest. After that we were okay with the routine of the 'first things first' dose of cod-liver oil. I never gave it a thought that this wasn't the most hygienic way to administer the potion, but the cod-liver oil sure kept us healthy!

After three weeks of unusual autumn days where we had been able to enjoy the out of doors, the weather took a nasty turn. Rain turned to sleet, and Mt. Esja was covered in white from her top down to the seashore. Rime covered the walkway to the school, and icicles hung from the metal pipes that formed a handrail.

I got my, regrettable, second revenge.

Sísí, Lilla, my friend Gógó and I had arrived at school all bundled up. We, carefully, walked up the icy steps as Óli and

two of his buddies gleefully kept their eyes on us. A metal flagpole was fastened at a slant to the iron rail. The Icelandic flag hung limply in the sleet. Óli had perched himself up on the rail and grabbed the pole with his, bare, left hand.

"Gógógógó... Íeda..." They started their taunting.

"Get your hand off of there, Óli!" Ínga's voice was shrill with alarm. She'd just stepped out to ring her school bell.

Startled, Óli slid down and slipped, still holding the pole. His hand was stuck. His face swung against the pole. He opened his mouth to yell, but all he could do was grunt. His eyes were bulging in terror. The tip of his tongue was frozen to the iron flagpole!

Other teachers came running when we all started screaming. Ínga was telling Óli not to move as she held his head tight to her chest. Boiling hot water was brought out and poured on the pole. In a short time, Óli was free. His left palm was sore for a few days and it was awhile before he was able to speak or eat properly. I behaved, I didn't sneer at all. The truth is, I felt sorry for Óli, and the whole episode was rather traumatic for all of us.

I can't say that I remember the teasing easing up a whole lot, but I do remember that from then on I didn't let it get to me like I used to. Perhaps it was because Mother started tutoring me a bit in the catechism of the Lutheran Church, dwelling quite a bit, I thought, on forgiveness.

Although Icelandic children are confirmed at age 14 and I was just going on eleven years of age, I guess I needed more time to get rid of my heathen ways and rid myself of the belief in this 'silly superstition of trölls and Hidden Folks.' It was easier to quit believing in trölls and ghosts than hidden

folks, after all we were being taught in church that 'many had entertained angels unaware.'

I thought that meant they were invisible and therefore 'hidden.'

CHAPTER 29
CHRISTMAS 1935

OF AT LEAST 27 public holidays observed in Iceland, our family celebrated only Christmas, New Year Eve, Easter, Bolludaginn (Bun Day), Ash Wednesday and Easter.

We didn't make anything of birthdays, never celebrating any of them.

—◉—

I vividly remember the Christmas of '35, probably because it was so unusual for Father to be home.

Father had arrived back home after a fishing trip to England. He was quieter than usual and speaking with Mother in a hushed voice about a war in Europe. I didn't pay much attention thinking that was far away and wouldn't affect our small isolated island. Right now we were as excited as could be; Father was taking us to a Seamen's Christmas Party held at the Opera House.

Our water line had frozen, but Gróa got a dishpan full of snow and melted it so we could to wash up. She took care

of the boys while we girls washed ourselves, with Mother's supervision. Then she brushed our hair and had us turn a few times to make sure we were presentable. We girls, wore our Icelandic dress-ups - ornately embroidered with gold thread, red vest over a white blouse, black skirt and tasseled cap on our head. The boys wore green jackets, their short breeches were tucked into their long socks just below the knees.

Bundled up against the winter blast until we looked like overstuffed sausages, we waddled downstairs to a waiting, decrepit taxicab that Father had so extravagantly called for.

All the church bells in the capital of Reykjavik were chiming at the same time, the Dómkirkjan [Lutheran Church, Iceland's state church] in down-town Reykjavik, the Catholic Church sitting high on a hill, and the Fríkirkjan [The Free Church], down by the lake, all were ushering the start of the Christmas Season. Our holiday started promptly at 6:00 PM on the 24th of December. The loud ringing of the bells added to the festive air.

The dark-blue sky was lit up with, pinkish-green, shimmering curtains of rapidly moving lights. The Aurora Borealis [Northern-lights] were in full display of red, gold, and purple streaks as the brilliant colors shot across the sky in a breathtaking show. Up and down, side-to-side the lights danced across the heavens. We kids craned our necks this way and that, pointing, *ooh-ing* and *ahh-ing* over each wonder.

In much excitement, we kids erupted out of the cab and into the entry of the Opera House. Father stopped to greet someone as Mother continued inside with us kids. Suddenly we stopped: The giant Christmas tree at the party was awesome, its top reached clear up to the vaulted ceiling. The few

trees we had in Iceland didn't grow to such massive height. I knew it had to come on one of the ships from some far-off country.

I threw my head way back to try to see the top. The hundreds of lighted candles flickered in the huge ballroom. Red, green, yellow and white paper-chains were wrapped around and around, from top to bottom. Various sized and intricately shaped bags were hanging from the branches, each bag bulging to overflowing with hard candy!

Rollicking accordion, and violin, music reverberated through the air. The place was already filled with children and their parents. We stood mesmerized, rooted to the wood floor that we could feel shaking, and crackling, like aftershocks of an earth quake. The kids had formed a circle and were hopping, clomping, and swinging in a dance around the tree. Sisi, Lilla and I grabbed hands that reached out to us as kids twirled by. Even Búddi joined the fun. But Frankel couldn't stop staring at the tree. He stumbled and tottered around, blue eyes scrunched half-shut, as he followed Mother.

"What's the matter with your eyes? Why are you closing them like that?" She was getting concerned.

Frankel was like one hypnotized.

"When I squeeze my eyes it makes hundreds and hundreds of lights, maybe millions, maybe gazillion trillion lights!" Not until the candy bags and oranges were handed out did Frankel quit his squinting.

We were a happy, but tired bunch that went home that night, chattering in excitement what tomorrow was going to bring.

We woke up Christmas morning with the kitchen

sending out an aroma of cardamom, cinnamon, and vanilla. Gróa was baking twist-cookies and pancakes. She'd spread the center of the pancakes with jam and topped them with dollop of whipped cream. Mother folded a cake in half and again in half, so it looked like a triangle. We needed forks to eat this rich, yummy treat.

After we had eaten and Gróa was clearing the table Father told Mother to have us sit down and wait, then he quickly disappeared into the bedroom.

My toes tingled in anticipation. We'd never had store-bought toys, but we always got something carved or knitted, just for us, and sometimes we had an orange each. We'd put the orange-peel in a glass of water with a spoonful of sugar and let it sit overnight. That was our next morning orange juice!

Father came out with his arms loaded with boxes, full of stuff from his trip to England. We started jumping as Búddi was handed a truck. He seemed speechless for a change. Then he whooped and fell to the floor with the truck. When Frankel got his, he inspected it from end to end, looked under it, and turned to Mother with his eyes sparkling.

"This is the biggest and the best." He breathed.

We, girls, each got an almost, life-size, plastic baby-doll. This Christmas was beyond our wildest dreams!

A few days later, Búddi was in the kitchen by himself. I heard him muttering. I crept closer. I was going to jump at him and scream just to scare him.

"Are you scared yet?" He asked.

I crept closer. Who is he talking to? I wondered, as I snuck up to the door and tip-toed up behind him. He had

a lighted candle in his hand and was holding it close to the nose of my doll. I could feel my eyes widen, ready to pop out of my head!

"Are you scared yet?" He bent closer as I opened my mouth to scream.

Suddenly, there was a sound of a hissing sizzle, then *pouf!* My plastic baby-doll disappeared, like a genie out of a bottle!

Shocked, my mouth still open. No sound came out of my throat. I stared at this tiny, weird-shaped, pink blob that had been my beloved Christmas present, then into the bulging eyes and white face of my brother, who slowly sank to his knees, then lay flat on the floor, unconscious.

That's when I started screaming. My doll was dead and I thought my brother was dead, too.

I don't remember getting another play doll. But later I was given a doll dressed in a black, ornately embroidered with gold thread, Icelandic National dress. She had long, curly brown hair on her china head. Her hands, and feet were also made of china. The cloth body was stuffed with cotton. For along time, the doll sat on a high shelf among my books.

A couple of days later Búddi was fine and so was I. Another adventure was already scheduled and our minds were now on the New Year's Eve festivities and New Year's Day Dinner.

The group of us kids, with Mother and Gróa, stepped outside. It was twilight-dark although it was only four in the afternoon. We caught the bus to go downtown. We were all looking forward to the exciting New Year's Eve event. Small bonfires were planned at various places in Reykjavik, but the BIG one was down at a cleared field. The pile of wood from

old or wrecked boats - old tires - anything burnable was, to me, scary-tall.

We found a good place to sit down on the ground and wait for the show to begin. I looked up into the dark-blue sky where a gazillion-trillion stars twinkled. In microseconds, that's one millionth of a second, there was a huge multicolored, spiral-curtain sparkling and moving very fast. Suddenly, purple and green streaked patches broke away from the curtain and leaped across the entire sky in an awesome show, for several minutes, then floated off and away... only to come back, move side to side in amazing display of bright colors that looked like fractured rainbows!

As the bonfire was lit and the huge pile was burning to the sky, people started dancing around in a huge circle, welcoming the New Year. Brennivín and coffee flowed generously.

People began belting out folk songs and singing at the top of their voices. I enjoyed the great spectacle, but thought that the Aurora Borealis was by far more impressive, and memorable, even though it's quite a frequent, and welcome, show during the long dark Icelandic winters.

It was our usual custom to go to our 'rich' Aunt's house on New Year Day for dinner. Aunt Þrúður, mother's sister, and her husband Jón. They lived in a beautifully furnished place above their store. They had a PIANO! Kalli, my half-brother, turned out to be the musician in our family.

The steps in the foyer, leading to the upstairs, had a brass edge that Sísí, Lilla and I got to scrub, and polish to a mirror-like finish each time we visited. After we were through polishing we'd tip-toe, and admire, each elegant step all the way up to the top.

Jón always sat at the head of the table and Aunt Þrúður at the other end. After a scrumptious dinner of smoked mutton, creamed potatoes, boiled eggs, and other goodies, plus cream-torte for dessert, each of us kids went to our hosts. Extending out our right hand, first to our Aunt and then to Jón, we girls would put our right toe behind our left heel, bend our knees while holding unto the hem of our dresses with our left hand, and give them a nice curtsy, while Búddy and Frankel bent deep from their waist and bowed quite elegantly.

Búddy NEVER acted up at Aunt Þrúður's home!

CHAPTER 30
JÓLASVEINARNIR
THE YULE LADS

IN PREPARATION FOR Christmas we kids had done our traditional ritual; we each, had placed a pair of our shoes on the window-sill, starting December the 12th . Very carefully, we made sure that we were extremely good. I was super-careful. Mother had told us many stories about Grýla and her terrible tröll family, who liked to chase, and grab a hold of naughty kids.

The tröll couple had at least 13 sons, there were supposed to be many more but these were the ones that seemed to delight in causing mischief among folks. The sons started out trying to snatch naughty children and stick them into the, huge, black, burlap-bag they had slung over their, grotesquely, lumpy shoulders. They would then take the naughty kids to their Monster-Mamma. [I tried to question this during a catechism lesson, but I didn't get very far. I got the 'LOOK'].

I never heard of any kids getting caught. They were either so good, or they could out-run the trölls.

Evidently, over the years the lads mellowed and became Christmas, or Yule-legends, and named Yule Lads. According to folklore; somewhere along the years they started leaving small presents in the shoes of the good kids. (We were, especially, thrilled if we got our own little candles)

But a piece of black lava-rock, or worse, a rotten potato would be in the shoes of the naughty children, as a reminder to be good. Just the thought of getting a rotten potato kept us kids behaving ourselves and anxiously checking our shoes.

These mischievous boys were not known for their good manners as their names indicate. How they had the nerve to leave rocks for naughty children when they themselves misbehaved was beyond me. But this was something I couldn't question either!

These are a few of the known names of the Jólasveinar, and their Poems;

Stekkastaur---Sheep-Cote Clod, the first Yule Lad comes to town December the 12th .The first of them was Sheep-Cote Clod...

He came stiff as wood,
to prey upon the farmer's sheep
as far as he could.
He wished to milk the ewes,
but it was no accident
he couldn't; he had stiff knees
-not to convenient.

Giljagaur -- December 13th came **Gully Gawk** (or Crevasse Imp) this lad likes to hide in gullies and wait for opportunity to steal milk.

> The second was Gully Gawk;
> grey his head and mien,
> He snuck into the cow-barn
> from his craggy ravine
> Hiding in the stalls,
> he would steal the milk, while
> the milkmaid gave the cowherd
> a meaningful smile.

Stúfur ---**Shorty**, or Stubby, the shortest of the brothers, arrived in the 14th.

> Stubby was the third called,
> a stunted little man,
> who watched for every chance
> to whisk off a pan.
> And scurrying away with it,
> he scraped off the bits
> that stuck to the bottom
> and brims - his favorites.

Skeiðisleikir--- Spoon-Licker came down from the mountains on 15th of December.

> The fourth was Spoon Licker,
> like spindle he was thin.
> He felt himself in clover
> when the cook wasn't in.
> Then stepping up, he grappled
> the stirring spoon with glee,
> holding it with both hands
> for it was slippery.

Pottaskefilll---Pot-scraper (or Pot-Licker) is expected on December the 16th.

> Pot Scraper, the fifth one,
> was a funny sort of chap.
> When kids were given scrapings,
> he'd come to the door and tap.
> And they would rush to see
> if there really was a guest.
> Then he hurried to the pot
> and had a scraping fest.

Áskasleikir---Bowl Licker, came to town on December the 17th.

> Bowl licker, the sixth one,
> was shockingly ill bred.
> From underneath the bedsteads
> he stuck his ugly head.
> And when the bowls were left
> to be licked by dog or cat
> he snatched them for himself
> - he was sure good at that!

Hurðaskellir---Door-slammer, came to town on December the 18th.

> The seventh was Door Slammer,
> a sorry, vulgar chap:
> When people in the twilight
> would take a little nap,
> he was happy as a lark
> with the havoc he would wreak,
> slamming doors and hearing
> the hinges on the squeak.

Skygámur---**Yogurt Gobbler**---On the 19th Yogurt Gobbler makes his appearance.

> Yogurt Gobbler was the eight,
> was an awful stupid bloke.
> He lambasted the yogurt tub
> till the lid on it broke
> Then he stood there, gobbling
> -his greed was well known-
> until, about to burst,
> he would bleat, howl and groan.

Bjúgnakrækir---**Sausage-Swiper**---shows up on December the 20th.

> The ninth was Sausage Swiper,
> a shifty pilferer.
> He climbed up to the rafters
> and raided food from there
> Sitting on a crossbeam
> In soot and in smoke,
> he fed himself on sausage
> fit for gentlefolk.

Gluggagægir---Window Peeper---This one starts his peeping on the 21st.

> The tenth was Window Peeper,
> a weird little twit,
> who stepped up to the window
> and stole a peek through it.
> And whatever was inside
> to which his eye was drawn,
> he most likely attempted
> to take later on.

Gáttaþefur---Door Sniffer, he comes around December 22nd.

> Eleventh was Door Sniffer,
> A doltish lad and gross.
> He never got a cold, yet had
> A huge sensitive nose.
> He caught the scent of lace bread
> While league away still
> And ran toward it weightless
> As wind over dale and hill.

———— ((O)) ————

Ketkrógur---Meat Hook---arrives on December 23ʳᵈ. St.
Thórlák's Day.

> Meat Hook, the twelfth one,
> his talent would display
> as soon as he arrived
> on Saint Thórláks Day.
> He snagged himself a morsel
> of meat of any sort,
> although his hook at times was
> a tiny bit short.

———— ((O)) ————

Kertasníkir---Candle Beggar---came on December 24ᵗʰ.
He longed to have his very own candle.

> The thirteenth was Candle Beggar
> -'twas cold, I believe,
> if he was not the last
> of the lot on Christmas Eve.
> He trailed after the little ones
> who, like happy sprites,
> ran about the farm with
> their fine tallow lights.

This popular poem about the Yule Lads was written by the late Jóhannes from Kötlum, and first appeared in the book "Jólin Koma" (Christmas is coming) in 1932.

CHAPTER 31
RANDOM MEMORIES
MARCH 1936
BOLLUDAGURINN
(BUN DAY)

THIS WAS ONE wonderful, yummy holiday in gloomy winter, two days before lent. Every store, cafe, and other eating/meeting places overflowed with Bollur (buns), and folks stuffing themselves before lent. The delicious cream puffs were filled with custard, jams or dipped in chocolate.

We kids tried to get up before Mother got up from her bed and Gróa got up from the divan where she slept. We'd run with our brightly decorated wands, called Bolludagsvöndur or [Bun Day Wand], gripped tightly in our hands. As many times as we were able to swat them before they were out of bed, we'd get that many buns!

The following day was called Spreingidagur (Bursting Day). How appropriate!

ÖSKUDAGURINN.
(Ash Wednesday)

We had pieces of colorful fabric scattered on the floor and table. Gógó and I were doing the cutting, while Lilla held the fabric steady. Ása and Sísí were sewing.

White, red, green and black spools of thread were on a chair. A large, red pin-cushion full of needles and straight-pins sat on the table. Next to the cushion lay a horseshoe-shaped magnetic bar which we used to pick up any stray pins that found their way to the floor.

Öskudagurinn was the next day and we were frantically trying to finish at least a dozen Ösku-pokar [ash bags]. We had big ones, little ones, cotton ones, and silk ones. Some solid colors, some print.

Each bag had a small amount of ash placed in the bottom. A drawstring closed the top, and a four-inch long string was left hanging on which we fastened a straight-pin that we bent in half, to form a hook. This we would then hang on the back of unsuspecting folks.

Several kids with the same purpose as we, were already downtown. All of us hid the bags in our sweaters and waited for our victims.

Some folks walking by had bags already dangling on their backs. Ása and Sísí went across the street and found a prime target right away. Lilla was too little to sneak up behind people and reach high enough to hook a bag on some-ones back so she carried my bags.

We got one great opportunity as a very dignified man walked past us. His long black overcoat made a perfect target.

With pick-pocket deftness I was able to add onto his back two of the gaudiest, and largest, bags we had made. My sister got her chance; since the coat almost reached to the back-top of his shoes, she was able to snag a small bag at the hem of his coat. It dangled splendidly at every stuffy step!

We were almost hysterical as we watched the gaudy bags swinging on the back of the pompous dignitary, who stalked ever so importantly toward the parliamentary building!

Lilla and I walked a few steps behind him and counted seven bags flip-flopping on his back. We were doubled up with laughter as Sísí and Ása ran up to join us in our giggles. What a fun day this had been!

In the days following, I thought back on those times, as reports on the situation in Europe steadily got worse. Rumors had it that German submarines were now in the North Atlantic, and were circling Iceland.

CHAPTER 32
WORLD WAR II, 1939

STORIES WERE BEGINNING to be heard in Iceland how the power hungry Nazi leader of Germany, Adolph Hitler, was bent on conquering the continent. The superiority of the German army seemed unquestionable as they invaded country after country; Denmark, Sweden, Norway. Then France and the Netherlands were overtaken.

When the Nazi invaded Poland, an ally of Britain, the British entered the conflict and a full scale conflict now raged in Europe. Iceland declared neutrality.

Father was still traveling to England and we were constantly on edge for his safety. Our remote country was not as immune to the war as I had once thought; reports of German submarines circling in the Atlantic off of Icelandic coasts intensified as the European war escalated.

Now, at the age of fourteen, I was on my way to Vopnafjörður (this turned out to be my last trip there.) We traveled with great trepidation and fear of the German submarines but arrived without an incident. Grandpa was at my

Aunt's house to meet me, and he had everyone in an uproar, insisting that Ólafur check the whereabouts of Kristján, Finna's dad, to make sure that his, Grandpa's, and Kristján's paths wouldn't cross.

Rumor had it that several men, including Kristján were sympathetic to the Nazi party.

"I wouldn't put it past him and his cronies to be signaling the Germans off of Lánganes." Grandpa fumed. I never heard of that and spent an uneventful summer; first with my Aunt and then at Hámundarstaðir with my Grandparents.

Grandpa had his ears pretty much glued to the radio that was almost impossible to understand due to crackling and static. The information we were able to get were unsettling and between that, and Grandpa's tirade, I got quite uneasy about sailing back home in the Fall.

But when that time came we arrived in Reykjavík without any trouble. The town was abuzz about grim reports on how Jews were being annihilated in gas chambers. We found that hard to believe, we knew the Germans to be good people, but it seemed that Hitler and the Nazi party were changing that.

We also heard a report that the Germans were building a new warship; the *Bismarck* with its eight 15" guns was the largest and the most advanced battleship built at that time. In 1940 the *Bismarck* was launched and soon became a terrible threat on the oceans.

Iceland was in a very strategic place between Europe and North America, and the Brits were getting concerned over Hitler's interest in Iceland. Britain was unable to get the Icelandic government to join them in a pact against Germany so they invaded our island. The North Atlantic soon became

a battleground as the British chased the German warships, and submarines, that Hitler sent with orders - to destroy Allied convoys that were in transit to Britain.

In 1941 a fierce fight broke out in the Denmark straits - the ocean between Iceland and Greenland which became known as "Torpedo Junction" - and the *Bismarck* sank the battle cruiser *HMS Hood,* the pride of the British Royal Navy. Fourteen hundred and sixteen men went down with the ship. Prime Minister Winston Churchill promptly issued an order *"Sink the Bismarck!"* A relentless pursuit of the dreaded ship ensued. The Germans, temporarily, got away from their hunters and headed for a safe port in France, but Torpedo planes from the British Royal Air Force got the notorious menace before it reached safety and sank it. Twenty five hundred German sailors drowned.

The United States had now entered into the war and Winston Churchill is said to have "slept the sleep of the saved and the thankful" because "there was now no doubt about the outcome of the conflict." It was no longer just a European war but had now become World War II and American service men and women were sent all over the globe.

As the war went on, Icelandic fishing boats were being attacked and sunk by the Germans. Then we heard that the trawler *Max Pemberton,* the ship Father had previously been on, disappeared without a trace in the Atlantic. Pétur Maack and his crew were presumed drowned.

Our family was in constant unease when Father was out at sea.

Even with the loss of several fishermen, Iceland maintained neutrality, but did make an agreement with the U.S

Government to have Navy bases built there. The first troops arrived in our country shortly after the attack on Pearl Harbor in 1941. Most of the twenty five thousand Brits left and were replaced by forty thousand American Troops.

They, British and Americans, were not entirely welcome in our country as they outnumbered the, about, twenty thousand adult Icelandic males. The total population of the country was some hundred and twenty thousand at that time. Our Government frowned on the fraternizing of Icelandic women with the service men.

The U.S. did not allow their troops to marry, regardless of country they were stationed in. Both Iceland and the U.S issued a ban on marriage.

Eventually, even though the sailors were mostly confined to base, they did get to coffee shops and restaurants in town, causing a dating game to flourish. These American strangers were interesting; they spoke in a funny way. Laughing a lot, they seemed uncommonly cheerful. Quite different from the dour English and Scots.

Although not enthusiastically welcomed, the presence of the U.S. Troops gave a sense of "one could sleep the sleep of the saved..." as Churchill had said.

In Europe the advances of the Nazi army were slowing down, and the Allies were gaining ground. Rumors were rampant about Hitler. He was said to be in Iceland because a plane had been spotted to drop something down on a small village on the eastern shore. People speculated that the infamous Fuhrer had been parachuted into the country.

U.S. Troops hunted for him where he was thought to be

hiding, a place called Skríðuklaustur in Djúpivogur. People there called the idea "ludicrous". The folks were right, he was still in Berlin where he later hid in a bunker and took his own life in Spring of '45.

CHAPTER 33
DEL COMES TO ICELAND, 1943

SEVENTEEN YEAR OLD , Del, stood shivering at the rail of the camouflaged troopship.

The biting north wind, mixed with rain and sleet, stung through his Navy Pea-jacket like the piercing of dozen needles. Cupping his hands over the tip of his freezing ears, he squinted through the murky air. Morosely, he felt the ocean's slow heaves gently lifted the ship in hypnotic moves.

It had just been announced that the troopship was on its way to Iceland, and he had been told that's where he was being deployed. Sure wouldn't have enlisted if I'd known where I'd end up. Del dried a dribble at the end of his nose, as he, enviously, thought of his two brothers, who were somewhere in the South Pacific.

Of all the places in the world he could have been sent to, he had to go to a forsaken place called Iceland! Just the thought of it was enough to give one the chills. Del shivered again. As if that wasn't bad enough, he grumped to himself, they were now traveling in a strait named 'Torpedo Junction,'

because of the fierce fighting going on between the Brits and the Germans, and the proliferation of German submarines circling the island like hungry sharks.

"Nasty weather!" Someone chuckled behind him. "Far cry from Illinois, where I am from." Continued the owner of the cheerful voice. A hand clapped Del slightly on the shoulder. "My name is Curtis, what's your name, mate?" Without waiting for an answer he chuckled again. "Iceland! I can't imagine a worse place to be sent to."

Del turned in surprise, and exclaimed; "Illinois! Hey, what are the odds of that?" Reaching out and shaking the hand of a sailor, who looked about twenty.

"My name is Del, and I, also, am from Illinois!"

Grinning at each other as they reminisced about their hometowns, the ship continued its full steam ahead. (They couldn't have know that they would become close friends, and Curtis would end up in being the best man at Del's wedding to an Icelandic girl, a year and a half later.)

Suddenly, Curtis pointed to a pod of orcas shooting up from the ocean.

"Have you ever seen anything like that?"

They were in awe as other sailors joined them to enjoy the show. After a few exited remarks they fell quiet and stared at the horizon, where a massive, ice-covered, mountain range appeared.

As the ship sailed closer and entered the sheltered harbor Reykjavik, they were astonished to see a rather modern looking buildings, no highrise, but still a pleasant surprise.

"I guess I was expecting Icelanders to be living in igloos." Del, said, sheepishly.

"I was thinking the same thing." Curtis mumbled. "Maybe this won't be quite as awful as we had anticipated." He scratched his head and blurted. " Frankly, what I see so far, the name 'Iceland' seems misleading." Then jumped as orders blared out. Time to go ashore.

A nice surprise awaited them; the Leathernecks who had arrived the year before had worked swiftly, and hard, with military smartness to build barracks in which the men had to live.

Camp Knox, as the base was called was on the edge of Reykjavik

Arriving in September, as they did, it took a while for Del and Curtis to get used to the gloomy days that stretched over winter as a one, long, dark, night. From noon, to about four in the afternoon it was like living in a twilight zone.

One day Curtis came running to Del and hollered.

"How about going to a dance tonight?" He waved a piece of paper into the face of his friend. "Marlene Dietrich, and troupe are going to be at White Rose Hall."

When Del started to shake his head, Curtis growled at him.

"Come on, it's Spring let's celebrate!" After several urgings, Del reluctantly agreed to go. He was surprised that he actually was enjoying the evening. The actress' show was well received. She was not a great singer, but her sultry voice was intimate. She had a way of making the guys feel like she was singing for each one only.

Del was scanned the crowd of service men when his eyes became riveted on the front entrance of the dance hall.

"Hey, Curtis, you've been here before, have you seen that

girl before." Del nudged

"Who? Where?" Curtis craned his neck.

"At the door, the one with the long, dark hair, she's with the red-head and blonde." Del hitched his head in the direction of the three girls that were just coming in. Suddenly he made a beeline for the young girl, who had made a move as to leave. Almost colliding with her in his haste, he reached out.

"Dance?" He asked. "I'm not very good at it, but I'd like to dance with you." At her confused look, Del realized the girl's knowledge of English was limited. Quickly deciding fewer words were better he gave her an entreating look, and merely said;

"Please?"

That much she understood, and said "Okay."

Dancing most of the evening with few words, Del was totally smitten. When he asked her to come back the next night, she agreed. It was a very happy, young man that went back to the base that night.

CHAPTER 34
SPRING, 1944, DEL AND I MEET

IN 1944, IN the capital of Iceland, Reykjavík, I met my husband to be, Del. He was in the United States Navy. Being color-blind, he was assigned to the "Sea Bee's" (the Construction Battalion). We both were nineteen years old. Two girlfriends of mine persuaded me to go downtown with them to an USO dance, at a place called White Rose Hall. As we entered my two friends deserted me to meet their boyfriends.

All around me was loud chatter, mostly American accents, but mixed with few British and Scottish brogues. Feeling un-expectantly shy, knowing very little English, I turned to leave and almost collided with a young, very good-looking, dark-haired, slim sailor, who had a huge smile on his face.

"Dance?" He said something else that I didn't understand. I shook my head.

"Please?" Something about that plea, and the entreaty in his soft hazel eyes made my heart do a flip-flop. These were

difficult times no one knew who would come back when sent out on a mission; ships were torpedoed, airplanes were shot down and many service men were losing their lives.

"Okay." I knew that one word; it was as universal as "Coca-Cola". As we danced that evening it was like we'd both been hit by a bolt of lightning! No need for words, just looks and - for me anyway - silly smiles.

We met again at the dance hall the next evening, and as we danced he asked me to marry him. I looked at him, thinking I knew what he was asking, but not quite sure. Del asked again, taking my left hand and acting like he was putting a ring on my finger. Then I knew, and said "yes." We were serious! The next day we told Mother.

"YOU WANT TO DO WHAT." My soft-spoken, easy going, Mother shouted! This was not good. Mother never raised her voice; not at us kids, not at my Father, no one. And now she had really raised her voice!

"Hermann and I want to get married." I repeated. (Later, in my family Del was always called Hermann, I guess it rolled easier of the tongue).

Mother had her face buried in both hands, rocking from side to side. She was quiet for a moment then she looked up, wide-eyed shock still on her face.

"Íedamín, will Hermann live in Iceland? Or, heaven forbid, are you going to move to Amerika? Do you realize how far it is? We don't know anything about his family. We don't even know what part of the country he's from. It's a huge country. You could get lost, then what?" Mother nervously twisted her fingers, then dabbed at her eyes with a hankie.

Del had been holding my hand and trying to follow

a conversation he couldn't understand. He didn't speak Icelandic, and my mother didn't speak English. My English wasn't a whole lot better; we got by with hugging, kissing and holding hands! Del squeezed my hand. He could see that this wasn't going as well as we had hoped.

I said something like, "You home Amerika?" He looked at me a little puzzled. I tried again.

"You Mamma, home, Amerika?"

Del smiled that great smile of his and said: "Chicago"

Mother about fell off of the sofa, gasping. "Chi-ka-ga? Gangstar Chi-ka-ga?!?"

It didn't come out "gangster," but close enough. We had some explaining to do and it wasn't going to be easy!

As usual - in Icelandic households - the coffeepot was steaming. I got up and placed three cups and saucers on the table to give Mother time to get over her shock. As I poured the coffee, I grinned at Del, a little wickedly I'm afraid. I knew he detested the drink but would pretend to like it for the sake of being polite. You haven't tasted *coffee* until you've tasted the way we used to make it, strong enough for the teaspoon to stick straight up out of the cup! I put the sugar-cube bowl out and sat down as a grateful Del scooped up a handful of cubes.

After a while Mother sighed and gracefully accepted the situation.

"Hermann is nice enough, Íedamín." Mother acknowledged, and then she shook her head and smiled. "Well, I guess I'd better get to know this young man of yours!" And that's how she took the news.

Father had been out at sea and when he came home

we shared the news. He was quiet but he also accepted our wishes.

Now that my parents had agreed to our marriage, it was time for Del to tackle the "powers" that be. Wearing down layers of authorities by unwavering persistence he got the ban lifted and was the first U.S. Service man to marry after that. On March 25, 1945 we were married in the *Dómkirkjan*, in downtown Reykjavík. Mother gave me away. Father was out at sea and was spared the embarrassment of being present when a daughter of his was marrying an army man. My two sisters attended, but not my brothers. Icelandic folks, especially men, were upset when girls started dating the "foreigners."

The church was full of various army personnel; American, English and Scots…most of them strangers to us. A virtual floodgate opened up as service men later rushed to tie the knot!

Mother was right, aren't mothers *always* right?. What was I thinking? I knew next to nothing about America. Of course I knew Leifur Eiríkursson had discovered America long before Columbus. I'd heard about New York, glamorous Hollywood where the famous stars in the movies lived and Chicago, where all the gangsters were.

Del said he didn't live in that city but in another one not to far away. How would I get there? Would I travel by myself like I would to New York? He had to stay in the Navy until Fall, at which time he would be discharged.

"Not a problem," he said. "My mother will meet you in New York."

"Your mother drives a car?" I was impressed. In our town

we had buses and a few dilapidated "taxis." Otherwise we traveled by horses or ships.

"Mother doesn't drive." Del laughed." She'll take a train to New York, and you'll go back with her to Illinois on one." I'd never seen a train! Mind you, this was all carried on by many hand gestures, and 'pidgin-English' by me.

As time went on I learned more English words and I tried to teach Del Icelandic, without much success. We took walks, hand-in-hand, around the lake in the center of downtown Reykjavik. Del would point and say *"water"* I'd say *"vatn."* He would say *"birds,"* I'd say *"fuglar."* Although he just couldn't get THOSE pronunciations he did quite well with the words "Elska mín" translated "My Love. "

Coming from totally different worlds as we did, I had a fleeting doubt, and then pushed it away, I was in love.

REYKJAVIK, ICELAND

MARCH 25ᵀᴴ, 1945

CHAPTER 35
COMING TO AMERICA

THE ENORMOUS, BATTLE-SHIP GREY, troop-transport, *USS Merak,* was anchored out in the bay, past the two flashing light-houses that guarded the entrance to the harbor of Reykjavík. The ship had sailed in from Europe the night before. It was to leave early this morning.

Mount Esja had snow scattered across her top. The sharp wind was nippy and the billowing clouds whipped across the ice-blue sky. The sea moved in shallow heaves and sloshed against the ship. The huge hunk of metal barely moved.

It was June 6, 1945. I was standing on the pier with Mother, Sísí, Lilla and Del. My bags were already stored aboard the landing boat, with hundreds of assorted boxes and belongings of dozens of troops who were heading back home to the United States, after completing their tours of duty in Iceland. Unfortunately my husband wasn't among them. We wouldn't see each other until September. I was going by myself to America. I'd never been out of this isolated island.

I was clueless.

The sailors hurried back and forth with the collar of their Navy pea-coats turned up against the biting wind. It was time to go. Giving my family a hug I boarded the boat that would take me out to the ship.

This time, unlike my previous journeys, there was no jumping, no shouting, just flurries of white hankies waved by Del, my Mother and two sisters, as the boat slowly veered away from the dock.

As we neared the gargantuan ship I felt the first twinge of unease, but then the boat went smoothly up to steps fastened at the side of the ship. Hands reached down, steadying me, holding mine with firm grips and guiding me to the deck. A smiling woman, with a Red Cross band on the arm of her U.S. Navy Uniform, guided me to the rail where I could look for my family. I could hardly see them because of the distance, and my eyes were now blinded with tears.

Suddenly, the noise of the ship's engines starting up. The ocean churned up like the cauldron of the Geysers as they roiled, bulged and boiled before erupting. *The USS Merak,* slowly, eased its way out of the harbor.

I stared a moment at Mt. Esja and the island of Víðey, then slowly turned and looked at the town of Reykjavík. My family was barely visible on the misty pier. When would I see my home again? Would I ever? Nausea squeezed through my stomach. I swallowed hard, watching the mountains and glaciers, slowly fade and blend with the sky and ocean on the eastern horizon. With mixed feelings of excitement, and unease, I saw my country disappear from my view. I shivered and wrapped my sweater tight around my shoulders.

On the north horizon a long trail of black smoke from a trawler billowed into the sky and slowly blended with the grey clouds. Soon the ship faded out of sight. I wasn't aware how long I stood there looking on an infinite plain of undulating water.

A sailor gave me a soft tap on the shoulder saying.

"Food."

He said something else I didn't understand, but by his motion I knew to follow him to the dining area. This first day went fast; there were so many new and different things to learn, mainly trying to follow the language.

In the following days I got to know the routine of breakfast, lunch and supper. The food was totally different than what I was used to, and the manner of dining even more so. To say that I felt out of place is putting it mildly. I was like a fish out of water!

The second morning I got up feeling tired. I hadn't slept well, tossing and turning all night with questions and doubts churning inside of me like wriggly worms. Listlessly, I took a shower and got dressed, skipping breakfast - not sure it would stay down with all the turmoil going on inside.

I'd decided I'd changed my mind. I didn't want to go to America after all. I didn't want to leave the only home I had ever known. But how in the world was I going to get back? I felt trapped. Grabbing a pillow I scrunched it tight against my chest. After fighting utter panic for a few moments, I started scolding myself, like I used to do as a little child when terror gripped my heart.

"Come on, you're a grown married woman now... and where is your 'explorer spirit'?" I jeered at myself as I fought

for control. I couldn't remember being this wretched since Hanna died. Why did I have to think of that? I was just a small child then; ten years ago, seemed more like hundred!

Miserable, I tottered up to the deck and leaned over the side of the rail. Nothing but ocean and sky met my eye. Suddenly, my heart started hammering at the sight of familiar white sprays shoot up into the air as a pod of whales cavorted in the ocean. Then two dolphins followed us. They swept up and down in the wide wake of the troopship. After a short time they all turned and headed north.

All of a sudden, it was as if a line had been drawn in the water. The whales and dolphins were gone. There was nothing to see. They'd just said "Goodbye".

Turning in a complete circle, I stared where the sky met the sea. The horizon looked the same in all direction. I retreated below deck, emotionally spent.

The whole next day was spent reading and knitting. I had awakened suddenly in the early morning. For a moment I felt disoriented and wondered what I was sensing. Then I felt it - the ship was lifting up, up, up, hovering still for a moment before shuddering and groaning its way down, down, down - I looked through the porthole; the ocean was wild from roaring wind and driving rain. Going top-side that day was of no interest.

The weather was much the same on day four. I meandered into the dining room where sailors, both men and women, were sitting at tables playing cards. Guitar music with sad-sounding vocals were coming from a Jukebox. I didn't understand the words, but the voice seemed heart breaking. Not needing that, I left. Back in my room and started aimlessly

assembling my six-inch, crochet, squares together. I was half-way to making a full size bed throw for my mother-in-law.

On the fifth day of traveling on the Atlantic with nothing but ocean and the heavens, I noticed that the air was much warmer, the sky bluer, and the sun hotter. Even the sea was calmer than I was used to. Feverish activity aboard ship began. Everything was being 'spit' polished and shined. Whistling, smiling sailors began scrubbing and hosing down the deck with new enthusiasm and energy.

We would be arriving in America in the morning.

I was up at sunrise, eager, but at the same time very scared as I thought of what was ahead of me. The sailors had now changed into liberty whites and were lined up along the troopship's rail. The immense Statue of Liberty loomed magnificently against the cloudless, vivid blue sky. Her right hand thrust up into the air holding a beacon of light and her left hand clasped a book to her chest. In the background towered rows of the tallest buildings I had ever seen. No mountains, just black and glass and one massive skyscraper after another. My jaws clamped tight. THIS was scary!

Since my passport and all proper papers were in order, there was no delay for me at the Ellis Island, Immigration Port. But I could see that some were not so fortunate; I looked at the masses of suitcases, boxes and children that were scattered about the motley crowd, huddled in long lines. Most of the men and women looked worn and tired, but some were smiling. A few had a hunted, frightened look. Maybe I thought that because I was now feeling really scared, but then I was met by a very friendly Red Cross lady, who patted my arm as she waved for a taxi for us. I felt a little better. We

started to get in, but not before a reporter from a New York newspaper poised his pen over his notepad and hollered at me.

"What do you think of New York?" Stepping up a little closer, as the Red Cross lady tried to shield me.

"Too much hot." I mumbled as I stumbled into the cab.

And off we went, with the cabbie driving like a maniac. I was sure he was going to run over people that were just simply everywhere. Gritting my teeth, I clenched the side of my seat with both hands, my eyes riveted on the rivulets of sweat that ran down the side of his face. The heat was suffocating. When I left Reykjavik the temperatures had been in the lower 50s, beautiful, crisp June weather. I was tremendously relieved when the crazy driver pulled up in front of a tall building and stopped. Stepping out, I craned my neck trying to see the dizzying top. I couldn't. My head was spinning.

The driver got out of his cab and opened the door for us. Trembling, I cautiously stepped out as the driver opened the trunk to get out my bags. After setting them down he wiped his face with a grimy hankie.

"It's hot enough to fry an egg on the sidewalk!" He grumbled. I thought I got the gist of what he was saying and instinctively lifted up my foot not wanting to step into someone's eggs!

The Red Cross lady asked how much the fare was and pulled out bills to pay the man. He carefully folded it up and placed it into a small black bag on the seat. Then she reached out and handed him extra money. I was aghast. By Icelandic customs, she was insulting the man by implying he couldn't take care of his family. I expected him to spit on the sidewalk

and haughtily upbraid her; 'I can take care of my own, I don't need a hand-out!' Instead he gave her a huge grin. Touching his cap he repeated his thanks and stuck the money into his pocket. I couldn't believe my eyes; this was so different from how I'd been brought up. My mind was in turmoil and I began to feel like a zombie.

My mother-in-law was standing by the hotel desk and turned toward us as we entered. She was a very short woman, dressed in a bright, blue-flowered dress. Her light brown hair, pulled back into a tight bun, was slightly grey at the temples. Her light-blue eyes sparkled behind large, silver-framed glasses. The small, blue, flower on her white straw hat bobbed, as she, with a quick step and a wide smile, came up to me and gave me a tight hug.

"I'm Mary, Del's Mom. Everything will be alright." She said in a soothing voice.

I must have looked as terrified as I felt. She, of course, didn't speak Icelandic, and my English was still pitiful. Somehow we managed to communicate with much babbling and pointing. I felt her kindness.

The three of us walked into the, rather elegant, dining room where waiters bustled about covering tables with white cloths. Chrystal vases with red flowers complimented the red velvet upholstered chairs. The window swags and drapes matched the red velvet on the chairs. I loved the look of the golden fringe and tassel tiebacks.

Mary picked up the menu and ordered a meat dish, she called it "meat-loaf," for the two of us. The Red Cross lady ordered fried CHICKEN! I was horrified when I saw her carefully pick up a chicken leg and scrape off a piece of

the meat with her fork. I looked at Mary who had cut up her food like she was preparing to feed a baby! I sat there, dumbfounded. I had my knife in my right hand and the fork in my left, as I'd been raised. Just then, the Red Cross lady picked up the chicken leg and daintily took a bite. I tried not to stare, but furtively looked around to see if the other diners had seen this uncouth behavior! No one was looking. I sighed, embarrassed.

After saying goodbye to the Red Cross lady, Mary and I followed a young man who was thoughtful enough to carry my two large suitcases. We entered the tiniest room that, without warning, moved and shook under our feet. The metal grinding all around was as bad as the screeching of ships cables in a fierce storm. I held on with a white-knuckle grip while the little room groaned, swayed and rumbled toward the heavens.

I stared at the young man who was nonchalantly chewing gum. American soldiers had introduced Wrigley's chewing gum to Icelanders. Younger folks and kids loved it but were forbidden to chew it because it looked like "cows chewing their cud" the older folks said. Mary seemed equally at ease as the young man did in this weird surrounding. I began to relax as the moving room slowed down, stopped and the clanking door opened.

The young man opened the door to a room and set the suitcases down. Mary reached in her purse and gave the man money. I waited, curious this time. Sure enough, he had the same reaction as the cab driver - a big toothy grin and thanks! This must be the way people do it over here.

Grandpa would fume, and Great-Grandpa would turn

over in his grave!

Our room was like an oven. I went to get a drink out of water out of the tap, took a big gulp and gagged; it smelled like volcanic fumaroles, or rotten eggs! I spit it out and ran to the window to get fresh air. I looked down; the cars below looked like small toys. I felt light-headed. Trying to get my head together and the bad taste out of my mouth, I chewed on an old, dried piece of kleinur I found in my pocket. Comforted by the familiar taste, I pondered what I had gotten myself into; what kind of country is this anyway? How can people survive this putrid tasting water! Baffled, I looked at Mary. She seemed healthy enough.

Departing from New York City, we journeyed toward the American heartland of the Midwest. The first leg.

The troop train was equally scary. This was my first train ride - I had never even seen one before! Everyone on the train was dripping with sweat in the overpowering heat as we entered Grand Central Station in Chicago. There we switched to the train that took us to the train station in Bloomington, Illinois. Then, on the final leg of our trip, we took a bus to Mary's house on Franklin Avenue in Normal.

Finally, my long and arduous journey, eleven days in all, was over and I had arrived in my new homeland. The house was a small, one story, white painted home in a row of other similar homes in an older neighborhood. That evening I stood in the yard and looked around, familiarizing myself with my new surroundings.

Across the street from Mary's house was an Assembly of God Church. I was looking at the church and thinking how strange it was - almost middle of June and very dark outside.

I was used to seeing part of the sun all night at midsummer. Then I saw these little sparks - like the embers shooting up out of a volcano - but I didn't feel any shaking of the ground. Something wasn't right. The church must be on fire!

I ran inside and tugged at Mary's dress. "Hey-you, kirk-jan [church] fire, fire!" I stuttered. Still not used saying Mary or mom, so I often called her 'Hey-you.' I pulled her to the front door and pointed. The sparks were even thicker than before and coming dangerously close to us!

"Fire?" She stared out and then looked at me, puzzled. "Where? I don't see any fire." She cocked her head at me, trying to understand my fear.

Frantically, I pointed. "See there, there!" I was twenty and acting like a six year old.

Turned out this was my first encounter with fireflies. Bugs with their own lights! Startling, and scary, I thought as I watched these little sparks land in grass and bushes, and not starting any fire. Del's Mom had quite a time educating me.

About three weeks later it was 4th of July. When I stepped outside of Mary's house, all up and down the street American flags were flying; big ones with halyards on poles which were landscaped around in the middle of immaculate, green lawns, small ones lining the walks, flags in every window, on the mail-boxes, in children's hands, flags everywhere! We Icelanders love flying our flags, and do so at every opportunity. I was extremely happy to see that the American people felt the same about their flag. This will be a great country to raise a family I thought, as I walked back into the house and a new beginning. I was beginning to feel at home

in America.

A few years later, I became an American officially. August 22, 1956 was a proud day for me. In Peoria, Illinois, I was administered the oath and sworn in as a *CITIZEN OF THE UNITED STATES OF AMERICA!* At that time, I was thirty and a mother of five.

EPILOGUE

Appendix A - Perils at sea; Father loses trawler *ICELAND II.*

Appendix B - Hard times in Eyjafjörður, from the diary of Sveinn Þórarinsson, magistrate´s clerk, 1869.

Appendix C - Earthquake in Dalvík, 1934.

APPENDIX A

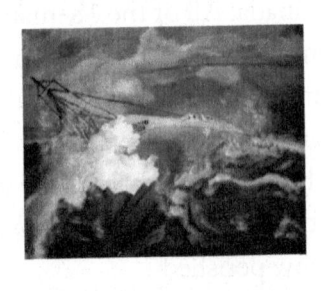

PERILS ON THE SEA

FOR CENTURIES THE sea has been a generous giver of life to Icelanders as well as other countries around the world. Yet at times, terribly cruel, cold, and dreadful to the seaman who's life and love is the ocean. For the countries in the northern hemisphere, blinding winter snowstorms can come up without warning and turn the ocean into a merciless enemy.

My father, Jónas Björnsson, was passionate about the sea, calm or roaring, it was his life. Not only did he fish around Iceland, but also England and Canada. Among the fishermen he was fondly called *"King of the Fishermen"*. He had an uncanny ability to know where the fishing was best and set

many catch- records on the east coast of Canada.

*The cruelty of the ocean caught up with the trawler in the horrible winter storm of 1967. The week that started Monday, February 20th, was one of the most tragic and terrifying ever known to fishermen. Early morning on February 21st, a trawler, *Cape Bonnie*, went aground on Woody Island, Newfoundland, Canada. All of the 18-man crew aboard perished. Prayers went up "for all those in peril on the sea... " as other ships were in danger from the brutal winter storm.

Desperate search was on for the Lockeport long-liner *Polly and Robbie*, but only the side of the deckhouse with a life-ring bearing the name *Polly and Robbie* was ever found. Seven more had now perished.

The *Iceland II* had left North Sidney, Cape Briton Island, on Sunday, February 19th, after unloading a cargo of fish. On her way back to the fishing grounds, she became trapped in ice off Glace Bay and didn't get free until late afternoon on the 20th. On the 23rd when the storm hit, with winds reported up to 100 miles an hour, the *Iceland II* went off course and slammed into the rocky shore near the village of Fourchu, Prince Edward Island, where the wreck was discovered. Later, two dories and a rubber raft were found on the rocks nearby. Ten more names were now added to the awful list.*

Father had gone to Iceland for New Year's Day and turned the ship over to a Canadian captain. At age 77 his ship gone, his crew dead, he never went back. He lived to the age of 96.

*Information gathered from The Canadian Fisheries Museum of the Atlantic Nova Scotia correspondent: Bonnie Purdy.

Trawler *ICELAND II* Went Down, Crew Drowned.
(Translated from the "Morning Paper", Reykjavik, Iceland - Tuesday 28, February 1967.)

Trawler owner Jónas Björnsson lost another ship 3 year ago and now considers quitting fishing. A tragic accident at Cape Breton, Nova Scotia last Saturday when the trawler *Iceland II* went down with the crew, ten men, drowned. Late Saturday men noticed that the trawler was stranded. Due to weather the rescue crew could not do anything, they had both boats and a helicopter. Sunday the bodies were found.

The Morning Paper contacted Jónas Björnsson the owner of the trawler who is here in Iceland now, some of his children live here. This is what he had to say:

---The trawler Iceland II was a 200 t. I came home to Iceland on New Year's Day and then the captain was waiting for the weather to change. He was going to leave after New Year's Eve but the weather was bad for many days. The crew consisted of rather young men, the captain was 35 years old, and they were both family men and single. I do not have much to say about who were hired on the ship, the captain did that. He was my first man last summer. There might have been some changes with the crew since I sailed with them.

---Yes, I have been in the trawler business 7-8 years. I went west in 1957. My first trawler, *Iceland I*, sank because of ice three years ago. The crew was rescued. It was steered towards land. I know very little about the accident with *Iceland II*. I phoned last night but could not reach those who are at the scene and the information I got is very little, except that last Friday the captain on *Iceland II* told another captain that they were going to harbor in Lais City. Everything was ok onboard. That is the last that was heard from the ship whatever happened after that.

---I do not know of any Icelanders onboard. I had an Icelander in my crew for two years but he left six months ago.

---I started in the trawler business in 1954. The trawler *Iceland II* was built in 1964 Bathhurst, New Brunswick. Last winter I was not fishing and therefore came to Iceland over the New Year. After this incident I do not think I will continue in the business.

It has been very windy by the coast of Nova Scotia and Newfoundland all last week. 18 crew members were killed when the trawler *Cape Bonnie* went down last Thursday in St. Lawrence Bay. Also two small fishing boats are missing since last Wednesday. On these boats there were seven people.

APPENDIX B

Íslandssöguvefurinn: Vesturfararnir.
The Icelandic Immigration.

HARD TIMES IN EYJAFJÖRÐUR (AKUREYRI)
From the diary of Sveinn Þórarinsson, magistrate's clerk,
1869

————⋙⋘————

ONE CAUSE OF the mass migration West, was the brutal climate conditions during the 1860s. The following is an
excerpt from the diary of Sveinn Þórarinsson, magistrates
clerk, detailing the effects of the severe weather at that time.
From Sveinn it is possible to trace a path to the New World.
Sveinn was the father of Jón Sveinsson, called Nonni, an in-
ternationally known children's book author from the early
part of the twentieth century.

Sveinn Þórarinsson was a gifted man, a carpenter and
bookbinder, a lover of music, a talented writer, an aesthete

and connoisseur of many things. The following portion of his diary spans the period from May 24ᵗʰ to June 24ᵗʰ, 1869. The diary ends on the tenth of July of the same year; Sveinn died only a few days later.

—————⊙—————

May 24. Frigid northerly breeze. The Pollur inlet is becoming choked with ice. Everywhere news of people near death; starving men slaughter starving sheep to save their own lives. Domestics wander from farm to farm begging for work in return for food and shelter. There is a general exodus of farmers in Skagafjarðasýsla and Þingeyjarsýsla. A general census meeting was held here today: I was present for part of it. Páll Magnússon and Ólafur from Espihóli came by. Before they left I gave Ólafur and P. Johnson a chunk of snuff to chew. Men complain of sore throats and other physical woes due to lack of tobacco.

May 25. Hellish north wind, snowstorm. The ground white with snow down to the sea. I got 17 Pollack from Johnsen for two inches of snuff. Chopped a tree for firewood, made a table for the dormer window. I´m running out of hay for the cow. Polar ice filled the inlet and grounded six shark boats that were lying there.

May 26. Calm but frigid weather at first, then chilly southeast winds for awhile. Polar ice floating at the bottom of the fjord. Walked into town and up to Eyraland in search of hay,

but to no avail. Hung a couple of bundles of small herring to dry. Elin Gunnarsen moved here into the north end of my house. They began laying the footpath to the church. People are hoeing every square inch of their garden in a frenzy of hope and hopelessness.

May 27. Northwest snowstorm, freezing gale-force winds. I did some repair but then had to lie in bed for a long time due to the cold; no fires anywhere for the lack of firewood. I got three barrels of hay for one Danish dollar and 56 shillings and got temporary relief from that problem. Ever-increasing shortages, and general scarcity of food. Total lack of coffee and tobacco everywhere; no victuals to be had except what little we can get from the sea. Havsteen, the merchant has nothing but moss and old tobacco slime in place of snuff; men use any and all kinds of surrogates for tobacco and coffee. I still have some tobacco left, and a little bit of food - dolphin meat and blubber, fish, beans, grains - but only enough for a few days. Others are no better off. I drink coffee made of beans and grain, sweeten it with molasses, which is still available. My cow only milks about 2.5 litres now.

May 28. Southwest gusts, slightly less cold. Northwest wind out of the fjord. Ice floating here at the bottom of the fjord again and gathering at Hrísey Channel. Our fishing nets catch nothing. I fixed my tools and work bench, then walked down with a bite of snuff for P. Johnsen, half out of his mind for lack of tobacco. Church path is finished. All ships on their way here, and others besides, get stuck in the ice on the east coast (Gunnólfsvík, Berufjörður). Norwegians have

arrived at Seyðisfjörður full of pomp and self-importance.

May 29. Icy northwest gale. Fog. Fjord full of ice all the way to Leira. I made some wooden lids, a mouse-trap, and a few other things during the day. Provisions are virtually exhausted by now in homes; no victuals left in stores. I sent Havsteen the merchant a little cut of snuff wrapped up in a cornet.

June 3. Northern windstorm, intermittent gusts of fog. Ebb tide pushes the ice further out of the fjord a bit though. I stayed home, puttered around, cured some herring. Starvation and the lack of hay are the news from all directions: it's said today that two children are dead of hunger in Ólafsfjörður. The snow is so deep in Fjörður and out in the surrounding countryside that only bare patches can be seen in the fields.

June 4. Cold northeasterly breeze. The air foggy and threatens snow. Couldn't work much because of the cold. Walked into town apothecary, bought a pound of chocolate and licorice and some dandelion root.

June 5. Devilish northeastern gale and snowstorm. Snow blanketed the ground down to waterline. I couldn't work. Sawed my last log for firewood and had to lie in bed to escape the cold. All my firewood gone. A couple of men rowed out yesterday and came back with a pitiful catch.

June 6. Calm clear weather, but still very cold. Árni Sólvason came from Þistilfjörður, having been on board the boats that are stuck in Finnafjörður on their way here and can't move

because of ice around Lánganes. Several of us here in town sent a man to Vopnafjörður for tobacco. I put in 60 shillings for ½ pound of snuff. Yesterday I cut the last smidgen of tobacco that I owned. No fish to be caught; the nets drag nothing. Hunger closes in on us all, rich and poor alike.

June 7. Warm southwesterly wind. Most of the ice streamed out of the fjord, kindling hopes that a ship might come. Ólafur from Espihóli came, wanting to buy barley, but it wasn't available any more than anything else; finally he managed to get the last of some rye that had gotten soaked in kerosene. Several people have bought it for a Danish dollar a bushel out of sheer desperation. I figured out that the best way to cure my herring was to smoke it a little after marinating it in brine. Cows are being let out for the first time in the neighborhood, but I kept mine inside. Everyone has begun planting potatoes.

June 8. Northwest gale-force winds with cloudy streaks in the sky.

June 9. Still weather, warm and cloudy early in the day; southerly winds by evening.

June 10. Southerly gale force winds, but northwesterly winds high in the sky. Seemingly calm at the mouth of the fjord. By now everyone is close to perishing from hunger. Many have begun slaughtering their stock to save their lives. No hope of ship's arrival at this time.

June 11. Hellish northerly gusts with intermittent snowstorms. Cows inside again, mine starving-hungry. Heavy snowfall. Conditions worsen steadily. I begged my way to ½ pound of juniper berries to eat. Lay in bed mostly due to the cold.

June 13. Northern frostbite gale. Ice ran all the way to Sigluvík. The cold is unbearable. Hunger sharpens. The magistrate and a couple of others from Möðruvellir came here and went home again. It is said that the magistrate got some grain from Möller, that both Möller and Steincke have several casks of meat, bread, and grain which they are hoarding while death from starvation threatens all around them. I got a barrel of lousy hay from Friðjórn Steinsson for the cow.

June 14. Northern blizzard. Mountains snow-white. I was forced to kindle to stay alive. Ice thick all the way into Leira. A courier came from Siglufjörður to fetch the sheriff. The ship *Íris* from Hofsós was stuck there in the ice; *Rachel* lay in a hole in the ice out beyond Siglufjörður and couldn't move. The barque that was to come here lay in ice out by Höfðastekkur; Möller the merchant rode out immediately to get news of it, while Steincke sent out to Siglufjörður for news of *Rachel*. Blizzard winds and heavy snow during the evening. I got a half-barrel of foul hay from Apothecary Ó. Þórarensen for the cow. Magnús came from Vopnafjörður with tobacco. I got ½ pound of snuff.

June 15. Bitter northern gale; skies heavy as mid-winter. I heard that the last barque turned around and sailed back East, so Möller the merchant came home last night. I sat,

updating the election records, sick from hunger. I haven't had any food other than a little plaice and salt-fish for a very long time. Eggert Gunnarsson was here in a fury trying to ensure that the people from Skagafjörður could get to the shipwreck in Siglufjörður. Dolphins in a hole in the ice at Oddeyrarbót. Men were chasing them and managed to get a few. Cows were let out door for awhile today.

June 16. Clear and sunny; warm southwesterly breeze. The news is that the barque got trapped in the ice near Hvanndalabjarg and is in danger. Möller sent a request to Sigurðurat Boggverstaðir to get news of it. The ice floated out of the fjord as far as Höfði

June 17. South breeze, warm weather. Calm out in the fjord. Traces of westerly winds in the clouds. It rained in the evening for the first time this spring. I lay feeble and starving in my bed for most of the day. Had nothing for food except a bite of salt-fish and some fried fish skin, nothing to drink except some wild thyme water. The ice is mostly out at the mouth of the fjord now. Various reports of ships out beyond. I gave Þórleifur Bjornson a chunk of snuff.

June 18. Still, calm weather; warm thick air. This morning the sheriff's horses were sent from Svarfaðardalur, accompanied by notice of the auction of goods on the shipwrecked *Íris* on Monday the 21st of this month. The sheriff had sent the magistrate grains, coffee, and a keg of spirits, and so it seems that Herod and Pilate are becoming friends again. Friðbjörn Steinsson sent his wife a pound of coffee, and I got

a taste of it. The men from here decided to go to the auction in two boats; I went with Steinn's boat, for Björn the editor gave me bread and sausage (rúllupylsa) to eat on the way. I prepared for the trip as well as I could. The barque was said to have been seen in the ice at Látrar.

June 19. Still, sunny and hot at first, then a sea breeze, I waited for my travel companions out beyond Siglufjörður until 12:00, and we embarked in Steinn's boat in light winds. Reached Hjalteyri at 3, Syðstibær on Hrísey at 8, the cape of Ólafsfjörður at 11, lake Hvannadalsvatn at 12, approaching Héðinsfjörður at 2, and landed at Ýtrikrókur on Siglunes at 3, after rowing along the coast for fifteen hours, through the ice which virtually blankets the sea along the entire northern coast of the country. We landed the boat, offloaded, pitched tents, and got a little bit of rest. News today is that the barque *Emma* lay fast in a plate of ice out beyond Mána Islands. The stranded *Íris* lies here far from land, mostly sunken, with sea-soaked food and other provisions all over the beach, spread out on a sail.

June 20. Calm and very warm. We walked to Siglunes to get some coffee; what we got was thin and poor. Then Ólafur from Espihóli walked in over Skríður (stony and gravel slopes) into town, but I didn't feel up to accompanying him. The sheriff and Snorri the merchant came out to the headland to prepare the auction. At midday I got a ride to Eyri on a little boat. *Rachel* lies there in the harbor along with several shark boats. I stayed the night in town with Ólafur and several others. Did some drinking during the evening. Jón Mýrdal showed me around.

June 21. Warm, foggy and still. The fjord of Siglufjörður is entirely choked with ice. I went with a few others out to Siglunes in a skiff; sometimes we had to drag the boat over the ice. We decided that Fríðbjörn Steinsson should bid at the auction as our proxy. The auction began, but Fríðbjörn did not do well by us. We got both fewer and more expensive things than necessary. The throng here is immense, most of them hungry people who constantly boil sea-soaked grains and shovel it, half raw, up into their mouths with shells, sticks, or whatever else they might find. We lay wet and exhausted in our wreck of a tent during the night. I slept little.

June 22. Cold, rainy easterly breeze. Auction continued today and ended at 4. We loaded the boat and embarked for Siglunes at 9:00, threaded our way along the coast in zigzag pattern due to the pack of ice and other obstacles, came to Hrísey and were able to sail along Árnarnesnafir, reached Akureyri at 6 p.m. on the 23rd, after a 21-hour trip.

June 23. Sea breeze with light fog. We immediately divided up most of what we had bought and went to sleep. Ólafur from Espihóli went home. The last few days there have been good catches of whiting, Pollack, herring and plaice, which has greatly eased the severe hunger and helplessness of all here.

Credits:
Editors: Víðar Hreinson and Jón Karl Helgason.
Text author: Víðar Hreinson
English translation: Verba-Translation.

APPENDIX C

EARTHQUAKE IN DALVÍK 1934
As recorded in the "*Öldin Okkar*" ("*Our Century*")

ON SATURDAY THE 2nd of June at 12:42 p.m local time a quick earthquake shook Eyjafjörður. It is thought to have been at 6,2 to 6,3 on Richter scale. The earthquake was noticed from Búðardalur in the west to Vopnafjörður in the east. It has been called the Earthquake of Dalvík for it was the most powerful in that area. This is the biggest earthquake remembered in this region. The source of the quake is thought to have been about 1 km east of Dalvík. Only the inhabited area nearest to the source was ruined.

The first shock was the longest and the strongest and followed by such noise that people thought it was an explosion. But they soon realized that it was an earthquake because houses trembled and things were thrown about. They were damaged or even destroyed. 'This shock must have lasted a minute and a half." (Öldin okkar 1931 - 1950bls.47) People ran out of their houses when the disturbance began,

but sometime it was impossible because exits and doors were stuck; still no lives were lost.

Sigurður Þórarinsson, then a geology student, thought the quake occurred at an apt time, when people were eating and less exposed to danger. Everything was thrown about, windows broke, walls cracked, split an fell. Great cracks formed and indicated that the source of the earthquake was in Böggvistaðarfjall in the west of the village. The disturbance was such that potatoes recently planted were tossed up. Following are a few narratives;

Bjarki Elíasson, later a superintendent in Reykjavík, was a child when the earthquake began: *When I came home to Víkurhóll the whole house and the hill it stood on was cracked. My grandparents lived upstairs but my grandfather was blind and bedridden. People were helping him out when I arrived. My father was not at home, he was working as a carpenter in Svarfaðardalur. I went to fetch him on my bicycle because I thought he did not know about the earthquake. I did not get further than to the new primary school because of a crack in the road. I did not dare cross it. There I stood crying when my father came on his bicycle. When we came home my father went quiet, observed the damages and said: "This is a bad sight, the house will not be inhabitable again.*

In the year 1965 an article on the earthquake appeared in the Christmas edition of *"Dagur"* by Hjörtur E. Þórarinsson. "When the earthquake began he was in the sheep-cote at Tjörn. He stood in the doorway when the quake began. He heard a loud din and felt in an instant that the earth was moving under his feet, first slowly but then more violently. It was as he was standing on a carpet two men were pulling

back and forth. A loud noise came from the roofs. He saw two boys who were working in the sheep-cot slipping their feet, then he fell. This disturbance only lasted a few seconds. He looked up to the mountain and saw the snow was now striped of mud slides. Everything went quiet but he felt that the peace was treacherous and he wished that the wind would increase or at least it would rain.

In *Öldin Okkar* 1931 - 1950 is written: In a house in Dalvík a woman had just given birth to her child. This house made of stone was greatly damaged. A wall collapsed and splinters from it fell over the woman in her bed but she and her baby were unharmed. Her calmness is thought to have helped a great deal.

In the mouth of Eyjafjörður ships were endangered. One captain said there was a sudden blow on his ship and that the crew below ran on deck because they thought the ship had stranded. Gigantic waves rose and seemed from the ship to be as tall as the mountains. The shock was the strongest in Dalvík and the damage according to that. The scene was terrible after the quake.

People hardly knew what hit them but soon they started to rescue things out of their houses which were more or less damaged, half collapsed or cracked. Gables had fallen in some houses and open cracks were visible, but even so most roofs were still in place. It was too risky to enter some of the houses because they could collapse anytime. Inside them almost everything breakable was smashed all over the place. Fireplaces were displaced and chimneys were broken. One house was caught on fire because of that.

After the incident when people had realized what had

happened they went calm and more accurate in the rescue. Generally people were very calm. One could expect more strong shocks and people wanted to save more from the houses before they would totally collapse.

During the night the inhabitants tried to get as comfortable as possible. About 200 people were homeless because it was not presumed safe to sleep in the houses if further earthquakes would occur. After the first shock the quakes were constant for the next hours. Therefore people made their homes in sheds and tents.

Neighbors from nearby areas came and tried to assist as much as possible. The weather was nice which made everything easier. Crockery and other equipment for the kitchen were damaged so handling of food was particularly difficult. A week after the first shock, aid came from everywhere due to the government's encouragement.

GLOSSARY

A, Á
Akureyri; Second largest town in Iceland, situated in the north.

B
Breiðifjörður; Wide fjord (bay), west Iceland

D, Ð (say soft 'th')
Djúpivogur; Deep Cove

E É
Eldfell; Fire Mountain
Eyjafjallajökull; Island Mountain Glacier.
Eyjafjörður; Island Fjord

F
Flatey; Flat Island
Færeyjar; islands situated in the Atlantic Ocean between Iceland and Norway.

G
Gullfoss; Golden Falls
Goðafoss; The Falls of The Gods.

H
Heimaey; Iceland's largest island
Helgafell; Holy Mountain
Höfn; Harbor

I Í
Ísafjörður; Fjord of Ice

J
Jökullsár; Glacier River
Jökullsárlón; Glacier River Bay.

K
Kría; Arctic tern.

L

Lagarfljót; Lake Handsome.

Lagarfljótsormurin; The Worm of
Lake Handsome.

Lögberg; Law Rock (situated at
Þingvellir)

Lækjartorg; Down-town square
Reykjavik

M

Mývatn; Midge Lake (no mos-
quito in all of Iceland!)

Mýrdalsjökull; Glacier of Mýrdal

P

Papey; Pope (or Monk) Island

Vestmanneyjar; West Men Island

Vopnafjörður; Fjord of Weapons

Þ (say hard th)

Þing; Parliament

Þingvellir; Old time meeting
place of Parliament, congress.

Æ (say "I")

Æðarfugl; Eider bird (Eider
duck).

Ö

Öræfarjökull

R

Reykjavik; Capital of Iceland

Reyðarfjörður; Red (?) Fjord

S

Snæfellsjökull; Snow Mountain
Glacier

Smörfjell; Butter Mountain

Siglufjörður; Fjord of Sails.

Skjálfandi: Trembling (shivering)
Bay

V

Vatn; Water.

Vatnajökull; Glacier of Water.

As a citizen of Iceland I enjoyed the odd beauty of my country; the mountains, the glaciers, and the fjords, yes, even the eruptions of awesome volcanoes.

As a citizen of the Beautiful and Amazing United States of America, it's been my pleasure to travel from the west coast of the Pacific, to the east coast of the Atlantic Ocean. And from the north: The Canadian border, to the southern tip of Florida, the Florida Keys, traveling many States in between.

As a citizen of Heaven for almost sixty years I am looking forward to the day I will get to explore and enjoy this, most beautiful country of them all...

Oh Lord my God
When I in awesome wonder
Consider all
The works Thy Hand hath made
I see the stars
I hear the rolling thunder,
Thy power throughout
The universe displayed.

When Christ shall come
With shouts of acclamations
And take me home
What joy shall fill my heart!
Then I shall bow
In humble adoration
And there proclaim
"My God how great thou art!"

Carl Gustaf Boberg, 1859–1940

BIOGRAPHICAL SKETCH

Íeda Jónasdóttir grew up in Iceland, a country often called *The Land Of Fire And Ice.*

In 1944, at age nineteen, she met and eventually married an American service man, Del Herman, who was stationed in Reykjavik. After WWII, she came to the United States, where she and her husband made their home in Illinois. Over the years they became parents of three boys and seven girls that Íeda enjoyed entertaining with many folk-tales of her mysterious homeland. The children were especially intrigued with stories of the '*Hidden People*' who were known to be helpful folks, but did not take kindly to naughty children climbing on top of lava rocks that were known to be the '*Hidden's*' castles!

Íeda's love and creativity in decorating her home on a small budget inspired her to enroll at Chicago School of Interior Design. After graduating, she owned and operated her own design shop. Ms. Herman wrote numerous decorating articles that were published in local newspapers and magazines. She also prepared a handbook; *How To Decorate With Sheets And More*, which was made available at the

numerous seminars at which she spoke: schools, women's clubs and church groups.

After retiring in 2009, and her family grown, Íeda's writing on decorating lead to writing her memoir for her family; *Trölls - Monster Worm - Hidden People.* Not one to stop there, Íeda enrolled, and graduated from the Institute of Children's Literature, West Redding, Connecticut. At the present time she is writing an adventure book for teenagers.

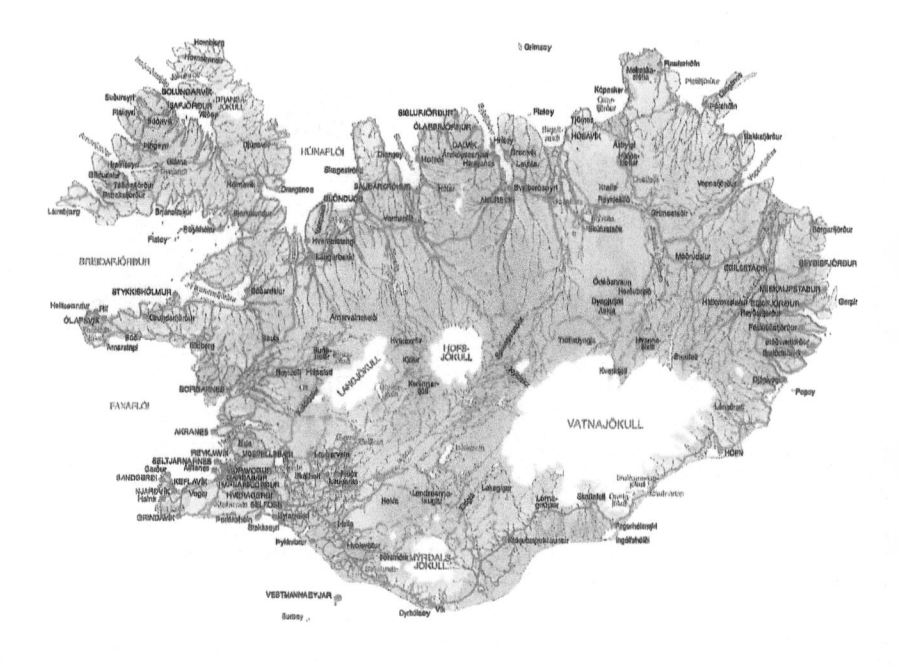

PRONUNCIATION

Áá,	say like in	<u>ou</u>ch - h<u>ow</u>
Ðð	"	<u>th</u>is - <u>th</u>e
Éé	"	<u>ye</u>t - <u>y</u>ell
Íí	"	<u>ee</u>k - <u>ee</u>l
Óó	"	<u>o</u>ver - n<u>o</u>
Úú	"	l<u>oo</u>t - m<u>oo</u>t
Þþ	"	<u>th</u>ing - <u>th</u>orn
Ææ	"	I - <u>I</u>ce
Öö	"	h<u>u</u>rry - h<u>u</u>rt.

The letter "C" is not used in any Icelandic words.

ACKNOWLEDGEMENTS.

Thanks to, Del, my husband, and all of our children; Lucille, Del, Marian, Peggy, Christine, Myra, Jonathan, Timothy, Della and Heidi, who have been so encouraging as I've been writing my memoir. Also, to all of our Grandchildren, a very special thanks. All of you, at one time or another, have expressed interest in knowing more about my life growing up in Iceland, which started me down this memory lane.

To my two sisters; Sisi and Lilla, thanks for your input, so enjoyable to re-live some of our fun moments.

EXPLANATION OF SOME TAG ENDINGS.

At the end of word like ----fjöll

----fell	mountain (s)
----fjall	
----fjörður	fjord
----vogur	
----vík	bay,cove
----flói	
----ey	island
----eyja	
---- jökull	glacier

Eyjafjallajökull Eyja - fjalla - jökull --- Island mountain glacier.

CONTENTS.

THE LEGEND OF THE ICELANDIC COAT OF ARMS.

"SKJALDAMERKI"
("COAT OF ARMS")

Denmark's King, Harald, planned to invade Iceland and sent a magician to check out a way to do that.

The magician turned himself into a whale, and swam to Iceland. He tried to enter the Eastern shore, but he met a Dragon protecting the island.

Then he tried the North coast, but there met with a Gigantic Bird with huge wings that scared him away.

In the West he was frightened away by a Bull, that waded into the water, snorting and bellowing.

Then the whale-magician swam to the Southern shore, where he was met with a mighty Giant with an iron rod in his hand.

No matter where he tried to come ashore he was turned away in fear, and had to slink back to Denmark.

This is the way The Guardians protected Iceland.

Outskirts Press, Inc.
http://www.outskirtspress.com

Paperback ISBN: 978-1-4787-0008-1
Hardback ISBN: 978-1-4327-9937-3

Outskirts Press and the "OP" logo are trademarks belonging to Outskirts Press, Inc.

Ieda J. Herman

Fond Memories of Iceland

Worm-Hidden People
Trolls-Monsters

5 Creating and using selections

6 Cropping, resizing, rotating, flipping and zooming

7 Layers

8 Working with shapes

9 Drawing, patterns and gradients

10 Working with type

11 Enhancing your photographs with blur and sharpen techniques

Top 10 Photoshop Elements Problems Solved

Top 10 Photoshop Elements Tips

Tip 1: Getting photographs from a camera or memory card

1 Connect your camera, or the memory card itself, to your computer – in whichever manner is particular to your camera, card and computer.

2 In the Organizer, click the File... Get Photos and Videos... From Camera or Card Reader menu item.

3 The Photo Downloader dialogue box opens. Select the source using the Get Photos from the dropdown.

4 Select the destination for the photographs by using the Browse feature and making a selection in the Create Subfolder(s) dropdown. If Custom is the choice, then enter a name for the folder underneath the dropdown.

5 The image files being copied into your computer can retain their original names, or you can set up a sequential naming scheme. To do this select Custom Name from the Rename Files dropdown. Enter a name in the box underneath and a starting number. As an example, if Chess is entered as the custom name, the files will be renamed to Chess_0001, Chess_0002, and so on.

6 If desired you can instruct Photoshop Elements to delete the files from the card after they are imported to the computer. To do this, select the After Copying, Delete Originals option from the Delete Options dropdown. Otherwise leave the setting at After Copying, Do Not Delete Originals.

7 Click the Get Photos button.

Tip 2: Backing up your photographs

It might be mundane but backups are like insurance. You don't need them until... you need them! And if you didn't create any backups it's too late. So, it's good to get the backup habit.

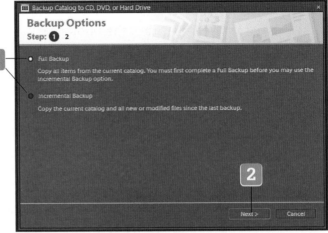

1 In the Organizer, click the File... Backup Catalog to CD, DVD, or Hard Drive menu item. Before the proper dialogue is displayed you may receive a dialogue about missing files. This appears if you moved files around during the current session.

2 The Step 1 Backup dialogue is displayed. In this step you decide on a full backup or an incremental backup. Click Next.

3 In Step 2 select the destination drive and path. Select the drive from the list. Use the Browse feature to select the path. Click the Done button and the backup operation runs.

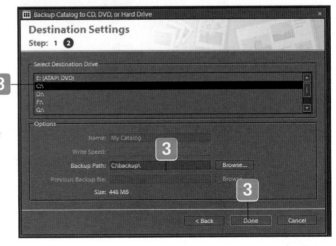

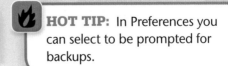

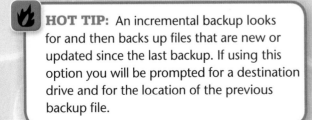

HOT TIP: An incremental backup looks for and then backs up files that are new or updated since the last backup. If using this option you will be prompted for a destination drive and for the location of the previous backup file.

HOT TIP: In Preferences you can select to be prompted for backups.

Tip 3: Assigning a keyword to a photograph

1. In the Organizer, keywords can be dragged onto photographs. While doing so the mouse pointer turns into a hand holding the keyword's icon.

2. Once tagged with a category and possible sub-category, and a keyword, the tagging is listed underneath the photograph.

category, sub-category and keyword

Tip 4: Creating a photo album

1. In the Organizer, in the Albums palette, select the dropdown next to the plus (+) sign and select to create a New Album.

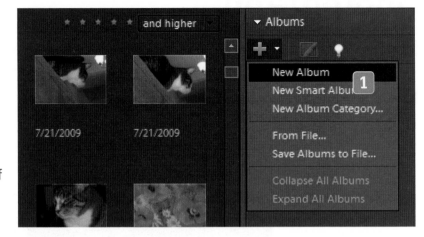

2. Enter the name of the new album. Click Done when finished.

3. The album is created and photographs can be dragged to the album. When this is done, clicking on the album icon displays the photographs that are in the album.

Tip 5: Reversing changes

There is much that literally meets the eye when altering an image and you might not like what you see. Adobe® Photoshop® Elements provides the Undo and Revert commands to reverse changes you made.

1 Undo: A history of changes is kept, and using Undo back-steps through them as many times as you click Undo. You can click on the Undo arrow to the right of the menus or click the Edit… Undo menu item. Using the menu, the phrase of the menu item will change based on what step is being undone.

2 Revert: This removes all the changes in one click. Whereas the single-step Undo is useful to return to a midpoint in the history of changes, Revert sets the image back to its original state.

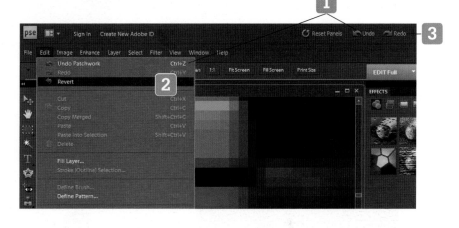

3 Redo: This is the opposite of Undo. Clicking Redo steps forward through the history of changes.

Undo, Redo and Revert are enabled only when there is a history of changes. When a photograph is first opened, none of the options are available. After the first change, Revert and Undo are available. Redo becomes available only after an Undo operation – it would reverse the Undo.

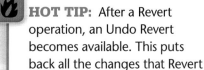

HOT TIP: After a Revert operation, an Undo Revert becomes available. This puts back all the changes that Revert pulled out. Neat!

Tip 6: Adding to a selection

While a marquee is displayed on an image, you can apply another marquee and have the two join together.

1. Draw the first selection.

2. While holding down the Shift key, draw another selection. Make sure it touches the boundary of the first selection, or even have it start from within the boundary of the first selection.

WHAT DOES THIS MEAN?

Marquee: this is a frame which identifies a selected area of an image. The frame is usually displayed with a flashing, dashed line.

Tip 7: Changing the background to a layer

The effects and changes that can be applied to the background are limited. As you become familiar with what layers offer, you may want to apply these to the background. The trick then is to change the background to a layer.

1 Right-click on the background in the Layers palette. In the context menu select Layer From Background.

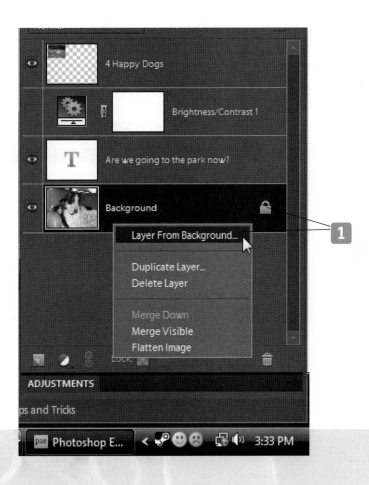

Tip 8: Saving for the web

The number one consideration for images on the web is file size. This applies both to the physical size and the file size in bytes. The physical size matters because the image takes up space on a web page. The file size matters because it affects how fast a web page is loaded. This is not overly important for an image or two. However, if a web page has many images, the page could have a delay in appearing in a web browser. This usually annoys people.

1 Click the File… Save For Web menu item. The Save For Web dialogue is displayed.

The dialogue has two panes – the before and the after. On the left is the image in its current format, and the right pane shows what it will look like based on selections made in the dialogue. You are not likely to notice much difference in the appearance between the panes. Changes to the image would have already occurred during editing. This dialogue is focused on how to save the image for web page presentation.

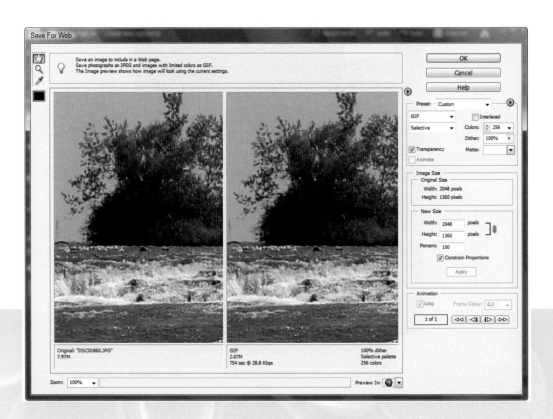

2 Reduce the size of the image and click the Apply button. Select the output file format.

An image for the web should not be exceedingly large. It is not unreasonable to reduce the image by a large percentage. Of course this depends on the original file size. In this example the original size is 2048 × 1360 pixels. This is greater than a standard computer screen. Here, the image is being reduced to a width of 300 pixels. The file format being selected is GIF.

3 Click the OK button. The Save Optimized As dialogue opens. This is a typical Save dialogue. Navigate to the folder of your choice and click the Save button.

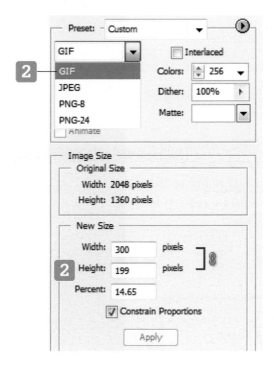

 HOT TIP: Leave the Constrain Proportions tickbox ticked. This ensures that changing any single size attribute – the width, height, or percentage – forces the other attributes to adjust accordingly. Bottom line – the image will retain its appearance, just resized. There will be no squeeze or stretch in the adjustment.

Tip 9: Emailing photographs as attachments

Sending attachments is the alternative to sending embedded photographs. Attachments have a benefit. The recipients can save them in their computer system and view or use them without having to reopen the email message.

E-mail Attachments

Items:

3

3 Items

☑ Convert Photos to JPEGs

Maximum Photo Size:

Small (640 x 480 px)

Quality:

10 - Maximum

Estimated Size:

~289 KB, 2 min @ 56Kbps

Next   Cancel

1 In the Organizer, click the Share tab.

2 Click the E-mail Attachments button.

3 Drag images from the Organizer into the E-mail Attachments pane.

4 If the images are not in JPEG format, then a tickbox provides the option to change them to JPEG. Other settings relate to the size the photographs should be resized to and the quality of the JPEGs.

? DID YOU KNOW?

JPEGs are the standard for sharing photographs. The quality rating is a measure of how much definition remains in the image. The highest rating retains all information, but creates the largest file size. The lower the quality setting, the smaller the file size. It's a subjective balance of quality vs. file size. Factor in how many images are being attached to the email. Best advice is to stay at the top quality or close to it.

 HOT TIP: If you wish to attach many image files then use the small or very small size. This ensures you won't be sending an enormous-sized email to the recipients.

5 Click the Next button. The following screen is where you select recipients. When finished selecting recipients, click the Next button. An email message is created in your computer's email program and is ready to be sent. The photograph files are attachments to the email.

Here are the files that I want to share with you.

File   Edit   View   Insert   Format   Tools   Message   Help

Send

To: James Tellerton <jamestellerton@yahoo.com>;

Cc:

Subject: Here are the files that I want to share with you.

Attach: Cats2_0020.jpg (92.0 KB)   Cats2_0023.jpg (90.1 KB)   Cats2_0026.jpg (98.3 KB)

Arial   14

Take a look at the great cat pictures!

Tip 10: Setting a photograph as the desktop wallpaper

See a photo you are just in love with? Family, friends, pets, or the moon? Whatever it is, you can easily have that photograph become the desktop wallpaper on your computer.

1 Right-click on the photograph.

2 Select Set as Desktop Wallpaper.

Yes, it's that simple.

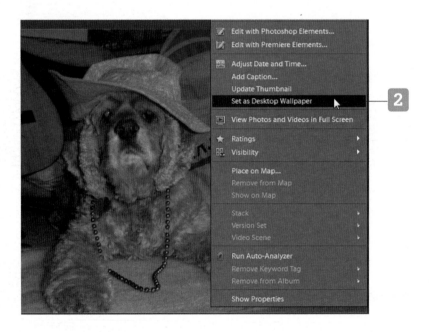

 HOT TIP: You can revert back to the previous wallpaper by right-clicking on the desktop and following the prompts to find and select the previous image.

 DID YOU KNOW?

When the image being set as the desktop wallpaper image is small, the single image can be centred on the desktop or it can be tiled to show a repeating pattern. Right-click on the desktop and follow the prompts.

1 Getting your photographs into Photoshop Elements

Introduction

Photoshop Elements serves two general functions: organising photographs and editing photographs. Each of these functional areas has a lot of power to perform the relevant tasks. Before any of this can happen though, you need to get the photographs into the program!

The Organizer is the half of this dual-purpose program that organises, catalogues, lets you add captions and ratings, and much more. The method for getting photographs in is much more robust in the Organizer. This chapter therefore shows how to gather up your snapshots and bring them into the Organizer. Rather than confuse the issue as to where photographs are actually kept, the terms used here about getting the photographs into the Organizer are a figure of speech. The actual image files themselves do not reside in the program. They reside on the hard disk of your computer, or on a CD/DVD, memory card or anywhere else that files are generally kept. It's their representation and presentation that are handled in the Organizer.

Make sure the Organizer is open. If you are in the Editor, you can click the Organizer button in the upper right part of the screen. Chapters 2 and 3 (about the Organizer and the Editor) show layouts of the respective screens.

Getting photographs from a memory card

The most likely place you will get your photographs from is your camera of course! The odds are that the files in your camera are actually on a memory card in the camera.

In these steps you will connect your camera or card to your computer. If an automatic file download starts then enjoy the experience, and afterwards set the preferences for this not to happen next time, if that is what you prefer. (See the *Setting Preferences* section in this chapter.) The following steps are used when the automatic download is not enabled.

1 Connect your camera, or the memory card itself, to your computer – in whichever manner is appropriate for your particular camera, card and computer.

2 Click the File... Get Photos and Videos... From Camera or Card Reader menu item.

3 The Photo Downloader dialogue box opens. Select the source using the Get Photos from dropdown.

4 Select the destination for the photographs by using the Browse feature and making a selection in the Create Subfolder(s) dropdown. If Custom is the choice, then enter a name for the folder underneath the dropdown.

5 The image files being copied into your computer can retain their original names, or you can set up a sequential naming scheme. To do this select Custom Name from the Rename Files dropdown. Enter a name in the box underneath and a starting number. As an example, if Chess is entered as the custom name, the files will be renamed to Chess_0001, Chess_0002, and so on.

 HOT TIP: When selecting Create Subfolders, avoid using any of the Short Date options. A folder named as a date is not intuitive for indicating what files are in the folder.

6 If desired you can instruct Photoshop Elements to delete the files from the card after they are imported to the computer. To do this, select the After Copying, Delete Originals option from the Delete Options dropdown. Otherwise leave the setting at After Copying, Do Not Delete Originals.

7 Click the Get Photos button.

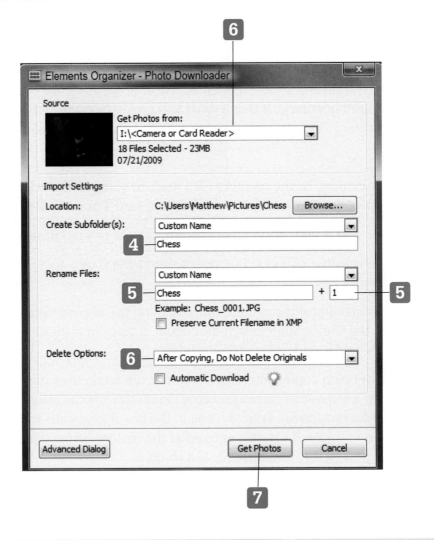

Getting photographs from a scanner

Do you have great artwork that is not in a file? Have a scanner? You can easily run the scanning and file saving direct from Photoshop Elements.

1 Click the File… Get Photos and Videos… From Scanner menu item. The Get Photos from Scanner dialogue box is displayed.

2 Select the scanner from the dropdown. Browse to select the folder where the scanned image will be saved. Select the Save As file type (jpeg, tiff, or png). If a jpeg file type is selected, you can use the slider to set the quality.

3 Click the OK button. The software that runs the scanner will start up. After the scan is complete and the scanner software is closed, the file will be in the selected folder and will also be found in the Organizer.

? DID YOU KNOW?
With the jpeg file type, the higher the quality, the larger the file size. The only reason to consider anything less than the best quality is if the file will be used on a web page or sent via email. In such cases file size matters.

HOT TIP: If your scanner is not found in the dialogue it probably means you have to load the driver software for the scanner. Check the scanner manual.

Getting photographs from a folder

It's quite possible that image files are already in your computer but not found in the Organizer. In this case the files are not being copied but will be represented in the Organizer, which of course lets you do all types of fun things, as you will see in Chapter 2.

1 Click the File… Get Photos and Videos… From Files and Folders menu item. The Get Photos and Videos from Files and Folders dialogue box is displayed.

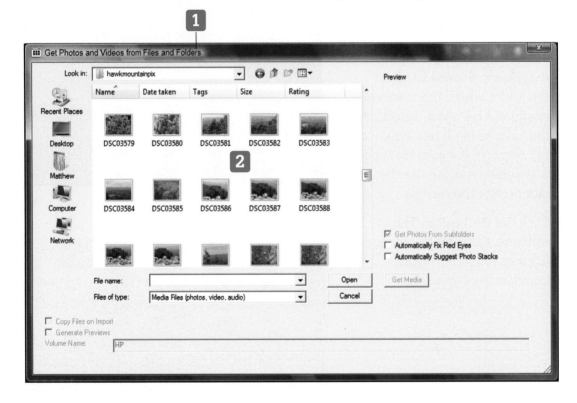

2 Browse to the desired folder and select the files you want. Then click the OK button.

HOT TIP: You select more than one file by holding down the Ctrl key while clicking on file names.

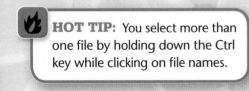

The Photo Downloader

The Photo Downloader is the powerful 'get all the media from wherever it might be' utility. In the Advanced Dialog view are all the options you need. Later in this chapter you will see where to set preferences to have the Photo Downloader run automatically. You may decide to turn this feature off, but if left on then here is what you do.

1 Insert the memory card or attach the camera to the computer. The Photo Downloader starts copying photographs to the computer. The destination folders are based on how they were selected in a prior session using Photoshop Elements.

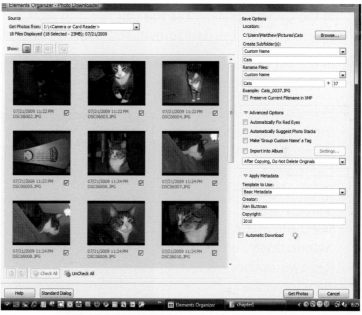

2 Watch the import process if you wish. There is nothing else you need to do. However, you can stop the process if necessary. While the Photo Downloader is running a progress window is displayed, on which is a Stop button.

 HOT TIP: If you know how to delete unwanted single images in your camera, do so first. This saves having to delete them in Photoshop Elements.

Setting Preferences

There are several facets of Photoshop Elements that you can set to desired default properties or actions. Some of these involve the copying of image files.

1 Click the Edit… Preferences… General menu item to display the Preferences dialogue. The initial view is the General preferences.

In the General preferences you can select to work in inches or metric measurements, the date format, and a few other settings.

2 In the left side of the Preferences dialogue click on Files. A variety of options is available relating to how and where files are saved.

3 In the left side of the Preferences dialogue click on Camera or Card Reader. Here is where you select the useful Automatically Fix Red Eyes option. Here too is the option to have the Photo Downloader start when a memory card or camera is attached to the computer.

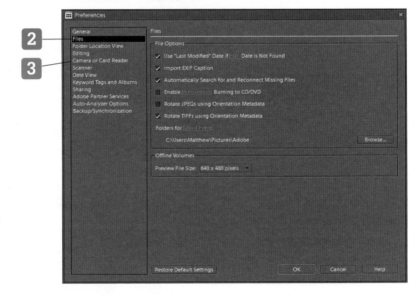

Along with the start option are the choices for how to create folders to hold incoming files.

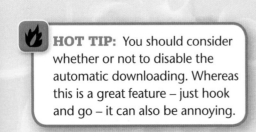

HOT TIP: You should consider whether or not to disable the automatic downloading. Whereas this is a great feature – just hook and go – it can also be annoying.

Moving files

You can move files from one location to another from within the Organizer.

1 Select one (click on the photograph) or more photographs to move (holding down the Ctrl key, click on multiple photographs).

2 Click on the File… Move menu item to display the Move Selected Items dialogue box.

3 Use the Browse feature to select a destination folder.

4 Click OK to close the Browse For Folder dialogue. Then click OK to close the Move Selected Items dialogue. The files are moved to the new folder.

2

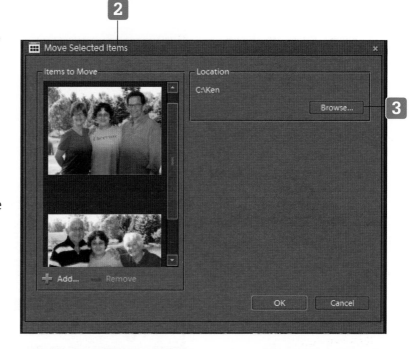

3

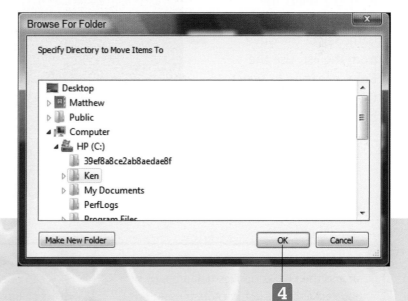

4

Backing up your photographs

It might be mundane but backups are like insurance. You don't need them until… you need them! And if you didn't create any backups it's too late. So, it's good to get the backup habit.

1 Click the File… Backup Catalog to CD, DVD, or Hard Drive menu item. Before the proper dialogue is displayed you may receive a dialogue about missing files. This appears if you moved files around during the current session.

2 The Step 1 Backup dialogue is displayed. In this step you decide on a full backup or an incremental backup. Click Next.

3 In Step 2 select the destination drive and path. Select the drive from the list. Use the Browse feature to select the path. Click the Done button and the backup operation runs.

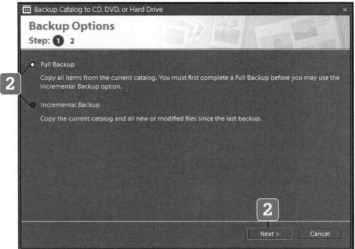

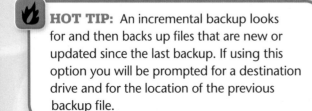

HOT TIP: An incremental backup looks for and then backs up files that are new or updated since the last backup. If using this option you will be prompted for a destination drive and for the location of the previous backup file.

HOT TIP: In Preferences you can select to be prompted for backups.

2 Working with the Organizer

Introduction

With the ability to take and store hundreds or thousands of pictures comes the need for ways to organise them. Photoshop Elements provides this capability with the Organizer. Photoshop Elements is basically a dual application: the storing and organisation of artwork, and the creation and editing of artwork. The latter is done within the Editor, which is described in several later chapters.

The Organizer, though, is what you will use to categorise your artwork. Besides divvying up photographs into categories, you can add captions, keywords, rate them with a 0–5 stars system, and more. You can even associate a photograph with a place on the globe by using the provided map feature. To help you follow the steps, a full screen shot of the Organizer is shown here with a key to major areas:

1. Photo Browser
2. Albums palette
3. Keyword Tags palette
4. Thumbnail size slider
5. Display options
6. Go to the Editor (used throughout later chapters).

Adjusting the thumbnail view

The Organizer displays thumbnails of your photographs. The thumbnail size is controlled by a slider near the top of the Organizer. By adjusting this you can have the Organizer display anything from a single large thumbnail image to dozens of smaller thumbnails.

1 Using the mouse, move the slider to the left to show many small thumbnails, or move the slider to the right to show fewer but larger thumbnails, up to displaying just one large thumbnail.

2 With the slider all the way to the left, many small thumbnail images are shown.

3 Putting the slider all the way to the right displays a single large thumbnail image.

Even with a single large thumbnail in view, you can scroll through the images using the scroll on the right side of the viewing area.

DID YOU KNOW?

To the left of the slider is a group of four small blue boxes. Clicking on this group will instantly change the view to display small multiple thumbnails. To the right of the slider is a single blue box, that when clicked instantly changes the view to a single large thumbnail.

Sorting thumbnails

With many thumbnails displayed in the viewing area of the Organizer, it's helpful to sort them. You can sort the images by date, either from newest to oldest or from oldest to newest.

1 To the right of the thumbnail view slider is a dropdown with the two options of how to sort by dates.

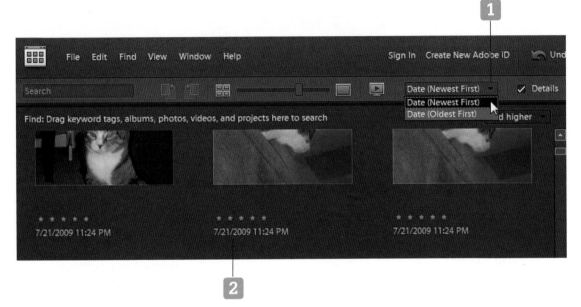

2 Each image has an associated Date Stamp. This is the date used for the sort. The date is part of the metadata stored with the image file.

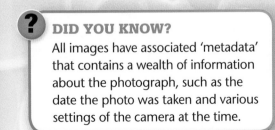

? DID YOU KNOW?

All images have associated 'metadata' that contains a wealth of information about the photograph, such as the date the photo was taken and various settings of the camera at the time.

Adding a caption to a photograph

A caption can be assigned to a photograph. This does not change the file name. The caption becomes a part of the photograph's metadata.

1 Right-click on an image to display the context menu.

2 From the context menu, select Add Caption.

3 Enter a caption and click OK to save it.

 HOT TIP: You won't see the caption unless the display is set to show the single thumbnail in the viewing area. Then the caption is seen underneath the image.

Creating a category

Categories provide a way to associate photographs that are similar in some respect. For example, a category named Animals could associate all the photographs you took at the zoo last year, or a category named Bahamas vacation for well... you get the idea. Here is what you do:

1 In the Keyword Tags palette, click the arrow to the right of the green plus (+) sign, to open a context menu.

2 Enter a name for the category and select an icon.

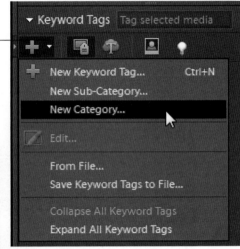

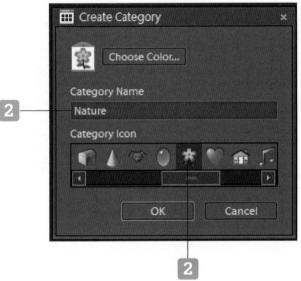

? DID YOU KNOW?

You can also click the Choose Color button. This displays a colour picker from which you select the colour for the icon's appearance.

Creating a sub-category

Any created category can have sub-categories. A category named Nature could have a sub-category named Flowers. A category named Family could have several sub-categories – one for each family member.

1 First right-click on the category for which a sub-category is being created. A context menu appears. Select Create new sub-category in (name of category) category.

2 The Create Sub-Category box appears. Enter the name of the sub-category and click OK. The Keyword Tags palette shows the categories and sub-categories.

In this example the category Nature has the Flowers sub-category.

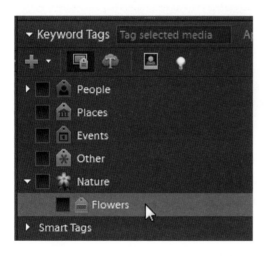

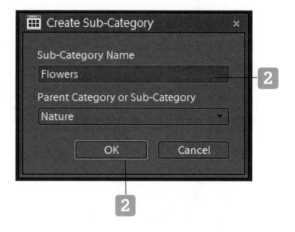

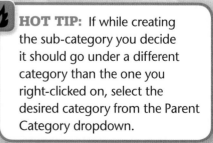

HOT TIP: If while creating the sub-category you decide it should go under a different category than the one you right-clicked on, select the desired category from the Parent Category dropdown.

Adding a photograph to a category or sub-category

Now that you have categories and possible sub-categories, the task at hand is to associate photographs with the categories and sub-categories. This is easily done by dragging photographs and dropping them directly onto the category or sub-category. In fact the dragging and dropping can go in either direction: you can drag one or more photographs onto a category or sub-category, or you can drag the category or sub-category onto a photograph.

1 Select one or more photographs. Here, three photographs of Niagara Falls are selected (they have a blue border – indicating they are selected).

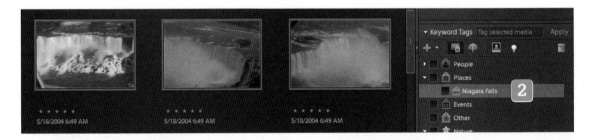

2 Click and hold down the mouse button. Drag the photographs over to the category or sub-category. While doing this operation the mouse pointer looks like a hand holding a stack of photographs. The three photographs now display the icon of the Niagara Falls sub-category.

? DID YOU KNOW?

If you select multiple photographs prior to dragging the category over, then all the selected photographs will become associated with the category.

Creating a keyword

Keywords are similar to categories and sub-categories. In fact, as you probably noticed, categories and sub-categories have been created inside the Keyword Tags palette. Keywords must belong to a category or sub-category. An advantage in associating photographs with keywords is the ability to search on keywords.

1 Right-click on either a category or sub-category and select it to create a new keyword. A dialogue box appears in which you enter the name of the keyword. You can also edit the keyword's icon.

The keyword name belongs to the category or sub-category.

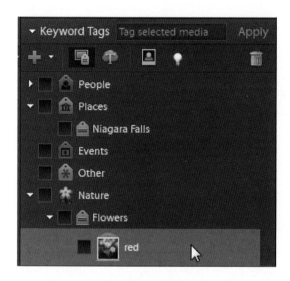

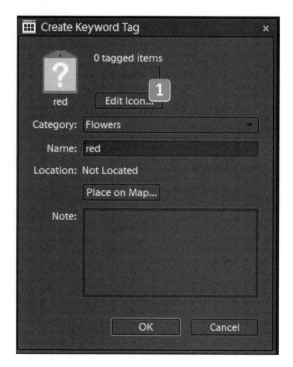

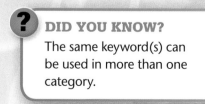

? DID YOU KNOW?

The same keyword(s) can be used in more than one category.

Searching for photographs

Just above the thumbnails, on the left side of the Organizer, is the Find area where various items can be dragged to facilitate a search. Keyword icons and category/sub-category icons can be dragged here. A useful attribute of this type of searching is the ability to mix different keywords and/or categories. This example does just that.

1 The Family sub-category icon is dragged to the Find area. This is done by clicking on the icon and holding the mouse button down while dragging the icon to the Find area. Then, letting go of the icon updates the display to show just photographs tagged with the Family sub-category.

2 Another sub-category, Flowers, is dragged to the Find area. The display now shows photographs tagged as Family or Flowers (or both of course!).

3 An additional search feature is pulled into the mix. This is the Date Range selector. This dialogue box is displayed by using the Find... Set Date Range menu. Using it to limit photographs to those dated as 2007 and 2008 only reduces the number of displayed photographs.

? DID YOU KNOW?
Under the Find menu are other methods for finding photographs, such as by caption or file name.

Using the Timeline to find photographs

The Timeline provides a fast way to zero in on photographs taken on a given date or a range of dates. The Timeline works a bit like a chart. Along the horizontal bottom of the Timeline are date markers, and above them are columns that are as tall as the number of photographs attached to the date. (Think of this as a simple bar chart that you may have come across in school maths lessons.)

1 Use the Window… Timeline menu to display the Timeline.

2 The Timeline has a small selector window that is dragged across the Timeline and determines the photographs, by date, that will be displayed in the Photo Browser. On each end of the Timeline are margin markers that limit how much range the selector window can travel back and forth. Along the Timeline are bars, at certain 'places in time', determined by the photographs. The more photographs at a given date, the higher the bar will be, and therefore more photographs will be displayed.

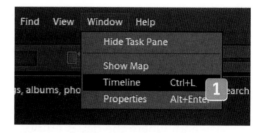

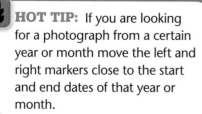

HOT TIP: If you are looking for a photograph from a certain year or month move the left and right markers close to the start and end dates of that year or month.

Using Date View to find photographs

A very useful date-based search utility is the Date View. The Date View is a calendar-based interface that shows which days have photographs that are dated as such. As with any sophisticated calendar, you can change the view between year, month or day, and you can scroll through any of these date delineations.

1 Use the Display options dropdown to select the Date View for display.

2 Select the type of display you desire – year, month or day – and then scroll to the year, month or day you wish to look at. Here is a month view that shows some days have photographs dated to the particular day and, where the day is empty, no photographs in the Photo Browser have a creation date that matches.

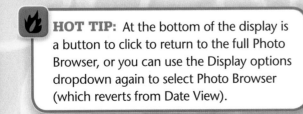

HOT TIP: At the bottom of the display is a button to click to return to the full Photo Browser, or you can use the Display options dropdown again to select Photo Browser (which reverts from Date View).

Creating an album

An album is another tool for getting your photographs organised. An album is similar to a category in that you set desired photographs to be brought together based on some commonality.

1 In the Album palette, select the dropdown next to the plus (+) sign and select to create a New Album.

2 Enter the name of the new album. Click Done when finished.

3 The album is created and photographs can be dragged to it. When this is done, clicking on the album icon displays the photographs that are contained in that album.

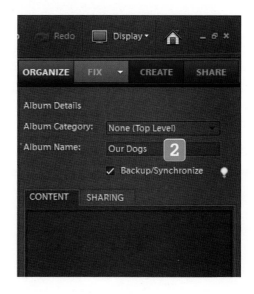

 HOT TIP: Click on the album icon again to have the Photo Browser return to displaying all photographs.

Creating a Smart Album

Another way to create an album is to use the Smart Album feature. This lets you create an album by running a search through all the photographs in the Photo Browser and having those that meet the criteria you stipulate become photographs that belong to the album.

1. In the dropdown next to the plus sign (+) in the Album palette, select to create a New Smart Album. In this example an album titled 2008 will contain all photographs that are dated after December 31 2007 and before January 1 2009.

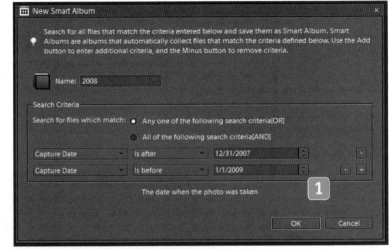

2. The 2008 album is created and populated with all the photographs that match the criteria.

Using Folder Location view

Folder view is another method of arranging photographs in the Photo Browser. Viewing by folder makes it easy to track down photographs that exist within known folders. Although there are many photographs in the Photo Browser, the files actually reside wherever they can in your computer system.

Folder location provides two views by folder. On the left of the Photo Browser is an expandable/collapsible hierarchical list of folders in your computer. In the main area of the Photo Browser are the photographs, only now separated by folder.

1 Select Folder Location from the Display options dropdown. To revert to the normal Photo Browser view, use Display options again and select Thumbnail view.

Displaying properties

There is a wealth of information incorporated into your digital photographs. General information, keyword tags, history data and metadata are available to view by displaying the properties of a photograph.

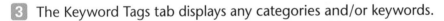

1 Right-click on a photograph and select Show Properties from the context menu. The Properties window has four symbols: clicking each shows a tab of available information. The first Properties view displays the General settings.

2 The Metadata tab indicates the photograph's conditions: the exposure time, F-stop, whether the flash fired, and more. There are two ways to view metadata – brief and complete. This choice is made at the bottom of the Properties window.

3 The Keyword Tags tab displays any categories and/or keywords.

4 The last tab – History – displays just a brief bit of information about modified and imported dates.

HOT TIP: You can leave the Properties window open and click on different photographs. The Properties window will display the properties of the selected photograph.

? DID YOU KNOW?

The exposure time is the amount of time the camera shutter stayed open when taking the photograph. A longer amount of open time allows more light in, but can introduce blurriness if the camera isn't held rock steady (or put on a tripod). The F-stop is the size of the shutter opening (which can change). Varying F-stop values and exposure times creates a world of possibilities.

Deleting a photograph

A photograph can be removed from the Photo Browser. It is up to you whether you delete it altogether from your computer.

1 Right-click on the photograph you wish to delete. Select Delete from Catalog from the context menu. The Catalog is the collection of photographs in the Photo Browser.

2 The Confirm Deletion from Catalog dialogue appears. There is an optional tick box that also allows you to delete the photograph from the hard drive of your computer. Use that option with care.

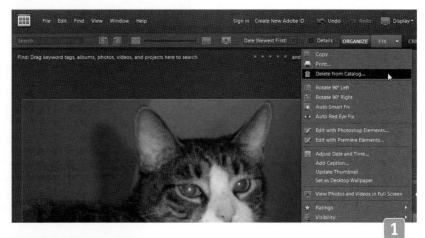

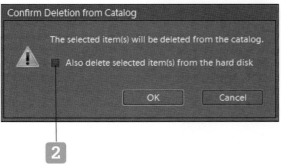

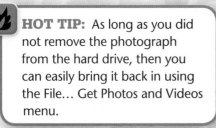

> 🔥 **HOT TIP:** As long as you did not remove the photograph from the hard drive, then you can easily bring it back in using the File… Get Photos and Videos menu.

Viewing a photograph in Full Screen

In the Organizer is a button that when clicked presents the currently selected photograph in full screen mode – that means it will occupy the full area of your computer monitor. This can be quite striking!

1 Click the Full Screen button located along the top of the Organizer.

2 The image appears in full screen. Some optional dialogues can be used, such as for quick editing. There are other options to cycle through photographs or to watch the photographs as a slide show.

 HOT TIP: When running through your photographs as a slide show, you can select how the photographs transition as they change.

3 Working with the Editor

Introduction

In the previous chapter you learned how to organise and categorise photographs. Additionally, keywords, albums, captions and other information were put to use. In this chapter, and in all those after it, you will learn how to edit or change facets of photographs. This is the real meat and potatoes of Photoshop Elements.

All photo manipulation is done within the Editor – the part of Photoshop Elements that provides all the tools needed to alter and enhance your works of art. Knowing the various areas of the Editor is key to using it effectively. This chapter introduces the Editor screen and how to work the Editor to get your creative ideas to fruition. First, a full screen shot of the Editor is shown here with a key to the major areas.

1   Active image area

2   Project Bin

3   Layers

4   Palettes

5   Palette Selector

6   Toolbox

7   Tool options

8   Display the organizer

9   Edit options

Adding a photograph to the Project Bin

It is possible, and often useful, to have more than one photograph image open in the Editor. Why? You might be combining parts of different images (a collage), sampling a colour from one photograph to use in editing another or any other numerous reasons.

The Project Bin, at the bottom of the Editor, displays thumbnails of each open photograph. To open the first photograph or an additional photograph:

1 Use the File... Open menu to select a photograph to open. The Open dialogue is displayed and a photograph can be browsed to and selected to open.

2 The photograph joins others in the Project Bin. It also is displayed as the active image.

To remove a photograph, right-click on the image in the Project Bin and select Close from the context menu.

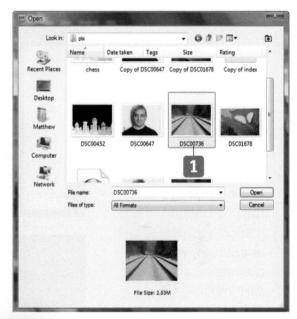

HOT TIP: Other options in the File menu provide other ways to bring photographs into the Editor. You can select a file from the Recently Edited Files list or import a frame from a video file.

Displaying multiple photographs

When more than one photograph file is opened there are numerous thumbnails displayed in the Project Bin. You can bring them all into the active image area as tiled or cascaded images.

1 Use the Window... Images... Tile menu to display tiles of the images.

2 To display the images in a cascade, use the Window... Images... Cascade selection.

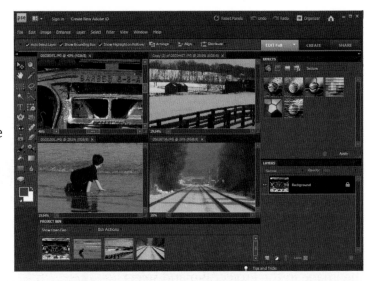

3 For full control of how many photographs to display in the Active Image Area, use the minimise, maximise and resize controls in the upper right of any or all of the images. This way you can individually move the photographs in any manner you desire, such as putting two photographs next to each other.

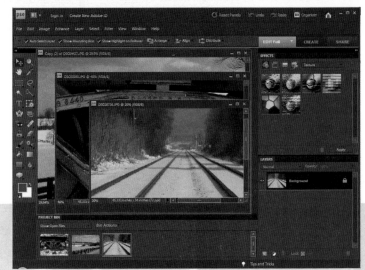

Selecting a tool from the Toolbox

The Toolbox contains many of the items you need to work with your images. One tool is selected at a time.

1 Click on the desired tool in the Toolbox. The tool is activated and ready to be used. When a tool is selected, the Tool Options change accordingly to offer the options available for the selected tool.

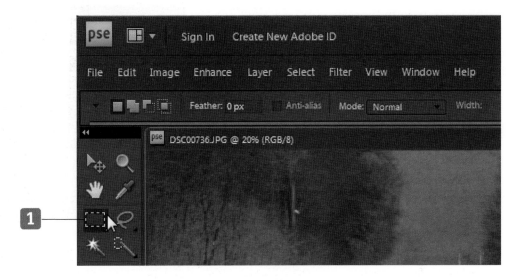

HOT TIP: Once a tool is selected it remains active until you select another tool. Most tools change photographs in some aspect, so to be on the safe side, when done with the altering tool, select a passive tool such as the hand or move tool.

Selecting a palette

In the Palettes area are selections for four types of palettes:

- Filters
- Layers
- Photo effects
- All – this makes all the palette choices available.

Within each palette type are sub-selections. These are found in the dropdown to the right of the Palette Selector. (When All is selected the dropdown is not visible, as all options are displayed as thumbnails in the palette.)

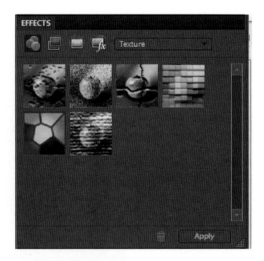

1 Select a palette. The items in the dropdown change to match the palette selection.

SEE ALSO: Applying the effects and other stylisations are explored in greater detail in later chapters.

Using Quick Editing

1. Click on the dropdown arrow on the EDIT button and select EDIT Quick from the list. The palettes are replaced with a series of slider controls, organised by type of editing: Lighting, Color, etc.

2. Click the arrow on the EDIT button and select EDIT Quick from the dropdown list. The palettes are replaced with a series of slider controls.

3. Try out different settings with the slider controls. The effects are instantly seen in the image. A tick mark icon and a cancel icon appear when a change is made. You can then commit (click the tick mark) or drop (the cancel icon) the changes. Notice also that the number of tools in the toolbox is reduced.

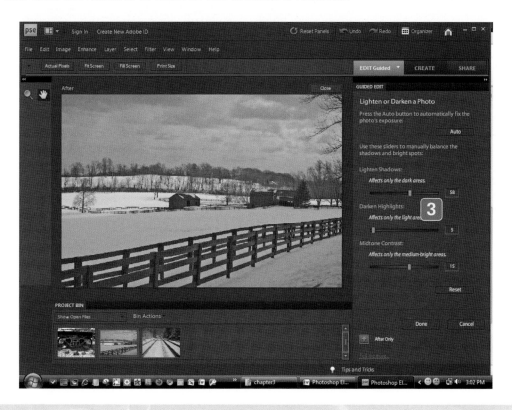

? DID YOU KNOW?

Quick edit mode gives you the best of both worlds. In Quick edit mode you control the essential editing properties and Photoshop Elements keeps the rest out of your hair.

Using Guided Editing

Guided Editing is the easiest editing mode as Photoshop Elements walks you through the steps.

1 Click on the arrow on the EDIT button and select EDIT Guided from the dropdown list. Note that the Toolbox is empty except for two passive tools – the Zoom tool and the Hand tool.

2 Click on an item in the Guided Editing list. Photoshop Elements will take you step by step to achieve the editing focus you selected.

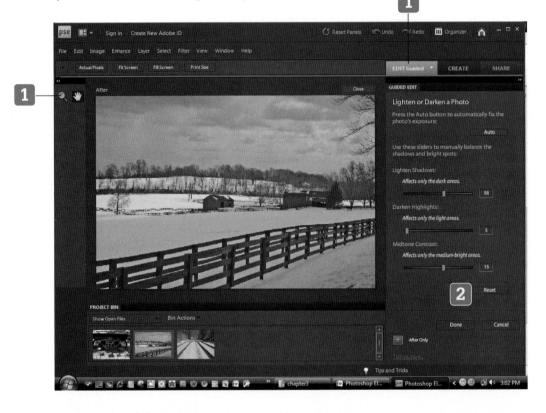

4 Adjusting colour, contrast and lighting

Introduction

Colour is an essential part of any image. Colour appearance though is comprised of more than just the colour itself. The contrast and lighting applied in an image affect colour. Contrast affects how strong or washed out colours may look. Lighting alters colours as well: if a picture is made lighter then all the colour in it will appear lighter as well. Yet changing lighting may change contrast, so coordinating these various aspects really is an art.

Photoshop Elements provides a wealth of tools and methods to manipulate colour, contrast and lighting. The appearance of colours can be altered slightly in just those areas that need a 'touch-up' or as drastically as reversing all the colours in an image.

Briefly, there are the three primary colours – red, green and blue. These are 'additive' primaries: adding them together produces an increasingly light colour. With fully applied red, green and blue the resultant colour is white. Removal of all three primary additives results in black or, in other words, the absence of any colour. The acronym RGB, used in computer application colour settings, literally means Red, Green, Blue, and these three colours are each set anywhere between 0 and 255 inclusive (256 options of each). This produces a range of more than 16 million colours.

A second set of primaries is 'subtractive' colours: cyan, magenta and yellow. These are also referred to as the secondary colours. The additive and subtractive primaries are best understood by looking at the colour wheel. In the colour wheel, each additive is set opposite its complementary subtractive. Red faces cyan, green faces magenta, and blue faces yellow. In practice, the increase or decrease of an additive causes the decrease or increase of its complement.

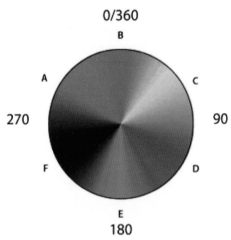

For example, reducing blue increases yellow; reducing yellow increases blue.

In the image of the colour wheel:

A is magenta

B is red

C is yellow

D is green

E is cyan

F is blue.

Knowing how additives and subtractives work is not strictly required to use Photoshop Elements. Being aware of the interplay of colours, however, will help you understand how colours are altered and how to approach their alteration. For example, applying a magenta filter will reduce green to a great degree, applying a cyan filter will also alter green but to a lesser degree.

The RGB approach is centric to a computer and equipment. An alternative approach to colour settings, HSB (Hue, Saturation, Brightness), is considered the more 'human' paradigm. Hue is colour and saturation is the strength of the colour. Hue is measured on a 0–360 scale, which represents a place on the colour wheel. Saturation is measured from 0% to 100%. At 0% saturation, an image is greyscale – no colour is present. Finally, brightness (or lightness) is a measure which runs from total darkness at 0% to full brightness at 100%. At the minimum, an image is completely black; at the maximum it's completely white.

Using Auto Color Correction

Photoshop Elements provides many automatic types of image correction or alteration and these are very handy. You just select the action or method you want and Photoshop Elements does the rest! Here, the colour is altered in just a mouse click to what an internal algorithm concludes is best.

1 Click the Enhance… Auto Color Correction menu item.

2 The photograph is corrected according to built-in methods. In this example the colours appear brighter and fuller.

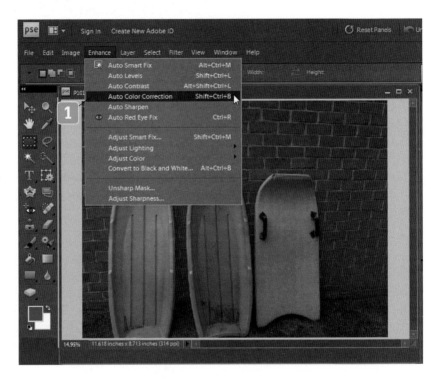

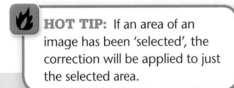

HOT TIP: If an area of an image has been 'selected', the correction will be applied to just the selected area.

SEE ALSO: Creating and using selections is covered in Chapter 5.

Using Auto Contrast

Contrast is used to alter how distinct the different portions of an image are to each other, such as between light and dark areas. Contrast is useful in adding life to a dull-looking image. Auto Contrast instructs Photoshop Elements to alter the contrast automatically.

1 Click the Enhance... Auto Contrast menu item.

2 Contrast is applied and the photograph looks lively. In this example the fence is more prominent against the snow.

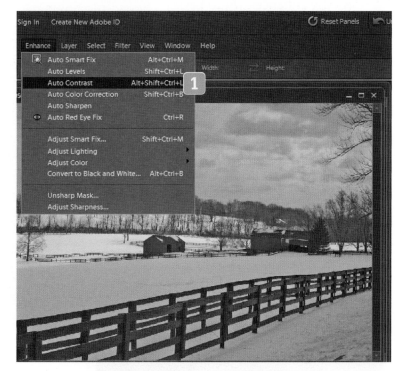

 HOT TIP: If the Auto Contrast feature does not produce a pleasing result, use the manual contrast setting in the Enhance... Adjust Lighting...Brightness/ Contrast menu.

Using Auto Levels

Level is a measure of luminance or brightness. Auto Levels correction will balance the level of a photograph, based on the range of level found in the image.

1 Click the Enhance… Auto Levels menu item.

2 The brightness is changed. In this example the image has been made brighter.

Using Auto Smart Fix

Auto Smart Fix applies the colour, contrast and level corrections all in one operation.

1 Click the Enhance… Auto Smart Fix menu item.

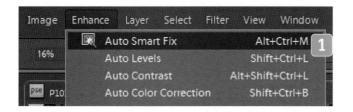

HOT TIP: Using Auto Smart Fix takes care of all corrections in a single mouse click!

Reversing changes

There is much that literally meets the eye when altering an image and you might not like what you see. Photoshop Elements provides the Undo and Revert commands to reverse changes you have made.

1 Undo: A history of changes is kept and using Undo back-steps through them as many times as you click Undo. You can click on the Undo arrow to the right of the menus or click the Edit... Undo menu item. Using the menu, the phrase of the menu item will change based on what step is being undone.

2 Revert: This removes all the changes in one click. Whereas the single step Undo is useful to return to a midpoint in the history of changes, Revert sets the image back to its original state.

3 Redo: This is the opposite of Undo. Clicking Redo steps forward through the history of changes.

Undo, Redo and Revert are enabled only when there is a history of changes. When a photograph is first opened, none of the options is available. After the first change, Revert and Undo are available. Redo becomes available only after an Undo operation – it would reverse the Undo.

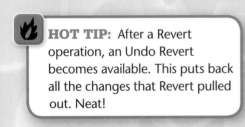

HOT TIP: After a Revert operation, an Undo Revert becomes available. This puts back all the changes that Revert pulled out. Neat!

Selecting the Color Settings

The colour setting tells Photoshop Elements how to treat colours with regard to where they are being viewed: on the computer screen or on paper. For most purposes you will want the setting to be optimised for the computer screen.

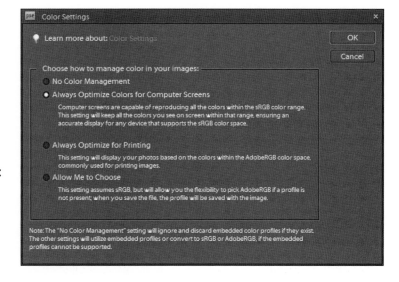

1 Click the Edit... Color Settings menu item to display the Color Settings dialogue box.

There are four options:

- No Color Management: The colours appear as they truly are in the image file.

- Always Optimize Colors for Computer Screens: This is the best all-purpose choice.

- Always Optimize for Printing: This setting is best if you print many of your photographs. This setting involves using colour profiles for different types of equipment (cameras, printers, etc.). This is an advanced feature that can be ignored since Photoshop Elements provides a default colour profile.

- Allow Me to Choose: This setting involves using colour profiles for different types of equipment (cameras, printers, etc.). This is an advanced feature that can be ignored since Photoshop Elements provides a default colour profile.

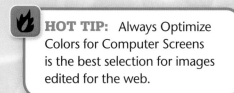

HOT TIP: Always Optimize Colors for Computer Screens is the best selection for images edited for the web.

Working with different image modes

The image mode sets the foundation for the work you will do with colour.

1. Click on the Image… Mode menu item. The choices of mode are available as sub-menu items.

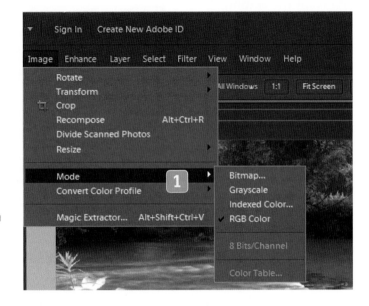

- Bitmap: In bitmap mode images are comprised of black and white pixels. Only two resolutions are available: 72 ppi (pixels per inch – for web work) or 300 dpi (dots per inch – for print work). This provides some limited but interesting effects; however, all is still in black and white (with no greyscale to blend black and white).

- Grayscale: This displays images in 256 levels of grey. This is a good way to leave out the colour but retain contrast.

- Indexed Color: This is a setting used primarily for the web. This provides up to 256 colours. Layers are not supported (see Chapter 7 on layers).

- RGB color: This is the default colour mode. Over 16 million colours are available, providing the richest work environment.

HOT TIP: Working in Grayscale can produce stark but stunning images, especially with images that contain significant contrast of light and dark areas.

Adjusting Brightness and Contrast

The overall brightness and overall contrast of an image are changed via two slider controls.

1 Click the Enhance… Adjust Lighting… Brightness/Contrast menu item. The Brightness/Contrast dialogue box is displayed.

2 The initial value for both brightness and contrast is zero, with the sliders set at the midpoint. Adjusting the image using the sliders provides more or less brightness or contrast, relative to the level of brightness or contrast in the image to begin with. Therefore there are no fixed values to enter or slide to, but any value selected is an offset for that particular image. So what has been brightened in one image may still be darker than the average state of another image.

SEE ALSO: Adjusting the brightness and contrast or adjusting the Lightness (see page 62) can produce similar results.

Adjusting Hue, Saturation and Lightness

1 Clicking the Enhance… Adjust Color… Adjust Hue/Saturation menu item, or using the Ctrl+U keyboard shortcut (in Windows), displays the Hue/Saturation dialogue box.

2 This dialogue is used to alter components of the HSB model. Each individual component alters the image in a different way:

- Hue – adjusts the colour spectrum in the photograph.

- Saturation – adjusts the level of colour. The lowest setting removes all colour, leaving a greyscale image.

- Lightness (brightness) – adjusts how dark or light the image will be. At the lowest setting the image is completely black. At the highest setting the image is completely white.

3 When initially displayed the hue, saturation and lightness values are all set to 0. Also, the choice of which colour(s) to edit is set to Master – which is the complete range of colours in the image.

4 Changing the settings alters the image. The changes affect the complete colour spectrum since the Edit dropdown is on Master.

5 In the Edit dropdown, besides Master, are choices for additive and subtractive primary colours.

6 Selecting Yellows in the Edit dropdown and lowering all three components changes the gold-looking rust part of the caboose to a shade of grey. Note that only yellow is affected. Therefore although the Lightness setting is approaching its minimum value, the overall image stays intact.

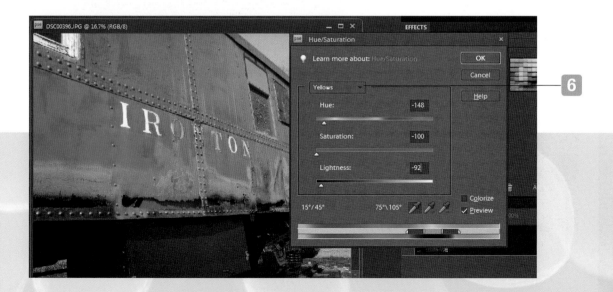

Correcting over- and under-exposure

Shooting photographs is a complex undertaking. You, as the picture taker, decide what or whom the subject is, how close or far to be, which direction to face, and so on. The camera, if on an auto setting, handles shutter speed, shutter size and whether flash is used. On manual settings you make some or all of those decisions. In a nutshell, a lot goes on when the picture is snapped, and the photograph may not turn out to be at all what you thought it would be.

One area that is prone to being out of kilter is the brightness (exposure) of the picture. Whereas brightness can be altered with the Hue/Saturation/Lightness settings, there is another approach that provides more options to correcting the exposure. This is handled by altering shadows, highlights and the tone.

Here is a photograph of a friendly reptile looking with excitement at his supper (peach baby food!). The photograph is under-exposed, it is too dark.

To improve the exposure the shadows, highlights and midtones can be altered.

1 Click the Enhance… Adjust Lighting… Shadows/Highlights menu item to display the Shadows/Highlights dialogue box.

? DID YOU KNOW?

Most digital cameras have a 'bracketing' feature that shoots three pictures at once of the same image, each with a different exposure setting – so you can use the best one.

2 Experiment with various combinations of the shadows, highlights and midtone settings:

- Lighten Shadows – brightens dark areas.

- Darken Highlights – darkens light areas.

These two choices may seem to cancel each other out, but not quite. Lighten Shadows applies brightening to shadowed areas. Darken Highlights works on highlights, the opposite of shadows. So in effect these settings are complementary.

- Midtone Contrast – affects the amount of contrast in the middle tones of the image, but not the image overall.

There is no magic 'fix it all' for these settings. Each image will make best use of its own mix of the settings. Here, the lizard is brighter and there is an increase in contrast. Considering it's a brown lizard on a brown stick the added contrast to midtones is useful. The bowl of baby food looks as appetising as ever.

▶ **SEE ALSO:** Adjusting overall brightness and contrast can help with under-exposure – see page 61.

Adjusting shadows, highlights and midtones

These attributes were used earlier in this chapter in the correcting over- and under-exposure instruction. Here these settings are used in a more general way to balance a photograph that has light and dark areas.

In this photograph the reflection of the trees in the river is pleasing to look at. The contrast and colours are nice, and yet can be enhanced to be more dramatic.

1 Click the Enhance… Adjust Lighting… Shadows/ Highlights menu item to display the Shadows/ Highlights dialogue box. The goal is to adjust shadows and highlights to bring out even more contrast and beauty of the trees' reflection.

2 The Lighten Shadows setting is decreased to bring more clarity to the reflection in the water.

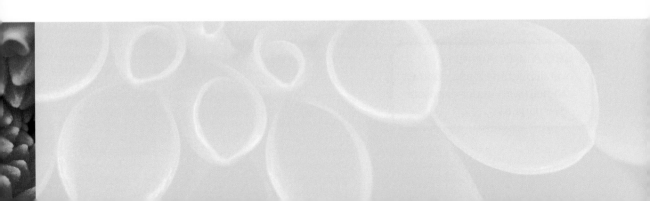

3 The Darken Highlights and Midtone Contrast settings are increased to accentuate the contrast of the trees.

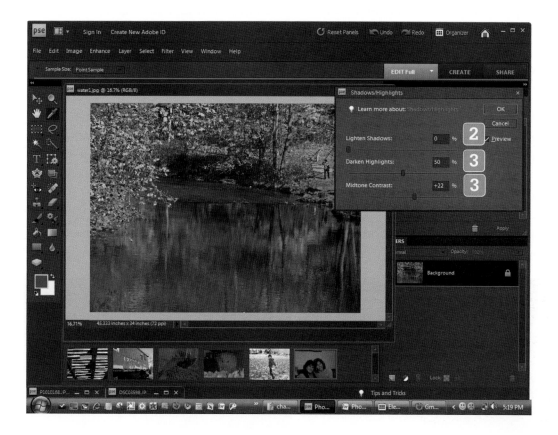

WHAT DOES THIS MEAN?

Contrast: contrast is the difference between light and dark areas in a photograph. The wider the range of light to dark, the higher the contrast.

HOT TIP: To avoid a disparity of light and dark areas, stand further away when shooting a photograph. The photo may come out darker overall, but then it is easier to edit by adjusting the overall brightness.

Removing colour cast

Here is a photo which has an over-abundance of a tan-yellow look to what in reality is lightly shaded porcelain. These steps help correct this off-colour:

1 Click the Enhance... Adjust Color... Remove Color Cast menu item to display the Remove Color Cast dialogue box.

2 This dialogue works by using the 'eyedropper' tool to sample a colour in the photograph. Click on the eyedropper icon in the dialogue, and then click on a part of the image that needs help. A few clicks on the image will cycle through variations, as each click with the eyedropper alters the image based on the colour where you clicked.

Comparing the before and after images, the colour of the sink rim is now a bit less discoloured.

WHAT DOES THIS MEAN?

Colour cast: the unintended appearance in a photograph that non-natural lighting can create. Fluorescent lights tend to cast a green shadow in a photograph, and other lighting can also play havoc.

Adjusting for skin tone

The approach is to use a person's skin tone as a guide to adjust the overall colour balance of the image.

1 Click the Enhance… Adjust Color… Adjust Color for Skin Tone menu item to open the Adjust Color for Skin Tone dialogue box.

2 In the figure the eyedropper is poised over the cheek of the man on the right side of the image. His skin will be sampled when the eyedropper is clicked.

Photoshop Elements alters the photograph to best match the sampled skin tone. The slider switch controls can be used to further alter the tonal balance of the image.

Changing colours

Photoshop Elements provides a powerful set of actions that lets you change colours. You can specify which colour to replace, which colour to replace it with, and of great use – decide a range of colour to apply the change to.

1 With a photograph in the active image area, click the Enhance… Adjust Color… Replace Color menu item to display the Replace Color dialogue box.

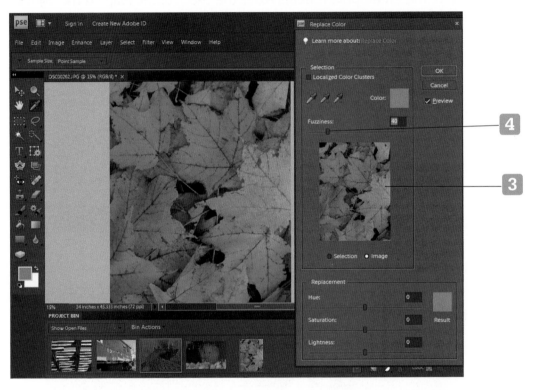

2 Using the eyedropper, click on a place on the image where you want to replace the colour.

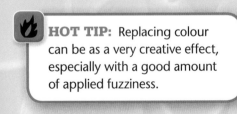

HOT TIP: Replacing colour can be as a very creative effect, especially with a good amount of applied fuzziness.

3 In the Replace Color dialogue, click in the middle section to show the Selection. The image changes to a black and white representation of the colour you clicked with the eyedropper.

4 Using the Fuzziness slider, add or subtract how much of a tonal range around the selected colour to include. This slider is what helps take away the need to click in a very precise spot with the eyedropper. Increasing the Fuzziness allows more of a colour range to be included in the selection.

5 Using the sliders in the Replacement section of the dialogue, determine the desired colour to have the selection change to.

6 Click OK to close the dialogue. The selected area of the photograph displays the new colour.

HOT TIP: You can also click on the Result box and use a colour picker to target the new colour.

Changing colour in large portions of an image

The Paint Bucket tool is helpful to place a colour in a large area of an image.

1 Select the Paint Bucket tool in the Toolbox.

2 Select a foreground colour by clicking on the foreground indicator box and using the colour picker dialogue.

There are several factors that affect how the colour selected to be used with the paint bucket will affect the image.

In this image, a yellow colour is selected, and the paint bucket is used to turn the jacket from red to orange. In the tool options area a number of options are selected:

3 The type of colour change is Soft Light. There are many other choices.

4 The opacity is at 100%.

5 The tolerance is at 40. The tolerance controls how wide a range of image colours will absorb the new colour. The tolerance can be set from 0 (no effect) to 255 (the entire image is painted). With a reasonable tolerance setting, the paint bucket effect will stop at boundaries where the colour changes.

Previewing changes with Color Variations

Here is a dialogue box that displays many options at once. This lets you experiment with a number of different changes with the ease of a few mouse clicks here and there.

1 Click the Enhance… Adjust Color… Color Variations menu item to display the Color Variations dialogue box.

2 Select Midtones, Shadows, Highlights or Saturation on the left side of the dialogue.

3 Adjust the Intensity using the slider switch. This creates various thumbnail options in the bottom part of the dialogue.

4 Click on one of the thumbnails and the 'After' image in the upper right of the dialogue displays the selected change.

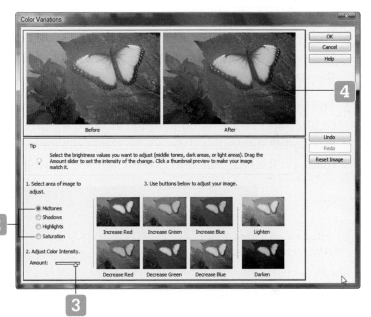

HOT TIP: The Color Variations dialogue has Undo, Redo and Reset buttons. Each time you select a variation, it's applied to the previous variation. This becomes a history of variations and you can move forward and back through them with Undo and Redo.

DID YOU KNOW?

The effects created by settings such as 'Increase Red' or 'Decrease Green' can also be made by using photo filters – in the Filter…Adjustments… Photo Filter menu.

DID YOU KNOW?

Although there are slider controls to adjust red, green and blue these do not add or subtract these colours. Instead, the sliders are setting how much of the original colours are used to alter the equivalent part of the grey shading in the image. The best way to get familiar with how this works is to experiment with a variety of images that are centric around different colours.

Eliminating colour

When colour is removed, a black and white, or greyscale, image is the result. Often used as an artful technique, black and white images make clear the contrast of subjects in the image. There are three ways to remove colour:

1 In various dialogue boxes that are used to affect colour, Saturation has been one of the components that can be altered. Bringing Saturation down to the minimal amount removes colour.

2 The Enhance… Adjust Color… Remove Color menu item instantly removes colour, leaving a greyscale image behind. The keyboard shortcut, Shift+Ctrl+U, performs the same action.

3 The third method gives you control over colour removal. Use the Enhance… Convert to Black and White menu item to display the Convert to Black and White dialogue box. In the dialogue a style is selected in the lower left, and then adjustments can be made on the red, blue and green channels, as well as to the overall contrast.

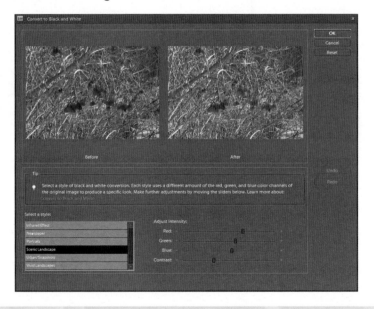

 HOT TIP: The keyboard shortcut Shift+Ctrl+U also instantly removes colour to leave a greyscale image.

 HOT TIP: Grayscale is not the same as Black and White. With Grayscale there are gradations of shades between black and white. Simple Black and White images have just those two colours.

5 Creating and using selections

Introduction

Selections are designated editable areas of an image. When a selection is put into an image, changes can be made on just the selected area.

There are many types of manipulation that can be done with selections. This chapter is about how to create selections. Making use of selected areas is explored throughout the rest of the book.

Selecting an area with the Rectangular Selection tool

The basic selection is a rectangular area.

1 Right-click on the selection tool in the Toolbox. The two types of selection tools are there for the choosing. Click on the Rectangular Marquee Tool.

2 The mouse pointer changes to a cross. Click on the image in a desired corner of where the selection will go. Hold down the mouse button and draw the rectangle over the area of the photograph.

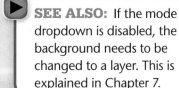 **DID YOU KNOW?**

Although the terminology is about selecting and selections, the tools are named as marquees. When a selection is drawn onto a photograph it looks like a marquee. Therefore selection and marquee are interchangeable terms.

SEE ALSO: If the mode dropdown is disabled, the background needs to be changed to a layer. This is explained in Chapter 7.

Selecting an area with the Elliptical Selection tool

Using an elliptical tool lets you draw selections that are ovals or circles.

1 Right-click on the selection tool in the Toolbox. The two types of selection tools are there for the choosing. Click on the Elliptical Marquee tool.

As with the Rectangular Marquee tool, the Elliptical Marquee tool has three modes: Normal, Fixed Aspect Ratio and Fixed Size. Normal lets you draw an oval shape. Fixed Aspect Ratio forces the marquee to a circle, as shown here.

Adding to a selection

While a marquee is displayed on an image, you can apply another marquee and have the two join together.

1 Draw the first selection.

2 While holding down the Shift key, draw another selection. Make sure it touches the boundary of the first selection, or even have it start from within the boundary of the first selection.

? DID YOU KNOW?

You can do this repeatedly, and can mix and match the rectangular and elliptical marquee shapes.

Setting the Feather

The Feather is the size, in pixels, of the edge of the selection marquee. At a low setting, such as 0 or 1 pixels, the selection will have a hard edge. Increasing the Feather produces a larger edge. The edge therefore has enough pixels to create a smooth transition around the marquee boundary. The effect of this is evident when the selection is put to use.

1 Select the Elliptical Marquee Tool. In the tool options area set the Feather to 0px (pixels).

2 Draw a selection in the image.

3 Click the Edit… Copy menu item to place the selection on the clipboard.

4 Create a new file. Use the File… New… Blank File to open the New dialogue.

5 The defaults presented in the New dialogue are fine. Just click the OK button to create a blank image.

? DID YOU KNOW?

You can change the size of the Feather after drawing the selection by using the Select…Feather menu.

6 Click the Edit... Paste menu item. The selection is pasted into the new blank image.

The edge of the pasted selection is abrupt, since the Feather was set for 0 pixels. Next, repeat the process, but use a Feather of 25 pixels.

7 Bring the original image into the active image area by double-clicking it in the Bin.

8 Click Undo to remove the marquee.

9 In the tool options, set the Feather to 25px.

10 Repeat drawing a selection, copying it, creating a new blank image and pasting the selection. Now the pasted selection is softer around the edges.

Creating freeform selections

The rectangular and elliptical selections are easy to draw onto an image, but often the desired focus areas of an image are not of such perfect proportions. A set of tools lets you select in a number of ways that will capture the portion of the image you need. The first of these is the Lasso tool.

1 Right-click on the Lasso Tool and select the Lasso Tool.

2 Freeform draw around an area of the image. While doing so the mouse pointer looks like a lasso.

3 Complete drawing the marquee by joining the freeform line with the beginning. Release the mouse button. The selection is now complete and will be a self-contained area.

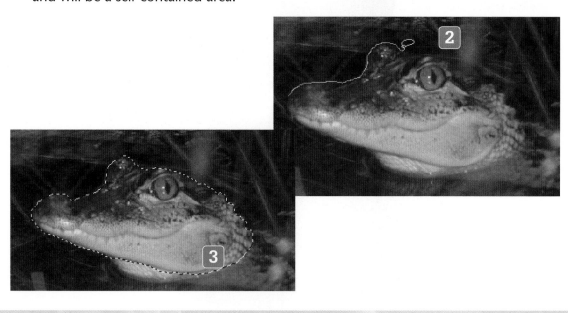

Using the Polygonal Lasso tool to create shaped selections

The Polygonal Lasso tool creates a line-to-line selection. The process is two-step. You draw a line, then click the mouse to end that line and start to draw the next line, directly from where the last one ended. In this manner the selection is continuous but the shape of the selection is the result of the individual lines and the angle of each one. Each line is a straight line but at each stop and start point the new line goes in the direction you draw.

1 Right-click on the Lasso Tool and select the Polygonal Lasso Tool.

2 Start drawing around the subject. Each time you need to draw in a different direction, click the mouse and then draw some more.

3 When the selection is drawn back to where it started, double-click the mouse to end the process. The image retains the completed selection.

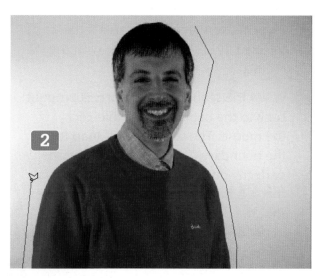

Creating irregular shaped selections with the Magnetic Lasso tool

The Magnetic Lasso tool works by snapping to a boundary that you define with a series of mouse clicks.

1 Right-click on the Lasso Tool and select the Magnetic Lasso Tool.

2 Place markers around the area to be selected by clicking around it with the mouse.

3 When the sequence of markers is brought back to the beginning, double-click the mouse. The selection will snap to the boundary. The selection can be so perfectly on the area set by the markers that it is hard to see. In the second screen shot the flower is selected, although it might be hard to tell since the selection is perfectly shaped to the flower.

Fast selecting with the Magic Wand

In a rush? Use the Magic Wand to make the selection.

1 Click on the Magic Wand Tool in the Toolbox.

2 Draw a quick line over the area to be selected. No need to try to draw around the boundaries: the Magic Wand will figure it out.

? DID YOU KNOW?

The tolerance setting, in the tool options area, controls how sensitive the Magic Wand is to boundaries found in the image. The higher the tolerance, the less detailed the selection will be. At a high enough tolerance the entire image will be selected (the marquee goes around the edge of the image).

Painting a selection

All the selection tools thus far have been focused on defining the selection around boundaries. Sometimes this is not necessary. Perhaps all you need is a sample from an image area. The Selection Brush Tool is the tool of choice for this chore. The Selection Brush Tool creates a selection that has nothing to do with boundaries. It simply creates the selection where you paint it on the image.

1 Choose the Selection Brush Tool from the Toolbox.

2 Using the mouse, paint in a desired area of the photograph. In this example, a selection has been made of the bird's beak. The colour of the beak was the desired part of the image, not the beak itself.

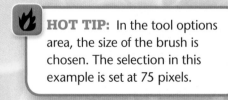

HOT TIP: In the tool options area, the size of the brush is chosen. The selection in this example is set at 75 pixels.

Saving a selection

Creating a selection can be tedious and time-consuming. If the selection is one that can be used again – whether in the same photograph or a different one – then saving it is a great idea.

1 Create the selection in the image.

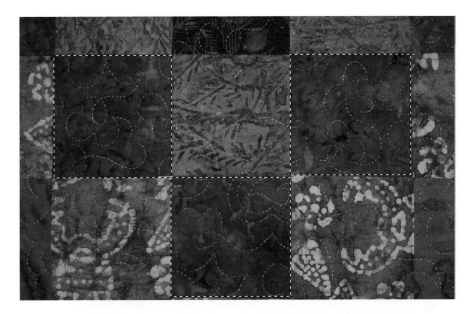

2 Click the Select… Save Selection menu item to display the Save Selection dialogue box. In the dialogue enter a name for the selection and click the OK button.

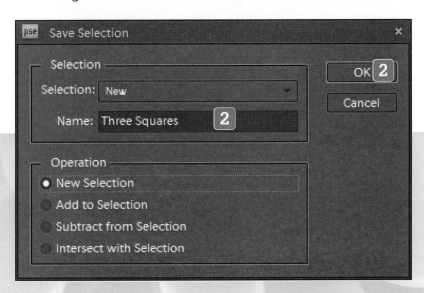

Inverting selections

When an area is selected in an image any changes are applied to the selection. What if you need to apply changes to the area that is not selected?

Easy! In the Select menu is an item to invert the selection. The selection in the image will swap with the rest of the image.

1 Create your selection.

2 Click on the Select… Inverse menu item.

3 The appearance might seem as if nothing has been inverted but the image now has a marquee around its edge.

SEE ALSO: After the painstaking work of making multiple selections, save them! See page 87.

4 The ducks still have marquees but now they serve to isolate the ducks from the selection. This becomes evident when a change is applied. Here, colour has been removed from the image, but the ducks are unaffected.

3

4

HOT TIP: Drawing a marquee around the subject, and then inverting the selection, is the best way to select everything but the subject.

Loading a selection

When you need to reuse a selection, if there is a saved selection that's associated with the image in the active image area, then the Load Selection menu item will be enabled.

1 Click on Select... Load Selection to display the Load Selection dialogue.

2 If there is just one selection associated with the image, simply click the OK button. If there is more than one selection associated with the image, first choose the desired selection from the dropdown list.

3 Click the OK button. The selection will snap into the place in the image where it was saved from.

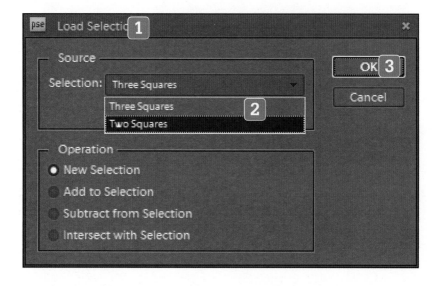

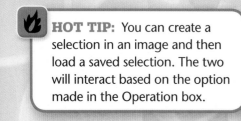

HOT TIP: You can create a selection in an image and then load a saved selection. The two will interact based on the option made in the Operation box.

6 Cropping, resizing, rotating, flipping and zooming

Introduction

Cropping a photograph is the action of removing a portion and just leaving the desired part of the image intact. Essentially cropping is like taking a pair of scissors and cutting a photograph down to a smaller size.

The other tasks in this chapter – resizing, rotating and flipping – are just as they sound. Resizing is usually used to make an image smaller. Making an image larger will take away its clarity, although a slight enlargement will not do any harm. Rotating is necessary for when you turned the camera sideways to take a shot and hence the photograph appears to be lying on its side.

Flipping is not the same as rotating. Rotation occurs by turning the image. Flipping is like viewing the image in a mirror, or as if you have turned it over and now see it through its back. Setting the zoom is simply increasing or decreasing magnification – used often to get in close for touch-up work, such as at the pixel level.

Plain old cropping

Sometimes a golden moment presents itself and you run for the camera and click away. Come what may, with digital cameras you can shoot to your heart's content, or at least until the batteries run out. And while you catch those beautiful shots, you can also get some annoying or distracting items in the photograph.

This is what cropping is for. Cut out the clutter and keep the best. Here is a photograph of a rainbow, and it was one of those moments when you have minutes, perhaps only seconds, to catch the beauty, along with the undesirable spotlights at the top left.

Those spotlights must be removed.

1. Click on the Crop tool in the Toolbox.

2. Drag the mouse in the image to create a line between what to keep and what to discard. The mouse pointer looks like the Crop tool while doing this.

3. When the mouse button is released a preview of what the image will look like appears. Just below it are commit and cancel icons.

4. Clicking the commit icon (the tick mark) displays the updated image.

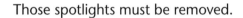

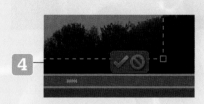

Cropping to a preset size

When the Crop tool is active, an Aspect Ratio dropdown is enabled in the tool options area.

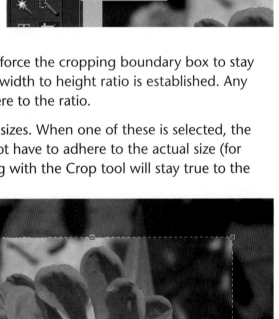

The options are:

1 No Restriction: The cropping tool draws rectangular shapes freely in the image.

2 Use Photo Ratio: With this choice, the width and height options are used. The width and height settings do not strictly force the cropping boundary box to stay at those exact measurements. Instead, a width to height ratio is established. Any drawing with the cropping tool will adhere to the ratio.

3 The rest: All the other options are preset sizes. When one of these is selected, the width and height ratio is fixed. You do not have to adhere to the actual size (for example, 4 × 6 in), however, any drawing with the Crop tool will stay true to the ratio, as in this example of keeping to a 4 × 6 aspect.

Clicking the tick mark commits the crop (although there is always the Undo to fall back on).

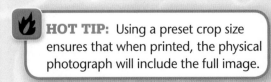

HOT TIP: Using a preset crop size ensures that when printed, the physical photograph will include the full image.

Moving, rotating and resizing the cropping box

When an area is in the stage of being cropped, the box can be moved, rotated or resized.

1. In the middle of the crop box is a handle. Clicking on it and holding down the mouse button lets you move the box to another part of the image.

2. Outside of the box is a handle in the shape of two opposed arrows. Clicking on this and holding down the mouse button lets you rotate the box.

3. Around the box, in the corners and at the midpoints of the sides, are handles that are used to resize the box.

? DID YOU KNOW?

Rotating the cropping box only changes the dimensions of the cropping action. The image within the cropping box is not rotated.

Cropping to a selection

1 An alternative way to crop is to first put a selection into the image, using one of the selection tools. Then to complete the operation click the Image... Crop menu item.

2 When the selection is not rectangular, the cropping operation will still crop to a rectangular shape, padded by 50 pixels where the non-rectangular selection was situated.

? DID YOU KNOW?

Cropping an image with multiple selections results in a cropped image that is as large as the range of selections.

Cookie Cutter cropping

1. In the Toolbox is a tool called the Cookie Cutter. When this tool is selected, a dropdown palette of shapes is enabled in the tool options area.

2. This tool skips the preview step and goes right to display the cut shape as a new image. You still can choose to commit or cancel the operation.

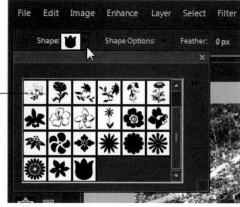

 HOT TIP: In the Shapes palette, click on the small double black arrow and many shape categories appear in a list – select one and the palette updates to the shapes of the selected category.

Resizing an image with the Image Size dialogue

For precise image resizing the Image Size dialogue provides full control.

1 Click the Image... Resize... Image Size menu item. The dialogue is displayed.

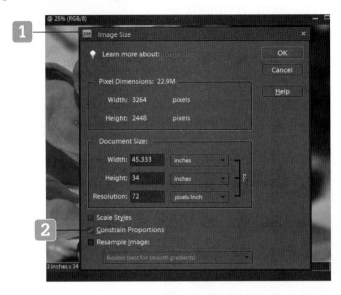

2 Initially the Document Size can be changed. Putting a new width or height and clicking the OK button will resize the image. Near the bottom left of the dialogue the Constrain Proportions option is ticked (the default). This forces the width and height to maintain a constant ratio – probably what you want, unless you purposely wish to distort the image.

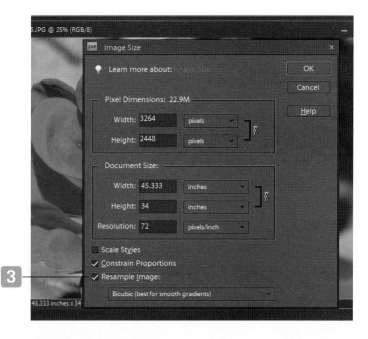

3 Ticking the Resample Image option in the lower left of the dialogue enables the Pixel Dimensions. Now the image can be resized by changing Document Size or the Pixel Dimensions.

4 An easy way to resize an image is to do so by a percentage. In the dropdowns, percent is one of the choices. Here, the image starts at 100% width and height. So for a quick resize to half the size, simply put the percentage at 50%.

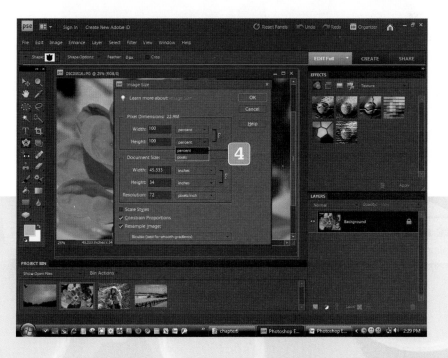

Resizing an image using the Scale feature

The other resizing method is to resize visually using handles around the image.

1 Click the Image… Resize… Scale menu item.

2 You may be presented with a suggestion to apply this type of change to a layer. If so, click the OK button.

3 The image now has handles around the edges, as well as the commit and cancel icons. Click on a handle, hold down the mouse button and drag to resize the image. When the image appears to be at the desired size, release the mouse button. Then commit or cancel the change.

SEE ALSO: Layers are explained in Chapter 7.

Rotating to a preset angle

Rotating an image may be necessary if the camera was held sideways to shoot the picture. For other images, rotating offers a different view, perhaps for an artistic effect.

With a photograph open in the active image area:

1 Click the Image… Rotate menu item. Several choices are presented.

2 Select a rotation method. Here, the image is rotated 180 degrees.

? DID YOU KNOW?

Rotation is based on the 360 degrees of a circle. A 180-degree rotation turns an image upside down.

Custom rotating

1 If you select Custom, the Rotate Canvas dialogue box is displayed. In this dialogue you enter an angle (in degrees from 0 through 360) and select the direction.

2 Here, the photograph has been rotated 45 degrees to the right.

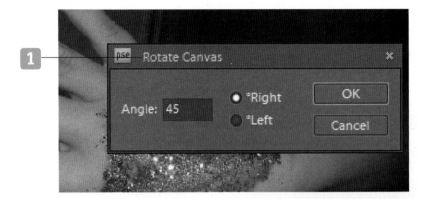

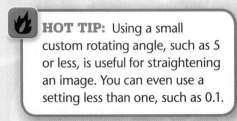

HOT TIP: Using a small custom rotating angle, such as 5 or less, is useful for straightening an image. You can even use a setting less than one, such as 0.1.

Flipping the image

Flipping is similar to viewing an image in a mirror. Whereas rotating is analogous to movement around a clock, flipping is like turning an image over and viewing it from the other side.

1 The flipping options are horizontal and vertical, and they are found in the Image... Rotate menu choices.

2 Here is how the hands photograph appears when flipped vertically.

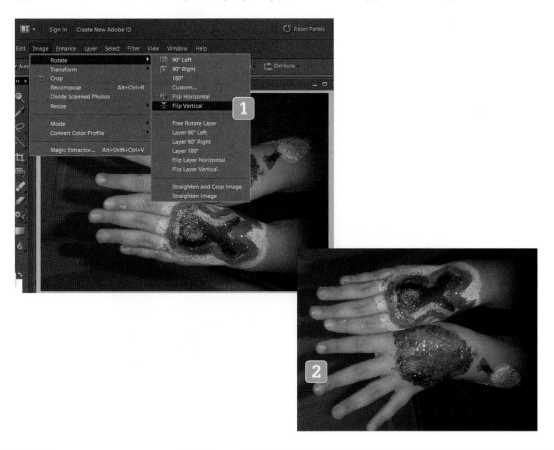

Resizing the canvas

An image sits on a canvas. The canvas is not always seen, depending on how much of the photograph is present in the active image area. If the photograph is larger than the active image area then the canvas is not seen. When zooming out (making the image smaller) the canvas will appear around the image. Although editing is done primarily on the photograph, there is the facility to make changes to the canvas.

1 If necessary change the zoom out so the canvas is visible around the image.

2 Click the Image… Resize… Canvas Size menu item to display the Canvas Size dialogue box.

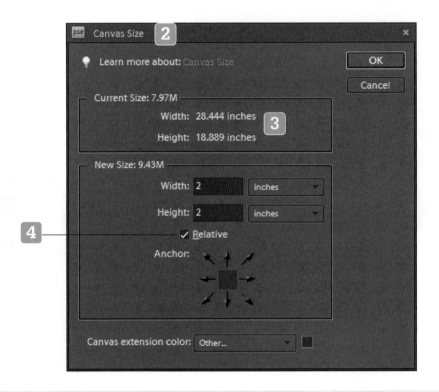

3 In this dialogue there is an area that reports the current canvas size and an area to set the new size. The new size can be set with fixed values, or relative to the current values.

4 To use the relative method, check the Relative tickbox. New width and height amounts are entered, and dropdowns provide a choice of measurement type (percent, inches, pixels, centimeters, etc.).

5 At the bottom of the dialogue is a dropdown to select a colour for the canvas. In this operation any colour selected here will apply to the extended part of the canvas, not the entire canvas. (Conversely, when creating a new image the colour of the whole canvas is selected.) Here, a deep red colour has been selected, and the colour extends out 2 inches.

By the way, the view of the image is not at 100%, it is zoomed out. The canvas extension of 2 inches is created as 1 inch on each side. It looks much smaller but a glance at the ruler bears out the truth. The image as viewed here is 20% of its real size.

Zooming

Just as the zoom lens on your camera lets you get closer to or further away from the subject, when editing the same function is necessary. Touch-up work often requires focusing on a portion of a photograph, and getting very close up to it as well. Some editing chores have to be done on a pixel by pixel basis, and that means zooming way in – much more so than what your camera can do.

Zooming back out of course is necessary to view the whole picture. So a good amount of back and forth could be on the plate for certain editing needs. Photoshop Elements provides ease when zooming.

1. Selecting the Zoom tool in the Toolbox displays the Zoom tool options above the image. To the left are zoom in and zoom out buttons (the + and – buttons). Click on one and then move the mouse over the image. The mouse pointer changes to a magnifying glass. Click on the image to apply the zoom.

2. Zoom can be selected as a percentage. 100% is the true size of the image. Increasing the number zooms in and decreasing the number zooms out. When you click on the percentage box a slider control opens beneath it and can be used to slide to a percentage.

? DID YOU KNOW?

Since 100% is the true image size, and most images are larger than can fully be seen in their entirety, images are often viewed at a smaller percentage of zoom so the whole image can be seen.

3 Clicking on the 1:1 button instantly reverts the image to 100% – the true image size.

4 The percentage can be set to many thousands above the true size. Here is an example of using the zoom at 1200% – to work at the pixel level.

5 The Navigator provides another way to zoom in and out. The Navigator is a small window that can stay open and be moved out of the way of the image. In the Navigator is a slider to control the zoom.

6 Click the Window… Navigator menu item. The Navigator is displayed.

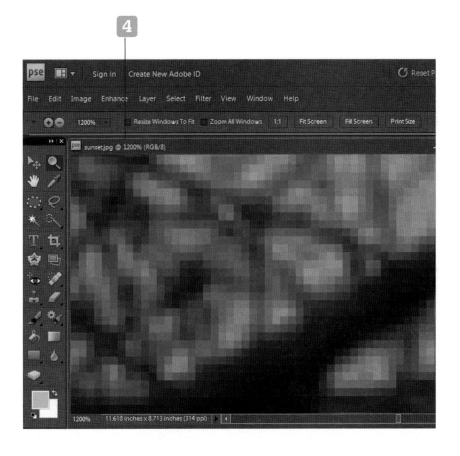

 HOT TIP: The Navigator has a red box that sits on top of the image preview. The box shows which part of the image is displayed in the active image area. You can drag the box around and the image will follow along to display the area you moved the box to.

7 Layers

Changing the background to a layer

The effects and changes that can be applied to the background are limited. As you become familiar with what layers offer, you may want to apply these to the background. The trick then is to change the background to a layer.

1. Right-click on the background in the Layers palette.
2. In the context menu select Layer From Background.

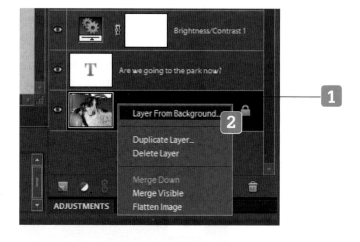

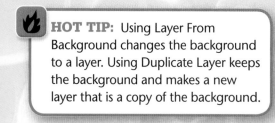

HOT TIP: Using Layer From Background changes the background to a layer. Using Duplicate Layer keeps the background and makes a new layer that is a copy of the background.

112

Adding an image (shape) layer

A shape (or image) layer is really just the basic layer, and is usually referred to as a layer – plain and simple. When this type of layer is added, you can use it to add shapes to the overall image, or a part of or the whole of another photograph.

1 Click on the Create a New Layer button.

   A new layer is now shown in the Layers palette, here simply named Layer 1.

   On this type of layer visual elements are added: shapes, other images, and so on. Here, we will add a shape, a heart.

2 With the layer selected in the Layers palette, click on the Custom Shape tool in the Toolbox.

3 Draw the shape where desired.

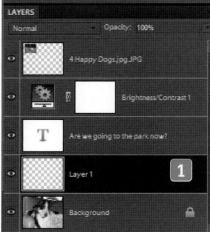

HOT TIP: Before drawing a shape don't forget to select a colour, by clicking Window… Color Swatches, or just double-clicking the forecolour box.

Adding an adjustment layer

Adjustment layers affect image layers. There are a number of adjustment types. The selected adjustment type alters just the layers that are below it.

1 Click the Create Adjustment Layer button in the Layers palette. A context menu appears and an adjustment layer type is selected. The names of the types are pretty clear about what they can adjust.

In this example, a Photo Filter adjustment type is selected. This action displays the appropriate dialogue for the Photo Filter selection.

2 The adjustment filter is now in the layer stack. If/when a change to the Photo Filter settings (or the settings for whatever type of adjustment layer it is) is required, double-click the layer thumbnail. There are two thumbnails in the adjustment layer: the layer thumbnail on the left and the layer mask thumbnail on the right.

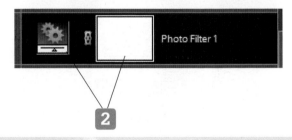

? DID YOU KNOW?

Each type of adjustment layer has its own settings and applies its own type of adjustment. The adjustments affect the layers beneath the adjustment layer. The layers can change position, explained further in the chapter. This action changes which image layers are affected by which adjustment layers.

Adding a fill layer

Fill layers are a subset of the adjustment layers. There are three fill layers:

1 Solid Color: You select a colour and the colour blankets all the layers beneath the fill layer.

2 Gradient: You select a gradient and can make several selections about how the gradient appears.

3 Pattern: A pattern is selected for the fill.

This shows the image with a gradient fill. Note the placement of the layer. The gradient affects the dog, heart and type – these are layers that are beneath the gradient layer. The small image inset in the upper left is not affected by the gradient – it is situated as the top layer.

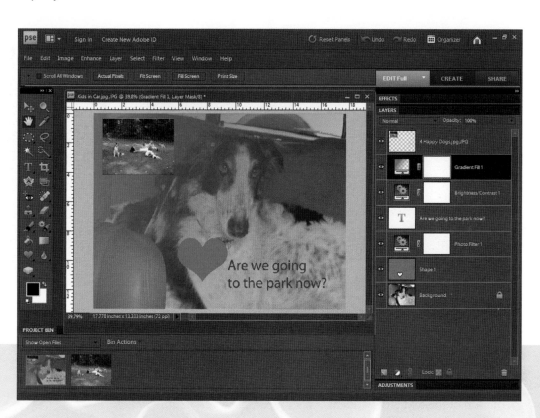

Adding a type (text) layer

A type (text) layer is added automatically when the Type tool is used. Start typing and the layer is there. In fact you may end up with several layers of text if you broke up your text entry with other activities. Later in this chapter are instructions on how to merge layers. That might be a desired action if the text came out on several layers.

1 Select the Type tool from the Toolbox. Select any options from the tool options area. For text, you can select the font type, size and other attributes.

2 Click in the active image area and type away! A type layer is created.

3 If/when you need to edit the text or its attributes, double-click the text layer thumbnail. This highlights the text and brings the Type tool options into the tool options area. Make changes and they are saved in the layer.

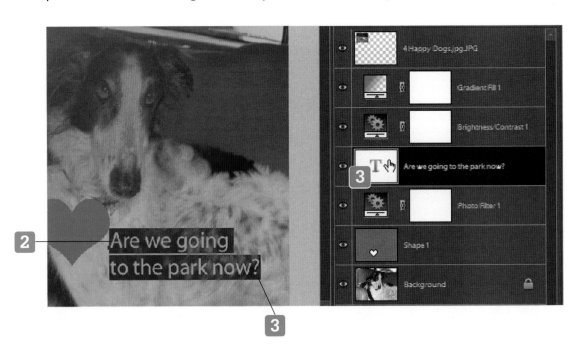

? DID YOU KNOW?

The size of the text is dependent on the zoom setting of the image. Therefore a large font, such as 72 point, can appear tiny when typing it in.

Renaming a layer

Photoshop Elements provides all new layers with a name – a functional name such as Layer1, Shape2, and so on. This is adequate if a handful of layers is being used. With more sophistication – and therefore more layers – the ability to rename the layers is helpful. You can name them with distinctive monikers such as 'The Blue Tree', or 'Layer to control contrast of the trees'.

1 Simply right-click on the layer name. A context menu appears; one choice is Rename a Layer. When clicked a dialogue box opens and the name can be changed in the dialogue.

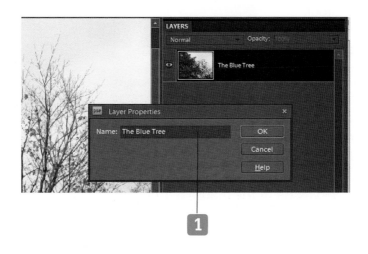

1

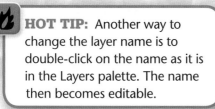
HOT TIP: Another way to change the layer name is to double-click on the name as it is in the Layers palette. The name then becomes editable.

Selecting, moving and resizing content on a layer

The biggest advantage of using layers is that you can make changes to a piece or portion of an image and not disturb anything on the other layers. Adjustment layers of course do affect image layers, but that is passive. If you remove the adjustment layer, the image layer no longer has the enhancement delivered through the adjustment. Here is how one part of an image, on its own layer, can be moved and resized while the rest sits blissfully by.

1 In the Layers palette, click on an image layer.

2 In the active image area, click on the Move tool. This puts a marquee and handles around the section of image that is on that layer.

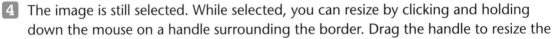

3 Move the mouse to the centre of the image. Click and hold down the mouse button. Drag the image to another location and let go of the mouse button.

4 The image is still selected. While selected, you can resize by clicking and holding down the mouse on a handle surrounding the border. Drag the handle to resize the image. When you let go of the mouse, the commit and cancel icons appear. Select one.

HOT TIP: You can rotate the image by using the rotate handle at the bottom of the image.

Creating a layer from a selection

A handy technique is to turn a selection into a layer. This is useful for duplicating part of an image.

1 In an image, select a desired element. In this example, the Magic Wand tool is used to select a zebra.

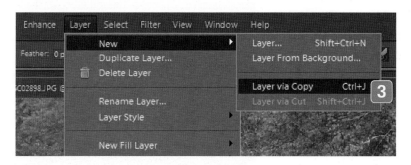

2 Copy the image by clicking the Edit… Copy menu item.

3 Click the Layer… New… Layer via Copy menu item. This creates a new layer that contains a copy of the selection.

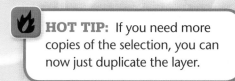

HOT TIP: If you need more copies of the selection, you can now just duplicate the layer.

Duplicating a layer

Duplicating a layer provides an easy way to add more images. Take one tree on a layer, duplicate the layer a few times, then one by one, work with a single layer and tree to move and resize the individual tree – and finally you have a forest!

This example follows the previous task of creating a layer from a selection. There is now a layer with just a zebra on it.

1 Right-click on the layer and select Duplicate Layer from the context menu.

The Duplicate Layer dialogue box is displayed and a name can be given for the new layer (here Zebra2).

2 Working with one of the identical layers, select the layer and then select the Move tool.

3 Use the Move tool to move and resize the duplicated zebra.

4 Taking it a step further, you could use the handles around the zebra to turn the zebra around. Now the overall image does not look as if a zebra was duplicated.

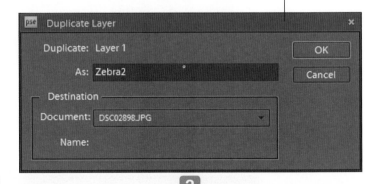

 HOT TIP: You can duplicate many layers at once. Select more than one layer then right-click on one of them and select Duplicate Layer. The number of layers you selected is the number of layers that are duplicated.

Reordering layers

With a number of layers making up the full image, options are available for how to stack the layers. Some layers will block out others; some add a new feature that appears correct in placement and therefore doesn't detract from the overall image. Adjustment layers alter only the layers underneath. So there are many variations that reordering the layer stack will create.

1 Take an image and work up a number of layers. No need to create a super work of art here. Just have at least a couple of image layers and at least a couple of adjustment layers.

2 Click on a layer and hold down the mouse button. Drag the layer up or down, whatever the case might be. Release the mouse button.

With the zebra example, the brightness/contrast and Photo Filter adjustment layers affect just the background. One of the zebras is treated with the adjustment. The other two zebras are on layers higher up in the stack.

? DID YOU KNOW?
The background layer must stay on the bottom of the layer stack.

Linking layers

Layers can be grouped. This provides the advantage of keeping associated layers attached so that changes will affect the linked layers together.

1 Click on a layer to select it.

2 Holding down the Ctrl key, click on one or more other layers.

3 Right-click on a selected layer and click on the Link Layers option in the context menu.

The individual layers are now treated as one. In this example, the two zebras are linked and the marquee now encases them together.

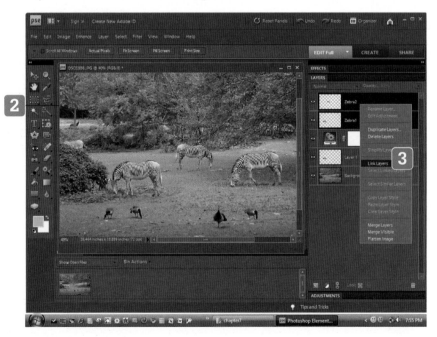

Any changes will be applied to the joined layers as if they were a single layer.

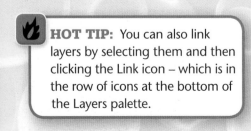

HOT TIP: You can also link layers by selecting them and then clicking the Link icon – which is in the row of icons at the bottom of the Layers palette.

Hiding and showing layers

The ability to isolate a layer is helpful when enhancements are to be made to just the content on that one layer. Conversely there are times when hiding some layers and letting others stay visible is desirable. Here is how to do both.

1 In the Layers palette, each layer has an eye icon to the left. These toggle the visibility of the layer. Clicking on a layer's eye initially makes the layer invisible.

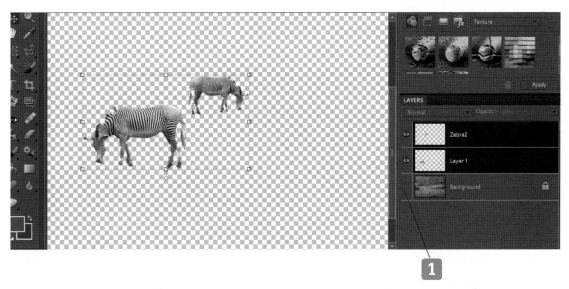

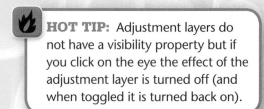

Note that when the layer is invisible the eye icon is not visible either. In this example the background layer is not visible, just the two zebras are seen.

2 To isolate one layer to be visible and all other layers invisible, either click the eye icon of each layer that should be invisible (the tedious method), or better – right-click on the eye of the layer you want to be visible by itself. A choice context menu appears. The two choices are complementary. Hide the layer, or leave the layer visible and hide every other layer.

HOT TIP: Adjustment layers do not have a visibility property but if you click on the eye the effect of the adjustment layer is turned off (and when toggled it is turned back on).

Selecting the blend mode

Layers are stacked and therefore there is an order to how the overall image appears. Adjustment layers offer enhancements and effects that affect the overall image depending on their settings and where they are in the stack. Another method of controlling the overall image is by using blends.

Blends are settings of how the image layers will affect each other (not the adjustment layers). Normally one layer will cover up the next assuming the upper layer is set at 100% opacity. This is what happens when the blend mode is 'Normal'.

However, there are many blend modes and they can be put to use to alter the overall image. Blends are selected from a dropdown list just above the layers.

Each layer can have its own selection of blend mode. This creates numerous possibilities for creative work.

 HOT TIP: Experiment with the blend modes. There are many variations and the best way to become familiar with them is to try them out – on different layers, with different modes and with ample time to get elbow deep into the feature.

Selecting the opacity

Opacity is a measure of how solid an image element appears. At 100% opacity, the element is opaque – it has no transparency and anything underneath will not be seen. At 0% opacity, the element is completely transparent and anything underneath is seen in its entirety. Adjusting opacity provides more options of what artistic technique to apply to the overall image.

Opacity is set per layer. There is a slider just above the layers and the selected layer(s) receives the change in opacity. This example shows three boxes – blue, green and red. They are offset from each other but with some overlap. The layer stacking order, top to bottom, is blue, green and red. Blue and green are set at 50% opacity. Red is at 100%. The blue and green layers show a blending effect with each other and the red layer, producing other hues. Red is left at 100% since it is the bottom layer. Nothing is underneath the red layer that could be rendered unseen.

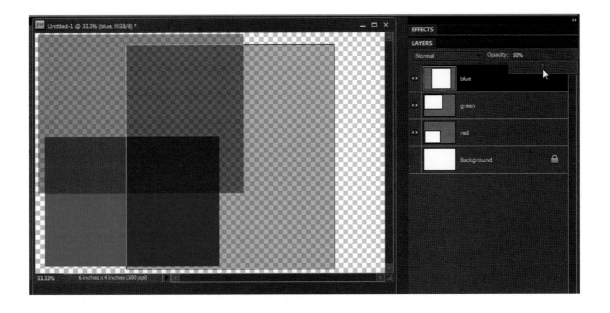

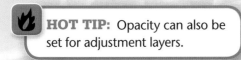 **HOT TIP:** Opacity can also be set for adjustment layers.

8 Working with shapes

Introduction

Besides managing and editing photographs, Photoshop Elements has a robust set of tools and methods for working with shapes. With rectangular, elliptical and a slew of custom shapes, the palette of your imagination can make image magic. There are many ways to alter, resize, line up, change colour and do more with shapes. Throw using multiple layers into the mix and you can create 3-D images.

Creating a new image

Underneath any image is the canvas. When you open an existing image file the canvas is there but not noticeable. With a new image though, the canvas has to be created. The task of creating a new image is synonymous with creating a canvas or with creating the background. The 'blank' that shapes or images are placed upon might be called the background or the canvas. (The terms are interchangeable.) So the first step in creating any new image is to create the canvas.

1 Click the File… New… Blank File menu item to display the New dialogue box.

2 In the New dialogue, enter a name for the new work of art. Size also is selected here. There is a dropdown with standard preset sizes, such as 640 × 480 pixels to match the minimum common monitor size (this is called the Web preset). The resolution is also selected or left at the default. Selecting a preset size and resolution does not lock you in. You can change the width, height and resolution, and colour mode can be selected as well.

3 Of a bit more pertinence is the background colour of the canvas. It often is left at the White default, but there are other options. The canvas can be set to the current background colour, or can be left transparent.

4 When all the desired attributes are selected or entered, click the OK button.

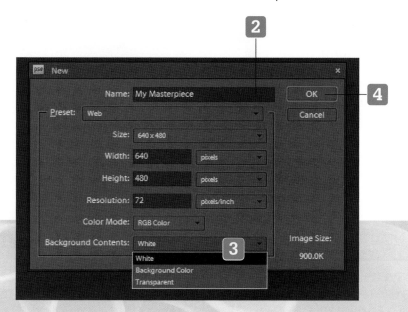

Selecting the colour for a new shape

A shape has size and colour. The colour can be selected before the shape is drawn by changing the foreground colour, or the colour can be changed after the shape is drawn on the canvas.

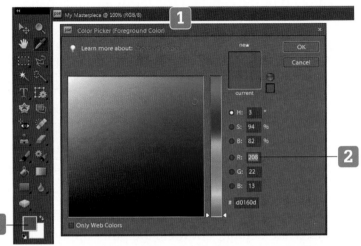

1 Click on the foreground colour box to open the Select foreground colour dialogue. The current foreground colour is displayed in the dialogue.

2 Use the hue and luminance controls to select a new colour, or enter values in the HSB, RGB, or hex # boxes. The colour box towards the upper right of the dialogue displays the new colour being selected (on top) and the current colour (on bottom).

3 Click the OK button. The selected colour is now the foreground colour, and is reflected as such in the foreground colour box.

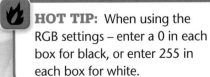

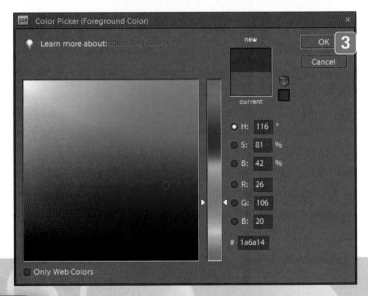

HOT TIP: When using the RGB settings – enter a 0 in each box for black, or enter 255 in each box for white.

Adding a shape to the image

Shapes are selected with the Shape tool in the Toolbox. There are several variations of the tool.

1 Right-clicking on the tool displays the choices. In this example the Rectangle Tool is selected.

2 Click on the canvas, and while holding down the mouse button, draw the shape. When done, release the mouse button. The shape appears on the canvas, in the selected colour and shape. Also, a new image layer is created.

HOT TIP: When the Custom Shape Tool is selected, a dropdown of various shapes is available in the tool options area.

Applying a style to a shape

In the tool options area is a dropdown to select the styling of the shape.

1 Click the Style button in the tool options area. A palette of styles opens. The palette displays styles that are grouped by a category, such as bevels or drop shadows. In the dropdown is a set of double black arrows at the upper right. Clicking here in turn opens another dropdown of the style categories.

2 Another category can be selected.

3 The style selections update to the selected category. Then a particular style is clicked and the shape updates to the style.

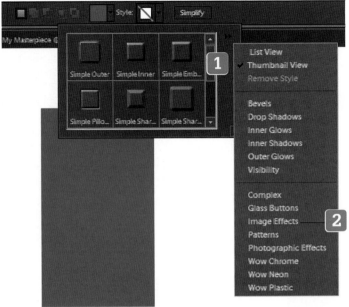

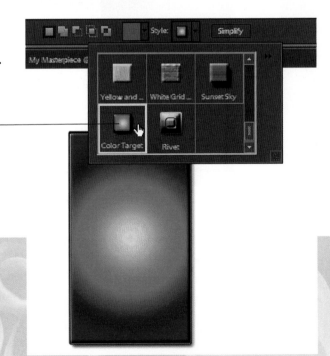

Removing a style from a shape

To remove a style, the style palette and dropdown list are used, but the particular selection of choice is Remove Style.

1 Click on the Style button in the tool options area. Click the double black arrows in the style palette to display the style categories. Click on Remove Style.

2 All style is removed. The shape now has a flat appearance, in its original colour.

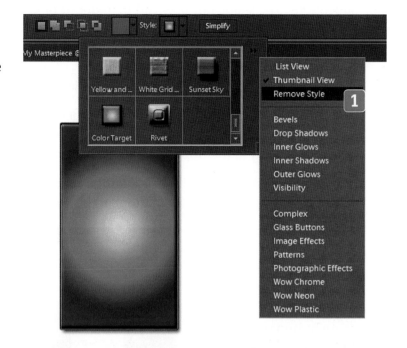

 HOT TIP: Duplicate a layer that has a shape and style, then remove the style from the shape on the new layer. Now you have two versions of the shape – one with the style and one without. You can toggle the visibility of the layers to show or hide the style.

Resizing a shape

A shape can be resized when it is selected. Once the shape is in a selected state, it has handles around the edges. These can be clicked on and used to drag the shape into new dimensions. The shape not only can be reduced or enlarged with a fixed ratio of width and height, but can also be resized such that the ratio is altered. This means that a rectangle can become a square, an oval can become a circle, and so on.

1 The shape has to be selected. Here are a couple of ways:

- Click on the Shape Selection tool in the tool options area. Then click on the shape. Handles appear around the shape. The Shape Selection tool looks like an arrow pointing to the upper left.

- Click on the Move tool. Then click on the shape. Handles appear around the shape. The Move tool is the first tool in the Toolbox – top left.

2 Click and hold down the mouse on one of the handles. Drag the mouse and the shape will change accordingly. Release the mouse button when done. The shape will now have the commit and cancel icons. Click the tick mark if you want to keep the change in shape.

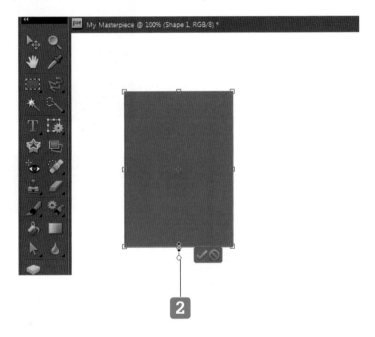

2

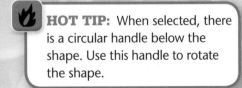

HOT TIP: When selected, there is a circular handle below the shape. Use this handle to rotate the shape.

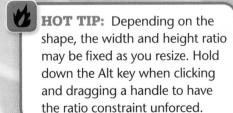

HOT TIP: Depending on the shape, the width and height ratio may be fixed as you resize. Hold down the Alt key when clicking and dragging a handle to have the ratio constraint unforced.

Adding to a shape

Even though there are several preset shapes to choose from, there are methods to alter a shape by adding to, or subtracting from, the shape.

1. Make sure the shape tool options are displayed in the tool options area. If not, click on the Shape tool in the Toolbox.

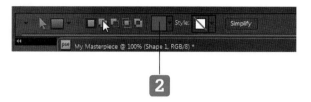

2

2. Click on the Add to Shape button.

3. Draw an additional shape that overlaps the first shape.

4. The shapes are combined, but still in a selected state. Click the Select… Deselect Layers menu item.

5. Once the selection is removed the result is a single custom shape.

3

4

> ▶ **SEE ALSO:** A style can be applied to the combined shape. See page 132.

Subtracting from a shape

Subtracting from a shape removes a part of the shape – which results in a custom shape.

1 Make sure the shape tool options are displayed in the tool options area. If not, click on the Shape tool in the Toolbox.

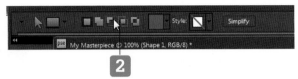

2 Click on the Subtract from Shape button.

3 Draw an additional shape that overlaps the first shape.

4 The shapes are combined, but selected. Click the Select... Deselect Layers menu item. The result is the custom shape – the original shape with part of it removed.

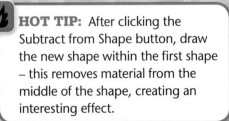

HOT TIP: After clicking the Subtract from Shape button, draw the new shape within the first shape – this removes material from the middle of the shape, creating an interesting effect.

Intersecting shape areas

Intersecting shapes removes all sections of the shapes that do not overlap. The remaining custom shape is the shape of the overlapped area.

1 Make sure the shape tool options are displayed in the tool options area. If not, click on the Shape tool in the Toolbox.

2 Click on the Intersect shape areas button.

3 Draw an additional shape that overlaps the first shape.

4 The shapes are combined, but selected. Click the Select... Deselect Layers menu item. The result is the custom shape – just the areas of the two shapes that overlapped.

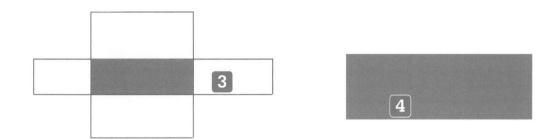

HOT TIP: After clicking the Intersect shape areas button, draw the new shape within the first shape – this reduces the combined shape to be the same as the new shape.

Excluding overlapping shape areas

This technique retains the parts of the images that do not overlap and removes the overlapped area.

1 Make sure the shape tool options are displayed in the tool options area. If not, click on the Shape tool in the Toolbox.

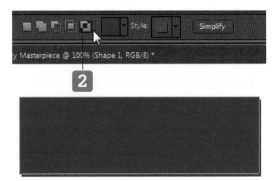

2 Click on the Exclude overlapping shape areas button.

3 Draw an additional shape that overlaps the first shape.

4 The shapes are combined, but selected. Click the Select... Deselect Layers menu item. The result is the custom shape – the combination of the parts of the shapes that did not overlap.

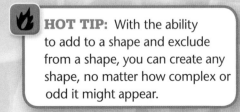

HOT TIP: With the ability to add to a shape and exclude from a shape, you can create any shape, no matter how complex or odd it might appear.

Changing the colour of a shape

In the tool options area is a colour selector.

1 Make sure the shape tool options are displayed in the tool options area. If not, click on the Shape tool in the Toolbox.

2 To the left of the Style button is a button with a colour on it. Either click on the button to display a colour selector dialogue, or click on the arrow next to the button to display a colour swatch.

3 Click on a new colour and the shape is set to that new colour.

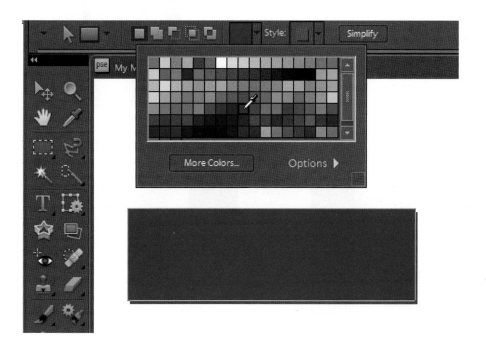

? DID YOU KNOW?

Clicking Options lets you select other colour swatches, such as Photo Filter Colors and Web Spectrum.

Aligning shapes

Aligning is the action of lining up shapes. Aligning can be to the left, right, centre, top, bottom or middle.

1 Have more than one shape visible in the active image area.

2 Select the multiple shapes by selecting the associated layers, or use the Move tool to group them together.

3 When selected together a bounding box is visible around the group. In the tool options area, the Align dropdown is enabled. In the dropdown are the various alignments.

4 In this example, the Left Edges alignment is selected. The shapes are lined up on their left sides.

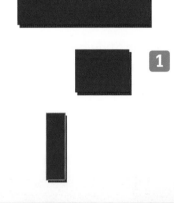

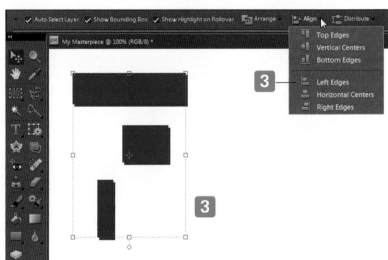

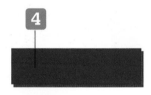

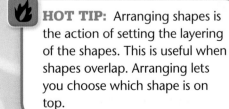

HOT TIP: Arranging shapes is the action of setting the layering of the shapes. This is useful when shapes overlap. Arranging lets you choose which shape is on top.

Distributing shapes

Distributing is the action of creating an equal amount of space between multiple shapes. The choice of how to distribute the shapes is the same as when aligning shapes.

1 Have at least three shapes visible in the active image area.

2 Select the multiple shapes by selecting the associated layers, or use the Move tool to group them together.

3 When selected together a bounding box is visible around the group. In the tool options area, the Distribute dropdown is enabled. In the dropdown are the various distributions.

4 In this example, the Vertical Centers distribution has been applied.

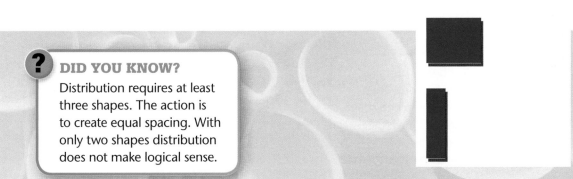

? DID YOU KNOW?

Distribution requires at least three shapes. The action is to create equal spacing. With only two shapes distribution does not make logical sense.

Combining shapes

With the versatility of layers it's a breeze to combine shapes. Since each shape is on its own layer, colour, position and every other attribute can be applied to one shape without affecting others. Here is an example of placing one shape over another and then merging them into one.

1 Place a shape on the canvas. This action creates a layer for the shape.

2 Place another shape onto the canvas. As the second shape to be added, its layer sits on top of the first shape's layer. Note that each shape is on a separate layer.

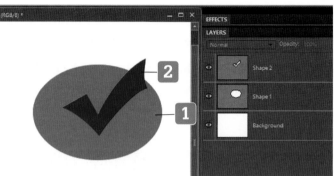

3 With both layers selected, click the Layer... Merge Layers menu item (the same option is available with a right-click on one of the selected layers).

4 The two layers are merged – the two shapes are one composite shape. Note that the two shapes are now together on one layer.

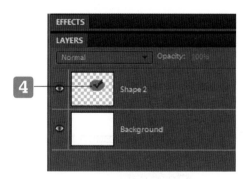

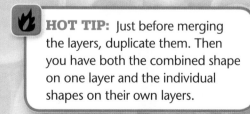

HOT TIP: Just before merging the layers, duplicate them. Then you have both the combined shape on one layer and the individual shapes on their own layers.

Simplifying a shape

In Photoshop Elements the Simplify action converts a vector shape to a raster shape. A vector shape is based on a mathematical calculation and has the same quality at any size. A raster shape is based on pixels. Detailed editing work is often done at the pixel level.

1. Draw an image on the canvas. Click the Simplify button in the tool options area.

2. The shape is now based on pixels; this is clear when the shape is zoomed in on.

3. The shape can be altered at the pixel level. This makes for very detailed touch-up work.

9 Drawing, patterns and gradients

Introduction

For those with an artistic flair, Photoshop Elements provides a wealth of drawing tools. The all-purpose brush is the tool of choice for most drawing needs. A brush can be tailored to be blunt, soft, large, small and a number of settings in between. The Pattern Stamp puts cool patterns right where you need them. And gradients – well, you'll just have to see these amazing visuals for yourself.

Drawing with a brush

In the Toolbox, the Brush tool has four variations: Brush, Impressionist Brush, Colour Replacement and Pencil. To start a basic drawing the prudent course of action is to use a basic brush – the plain Brush tool.

1 Right-click on the Brush tool in the Toolbox and select the Brush tool.

2 The tool options area has several settings for the brush:

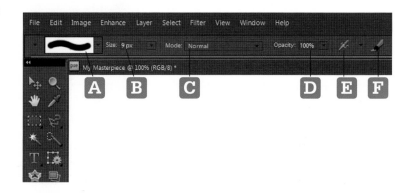

   A Brush type

   B Size

   C Mode

   D Opacity

   E Airbrush

   F Additional options

3 Without changing any settings, move the mouse into the active image area, click, hold and drag the mouse around. Release the mouse button. You have created a basic brush stroke.

SEE ALSO: Techniques presented in this chapter are used with a blank canvas. See Chapter 8 for details on creating a new image canvas.

HOT TIP: As you draw with the brush, pause, release the mouse button, then press the mouse button down and continue. This makes it easy to undo a mistake right when you make it without having to start the whole drawing over again.

Selecting a brush type

There are more brushes here than Van Gogh could possibly use, but this is the digital age, so any art program worth its salt must present a near endless variety.

1 In the tool options area, click the Brush type button. A set of brushes is available in a palette.

2 In the brush palette is a dropdown that lists several categories of brushes. Clicking on any of the categories loads the palette with the associated brush types.

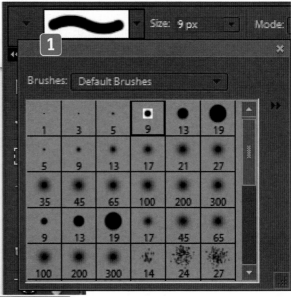

HOT TIP: One of the categories is Special Effect Brushes. These provide shapes, such as a flower and a butterfly, which can be entered into an image. Drawing with one of these brushes creates a stream of shapes, such as a group of butterflies flying together.

Selecting the brush size

1 Clicking on the Size box in the tool options area displays a slider control for selecting the brush size.

2 The brush size can be significant. This shows three lines, respectively sized at 50, 100 and 250 pixels.

 HOT TIP: In the tool options area, to the left, is a dropdown that displays several preset sized brushes to select from.

Altering a drawing with the Impressionist Brush

The Impressionist Brush applies a softening effect to an image.

1. Draw or open an image.

2. Right-click the Brush tool in the Toolbox and select the Impressionist Brush. A new button is displayed in the tool options area. Clicking it opens a dropdown with a variety of styles to select from.

3. Experiment with the various settings to see the effect they produce. Here, the chimney and the tree are altered. A small brush size was used to keep the affected area small.

4. Using an Impressionist Brush with a large brush size can alter the entire image with one stroke.

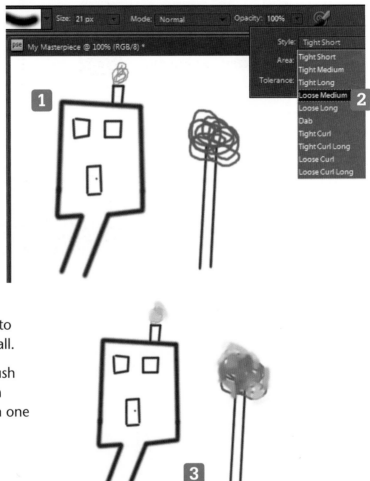

 HOT TIP: Becoming familiar with blending modes will greatly increase your versatility in creating great art. It's useful to print out the description of blend modes and keep it near your computer for quick reference.

Using the Eraser

As expected from its name, the Eraser clears wherever it is applied.

1 Right-click on the Eraser tool in the Toolbox and select Eraser Tool.

2 Drag the Eraser over the image. The image is erased where the Eraser is dragged over. The Eraser can be sized just like the brushes.

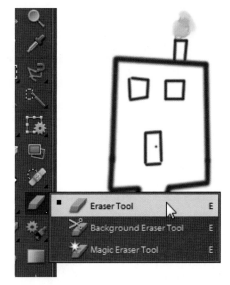

HOT TIP: If you need to erase a defined shape or colour, use the Magic Eraser Tool (one of the Eraser Tool types). With a click this will erase entire areas – with the area being defined by the tolerance setting.

Using the Pattern Stamp

This interesting tool paints a pattern in the image. The pattern can be geometrical, scenes from nature, artistic surfaces and many other textures.

1 Right-click the Stamp tool in the Toolbox and select the Pattern Stamp Tool.

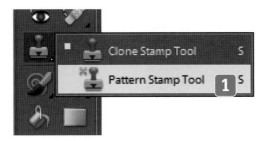

2 In the tool options area is a button to select a pattern. Clicking the button opens a pattern palette, and clicking the double black arrows displays a list of pattern categories.

3 Patterns are stroked across the image area, similar to the brush. This size can be changed just like the brush. Here, the image is being filled with a rock pattern.

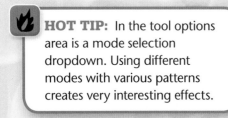

HOT TIP: In the tool options area is a mode selection dropdown. Using different modes with various patterns creates very interesting effects.

Using the Gradient tool

Gradients are blends of colours. The number of colours, the ratio of blending between colours, the smoothness of the blends, and the direction of the blend are all options when using gradients.

1 Click the Gradient tool in the Toolbox. The tool options area displays selections particular to manipulating gradients.

2 Click in the image area and drag the mouse. A line is drawn.

3 When the mouse button is released, the gradient appears.

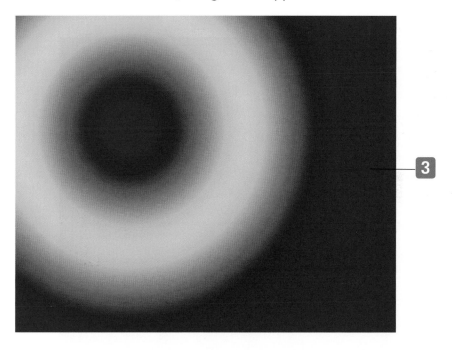

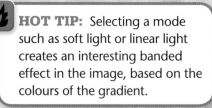

HOT TIP: Selecting a mode such as soft light or linear light creates an interesting banded effect in the image, based on the colours of the gradient.

Selecting the Gradient pattern

In the tool options area, on the left side, is a button with a dropdown arrow. Numerous gradient patterns are available in the dropdown.

1 Click the arrow next to the gradient sample. A palette with gradient samples is displayed.

2 Click the double black arrows in the palette for a choice of gradient categories.

3 Select a gradient. Then drag the mouse across the image area. When the mouse button is released the new gradient appears.

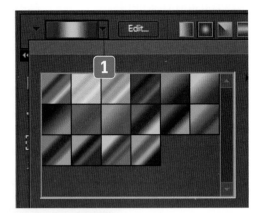

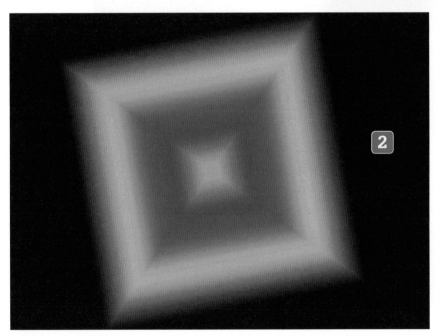

? **DID YOU KNOW?**

A gradient can be made from two or more colours. Many of the gradient categories have gradients made up from numerous colours. One category, Simple, has gradients made from just two colours.

Selecting the Gradient direction

1 In the tool options area are five buttons for selecting the direction of the gradient.

A Linear Gradient

B Radial Gradient

C Angle Gradient

D Reflected Gradient

E Diamond Gradient

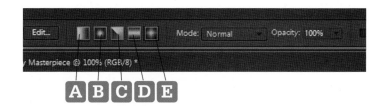

2 Each gradient direction paints a different picture, literally. Here, for example, is an Angle Gradient.

HOT TIP: With the Radial and Diamond Gradients, the shape of the circle or diamond matches the length of the line drawn with the tool.

Using the Gradient Editor

In the tool options area is an Edit button. Clicking it displays the Gradient Editor.

The Smoothness percentage factors how smoothly one colour blends into the next.

Opacity stops and Color stops are used to alter the dynamics of the gradient. The Opacity stops are the black boxes above the colour strip. The boxes below the colour strip are the Color stops, and each displays the colour it controls.

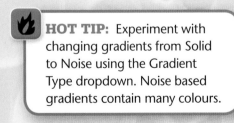

HOT TIP: Experiment with changing gradients from Solid to Noise using the Gradient Type dropdown. Noise based gradients contain many colours.

1. Click just above the colour strip to set a new Opacity stop. This determines a position where the opacity level can be changed. The percentage of opacity is set in the Opacity box (clicking the arrow provides a slider switch).

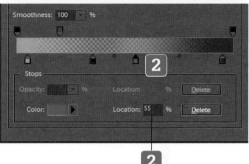

2. Clicking on a Color stop allows you to alter the colour by using the Color box. The position of the Color stop can be changed by entering a value in the percentage box or just dragging the stop itself.

3. Clicking just below the colour strip sets a new Color stop. To remove a Color stop, click on it and drag it away from the strip. Here, the red Color stop has been removed.

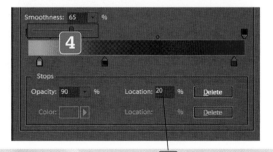

4. The smoothness is changed with a slider control. The percentage determines how hard or soft the blend is between colours.

5. Click the OK button to close the Gradient Editor.

6. Drag the mouse across the image area. Release the mouse button and the gradient will update to the customised look.

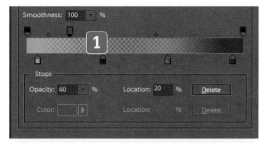

10 Working with type

Introduction

A picture says a thousand words. Can words replace pictures? They certainly can be used with pictures for enhanced impact. Photoshop Elements manages text in much the same way as images themselves. Text is editable, text goes on layers and there are text effects to use. One thing it won't do is help you compose what you wish to say.

Entering horizontal text

Left to right is the most common and familiar way for text to appear.

1 Right-click on the Type tool in the Toolbox and select the Horizontal Type Tool.

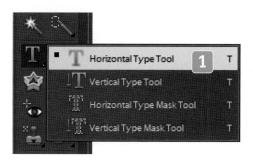

2 Click in the image area and type.

3 To complete the entry, click on the commit button on the right in the tool options area, or just click on the Type tool.

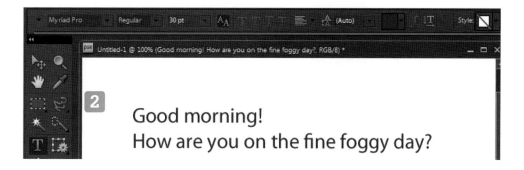

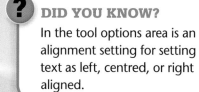

▶ **SEE ALSO:** Techniques presented in this chapter are used with a blank canvas. See Chapter 8 for details on creating a new image canvas.

? **DID YOU KNOW?**
In the tool options area is an alignment setting for setting text as left, centred, or right aligned.

Entering vertical text

Getting fancy in your graphics? Vertical text is a pleasing alternative for short snippets of type.

1 Right-click on the Type tool in the Toolbox and select the Vertical Type Tool.

2 Click in the image area and type.

3 To complete the entry, click on the commit button on the right in the tool options area, or just click on the Type tool.

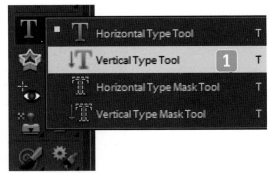

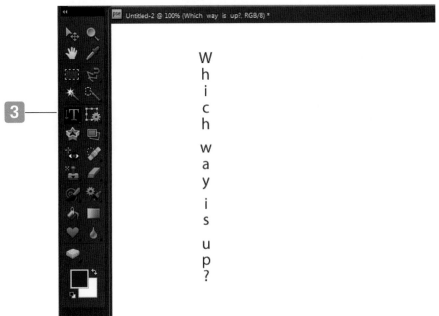

? DID YOU KNOW?

You can combine horizontal and vertical type for an interesting effect. Enter a word or phrase as horizontal type. Duplicate the layer. On the new layer change the type to vertical. Then move the text so the first letter lays on top of the first layer in the horizontal type layer.

Editing all the text on a layer

1 Select the layer the text is on.

2 Click the Type tool.

3 Make the desired changes using the selections available in the tool options area. There are several things you can do: change the font; change the size of the font; set bold, italic, underline, and strikeout attributes. You can change the colour of the text by clicking on the foreground colour box and selecting a new colour in the Select foreground colour dialogue box.

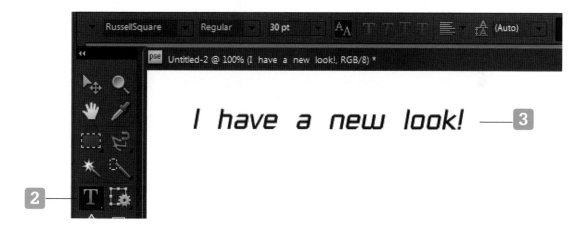

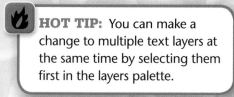

HOT TIP: You can make a change to multiple text layers at the same time by selecting them first in the layers palette.

Editing some of the text on a layer

If a section of text is selected (highlighted), then editing changes will be applied to just the selected text.

1 Select the layer the text is on.

2 Click the Type tool.

3 Drag the mouse over part of the text. While the text portion is selected, make any needed changes. Click the Type tool again to finish editing. Here, the three words (Apple, Banana and Pear) are each of a different font and colour.

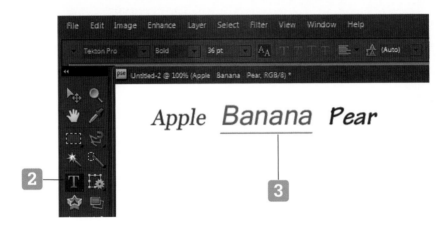

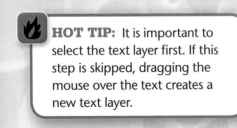

HOT TIP: It is important to select the text layer first. If this step is skipped, dragging the mouse over the text creates a new text layer.

Wrapping text

When entering text, the text will continue in a line, even past the image area! There are two ways around this. One is to press the Return key while you type. Better though is to have the text wrap to dimensions that you create.

1 Click the Type tool and instead of clicking where the typing should begin, drag the mouse. A bounding box will appear.

2 Type away! As you type the text will wrap to the dimensions of the box.

3 The dimensions can be changed by using the handles around the edge of the box.

4 Click the Type tool to remove the appearance of the box. The text will stay in place.

I am text that is inside a box. The box keeps me wrapped up like this. I like the way this works. I don't worry about running off the image area.

2

I am text that is inside a box. The box keeps me wrapped up. I like the way this works. I don't worry about running off the image area.

3

HOT TIP: You can wrap the text from the right side by selecting right alignment in the tool options area.

Setting the leading

Leading is the space between lines. In particular it is the spacing between the baselines of text on wrapped lines. In Photoshop Elements the leading can be set to Auto (and the program will properly space the lines), or you can manually select the leading for artistic effect.

1 Here are three lines of text that are a bit squeezed. The font size is 18pt and the leading is set at 14pt (seen towards the right in the tool options). The leading is set from a dropdown that opens when the arrow to the right is clicked. One of the options in the dropdown is Auto.

2 Selecting a different leading size moves the lines closer or further apart. Here, the leading has been increased to 30 points.

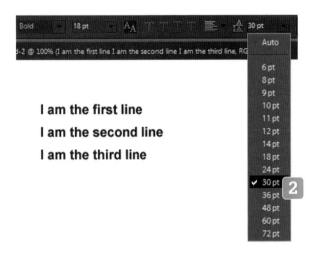

I am the first line
I am the second line
I am the third line

HOT TIP: If the leading size is smaller than the text size, then the lines of text will overlap. You can use this peculiar effect in some creative way.

Moving text

To move text to a new position on the layer, follow these steps.

1 Click on the layer to select it. Then click on the text itself.

2 Move the mouse away from the text. The mouse pointer changes shape.

3 Click and hold down the mouse button. Drag the mouse and the text block will follow.

4 Release the mouse button when the text is repositioned.

I am the first line

I am the second line

I am the third line

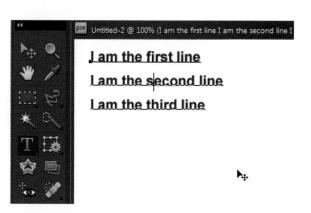

Applying artistic styling

1 Towards the right side of the tool options area is a Style dropdown. Clicking this opens a palette of styles.

2 Clicking the double black arrows on the right side of the palette displays a dropdown with numerous style categories.

3 Select a category – the palette updates to the styles of the category – and then click a particular style. The text is altered to appear in the selected style.

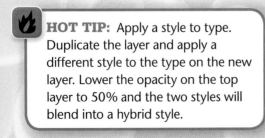

HOT TIP: Apply a style to type. Duplicate the layer and apply a different style to the type on the new layer. Lower the opacity on the top layer to 50% and the two styles will blend into a hybrid style.

Warping text

Towards the far right of the tool options is a button with a letter T sitting over an arc. Clicking this button opens the Warp Text dialogue box.

1 In the dialogue is a dropdown with numerous warp effects.

2 When a warp style is selected, the dialogue has other settings to further refine the warp effect.

3 When the desired warp effect is achieved, click the OK button to close the dialogue. The result is warped text.

? **DID YOU KNOW?**

The shadow effect is added by applying a style selection in the tool options area.

11 Enhancing your photographs with blur and sharpen techniques

Introduction

Blurring may sound like a non-useful technique at first, but applied with thought can produce some very interesting images. In fact blurring can bring focus to your photographs. If that sounds contradictory, consider that if part of an image is made blurry, the part left intact gets the focus – in terms of a viewer's attention. You will see this technique in the Getting Sharp task.

Applying sharpness is the other side of the coin. If you have something in an image that is blurry but should not be, adjusting sharpness is just what you need.

Applying Average blur

Average blur, simply put, takes the colour values of the pixels in the selection, calculates the average colour, and then applies it to each pixel. The result is a single colour area. The resultant area does not appear blurry; it appears devoid of any variation. As such its use is limited at best to small areas. Applying an Average blur to a full image would just make one solid colour out of the image.

1 In a photograph look for a small area that needs a touch-up – perhaps a spot of glare or a blemish on a person's skin, etc. In this example, there is a small reflective spot produced by the flash reflecting off an earring. The earring is not seen, but the reflection is.

2 The Zoom tool is used to get the image blown up to the pixel level.

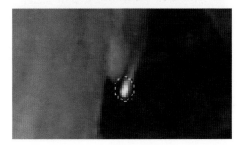

3 Select the Elliptical Marquee tool. Set the feather (in the tool options area) to 3px, and then draw an oval around the glare spot.

4 Average blur is applied. It is the Filter… Blur… Average menu item. Once the blur is applied the Select… Deselect menu item removes the marquee.

While still zoomed in the appearance might look a bit odd or uneven. However, once you return to normal view the change will show the desired effect – the glare is gone.

 HOT TIP: If a colour flattened area is produced with the Average blur, it can be further worked on to blend in using the smudge tool, clone stamp or other blur methods.

Blur and Blur More

Blur and Blur More work in the same way, except that Blur More applies the effect to a greater degree. Blur and Blur More work by averaging colours along the edges of clearly defined lines and shading. This differs from Average blur which simply averages all colours.

1. Find an image or area of an image that could benefit, perhaps for an artistic effect, with being blurred. If it's an area within an image, draw a marquee around it with a selection tool.

2. Click the Filter... Blur... Blur (or Blur More) menu item. This step can be done repeatedly until a satisfactory level of blur is reached.

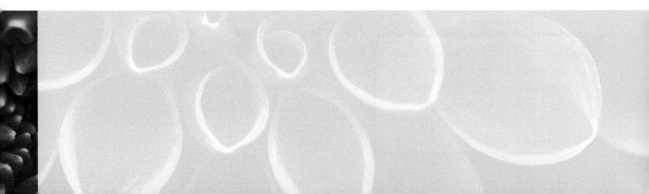

Using Gaussian Blur

Gaussian Blur provides more control over the blurring effect. A dialogue box provides a slider control to set how dissimilar pixels have to be for the blur to be applied. Generally the higher the setting, the more of the blur effect is produced.

1 Click the Filter... Blur... Gaussian Blur menu item to display the Gaussian Blur dialogue box.

2 Set the Radius – the width of pixels that the blur is acting upon. A larger number contains more pixels and therefore produces more blur.

3 Click OK to apply the blur and close the dialogue.

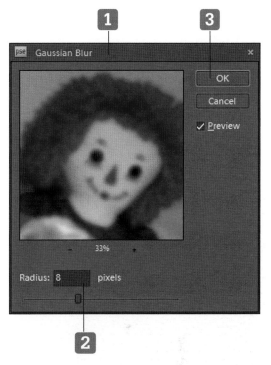

HOT TIP: This blur effect is very useful when applied to a section of a photograph. In this example, the hippopotamus's face was placed as a selection using the Magnetic Lasso tool. Then the selection was reversed using the Select... Inverse menu item. The blur therefore was applied to the whole image, except the face. The result is a blurred image with the non-blurred face.

Using Motion Blur

Motion Blur works by setting the blur effect in a selected direction (the angle of the blur).

1 Click the Filter... Blur... Motion Blur menu item to open the Motion Blur dialogue box.

2 Set the angle – the direction of the blur.

3 Select a pixel distance – the width of pixels used for the blurring method. A higher number creates more blur.

4 Click OK to complete the blur and close the dialogue box. The result is as shown.

> ▶ **SEE ALSO:** This technique is used quite a bit in action scenes – sports, for example. Applying a selection around the moving figure, you can apply the blur to the subject (the background stays sharp), or apply the blur to the background (the subject stays sharp).

Using Radial Blur

Radial Blur is a neat tool. It blurs in a circular motion. This creates many possibilities such as the appearance of tyres in motion or a globe being turned. Here, a clock is used for the effect.

1 Click the Filter... Blur... Radial Blur menu item to open the Radial Blur dialogue box.

2 In the dialogue is a blur choice of Spin or Zoom. Zoom creates the effect of the blur radiating out from the centre. Spin creates the circular blur. This example shows the effect applied to a clock.

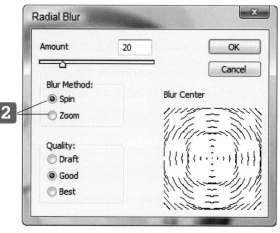

HOT TIP: Using a mix of Motion Blur and Radial Blur you can take a photograph of a parked car and make it look like it is speeding along. Motion Blur is used to simulate the blurred background and Radial Blur is applied to the tyres so they appear to be spinning.

Using Smart Blur

Smart Blur provides a variety of settings together in one dialogue:

- Radius: a measure of how many pixels are used to calculate the blur effect.

- Threshold: determines how different the pixels have to be for the blur to include them in the effect. A higher threshold results in a higher degree of blur.

- Mode: Normal works on the entire image; Edge Only and Overlay Edge work on where significant contrast occurs, typically along defined lines.

1 Click the Filter... Blur... Smart Blur menu item to open the Smart Blur dialogue box.

2 The interplay of the settings can create effects from subtle to wildly artistic. First, here is an example of applying Normal mode with a high threshold.

3 This next example is created using the Edge only mode.

Normal mode with high threshold

Edge Only mode

HOT TIP: Using the Edge Only mode, the amount of edge detail is controllable. There could be a good amount of edges showing – and that makes it clear what the subject is. Applying the setting to display less detail could leave the 'suggestion' of an image – a very useful artistic effect.

Getting sharp

Blurring a photograph is one thing. Getting a blurry photograph to look sharp is quite a different animal. A blurred original can, at best, get clearer with some techniques, but there is no magic to making it all clear and sharp.

Photoshop Elements provides a handy enough utility to get a good crack at improving a blurry image. This is a dialogue of selections to essentially reverse a blur. This is adequate, or not; it depends on the original and how close to perfect you need it to be.

1 Click the Enhance… Adjust Sharpness menu item to display the Adjust Sharpness dialogue box.

2 In the dialogue are settings for the amount of 'unblur' to apply, and the radius – the width of pixels used to calculate how the effect is applied.

3 Beneath these settings is the Remove dropdown, with three types of blurs. What is suggested is to select the type of blur the photograph appears to have. A Gaussian Blur is the best choice for a generally blurred photograph. Lens Blur sharpens along lines of contrast. Motion Blur is used to correct a shot made with a shaky camera or a subject that would not stay still. With the Motion Blur setting, you set the angle of the blur as well.

 HOT TIP: Make repetitive small adjustments. Each sharpening adjustment builds up from the previous one. This leads to a better appearance than trying to get it all done in one strong adjustment. Another helpful approach is to make the repetitive adjustments on a sequence of layers. Each adjustment is done on a copy of the layer used for the previous adjustment. This leaves you with several steps to fall back on.

12 Repairing images

Introduction

When you consider that a photograph is a 2D representation of a 3D world, it's a wonder that so much imagery depth is kept. At times the photography process creates distortion – a bad angle, an odd sense of perspective, a crooked picture – but these can be corrected using Photoshop Elements.

Then there are the popular improvements in facials – goodbye red eye, removing blemishes, ironing out wrinkles. And the old standard photographer's nightmare: getting a group of people to all smile and keep their eyes open at the same time. That is handled here too.

Correcting camera distortion

When shooting up, down or at any angle that is not straight ahead, the photograph may have a distorted view. Photoshop Elements has a utility to correct the distortion.

1 Open a photograph that has some distorted perspective. Here is an example – the fence appears to arch inwards. In reality the fence is straight.

2 Click the Filter... Correct Camera Distortion menu item to display the Correct Camera Distortion dialogue box.

3 The Vertical Perspective slider is used to lower the perspective setting – this effectively straightens the fence. Lower the Vertical Perspective using the slider control.

The fence is now straight, but the reorientation of the image has left an empty area around the bottom half of the image. This is filled in by using the Edge Extension setting.

4 Increase the Edge Extension using the slider switch. Then click the OK button to keep the changes. The result is the image with a fence that stands straight.

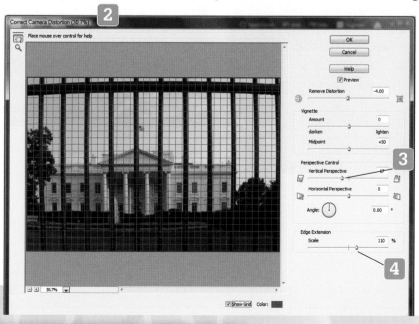

HOT TIP: In the dialogue, a screen is placed over the photograph that helps when reorienting the perspective. This screen can be turned off by unticking the Show Grid tickbox at the bottom of the dialogue.

Automatically Remove Red Eye

When light hits the retina, a colour can be reflected back that is not natural. In humans, this distortion is known as red eye (pictures of animals can result in other eye colour distortions).

1 Open a photograph that shows a face with red eye(s).

2 Click the Enhance… Auto Fix Red Eye menu item. The change is run automatically – no dialogue appears to adjust settings. In a moment the photograph is altered to show true eye colour.

WHAT DOES THIS MEAN?

Red eye: a side effect seen in photographs in which the flash was used. The light of the flash can reflect off the eyes' retinas. It is not a natural occurrence. It only appears with flash photography.

Using the Red Eye Removal Tool

The Red Eye Removal Tool is great when the Auto Remove Red Eye doesn't get the job done. The Red Eye Removal Tool provides adjustments so the change can be applied in the best way.

1 Open an image that has eye colour distortion. For variety, the change in this example is applied to a friendly and lovable cocker spaniel, but one whose eyes are like mirrors when a flash photo is taken.

2 Click on the Red Eye Removal Tool in the Toolbox. A pair of settings appears in the tool options area.

3 The Red Eye Removal Tool is used by drawing a box around the eye or just clicking on the eye. The Pupil Size percentage setting is meant to drive how much of the pupil is altered, but this is a sensitive setting. Every application of changing a pupil's colour is unique. The percentage setting alters each image in a unique way. Here, the dog's eyes have been reverted to the real colour.

 HOT TIP: When a box is drawn around the eye, instead of just clicking on the pupil, the size of the box affects the way the Pupil Size percentage affects the image. Experimentation is best to reach a happy medium.

Using the Healing Brush

The Healing Brush tool removes imperfections by applying a sampled area of the image that is similar but free of the imperfection(s). The Healing Brush is useful in both large and small images. Since it works by sampling one area to replicate in another, the important point is that the sampled and altered areas are meant to appear the same.

Here is a photograph of a sprightly young man, with a blemish (a liver spot) on his forehead. The blemish has to go. Here's how.

1 Right-click the Healing Brush Tool in the Toolbox and select the Healing Brush Tool.

2 Right-click in the image to display a dialogue with an assortment of settings. In the tool options area there are other settings too.

3 After any settings are made, the tool needs to know where in the image to sample. Do this by holding down the ALT key and clicking in the image – on a part of the image that has the definition of what the corrected area should look like.

4 The Brush is moved over the blemish.

5 One click and the blemish is gone.

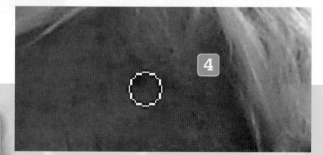

Using the Spot Healing Brush

The Spot Healing Brush tool also removes imperfections but using a different method. Spot healing works by matching pixels that are in the bounds of the area the tool touches when used.

1. Right-click the Healing Brush Tool in the Toolbox and select the Spot Healing Brush Tool.

2. The tool options has two types of match methods. Each of these occurs once the area to correct is clicked on. The brush size should be larger than the area being corrected:

   - Proximity Match – uses pixels around the edge of the brush area to determine a usable sample to cover the area being corrected.

   - Create Texture – uses pixels within the brush area to determine a usable sample to cover the area being corrected.

   In a nutshell, the methods are similar; they differ just on where the sampled pixels are used. The choice of which type to use depends on the image. Try them both to see what looks best.

3. In this example the man's wrinkles will be removed.

   A brush size slightly larger than the area of the wrinkles above the eyes is selected. Then the image is clicked on the wrinkles. The wrinkles are removed.

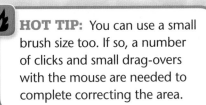

HOT TIP: You can use a small brush size too. If so, a number of clicks and small drag-overs with the mouse are needed to complete correcting the area.

Cloning out trouble spots

Got a great shot, only to find there is something in it that doesn't belong? The Healing and Spot Healing brushes give you one way to fix this type of problem. Here is another method. This is useful for covering up large areas, but of course it all depends on what is in the image to start with. Here is a nice shot, but unfortunately someone threw some rubbish to one side of the flowers – the red circle indicates the litter.

1 Right-click on the Clone Stamp tool in the Toolbox and select the Clone Stamp Tool.

2 Looking at the place where the litter is, see if a nearby area in the photograph has the imagery that should also appear where the litter occurs. Select an appropriate brush size in the tool options area and ALT-click on the area with the correct imagery.

3 Draw over the litter. The tool clones the ALT-clicked area and overlays it on the area being drawn. Since the sample of ground is varied and choppy it blends well when drawn over the litter. The result is a clean image with no telltale distinction where the new material was drawn.

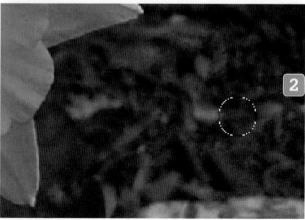

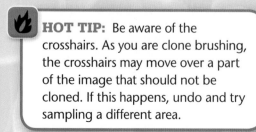

HOT TIP: Be aware of the crosshairs. As you are clone brushing, the crosshairs may move over a part of the image that should not be cloned. If this happens, undo and try sampling a different area.

Removing scratches

Scanned photographs are susceptible to imperfections appearing because of a scratched, dirty, dusty or hair-covered platen. The same could be true of the physical photograph itself. These imperfections are carried directly into the image file. Here's a way to remove a scratch.

1. Open an image that has a scratch or similar imperfection.

2. Use the Selection Brush tool to draw over the scratch. The Selection Brush tool is great for creating a selection along a line.

3. Click the Filter... Noise... Dust & Scratches menu item to open the Dust & Scratches dialogue box.

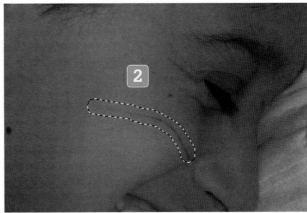

4. Adjust the Radius and Threshold while viewing the preview of the change. The Radius is a setting of how wide the affected area extends past the selection. The Threshold controls the pixel level at which the effect is applied. A lower threshold produces the effect more easily – less differentiation is needed between the selection and the surrounding area. When an acceptable balance is seen in the preview, click the OK button. Then deselect using the Select... Deselect menu.

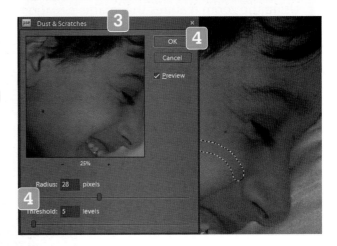

 HOT TIP: The result of scratch removal may still leave a noticeable imperfection. Continuing with another tool, such as the Spot Healer Brush, will finish the scratch removal.

Working on pixels

The ability to zoom in and get down to the finest detail in an image lets you make the finest adjustments. The technique is to magnify greatly the image and use various tools to adjust imperfections that are best handled with changes on a few pixels.

1 Open an image with an imperfection. Here, the man's spectacles caught some glare.

2 Using the zoom features the image is magnified and centred on the bright spot of the spectacles.

3 The technique is to change the off-colour pixels to blend in with the correctly coloured ones around them. Click on the Eyedropper tool and click on a pixel with a correct colour. This colour becomes the forecolour, as seen here in the forecolour box – on the left.

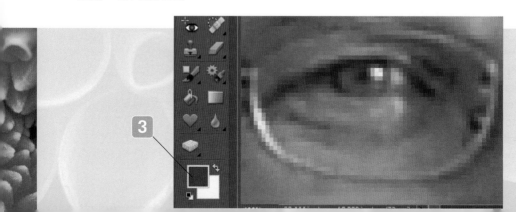

4   Next select the Brush tool and size it to 1 pixel. Click on the pixels that need colour replacement.

5   Repeat steps 3 and 4, each time using a slightly different colour (from differing pixels). At this magnification there are many similar colours spread around the surrounding pixels. When a bit of good colour variety has been put into the off-colour pixels, the result will appear as a nice blend of colour.

? DID YOU KNOW?

Working on images at the pixel level opens the door to many possibilities. The ability to alter images by the pixel is something that no other tool can do. Creativity is not hindered working at the pixel level.

Correcting a group shot

Getting people to smile, not blink, and to stay still for a few seconds can be a chore. Historically the way around this has been to take multiple shots of the same group pose. One of them has to be good, you hope. But now there's a way to take the best and combine them.

Here are shots of two people: in one shot the woman's eyes are shut and in the other shot the boy's eyes are shut.

1. Select the two images in the Project Bin.

2. Click the File... New... Photomerge Group Shot menu item. One image will appear open on the left in the active image area.

3. The other photograph is dragged from the Project Bin area and placed on the right.

4. The two images are aligned by using the Alignment Tool in the Palette Bin.

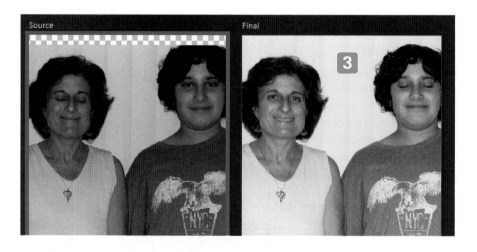

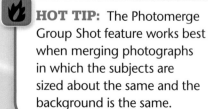

HOT TIP: The Photomerge Group Shot feature works best when merging photographs in which the subjects are sized about the same and the background is the same.

This tool works by setting three points in each image that guide how the images are to be lined up. This means that if you are replacing an eye for an eye, the eye will not accidentally end up over an ear or somewhere else. The Alignment Tool is clicked in the Palette Bin and as the mouse moves over an image three crosshairs appear. These are easily moved with the mouse and are meant to pinpoint the same features in each image.

5 Click the Align Photos button to confirm the alignment.

6 Using the Pencil Tool in the Palette Bin, draw over (or around) the areas in the image on the left that should overwrite the equivalent in the image on the right.

When all desired areas have been copied over, click the Done button in the Palette Bin. The result is the combined image: here, both people have open eyes.

? DID YOU KNOW?
Photomerge Group Shot can combine parts of up to 10 images.

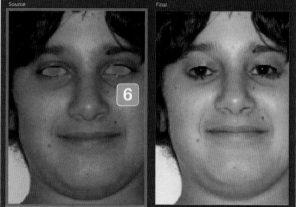

Straightening an image

It happens – you take a shot, it's great, except it's crooked. There might have been a time when such tragedies were discarded, but no more! Photoshop Elements has a utility to set it all straight.

1 Open a photograph in which the angle of view is not aligned with the edges of the image itself – in other words, crooked.

2 Select the Straighten tool from the Toolbox. Draw a line in the image, along an angle that should be the horizontal bottom edge of the image. Often there is a clear guide to do this based on the subject(s) in the image. Here, the bottom of the guitar serves as the angle to correct, so the line is drawn parallel with the guitar base.

3 The image straightens but in doing so exposes the canvas underneath. What is needed now is to crop the image. Using the Crop tool the inner part of the image is retained and is a full image itself, aligned with its edges.

 HOT TIP: An alternative straightening method is to use the Image... Rotate... Straighten menu item. Going a step further is the Image... Rotate... Straighten and Crop Image menu item. The latter straightens and crops in one automated operation.

13 Saving, printing, sending and sharing

Introduction

With all the techniques, tricks and 'ooh-aahs' you've learned and used, one thing remains to be done – get your masterpieces in front of others. Photoshop Elements helps you prepare and output your images in a variety of ways. Now it's time for family and friends to see, and even get the world to take a look – on the internet.

Saving a file in Photoshop format

There are a number of standard image file types and when an image is used on the web, in print or sent in an email message, the photograph should be in one of the standard types. Prior to that, when editing an image, Photoshop Elements will manage the file in the native Photoshop format. When saving the file, it is necessary to keep the image in the Photoshop format if there are layers. Standard formats do not support layers. When an image is saved it can be flattened into a single layer – which does allow the image to be saved in a standard format. However, if you are working on and off editing an image, then you must save it in the Photoshop format between editing sessions.

1 Click the File... Save menu item. The Save As dialogue is displayed. In the dialogue is a dropdown of file types. Select Photoshop (*.PSD).

2 There are a couple of key options in the dialogue. If you wish to have the image available for view in the Organizer, tick the Include in the Elements Organizer tickbox. If your image has layers, tick the Layers tickbox.

3 Navigate to the folder where the image should be saved and click the Save button.

HOT TIP: You must keep the Layers tickbox ticked to avoid flattening the layers into a single one.

Saving a file in a standard image format

Saving an image file in a standard format is necessary to enable the file to work in any application or place where Photoshop format files are not recognised. The most popular of these formats is the JPEG format, as most images on the web are of this type. Other popular types are GIF, TIFF and PNG.

1 If the image contains layers they must be flattened into a single background. Click on the Layers... Flatten Image menu item.

2 Click the File... Save menu item. The Save As dialogue is displayed. Select JPEG as the format.

3 Navigate to the folder where the image should be saved and click the Save button. The JPEG options dialogue box opens.

4 Make any appropriate selections and click OK.

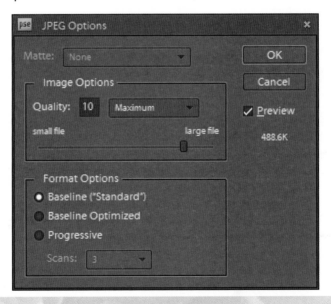

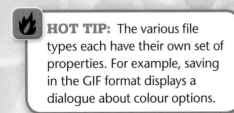

HOT TIP: The various file types each have their own set of properties. For example, saving in the GIF format displays a dialogue about colour options.

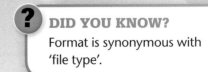

DID YOU KNOW? Format is synonymous with 'file type'.

Saving for the web

The number one consideration for images on the web is file size. This applies both to the physical size and the file size in bytes. The physical size matters because the image takes up space on a web page. The file size matters because it affects how fast a web page is loaded.

1 Click the File… Save For Web menu item. The Save For Web dialogue is displayed.

The dialogue has two panes – the before and after. On the left is the image in its current format, and the right pane shows what it will look like based on selections made in the dialogue.

2 Reduce the size of the image and click the Apply button. Select the output file format. An image for the web should not be exceedingly large. It is not unreasonable to reduce the image by a large percentage.

3 Click the OK button. The Save Optimized As dialogue opens. This is a typical Save dialogue. Navigate to the folder of your choice and click the Save button.

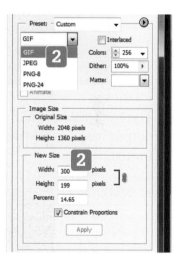

 HOT TIP: Leave the Constrain Proportions tickbox ticked. This ensures that changing any single size attribute – the width, height or percentage – forces the other attributes to adjust accordingly. Bottom line – the image will retain its appearance, just resized. There will be no squeeze or stretch in the adjustment.

Printing a photograph

Most people have colour printers. Printing a photograph in colour is an obvious choice.

1 Click the File... Print menu item to display the Print dialogue.

2 The Print dialogue has many settings. The left side has a thumbnail image of the output. You can add additional photographs to be printed by clicking the Add button.

3 In the middle of the dialogue is a preview in which you can flip the image and also zoom in and out using the slider switch. When multiple photographs are selected for printing, you can cycle them in the preview.

4 The right side of the dialogue offers further options. Here you select the printer, paper size, number of copies to print and other settings. When finished click the Print button.

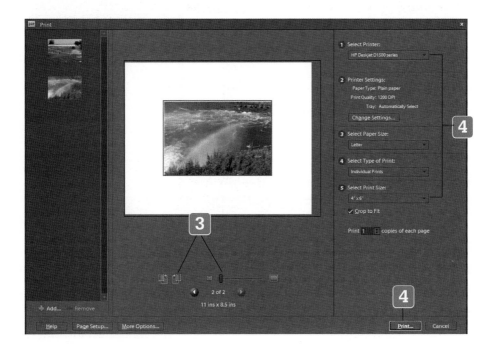

 HOT TIP: If you find the need to print an image during editing – to see how it looks on paper – it's beneficial to print it at a small size to save ink.

Emailing photographs

The email function in Photoshop Elements offers two methods – embed the photographs in the body of the email or attach the files. This describes the steps for the former.

1 In the Organizer, click the Share tab.

2 Click the Photo Mail button.

3 Drag images from the Organizer into the Photo Mail pane.

4 Click the Next button.

5 The next screen is where you compose a message for the email and select recipients.

6 Type your message in the dialogue box. If no recipients are listed, or you wish to add additional recipients, click the icon of a person to the right of the Select Recipients label.

7 The Contact Book dialogue opens. In here, you can enter, edit and delete contacts. Click the OK or Cancel button to close the Contact Book.

 HOT TIP: You can use the plus and minus symbols to add or remove images.

8 Click the Next button. The Stationery & Layouts Wizard dialogue opens.

This two-step dialogue lets you customise the appearance of the images by inserting a background, borders, a caption and a layout. When finished with these selections, click the Next button on the second wizard screen.

9 An email message is created in your computer's email program and is ready to be sent.

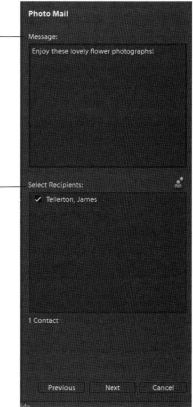

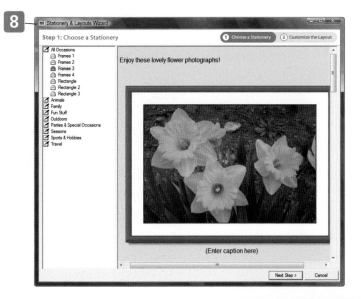

Creating a CD or DVD

A CD or a DVD can store hundreds of images. This is a handy way to back up your photographs, or share them, when the number is too great to send via email.

1 In the Organizer, click the Share tab.

2 Click the Burn data CD/DVD button. The Burn data CD/DVD dialogue box opens.

3 Select the Destination Drive in the list inside the dialogue. Another dialogue will appear prompting you to insert the disc.

4 Insert the CD or DVD. Close the drive door. Select the Write Speed (or leave it at the default).

5 Click the OK button.

6 When the process is complete, a friendly message appears.

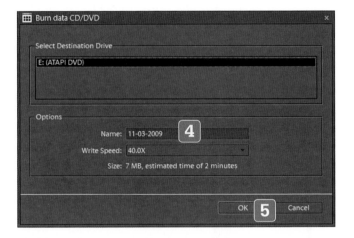

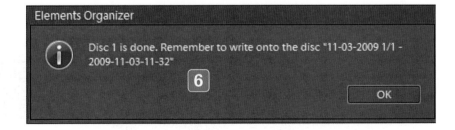

 HOT TIP: It's best to put the photos you want on the CD/DVD into an album, and have the album displayed in the Organizer. Otherwise you might put all your images on the CD/DVD – probably not your intention.

Creating a Photo Book

A Photo Book is an assembled set of photographs, organised into a formatted album. The Photo Book can be created and then ordered via the Adobe Photoshop Services.

1 In the Editor, click the Create tab.

2 Click the Photo Book button. If no images are in the Project Bin, then open several images. Rearrange the images in the Project Bin so the first is the one you want to be on the title page. You can drag the images in the Project Bin with the mouse. The first image appears in the Create pane as the Title Page Photo.

3 Select whether to Print with Local Printer, or to use one of the offered online services. This assumes printing to local printer by clicking the Print with Local Printer button. Select the layout option. If you select a Random Photo Layout, choose the theme as well. Tick the Auto-Fill with Project Bin Photos option to have the open photographs placed in the book pages.

4 Click the Create button. Photoshop Elements creates the Photo Book. The process may take several minutes. When the process is complete you can make further refinements such as changing the background.

5 You can save the Photo Book as a file by using the File…Save menu.

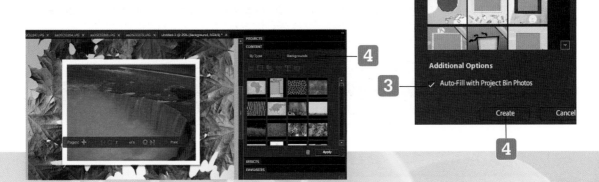

HOT TIP: If you select the Choose Photo Layout option, then on this screen you select the layout, and on an additional screen you select the theme and the number of pages.

Creating a slide show

A great attention grabber is the slide show. Besides its thematic appeal, the use of transitions between slides is always a crowd pleaser.

1 In the Organizer, select an album with a reasonable number of images. Click the Create tab.

2 Click the Slide Show button. The Slide Show Preferences dialogue is displayed.

3 Select the Static Duration, Transition type, Transition Duration and any other desired settings. Click the OK button. The Slide Show Editor is displayed.

In this dialogue more properties can be set for the slide show. Here you can select a different transition between each slide, reorder the slides, add slides, and more. Using the VCR buttons you can preview the slide show.

4 When finished editing, click the Save Project button in the upper left corner of the dialogue. The project is saved in the Organizer, with the current date.

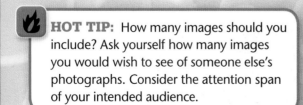

HOT TIP: How many images should you include? Ask yourself how many images you would wish to see of someone else's photographs. Consider the attention span of your intended audience.

5 With the Slide Show Editor still open, click the Output button. A set of save options is presented in the Slide Show Output dialogue box.

6 Make the appropriate selections and click the OK button.

7 A standard Save dialogue opens, letting you navigate to the folder where the slide show should be saved. When done, click the Save button.

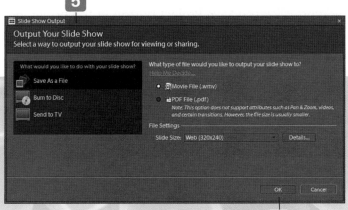

Creating a collage

A collage is a grouping of photographs for the pleasant artistic effect.

1 In the Editor, click the Create tab.

2 Click the Photo Collage button.

3 In the Create pane, select the page size, theme and layout.

4 Click the Done button. Photoshop Elements assembles the collage. Photographs from the Project Bin are placed in the collage.

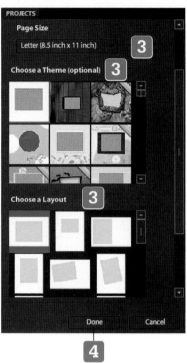

PROJECTS

Page Size

Letter (8.5 inch x 11 inch)   **3**

Choose a Theme (optional)   **3**

Choose a Layout   **3**

Done   Cancel

4

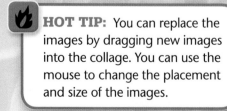

HOT TIP: You can replace the images by dragging new images into the collage. You can use the mouse to change the placement and size of the images.

Creating an Online Album

An online album is meant for the web. If you have access to a website, here is a way to get your photographs available to one and all.

1️⃣ In the Organizer, click the Share tab.

2️⃣ Click the Online Album button. Existing albums are displayed. There is also a choice to create a new album. These steps show how to use an existing album.

3️⃣ Click on the desired album.

4️⃣ Select where to share to. Since this is for the web, Export to FTP is a good choice.

5️⃣ Click the Next button. In the next screen, select a category and a template. The template updates when a category is selected.

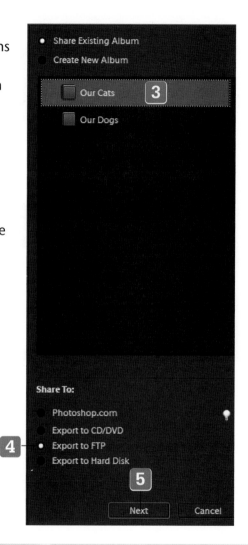

DID YOU KNOW?

FTP (File Transfer Protocol) is a method for moving files from a computer to a web server.

6 Enter the necessary FTP information. You can choose the look from the variety of templates shown at the top of the screen.

7 Click the Done button. The Online Album is created as a directory on the web saver.

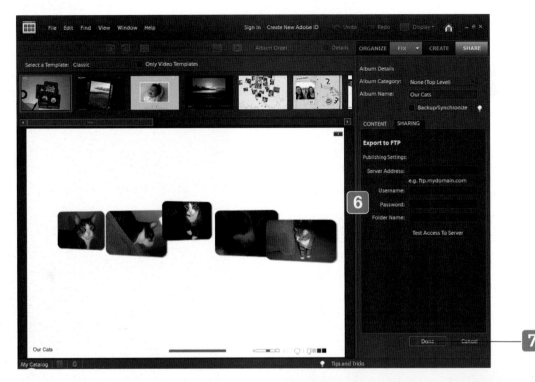

HOT TIP: If you know how to use FTP, enter the settings and upload the album! If FTP is a mystery, maybe there's a neighbourhood tech lover or a clever relative to help.

Top 10 Photoshop Elements Problems Solved

Problem 1: The colours don't look good in this photograph

Photoshop Elements can enhance an image to have the best colour range and balance.

1 Click the Enhance… Auto Color Correction menu item.

2 The photograph is corrected according to built-in methods. In this example the colours appear brighter and fuller.

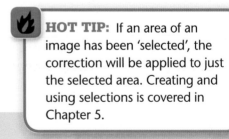

HOT TIP: If an area of an image has been 'selected', the correction will be applied to just the selected area. Creating and using selections is covered in Chapter 5.

Problem 2: How do I select the foreground and background colours?

Some photo editing work involves directly adding colour as if painting it into the photograph with a brush. But before painting, how do you select the colour?

Below the Toolbox are the colour indicators. These appear as one box overlapping the other: the top box shows the foreground colour and the bottom one shows the background colour. The use of foreground and background colours depends on the image change that is being done. Some changes require a setting for both colours – such as the colour of text on a background of a different colour. Other colour change operations may need just one of the colours.

To change a colour, simply click on it, which opens up the colour picker dialogue.

In the dialogue you can select the colour by moving the mouse around in the large colour box, along with moving the mouse up or down in the vertical colour bar. The large box is a blend of the brightness and saturation, and the vertical bar is the hue. Alternatively you can enter known values:

1. The three settings for hue, saturation and brightness.

2. The three RGB values for red, green and blue.

3. The hexadecimal number for the colour (used in web page settings).

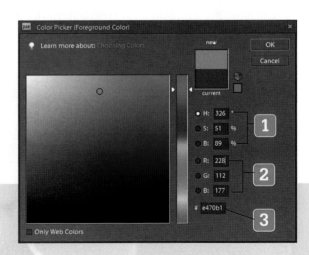

 HOT TIP: You can quickly swap the colours by clicking on the small two-way arrow to the upper right of the two boxes.

Problem 3: There is too much extra space and unwanted things in this photograph

Sometimes a golden moment presents itself and you run for the camera and click away. While you catch those beautiful shots, you can also get some annoying or distracting items in the photograph. This is what cropping is for. Here is a photograph of a rainbow, along with the undesirable spotlights at the top left. Those spotlights must be removed.

1 Click on the Crop tool in the Toolbox.

2 Drag the mouse in the image to create a line between what to keep and what to discard. The mouse pointer looks like the crop tool while doing this.

3 When the mouse button is released a preview of what the image will look like appears. Just below it are commit and cancel icons.

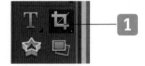

4 Clicking the commit icon (the tickmark) displays the updated image.

Problem 4: I'm using the Type tool to enter text but it just keeps going right past the image!

When entering text, the text will continue in a line, even past the image area! There are two ways around this. One is to press the Return key while you type. Better though is to have the text wrap to dimensions that you create.

1 Click the Type tool and instead of clicking where the typing should begin, drag the mouse. A bounding box will appear.

2 Type away! As you type the text will wrap to the dimensions of the box.

3 The dimensions can be changed by using the handles around the edge of the box.

4 Click the Type tool to remove the appearance of the box. The text will stay in place.

I am text that is inside a box. The box keeps me wrapped up. I like the way this works. I don't worry about running off the image area. 2

I am text that is inside a box. The box keeps me wrapped up like this. I like the way this works. I don't worry about running off the image area. 3

Problem 5: Yikes, my photo came out blurry!

Photoshop Elements provides a handy enough utility to get a good crack at improving a blurry image.

1 Click the Enhance... Adjust Sharpness menu item to display the Adjust Sharpness dialogue box.

2 In the dialogue are settings for the amount of 'unblur' to apply, and the radius – the width of pixels used to calculate how the effect is applied.

3 Beneath these settings is the Remove dropdown, with three types of blurs. A Gaussian Blur is the best choice for a generally blurred photograph. Lens Blur sharpens along lines of contrast. Motion Blur is used to correct a shot made with a shaky camera or a subject that would not stay still.

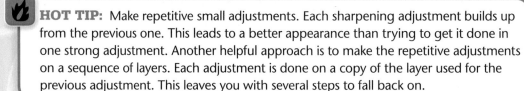

HOT TIP: Make repetitive small adjustments. Each sharpening adjustment builds up from the previous one. This leads to a better appearance than trying to get it done in one strong adjustment. Another helpful approach is to make the repetitive adjustments on a sequence of layers. Each adjustment is done on a copy of the layer used for the previous adjustment. This leaves you with several steps to fall back on.

Problem 6: Aunt Sally has red eyes!

When light hits the retina, a colour can be reflected back that is not natural. In humans, this distortion is known as red eye (pictures of animals can result in other eye colour distortions).

1 Open a photograph that shows a face with red eye(s).

2 Click the Enhance… Auto Fix Red Eye menu item. The change is run automatically – no dialogue appears to adjust settings. In a moment the photograph is altered to show true eye colour.

❓ DID YOU KNOW?

Your camera may have a feature that removes red eye when the photograph is being taken.

Problem 7: The subject in the photograph seems warped

When shooting up, or down, or at any angle that is not straight ahead, the photograph may have a distorted view. Cameras try to capture the image in the best way, but that is where 2D can confuse a 3D reality. Photoshop Elements has a utility to correct the distortion.

1 Open a photograph that has some distorted perspective. Here is an example – the fence appears to arch inwards. In reality the fence is straight.

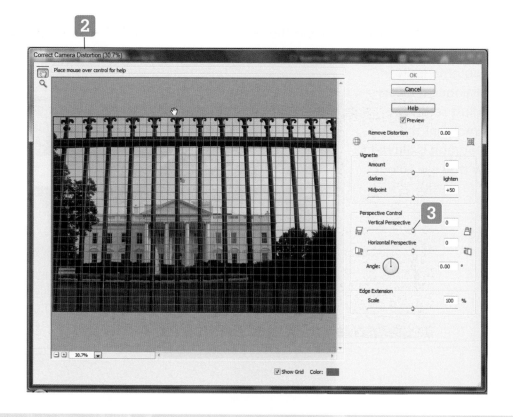

HOT TIP: In the dialogue, a screen is placed over the photograph that helps when reorienting the perspective. This screen can be turned off by unticking the Show Grid tickbox at the bottom of the dialogue.

2 Click the Filter... Correct Camera Distortion menu item to display the Correct Camera Distortion dialogue box.

The dialogue has controls to correct the perspective vertically and horizontally, to correct if the perspective distortion is one of a bowing in or out, or if the perspective is based on lighting differences around the edge of the image. In this example, it's the vertical perspective that needs correction. The Vertical Perspective slider is used to lower the perspective setting – this effectively straightens the fence.

3 Lower the Vertical Perspective using the slider control.

The fence is now straight, but the reorientation of the image has left an empty area around the bottom half of the image. This is filled in by using the Edge Extension setting.

4 Increase the Edge Extension using the slider switch. Then click the OK button to keep the changes. The result is the image with a fence that stands straight.

Problem 8: How can I get rid of skin imperfections?

The Spot Healing Brush removes imperfections by matching pixels that are in the bounds of the area the tool touches when used.

1 Right-click the Healing Brush Tool on the Toolbox and select the Spot Healing Brush Tool.

2 The tool options are two types of match methods. Each of these occurs once the area to correct is clicked on. The brush size should be larger than the area being corrected:

- Proximity Match – uses pixels around the edge of the brush area to determine a usable sample to cover the area being corrected.

- Create Texture – uses pixels within the brush area to determine a usable sample to cover the area being corrected.

The choice of which type to use depends on the image. Try them both to see what looks best.

3 In this example the man's wrinkles will be removed.

A brush size slightly larger than the area of the wrinkles above the eyes is selected. Then the image is clicked on the wrinkles. The wrinkles are removed.

 HOT TIP: You can use a small brush size too. If so, a number of clicks and small drag-overs with the mouse are needed to complete correcting the area.

Problem 9: My scanned-in photograph has a scratch. How can I remove it?

Scanned photographs are susceptible to imperfections appearing because of a scratched, dirty, dusty or hair-covered platen. The same could be true of the physical photograph itself. These imperfections are carried directly into the image file. Here's a way to remove a scratch.

1. Open an image that has a scratch or similar imperfection.

2. Use the Selection Brush tool to draw over the scratch. The Selection Brush tool is great for creating a selection along a line.

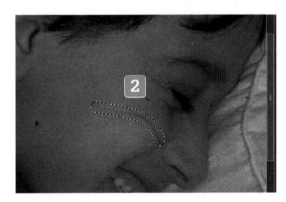

3. Click the Filter... Noise... Dust & Scratches menu item to open the Dust & Scratches dialogue box.

4. Adjust the Radius and Threshold while viewing the preview of the change. The radius is a setting of how wide the affected area extends past the selection. The Threshold controls the pixel level at which the effect is applied. A lower threshold produces the effect more easily – less differentiation is needed between the selection and the surrounding area. When an acceptable balance is seen in the preview, click the OK button. Then deselect using the Select... Deselect menu.

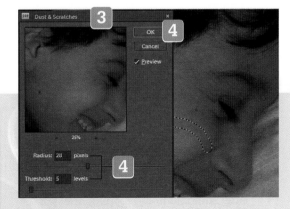

 HOT TIP: The result of scratch removal may still leave a noticeable imperfection. Continuing with another tool, such as the Spot Healer Brush, will finish the scratch removal.

Problem 10: The photo came out crooked, now what?

It happens – you take a shot, it's great, except, it's crooked. There might have been a time when such tragedies were discarded, but no more! Photoshop Elements has a utility to set it all straight.

1 Open a photograph in which the angle of view is not aligned with the edges of the image itself – in other words, crooked.

2 Select the Straighten tool from the Toolbox. Draw a line in the image, along an angle that should be the horizontal bottom edge of the image. Often there is a clear guide to do this based on the subject(s) in the image. Here, the bottom of the guitar serves as the angle to correct, so the line is drawn parallel with the guitar base.

3 The image straightens but in doing so exposes the canvas underneath. What is needed now is to crop the image. Using the Crop tool the inner part of the image is retained and is a full image itself, aligned with its edges.

HOT TIP: An alternative straightening method is to use the Image... Rotate... Straighten menu item. Going a step further is the Image... Rotate... Straighten & Crop Image menu item. The latter straightens and crops in one automated operation.

USE YOUR COMPUTER
WITH CONFIDENCE

Laptop Basics

9780273723486

Windows Vista

9780273723493

Computer Basics

9780273723479

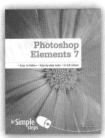

Photoshop Elements 7

9780273723523

Web Design

9780273723530

Photoshop CS4

9780273723509

Excel 2007

9780273723547

Office 2007

9780273723554

Windows 7

9780273729136

Mac Basics

9780273729297

Windows 7
FOR THE OVER 50'S

9780273729181

Laptop Basics
FOR THE OVER 50'S

9780273729129

Computer Basics
FOR THE OVER 50'S

9780273729174

in Simple steps

Practical. Simple. Fast.

PEARSON